khwab nama

khwab nama

Akhtaruzzaman
Elias

Translated by
Arunava Sinha

PENGUIN

An imprint of Penguin Random House

HAMISH HAMILTON

USA | Canada | UK | Ireland | Australia
New Zealand | India | South Africa | China | Singapore

Hamish Hamilton is part of the Penguin Random House group of companies
whose addresses can be found at global.penguinrandomhouse.com

Published by Penguin Random House India Pvt. Ltd
4th Floor, Capital Tower 1, MG Road,
Gurugram 122 002, Haryana, India

First published in Hamish Hamilton by Penguin Random House India 2021

Copyright © Andalib Elias 2021
English Translation Copyright © Arunava Sinha 2021

ISBN 9780670087211

Typeset in Adobe Garamond Pro by Manipal Technologies Limited, Manipal
Printed at Replika Press Pvt. Ltd, India

www.penguin.co.in

This is a legitimate digitally printed version of the book and therefore might not
have certain extra finishing on the cover.

Author's dedication
To Mahbubul Alam

Translator's dedication
To the nation of Bangladesh

1

The spot where Tamiz's father stood with his feet planted in the mud, craning his neck as high as possible, stretching his nerves taut, and waving his jet-black arms to dispel the grey clouds, needs to be noted carefully. A long time ago, when leave alone Tamiz's father, even his father had not been born, when his when his grandfather Bhaghar Majhi's birth was still a long way in the future, when Bhaghar Majhi's grandfather's father, or was it *his* grandfather, had barely been born, or not, and even if he had, was only crawling about on the newly-laid earth in the home built by clearing a part of the forest, on one afternoon during those days, while he was speeding towards the Kartowa River to visit the Mahasthan Killa with several of Majnu Shah's fakirs, Munshi Barkatullah Shah was flung from his horse after being shot dead by Taylor, the commander of British troops. The hole left in his neck by the bullet was never filled. After his death, with a chain around this neck and his body smeared with ash, and holding an iron pan with fish motifs carved on it, he perched on the fig tree on the northern side of the Katlahar Lake. Ever since then, he became the sunlight during the day and spread himself all over the lake and reigned over the lake all night from the fig tree. Tamiz's father waved his arms to get rid of the clouds in the sky in the hope of catching a glimpse of Munshi. Which was all very well, but two or two and a quarter years from now, or maybe two and a half or even three, after drowning to death in the quicksand in one corner of the bank recently sprung from the receding waters of the lake, where would Tamiz's father surface? Who was going to make room for him? The large jackfruit trees had long been cleared out by the fangs of the big flood, and once Sharafat Mondol's son had set up his brick kiln, the remaining trees would also be swallowed by the kiln. What would happen then? Where would Tamiz's father float up? The lake dried up rapidly, the dry land was cultivated, and people built their homes along the perimeter of the land. Would there be room for a large tree any more?

By daylight it was clear to the eye—to the west, the land between the western bank of the lake and the edge of the creek here was still empty. Majhipara—where the fishermen lived—began at this point. Not that the people of Majhipara referred to their enclave as a neighbourhood, for they used to occupy the entire village once. Now, though, 60 or 70 per cent of them were peasants. Several families of Kolus had lived here, extracting oil for a living, but within three years of Tabibar Muktar's Rahman Oil Mills being set up in the town, 8 miles to the west, more than half of them had left for the bank of the Jomuna to the east. The few who had remained were more inclined towards farming.

A large expanse of the land across the lake was given over to cultivation; beyond, on the other side of the narrow creek, lay Chashapara, the cultivators' village. Next to each of the houses stood a tethered ox, a battered pile of yellow hay blackened by the rain, cow-dung manure beside shrubs of Barbados nut, rows of banana trees, screens of dried banana leaves behind which the women could stay out of view, and a plough, a yoke and a harrow. The other side of the lake was clearly visible from morning to afternoon, and in the month of Asharh, even at twilight when it didn't rain. Fishermen came from far afield, paying a rent to Sharafat Mondol for the right to fish in the lake. The peasants and even their womenfolk lined up to watch. There would be pandemonium around the lake on such days. But it wasn't as though there were many fishermen. In fact, there were three or four times as many urchins jumping up and down and screaming on the bank. Whether it was people or cattle, women or children, fish or snails—all, all the brazen buggers would dance, flaunting their nakedness.

It was night now, but a different sight presented itself. A faint, fine, black fishing net drifted down to the water as evening fell, widening its expanse as the evening developed into night. The darkness intensified, and the entire area was finally captured in the net. The night deepened, then deepened further, and before anyone realized, the net began to be drawn in. There was a tug on the rope from the fig tree, and gradually the entire lake, along with the villages on either bank, was pooled in the centre, its waters trembling. On purnima or amaboshya or ekadoshi—when the moon was either full or new or in the eleventh day of the cycle—Girirdanga and Nijgirirdanga, the two villages flanking the Katlahar Lake, flowed into each other and became one within the lake. When you looked, you couldn't tell them apart any more. The fig tree cast a giant shadow on the water then, and as the night deepened, its shadow kept growing, kept growing. Wrapping this gigantic shadow around themselves in the dense darkness of the new moon night or by the yellowish beams of the full moon or the murky red glow of the waning moon, Katlahar Lake, the villages on either side, the creek next to the lake, the clearing with the fig tree at its head, Sharafat Mondol's tin-roofed hut to the south and the white silk-cotton tree to the east of the hut shrouded in storks—all of them, all, sighed constantly, like the young boy from the fishermen's neighbourhood who had fallen asleep weeping, his body entangled in a fishing net when his pleas to his mother for some food fell on deaf ears. Their breath held the lingering notes of someone crying. It was the perfect time to take all of these things in at one glance. That was when Munshi Barkatullah Shah walked into the sky over the middle of the lake, pulling on the ropes of the net. A flock of sheep swam forward, leading the way. Tamiz's father came here for what could only be a momentary glimpse of this scene, for Munshi never stayed very long. The sky above and the water and the land below all became one then, and Munshi moved about everywhere at will. Setting everything and everyone in their place for a moment, he soared away with the net to the north, where a narrow stream from a river had lost its way to flow into the lake. Perched on the fig tree at the head of the lake, Munshi slipped into the eye of a vulture every morning and watched the motion of the sun across the sky, merging into the sunlight without warning, becoming the sunlight himself to warm the chilled bodies of the catfish, the carp and the small fry in the lake. And when he grew exasperated, he would turn into a tiny ball of fur beneath the wing of a green pigeon behind the dense foliage of the fig tree to sleep all afternoon in the warmth of the tender flesh.

Mind you, everything farther north of the head of the lake was also under Munshi's control, he reigned there too. And Tamiz's father had been there, of course he had. Sharif Mondol had arranged for the years-old thick forest of kaash here to be cleared for cultivating jute. It was the month of Poush. Some of the people from the fishermen's neighbourhood on this side of the lake joined the peasants from Nijgirirdanga in two boats very early one morning under the blanket of mist, and Tamiz's father went on board too as a hired hand. This time of the year had been chosen because the kaash forest was usually free of stagnant water now. But no, there was not a single dry patch to be found anywhere—there were still puddles beneath their feet. Thousands of leeches were sunning themselves on the kaash stalks to rid their bodies of the freezing cold, the plants bending beneath their weight. When so many people marauded into the forest with their sickles and spades, the starving leeches fastened themselves to the men's stomachs and bellies and thighs and cocks and buttocks—even to their arses—clamping their teeth on whatever gave them some purchase. Although the peasants of Girirdanga and the fishermen of Nijgirirdanga did not exactly experience fear at this attempt by the leeches to assuage their pent-up hunger, they extricated themselves with urgency, returning home with entire leeches or wounds from the leeches on different parts of their bodies. So Sharafat Mondol had to wait several years before he could use that particular bit of land.

Moreover, it wasn't him but his eldest son who was to eventually take a lease on it, when there was not a single stalk of kaash left. Even before the love bites of the leeches had disappeared from the bodies of the peasants and the fishermen, Ramesh Bagchi, a lawyer from the town, had taken charge of the kaash forest. But he was a town-bred toff—cultivation was not ordained for him. Ramesh-babu had no faith in his nephew Tunu-babu when it came to taking responsibility for the land. He was looking for a hard-working, trustworthy and unintelligent person to help Tunu-babu as well as to keep an eye on him. Tamiz's father could have seized the opportunity—if only he had wanted to. By the time he came to know of it he was practically starving, with Tamiz's mother being eight months pregnant and unable to work.

But Sharafat Mondol said, 'The northern bank of the lake is not a safe place. You'll have to be on your guard.' Mondol was not lying; Munshi was indeed a little short-tempered. Anyone who got into his bad books once would not be allowed to work ever again in his life. It didn't matter that he might be married, that he might have children to feed. Tamiz's father, the ignorant son of a fisherman, could not tell the pure apart from the impure. What if he made a mistake of some kind? So he withdrew in apprehension. When Tamiz's mother dropped a dead girl at the end of the eighth month and took to her bed like the women from the Mondol family, Mondol's second wife warned him in a low voice, 'Don't even think of going to the head of the lake, Tamiz's father, who knows what new trouble you'll invite.'

Calculating when all this had happened, or how long it had been since then, was beyond Tamiz's father. And look, these days he woke up from his sleep in the middle of the night to take the same road to the lake, driven by his longing for a glimpse of Munshi. The night was of course the right time if you were to have any hope of spotting him. The currents of air generated by Tamiz's father's swinging arms were turning the dark grey of the clouds to a lighter shade of ash. Now the flock of sheep would swim in the lake, gasping for breath all the while. The clouds would shed their grey colour, disappear completely. It was easy to identify the creatures as sheep then by the coats of grimy white wool on their bodies. But the bloody clouds were refusing to disperse. Only after they vanished would Munshi make an appearance behind the flock of sheep, holding an iron pan with fish motifs carved on it. The pan was attached to his palm, protruding from it like a large finger. Although the bellows projecting out of the slit in his throat were shrinking by the day, their power still made you tremble in fear. Munshi could not talk because his throat had been slit, but the puffs of air that emerged from the opening with great force were powerful enough for the sheep to understand his instructions. Flailing their legs, they swam, all but drowning. Complying with the commands roared out by the gusts of wind, they sank and floated, advanced and retreated, all night long, touching the earth and the water between the fig tree in the north and the silk-cotton tree in the south, and even as far afield as the Poradaho field in the north-east. All the fish in the lake made way for their savage expedition. The senior devilfish and catfish marshalled their families and dived deep beneath the surface to rest their breasts on the moss or on an oar that had slipped out of a fisherman's hands during the flood that had followed the earthquake a hundred and twenty-five years ago, waiting for Munshi to restore the sheep to their original form and return them to their appointed place in the lake. After which he would climb to the crown of the fig tree. And then? The next day he would turn himself into the sharp eye of the vulture, slicing the sky into strips all day long. If he was in an affable mood, he would merge into the sunlight to become the sunlight himself and warm the water of the lake. And if he was tired he would turn into a chick and tuck himself into the fur on the wing of the green pigeon behind the dense foliage of the fig tree, sleeping in the warmth of its flesh all evening.

Which was all very well, but right now, having sleepwalked all this way, Tamiz's father could not see Munshi anywhere, where was he? It was impossible to catch sight of him when awake, but was he going to remain behind the veil of dreams forever? This

Munshi was not a good man. Not a good man, this Munshi. He was far too adroit at hiding. But oh, was Munshi even a man? Forgive the thought! He would create all kinds of problems if he were to be included among the ranks of humans. Possibly he had been a human till the moment of his death, but it wasn't just the other day that he had died, was it? It was in another era altogether that he had fallen off his white horse, shot dead by Taylor, the commander of the English troops, late one afternoon before the sun had set, while galloping towards the Kartowa with thousands of Majnu Shah's band of fakirs. Who knew where the horse, with arrows impaled in every part of its body, had flown off, while Munshi's corpse, languishing in the mud here, blazed with red, blue and black flames. For three days no one dared touch his burning body. When Munshi saw that the ceremonial shroud and burial were all in abeyance, what could he do but climb to the top of the fig tree with his throat slit open by the bullet. Ever since then he had been a creature of fire. His entire body, his flowing beard, his black turban, the chains on his chest, the pan in his hand— all of them seemed to burn perpetually. Tamiz's father trembled every now and then, struck by fear and regret at having considered such a being a mere man. Maybe it was this trembling that nudged him out of the impenetrable darkness of his sleep. He took a step forward, like someone who had woken up abruptly, and confused the splashing of his feet in ankle-deep water with stifled groans emerging from Munshi's throat. His heart fluttered in hope; maybe he'd catch a glimpse any moment now. His heart pounded in fear; maybe Munshi would descend any moment now. When his feet touched the roots of the water lilies in the lake, he stooped to clutch their stalks, although the vines couldn't possibly bear the weight of his body. Still, the mud was hard enough to support him. The torn-off, crumpled lily petals were resting in his fist now. Although the soft touch of the ripped petals peeled off a few layers of sleep, not all of it left him. He stumbled off homewards, still slumbering, clutching the torn petals in his hand, the fishing net dangling from his shoulder. And well before his sleep could wear off, the rhythm of his footsteps took him deeper into sleep.

But it didn't turn out the same way every time. No, on some nights an unbroken sound woke Tamiz's father up completely. Someone was speaking in a hoarse drawl far in the distance—where else but the fig tree:

> Munshi lives in the fig tree to the north
> Beneath him swim all the fierce murrels
> Late at night, only on Munshi's command
> All the murrels take the form of sheep.

But because Tamiz's father started violently, the verses from afar did not remain audible, although they gave him a violent itch on his scalp before subsiding. It was possible that tingling he had been feeling all over his body had been caused by the droning of these verses. No sooner had it acquired the form of words, however, than Tamiz's father woke up, by which time the sounds had returned to the fig tree. A violent gust of the same wind on which they had flown in now blew them away to the yard of the Mondols' home in the south, which in turn awoke the flock of white storks on Sharafat Mondol's silk-cotton tree. These storks were favourites of Sharafat's, whose influence in the area ensured that they survived. It was because of his strict instructions that not even the thousands of people who visited the village fair at Poradaho on the last Wednesday of the month of Maagh every year dared to throw rocks at the tree. Like Sharafat Mondol, the ancestors of the storks too had their original home in the village of Nijgirirdanga. Across the creek adjoining Chashapara lay Kamarpara, where the blacksmiths lived, marked by Dasharath Karmakar's arjun tree. Dasharath's forefather may not have been Mandhaataa himself, but in those ancient times, the mythical king Mandhaataa's era, when, leave alone Dasharath, not even Grandfather had been born, and even if he had, was barely crawling about near the warm bellows set in the newly built house in the settlement created by clearing a part of the forest, that was the era when the storks had set up their household on the arjun tree. The blacksmiths and the storks had proliferated next to one another. When the blacksmiths began to die in hordes during the last famine, several storks died too, beneath the arjun tree. During the famine, half the land owned by the blacksmiths was about to pass to Jagadish Saha when Sharafat Mondol sent for the blacksmiths and gave them money which they paid Jagadish to prevent their land from being confiscated. But Sharafat himself became the owner of the land in this way. When the blacksmiths moved to the town, Mondol's hired hands went over to plough their land, which was when the swarm of storks on the arjun tree flew across the lake to perch on the branches of Sharafat Mondol's silk-cotton tree. Sharafat offered shelter to the helpless birds with great tenderness. God is merciful, nothing escapes his eye, and so Sharafat was rewarded plentifully for this act. His flourishing household kept swelling with children, women, cattle, ducks and hens, land and hired hands. But a question—could birds from a Hindu village possibly turn anyone's luck so much? Although the villagers hesitated to say it in as many words, the truth was that they knew that the storks were slaves to Munshi's wishes. Which was why Tamiz's father trembled uncontrollably at their slow flight. This trembling could, however, also be the remnants of the incantations he heard in his sleep or was woken up by. Did these incantations also emerge through the hole in Munshi's throat to be borne on the air? Or was it the voice of someone he knew that had attached itself to his hairy ear, buzzing like a bee? When the buzzing spread everywhere, seven or eight storks flew in circles over the lake to measure it, looping around Tamiz's father's head to gauge whether he was pure or not. Just a short while ago, Tamiz's father was waving his arms to disperse the clouds in the sky so that he could see how Munshi commanded the flock of sheep to take on the appearance of murrels. Now he clamped his hands over his own head. If the storks were to notice his scalp, covered in hair like tendrils of hemp, there was no escaping Munshi's wrath, no escaping it at all. Turning his head away, Tamiz's father struggled up from the mud to climb back on shore, and set off for home directly. Staggering as he walked, several times he trod on goathead thorns, some of which lodged themselves in the thousands of apertures left in his soles by thorns that had pricked him earlier. Pulling the thorns out as he walked, and increasing his pace despite the risk of stepping on more of them, he raced homewards. On many such occasions in the past, Tamiz's father had retreated out of fear at the sight of thin grey clouds scudding across the sky while he was trying to dispel them to catch a glimpse of Munshi, abandoning the fishing net draped over his shoulder by the side of the lake— sometimes in the mud, at other times on the rain-soaked earth.

2

When hunger jabbed open Kulsum's eyes, she noticed that one side
of the door was wide open. Tamiz's father had left a muddy footprint
on the doorstep. Had a kick from the same foot opened the door?
How could that be possible? The foot wasn't strong enough. He was
lying on the floor; so the man had obviously been outside at night.
Which meant that the swamp of Katlahar had sucked out at least a
little bit of blood from his feet. It was doubtful whether he would be
able to walk before it was afternoon. His numb right foot lay near
the side of the door that was still shut. His faded lungi was hoisted
halfway up his legs, though the garment was not in its place. A long
time ago, when Tamiz's mother ran the household, a murrel had
bitten off an ounce of flesh from his thigh one new moon night when
he entered the waters of Katlahar Lake. With his lungi raised, the
scar was visible now. Below it was the inflamed wound from about
a year ago, earned when he was stabbed by a fishing hook. Tamiz's
father had been fishing beneath the sandpaper tree at Fakir's Ghat.
When a huge catfish was caught on the hook, he tugged hard at the
rod. The hook flew out of the water, the catfish still attached to it,
and struck him on the knee, impaling itself in his flesh while the fish
was flung upwards to a low branch of the tree. The fish was never
found—nor did Tamiz's father discover any sign that it had returned
to the lake. Whose signal had it responded to, then, to launch itself
out of the water and perform the manoeuvre that had ensured his

wound had not healed yet? The scar from the bite of the murrel from the time when Tamiz's mother was alive and the recent wound from the fishing hook remained adjacent nevertheless. The wound kept spreading, threatening to encroach on the scar from the murrel bite at any moment. But having reached the edge, the bloody thing refused to advance, showing no signs of climbing farther. But it did not heal either, the pus making it swell without allowing it to grow sideways.

The mud stains persisted beneath the knee. A little higher and the moist tang of Katlahar Lake would have combined with the fishlike stench of the wound to create a completely different smell, one that was very familiar to Kulsum. When she sniffed deeply, wrinkling the nose on which she had still managed to preserve the stud she wore, her nostrils were beset, along with the slightly moist, slightly stale, and slightly fishlike smell of the lake, with a lighter scent. A scent of what? Clambering up on the maacha, the rough-hewn platform of bamboo logs attached halfway up the wall, Kulsum threw a glance to her left, and another to the right. Finding her bearings with the help of the scent, she discovered the object. What was it, then? Nothing but crumpled and torn lily petals peeping out from beneath Tamiz's father's coal-black, bony frame. Along with her nose, Kulsum's entire belly and breast were now pressed into service for sniffing. She made the inhaled air circulate through the length of her body, turning even her short and medium breaths into a single long one which could actually be called a sigh. If the sigh were to be passed through a strainer, the words that would emerge would be something like this: if only the old coot had picked some lily stems. What then? Then Kulsum would have cooked a delicious dry dish with them, adding chillies and some diced garlic pods. When she made this dish, Tamiz's father gobbled up three platefuls of rice with it, with some roasted chillies on the side. Waking up late in the morning after trudging all night through the mud and water, he could consume an enormous quantity of rice. Where did the old fellow stow away so much food in that scrawny body of his?

For Tamiz's father, certainly, but for herself too, she should cook the rice early. It had been raining incessantly since last afternoon, and the clay oven in the yard was brimming with water. She had kept some of the rice she had made the day before yesterday, soaking it in water to prevent it from spoiling. Yesterday afternoon Tamiz's father had put. After his meal, he drew a few times on his hookah, climbed on the maacha and sank into such a deep sleep that, oh Allah, the storm in the evening, the rain that followed, then the sky resting for a while before the drizzle began again—he slept through it all. How the old man could sleep when his stomach was full!

Kulsum had bailed her belly out yesterday morning with two or three potato-like shankalus. That was all that she had got. She hadn't eaten a morsel since then. How would she sleep? They did have a stove inside the house too, but where would tomorrow's rice come from if it rained again the next day? So Kulsum had only sniffed the rice stored in the pot and then curled up next to her husband. Absorbed in the joy of a freshly thatched roof that did not leak anywhere, she had not realized that all the sleep in the world had descended on her eyes. When had Tamiz's father woken up and gone outside? When had he returned to go back to sleep? Kulsum had been oblivious to all this. No matter how long Tamiz's father slept now, when he did wake up, late in the day, he would stare greedily at the vessels stacked in the corner of the room with rheum-lined eyes. And if he wasn't fed at once, his entire body would revolt, voice thick with phlegm, making it impossible to go anywhere near him.

But it would be a while before this voice would be heard, for the old man was sleeping like the dead now. Kulsum seized the opportunity to remove the clay lids covering the two aluminium pots in the room and breathe in the fragrance deeply. She had not had to descend to the floor for this, for the things that lay at one end of the maacha could be reached from where she was. Plunging her nose into the containers filled with a seer and a half of rice and taking three or four deep breaths released the fragrance it gave out when being cooked. This gave rise to a tingling feeling in her stomach and then in her abdomen, which then travelled back up from her abdomen to her stomach and then to her breast and finally to her tongue. But instead of wilting under the agitation in her belly at the aroma of cooking rice, Kulsum felt physically invigorated. Responding to this call from her body, she began to do a bit of this and a bit of that. For instance, lifting the earthen lid off a large aluminium pot that Tamiz had brought from town a few months ago, she gingerly took out a vial of medicine from the time Tamiz's mother was alive and ran her calloused fingertips across its smooth glass walls. Holding the small circular mirror in her right hand, she looked at her left profile and then the right one, followed by her chin, several times over. There was not much difference between her right cheek and her left, the brownish complexion of her skin turning paler in the mirror, making it appear almost fair. Even if it wasn't sharp, her nose was on the whole pointed, and a little elongated. Her lips were not as thin as her brother's, but when she had had a paan they looked just as red. Her brother would have a paan tucked away in his mouth all the time, but how could Kulsum afford paan? Having examined herself thoroughly in the mirror before putting it away, Kulsum took out Tamiz's old long shirt, lungi and skullcap one by one, holding them up to her nose and breathing in their smell deeply. There was a gash at the back of Tamiz's shirt, which hadn't been washed since he had left. The scent of perspiration on the front of the shirt was so faint now that it might well be swept away under the force of Kulsum's breath. Or was it actually her breath that had still kept the smell alive?

Completing her daily morning rituals, Kulsum looked at the floor out of the corner of her eye. No, Tamiz's father was still sleeping like the dead. Now she took out the oldest object in the room from where she had hidden it behind all the pots, pans and sacks on the maacha and breathed in its aroma deeply. The book belonged to her father's father, but Tamiz's father guarded it like treasure. What did the unlettered son of a fisherman know of books? And yet he glared angrily at Kulsum whenever he found out that she had picked it up.

Allah alone knew what Kulsum's grandfather had deciphered from the pages filled with squares and gibberish—she did not fret over it. But for all that it had belonged to her grandfather. If she sniffed at it long enough his image appeared in the door frame. Where was the time to feast her eyes on him, though? The pressure of Kulsum's puffy feet on the floor elicited a response, even if slight, from Tamiz's father's scrawny dark body. Muttering incomprehensible words, he raised his lungi farther. All this time only the wound on his knee had been visible, but now the scar from the time Tamiz's mother was alive was exposed too. If the lungi were to be lifted farther, the old coot's limp cock above his jet-black balls would pop out as well. What use was this sight for Kulsum? But instead of adjusting her husband's lungi, she just sat there in silence. Her ears pricked, she focused her entire attention on comprehending the words from the words that Tamiz's father was muttering. When words that sounded like 'talat tajol tachh', thick with spit, splashed out of his lips, Kulsum began to listen even more closely. What was Tamiz's father dreaming of now? Was it 'kajol' he had meant to say when he had said 'tajol'? Her grandfather used to say that when you dreamt of kohl, children warmed their parents' hearts. Since Tamiz's father did have a son, he could well have such dreams. Resting her hand in her empty lap, Kulsum surveyed her husband from head to toe. Had this foolish man ever considered that his wife was childless? Was he even aware of it? Dead to the world, Tamiz's father mumbled again in his sleep, whereupon Kulsum began to listen closely once more. But as before, this time too his words emerged from his mouth only to slide down his food pipe and burrow all the way down in his belly. Kulsum could never reach them. During the day, or even when he was awake at night, Tamiz's father lost the ability to chant verses. However much you might nag him, 'Come on, what was that you were muttering in your sleep?' he would only stare blankly. If Kulsum coaxed and cajoled him insistently to find out what went on while he slept, he either frowned or, if he was in a good mood, tried to recollect his dream or the verses he had mumbled, dozing off during his attempts, his voice becoming softer with the exhaustion of his effort, and he murmured, in much the same way that he did while slumbering, 'Who remembers what he says in his sleep? I don't know what I said or what I saw.' When Kulsum pleaded with him even more to remember what he had dreamt of, he grew testy and chided her, 'Stop this nonsense. Food. Give me food. Got to go to work.' Still Kulsum wouldn't give up, her husband's scolding making no impression on her. She barely cared even when Tamiz's father gave her a beating. Sleeping people talked with Munshi, or with jinns and nymphs, while innocent children conversed with angels. Tamiz's father must be communicating with creatures of fire. Her grandfather used to say, 'He may look like an idiot, he may be the son of an illiterate fisherman, but there's a hidden gift he has, a fire burns inside him somewhere.'

Was it to stoke the flames beneath this blackened heap of ash that her grandfather had handed her over to him and disappeared? Couldn't Tamiz's father do anything at all to search out her grandfather? He had spent so many years in Cherag Ali's company; they had whispered and conspired together so much— hadn't Tamiz's father picked up anything at all from Kulsum's grandfather? This torn and tattered book of his, with all sorts of signs and symbols, squares and gibberish—her grandfather had studied them all and drawn lines on the ground and interpreted so many people's dreams, helped find things that were lost, told countless men how to make love to the women of their dreams. It wasn't proper to say it now, but Kulsum had heard that in his prime her grandfather had used this same book to break families for money. And this was the book that had remained with Tamiz's father—yet he could not ferret out any information of Kulsum's grandfather's whereabouts. He went off somewhere in his sleep, he talked while he slept, sometimes stammering out her grandfather's verses—how could he not have received any signs at all? But no, Kulsum had no hope whatsoever of deciphering anything he said. And here he was—no sooner had these words escaped his lips than

Tamiz's father began to snore softly again. Who knew when he would stop? The way the old man was sprawled on the floor made it difficult for Kulsum to get off the maacha. There would be hell to pay if her feet touched any part of his bony frame, for the old coot would create a horrible scene. She had suffered in no small measure the one time it had happened.

But then all this had taken place a long time ago. She had been married for maybe two years then. Tamiz's father was eating in the darkness of the night, the room stilled in the blackened light of the lamp. Tamiz was smoking in the moonlit yard outside. Maddened and a little drunk on the tobacco smoke, the moonlight had taken advantage of the door being left ajar quite a long way to enter the room and add yellow to the reddish-black colour within, possibly making Kulsum's senses reel a little. At that very instant, wolfing down his rice and catfish curry, Tamiz's father had demanded an onion. Rising to her feet to retrieve it from the clay pot on the maacha, Kulsum had just bent over to put it on his plate, or perhaps she had been about to squat opposite him, when her left foot had brushed Tamiz's father's right elbow. This had tilted his rice plate. Kulsum was a little clumsy when it came to mopping and cleaning the floor—if only she could balance herself somewhere! And so a little daal had spilled from Tamiz's father's plate on the floor. Nothing else. The spilled daal had included only a few grains of rice. The remnants of the fish or the aubergine slices or the half-consumed pieces of roasted chilli had all stayed on the plate as before. But still the man had lost his temper. Abandoning his meal to spring to his feet, he had begun screaming. 'You kicked my food away? How do I eat this now that your dirty feet have touched it?' All the while he rained blows on Kulsum's back with fists that still had crumbs on them. Oh, how fierce the old man had become now that he had eaten some fish after a long time. He wouldn't stop beating her up. Meanwhile Tamiz had paused his smoking under the moonlight to appear at the door and add fuel to the fire of his father's rage. 'You actually kicked away my father's plate of rice? How can you do this? How can you put your feet on the food that passes through his mouth? This is like kicking the goddess of fortune. What sort of woman are you?'

Having secured his son's support, the father had dragged his wife by her hair out to the yard, saying, 'You're as slippery as a fish! Can't you do your work carefully? Shameless whore, is it the itch that's making you jump about all the time?' And the young man Tamiz, without knowing or understanding anything of what was going on, had twisted things further, 'You've never had to earn any money, your father's a fakir, what do you know how hard it is to work for a living? No wonder you can kick away a man's plate of food.' But Tamiz's unhappiness had not stoked his father's anger further. He had gone back to stuffing handfuls of rice into his mouth, the lines around which were stricken with the loss of a few grains, and had sat down on the doorstep, facing the yard, his heart heavy with the grief of remaining only half-fed. The tiny clear space in the yard had levitated a little in the pale, weightless moonlight—staring at this ascending void, he had roared, 'I want to smoke!' The agitation from chastising his wife was making him pant, which had turned what was meant to be a bellow into a sickly rattle, a sound that did not cause the slightest crack to appear in the moonlight, so that even Kulsum had stomped into the house without a care for his command, or for Tamiz's mild dissatisfaction, or for the restless void touched by the moonlight. Now that she had come in and lain down on the maacha, she would not get up all night. The pot of rice would stay uncovered on the floor, and the plate of food and the bowl and glass of water would remain strewn about. Once she had fallen asleep without a meal, not even kicks or screams would be able to rouse her from the maacha. A couple of seers of rice had to be fetched from the Mondols' home; it was no small task. Who was going to get this whore out of the maacha now? Because he did not have the power to get his wife to stir, and because he no longer sounded as bellicose as he used to, Tamiz's father had been forced to keep up his rant. But there was more discontentment in it now. 'It's not good for women to be so angry, not good. As slippery as a fish, jumping all the time, a woman will have to pay for it, her home will be destroyed.'

Listening to all this from the maacha, Kulsum had actually had the impulse to jump. Did the old fool have any idea of her abilities? Tamiz had been on his way back home the previous evening after harvesting rice all day in the Khiyar. This was the first time he had gone outside the village to work for a living. He had brought back at least two rupees, less three annas. Two years before the famine, it was not a small sum at all. He had got 8 seers of rice too. Kulsum was at the Mondols' when Tamiz had got home that evening. Returning a little early the next morning, she had found that her stepson had gone to Nijgirirdanga to inspect the crop and the harvesting on the Mondols' field, after which he had been to the Katlahar Lake with the fishing net, returning late in the afternoon with a catch of catfish. He might be a fisherman's son, but when it came to fishing he was not exactly an expert. The fine rice of Khiyar was crying to be eaten with fish, though, which was why he had been to the lake with the fishing net. A slender-grained rice, a spicy preparation of fish with diagonally sliced aubergine, a daal, and a mash of tender potatoes— the excitement of cooking such an elaborate meal had led Kulsum to be more garrulous with Tamiz than she usually was. Maybe they had laughed together a little excessively too. But then why blame Kulsum? Her husband made demands of her constantly, leaving her with no opportunity to share a light moment with her son. Right from the beginning he had been entertaining her with stories about Khiyar, where every landowner had a hundred-and-fifty, two hundred, five hundred, even a thousand acres. If you stood on their land, you could only see paddy stalks as far as the eye could see. Traders came from distant lands to buy rice there, packing hundreds of seers of it in sacks and leaving again on the train for faraway places. Talora, Kahalu— these were the places with railway stations, where sacks of rice were piled up on verandas. But despite the bountiful harvest, the people of Khiyar were supposed to be such misers that they offered none of it to those who came begging for food, even barring their doors at night to travellers. When a land has no water, its people usually have a dearth of kindness in their hearts. Here there were no rivers or canals, only large lakes. But these were not Allah's gifts, for they had been dug by men. When there were no rivers, how could there be floods? Kulsum had not been able to stop laughing when Tamiz made a droll imitation of how a sharecropper's daughter-in-law had jumped out of her skin, screaming, on being told that the bite of floodwater could gouge out wounds on the leg, 'What do you mean? How can water bite? Does it have teeth?' But the happiness of Khiyar's people might be short-lived. New waves were rolling in from the north and the west, and the sharecroppers, who cultivated the land on behalf of the jotedars, as the middlemen were known, were closing ranks to store all their rice in their own homes. 'What are you saying?' Encouraged by Kulsum's astonishment, Tamiz had turned grave, reassuring her that there was a war on somewhere, which everyone was troubled by, so that the leaders of the sharecroppers were unable to decide on a course of action. But what did they have to do with the war? Tamiz had found it a little difficult to answer this question of Kulsum's. Still, he had informed her that the war was driving prices up. He had seen for himself that beef was now being sold at four annas a seer in the town. He would have brought back a seer or so of beef two days ago had it not been so expensive. Kerosene had disappeared from the shops—that the Mondols had to buy the kerosene for their lamps in the town at a high price on the black market was all on account of the war. Why should prices rise because of the war, though? Instead of responding to Kulsum's curiosity, Tamiz had resorted to telling stories about things in the town, which he had to pass through when travelling to and from Khiyar. The people there all drank tea at roadside tea shops, where the hot tea was served in small earthen pots. Apparently white sugar had become scarce because of the war, and so they drank tea made with brown sugar, two paise a cup. Tamiz had learnt his lesson after trying a cup and scalding his tongue, never again. The town people weren't straightforward, they fooled one another with clever words, charged eight annas or ten for what should cost four annas. The restaurants there served many different kinds of food—they slaughtered dogs and passed their meat off as mutton. That was why, whatever else Tamiz might do in the town, he never ate beef. He couldn't be fooled, even if he was from the eastern villages—it hadn't taken him long to become wise to the tricks there. Then take the women. How they talked, how they rolled their hips when walking, all women of marriageable age who would have had two or three children by now had they been married, they went to school clasping their books to their breasts, in the rickshaws they wrapped themselves in their saris like veils and yet peeped at the sights and talked to one another—Tamiz had given all these details, accompanied by exaggerated movements of his body that made Kulsum break into giggles. But how was Tamiz's father supposed to be interested in all this? When he was home he slept most of the time, or else drew on his hookah, or dozed on the doorstep. The one time that Tamiz had returned home after a long gap was after his first journey outside the village. Wasn't Kulsum supposed to be happy that her son had come back home with the money he had earned? So what if he was her stepson, so what if he was the son of her rival, so what if she hadn't given birth to him—he was still her son, wasn't he?

All these memories from long ago, the exuberance from the past, the happiness before the famine—all of them surged through the troubled times that had passed since then to bubble up in Kulsum's heart. She had not given birth to a child from her own womb. So whether you talked of a son or of a daughter, Tamiz was both of these for her. When this surge of emotion spilled out of her heart, her entire body thrilled to it, and to escape this infestation she suddenly grew desperate to find fault with Tamiz. But then she was an illiterate woman, the daughter of a fakir; how was she to find a flaw in the strapping young man that Tamiz was? Instead, she took advantage of Tamiz's father sleeping like the dead to steal some of his anger with his son and taste it—do you *have* to go to Khiyar in search of work? But there was less and less of work to be had with every passing day, this was true too. Not too long ago, even eleven or twelve years ago, old-timers used to say, sowing, weeding, reaping—all sorts of jobs were available right here in Girirdanga and Nijgirirdanga, on both sides of the lake. Apparently there weren't enough people looking for work then. And in case something needed to be done at short notice, Pocha's son Kasimuddi, who lived across the lake, had to be sent for. He was as stupid as his father, didn't own even a sliver of land, and lived in other farmers' huts or cowsheds or verandas. People would beg and plead with him when they needed a tree trimmed or a house repaired. And look, since then a thousand Kasimuddis had sprung up in every direction. All the bastards were in search of work. So many people died in the famine, so many more sold their house and land and went away, but still the number of people never decreased. All those who had sold their land and house but not left the village were desperate to work as hired hands. But where was the work? Earlier the sharecroppers hired daily labourers, but now they even set their own babies in arms to work in the fields. All right, all understandable. What choice did Tamiz have but to go to Khiyar for work? But consider what his father was saying, consider it well. Why all this flirtation with women when you go to Khiyar? Tamiz's father knew everything, Kulsum could imagine too, they weren't good people over at Khiyar. Whenever they spotted young men, working men, they set their daughters to trap them. They got their daughters to marry these men and then kept them in their own homes, forcing the grooms to work on the land that they had taken on lease, to look after the cattle, to build their houses for them. Kneading clay and making walls with it was hard work. The young men became permanent members of their families. The witches cast their spells and the men passed their entire lives as their slaves, not even remembering their own parents any more. A man settling down in his wife's home—the whole thing suddenly appeared intolerable to Kulsum. Not for nothing had Tamiz's father become despondent. Let me tell you, he was no ordinary man. No one knew whose call he answered in his sleep when he walked out at night, or where he went, or how far. People said so many things about Tamiz's father, but no matter what he did in his sleep, there was no match for him when it came to hard work. It was the people of Majhipara who used to enjoy the fish that Tamiz's father caught in Katlahar Lake before it passed into Sharafat Mondol's control. Back then Tamiz's father could snare carp weighing 6 or 7 seers each even with his ripped fishing net. Those little nets would often sink to the bottom of the lake under the weight of the fish, forcing him to wade neck-deep into the water to reel the net back in. The veteran fishermen would say, 'You'd better be careful going in there. All the fish come running when you cast your net. Not a good sign.' Some of them frightened him further. 'You'll be in serious trouble if even a single murrel is caught in your net.' Some had observed that his grandfather Baghar Majhi's extraordinary abilities flowed in his blood. But then all this was a long time ago. Tamiz's mother ran the household then, or perhaps it was even earlier, when Tamiz's father was not even married. But Kulsum's grandfather Cherag Ali knew the truth, which was that Tamiz's father's ancestors had nothing to do with it. He drew his strength from the fig tree. But with Katlahar Lake under Mondol's control now, where was he to demonstrate his fishing prowess? How was Kulsum to believe her grandfather? Ever since she had come here, long before her marriage, she had always seen Tamiz's father either drowsy or asleep. Mondol had leased the lake just the other day, the year after the famine, but Tamiz's father had been this way even earlier. But yes, apparently he was a changed man when he began to work—on the land, he toiled as hard as three labourers. And when the same man came home, he slept and then sleepwalked. But then sleep for Tamiz's father didn't mean just closing his eyes and snoring; he moved about, he walked, he did many things. People admired him greatly, but for all their respect and fear of him, his son didn't bother to obey him. Why? Since his father didn't like it, why did Tamiz have to run to Khiyar every year for work? He had been away for some twenty days now; who knew what he was doing in the rains there? The aush paddy was being harvested on Mondol's land here across the lake, with Harmatullah having taken on the

entire land for sharecropping. Amon paddy seeds would be brought
from Beejtola for sowing after the harvest. There was no dearth of
work, but Tamiz was too full of himself. He had wanted to sharecrop
Sharafat Mondol's land here, but when Mondol didn't agree, he had
stomped off to Khiyar. But then you were only going to be a daily
labourer there, no one was going to let you sharecrop their land.
There too you'd have to work on the fields through the day, getting
drenched to the skin all the while. Maybe he was being served his
meals on the veranda of a sharecropper's house by his plump wife or
coquettish daughter, but it wasn't as though the whores were feeding
him out of generosity. Obviously they were spinning a web around
him, tying him to the post. Kulsum knew full well all the tricks they
would be up to.

A lizard confirmed her surmise with approving clicks. Actually
it was probably not a lizard at all, but, more likely, Tamiz's father
mumbling his support of her suspicions while turning over on the
floor. What was he saying? Whom had he discussed things with
when he went out last night? Had Kulsum's grandfather appeared in
Tamiz's father's dream with a sign? If only she could make out what
he was saying! Kulsum lay on her stomach on the floor, bringing her
ear close to Tamiz's father's lips to listen closely. Without waking
up, Tamiz's father raised his lungi a little higher, placing his hands
on his knees, and began to snore loudly instead of mumbling. When
Kulsum tried to lower his garment, he stopped snoring and smacked
his lips as though he had tasted something delicious. Had Cherag Ali
slipped away from Tamiz's father's dream then? Or was he rolling
all his words back into his throat himself? As Tamiz's father noisily
swallowed all that he had said, the words faded, taking their place
deep inside the kernel of a dream beyond Kulsum's reach.

Instead of the words reaching Kulsum's ears, it was the rotten
smell of fish from Tamiz's father's mouth that drifted up her nostrils.
Climbing up her sharp, if not quite hooked, nose, the familiar stench
from his mouth penetrated her stomach. Not only did it hit her throat,
but she also felt it nudging her brain. The odour of putrefying fish

was all over her tongue now. Spitting repeatedly beneath the maacha to get rid of it, Kulsum brought her nose close to her husband's. This should have dulled her hunger, but it had just the opposite effect. Her inert appetite began to whirl in desperation, moving down from her stomach to her abdomen and then to her chest via the stomach again, even climbing to her throat. Not that all these different parts of the body were shaken and stirred at the same time—with each blink of her eyes, it was a different organ that conveyed its hunger to her. But then Kulsum knew a trick to overcome this man-eating whorish hunger of hers. She had known how to do it in other ways ever since she was born, but had acquired this new trick a couple of years ago, during the famine. What sort of trick? If only she could get her fill of a strong smell of some kind, her stomach felt bloated. But she must not spit. Every time the saliva rose in her throat she had to let it gather and then swallow it—this would be as effective as eating a light daal. She would feel as though she wanted to throw up, but she must not, for vomiting would empty her stomach out again.

The very thought of it made the vaporous flavour of paan and tobacco play in Kulsum's nostrils. This aroma from Boikuntho's mouth, Boikuntho from the market at Golabari, arrived without the person, but then this happened quite often, though it did not satiate her hunger. Entering through her nose, the smell dropped as far as her throat before rising to her brain, which became redolent with the scent for a long time, before it disappeared without Kulsum's knowledge.

In the yard the ashes in the oven covered with a clay pot had turned to slush after last night's rain. But she was no longer in a hurry to extract a couple of lumps of coal from the sludge and put them in the room before going into the yard again and then to the pond to assuage her hunger. A narrow path ran uphill on the other side of the pond for some distance before joining the main road to Golabari built by the district board. Was that a faint aroma of paan and tobacco borne in by the monsoon wind? The front door of their house faced east. Her grandfather used to say, 'The doors of kings are to the south, eastern doors are down in the mouth.' Like in Madaripara and Dargatola on the banks of the river Jomuna, the front doors of houses hereabouts also faced east. Cherag Ali was delighted to have found a hut with a thatched roof and an east-facing front door in Kalam majhi's bamboo grove. 'Doesn't it look just like one of those houses?' Then, when she shifted to Tamiz's father's house on the other side of the pond after her marriage, its front door turned out to be facing eastwards too. Even the slightest of breezes outside cooled the house. The combined smells of the grass and leaves and moss, of the small fry in the shallow water, the fresh fishlike smell of the carp who had set up their household by the mudbanks, human shit and cow dung—dried under a scorching sun or soggy in the rain—percolated into the room all the way to the maacha, sometimes making the confined emptiness on the earthen floor or in the entire room feel lighter, and sometimes heavier.

These smells were far from new to Kulsum. Long before her marriage to Tamiz's father, when she lived in her father's thatched hut, all the washing of clothes and dishes, cleaning of teeth, the after-shit rinsing, the bathing—all of it was done here at this pond. Before they sank a draw-well at Kalam majhi's house, even the water they drank came from this pond. It used to be a lake then, however. When the northern half was filled with silt from the great flood, Kalam majhi laid more soil on top of it and started growing capsicum and aubergine, claiming the land for himself. All this had happened in front of Kulsum's own eyes. But, oh Allah, even marriage did not change her routine.

Sitting by the pond, she could make out even with her eyes shut that the Sakirdars' son, who went to school, was cycling along the narrow path on the opposite side. And Ahid Poramanik was on his way to the Mondols' with a load of paddy.

Sitting beneath a palm tree, Kulsum was crouched over the pond, rinsing out her mouth, the murky water not changing its colour even after she spat out the powdered mixture of ash and coal she used to clean her teeth. Gazing at the unchanged shade of

the surface of the pool as she noisily rubbed her white teeth with
the index finger of her right hand, rinsing her mouth periodically,
Kulsum realized unerringly that Gofur kolu from Dokkhinpara was
on his way to Golabari with an entourage. It made no difference
to her whether it was Gofur kolu or not—she would continue to
splash as much water as possible on her brownish face to make it
appear fairer. But Gofur kolu was an unapologetic conversationalist,
and Kulsum was in any case dying to hear what he had to say. But
then, even though he was garrulous, Gofur bhai was an efficient
man. When his father had fallen too ill to operate the oil press any
more, they had practically been reduced to begging. But Gofur had
ignored the traditional business of his clan to trail after the younger
Mondol son, Kader. Joining the frenzy over Kader's political party,
the Muslim League, had reaped big benefits for him. He had got
himself a job at Kader's shop. Sharafat Mondol had been the first to
set up a kerosene shop in this area; Kader ran the shop. Within a year
he had expanded the business. Earlier a horse-drawn carriage would
ferry six or seven tins of oil from the town twice a week; now, not
even entire overloaded ox carts could meet the demand in the area.
Gofur was in charge of all this. But he didn't brag about it—nor did
he nurse a grudge over the fact that, like everyone else in Majhipara,
Tamiz's father also referred to him contemptuously as the son of an
oil grinder. Whenever he ran into Kulsum he would stop for a few
minutes, tell her what was going on at the Golabari market, ask after
Tamiz's father, inquire when Tamiz would be back, and give one
or two examples of how Kulsum's grandfather interpreted dreams.
These days he was inevitably accompanied by a couple of youngsters.
The League was becoming quite popular, and he had drafted them
to the cause, often accompanying Kader when the workload at the
shop wasn't heavy. Which is fine, for you have to comply with your
employer's whims, after all, but why are you taking that bitch along
today? Where was Bulu majhi's starving wife Abiton off to at the
crack of dawn, stuck to the oil grinder's arse? You brazen whore,
you're about to be divorced by your husband any day, how dare you

walk on the road today clinging to the underarm of a man from a different sect? Have you no shame at all?

'Didn't you lock the door last night, Kulsum?' Before she could answer, Gofur continued, 'The water was knee-deep at Taltala, so I had to make a detour and go past your house. I found the door open. When I peeped in I saw you were asleep. No sign of Tamiz's father.'

As he spoke he transferred the bundle from his right hand to his left. 'I assumed he had gone to the bamboo grove. But when I passed the grove I didn't see him. Did he leave you alone at home?'

No sooner did Kulsum feel a pang of uneasiness at the thought that this man had peeped into the house in Tamiz's father's absence and seen her asleep than Abiton the famished wife snarled at her, 'Why do you sleep with the doors and windows open? It was different in your father's house. What did you have there anyway? There was nothing for a thief to steal. But here you have utensils if not anything else. If the few fishing nets Mamu still has are stolen, even selling you will not fetch their price, you know.'

Abiton was a fisherman's daughter. Tamiz's father was bound to be some sort of uncle or grand-uncle or cousin or something of hers—a connection she had used to be snide about Kulsum's parents' house. You daughter of nothing but a fisherman, you're going to marry an oil grinder's son a few days from now. We'll see where your kinship with Tamiz's father goes then. Kulsum could have said something nasty to her face right now, but Gofur kolu urged Abiton to leave. 'Let's go. I have to meet Kader bhai in Golabari by nine. The meeting at Joragaach is at ten. We won't get there in less than an hour, come on now, hurry up.'

Oh lord! How much more was Kulsum to be witness to? Now that he was employed at Mondol's shop, Gofur kolu set the time by the watch these days. Now he even attended meetings. The son of an oil grinder would always be the son of an oil grinder, but just look how he bragged. The sting in Abiton's reproaches made Kulsum angry with Gofur kolu. Her grandfather used to be extra deferential to his father, listening to the details of his dreams with great concentration in the hope of getting a quarter-litre of oil in exchange. And now the son of an oil grinder was strutting about with a fisherman's wife. No one even bothered to shame them in this accursed village.

3

Still, raging at Gofur kolu would not wipe out the sting in Abiton's taunts. Kulsum rose from the pond to go back home, stomping her feet harder than necessary. But not a single one of her heavy steps descended on Abiton's buttocks in the form of kicks. On the contrary, the whore's invectives seeped into Kulsum through her feet to raise a wave of acute discomfort in her body. No matter how furious she might be with the starving bitch, Kulsum could not vent her anger like all the other women in the village. Since her father was gone and had always been gone, what right did she have to retaliate at the barbs about her family's poverty? The father she had never known had died vomiting his guts out one full moon night in the month of Choitro or Boishakh, when she was so young that she had barely started crawling. Then, she no longer remembered how many years later, her mother took the hand of a peasant who lived east of the Jomuna, took Kulsum in her arms, and moved to a sandbank on the eastern side of the river, a sandbank whose name Kulsum still did not know. Soon after she grew out of her mother's arms, she began to walk around clutching her grandfather's fingers. Cherag Ali the fakir used to wander through different lands, singing. Perhaps he had run into his dead son's wife on that sandbank on the Jomuna, perhaps it had been Kulsum's mother who had handed over her daughter to the father of her first husband, wiping her eyes with the end of her dirty green sari. But no one brought up the matter of which village her grandfather belonged to. Not only was he assured of alms at certain houses, but it was also given that if he visited a family at any time on Friday before the prayers, he would be given half a wicker potful of rice to put in his sling bag. On Eid he was bound to get a lungi—old or new—from someone. Normally he would have had to go alone, but Cherag Ali never accepted an invitation unless it included his granddaughter. In Chandandaha, across the canal to the west of Madaripara, in the house where the Akanda family lived, Inspector Hafiz's mother had once dreamt, in the early hours of the morning following the night of the Muharram moon, of Hafiz's father eating beef curry and rice, after which she had decided to offer the same meal to three fakirs. Cherag Ali was one of the three. Spotting Kulsum with Cherag, the long-standing maid of the family began to grumble, 'Look, he's brought his granddaughter along. Has your granddaughter been invited too, fakir?' The deep, hoarse voice of the bitch of a maid turned the aroma of the beef curry with chickpeas wafting out of the huge kitchen by the yard into dry thistles that split open Kulsum's belly and throat—what if they were forced to go back without a meal? But her grandfather Cherag Ali cared for no one. He spoke directly to the woman of the house. Addressing Hafiz's mother, he said, 'My granddaughter is with me. We're fakirs from Madaripara, we're forbidden from accepting invitations alone. If we eat alone our prayers are not accepted.' Another thing, as long as they lived in Madaripara, it was considered repugnant to speak during the Friday afternoon meal—he would have to be silent. Kulsum would take the responsibility on her grandfather's behalf for asking for more rice, or another piece of meat, or an extra spoon of daal, or some more jaggery to go with the curd. Whether it was fate or a vow, whether it was a matter of offering food to fakirs, or even circumcisions, post-death rituals, and feasts, all of these were usually held on Friday. How was Cherag Ali to eat well without his granddaughter nearby? Well-off people lived in the villages beyond the Madaripara canal—Chandandaha, Shimultola, Shakda, Goswamibari, Bhabanihat, Dargatola. Chandandaha, for instance, was crammed with houses with actual tin roofs and walls. In Shimultola the Talukdars lived in an enormous brick house with corridors. The Sarkars lived in a brick house too in Bhabanihat. There were always naming ceremonies or circumcisions or funerals or forty-day observances or weddings at these places. Shah Shaheb's dargah at Dargatola was practically Cherag Ali's second home. On Thursday evenings he was assured, at the very least, of dates and milk or a thin treacle of rice and jaggery.

The shrine was always redolent with the scent of jaggery along with the fragrance of joss sticks. Kulsum had never been ignored for being a fakir's daughter. Or had she? She didn't know. But even if she had, she had faced no trouble getting her share of the sweet shirni.

The rainy season meant suffering. It was difficult to go out, and moreover, people did not want to offer alms till the aush paddy had been harvested in the month of Bhadro. They didn't even have dreams in this period. After the harvest there was an epidemic of dreams. People rushed to Cherag Ali whenever they had a nightmare. 'Fakir, tell me, last night I dreamt that the water in our well had turned hot. My back burnt terribly when I drew the water in a bucket and poured it over myself. What does this dream mean?' Taking his book out of his sling bag, Cherag Ali turned over the pages slowly. Touching his tongue with his fingertip before turning a page, he would say, 'At what time exactly did you have the dream?' If the dreamer stumbled over the answer, Cherag Ali would fire the next question, 'Which side were you sleeping on last night, left or right?' Putting the book down without taking his eyes off the pages, he drew squares on the floor of the yard with a small stick, all the while continuing with his barrage of questions, and, despite half of the two dozen or so questions he had asked remaining unanswered, explained the dream perfectly. Warm water in the well was an assurance of coming into some money. Explanations such as these always earned him some cash, no matter how little. But people stopped having dreams during the rains and then in the months of Kaartik and Aghran. Their hardship never eased in Kaartik. But no adversity could overcome

Cherag Ali. Whether he was starving or not, his explanations never lost their acuity. To him Kaartik was a pregnant month.

A pregnant woman grows lean with a son
The mother's blood makes the boy grow.

Kulsum hated all this when she was famished. 'What drivel is this!'

'It's not drivel, try to understand.' Cherag Ali explained. 'The earth is pregnant now. A two-month pregnancy—Kaartik and Agrhan. A pregnant women withers as the baby in her womb drinks up all her blood. Once she has given birth in Poush, though, all her sufferings come to an end.' As he spoke, the misery drained away from Kulsum's grandfather's face, for he was delighted that the austerity of Kaartik was nothing but preparation for prosperity. But Cherag Ali wasn't one to squander his happiness languishing at home. Jumping to his feet without warning he drew his sling bag to himself, saying. 'Come bubu, let's go for berakura. At least we'll get one meal.' Going for berakura meant begging—it was the word used by the people of Madaripara. No one looked askance at him for the way he earned a living. On the contrary, it was him they turned to during minor crises, or when difficulties arose, or to have their dreams and nightmares interpreted. But this was Kalijug—Judgement Day was not far away, the number of people who paid generously for advice had dwindled, and the fakir was forced to beg. This should not have been anything to be dismissive of, but people seemed to be looking at them with contempt, although Kulsum wasn't sure. Her grandfather walked ahead, a black cap on his head, dressed in a robe that might also have been black once, but had so many patches of different colours now that it was virtually impossible to discern the original shade. A faded sling bag hung from his shoulder, with his book in it. And when householders offered him rice, or shopkeepers at the market gave him potatoes and onions and gourds and chillies and seasonal mangos or bananas, he held out the same bag. Kulsum carried a tin plate for the coins. The fakir walked swiftly, his reedy

legs like stilts. Many confused the stick in his hand for a third leg.
Kulsum had grown used to skipping alongside her grandfather, and
she could no longer slow down even if she tried. But then no one had
faulted Kulsum for the way she walked when she lived in Madaripara.
Or had they? Kulsum didn't know. Ever since she had moved here,
particularly after she began to run Tamiz's father's household, she
began to confuse some of the criticism from the women of Majhipara
with what the people in Madaripara used to say. It was also possible
that she had attributed all the sarcastic comments she had heard in
the past to the women of Girirdanga and Nijigirirdanga. It wasn't as
though Madaripara was perfect in every respect. No one there was
well-off. There was scarcity all the year around, permanent hardship.
They wouldn't get a meal all day unless they crossed the creek to
beg for food on the other side. Theirs was a tiny village, with only a
handful of houses, each occupied by a relative of Cherag Ali's. The
Jomuna was to the east, with 2 miles of farmland in between. Barring
a few acres, all of it belonged to the Akandas of Chandandaha, the
Talukdars of Shimultola, the Khans of Rouhadaho, and the Mondols
of Goswamibari. The majority of the fakirs of Madaripara were
either sharecroppers or daily labourers. They owned tracts of fallow
land, which they boasted about frequently. But what was there to be
proud of? The old graveyard was situated there. An enormous siris
tree, several rohituka trees, and two sandpaper tree. Dens of djinns
and spirits. When anyone from the fakirs' clan died this was where
they were buried; but the living returned hastily after the burial, no
one dared visit the grave to pray afterwards. There was no sign of the
graveyard now.

Before the river changed its course, you had to walk 2 miles from
Madaripara to reach the Mulbari Ghat on the Jomuna. Cherag Ali
used to say that there hadn't even been a river there when his great-
grandfather's great-grandfather had been alive, that the Jomuna was
just a shy, slender creek then. Apparently the Madaris used to ride
across it on horseback whenever they wanted to fight the Christian
Englishmen. Eventually the British had won, about fifty or sixty

years after which the curse of a leader or fakir of the Madaris, or
perhaps a pir or a prophet, issued from this very graveyard, caused
an earthquake, a calamitous one, which turned the creek into a river.
Cherag Ali had never clearly revealed what the curse was, why it had
been delivered, or who had been cursed. When Kulsum asked, he
would hum one of his verses.

> A wild fury split the earth wide open
> All the lakes and rivers were in turmoil
> The Brahmaputra flowed into the Jomuna
> The Kartowa became a shadow of itself
> A majestic river had turned to mud
> The fakir found his address close to the lake

So when the creek-turned-river began to flood its western bank,
Cherag Ali rumbled, 'Let the whore flow this way to Madaripara.
We'll see then.' When the current still didn't slow down, he issued
a warning. His teacher and followers, his family and his relations,
whose curses had converted the creek into a river, were all buried
here in this graveyard. Cherag Ali promised to bequeath his name
to a street dog if the river dared to flow a mere foot beyond the
graveyard. But even after it had swallowed the entire cemetery with
the graves of Cherag Ali's ancestors and relations and the siris and
rohituka and sandpaper trees with their resident djinns and spirits,
the Jomuna showed no signs of receding. Even the dogs glorified
with Cherag Ali's name were wiped out. But then the river did come
to an abrupt halt at the edge of Madaripara. Everyone realized that
the Jomuna had only paused for a rest—the bitch would resume
devouring everything in her path as soon as she shook off her
lethargy. So the people of Madaripara began to move out while they
still could. But who would persuade Cherag Ali to budge? He seemed
to have received a divine revelation to the effect that the Jomuna
was completely satiated, that even one more clod of earth would
give it indigestion. The whore would never dare digest Madaripara.

But Cherag Ali was plunged in doubt when his nephew Samad Fakir came to him for a reading of his early-morning dream, in which he had drowned in the muddy currents of the Jomuna. It was not good to dream of murky water. This was a portent of illness, you know. It could signify sickness, disease, harassment, even imprisonment. But Samad was a good swimmer, why would he dream of drowning? Dreams like these never spelt anything propitious. To keep the implication of Samad's dream at bay, Cherag Ali told everyone he set eyes on, 'Madaripara might be a small village, but it goes back a long way. Our great-grandfather's great-grandfather fought against the Christian Britishers to protect the honour of the shrine. The blessings of our guardians are with the village. Powerful blessings. The river won't dare harm us, you'll see.' Nullifying the blessings of the ancestors, of Cherag Ali's own auspicious dream at dawn while sleeping on his right side, and of all his prophecies, the river rested for less than a year before striking in the middle of the rainy season at the eastern areas of Madaripara. Within a few days it had swallowed the land to the north, the south and the east before stopping at the edge of the creek. But Cherag Ali's cousin's three-month-old son, Samad Fakir's young calf, a flock of newborn ducks belonging to Bhulu Fakir, and a scuttle of rice belonging to lame Laimuddin could not be saved eventually. Everyone else stood on the Akandas' land on the western bank of the canal with their utensils, their bamboo posts and fences, their pillows and rugs, screaming as they watched the scale on which the Jomuna feasted. Cherag Ali's alertness had come too late to save his house of bamboo. But from the black cap on his head to his multicoloured patchwork robe, from his walking stick to the iron chains wound around his neck and hanging down to his chest, from his two-stringed dotara and sling bag with the book to Kulsum—none of these had been lost. He spent a few days with his possessions on the Akandas' land, beneath a thatched roof put up by Inspector Hafiz's mother, after which he lived for several days at the shrine at Dargahtala. A number of new devotees gathered there, reading the namaz five times a day and converting the shrine into a mosque. They wouldn't even allow feasts. Cherag Ali belonged to the Madari school of fakirs—how was he to survive all these rules and regulations of the Shariat? But Kulsum knew that her grandfather wasn't obstinate about following the traditions of his clan. It was just that if he had to read the namaz five times a day, observe the roza and listen to the sermons of the maulanas, he would have no time to wander about all day as he liked to. And how, for that matter, would he make a living? That explained why Kulsum's grandfather had given up the luxury of sleeping beneath a tin roof on the paved veranda of the shrine and moved to this hovel with a woven roof of grass set amidst tall reeds in Kalam majhi's bamboo grove in the village of Girirdanga.

But the old coot alone knew what attracted him to this place. It wasn't even a village to speak of. In the early days she had had to hear comments like 'how can such a small child have such a big appetite?' or 'brazen girl!' if she happened to ask for some more rice at a meal with her grandfather. Whenever there was an altercation, she was dismissed as a 'fakir's daughter' or 'fakir's granddaughter'. All right, you couldn't stand living in the shrine, but couldn't you have stayed with the others who had settled down for all those months on the Akandas' land in Chandandaha? Soon his relatives moved deep into the area around the river, some to the island in Gobindopur or Dharabarsha, others even farther to Madarganj and Sarishabari on the eastern side of the Jomuna. He would at least have got some land to farm if he had moved with them. It was best for people who belonged to the banks of the Jomuna to live under its protection. But who was going to tell him that? Whenever anyone suggested moving, Cherag Ali was full of bravado. 'We were never migrants. What should I move somewhere else for?' But all this was talk. Nothing but an excuse to chant his rhymes and beg for a living—he was so lazy that he had never tried to work on the field. Kulsum's grandfather was drunk with joy at having found shelter in Kalam majhi's bamboo grove. In the monsoon, it rained every day, during which time the old man curled up and revised his verses. There was Katlahar Lake, near whose head lived a djinn or spirit of some sort, Cherag Ali's father or relative or some such person—Cherag Ali seemed to have dedicated all the verses he knew to him.

Kulsum was not happy with anything. The people of Majhipara weren't generous, didn't invite them to meals often, and she wasn't even sure whether they circumcised the boys. And their departed ancestor seemed to have a heart of stone, never appearing in his descendants' dreams. Market day at Golabari was twice a week, and once at Jorgachha. Even if grandfather and granddaughter went along on all three days, shouting at the top of their voice, what they earned was not enough. They starved quite often. On top of which, whenever a wind sprang up at night, the bamboo trees began to knock against one another. When they lived at Madaripara Kulsum's grandfather did not ever have to pass the bamboo grove at night. Once darkness fell each of the bamboo shafts was occupied by a spirit. And here the grove was their permanent residence. But whenever she mentioned this the fakir would launch into a lecture. 'Have you seen how rich everyone in this area is? Our forefathers had settled down here, so many of them died here, their spirits still move about here, this isn't just another village.'

'Didn't you say your forefathers are buried in Madaripara? How many graves can one man have?'

'You think one man can't have more than one grave? Of course he can.' Cherag Ali offered examples. 'In Sherpur the same pir has two resting places, two shrines. One of them holds his head, and the other, his body. The pir's enemies had cut him into two pieces, and so he was buried in two places too. Two miles apart.'

'Were all your forefathers cut up into two or three pieces after death?'

Upset by such a cruel comment, Cherag Ali would warn Kulsum softly, 'Not so loud, bubu. The ancestors can hear everything.' But then he knew the technique for cheering her up too, which he applied immediately by reciting one of his rhymes.

Munshi lives in the fig tree to the north
Beneath him swim all the fierce murrels

'You made up this rhyme when you saw the lake.'

Cherag Ali smiled at the innocent girl's suspicion, for he did not have the ability to make up new couplets. A man's heart held so many different kinds of sounds, some of which emerged when he was sad, and others, in moments of fear. Sounds of grief were different from those of pleasure. Innumerable verses were stored in the layers of his body, having flown in with the tide from the blood of his grandfather and great-grandfather. Which of them he would sing at any particular moment was not his own choice. Kulsum realized that her grandfather was right—how could he have composed so many verses all by himself? He had inherited all of them. Kulsum had heard some of them often enough to have memorized them. Cherag Ali sang them on the streets, and at markets and fairs, accompanying himself on the dotara. Kulsum had to complete the song when he stopped halfway. Sometimes history dripped from her grandfather's verses, with lines from other poems slipping in—Kulsum caught him out every time. Lots of people at Dargatola in Madaripara knew these songs. Sometimes they ran into listeners who could even hum along during the first few lines, though only Boikuntho from Golabari knew some of the songs in their entirety, and half or quarter of the others. It was he who had taken them to Kalam majhi's shop in the Golabari market. It was on his instigation that Kalam majhi had made room for grandfather and granddaughter in a hut in his bamboo grove. Kulsum may have been young then, but she remembered everything. The Hindu man had ruined her future by arranging for them to stay here. What Gofur kolu said nowadays after all the meetings he had attended with Sharafat Mondol was right—'Hindus are one race, Muslims, another.' Why else would Boikuntho have ensured her utter ruination by arranging for them to stay here permanently only so that he could listen to Cherag Ali sing?

Bulu majhi's starving wife Abiton had gone far away by now, but Kulsum's rage with the people of Girirdanga and the climate of Girirdanga would not abate. She kept rubbing the end of her stained sari on her face. The constant rubbing made the tip of her nose smart, but it also made the smell of the grass and leaves and moss from the pond and of the shit and cow dung and the earth, along with the fish-like stench of the small and large fish, fade gradually and disappear. The fragrance of paan and tobacco on Boikuntho's breath took this opportunity to enter, making her senses reel. Accompanying the heady scent, the twanging of Cherag Ali's dotara made acidic clouds gather to Kulsum's left and right, in front of her and behind her, and even overhead. Amid the staleness of the smell and the sound, the rain fell on her head. Long, long ago, they had raced through just such a spell of torrential rain to take shelter in Kalam majhi's shop. It was market day at Golabari, and the rain was pelting down in the evening. Responding to Boikuntho's calls, her grandfather and she, clutching his hand, ran helter-skelter between Mukunda Saha's and Kalam majhi's shops. The skies had opened up. The signs were not good in any respect. Her grandfather knew so many things, how could he not have realized that there was no sense in staying outdoors or moving into a new house on that dark, stormy night? In fact, often it had so happened on rainy mornings in Madaripara that, lying face down on the floor and strumming his dotara, Cherag Ali would try to send Kulsum over to the neighbour's. 'Go to Samad's mother, bubu, and ask for a bowl of rice. We aren't going out today.' But Kulsum wasn't willing to be shouted at. When she pleaded for them to go to the Akandas' in Chandandaha across the creek instead despite the rain, Cherag Ali told her, 'We must stay indoors when it rains.' The thin rain brought forth a song in his baritone.

> Clouds gathered in the sky, a throne on an elephant
> Majnu stayed at home, his murmurs calling Allah's name
> Do not go out, any of you, for a month or even two
> The wanton rains will force us to starve in the future.

But then if all this was Allah's doing, why would Cherag Ali have been evicted from the paved veranda of the shrine? The new set of disciples had been unhappy with his heretical ways right from the beginning, and besides, there was a mosque on the spot, which meant no blasphemy would be tolerated. But then if all it took to get permanent shelter on the veranda was to make a vow to read the namaz, shouldn't Cherag Ali have done just that? The imam of the mosque wouldn't have allowed women to sleep in the shrine, though. Was Cherag Ali supposed to abandon his granddaughter, then? Of course, he would aver loudly, 'These bastards are a different sort, they've captured our shrine, I wouldn't stay here even if they begged. We didn't become fakirs overnight. We're Madaris, our ancestors will curse us if we eat anything other than what we get as alms.' And yet all his bluster was never in the presence of the imam or the devotees, not even within the shrine, but outside, on the road, when no one but Kulsum was with him. Still, no matter how much the old man feared the new disciples, no matter that he had left the shrine out of his fear of the imam, when he said all this he would start singing. The twanging of his dotara rang so loudly in Kulsum's head even after all these years that the haze of the tobacco vanished, as did the figure of Tamiz's father lying spreadeagled on the floor—from both her sight and her mind. As she took some rice from the maacha to cook, verses emerged from her throat, in tune with the notes of her grandfather's dotara.

4

'What's this, you're still sleeping? Wake up.'

It had been so late by the time she had gone to bed last night that the accursed sleep refused to abandon her now. Shoved unceremoniously by Bulu majhi, Kulsum shook herself awake, which reminded her that Bulu majhi had died last afternoon, and Tamiz's father had returned late at night after his burial, going to sleep without demanding food, for he had already eaten his fill at the Mondols'. Sharafat Mondol had given Bulu a posthumous reward by feeding the nine or ten members of the burial party to their hearts' content. The rice was from the land that Bulu had farmed with his own hands—it was delicious. Bulu had taken 4 acres of Mondol's land for sharecropping for the first time this year. Mondol, who had been very pleased with the aush harvest on it, had hesitated initially about giving the land to Bulu, because Bulu himself used to be the owner of the land, but had been forced to sell it to Mondol two and a half years ago during the famine. This year Bulu had implored him earnestly, and when Mondol's youngest son in particular pleaded his case, Mondol had relented. And then Bulu had produced a spectacular crop. All things considered, it was his own land, adjacent to the family house going back generations—how could it not respond to the superhuman labour he had put in despite his frailness? Maybe Allah had given him a lease of life for one more year just to ensure the aush harvest on his land. Or else his abdominal disease should have killed him long ago. His wife had escaped even earlier. Sharafat Mondol stood by for some time watching the pall-bearers eat, and Bulu's son Afaz was given several helpings of rice at his behest. Everyone got a single piece of fish, but Afaz was served two succulent slices. Famished after their hard work, the members of the burial party stuffed themselves. The sheer satisfaction of a sumptuous meal of fish curry led Tamiz's father to recount his grief and regret at Bulu's death with great relish to Kulsum. When his lament faded gradually and turned into the unbroken drone of snoring, all that Kulsum could do was to squat on the floor and polish off all the rice in the pot all by herself. Lying down next to Tamiz's father on the maacha, she found sleep eluding her. Bathed by the rain, moonlight flooded the yard, trickling in through the corner of the roof to lighten the darkness in the room. The rain had worn away much of the thatching this monsoon. When the roof had a hole, the rainwater could at least be collected in pots and pans, but how would they stave off the cold? If only Tamiz bought Kulsum a new sari, she could use her tattered one, along with Tamiz's old lungi and some rags, to stitch a quilt. The fine red and blue and green thread fluttered before her eyes in the dark. The pleasure of sleeping in the warmth of a new quilt in the coming winter made sleep descend heavily on Kulsum's eyes.

Her heart trembled when she woke up at Tamiz's shouts. He had returned after a long time—she hoped he wouldn't start scolding his father at once. The door was locked from within, which meant that Tamiz's father had spent the entire night asleep here on this maacha; he hadn't sleepwalked at all. Was it the weight of his grief for Bulu that had made him sleep through the night? But no matter how soundly he was sleeping now, the fact that he hadn't tired himself out walking about all night meant that he would wake up soon. And as soon as he did, his son would give him a talking-to. Kulsum usually felt a sense of relief when Tamiz was busy upbraiding his father, for he would not have the time then to be caustic with her. Then again, the thought of Tamiz's father's disconsolate expression at his son's admonitions made her relief crack.

Meanwhile she could again hear Tamiz's voice outside. 'When was Afaz's father buried?' He must be talking to someone. Kulsum took the opportunity to lift the lid of the aluminium pan, whereupon the scent of Tamiz's old shirt rose from it like smoke. A feminine voice was answering Tamiz outside. Putting the lid back on the pot, Kulsum raised her head and listened closely, realizing instantly that it was Abiton. Did the whore have no shame? She had married Gofur kolu just six months ago, after which she was forbidden from even setting foot in Majhipara. How could she be so brazen today? Leave alone her own parents' home or Majhipara, she had been rejected from all of Girirdanga for the rest of her life. Forget about spending time with Gofur kolu, the fishermen didn't even sell him anything. Although he was much better off after getting a job at Kader's shop, none of the people at Majhipara ever asked him for a loan. Given this situation, how could Kader enlist him to work for the League? He had had several meetings with the leaders of Majhipara, telling them, 'Whether he's an oil grinder or not, he's Muslim, isn't he? Yes or no? What is Abdul Gofoor's religion? Islam. Islam does not make these distinctions. All Muslims must unite now, how can we fight the Hindus unless we're united?' But then the fishermen's clan were even more united. No matter what Gofoor's qualities were as a human, neither he nor his wife could be pardoned for insulting the clan by marrying each other. Kader was irked by their decision. 'You'll be ejected from the Muslim community if you believe in castes like the Hindus do—do your realize that?' Bulu himself had been present at one of these meetings; he had actually divorced his wife three or four months earlier. And now it was on Kader's recommendation that he was getting a chance to sharecrop on Sharafat Mondol's land. But he too sat in grim silence, fuelling the fire of his clan's anger. At the final meeting, Kalam majhi deflated Kader with a single last-minute verbal punch: 'Talk to your father. Will you ever marry into a fisherman's family? Why don't you tell us what you really think of us?'

Back home Sharafat Mondol had presented more or less the same argument to his son. 'You're supporting the marriage of a fisherman's daughter to Kolu today, very well. But will you agree if one of them were to send a proposal for your sister's marriage?' Kader had retorted, 'Why should I object if the boy is educated?' He said that his elder brother was held in high regard everywhere because he had got not only an education but also a job. People lined up on both sides of the road for a glimpse when he entered the village in a carriage. And then many people envied him too. The logic was infallible. But when Sharafat Mondol said, 'Listen to me, Abdul Kader mian,' Kader lowered his eyes and literally presented his ears to his father on being addressed by his full name and the respectful appellation that followed it. 'You're working for the League,' his father told him. 'Elections are coming. If you want votes you must follow the rules of society. Try to understand what people want. Talk of books. All this talk of yours will not earn you votes.' Bringing up the elections had its effect. Mondol was also compelled to keep Gofoor from campaigning for the League in Girirdanga.

A man like Gofoor had been thoroughly humiliated for marrying this whore who now dared to visit Majhipara with her husband barely in his grave. Shame! Leaping to her feet as soon as she heard Abiton's voice, Kulsum opened the door and went out. Although he had seen her, Tamiz asked Abiton, 'Afaz's father was carrying the poison in his stomach for a long time, wasn't he?' Abiton walked away quickly in the direction of Golabari without replying. Looking at her retreating back with blazing eyes, Kulsum told Tamiz, 'Go inside,' and set off for the pond. 'Are you asleep, bajaan?' said Tamiz on entering, addressing his father.

The question cut through Tamiz's father's fog of sleep like a sharp rebuke. He jerked awake. This was a long-standing problem. His heart always thumped as soon as he woke up: Oh no, had the hours already slipped down the white bodies of the storks perched on the silk-cotton tree in the Mondols' yard all the way to their knees even before he had rubbed the sleep out of his eyes? To relieve himself of this anxiety, or to dispel the exhaustion it brought about, he usually climbed up on the maacha if he had been sleeping on the floor, or turned over on his side if he was already up there. Not that he could go back to sleep, but he panted out of exhaustion at having slept all this time. After all, sleeping was a form of work for Tamiz's father—it could even be called his favourite profession. He had to put in hard labour in his sleep, for that was when he moved about, searched for things, pondered and worried, felt anxious and agitated, planned and plotted. What made things more difficult for him was that he had no clear notion of what he searched for or worried about, what the causes of his anxiety or his agitation were. Which was why, no matter when he awoke, he could not get to his feet until he had rested for some time. But how could he rest now? Tamiz was in the room. And yet, Tamiz's recriminations were buried by the constant pricking of a snake or a scorpion beneath his back, and in a bid to extend this exemption, he grew furious with the invisible reptile and, muttering 'bastard son of a bastard', reached for an almost inaccessible part of his body to pull out an unfamiliar creature. It had several pointed wings on either side. Holding it up for a close look, he found the image of last evening's burial floating up dimly. He had picked it up at a two-day-old grave at the cemetery. A palm branch from the graveyard was very efficacious, second in strength only to fire and iron—no one would dare trouble you at night if you had one. It would be wise to keep it with him during his expeditions to the fig tree at the head of Katlahar Lake at night. But he had spent the entire night sleeping. What a waste! Despite his dismay at having squandered the darkness, Tamiz's father shut his eyes with the expectation of regaining his wasted nocturnal vigour. Naturally, it worked. The flock of sheep swam about in Katlahar Lake, struggling to stay afloat, moving through the water with great concentration in the hope of assuming their natural form of murrels once more. As he saw all this, Tamiz's father glanced at his son. He did not notice his only living child's stern eyes—in his offspring's shaggy black hair he saw a black turban on a figure holding an iron pan, with a chain around his neck.

'Are you unconscious or are you dead? Why don't you wake up?' Although Tamiz's admonition held a hint of familiar rhymes, it sounded so brutal to Tamiz's father that the pan that had materialized disappeared instantly in Tamiz's arm, somewhere between his wrist and his elbow, the chain around the neck merged into Tamiz's collarbone, and the black turban hid itself in Tamiz's head of hair. Climbing on to the maacha, Tamiz's father said, 'Is everything all right?' To avoid the risk of being scolded by his son, he took the initiative to pass on important information, rubbing his face and eyes and beard with both his hands. 'Have you heard about Bulu? Can you imagine, as alive as can be, goes out after a full meal, rice with . . .'

'I've heard.' Relieved from the effort of talking by a single word from Tamiz that cut him short, deprived of the opportunity of giving a mouth-watering description of Bulu's final meal, and unable to decide what to do now, Tamiz's father suddenly climbed down to the floor and, saying, 'It's late,' went off towards the pond, muttering to himself, 'I'm supposed to work on Shamsher's land today. It's Wednesday, isn't it?'

'Since we don't even have a pinch of land of our own, why should we do unpaid labour for the jomidar who owns all the land?' When his father went out instead of answering, Tamiz said loudly, 'Can the owner of the land you work on help you? Where's your own land?' It was difficult to counter this challenge. There was no possibility of Tamiz's father getting any help in return from Shamsher.

While his father went out to clean his teeth, Tamiz went into the new room behind the original one. He had constructed this room in spring for himself with the money he had earned in Khiyar. When he went away Kulsum cooked in here on rainy days, storing her sacks of rice as well. She had put the hen in this room so its eggs could hatch. The chicks were down to two in number, the rest having died. The hen spent the night here with the two children. It was a cloudless day today, and moreover, Tamiz had come home. So Kulsum was washing the rice before cooking it on the oven in the yard. Tamiz handed her a gunny bag. 'I got some fish from Golabari.' When Kulsum took the bag from him without interrupting her washing of the rice, Tamiz began shouting all over again. 'I'd told Kalam bhaiya to send some bamboo and straw over, told both of you to put up a canopy over the oven. But no one's done anything.'

The last time Tamiz was home, he had repaired the walls of Kalam majhi's draw-well without charging money for the work. They had agreed to a payment of half a mon of rice. Tamiz already had plenty of rice at home—getting some more from Kalam meant giving his father the opportunity to go some more days without having to work. So Tamiz had asked Kalam for a couple of bamboo poles and some straw instead. It would be very convenient for Kulsum if Tamiz's father could use them to erect a canopy over the clay oven. Kulsum cooked under a blazing sun, and when it rained she had to run indoors to use the smaller oven in there. The idea behind the canopy was to relieve her from these troubles. But Tamiz had had to rush to Khiyar. He had instructed his father repeatedly before he left, but there was no canopy, nothing. Not even a post. Tamiz flew into a rage. 'Will no work get done if I'm not here?'

Tamiz had already ruined Kulsum's day by chatting with Gofoor kolu's legally wedded wife first thing in the morning. And now Kulsum's husband's first wife's son had begun ranting. Puffing her cheeks, she blew on the fire she had started beneath the stove with all her might to get it going properly. The flame shot upwards suddenly, her face turning purple with its heat. Her voice rang out loudly through the flames. 'First you turned me into a maid. Now you want me to be a labourer too?' Once she started, Kulsum wasn't known to stop, which meant she had to keep up her tirade. 'Do I have to cut the poles from Kalam majhi's bamboo grove myself? Do I have to fix them too?' Turning her face, crimson with both anger and the heat from the flame, towards Tamiz momentarily, Kulsum returned her attention to the stove. 'Do you think any of the women in our families have even seen kitchens in their lives, leave alone cook? We can burn under the sun or be drenched in the rain, we don't care.' She would now repeat the same sentiments with a different choice of words each time at least till evening fell. Soon more arguments would be added. Such as? 'It's our fate.' Why? After fire and iron there was now . . . she came from a family of fakirs, but had ended up with fishermen, who didn't even have enough rags to cover their arses— even the penniless cultivators of Nijgirirdanga wouldn't be seen in their company, never mind eating with them. How dare Tamiz taunt her for being a fakir's daughter when he himself was nothing but a fisherman? At least Tamiz's father never brought up Kulsum's ancestry to humiliate her. Whether he was a fool or just plain lazy, for several years he had accompanied Cherag Ali wherever the fakir went. Kulsum's grandfather must have passed on some of his gifts to the old coot. He went out in his sleep and returned home safely without waking up for a moment—how did he do it? Only because one of 'them' was protecting him. She would never have had to stand for her stepson's taunts had Cherag Ali been alive. Kulsum's eyelids grew heavy. But when the flames in the stove were fanned by the indistinct sounds of Tamiz's conversation with that flirtatious whore Abiton at the crack of dawn, they made her eyes smart, bringing forth angry waves of resentment. However, neither Kulsum's anger nor the heat from the flames affected Tamiz, who continued haranguing his father. About what? About the fact that during the famine, Tamiz's father had sold the only land he possessed, a 3-acre plot, to Sharafat Mondol in order to pay back what he owed Jagadish Saha, whose people had even taken away Tamiz's father's ox. And this had not settled the debt in its entirety, which was why Tamiz now had to work as a daily labourer for food. How could his father have been so greedy? Tamiz's father did not answer. Tamiz marched off towards the road without bothering to wait for a response.

Kulsum examined the pot to gauge when the rice would be ready. Tamiz was no longer in view. What kind of a young man was this who could leave home in the morning on an empty stomach? Maybe he would walk all the way to Sharafat Mondol's house. If he took on the land that Bulu used to sharecrop he could cultivate the amon himself. The sowing season had not yet ended. He had told his father of this plan while taking him to task, but no response was forthcoming. So he had rushed off.

Tamiz had vented his ire on Kulsum by skipping his meal. Whenever father and son quarrelled, both of them shouted at her. Her grandfather had made her life miserable by forcing her to marry into this family. The old coot had merrily disappeared, but didn't he remember his orphaned granddaughter at all? He frequented Tamiz's father's dreams regularly—couldn't he at least pop into Kulsum's line of sight sometimes? Who knew, maybe the horrid old coot had died. Actually, it might not be such a bad thing if he had. If he was still alive he would be near-blind by now. How did he walk all those miles on his own? Who would ask for an extra helping of meat or daal to be served to him when he sat down to eat? Topped by a black cap, Cherag Ali's face quivered in the steam rising from the pot of rice. Which fair or market or riverbank did the old man wander around these days, tapping his cane on the ground or playing his dotara and singing? The rice bubbled on the stove, the sounds shaping themselves into Cherag Ali's verses. But Kulsum could not decipher the words. The old coot began to pant with effort, just about managing to strum his instrument, without attempting to sing. Kulsum couldn't even hum the lyrics to give him a bit of relief, because she had no idea what the verses were.

Suddenly, from a distant, unfamiliar place, Tamiz's father's warning rose above Cherag Ali's incoherent singing. 'The rice is boiling over, can't you see?' Lowering the flame on the stove and setting the pot to drain out the starch, Kulsum felt her body breaking down, oh Allah, even if her grandfather was choking on the words, there was no one who could finish the song for him and let him rest a little.

5

After a long time, having stuffed himself at night with a meal of tender aush rice, beef curry, and the famous curds from Hatibanda, and, before that, a fish curry cooked with potato along with rice in the afternoon, and two rounds of puffed rice and sugar crystals before lunch and dinner, Tamiz's father had come back home stroking his belly and fallen asleep at once. Waking up with an abdominal pain in the middle of the night, he couldn't even go as far as the bamboo grove beyond the yard and had to squat well short of the pond. Before he could drag himself home after washing his soiled lungi perfunctorily along with his buttocks, thighs and legs, he was forced to squat again just outside the door, where he proceeded to vomit with loud sounds. The inconsiderate rules of the body had prevented him from tasting even a morsel of food in his rectum while passing his stool, but now the taste of delicious food as he brought it up revived him somewhat. The sounds emerging from his throat included the expression of regret at the loss of all the delicacies that were deserting him. The possibility that the noise also held some gratitude for Shamsher Poramanik was not ruled out. Shamsher belonged to the original line of peasants— he considered himself the son of a nobleman, no matter that his arse was perpetually bare now. He hadn't kept his promise entirely. When they had met the day before yesterday at Golabari market, he had assured Tamiz's father of at least two rashogollas from Naresh's shop. But no, the bastard had not offered any sweets. Not that Tamiz's father was particularly unhappy about this. Considering the amount of curds from Gopal Ghosh's shop in Hatibanda, along with sugar cane jaggery, that they'd been given, a sweet dish was not really necessary. But it was just his luck that none of these fine things remained in his stomach.

But then why blame the stomach? With his own son taunting him over his meals, how were the beef curry and the fish to rest comfortably for even a moment or two? This was food for the high-born, which had to be paid due respect. Tamiz kept harping on the same thing—how could a man without an inch of land of his own think of working for food? This same Shamsher had had to sell practically all his land to Mondol during the famine to settle his debt to Jagadish Saha, but he had refused to let one 2-acre plot go. Even if it *was* a low-lying plot, on which nothing but aush could be sown, Mondol had left no stone unturned in his effort to buy it. How had Shamsher managed to hold on to the plot? Since Tamiz's father could not answer this puzzling question after stuffing himself with food, Tamiz had to take on the task himself. It was simple—because Shamsher Poramanik belonged to the line of original peasants, he couldn't imagine not having a little land of his own to cultivate. And Tamiz's father was a majhi, whose family tradition was to catch fish for a living. There was a great deal of difference between a low-caste Hindu and a Muslim fisherman. How was a clan of fishermen to understand the respect that land commanded? A rumbling discomfort in Tamiz's father's stomach began to take shape as he listened to his son heaping insults on their own lineage.

Paying no attention to his father's unhappiness or stomach ache, Tamiz continued, instead of being so greedy about eating at other people's houses, his father should beg and plead with Mondol for permission to sharecrop the land that Bulu used to cultivate. Mondol wasn't willing. He had turned Tamiz away today, although he had asked him to come again tomorrow. Why couldn't Tamiz's father try too? Mondol would surely forgive Tamiz's father if cajoled.

But what had Tamiz's father done that needed forgiveness? Now his entire body rumbled with rage along with his belly. What crime had he committed?

'Don't you go to Katlahar Lake even if it's in your sleep?' The old man looked at his son uncomprehendingly. What was wrong with that?

'What do you go to the lake with a fishing net for? Don't you know that Mondol has officially leased the lake? No one is allowed to do anything in the lake without paying a rent to Mondol. And you go every single day to catch fish—what will you do if Mondol decides to have his guards arrest you?'

A cloud descended over Tamiz's father's eyes on hearing his son voice Mondol's accusation. 'All my forefathers made their living from the fish in that lake, and now . . .' Barely had the incomplete sentence passed his lips when it ran into a wall of darkness and bounced right back into his mouth, negotiating the gullet to nestle in the tender sanctuary of the rice, beef curry, fish, and curd-and-jaggery progressing towards digestion or perhaps indigestion. He did not look up at the ceiling, although his withered black frame shivered at the lonely flight of several of Mondol's white storks over his home. Much more important than protecting his head was to protect what was in his stomach from the ashen shadows of the storks. Clutching his stomach to shield the food from the covetous glances of the birds, he tried to escape into sleep even as Tamiz continued shouting at him. But if only sleep could wipe out the ever-widening darkness of the storks casting their grey shadows! Their evil eye ensured that his food did not stay in his belly. The grotesque sounds of vomiting as he was hunched by the door not only conveyed his lamentation at losing the beef curry, fish, puffed rice, sugar crystals and curds, but they also held, if anyone cared to dissect them, fragments of Cherag Ali's songs sung by Boikuntho:

All you Madari fakirs, Majnu roared,
Wrap those turban round your heads

Put your chains around your necks
Line your eyes with strips of kohl

'You know all of Fakir's verses, don't you? Do you realize these are
spiritual songs?' Boikuntho was undaunted by Shamsher Poramanik's
doubts. He wasn't leaving till he had sung five full songs. Dressed
in a dirty dhuti and a clean vest, his mouth stuffed with paan, he
had been on his way to the market in Sabgram to buy cumin for
his employer's shop and to order white turmeric from Bhaktodas
Kundu at Chhaihata to adulterate the cumin with. He would return
to Golabari only after evening had fallen, his bullock cart laden with
cumin and white turmeric. But, passing Shamsher's plot of low-
lying land on his way to the market, Boikuntho stopped when he
discovered that unpaid labourers were at work there, and settled
down beneath the mango tree on the raised verge of the land.

'What's all this, why don't any of you join me?' When Boikuntho
began singing Shamsher grew worried, for the man completely lacked
common sense—now that he had started singing there would be no
stopping him. What if the labourers slowed down?

'Weren't you going to Sabgram?' he began to urge Boikuntho.
'The shops have all been set up already.'

'I can buy the cumin any time. And anyway I'll have to plead
with that bastard Kundu for the white. The swine sells adulterated
stuff, but have you seen his swagger? Claims he will lose money if he
sells pure cumin.'

Boikuntho had forgotten all about the market, and the labourers
were far from unenthusiastic about his singing. 'The shops will be
open till the evening, sing some more.'

Another one added, 'How can we work without songs? We loved
to work on the fields when Cherag Ali fakir was alive. Whenever he
heard we were here, he would turn up to sing, and working became
easy.' But then Cherag Ali was one of a kind. He would always arrive
with his granddaughter wherever people were working without pay,
and sing a succession of songs, strumming his dotara. He wouldn't

leave until he and his granddaughter had had at least one meal. Boikuntho was not particularly concerned about food—you didn't often see him chewing anything other than paan.

He even put back the hookah leaning against the mango tree after picking it up, saying, 'No, I'd better not.'

'Will smoking here mean you'll lose your religion? In that case singing a Muslim fakir's song should make you lose your religion too.' Ignoring Shamsher's amiable rebuke, Boikuntho took a brass container out of the folds of his dirty dhuti and popped a pre-prepared paan into his mouth. There was another small container inside it. The air grew redolent with the aroma of sweet tobacco when Boikuntho turned it upside down on his palm. Chewing contentedly on his paan for a while and spitting out only a little juice like a miser, he said,

'Keep working, all of you. Singing makes hard work better. Wise men say, the mountain told the cripple that music would help him cross. And who is this mountain? Let me sing his song for you. You've heard it before, now hear it again.' Completing his preamble, Boikuntho hummed the tune and then brought his palms together in reverence to some invisible entity. Then he sang.

> The Giri clan is in the water
> To pick him up with love and care
> Like Radha holds Krishna in her arms.
> Let your hearts turn to stone today
> Weep, you Giris, weep all you can
> Bhabani Pathak is in this world no more.

The cadences of the devotional song dispelled the humidity, making the labourers' sickles sharper, and Tamiz's father sliced off thick stalks of paddy to the echoes of the last line. Even though Boikuntho's voice, thick with the paan juice he had swallowed, broke with grief at Bhabani Pathak's death, it was so full of rage at the assassin that everyone's sickles moved faster. The wind blew across the field once the song stopped, buffeting the leaves of the mango tree and the stalks of rice. It was past afternoon by the time Boikuntho left for Sabgram with an armful of puffed rice and sugar crystals.

Now, all this time later, there was not the faintest shadow of Boikuntho Giri anywhere near Tamiz's father as he vomited deafeningly loudly at midnight. He extracted the words of the song from the sounds of his vomiting. The song made his frail body tremble so violently that he did not have the strength to rise to his feet, tumbling over the doorstep in his attempt. His head was on the floor, touching the far post of the maacha, while his feet were in contact with the doorstep. Awakening from his sleep, Tamiz said drowsily, 'He'll die any day, but he won't stop his gluttony. Now you're suffering, Allah alone knows how many times I'll have to get up.' Tamiz's father must have heard his son grumbling in anxiety and disappointment, but the whining mosquitoes and the creaking crickets, the whistling of the wind in the bamboo groves and the stirring of the water caused by the startled fish in the pond, accompanied by Tamiz's slurring sleep-laced speech, reminded him of a tune with a ragged rhythm, which began to play in his ears.

The moon rises behind the grove
The wife and son are fast asleep.
Who knows where the fakir has flown
Bhabani Pathak is in this world no more.

6

Tamiz had to face a barrage of criticism for his insistence on sharecropping land in his own village instead of continuing to work as a labourer on farms in Khiyar. He had no oxen or plough or yoke or harrow, nor the money to buy seeds—how could anyone trust him with their land? Tamiz pleaded with joined palms. Couldn't Mondol give him all he needed now? After the harvest came he would pay it all back in the form of a higher share of the crops.

This was possible; it wasn't as though there was no precedent. But Sharafat Mondol's eldest son Abdul Aziz was a very cautious man. He lived in Joipur, where he worked as a clerk in the sub-registry office. He was in the know of everything related to land—from the measurement of plots to the intricacies and loopholes in rents. It was doubtful whether anyone even in the government offices at Lathidanga knew more than he did. He demanded half the price of the oxen, the plough, the yoke, the harrow and the seeds in advance. No oxen, no plough, but still want to be a sharecropper? All right, it's possible, but you must accept the conditions before you start work on the land.

Abdul Kader would say, 'These people have lived here a long time. Even their fathers used to work for us . . .'

But the excessive demands of the cultivators had crossed all limits. How long would it be before they went on the rampage here in the eastern parts as well? In Khiyar the tillers were demanding two-thirds of the harvest, they weren't ready to deposit more than one-third in the landowner's granary. Go ahead, then, there's no tax on making demands. But just one point—the land had not exactly fallen into the lap of the jotedar who had leased it from the jomidar. It wasn't a stork from the arjun tree in Kamarpara that had flown over the lake to perch on the silk-cotton tree in the Mondols' yard, now was it? Do you even know that for every little slice of land a man owns, a quart of his blood turns to salt? Abdul Aziz had witnessed the resoluteness of illiterate farmers in Khiyar. It wouldn't take long to stoke the same resolve amongst peasants hereabouts. There was no need to be considerate to anyone. Just follow the rules if you want to be a sharecropper. Go elsewhere if it doesn't suit you.

How could Tamiz counter these anxieties and prophecies of Abdul Aziz's? Even Abdul Kader himself, who wrote his name in English with a single stroke of the pen, M.A. Kader, a man who attended meetings, who cornered people whenever he could to reveal the atrocities of Hindus, who exhorted everyone to unite under the banner of the Muslim League to save themselves from this tyranny— even he could only pick his nose and scratch his head. After all, his brother was employed at the sub-registry office in Joipur, receiving money both officially with his right hand and unofficially with his left. Now that he was home for a few days, the only use for his left hand was to wash his arse after shitting, resulting in an inactivity he avenged with constant use of his tongue and the roof of his mouth.

Tamiz had personally witnessed the exploits of the aadhiars, who wanted more than half of the crops they grew, when he went west to harvest grains, but he did not support their violent ways. The land was controlled by the jotedar, who had the authority to decide whom the crops would go to. Yet the aadhiars had taken up arms to get a greater share. To keep them at bay, some of the jotedars of Panchbibi had employed daily labourers for the harvest, which was how Tamiz had found work when he travelled west. The jotedar had apparently spoken to the police in advance. But then how many places could the police patrol? Tamiz had started work for a generous payment—though he would have to pay for his own food. He had worked himself to the bone in the fields—the rice had to be harvested as quickly as possible. But thankfully for him, he had run away in time when he heard an uproar from a group of men one afternoon. Even the wives of the cultivators had given chase with their brooms and ladles and kitchen blades and stirrers. Tamiz would certainly have faced the wrath of their brooms and ladles had he not raced away through the rice fields, leaping over—and sometimes stepping through— stacks of cut paddy. Not that anyone knew whether he had actually been attacked. Nobody announces that they have been beaten up by a woman. Still, after withstanding, or evading, the swipes of the women's brooms, Tamiz had already developed an aversion for the aadhiars' methods even before making it to the jotedar's yard. The land was the goddess of wealth, her children were the crops. Wouldn't it hurt the land if you battled over the harvest? It was at the centre of the landowner's existence—how was the poor fellow going to survive such a conflict? Tamiz felt very upset when they said that being the son of a fisherman, he would never understand how the land suffered. It was true that his father and grandfather and great-grandfather had all lived off fishing. Apparently, long before he was born, the largest fish at the country fair at Poradaho used to be delivered by his father's grandfather Baghar majhi. Which was why Tamiz's father had inherited the name of his venerated forefather, so much so that his real name was forgotten even by his own family. This fame had been handed down as far as Tamiz's father. Before Tamiz was born, everyone knew of his father as Baghar majhi's grandson, but his identity changed after his son was born. Everyone knew Tamiz as Tamiz, though.

But then the people of this family did cultivate the land once upon a time. Sovan Dhuma, who was Baghar majhi's father Budha majhi's grandfather or great-grandfather—or was he *his* grandfather? Who was it who had cleared half—if not half, a quarter—the land of Girirdanga of forests and settled down here on this side of the lake? Sovan Dhuma, of course. This area used to be overrun by jungles when Sovan's father had fled to these parts after causing trouble somewhere to the west of the Kartowa. Sovan had four mothers, and at least twenty-five or thirty siblings, most of whom were male. Very few girls had been born in their family before they had taken to fishing as a profession. Could women possibly have cleared out such a large tract of forest to create cultivable land on the western side of the lake? And what a forest! There were tigers, bears, wild pigs and snakes everywhere. Although they grumbled initially, the beasts were terrified of Sovan and his brothers. Eventually even the tigers didn't know where to hide when they got Sovan's scent. If he had caught one of the tigers Sovan would have planted a yoke on its shoulders and made it plough the land.

Later, who knows when, during the time of Sovan Dhuma's grandson—or his grandson's son—there was a huge earthquake in Assam or maybe Rangpur or was it in Delhi, no, it must have been Burma, after which the water from a wide river somewhere all flowed to the Jomuna in the east. What sort of river was the Jomuna before this? People laughed when asked, for it was nothing but a narrow stream. Its slender frame couldn't possibly absorb this sudden influx of water—where would it store it? Eating up miles and miles of land, along with all the tigers and bears and pigs and snakes and people and their homes and their poultry and their cattle, the river heaved and gasped, it wanted more. Suffering from indigestion, the Jomuna retched much of the murky water into the Bangali river. A furious current broke away from the Bangali to enter Katlahar Lake here. The lake was just a swamp then, on whose northern end Munshi had taken up his position in the fig tree in the time of Sovan Dhuma, or perhaps of his son. Who would have cleaned up Katlahar had Munshi not been there? His presence had made the water in the lake so pure that it was drunk by the people who had cleared the jungle in Girirdanga to start a settlement. But how could a swamp hold the breakaway flow of water from the Bangali in its tiny body? Girirdanga was flooded, as was Nijgirirdanga, which was still a forest, with the exception of Kamarpara. Unable to bear the sight of the people of Girirdanga being swept away, along with their farmland and cattle and poultry and wives and daughters, Munshi stretched his legs twenty-five or thirty yards, or maybe forty or fifty, to the south of the lake from his fig tree and delivered a mighty kick. The farmland and houses that had come up after the jungle had been cleared all those years ago crumbled at once, and the floodwaters rushed into the lake now that the bank had been demolished. Touching the feet of the fig tree in reverence, two separate streams from the Bangali river flowed in from opposite sides to meet in the lake. One of those streams had been wiped out long ago, though some of the earth behind the fig tree was still moist with its memory. Tamiz had heard his mother recount how Ramesh the lawyer from the town had leased the area covered by kaash flowers for cultivation. It seems he had wanted Tamiz's father to work on the land, along with his own nephew Tunu-babu. Had Tamiz's father accepted the offer he would have been the owner today of no less than 3 acres of land to the north of the fig tree. It was by gobbling up their land that the lake had swollen so much. Had the flood not come and Munshi not kicked the bank of the lake to save them, all this land would have remained in their possession. But then Munshi himself had arranged for the livelihood of the people whose land the lake had fattened itself on. When the bank crumbled at his kick and sank into the lake, the plough was lost in the water. At Munshi's request different kinds of fishing nets—the toura, the pyala, even the enormous ber—floated up on the surface of the lake.

And so Sovan Dhuma's progeny became fishermen at this signal given by Munshi. But now the lake had begun to die, shrinking under the silt deposited by the big flood eight years ago. Many of the fishermen had left for the Jomuna to the east with their fishing nets, their wives carrying the children in their arms. Some people had even tried to sink their ploughs into the new land that rose out of the water, but apparently all of it belonged to Sharafat Mondol, who had leased the entire lake from the jomidar. Still, Tamiz had his doubts about who really had the rights to cultivating this newly emerging land.

Try to make sense of it, he instructed himself. But he could not work it out clearly in his head. Still, even if you weren't the owner of the land you could sharecrop on it, couldn't you? His agitation and anxiety, and admittedly some regret too, were readying themselves to plead on Tamiz's behalf. But he couldn't bring himself to do it. Kader spoke up for him, however. 'Our harvest will be secure if we let Tamiz farm our land. The boy can work really hard. He's the son of a poor fisherman, he won't dare play tricks.'

Abdul Aziz had guessed as much. The son of a fisherman, and poorest of the poor besides. Even if Tamiz began farming now, it would take two generations more for his family to become proper farmers. Considering he would just be starting with the plough, he wouldn't have the time to be in cahoots with other cultivators. All right, but Abdul Aziz was a government employee, whose salary came from the district treasury. He had to follow the rules of the British government. You may say what you like about the British government, but it won't tolerate a breach of rules. You're desperate to drive them out—but wait and see what happens when they leave. The laws of the land are still in place, there are rules governing cultivation too. The harvest is still shared half and half. The capital invested should be half and half too, as has been the practice all this time. You may not have your own plough and oxen, but you must pay half the cost of hiring them.

When Abdul Aziz had finished Abdul Kader spoke up. 'Bhaijaan, do you expect cash dealings with aadhiars? You can get Tamiz to pay his share of the costs when the crops are harvested. Where will he get money now?'

'How far is Jagadish Saha's house?' Aziz advised, 'Let him have your cycle if he finds it difficult to walk.'

Either at Munshi's signal or because of a trick of the light and the shadows amongst the leaves of the mango trees overhead, Jagadish Saha's name took on the blurry form of an ox being dragged forward relentlessly by a rope tied around its neck. The owner of the hand holding the rope was not visible, or perhaps the person remained out of sight because Tamiz lacked the courage to find out who it was. His father's real-life ox had at least thrown several backward glances, but this blessed ghost of an ox had no such attachment. Tamiz had to struggle to stay upright when the ox kicked him on his tottering legs. Some of the strength he had used to remain on his feet gathered on Kader's tongue, which began to move spiritedly. 'The League is fighting for the formation of Pakistan in order to save us from Hindu landowners and Hindu moneylenders. These moneylenders are sucking Muslim peasants dry. And now you want to send this fellow to the moneylender? No need to make him a sharecropper.' Doubling the acidity in his voice, he instructed Tamiz, 'Go, Tamiz. You can't get this land. You're the son of a fisherman, go catch fish in streams and lakes. Get out.'

'Will you stop it!' Sharafat interrupted them as soon as the lake was mentioned. It was to keep the fishermen away from the lake that he was keen on turning them into sharecroppers. And now his son had brought up the subject of the lake. He didn't usually intervene in arguments between his sons. He was lying back in a maroon and green striped canvas easy-chair in the raised veranda outside the front room. Aziz and Kader were seated a few yards away beneath the mango tree, on a chair with armrests and a bench, respectively. Sharafat could hear their conversation clearly enough, but his eyes were on the land beyond the house, across the Katlahar Lake, behind the peasants' village, which was submerged in rainwater. Bananas had been planted this year on the one-and-a-half-acre plot abandoned by blacksmiths a few yards beyond the arjun trees deserted by the storks. Sharafat Mondol was the first in this area to plant bananas on such a large stretch of land. He wasn't discouraged in the least by the muddy sunlight falling on the tender green leaves of the plants, for he could see the actual colour of the leaves quite clearly even without his glasses. He was intimately familiar with everything that lay across the lake—the sunlight, the shadows, the rain, the vegetation, the lie of the land, the people, the cattle. He might be living on this side of the lake now, but he had been born on the other side. In every official document his address said, village: Nijgirirdanga. These days Abdul Aziz had started filling out his documents with Girirdanga as his current domicile. Sharafat's father had moved to this side of the lake after quarrelling with his co-owners, long before the lake had begun to die. Sharafat had been a mere baby then. And then something happened that year—who can understand Allah's will?—the fish in Katlahar Lake died in droves. Only dead fish turned up in the Girirdanga fishermen's nets. Eating the rotting fish led to an outbreak of cholera in Majhipara. When poverty forced many of the fishermen to sell their homes and land, Sharafat's father bought some of it and moved to this side of the lake. But it wasn't as though Sharafat Mondol had been quiet all this while because he was immersed in the memories of his father or forefathers, or deep in dreams of expanding his landholdings. His property on the other side of the lake was by no means small. By the grace of the lord he owned considerable land in his ancestral village. The land to the south of the ox pool had been theirs from the time of his father. They had farmed it themselves since then, handing it over to Harmatullah for sharecropping only five years ago. The entire land adjoining the ox pool belonged to the jomidar, all of it barren. To the north stood Harmatullah's house, the 3 acres of land next to which he had not let go of yet. South of his home lay what was known as Bhabani's field, a desolate span of nearly a mile. Cattle from the village on the other side grazed over there, and the jomidar never leased it out. After this came an entire stretch of Mondol's holdings—12 acres of land, a swamp, and another 4 acres in Kamarpara, where the blacksmiths once lived. He owned 48 acres in seven separate stretches to the south of the lake, most of which were sharecropped by Hamid Sakidar. The land he owned in Girirdanga was far from insignificant, but it was scattered. How could fishermen be expected to have organized their landholdings into contiguous blocks? Mondol never let go of an opportunity to buy land cheap, but his attention was centred on his property in Nijgirirdanga. Hamid Sakidar was quite a reliable man. His sons had not supported his decision to have half the land in the north farmed by daily labourers and give the other half to Harmatullah to sharecrop. They had wanted Hamid Sakidar to do it. But Sharafat's calculations were different—he had added a faithful subject to his flock in his ancestral village. Besides, Harmatullah would pay extra attention to this land along with his own meagre plot because it adjoined his house. Moreover, this distant relative of Mondol's would be kept under control in the process. But Sharafat alone knew why he refused to give the rest of the land to Harmatullah though he had pleaded for it. Still, if he could get a lease on the land to the north, east and west of the ox pool he would probably give it to Harmatullah. Sharafat had even had a conversation about it with the jomidar's manager at the fair at Poradaho last year. There was reason to hope. The jomidar was apparently losing interest in retaining his arable land with every passing day. His sons refused to budge from Calcutta nowadays, and they had no interest in land except to use it as a source of money, supposedly for their business ventures in Calcutta. The manager said that his employer was also becoming indifferent to his estate and his property, which he wanted to interpret as a growing detachment with material life. Sharafat began to walk faster with excitement and enthusiasm at this news, although he consciously kept his pace in check while strolling around the fair. Two days later, he went to meet the manager at his office in Lathibhanga with two fifteen-seer carps and three pots of the famous curds from Hatibandha to cautiously broach the subject of leasing the ox pool. The manager indicated that some investment would make it a possibility. Getting this lease would mean controlling a continuous stretch of about 10 acres around the lake coming under Sharafat's control. It was easier to keep track of things when the leased land was not fragmented, besides being a pleasure to behold. Meanwhile, Sharafat had already bought up most of Kamarpara over on the other side of the arjun trees to the south. Only Dasharath and Narod, and, farther down, Gourango, were clinging to their holdings of about 8 acres. If only they'd leave, Sharafat would have an unbroken expanse of 17 acres. Ah! He would then own more than half of his ancestral village. But if his sons were going to waste their time arguing over whether or not to grant sharecropping rights to the son of a fisherman, how would they ever preserve this vast estate? It wouldn't be long before the argument turned into a feud. The potential of being the owner of an immense stretch of land, combined with anxiety over the chances of a discord between his sons, kept him from savouring the comfort of his easy chair. It also compelled Mondol to be silent. Normally he would never have allowed a discussion or quarrel without participating in it, at the very least he would have shouted at the oxherd for not replenishing the feed for the oxen and for not noticing that the calf tied up beneath the jackfruit tree was refusing its salt-and-starch-flavoured water. The shrapnel from this explosion would have hit his sons as well. But Sharafat suddenly became so apprehensive that, sitting upright in his easy chair, he declared, 'Since we've given our word the land must go to Tamiz.'

Sharafat Mondol had not taken this decision to pacify his sons. The elder one spouted the law whenever possible, but you couldn't threaten sharecroppers with the law. There were no predetermined rules for how to protect your land and to increase your holdings. Abdul Aziz was capable of losing his temper, but several years of working for the government had choked his ability to nurture his rage. Sharafat found it easy to control this son of his. He concentrated on correcting Kader instead. 'Look, Kader, it's Jagadish's profession to lend money, he wouldn't have been able to recover the money his father had invested unless he had gone into the business himself. This is business, it's no use debating its good and bad sides. If you insist that no one can borrow money from Hindu moneylenders, where are they to go? If Jagadish stops lending today, hundreds of people will starve to death tomorrow. It's Jagadish who puts food in people's mouths on Kaartik.'

'You also know how he recovers the interest.'

'That's his business. People borrow from him knowingly. His religion doesn't forbid him from earning interest.'

Although Sharafat Mondol knew that Abdul Kader's silence did not signal acquiescence, he was not perturbed. He quite enjoyed indulging his younger son's whims. The boy was the only one in the family to have studied in college for three years. After passing his Intermediate exams on the second attempt, he had demanded to be allowed to study for a B.A. But that would have entailed going to Rajsahi, which not only meant paying his expenses every month, but also letting his son out of reach. Considering Abdul Kader's enthusiasm for attending and organizing meetings, he would have given up studies completely if he were to live away from home. He could go to as many meetings as he liked, Sharafat had no objection, provided he lived at home. Considering the times they lived in, there was no alternative. The idea of starting a kerosene shop at Golabari had occurred to him only because of the connections he had. His son treated the poor and low-class people in the village well. These things were important. No matter what Abdul Aziz said, Sharafat knew very well that things were far from peaceful. Following the law strictly would only mean losing everything eventually. Sharafat had to take the situation into account. Kader had given his word to Tamiz—if the young man were to be turned down now, he would either begin stealing fish from Katlahar Lake, demanding rights to the lake one day by virtue of all the fish he had stolen, or he would go away to Khiyar. And who could guarantee that he wouldn't lose his head and join the cultivators who were on the rampage?

Sharafat said there was no need to give Bulu's land to anyone else now. Let Tamiz sharecrop the land next to Harmatullah's across the Katlahar Lake. Mondol's oxen, plough, yoke and harrow were all in Harmatullah's house—Tamiz could use them. But he would have to pay an extra portion of his share of the harvest for whatever he used. Being a Muslim, Sharafat would not charge interest, but surely no one could object to his taking a share of the profits.

Abdul Kader did not concern himself over the question of whether charging interest was a problem for Muslims. He was not a

fundamentalist who had studied at a madrassa, he had a full-fledged
I.A. degree from a college—why should he be dogmatic?

Once the conversation veered round to Pakistan at the Muslim
League office in town, or at Ismail Husain's house in Sirail, or in
Sadeq the lawyer's drawing room in Jhautala, the hours for successive
namaz prayers passed without anyone paying attention. Abdul Kader
couldn't stand the tyranny of the Hindus. What did it have to do
with what Muslims considered sacred or profane? It was beyond
Kader to explain all this clearly, the way Sadeq the lawyer or Ismail
Husain did.

Ignoring his mumbles and Aziz's restless silence, Sharafat said,
'I'm giving you our best land, Tamiz. We've farmed it ourselves for
two generations. Perfect for amon.' There used to be no fertilizer
besides cow dung in his father's time—they considered it sinful to
use any other kind of manure. In his grandfather's era each acre of
this land had yielded six, even six and a half mons of paddy. 'When
my father took up the plough himself he never gave up till he had got
seven and a half mons.'

Neither Abdul Aziz nor Abdul Kader enjoyed the descriptions of
their grandfather ploughing the land himself. Aziz was a government
employee, and even if the job was not an important one, he kept the
company of educated gentlemen, who would look askance at him if
they came to know that his forefathers had personally ploughed the
land just two generations ago. And those among them whose fathers
still worked on the fields all day would taunt Aziz obliquely.

But Kader had no reason to be annoyed now. In fact, he was
overcome with gratitude to his father for offering the land to Tamiz,
who would now be under his control. The fishermen were still quite
influential in Girirdanga, but Tamiz was the only one among them to
make it a point to visit his shop when he went to Golabari, and spend
a long time there listening closely to what the members of the League
had to say. Kader would use him to gain the support of Majhipara.
At the same time he would be able to present Tamiz to the party as
a worker with unmatched abilities. Besides, if wedges were driven

between the fishermen and the peasants and the oil grinders, none of them would respond to the call for the formation of Pakistan. There was no need to be embarrassed by the fact of his father or grandfather tilling the land themselves. Still, he tried to appear indifferent to his father's reminiscences of their plough-bearing forefathers. And just as both the brothers began to be stricken with anxiety over how far their father would go, how low he would drag the family down, Abdul Aziz and Abdul Kader were rescued by a cry emerging from the house. Sharafat's second wife was asking, 'It's so late, none of you has even bathed yet, when do you plan to eat?'

7

The morning had almost passed by the time Mondol went into the house with both his sons. The rice soaked overnight in water that Tamiz had eaten in the morning had escaped by now in the form of sweat and wind, leaving him with a deflated belly. But still his entire body, including the collapsed stomach, yearned to take a round of the two acres and a bit of land in Nijgirirdanga. Tamiz borrowed Mondol's boat, moored on the bank, from Bulu's son, who was in charge of guarding the lake.

The water was ebbing now, and Mondol had made arrangements to confine the fish on the southern side of the lake, near his house. This was a good time to go fishing. The lake was almost full-term pregnant now, its womb holding everything from carp to catfish in different varieties. Someone was cooking fish within the lake, somewhere deep within, its fumes blurring Tamiz's vision. But then the steamy glare of the sun could have been to blame too. There were scattered clouds in the sky, drying up in the heat, so that the raindrops included the smoke emanating from the dirty clouds. The surface of the lake had turned turbid. Only in the month of Ashwin, when the rains had ended, would the lake look clean. But then, transparent or murky, it was under Mondol's control. The small fry in the water were up to mischief, nibbling at the oars; were the fish of Katlahar bidding goodbye to Tamiz now that he had become a sharecropper for Mondol?

Before Tamiz's boat had reached the eastern bank he could see Harmatullah Poramanik reading the namaz on the ridge between two plots of land. Jumping off his boat and dragging it on to the bank, Tamiz went up to the plot of land he would cultivate. Sharafat owned an unbroken stretch of four and a half acres just beyond the slope leading down to the lake. The ridge ran through its middle, a little wider than usual. Harmatullah sharecropped the western half, and Tamiz would work on the eastern half from now on. The ox pool was some distance away to the north. Harmatullah's home was another 5 or 6 acres of land away, to the north-east of the enormous circular lake which was not visible clearly because of its very high banks. Tamiz scanned the familiar land, measuring it in his head. Yes, Mondol had indeed given him an excellent plot. Flat and even, just like in Khiyar. Even the ridge separating the plots was smooth. Harmatullah was seated on the homespun towel he had laid out on the green patch beneath the jujube tree, his palms joined in supplication. Moulobi Kuddus had once complained after the namaz in the mosque in Majhipara that this was another of the Rafadanis' flaws, this joining of the palms to make a perch for the devil. Behind his palms and straggling beard, Harmatullah's blackened lips were muttering prayers. He could not stop asking for blessings even after he had lowered his hands, but as his voice became more audible, Tamiz realized that Harmatullah was no longer addressing Allahtaala, but Tamiz himself. What was he saying? 'So, you son of a fisherman, Mondol chose to give the land to you? Now tell him to get rid of me too. I cannot possibly work with a fisherman on the same land.'

Then began a continuous litany of regret about how long he had laboured for Mondol on the entire four and a half acres. Before him, his brother had worked here as a hired hand too. Harmatullah had asked for the entire land, whereupon Mondol had whispered, 'You must understand, it's true my sons keep asking me to turn the entire land over to sharecroppers, but look, my father was a farmer, after all. I don't plough the land myself, it's true, if I don't get it done with hired labour instead of giving the whole thing away, the earth will be displeased. Let me keep this bit, you can work on it as a hired hand like before.' But considering Mondol had given in to his sons eventually, how would it have hurt him to have picked Harmatullah? Abdul Aziz had in fact wanted to intercede with his father on Harmatullah's behalf—but no one knew whether he had. If Harmatullah had got this bit of land, he could easily have harvested the jute on his other plots a little early. And then he would have sown amon and shown everyone what farming was. His problem was that he himself belonged to a peasants' family—which used to be related to Sharafat's family even two generations ago. He hadn't been born into a family of tanners or blacksmiths or potters or oil grinders or fishermen, after all. Why should he beg and plead with Mondol's sons for sharecropping rights? 'I only asked Mondol once. And his younger son says, this land is going to Tamiz. What for? So that a fisherman can turn this earth to gold.' Harmatullah was overcome by a fit of coughing, making his efforts to imitate Abdul Kader's speech unexpectedly successful.

Tamiz knelt down without replying to pick up a handful of the soil on which he would be sharecropping. The ayush had been harvested down to the roots, stripping the land so bare that it looked like a head of closely cropped blackish-yellow hair. Rubbing the base of the stubble, his calloused fingertips encountered softness. As he rose to his feet and began walking around slowly, the soil, moist with rainwater, squelched beneath his feet. He would rise before dawn tomorrow, when it was still dark, put the yoke on the pair of oxen that Mondol kept in Harmatullah's cowshed, and run the plough across the soft land. He might be the son of a fisherman, but Tamiz had grasped the fact that the earth was yearning for the plough. Was this rainwater that had gathered in the soil? Or had the water rolled down the sloping riverbank? He would have to quench the thirst of the soil by ploughing as wide an expanse as possible on the very first day. Plough it again the next day, and the day after that too. Tamiz would plough the entire land as many times as possible. Even the roots of the stubble would blend with the earth and take on the colour of the soil. Once the earth had been turned into mush, he would sow his paddy seeds. Bulu had made a bed of seeds in Mondol's backyard. Tamiz had seen it today too. So beautiful—like a new rug of tender green. Who had laid it out? Who was that bent over the carpet? Tamiz's head began to spin when he realized that it was Kulsum's head that was lowered over the seeds. He felt an urge to return home at once, his innards twisting with hunger all over again. But then this was a fleeing sensation. He had to plough the land, it needed one, two, three runs with the blade. The seeds would suffer unless the soil was as soft as could be. He would have to leave plenty of room between each seedling—only then would the paddy grow quickly, shooting upwards without impediments. The saplings would turn into stalks and keep growing in the rainwater and the slush. The water would dry in the month of Aghran, when the crops would lower their roots deeper into the earth in search of moisture. They would grow taller too. This very same plot of land would turn arid if it didn't rain in the month of Kaartik. Then it would be a mad rush to water the stalks, uproot the weeds, loosen the roots at the base. Because these acts of servitude did not present themselves to Tamiz in chronological order—or, indeed, in any order at all—his agitation mounted. He felt a chill run down his spine, although he sensed a pleasant breeze as well. The frightening but liberating excitement included the pleasure of considering Sharafat Mondol's land his own, the anxiety of taking on, for the first time, the entire responsibility of farming a plot of land, and gratitude towards Abdul Kader, which had escalated into devotion. Tamiz was so nervous because of all this that he had to sit down next to Harmatullah, grabbing his hookah and taking long drags on it to fill his empty belly with smoke, an effective way of dulling his hunger. Letting the hookah remain with Tamiz, Harmatullah continued reaping the jute on his land. The old fellow was doing it all by himself. Looking at him out of the corner of his eye at first, then more openly, and finally directly, Tamiz forgot that he was smoking. He might be a jealous old fool, but he could work harder than any man. The sun was overhead, and he lived just

across the lake, but not once had he gone home to rest his back or
his limbs. Nor had he employed a single labourer. Did Harmat do
everything unaided? Did he have a pet jinn or something?

Harmatullah had never been known to associate with jinns. But
people said other things about him. Even though he did employ
daily labourers, once the back-breaking part of the work was done
he dismissed them and put his daughters to work on the land.
Harmatullah had three daughters. The eldest had been married,
but her husband had stopped taking care of her three years ago, and
so she languished in her father's home. The second daughter was
old enough to be married, though the youngest one was probably
quite young. Despite two marriages, Harmat had not been fortunate
enough to have a son. He had sent his second wife to her family home
during the famine, where she had died in her youth. But people said
each of his daughters was as good as a son. Not only did they do
all the work at home, but they also put in hard labour on this plot
of land to the south of the lake. All this jute that the old man was
growing—when it came to lining up the stalks, his daughters were
no less skilful than any hired hand. Tamiz surmised that they must
have been at work with Harmatullah, going home only because they
had caught sight of him. Harmatullah hailed him suddenly. 'This
way, son of a fisherman. You don't seem to have much work on your
hands, come help me with these.'

Tamiz held on to the reaped stalks while Harmatullah cleared a
space to stack them. The crop looked beautiful. Glorious, in fact. He
had delayed the reaping a little, but the jute had not been damaged.
How plump the stalks were! The golden glow of the fibre was already
peeping through the ripened skin. Harmatullah sighed when he saw
Tamiz marvelling at them. 'The jute grows well enough when Allah
wants it to. But what's the use, all of it just goes to Mondol. I've been
cultivating his land for five years now, what I take home at harvest
time is no more than what I would have got as a daily labourer.
I don't know how much I'm supposed to have borrowed or how the
calculations are done, but I get nothing.'

'Here are your stalks,' said Tamiz, 'I'm going home.'

'Just a few minutes more. I'll finish these and leave.'

'No, I can't stay. I'm hungry.' Tamiz walked along the ridge and came to a halt on his own land. This Harmatullah was obviously a very wicked old fellow. He should thank his stars for the chance to be a sharecropper on Mondol's land. The old coot would have had to turn to Jagadish Saha if Mondol hadn't lent him the seeds in Kaartik. He had no inkling of how the Hindu moneylender would have fleeced him. Instead of which his heart was breaking at the thought of giving the owner of the land his due share of the crop. Traitor! Traitor! He must mention this to Kader. But no, Kader was too soft-hearted to do anything about it. If Tamiz told Mondol, he wouldn't allow Harmatullah on his land any more. Tamiz would have to incite Mondol to evict Harmatullah. He would talk to Kader after that. If Tamiz could win him over and get Harmat's land, he could demolish the ridge and work on all four and a half acres by himself. He could not tolerate this treacherous Harmatullah's betrayal.

But Tamiz did not succeed in making his case to either Sharafat Mondol or his son. Where was the time! He had to go to Harmatullah's house well before sunrise to collect the plough and oxen and yoke. It drizzled at that hour almost every day. It would still be raining when he arrived north of the ox pool, covering his head with a towel. If only there were a torrential shower, that would ensure that the sky stayed clear till late afternoon. But no matter how early he went, Tamiz had never seen Harmat at home even once. The old coot was off to work on his land already. As soon as Tamiz arrived with his oxen and plough, the old fellow's eldest daughter ran off home, covering her face with the end of her sari. It would be no later than daybreak then. Tamiz's mood soured as he watched the old man harvesting the jute in the pouring rain, coughing fit to burst. Didn't the man and his daughters ever sleep? And what did she have to run away for when she caught sight of Tamiz?

Harmatullah sometimes appeared on Tamiz's land with his hookah during pauses in his own work. Tamiz would hear him speak suddenly, 'Look, fisherman, you'll find it hard to push the plough into the soil if you hold it that way. Can't you see your oxen tiring?' Taking the plough from Tamiz, Harmatullah demonstrated how to use it correctly on moist earth.

And so Tamiz had turned the earth into a bed of butter over the past few days. After a few showers in the morning, it hardly rained all day. When he sat on the ridge late in the afternoon, kneading the mud with both hands, the scent of the rain and the soggy earth and the hint of sunlight and the rhythmic movement of his arms made Tamiz drowsy. His entire body longed to stretch out on the ground. He may well have done just that, but that was the moment the bloody old coot decided to scream, 'Do you think the earth is a whore's tit, fisherman? What're you squeezing it for that way?' This admonition seemed to transform the land into a naked woman lying on her back, making Tamiz frantic with desire to swim across not just her breasts but also her entire length and breadth. He didn't even have the chance to be angry with Harmatullah, whose subsequent instructions dampened his arousal. 'You can't knead the mud with your hand. The soil needs the blade of the plough, don't you understand? She's worse than a whore, this bitch is a tease through and through. The slut won't be happy till she's been fucked by a plough. What can you do with your hands?'

Turning grimmer with every word, Harmatullah ignored a coughing bout to declare that if you kneaded the soil with your hands it became hard as soon as the sun rose higher. And hardened soil could not offer the comfort of a home to paddy seeds.

Tamiz rose to his feet, withdrawing his hands from the breasts. Still coughing, Harmat spat out gobs of phlegm without stopping his grumbling: How can the son of a fisherman serve the land? It's not just a matter of casting a net and catching fish by the dozen. They were cruel towards the fish, and they used the land only for their pleasure. How could you understand the true value of the earth unless you were born into a peasant's family? Harmatullah was a man in any case, but even his daughters could tend to the land in a way a fisherman burning with desire to be a farmer couldn't even dream of. Tamiz was burning with rage at being compared to a woman. The buxom figure who had lain down wistfully on his two acres and a bit of land was lost in the depths of the earth now, no longer visible.

Tolerating this Harmatullah was becoming impossible by the day. But it was difficult to be harsh with him—he knew farming inside out. When the old man's daughter slipped away on spotting Tamiz, she left behind work that was always perfectly done. He could never turn his admiring eyes away from the father-and-daughter duo's accomplishments to confront Harmatullah. But whether he was harvesting the jute or lining up the stalks, all the while abusing the clan of fishermen roundly and coughing uncontrollably, one of the old man's clouded eyes was always trained on Tamiz.

8

At home Tamiz's father never even looked at him. When he returned he found his father snoring on the maacha in the darkness. And in front of the clay oven in the tiny veranda attached to the room, her face looking strange in the light from the fire and the smoke and the shadows cast by them, sat Kulsum, staring at the darkness above her. Her practice of cooking some rice at all sorts of hours would not end till the grains that Tamiz had brought back from Khiyar ran out. Tamiz's father had no fixed time for his meals. Two years ago, when not even rice husks were available during the famine, he had become quite accustomed to starving. And now, whenever Tamiz brought some rice back from Khiyar, the man could not control his appetite. He may have gone to sleep late in the afternoon on a full belly, but if he happened to wake up in the early hours of the morning he would climb down from the maacha to rummage in the pot. After recovering from his stomach upset the other day, he had started eating much more than before. No matter what the quantity of the food that Tamiz put away, there was a pattern to his meals. After his morning meal of rice soaked overnight in water, he packed some rice when he went to work. And when he returned home, he ate just the one time. When he took a dip in the pond before his meal, there would always be a spot of mud sticking to him somewhere—on his arm or leg, or on his earlobe or the lines on his neck. When Kulsum pointed to it with great glee, Tamiz would demolish all her delight by rolling his eyes in his father's direction and asking, 'Was he home all day?'

Kulsum never answered this question. Exhausted with watching her husband sleep constantly, she would start yawning if she had to describe the whole thing. Kulsum did not like yawning in the evening. Engaged in stealing a whiff of the mud sticking to Tamiz's earlobe or the lines on his neck or his arm or leg from a distance, she evaded the question. Instead, she asked, 'Are you done ploughing?' or 'How many times more will you have to plough the field?'

Devouring his food, rinsing his hands, and squatting on the doorstep of his own room with his hookah, Tamiz took his time answering. 'It's too early. Doing it all by yourself is very hard work. This isn't the same as working as a hired hand on someone else's land. There you run the plough twice as agreed and sow the paddy seeds. This is amon, after all, if you work hard at it it'll grow as well as wild rice does, but if you don't, you'll get nothing.' Drawing on his hookah, he informed her that the land needed constant attention and was displeased if deprived. 'The land is like a bitch on heat . . .' He bit his words back at the last moment. This wasn't the right place to parrot Harmatullah. After a pause, a metaphor sprang up in his head on its own, perhaps out of the joy of imitating the old coot. 'Resentful soil is a terrible miser. Even more miserly than that bastard Jagadish Saha.' Kulsum rolled with laughter at this comparison of the parsimoniousness of land and humans. Whether Tamiz's analogy was the cause or the excuse for Kulsum's laughter was not clear to either of them, but Tamiz was encouraged by her response. He declared that the attention he was lavishing on the land now was bound to make that bastard Harmatullah eat his words in ignominy. It could be the expectation of a bountiful harvest, or the hope of watching Harmatullah eat his words, or the blackish-yellow glow of the lamp—but the purple flush on Tamiz's dark-skinned face made Kulsum's entire body tremble. If she could have converted this faint shudder into words, this is what Kulsum would have heard herself thinking: the same dark flush also appears on Tamiz's father's face now and then. But when? When does it appear? Kulsum began to take deep breaths in search of those particular days, as though she would be able to sniff out the smell of Tamiz's father at those moments on his son's face. It took her just a few of these breaths to locate the smell which signalled that Tamiz's father's face also glowed with a colour somewhere between a blackish yellow and purple at dusk. No, not every day, but occasionally. Which were those days? Kulsum took a few more deep breaths. Yes, it was on the evenings preceding the nights on which he went sleepwalking that his face blurred behind a curtain of these dark colours.

His son, though, spent all his time in the fields, and even at night Tamiz could think of nothing but his crops. Dreams that came in the night could never take control of him. Still, you couldn't be too careful about these things. This yellowish-purple flush on Tamiz's face must be wiped out at once to ensure that there was no chance of his sleepwalking too. It was probably with this consideration that Kulsum did not allow the discussion about Harmatullah to be interrupted. 'What can Harmat do to you? He's too old to cause you any harm.'

'Too old? You want to hear his tricks?' Stirred by the prospect of conveying the details of Harmatullah's objectionable behaviour, Tamiz stopped stuffing his hookah with fresh tobacco, sat up straight, and proceeded to complain in a progressively louder voice about how Harmatullah took advantage of his own peasant lineage to humiliate him, Tamiz, constantly and find fault with his work. 'He says, listen to me now, you're no more than a fisherman, but we've been farmers for generations, what our women know about farming is a million times more than you will ever learn even if you plough the land all your life.' What kind of talk is this? When he doesn't hesitate to bring the women of the family into the open, what right does he have to brag about being farmers? And they're supposed to be Rafadani Muslims. Even if Tamiz goes to the field at the crack of dawn he finds Harmat's eldest daughter working there. She slips away quietly when she sees him. Just imagine, Harmatullah allows such a beautiful young woman out in the fields in full view of males, will Allah stand for such things?

Tamiz kept talking about the brazen shamelessness of Harmatullah's pretty daughter, but Kulsum said nothing in response. Suddenly he realized that she had edged closer to him and was drawing deep breaths. With her breathing substituting for conversation, Tamiz was forced to stop talking and turn his attention back to his hookah. Whenever Kulsum lost something she sniffed around the room in search of it, which was something that Tamiz's father had scolded her about repeatedly, while Tamiz himself had made fun of it even before she married his father. Why was she sniffing Tamiz all over the same way now? His heart fluttered at the sound of her deep breaths; what had Kulsum lost? Whatever it was, could it possibly be lying within the shaggy mop of his hair or the mud-streaked lines in his neck or in the crook of his elbow? Had Tamiz stolen something of Kulsum's? With his original uncertainty now replaced by the anxiety to find out what it was that he may have stolen, Tamiz tightened his fingers around his hookah so grimly and clamped his thick lips around its nozzle so hard that his sucking motion made the entire water within it vaporize in the heat of the tobacco and enter his chest and lungs and even his abdomen in the form of smoke, darkening his insides. The gurgling of the hookah and the whistling of Kulsum's breath grew louder in equal measure. There was no risk of conflict between them, but no scope for harmony either. So Tamiz gave up soon afterwards and just sat quietly, laying his hookah down like a useless weapon by the door, leaning against the wall, and not looking at it despite the risk of its rolling away. He moved closer to the door, and, after achieving a reasonably safe distance, coughed a few times, spat in the direction of the yard, and even belched once. When the burp allowed his tongue a tobacco-flavoured taste of the rice, daal and spicy fish curry he had eaten a short while ago, Tamiz found a new strength in his body. As he rose to his feet and set off towards his own room, Kulsum took a couple of steps behind him, saying sharply, 'A woman from a peasant family will certainly do a better job than you of looking after crops. Harmatullah Poramanik said nothing wrong. Your father said the same thing yesterday. He said when a fisherman's son tries to plough the land, the fishing net gets snarled in it. There will never be a good crop, and the net will rot underground, which means that's the end of fishing.'

Kulsum's frenzied sniffing died under the force of her outburst. Released from her frenetic breathing, Tamiz regained his spirit and shouted back just as energetically, 'What do you know about it? Your father was so poor you had to go around begging people's arses for food, what do you understand of farming? Don't try your tricks with me. Give my father something to eat, he's old, he gets hungry. All you care about is stuffing your belly. How does a fakir's daughter talk so much?'

But each of these words turned around to land like someone's slap on Tamiz's face. And with every slap his tirade grew sharper. Tamiz had been in some sort of a trance from the time he crossed the lake before sunrise to collect the oxen from Harmatullah's shed, and it had strengthened through the day as he drove the plough into the earth. He had sunk deeper into it under the onslaught of Kulsum's sniffing, but now his own diatribe dispelled it completely, and at once he was overcome by exhaustion. Sleep assailed him then, and as he proceeded drowsily towards his own maacha he heard his father talking hoarsely in the other room. 'Shamsher is planting rice on the eastern side of his house. Go see him tomorrow. I've spoken to him. His seeds are better. Shamsher told me himself. Don't let him pay you less than he should.'

Unless Tamiz listened carefully to his father speaking in these short sentences in a voice still thick with sleep, he would not be able to draw the connection between them. Still, even in Tamiz's own sleep-laden brain Shamsher's bed of seeds began to undulate in a shade of light green, which in turn made him sleepier.

Meanwhile, Kulsum stood at her doorstep with her hands on her hips, screaming, 'I may be a fakir's daughter, but your father owns miles of land, doesn't he, so that I can learn all about farming from him? Even your mother used to spend the entire day at the Mondols' house. She must have learnt everything about growing crops as a maid. She must have been very happy working there. I don't want such happiness. I'd rather kick happiness like that on the balls.'

Through all this Tamiz's father kept talking about Shamsher and the power of his seeds. The combination of his phlegm-heavy rumble and her high-pitched shrieks made the light-green waves in Tamiz's head rock so hypnotically that they wrapped him in deep layers of sleep.

9

But Kulsum's vehemence banished all remaining traces of sleep in Tamiz's father. Tired from spending the entire day on his back, he didn't even have the energy to shout at his wife. If he sat on the floor and looked out through the open door, the indistinctly visible yard outside gradually gained a definite shape in the dim starlight, but his body still felt numb. Even the pond in front of the house had tucked its head into the yard. Had its water dried out, making its bed visible? Was Tamiz thinking of running a plough into this patch of newly awakened land? Its ownership would pass over to Mondol if that were the case. Was Tamiz going to spend his entire life as a sharecropper on Mondol's land? Over at Katlahar Lake the pool of water was shrinking rapidly, exposing new tracts of land every day. The lake might one day shrink into a pond as small as this one, gasping for breath. Tamiz's father knew that the bastard Mondol was up to no good. He was probably aiming to take control of the fig tree to the north of the lake. Suddenly Tamiz's father felt a sting in his eyes, something had got into them, he didn't know what. A vision of Katlahar Lake floated up in front of his eyes, though he had closed them because of the irritation. Drops of rain fell occasionally on the water overflowing the lake in the month of Bhadro, giving him an itching sensation inside his head. It was possible that whatever had pricked his eye had gone all the way into his brain, where he could feel an ache now. Perhaps the reverse pull of the clouds was sucking all the water of Katlahar Lake up into the sky so that it could turn into clouds too and then float all night, keep floating at sunrise, turning into flames under the heat of the sun and drying up every last drop of water in the lake. And then from the sky the fireballs would watch Sharafat Mondol's sharecroppers tilling the land left behind by the waterless lake. What would happen if Mondol ran his plough all the way to the fig tree? If all of it became Mondol's property, Munshi's pet murrels might turn into worms and wriggle under the newly exposed bed of the lake. Or would Munshi, unable to turn them into sheep, make iron rings out of them to be added to the chain around his neck? But it was not so simple! Cherag Ali had declared; in fact, Munshi had announced in through Cherag Ali's spirit, that anyone who disturbed the fish would never get another meal in his life. So tyranny against the murrels was out of the question. The blood began to course faster through Tamiz's father's veins, its movement making itself audible in the form of a verse.

Munshi's orders rumbled across the lake
The angel of death eyed the Company soldiers

But with Cherag Ali gone, who would relay Munshi's orders? Across distant villages and numerous sandbanks, some old and some new, dancing to the tune of the seven currents and forty-nine waves in the Jomuna, Cherag Ali's song spilled over into the waters of the Bangali river, took several dips, and then, losing its power as it traversed the fields of grain, negotiated the ridges between plots made slippery by the blood spilled in battles between jotedars and sharecroppers, and finally rolled into Katlahar Lake. By the time it emerged after floundering in its depths to wash ashore here in Girirdanga, the song had become much fainter, throwing its shadow in the rain-soaked starlight on the roof of Tamiz's father's house. Whose voice had made the journey possible in this fading light? A closer look revealed the shadow as the white horse near the fig tree. The enemies' arrows were impaled in his body, the arrowheads vibrating in tune with the

impatience of the horse for its rider. It began to gallop even before a
place for Munshi to sit could be identified amidst all those arrows, its
hooves striking up Cherag Ali's song.

> Your wife sleeps by your side
> The moon is awake in the sky
> Your son weeps in his dream
> The fakir does not know
> The pillow languishes near the head
> The horse appears at the door
> The fakir leaves on his steed
> No one knows where he's going

Who was that singing here? Was Cherag Ali back? Tamiz's father
might have had the answer had he looked outside, but he was resting
his chin on his knees, which were drawn up to this chest, listening to
the song with great attention, both his eyes and ears shut.

> The moon rises over the bamboo grove
> One by one its lays all the eggs
> The yellow yolk is everyone's home
> But the fakir is gone.

But no, it wasn't Cherag Ali singing after all. Who knew the fakir's
voice better than Tamiz's father? Who used to listen to Cherag Ali
singing almost constantly after his arrival in Girirdanga? Tamiz's
father, of course. Along with Cherag Ali's granddaughter Kulsum. But
then Kulsum was younger then. She would sing the songs she heard
from her grandfather, though she wasn't old enough to understand
what they meant. Not that she understood them now either. There
was no count of the number of people whose dreams Cherag Ali
explained, humming as he drew lines on the floor of Kalam majhi's
ramshackle hut. He would keep singing while he tried to interpret
people's dreams, or perhaps he sang them so that he could interpret

the dreams. He would also gather crowds at the Golabari market, singing and strumming his dotara, beginning his explanations of the dreams once he had a large enough audience. He would take a tattered book from his patchwork sling bag, but Tamiz's father did not know whether he read what was written in it, or whether he would simply listen to the lines drawn on its pages. Drawing all those lines was how he got to the meaning of dreams, but he drew them on the floor, not on paper. Everyone had a dream that they wanted explained. Someone might have dreamt of an ox, but a plump ox had a different meaning from a gaunt one. The meaning would change entirely if the ox was being slaughtered. Cherag Ali would smile when someone said he had been chased by a dog in his dream, for it meant that the man's enemy would receive his comeuppance. But then seeing just a dog in a dream was a warning of danger. Once, a frail old man who lived in a village across the Bangali river had walked all the way to meet Cherag Ali, throwing himself at his feet. Apparently, at least once a week he dreamt he was sleeping with his daughter-in-law. Despite confessing and begging pardon of Allah over and over again, the dreams had not stopped, which was why he was now at Cherag Ali's door. Then consider the fact that Kalam majhi's dream that he was leading the prayers was broadcast to everyone. But the details of many of his other dreams were known only to Kalam himself and to Cherag Ali. Even Sharafat Mondol had drawn Cherag Ali aside at the Golabari market one day to tell him confidentially of a dream he had had. Cherag Ali had not disclosed anything about the dream to anyone else. As for Boikuntho, he would recount a new dream every day. Tamiz's father was the only one who had not told Cherag Ali what he had dreamt. But why blame him? He was simple in the head, remembering none of his dreams once the sky lightened. At the Golabari market young Boikuntho would often ask him, 'Why don't you ever talk about your dreams, Tamiz's father? What did you dream of, tell me.' Considering that Tamiz's father got confused every time he tried to speak, how was he to talk of his dreams? It was the same Boikuntho who cornered him one day in

Cherag Ali's house. 'You have to tell us today, Tamiz's father. I hear you unlock the door and go out every night. Who calls out to you? What dreams do you have? You have to tell us today.'

Cherag Ali was drawing lines on the ground and humming as he sought the meaning of Boikuntho's dream. He kept pausing to ask Boikuntho for clarifications, and between his answers Boikuntho kept poking Tamiz's father. 'Well? Are you telling us or not?'

Tamiz's father looked around with dull eyes, staring outside for a long time. Kalam majhi's nanny goat was standing across the bamboo grove, dismayed at being unable to jump over the fence into the eggplant field. What could Tamiz's father see in her eyes? His own kept closing as he gazed at her. Should he take a nap in an effort to remember what he had dreamt last night? Eventually he had to respond to Boikuntho, who kept nagging him, with a 'yesterday'. After a pause he muttered, as though talking in his sleep, 'No, not yesterday, the other day.' Without specifying the day, he continued, 'I ate my rice with a chilli that evening, but there was a banana too. No, the banana was the day before.' He stopped again to recollect when he had eaten the banana. Unable to come to a conclusion about this, he looked helplessly at Boikuntho, who couldn't help chuckling.

'What happened that day?' Startled, Tamiz's father rattled off, 'I went to the lake that day with the fishing net. Got some fish, six or seven of them.'

When he stopped again, Boikuntho said in disappointment at this abbreviated account of the dream, 'How could this have been a dream? You go to the lake every day. Don't you catch fish there all the time?'

Sharafat Mondol had not taken a lease on the lake yet at that time. Why should Tamiz's father only have been dreaming about it, then?

Then what was the dream he had had that night? Tamiz's father remained sitting on the floor, his head bowed in thought, his still-black beard fluttering recklessly in the breeze. He felt sleepy as he mused on his dream, but there was not a trace of a dream in those sleepy eyes. He could faintly hear Boikuntho Giri singing along with Cherag Ali, his mouth stuffed with food, a powdery fog of puffed rice suspended in front of his lips. He had brought a mound of puffed rice to Cherag Ali's house, which everyone was eating—Cherag Ali, Kulsum, even Tamiz's father. When his throat felt parched with all the puffed rice and talking, Boikuntho told Kulsum, 'Give me a bite of that mango you've got, Kulsum.'

Kulsum had crossed the creek before sunrise to collect the mango from Bulu the fisherman's kitchen garden. She handed it over, her face falling at Boikuntho's demand disguised as a request. Boikuntho bit off a piece from the lower half of the mango, sucking on it and saying, 'It's sour, so sour.'

'Did I beg you to eat it?' Kulsum snarled at him. 'Who asked you to have a sour mango?'

'I'm thirsty, what do you expect?'

The trouble was that Boikuntho could not have a drink of water in Cherag Ali's house. Since they belonged to different faiths, he had no choice but to quenching his thirst with a mango instead of water so that he didn't break with his religion. Sitting here was allowed, so was eating puffed rice, not just with a side of jaggery, but even with a smear of salt and oil if he so desired. Water, however, was out of the question. It would mean breaking the rules of his faith. When Kulsum yelled at him again, Boikuntho said, 'God has given us our religion, how can I break out of it?'

'But your god has ordered you to eat mangos anywhere you want, isn't that right? What a greedy god, don't accept water, but no harm when it comes to mangos.'

'Stop vomiting out what everyone says. Your Allah is the same as my god. Different names, that's all. Isn't that right?'

Nodding to indicate his approval of Boikuntho's conclusion that Allah and god did not have separate identities, Cherag Ali drew a few more lines on the floor and, after staring at them for a few minutes in silence, asked Boikuntho, 'Did you dream you were eating those rice flakes in the morning? Was it before noon?'

'Hmm. Let me see, it must have been nine when babu took the road home. Or was it ten? No, can't have been earlier than eleven.'

It took him quite some time to estimate the hour at which his employer had left the shop. Then he proceeded to give an extended account of his own meal of rice, fish curry and milk. Nor was there any lack of fervour in his description of settling down for a nap after muttering a prayer but being unable to fall asleep in the seclusion of Mukunda Saha's shop in the silent market. Only when he had exhausted every last detail did he finally get to his dream, adding numerous minutiae to the picture he had already provided. None of this made any impression on Cherag Ali, who only kept adding more lines on the ground with every new fact revealed by Boikuntho. In the course of this exposition Boikuntho announced that in his dream he had consumed the rice flakes beneath his mosquito net. 'Are you sure?' asked Cherag Ali. 'Eating them under the net has a particular meaning, but it changes if you were sitting on the edge of the bed. It all goes wrong if you can't describe your dream perfectly. I have to take everything into account to explain the meaning.'

Encouraged by this question or observation or warning of Cherag Ali's, Boikuntho gave such a complicated but comprehensive account of just one night's dream that Tamiz's father was utterly fascinated. But the significance of Boikuntho's dream that Cherag Ali conveyed with movements of his eyes and strange twists in his lips made it clear to everyone that in sitting beneath the mosquito net and not outside it, Boikuntho had not only personally destroyed the possibility of acquiring wealth that he had originally created by consuming rice flakes, but he had also created a crisis for himself. At this indication of imminent danger Boikuntho sucked out the last drop of the sour mango juice with a loud noise. A pall of gloom descended over Cherag Ali's bearded face at Boikuntho's indifference. He felt hesitant about declaring that dreaming of a mosquito net signalled a coffin. He passed on this information directly to Tamiz's father instead, but not until three days later, at the Golabari market. All he told Boikuntho now was, 'Your dream is ominous, Boikuntho. You have to make a pledge with five annas to Munshi.' When Boikuntho laughed at this Cherag Ali scolded him. 'What are you laughing at? Your life is in danger.'

Five annas was no small sum. 'Where's the money going to come from?' said Boikuntho. 'Do you know Calcutta is being bombed? My babu's business is about to collapse, he can't sleep nights. You expect him to give me money now?'

The market was abuzz with excitement that day with news of the bombs falling on Calcutta and Japan's inevitable victory. Cherag Ali wasn't doing much business. Four annas from Boikuntho would have let him buy some rice, eggplant, salt and cooking oil. The pledge could always be made later. 'You find it funny?' said Cherag Ali. 'You still think dreaming of a mosquito net is a joke?' He began to sing dire predictions for people who dreamt of mosquito nets.

> Musa dreamt in his bed of a mosquito net
> Majnu burst out in tears when he heard
> My dearest son has no future, alas
> How will I live with the loss of my child
> The angel of death has given three days
> You must beg pardon at the shrine.

Today, as he sat on the floor of his house after all this time, gazing at the dim light thrown by the stars, Tamiz's father's thick head was buffeted by a series of waves that crested and crashed, his eyes growing heavy with sleep all the while. Ignoring the attraction of the rice and the daal laid out for him on a plate, he stretched himself out on the maacha, sleep descending on him as soon as he had fitted himself snugly next to Kulsum.

Cherag Ali's song did not fade in his sleep, however. On the contrary, it began to bubble loudly now. Cherag Ali had sung these verses earlier for Boikuntho. When he sang it a second time at the market, Boikuntho joined the chorus, along with Tamiz's father. He no longer seemed troubled by his employer's business losses or the fear of Japanese bombs. In fact, he seemed to have forgotten his dream from three nights ago, or perhaps it had been obscured by a newer dream. Asked repeatedly to sing Cherag Ali's new song,

Tamiz's father suddenly looked grim, saying with emphasis, 'Give him the money, Boikuntho. Your dream is a dangerous one.'

Paying no attention, Boikuntho asked Cherag Ali, 'New song? Never heard it before.'

'I don't compose these songs, haven't I told you before? These are handed down to us, not to us, we're not big enough, but to our ancestors, important people, all.'

Meanwhile, Kulsum piped up, looking at Boikuntho, 'Why can't you pay up? Don't you care for your life? It's just a matter of four annas, after all.'

'If I give anyone any money it'll be to you. That mango the other day was so sour, I have to pay you back for it, don't I? It'll come to eight annas with interest.'

Kulsum felt fear, not anger, at Boikuntho's witticism. Didn't the man have any fear for his life? Tamiz's father, who was sitting quite close to her, had seen the dread in her eyes. All this had happened deep in the past. And yet, see how Kulsum's anxiety for Boikuntho all those years ago still ate away at Tamiz's father's head. To get rid of it he lay down next to Kulsum, his head touching her chest. It was difficult to say whether there was any remnant of her concern for Boikuntho's dream of a mosquito net, or, even if there was, whether Tamiz's father could hear it. But the smell of mud in Tamiz's father's head and shoulders, in his thinning hair and his thick beard, made Kulsum's breasts swell. In Tamiz's father's ears, though, it was Cherag Ali's song that vibrated, and perhaps because Boikuntho Giri was singing along, his head turned heavy and rolled off Kulsum's chest. In this head he could now hear the clatter of Sharafat Mondol's wooden clogs. Had Munshi drawn in his large black fishing net at the sound? Did he not pay attention to anything? What was he doing now in his fig tree? Tamiz's father should find out. He clambered down from the maacha, his legs tottering, with the intention of walking to the lake for a quick glimpse of what Munshi was up to.

10

The month of Bhadro came and went, and so did the month of Ashwin, but Kaartik refused to leave. The amon crop was good this year, but because the land had been largely dry, there were silken streaks around the base of the grain. There was some water standing in the fields at the beginning of Ashwin. Before it drained into the soil, Harmatullah had sneaked up to make a breach in the ridge standing between his field and Tamiz's, so that the water would flow into his land. The soil in his field was still black, filling Tamiz's nostrils with the smell of moisture when he stood on the ridge, making him envious. Harmatullah had planted pepper in his field now.

Meanwhile, there were signs of cracks in the soil on Tamiz's field, their lips widening slowly in thirst. How long would it be before the cracks turned into gaping mouths? The rice saplings would no longer stand upright when that happened. And after that? Tamiz was overcome by thirst whenever he had to weed his field. Harmat had a bowl perpetually brimming with water, but he became distracted whenever Tamiz asked for some. Tamiz realized that the old coot was reluctant to let the son of a fisherman have a drink of water from his bowl—which meant he had to go to the ox pool. But now the parched land had parched Tamiz's throat too, and he did not have the patience to clamber down the steep bank of the pool and up again. So he walked along its eastern edge towards Harmat's house. 'Anyone home? Can you give me some water?'

Shortly after Tamiz had made his request loudly, Harmat's younger daughter appeared with a bowl of water. Tamiz had expected the elder one, however. He had seen her leaving the field early every morning when he went to work, which meant he was familiar with her from the back. Perhaps Tamiz was keen to see her face too. She had been standing by her father when he had breached the ridge with his spade to make the water flow from Tamiz's field to his own. So he could have used this opportunity to give her a piece of his mind. But Tamiz remembered none of this when the younger sister appeared. His thirst became sharper, and he tilted the bowl to pour its entire contents down his throat.

A curtain of dried banana leaves hung behind Tamiz, from the other side of which a dark-skinned hand appeared, holding out a slab of jaggery on a tender banana leaf. Tamiz took the leaf and devoured the jaggery, all the while cursing the ostentatiousness of a curtain concealing a bitch who was more like a man, the kind who makes a breach in the ridge protecting another man's field to steal his water. The water he had drunk was delicious now with the taste of jaggery. On his way back to his own field he belched delicately, which brought up both the flavour of sugar cane jaggery and the prick of envy. Ordinary people could barely put rice on their plates at this time of the year, and here was a peasant showing off with jaggery. Her father was a miser who never offered Tamiz any food while wolfing down his own lunch beneath the jujube tree. And here she was, the miser's daughter, flaunting their stock of jaggery. What was the need for a curtain if she was going to give him something to eat anyway? Where was the flourish of the veil when she joined hands with her father to breach the ridge and steal water from his field in the middle of the night? But then she had been living off her father for two years now, so what choice did she have but to work on his fields? Tamiz knew everything that had happened. In the year of the famine, Harmatullah's son-in-law had deposited his wife, a one-and-a-half-year-old son and a six-month-old daughter in his house and disappeared. The girl had died before the year was out,

while the boy's swollen belly kept expanding every day, his coppery
face turning yellow, even his eyes taking on a yellow hue. And even
though she was starving, Harmatullah's daughter's buttocks were
the size of little hillocks now. But her husband was nowhere to be
seen. Apparently half the people in his village had succumbed to
the famine, and the survivors' houses had been swallowed by the
Jomuna. Harmat had heard his son-in-law hadn't died, though—he
had gone away to Rangpur or Assam or Cooch Behar of Jalpaiguri or
Dinajpur or some such place, without leaving an address. He wrote
songs, it seemed, and Harmatullah was claiming that this work had
taken him to Calcutta or Dhaka or Delhi. Tamiz knew the truth.
The husband must have run away to Khiyar, where the daily wages
were much higher, at least five and a half annas or even six, even late
in Kaartik. There was plenty of work to be had over there. They took
good care of their land, and worked very hard on it too. There were
virtually no rivers to speak of in Khiyar, only large lakes, from which
they had dug canals to let the water flow to the fields to irrigate them.
The earth soaked up the water like a famished labourer lapping up
the last drop of starch from his rice. Tamiz's field here could do with
some irrigation. If he could convince Harmatullah of the necessity,
the old coot could talk to Sharafat Mondol about having a canal dug
from the ox pool.

But how was Tamiz to broach the subject? He could start by
advising Harmatullah to make inquiries about his absconding son-
in-law. Never mind all the talk about Calcutta or Delhi or Assam
or Jalpaiguri, the truth is that your son-in-law has gone to Khiyar.
It's very simple. Go into the town, get on a train, and then wherever
you get off all you'll see are rice fields. Some jotedar fed up with the
demands of sharecroppers must have hired Harmatullah's son-in-law
as a daily labourer on his best land. After the aadhiars started creating
trouble, daily wages had risen there. Why? Because of the risks
involved in working on the land. The sharecroppers were united,
and could attack the jotedars at any moment. Tamiz had been there,
barely three months ago. Even if it was three months, it felt like

yesterday. He had had to abandon the grains he had harvested to make a run for it when the aadhiars had given chase. Oh, how swiftly he had run! He was hit by a flurry of arrows—Tamiz had heard that Santhal peasants sometimes attacked jotedars with bows and arrows. Not able to run any more, pursued by all those bowmen, Tamiz had taken shelter beneath an acacia tree on a ridge between two fields. But how was a scraggy acacia going to provide protection? Tamiz had had no choice but to break off the prickly acacia branches and throw them at his pursuers. But some bastard must have cast a spell, because every one of those branches hit the jotedar instead. Sharafat Mondol was bleeding from his neck where the thorns had penetrated his skin. His sons Abdul Aziz and Abdul Kader were standing behind him. Tamiz tried his best to ensure that at least one thick branch with thorns hit Abdul Aziz on his face, but without success. He had broken off more branches. Those jotedars were bastards all the way, they were bloodsucking leeches. Tamiz had to deposit the fruit of all his back-breaking labour, the harvest of all the hard work he did, in their sheds. He finally looked around when the thistles from the branches of the jujube tree he was clutching began to press into his palm and fingers. Harmatullah was sowing pepper in the adjoining field. What acacia tree? When had he ever been chased by peasants in Khiyar and fought back? It was just that one time that he had run away from the rampaging aadhiars to hide in the jotedar's house, built on high ground, from where he had seen the Santhals fire arrows. But did that mean he had to join their ranks? Excuse me, for shame, how could he possibly lay a finger on Sharafat Mondol or his sons? He wasn't so ungrateful as to harbour such thoughts. Tamiz had graduated from being a daily labourer to a sharecropper thanks to Abdul Kader's recommendation and Sharafat Mondol's kindness. What then were these hallucinations in the middle of the afternoon right here on Mondol's own land? Had his father's illness come over him? Before he could understand what was going on, he heard Harmatullah say, 'Well? What's so amusing? Is the weeding done? Even the floods were useless this year.'

Tamiz could easily use this as a cue for suggesting a canal. But although he had not forgotten the matter entirely, the reckless waking reverie from a few minutes ago had left him confused about his preamble. How was it he had planned to start? He simply couldn't remember, but then, that wasn't surprising. His imagination was taken over by the flowing current in a canal leading from the lake to his field, the water making his land send up a dark green breeze into the sky, a breeze that sent a shiver of pleasure up and down Tamiz's body. It would make Harmat quiver with even greater joy. First his pepper field would turn a dense green, and then the green leaves would begin playing hide and seek with the tender green peppers. And finally, bursting through the canopy of green, the blood-red flames of the ripened chilli peppers would appear. Oh, Tamiz was ready to forgive the old man for all his faults at the sight of the fiery smiles of those ripe red peppers. As for Tamiz's own harvest of amon, it would be two and a half times as much as his Aush. How much of all this rice could they eat themselves? He didn't care for the amon, whose slender grains slipped through the teeth, never offering the satisfaction of real rice. Aush was much better. But why be so greedy? He would save some of the money he got from selling the amon instead of eating it all up. If only he could buy a pair of oxen, a plough, a yoke and a harrow, he would have no difficulty getting work as a sharecropper. It wouldn't take long—if he could just be a sharecropper for three years, planting and harvesting two crops a year, he would have the money to buy 15 per cent of the land. There was no harm in trying to get the field adjoining his house back from Mondol. Tamiz would try bringing it up with Abdul Kader. For a month or so now he had been visiting Kader's shop in Golabari every evening, joining the Muslim League supporters in shouting slogans at the top of his voice. Kader must be happy with him. Would he not put in a word to his father about the land Tamiz wanted to take back? Even if Mondol was not willing to sell it, let him work out a mortgage on it. Tamiz could get his father to work on the field then.

Tamiz's father was a dedicated worker. He was as good as ten men at his work, the only condition being that it should be the kind of work he enjoyed. Take those patches of land that had surfaced in the lake. If only Tamiz's father could become a sharecropper on them, he could show them what he was capable of . . . Before Mondol took a lease on this lake, Tamiz's father could get fish wherever he cast his net. A net in his hand always meant a catch of fish. Who knew the eccentricities of the lake better than him? The land rising out of the water would also bend to his will the same way. Was it for nothing that he trudged off in his sleep to the lake every night through the fields? If Munshi, perched in his fig tree at the northern head of the lake, gave Tamiz's father a little strip of land above the sandbar, there was no way the rest of it would not come to him too.

But when Harmatullah suddenly jumped to his feet and began running, never mind Tamiz's father, even the Katlahar Lake and the villages on either side of it and Munshi himself vanished in the sunlight. What had bitten the old man? Looking at his own house across the ox pool, Harmat pointed to the road on the east and shouted at the top of his voice, 'Phuljaan, Nobiton, Felani, look who's coming, see for yourself.'

A horse-drawn carriage was trundling along the road that ran south from Golabari, skirting Katlahar Lake on the east before going past the Mondols' house all the way to Kolupara. Behind it raced a swarm of children, most of them naked except for amulets around their waists and armlets to hang dented coins from. Four or five of the girls had homespun towels on, their amulets being displaced to their throats. There was the occasional rattling sound from the impact of the axle on the wheels of the carriage, while the clatter of the horses' hooves drew the women out from their houses, each of them holding a naked baby.

The reason for Harmat's excitement became evident once the passenger of the carriage was spotted. It wasn't easy to see clearly across the breadth of the lake, but still it was possible to identify Abdul Aziz sitting on a folded piece of cloth on the carriage. The boy next to him wrapped in a green shawl of coarse silk must be his son. And the girl opposite them couldn't be anyone's but Aziz's daughter. With the carriage coming closer, Harmat began to run towards the lake, but even if he crossed it on a boat the travellers would have gone a long way by then. So he came back instead, clambering up the steep bank of the ox pool to get as good a view as possible.

Harmat's daughters had joined him on the bank of the lake by now. The boy with the coppery yellow eyes in the eldest daughter's arms kept whining, so that her mother's efforts to draw his attention to the carriage were a complete failure. Harmat's younger daughter was sliding down the slope, and when her sister tried to hold her back the boy practically rolled out of her arms to the ground and proceeded to wail as loudly as he could. But his crying was faint—it seemed as though his bloated liver had consumed his vocal cords too.

Now that Harmatullah's daughter's son had slipped out of her arms, Tamiz could see her face and breasts clearly. Phuljaan's neck looked a little swollen beneath her round, coppery face. She was plump, though her waist was not very wide, and bursting with health. Why wouldn't a woman with a body like hers not work in the fields? That idiot husband of hers had not realized this, or else he could have taken his wife's help to become a sharecropper instead of working as a daily labourer.

Harmatullah returned to his position beneath the jujube tree on the ridge between the fields, panting, and, despite the bowl of water within reach, screamed at his daughters, 'Get me some water.' But he changed his instruction the very next moment, saying, 'What are you staring at like a hussy? Go home.'

Without checking on whether his daughters were obeying him, Harmat said, 'Must go to the Mondols.' Why is he here, need to find out.' Wiping his chest and back with his towel, he proceeded to hazard guesses about who the other passengers of the carriage might have been, guesses that he then felt doubtful about, which in turn led him to cancel them and make fresh guesses. Tamiz was disapproving of Harmatullah's excitement at the sight of Abdul Aziz going home in a carriage. But leave alone conveying his dissatisfaction, he couldn't even afford to nurse the feeling too long. Harmat was a favourite of Aziz's. Before Sharafat Mondol moved out of the village, Harmat used to be his neighbour. They might even be related. In fact, Aziz had wanted to hand over Tamiz's land to Harmat for sharecropping. 'He's an old hand at this,' Aziz used to say.

But no one knew what had happened to Sharafat Mondol—ever since he had taken a lease on the lake, he had begun to give his land out to the fishermen for sharecropping. Abdul Aziz didn't have much of a say in all this. After all, he lived away from home, which meant he didn't know the ins and outs of the village. But when it came to the accounts, Mondol had greater faith in his eldest son, which was why Abdul Aziz always had to take leave from his work to come home during the harvest. As long as he was on the spot, the aadhiars couldn't cheat, for he could see through all their tricks. But this wasn't harvest season. So why had Abdul Aziz come home suddenly? Was he here to make an estimate of the next harvest? Tamiz was worried—he was in trouble if Abdul Aziz was here to investigate his misadventures with the plough.

11

Mahadev himself had dug the ox pool with his trident, that too at goddess Durga's loving demand. A deep furrow ran through the manager's bushy eyebrows as he squirmed at the possibility of the god throwing a temper tantrum if the lake fell into the hands of people with questionable religious antecedents. Sharafat straightened in his chair, listening to the manager's devout wails, his spine quivering slightly in fear of Mahadev's—or his followers'—inordinate rage.

The manager allocated his fear and fervour equally between the deity and the jomidar. 'Sir is always thinking of you people, you know that, don't you? Most of his subjects are Muslims, just like you. And then another quarter are Namashudras. How many people of his own caste do you suppose live in this area? You know very well how few Brahmons and Kayasthos there are on the estate. As for sir's sons, they don't even believe in caste, they eat and drink and spend all their time with the British.' The manager was as proud of the revolutionary lifestyles of the jomidar's sons as he was staunch in his loyalty to the gods and goddesses. 'You must understand,' he continued. 'Don't get me wrong.' After a pause, he half-closed his eyes. 'Mahadev dug this lake himself, on Ma Durga's request. Not even Brahmons dare touch the soil here with their spades. How will Mahadev tolerate it if someone from another religion were to do it? Think about it.'

Although Sharafat had no idea how far Kailash was, he knew the manager, who was devoted to the inhabitants of Kailash, only too well. He belonged to the Ahle Hadis Jamaat, who, unlike oil grinders or fishermen or the people of the Hanafi Jamaat, never made a pledge to Hindu deities. But he did fear them. Here in the jomidar's office, he had neither the inclination nor the courage to be insolent with either the manager or the absent Mahadev. As long as he was there, he didn't allow his anxiety and his reverence to desert him, even though he was hearing for the first time in his life that the lake had been personally carved out by Mahadev. Was the tale that he had been told from his childhood, that Bhabani the hermit had dug the earth to form this lake so that he could clean the blade he had used to slice the British troops, not true then? But there was no point annoying the manager. So Sharafat left the office without bringing up the story.

Gofur kolu ran up to Sharafat from Kader's shop as soon as he dismounted from his Bhutanese horse at the Golabari market. Once Gofur had taken charge of the horse, Sharafat said, 'Find a spot in the shade behind the shop and tie him up. Send him back home with someone in the evening.'

As he gave Gofur his instructions Sharafat felt the fear he had experienced in the jomidar's office melting away. Kader was standing behind the cash box inside the shop. He hadn't stood up in deference to his father, he was on his feet out of agitation over his discussions with the League workers. A poster for the Muslim League's meeting in the town on Sunday was stuck on the tin wall behind him. On top of the poster the flag of the Muslim League was drawn diagonally, above it the words 'Long Live Pakistan' and 'Long Live Muslim League'. The other three walls of tin were covered in posters written with dark-blue ink on old copies of the *Daily Azad*. Filled kerosene tins were arranged near one wall, while the empty tins were scattered near the opposite wall. Sharafat ran his eyes over the empty tins to estimate the past two days' sales.

Abdul Kader had been talking to a dozen or so young men crowded on two benches facing him. Whenever Sharafat Mondol went to the shop these days there was always a group of young men. How would business thrive if Abdul Kader was going to hold court all day? Mondol's mood soured. You want to butt heads with Hindus? First learn from them how to run a business. There was Mukunda Saha's warehouse, still a ramshackle tin shed; it hadn't changed a bit since his father's time, he'd not even added a stool. But he was doing roaring business. It wasn't market day, and yet there were four or five horses tethered outside the warehouse, which meant suppliers had brought ginger, garlic and cumin. Saha never wasted his time gossiping. But look at Kader's shop, full of all these louts, thick with smoke. Wouldn't a self-respecting person hesitate to enter?

Still, Sharafat contained his annoyance and indignation, actually perking up when the young men jumped to their feet, flustered by his appearance. He asked for a glass of water, although he wasn't thirsty. When Gofur made to go to the handpump outside to fill the large gunmetal tumbler kept in the shop specifically for Sharafat's use, he said, 'Leave it.' Kader took the glass back from Gofur and handed it to one of the young men from Chashapara in Girirdanga. This time Sharafat had no need to postpone his drink of water. Draining the tumbler, he sighed in satisfaction and said, 'We can't dig a canal from the ox pool. Apparently it was made by some god or deity, the manager says Mahadev created it himself, the gods will be angry if Muslims take a spade to it.'

Kader exploded in fury. 'Hindus can't stand anything that benefits Muslims.' Since this could be said to be in continuation to what he was telling the young men earlier, he had no difficulty in keeping his diatribe uninterrupted. 'These Hindu jomidars talk big but suck the blood of their Muslim subjects. The lives and honour and property of Muslims are in danger unless Pakistan is formed.'

Meanwhile, Boikuntho Giri had appeared at the door, listening to Kader with close attention. He didn't leave when Kader was done speaking. On the contrary, he popped a paan into his mouth, strengthening his occupation of the spot with the scent of tobacco. As Sharafat and Kader were leaving for home, Boikuntho approached

Mondol, saying, 'Kaka, babu is looking for you, he has something to discuss with you.'

'Oh yes, I forgot.' Sharafat told Kader, 'Wait a bit, let me see what Mukunda-babu wants.'

Sharafat walked off towards Mukunda Saha's warehouse, but Boikuntho didn't follow him. 'Isn't there supposed to be a meeting, dada?' he asked Kader. 'There will be songs, won't there? What's a meeting without songs?'

The afternoon was winding down at Golabari market. A beggar woman had built a fire with a heap of leaves beneath a banyan tree and was making arrangements to cook. All the shops were closed, and a girl of seven or eight was asleep on a maacha in front of one of them—probably the beggar woman's daughter. Not even a flippant Kaartik shower could wake her up. It didn't interrupt her mother's cooking either.

Sharafat didn't close his umbrella even after the rain had ended. Walking along the road, he said, 'It won't rain any more. We need the rain, though, or the crops will die.'

But Abdul Kader was distracted. He grumbled about the tyranny of Hindu jomidars all the way back home. He was also upset about his father being insulted. 'Did the manager behave very badly with you, baapjaan?' he asked his father.

'Of course not!' Although Sharafat dismissed his son's apprehensions, he was still smarting from the statements made by the manager, who had sent for him in the morning, when he was washing his hands after a breakfast of flattened rice and bananas soaked in milk. Kader had not had his breakfast yet, for he was busy checking his nephew's temperature on a thermometer. That was when the manager's favourite office boy, one-armed Asimuddi, had turned up. Asimuddi did not convey a clear message, only saying that the manager had heard something about a canal being dug to take water out of the ox pool, and wanted to discuss it with Sharafat.

When he saw his father dress hurriedly to comply with the manager's orders, Kader threw him a sidelong glance and said, 'Humayun's fever is higher today.' Extending the thermometer towards Humayun's mother, he took a Jinnah cap out of his suitcase, placed it on the bed in front of this father and said, 'Put this on, baapjaan.'

But Sharafat blew into his own boat-shaped cap instead to unfold it before fitting it on his head. Still, he didn't return the Jinnah cap to his son, handing it to Aziz's wife instead and saying, 'Keep this, it should fit Babur.'

It occurred to Sharafat on the way back home with his son that the manager might have been a little more circumspect had he worn the Jinnah cap. In any case the manager had become mellower with age, and he was much more civil nowadays. But why had he been so aggressive today after all this time? Even before Sharafat could take a seat on the bench, he said, 'Well Mondol, we don't see you much these days. But then you're on good terms with important people, we can't match up to them. Is our time up, then?'

Sharafat was silent. The manager had said far worse in the past. But he was deflated because it was obviously not a good time to bring up the subject of taking a lease on the land on the eastern side of the ox pool.

'Your son is organizing meetings about Pakistan these days. Which is very good, after all, we'd be delighted if someone from the estate did well for himself. But we're also hearing he wants to abolish the system of jomidars. Look my boy, whether it's the jomidar's estate or his wealth, it's all temporary. Kortababu tells me, none of this will remain ours, Purno, the country will eventually belong to the lower classes. My only request is, don't take our caste away from us, what does a man have if his caste is gone?'

'How can you say such a thing, babu?' It wasn't clear even to Sharafat which of the manager's regrets he was responding to.

'You people are the kings now. The ministers, the judges, the bailiffs, all of them are your people. They've stopped giving jobs to the upper classes. Let some more time go by, soon you won't have anyone left to grow crops. The peasants will go to offices in hats and coats. But let them. God provides for us, if he has given us tongues, he will ensure we have food too. But if you're plotting to take away our caste, my boy . . .'

How was Sharafat Mondol to answer this incomplete threat? He was rescued by the manager himself, however. First he declared that Sharafat had not been wise to begin digging a canal leading out from the ox pool. Then he suddenly asked, 'You're an old man now, Mondol, you know everything hereabouts. Don't you know who made the lake and why?'

Was there anyone in the neighbourhood who didn't know? A katra had floated up on the water of the Katlahar Lake, close to the fig tree at its northern head, at about one-thirty in the morning on a new moon night in Asharh. The manager frowned as Mondol began his tale. 'Katra?' Mondol paused to explain. 'A katra is the wooden frame used to slaughter animals. Meaning . . .'

The manager raised his hand to stop him. 'The sacrificial stake, you mean?' When Mondol didn't answer because he didn't know what that meant, the manager said, 'But these are concocted stories.' But then it was that very same concocted story that had circulated for many decades. When the katra floated to the surface, a pair of goats were sacrificed, after which all diseases vanished on both sides of the lake. But then no one sacrificed goats nowadays, which was probably why the katra had become so angry that it didn't float to the surface of the water any more. How could goats be sacrificed these days? You weren't allowed to buy goats for this purpose, they had to be your own. That night not all the Munshi's pet murrels had been transformed into sheep, because he had made a pair of them swim along in the form of goats. A hermit had apparently turned up hereabouts hundreds of years ago. Fighting with British soldiers on the banks of the Manosh river, he had beheaded most of them before dying at their hands eventually. After his death he had made a habit of visiting the spot once a year, retrieving the wooden frame from the lake, sacrificing the goats provided by Munshi, and taking shelter beneath the banyan tree in the field at Poradaho, where hermits usually rested. Before leaving he had washed his blade in the water of the ox pool. There was no one nearby, for people were forbidden from going there at night. The next morning, the surface of the ox pool had turned pink.

The manager laughed at the story, as he did every time he heard it. Sharafat Mondol laughed too, for he did not believe these tall tales floated by Hindus. But it was different when it came to fishermen and oil grinders—in fact, Sharafat had his doubts about whether they were genuine Muslims at all. Not that there was any lack of people among his relatives who were ready to parrot these scandalous tales. But then the katra didn't float up on the surface of the lake these days, or, even if it did, it was doubtful whether anyone had seen it.

The manager was saddened by the ignorance and superstitions of the villagers. 'Mahadev created the lake, but these uneducated Namashudras claim some hermit did it. The lake came up on Durga's request, you think Mahadev will tolerate it if lower-caste people have anything to do with it? It'll be on the heads of not just the people of Girirdanga and Nijgirirdanga, but also on the head of the jomidar himself in Calcutta.'

But Sharafat Mondol couldn't reveal any of this to Kader. He was so hot-headed that he might do something reckless. If the jomidar was angry with Sharafat his dreams of leasing the land on both sides of Katlahar Lake would never be fulfilled. He couldn't afford to annoy the manager, who had mellowed now, but used to have a temper that Kader had never witnessed. None of the jomidar's managers had ever addressed Sharafat's father and uncle with anything but contempt. A long time ago, the previous manager used to refer to Sharafat's uncle Piarullah Mondol as Shiarullah, which turned into Shialu, an unsubtle reference to the word for fox. Since then he had never managed to shed that name, and all his descendants still entered their father or grandfather's name in forms and registers as Shialu Mondol. Despite being his nephew, Sharafat was addressed by his actual name by the manager, who also spoke civilly to him. By Allah's grace Sharafat had succeeded in leasing three large tracts of land, and replaced his father's hut in Girirdanga with a house of tin walls and large rooms. One of this two sons had passed the matriculation examination and had a government job, while the other one had studied in college for three years. All of this was thanks to the land he had leased, which would not have come his way if he hadn't been in the manager's good books.

Sharafat suddenly increased his pace when he was near Katlahar Lake, veering off the road to the ridge bordering the field on his right. He accelerated further as they walked towards the fig tree, and, sensing Kader's uneasiness, said, 'Might as well see what's going on in Harmat's field. We should find out whether he's doing a good job with the pepper. Mukunda said he'd pay a decent price for it.'

The afternoon was turning into the evening, but with the sky cloudless after the earlier showers, the sunlight was still quite strong. Kader was limp with hunger. And besides, the area around the fig tree was full of dense jungles—it needed a strong heart to walk through them just before dark. But his father had taken a decision, and it was impossible to change his mind.

When they finally reached the edge of the ox pool after braving the jungle and balancing on ridges between fields, Kader recovered his spirits, saying, 'So it's a sin for a Muslim to dig anywhere around this lake, is it?' Fired by his own question, he worked out an alternative. 'Why not make a breach in Katlahar Lake, baapjaan? Can't we get a canal flowing?' He became impatient when Sharafat didn't answer, saying, 'Munshi won't be angry, will he?'

Sharafat wasn't pleased with the taunts about Munshi, feeling a stab of fear. But he was definitely going to consider his son's proposal. Katlahar Lake was more or less his own property, considering the trouble he had gone to when getting the lease. He had had to bribe the manager in several instalments, and grease the palms of officers at every level at the Lathidanga court, including the messenger boys and guards. Not even the dogs and cats had been deprived. The manager had extracted several pots of the delicious curds of Hatibandha, claiming they were for the jomidar in Calcutta. Sharafat had even had to pay for them to be sent there. Considering the effort he had put in to secure the lease, why shouldn't he be allowed to dig a canal to irrigate his fields? Kader had given him good advice. He would be able to use Tamiz's services without paying him, since Tamiz was the one who had first shown enthusiasm about it.

But Tamiz was not to be found in the rice field, nor Harmat in the pepper field next to it. Harmatullah's hookah was leaning against the jujube tree on the ridge, a bowl of water next to it. Little piles of weeds lay on the field next door—but where had all of them disappeared? Sharafat examined the growth of the pepper plants, but he couldn't tell anything.

A little later Harmatullah was seen racing out of his own house in this direction. He had climbed the high bank of the ox pool with the idea of taking a short-cut, but this route was actually taking him longer. Panting on the crest, he screamed, 'Get some paan, Nobiton, get some paan.' The intensity of his instructions to his daughter made him hoarse, after which he had a coughing bout. This made it difficult to run, while running prevented him from coughing naturally.

Eventually Harmat arrived where Sharafat was waiting, and continued panting. He tried to say several things at the same time but, being unsuccessful, screamed again, 'Can't you hear me, Nobiton?'

'Where were all of you? Where's Tamiz?'

Harmatullah deemed it more important to look after Sharafat than to answer his questions. He tried to shout for his daughter again, but the combination of agitation and exhaustion robbed him of his voice. Despite the risk of being pierced by thorns, he leaned back against the jujube tree, mumbling, 'Are they all deaf? Why can't anyone hear me shouting?'

Meanwhile Tamiz returned from the opposite bank of the ox pool with the ingredients for paan arranged on a plate, along with tobacco leaves. After Sharafat had made himself a paan and popped it into his mouth, Tamiz told him that Phuljaan's four-year-old son had suddenly fallen unconscious during his meal, foaming at the mouth. Harmatullah and Tamiz had both rushed back on hearing Phuljaan, Nobiton and Felani shriek in chorus. It was thanks to

Tamiz's brainwave that they had kept pouring water on the four-
year-old boy's head for a long time. He was much better now, and
Phuljaan was feeding him his lunch.

'He fell unconscious?' said Kader. 'I don't like the sound of that.
Didn't I hear you say your grandson has kala-azar? Aren't you getting
him treated?'

Harmatullah began by heaping abuse on his fate and his
absconding, irresponsible son-in-law. When Kader urged him
for a suitable answer to his question, he let fly a description of his
grandson's treatment. 'I went myself to Jotin the ayurvedic doctor in
Lathibhanga last year to get pills, I spent six annas on the medicine,
the boy stopped after two pills. When I tried to return them, the
doctor wouldn't take them back or refund my money. Then, only
three months ago, I got some charmed water from the pir, not once
but twice, I had to pay four and a half annas, and there was the travel
cost too, three annas and fourteen paise, so how much is that?'

'You and your charmed water. How will he be cured without
proper medicines? Take the boy to the Sakidars' house in Chhaihata,
let Iman Ali Sakidar's son Karim examine him. He's a doctor with
an LMF degree, he's just passed his exams. Take him, don't delay
these things.'

'Why does he have to go to Chhaihata when we have Horen
right here?' Sharafat did not endorse his son's choice of physician.
'He treats everyone hereabouts.'

'It's true Horen has been seeing patients for a long time,' said
Kader with emphasis, 'but a young well-qualified Muslim is starting
a new practice as a doctor, how will he get by without some help?'

But Sharafat had no time to waste discussing the medical
treatment for Harmatullah's grandson. So he brought up the subject
of irrigating the land. 'There are cracks in the soil on your field,
Tamiz. A few days more and . . .'

Tamiz had been waiting impatiently for just this. He had barely
sunk his shovel into the land by the ox pool when he was asked to
stop. Who knew whether Harmatullah was behind it? But he was

extremely careful not to voice his suspicion about Harmat in any circumstance. After some thought, he said. 'A canal will mean better crops on all your fields. In Khiyar I saw so many . . .'

'No Tamiz, we can't dig around the ox pool,' Kader became agitated again at Sharafat's declaration. Preparing his arguments, he began, 'If the bastard jomidar cared for his subjects . . .'

Sharafat interrupted him before he could bring up the subject of Pakistan. 'I'm going to take a lease on the ox pool, all right? You think I will let it be ruined? A canal will just mean dirty rainwater flowing into the lake, that's what I told the manager.'

Abdul Kader listed to his father in astonishment. When he saw that Sharafat wasn't going to reveal the manager's evil plans, he had the urge to give his father a piece of his mind. But Sharafat was now engaged in discussions with his two sharecroppers about how to dig a canal from Katlahar Lake instead. Kader's rage escalated as he was unable to speak his mind. All he could do was to keep spitting on the ground.

12

Tucking taro leaves beneath the pillow, Sharafat Mondol's second wife was pouring water over the head of Abdul Aziz's son, all the while running her fingers through little Humayun's hair. The boy had his eyes closed beneath the constant stream of cold water. He might have even fallen asleep, but he turned his head to look at Sharafat and Kader when they entered. His eyes were a fiery red, pain written clearly in them. Kader could not bring himself to speak, and his appetite seemed to have died. After a quick glance at her husband and stepson, Sharafat's second wife continued pouring water over the boy's head. Aziz's wife Hamida was seated on the bed, stifling her sobs with the end of her sari. At the sight of her father-in-law and brother-in-law, she said, sobbing, 'Where has he gone? What do I do with this boy now in the middle of nowhere?'

Leaving his ailing son and only daughter at home, Abdul Aziz had gone to his workplace. His wife was here already—she had arrived during the aush harvest in Bhadro and would stay till the amon harvest. The children were to come after their annual examinations, which would mean being without their mother till then. But with his youngest son developing a recurring fever, Aziz was finding it difficult to look after him. How could a man handle such things? And then it was impossible to get decent fish over in Joipur. Only one or two varieties of vegetables were available properly, the rest being insipid. Vegetables bought at the market could never be tasty.

Here they had their personal lake for fish, and there was no counting the number of ducks and hens in the yard. Aziz had deposited his son here, confident that he would recover after being fed freshly caught fish from the lake, home-grown chicken, and vegetables from the kitchen garden. Thing were going well initially, the fever appearing on schedule but never lasting longer than three hours, and the afternoon fever not coming on till after the asr namaz. The boy was very fond of his grandmother, often leaving his mother when the fever went down at night to go into his grandmother's room and snuggle with her. He was well on the road to recovery. His grandmother had even fed him hilsa cooked with mustard one day, with no after-effects.

But the fever had risen suddenly this afternoon. During lunch in the kitchen he began to tremble uncontrollably, and would have fallen off the low wooden platform he was sitting on had his grandmother not caught him in time. Hamida had been a little worried when she found him sitting in the sun in the morning, asking Abdul Kader to check his temperature on the thermometer. Surely he would have told her had anything been wrong. No one but Kader knew how to read a thermometer, but it was clear from the boy's hot skin that the fever was back.

Sharafat Mondol's first wife, the mother of Abdul Aziz and Abdul Kader, had gone to bed in the room across the yard with the door on the east. This was her usual response to illness in the family. She was mumbling constantly like someone with a high fever, saying things that could not be dismissed as delirium. The lion's share of her monologue consisted of complaints against her husband. As her grandson's own fever raged, her grievances intensified into direct abuse. Sample: 'Land and property, that's all he thinks about all day. My son left his sick child here, no medicines for him, no charmed water, no visit to a pir even. Is a fever your hired hand? Is it your servant? Do you think it will leave on your orders?'

The first wife's rant floated across the yard to collide with Humayun's mother's laments. 'My son, my boy, how do you feel now, my son?'

Opening his eyes at his mother's frantic cries, Humayun slurred, 'Ma, will you give me an egg with my rice today, ma?'

Overcome with regret at not giving her son an egg with his rice during the half-yearly examination because of its resemblance to zero, Hamida began to weep unconsolably, determined to give her son two eggs every day once he recovered, not even stopping during his annual examinations. Ignoring his mother's tears and her decision, Humayun muttered feverishly, 'Let me just have the egg, ma, no need for the rice, we have a half holiday at school.'

Everyone panicked at his delirious state. Rummaging for the thermometer on the wooden shelves on the tin wall, Abdul Kader dropped Sharafat's sex revitalizer Madan Manjari pills, two tins of Chawanprash, and the mortar and pestle used to grind his medicine. None of them broke—in fact, not even the lids of the tins came loose. But Kader felt a tremor in his heart. Taking his time to shake the thermometer thoroughly to ensure that the column of mercury had gone all the way down, he tucked it under Humayun's arm. The pouring of water over his head had to be stopped, which made the anxiety in the room escape across the yard and arrive at the room with the door on the east. Once again Sharafat's first wife sharpened her criticism into invectives. 'The miserly old fool won't spend a paisa on anyone's illness. Who does the cheapskate save his money for? You think I don't understand? Now that you've taken a young wife in your old age, I bet you're planning to give her everything. You think I don't understand? What else do you go to the courts for so often? You think I don't understand whose name is on all those documents you're preparing? You'll be happy if your children and their children die, if the entire family's wiped out, so that you can live with your young wife.'

When her curses reached the sickroom, Sharafat's second wife handed the bowl of water to Hamida, saying, 'Hold this,' went out of the room, descended into the yard, and stood with her hands on her hips, facing the room with the door on the east. Then she began her monologue. 'Mind your tongue, Aziz's mother. I piss on your old husband's property, I piss on it.' She swung her hips in a way that suggested she was about to implement her threat. But though there was no rain, the thunder continued. 'Do you know how much land your old coot of a husband is buying with my father's money? He tells my father my name will be on the lease, and then puts his own name on the documents. If he dies today it's you and your children who'll get all his property.'

Shaking her anger off, she returned to her position next to the sick child and resumed pouring water over Humayun's head as before.

But Abdul Kader's face fell when he saw the temperature on the thermometer. He threw a glance at Hamida. All that water hadn't helped. A troubled Kader strode off, still holding the thermometer, to the room where Sharafat was reading the namaz. He waited impatiently, but Sharafat showed no signs of stopping, even if he was aware of his son's presence in the room, reading a succession of rakats. After a long time spent in a gesture of obeisance at the end, he got to his feet and said, folding the prayer book, 'Take the cycle and go to Horen. He will decide whether a different doctor is needed. But bring him here to examine the boy.' Sharafat went out into the veranda. Bulu's son was sharpening a stick beneath the mango tree to play with. Sharafat began to scold him. 'Every time I see you you're playing. Who's supposed to look after the oxen? The calf is licking the bottom of an empty trough, where did all the hay go?' Continuing in the same tone, he instructed his son in a low voice, 'Take one of the labourers with you. On my way back from the office I saw Ajit going somewhere on his cycle. Let Kaalu's father take the horse and go with you. Horen can ride the horse if Ajit isn't back in time with his cycle. He used to ride to patients' homes earlier, he only got the cycle the other day.'

Kaalu's father was working in the eggplant field opposite the house. Sending Bulu's son to fetch him, Sharafat suddenly remembered Kader's recommendation for Harmatullah's grandson. 'Weren't you talking about some other doctor, Kader? What was his name now, a Muslim doctor, you said, someone from Chhaihata.'

'Are you talking of Karim? Abdul Karim?' Kader got the name right, but dismissed the idea. 'No, baapjaan, Horen-babu is our old doctor, let him have a look first. Rushing off to a new doctor at this stage . . .'

'No need. I asked because you'd mentioned him.'

Horen visited two days in succession. The fever dropped a bit before becoming twice as high, after which Sharafat hired a two-horse phaeton from Rahmat Sheikh, who lived in the town, and had Dr Shishir Sen fetched. He was accompanied by Proshanto the compounder, who was carrying the doctor's bag. The carriage was followed by people from both the peasants' and the fishermen's colonies, besides some of the inhabitants of Golabari, and Gofur himself. There were plenty of women too, with naked babies in their arms and accompanied by a large number of children. The people from Nijgirirdanga across the lake had crowded around the Mondols' house, and even Harmatullah had torn himself away from his pepper field to be present, seeking out Abdul Aziz at regular intervals and engaging himself in praising his son and ruing his illness, expressing these sentiments in the form of a dirge. Abdul Aziz had arrived shortly after Dr Sen in response to a telegram, which was why not many people had been available to celebrate the speed of his carriage or to follow it.

Two of Harmatullah's daughters were there, Phuljaan and the youngest, Felani. Phuljaan's son moaned constantly, his feeble crying stopping at intervals when he fell asleep with his head on his mother's shoulder. Tamiz was hanging about behind Proshanto the compounder, holding out both his hands in an offer to lighten Proshanto's burden by carrying the doctor's bag, only to be rebuffed every time. Fobbed off rudely, Tamiz told himself it would be better to go back to the field or get going on the task of digging the canal, but the sheer number of people here, besides the attraction of the two-horse phaeton, the doctor and the compounder, and, above all, the bag in the compounder's hand, kept him glued to the spot.

It was the pretext of Humayun's illness that had provided the women of several villages a chance to catch a glimpse of the renowned doctor from the town, the Brahmon compounder carrying his bag, the two-horse phaeton, et cetera. Anxious to fulfil their responsibility towards Humayun, therefore, they gathered in the veranda outside his room, in the yard, at the door, and even inside the room. 'Do you think it's a circus?' said Proshanto, clamping a handkerchief on his nose. 'Go away.' Once Sharafat, Abdul Kader and Horen had managed to thrust them out of the way into the yard, Dr Sen examined Humayun thoroughly with his stethoscope, looking increasingly grim as his examination progressed. Occasionally he looked coldly at Horen, who had been apprehensive since yesterday. Humayun had urinated in his bed the day before. Spotting blood on his lungi, Hamida had screamed and fainted on the spot. The decision to fetch Dr Sen had been taken instantly. Although this was his first visit to the village, it was him that Sharafat Mondol's sons went to for treatment in the town. He knew Abdul Kader quite well—addressing the brothers by their first names had shrunk the distance between them. His use of endearments for Humayun— 'baba', 'babu', 'there's a good boy'—warmed the hearts of everyone in the family and earned their unfailing trust.

In the room with the door to the east, Sharafat's first wife could not see the doctor's expression but correctly gauged the seriousness of Humayun's illness from the sudden silence and, as she was wont to, immediately began lamenting Sharafat Mondol's indifference before heightening it to direct abuse. This high-pitched litany embarrassed and then annoyed Abdul Kader, although he busied himself checking the doctor and compounder's reactions to such slovenly behaviour. The doctor was impassive, but Proshanto the compounder contorted his face and kept throwing glances at the room across the yard, belching out his irritation in a voice too low for Dr Sen to hear, 'What's all this? How can a patient be examined with everyone shouting?'

Abdul Aziz was on tenterhooks about not angering the doctor. He brought a bucket, bowl and stool to the veranda for the doctor to wash his hands after examining the patient. Rummaging in the bag for a bar of soap when the doctor held out his hand for it, poor Proshanto was deeply flustered when he couldn't find one. He was making such mistakes frequently these days. The doctor was bound to bring it up when they went back. Trembling with fear, he asked Aziz, 'Is there a shop here where they sell soap?'

'Soap? Just a minute,' said Aziz, going into a room.

But Proshanto's doubts weren't dispelled. 'Do you have pink soap from the market?' he asked Kader. 'Not something you've used already.'

A furrow appeared between Abdul Kader's eyebrows. He looked at Proshanto with narrowed eyes beneath them. Meanwhile, Abdul Aziz brought a fresh bar of Lifebuoy for the doctor, who soaped his hands and rinsed them with the water poured from the bowl by Aziz. Taking his lips close to Proshanto's ears, Kader said, 'Will Lifebuoy do? Or do you need Lux or Palmolive?'

Proshanto smiled bitterly. 'You people are on top now. You buy new things every day. You can even afford to give Dr Shishir Sen a call. My god! He uses nothing but Pears at home. Do you have that as well?'

In the room for visitors, the doctor said in a low voice, 'You've left it too late, Sharafat mian. Let Kader come with me and get the medicines. Horen will give the injection. Let's see.'

Kader hesitated a little before ladling the home-made rice pudding from the giant gunmetal bowl on the large china plate with the floral design. But when the doctor said 'enough' after the first two spoonfuls, he was confident that the offering had been accepted, and added an extra spoonful in delight. He had got some Lipton tea and cream crackers in the town when fetching the doctor. After the rice pudding followed by a few biscuits, the doctor took a luxurious sip of the tea, saying, 'Aaaahhh. This is very good.'

But Proshanto, who was sitting in the veranda, could not be persuaded to eat anything. He didn't touch the tea out of apprehension over what else might have been cooked in the pan in which the water had been boiled. Neither Sharafat nor Aziz was perturbed about this. But Kader seemed determined that Proshanto should eat. 'How about a banana? Bananas don't smell of religion.'

Inside the room, the doctor chuckled at Kader's agitation. Calling him into the room, he said, 'Don't be angry, Kader. Proshanto is extra careful about these things. As a Brahmon he doesn't even eat at my house. Don't mind, all right?'

When Kader went back outside Proshanto lowered his voice and told him, 'Sir is practically British, he can do anything. We are poor Brahmons, no money, no prestige, what will be left for us if we break away from our religion?'

'You're obsessed with religion,' said Kader. 'It's because our religion is different from yours that we want to be on our own. Why does it hurt you people so much to let us have a separate country?'

The slim and fair Proshanto smiled sarcastically again. 'You think you can survive if you're on our own? Who's going to treat your brother in that case?'

Abdul Kader felt a rage coming on, against his father, his brother and, partly, himself too. If only he had applied himself to his studies in school he could have written his ISC examinations, got into medical college, and graduated as a doctor a long time ago. He could even have joined Campbell Medical School after his matriculation. Abdul Kader was deeply distressed at not being a doctor. This accursed Hindu compounder would not have been so scornful if there were a doctor in the family. Considering he'd put both his sons through school, why hadn't it occurred to Sharafat Mondol that at least one of them could study to be a doctor? All that he could think of were ways to get more land. Abdul Aziz's elder son Babur was a very good student, ranking fourth or fifth in class despite the preponderance of Hindu students at Joipur High School, defying the Hindu teachers' attempts to make him fail. If Babur could grow up to be a doctor it was this same Shishir Sen whose business would suffer. All the Muslim patients in this area would queue up at Babur's chambers in the town. Even this infidel compounder would ask Kader to recommend him for a job. Why not? But all his plans for his nephew to become a doctor who would snatch Dr Sen's patients from him and give Proshanto a job were aborted by Tamiz's cry: 'Bhaijaan!'

Startled, Kader looked at the yard and recoiled in horror. What was that ghastly swelling on Tamiz's shoulder? Then he realized that it wasn't a swollen gland or anything, just a head. Two heads stood on the bare-bodied Tamiz's shoulder, one of them with the familiar face of Tamiz, currently a sharecropper on their own fields, and the other with a coppery skin now turned pale, covered in yellowish-black spots and glassy eyes. Tamiz's mop of thick, black, curly hair had cascaded down on his second head like bleached red fibre. The glazed eyes, all but closed, in the second head were fixed on Kader's face. Confronting the dull, dimmed look in the dirt-rimmed pair of eyes was beyond Kader.

'Bhaijaan, this is Phuljaan's son. Harmatullah's grandson.' Kader felt it was actually the head that he had just been introduced to which was talking through Tamiz's lips. Only when Phuljaan's son began crying softly was Kader able to tell him and Tamiz apart. 'The boy's had a high fever since this afternoon, bhaijaan. He didn't collapse like the other day, but his body feels like it's on fire. He keeps falling over. I was hoping the doctor could see him too.'

Kader felt a shiver run down his spine. Suffering from kala-azar, followed by the high fever today, had given the boy a grotesque appearance. Who knew whether he was possessed or something? What if Mahadev or some other god had put a curse on him because of the attempt to dig a canal out of the lake? Or had the age-old inhabitant of Katlahar turned an evil eye on him? How could he request the doctor to treat the boy for being possessed?

Meanwhile, Dr Sen had descended from the veranda and paused on his way to his carriage to gaze in amazement at the red silk-cotton tree covered by storks. Abdul Aziz, who was by his side, barked in a low voice at Tamiz, who moved away only to take up a position next to the phaeton. Phuljaan's son was in his mother's arms now, though his appearance had not changed as a result. But Tamiz had been freed from his ghostly head. Relieved, Kader conveyed his gratitude to his sharecropper. 'I don't like the looks of the boy, Tamiz. Take him to Karim. Didn't I tell you? He won't charge you his usual fees if you mention my name.'

The doctor was holding a final conversation about the patient with Abdul Aziz before getting into his carriage, while Sharafat Mondol was personally supervising the task of transferring a heap of bananas into the vehicle. When Phuljaan tried to take a few steps towards the doctor he warned her sharply, 'Get away from here, you brazen bitch, get away.' Complying with his order, she ran into Proshanto, who put his hand on the child's forehead and said, 'He's got a very high fever, I could tell from his eyes.'

Phuljaan was gratified by this indulgence, her words rolling off her goitre as thickly as pus. 'This boy of mine is sick all the time, Doctor. Give him some medicine, please give him some medicine, I've brought the money.'

The coins she had gathered added up to fourteen and a half annas. Tamiz had taken eight annas from her to pay the doctor's fees. 'He won't even touch your boy unless you pay him,' Tamiz had told her. She had six and a half annas left now. Since Tamiz had failed, she had approached the doctor herself out of desperation. She would buy the medicine right now with cash, or else there was no chance of recovering the money from Tamiz later.

'You had to ruin my day, didn't you,' said Proshanto unhappily. 'Now I'll have to go home and bathe at this hour before I can eat.' But despite the risk of bathing on an autumn evening, Proshanto palpitated the child's abdomen and concluded, 'The liver's swollen. Has Horen let this happen?'

Not that Horen had ever been consulted, but Phuljaan still provided an account of the expenses incurred so far on her son's treatment. 'We've been to so many people, Doctor. The kobiraj took seven and a half annas the other day. Then we got the charmed water from the pir in Mahasthan before that, it cost four annas less one paisa for baapjaan to travel and to pay at the shrine. On top of that . . .'

'How long has he been ill?' Proshanto interrupted Phuljaan.

'He's ill round the year. He won't live.'

'Why won't he live?' To live up to the image of someone being addressed as 'doctor', Proshanto fired off a prescription. 'He needs Brahmachari's injection. Kala-azar is curable these days, just needs the injection. Bring him into the town, I'll give the injection. Your son will live.'

This reassurance about her son's survival made Phuljaan's goitre tremble, while her fat, coppery cheeks were tinged with red. Even if slightly, it cast a glow on the mottled skin and glazed eyes of the child whose face was pressed to hers.

13

Fulfilling Proshanto the compounder's prediction, Phuljaan's son lived on. His liver fattened itself on the blood in his body, and his belly seemed to swell a little more every day. He had neither been given the injection nor been taken to Karim. After Abdul Aziz's son Humayun died, Kader languished at home, heartbroken, for a week before galvanizing himself into a frenzy of activity for the League that left him no time for anything else. He had to cycle to distant villages these days, and go into the town five days a week. He was selling a lot more kerosene now that the fuel was not available anywhere else nearby. People from several villages lined up at his shop, which Gofur ran with aplomb, selling kerosene and delivering speeches on Pakistan. People had no choice but to listen, and that's all they did anyway, day and night. Phuljaan had no opportunity to meet Kader with her son.

Tamiz knew a little about injections. There was no guarantee that a needle could be extricated once it had been inserted into the body. Besides, he himself was a busy man. Everyone around was caught up in harvesting the amon, which was a relatively new crop in these parts. For three years now, people no longer left riverbanks and elevated plots of land uncultivated; they sowed amon on them instead. The harvest was quite plentiful on all of Sharafat Mondol's land in Girirdanga. His aadhiar Hamid Sakidar did have some land of his own, but it was not high enough to yield a reasonable harvest.

On Sharafat's fields, though, he had produced an impressive crop. Mondol did not allow sharecropping on a plot of land of about an acre and a half just beyond his kitchen garden, employing hired hands instead to farm it. He personally supervised everything from the sowing and the harvesting to the husking and the storage. On the highest spot of this land, which must have stretched for almost half an acre, he had cultivated autumnal paddy. This was his first time with the black-seeded grain. What option did he have? His daughter-in-law's family lived on the edge of the town, where they cooked pilau every fortnight. It was practically at his son's and daughter-in-law's desire that he had sowed this variety of paddy. Harvesting it all day filled Tamiz's senses with the fragrance of the rice from which pilau was made.

The harvest on Tamiz's land was bounteous too. He had transformed the soil by irrigating it with water from the canal he had dug. The cracks that had appeared on the earth in Kaartik had closed completely, and the soil was a rich black even in Poush. But look, the clay road next to his field was bone-white. The rice was growing densely on Tamiz's land, the stalks bent over under the weight of the ears, while the grains turned a deeper shade of gold with every passing day. Seasoned farmer or not, whoever went past the field had to stop and admire the sight. Standing on the ridge between the fields, Shamsher could not take his eyes off the crop. He was bubbling with joy. 'What have you done, my boy? You have magic in your fingers.' And Shamsher hadn't even looked beyond the ears. Tamiz was the only one who had seen the fat stalks beneath the golden canopy, close to the earth. Rice fields never revealed all their colours in entirety. At dawn, they shimmered beneath the dewdrops, and in the afternoon, when the sun grew brighter with hues borrowed from the sheaves of grain, they turned a little paler. And when the winter afternoons ended hurriedly, a grey hue spread over the field, while the same sheaves gazed at their own shadows. Finally, when the rice field tucked its head into the mist after dark, it was impossible to tell where its loyalty lay.

It got colder in the morning. Tamiz felt the chill even with a quilt wrapped around his shirt. The rice stalks shivered a little too, so that he could not distinguish his own trembling from theirs.

Having spent his day harvesting or supervising the harvesting of the rice in Sharafat's other fields, Harmatullah arrived shortly before evening to weed his pepper field. This side of the lake became deserted after sunset, while smoke rose from Harmat's house on the other side. But he didn't leave his field. Phuljaan brought his hookah sometimes, occasionally accompanying it with a charred sweet potato. She offered Tamiz one or two slices without letting her father know. Lowering her child to the ground and propping him up against the base of the jujube tree, she gave her father a hand on the field. When her son began to shiver uncontrollably in the cold, Tamiz put him in his lap to pass on the warmth of his body. His heart felt heavy, but he could not gauge whether it was from the weight of the child with the swollen belly. It was doubtful whether the light mist that hung over the pepper field allowed Phuljaan to see Tamiz with her son in his lap. Tamiz hoped it did.

Harmatullah's elder daughter had a heart of gold. She slipped Tamiz a charred potato or a chapatti or some home-made sweets whenever she could. It was hard to believe that a woman could be so adept at weeding. She was wonderful in all respects, expect one, which was that she held Tamiz in great contempt because he was the son of a fisherman. And one more thing. She could not forget for a moment the eight annas she had given Tamiz to pay Shishir Sen for her son's medicine. But Tamiz had ended up spending some of that money. No, not on himself—he had got holy water from the Kali temple at an expense of ten paise. Boikuntho had taken two extra paise for paan. Even a dead man leapt to his feet when given the holy water from the Kali temple in the town, but it didn't do Phuljaan's son any good. How could it? Gofur, that damned son of an oil grinder, had ruined everything. 'You think the fisherman's son will ever return your daughter's money?' he had told Harmatullah at the Golabari market one day. 'And I hear he's got some holy water

from a Hindu temple. How can a Hindu goddess save a Muslim?'
Phuljaan's heart was poisoned when she heard this, and it killed
her faith in the holy water. How was the boy to get better in such
a situation? After this she began to nag Tamiz continuously to
return her money. He promised to give it back after the harvest was
completed, but she wouldn't listen.

It wasn't as though Tamiz couldn't pay back some of the money
at once. The work he did on other people's fields meant his earnings
were far from meagre these days. There was rice for dinner every
day, and neither he nor his father left home in the morning without
eating their fill. He was making money in other ways too. Just the
other day Abdul Kader had given him a rupee to buy sweets and
paan for party workers, out of which he had spent only twelve and
a half annas. Abdul Kader wouldn't even ask any questions if Tamiz
had kept the entire change of fourteen paise instead of returning two
annas. On Monday Boikuntho had sought his help to carry sacks
of ginger into Mukunda Saha's warehouse. The two of them had
unloaded twelve sacks from the bullock cart and put them into the
store, after which Boikuntho had drawn him aside and pressed three
annas into his hand. He must have got a lot more from his employer,
but that didn't matter. Three annas was not a small sum. If only he
had not splurged two annas from it on fish, he could have used it to
reduce this debt to Phuljaan.

Immediately after market day the rice was harvested on Sharafat
Mondol's land in Kamarpara, where the blacksmiths lived. Judhisthir
Kamar was the aadhiar, which meant the son of a blacksmith was
sharecropping on his own land. Tragic. Judhisthir's father had
borrowed rice from Jagadish during the famine, and then, in order to
pay him back with interest, he had had to sell his land to Sharafat. It
was impossible to understand Sharafat. He was willing to let the son
of a blacksmith be a sharecropper on his own land, but he wouldn't let
Tamiz do the same on the land adjoining Tamiz's father's house. Did
he think Tamiz or his father would create trouble? Judhisthir had put
up stiff resistance. The sequence of cutting, threshing and winnowing

the crop he wanted to follow was not acceptable to Sharafat, who did not want, as Judhisthir had suggested, to leave the bundles of paddy in the blacksmith's yard for even a day, because he suspected that some of his grains would be stolen. Even if it was an inferior kind of rice that they were cultivating here, cheaper than the other varieties, Sharafat wasn't going to be deprived of his due. Judhisthir had to give in to the jotedar eventually, although he had been quite insolent with Sharafat Mondol in the process. Apparently, some of the white storks on the silk-cotton tree in the Mondols' yard had accompanied Judhisthir back home, which had infuriated Sharafat even more. The swarm of storks had arrived from Kamarpara in the first place— was Judhisthir doing some black magic to lure them back? But that night Tamiz's father had told Tamiz, slurring his words, that the treacherous storks had actually flown to the blacksmith's house to inspect whether any of Mondol's rice was stacked there.

Anyway, let Judhisthir and Mondol do as they pleased, what business was it of Tamiz's? Judhisthir was a decent man. He had paid his daily labourers fairly, and fed them properly too. The money that Tamiz had earned from him would have left him with plenty even after paying back Phuljaan, but then it was important to save for the future. How would he ever buy his own oxen if he kept splurging on fish and sweets and paying people back? Still, Phuljaan's taunts sometimes made him feel, to hell with it, let me pay her back. But Phuljaan would have no reason to talk to him in that case.

Harmatullah didn't pay much attention to these little exchanges between his daughter and the fisherman's son. After all, she was married, so how far could she go? But he was much more careful when it came to Nobiton; he didn't allow her to go anywhere near Tamiz. She was conscious of her appearance, being someone who, despite stitching quilts all day, starched her clothes frequently and combed her hair every day. But then she did not care for the men from the fishermen or oil grinder communities, which was reassuring for Harmatullah. Nor did he treat Tamiz badly, for after all, the young man had been of great help to him. He had more or less single-handedly dug the canal that brought the water from the lake to the fields. Harmatullah's pepper crop would, Allah permitting, be better than ever before. Considering the rate at which they were growing, he would be able to harvest them as early as the month of Phalgun. He was expecting Mukunda Saha to pay Mondol a good price. Even if he could not grasp the entire picture, Tamiz could guess some of its elements. He could see Harmat's eyes becoming heavy-lidded as he weeded his pepper field, but he could not tell whether it was out of happiness at the profits Mondol would make from the pepper or out of exhaustion.

Tamiz's eyes never closed without reason, always staying open so long as he was awake. Today, however, his heart leapt into his mouth as he was unloading the bundles of grain he had harvested on Shamsher's land. He couldn't tell who was making his heart thud now, or why. He never experienced such casual discomforts. Tamiz found out the reason when he sat down to eat that evening.

'You work on other people's crops every day. Will you never grow your own?' Kulsum's simple question made Tamiz realize why his heart had been behaving erratically. Was he late with his harvesting? Harmatullah said they had sowed later than usual, which was why they should not be harvesting the grain for another week. But could he be trusted? It would be disastrous if he left it too late. Harmatullah would have him evicted from the land and take it under his own control. He was a devil, that one. Although it had been a long day, Tamiz felt uneasy suddenly. His field was brimming over with paddy, but he hadn't been there even once today. Who knew whether someone had cast an evil eye on it? Who knew what was going on there? He couldn't get any sleep, or, even if he did, the curtain it drew over him was so light that he kept tossing and turning beneath it. His father was asleep in the next room. Kulsum was sitting at the open door leading into the backyard, humming. Half-asleep, or dozing, or perhaps awake, Tamiz heard her monotonous drone. It was this that unravelled the knot in his head.

The sun bids goodbye, stricken with cold
The grain in the stalks quivers alone

Jumping up, he opened the front door to go out into the yard. 'Where are you going in this cold?' asked Kulsum. 'Has your father passed on his illness to you?'

'I don't suffer from illnesses like these. Only fakirs like your father get them, he's the one who gave it to my father. I have to go check on my crop.'

'In this weather? All you have on is a shirt, aren't you going to freeze?'

'I have to go. I didn't have time all day.'

No sooner had he taken a step than Kulsum's cotton shawl fell on his back. 'Put that on,' she told him.

She had got the shawl thanks to Abdul Kader's munificence. A Red Cross team had turned up with powdered milk, cotton shawls, quinine tablets and matchboxes. Kader knew the leader of the team—he was a Muslim League leader from the town. 'An educated man, used to be a student leader,' was how Kader described him. 'He's back home now.' He was young, thirty-one, thirty-two at most, but greying at the temples already. Tall and dark, he was dressed in a long, loose, buttoned-up upper garment. An achkan, Kader called it. Although the man in the black achkan and white pyjama always had a cigarette hanging from his lips, Tamiz liked to hear him talk in his deep but liquid baritone.

He spoke affably to everyone. Why, he even told Mukunda Saha while handing out relief material, 'There you are, Saha-babu, I hear you've complained to Calcutta about me. You could have just told me directly.' It wasn't Mukunda Saha who had complained—Nalinaksho-babu, the Congress leader in the town, had passed off his own accusation as Mukunda Saha's. And what was his grievance? That the Red Cross relief was being distributed in Golabari from the Muslim League office. Kader's shop had a signboard of the League over its door. The material belonged to the Red Cross, but it was

the League which was earning the goodwill. Was this right? Before
Mukunda Saha could elaborate on the complaint, the Red Cross man
said, 'Very well, why don't you let us operate from your shop? You can
put up the Congress's signboard or the Hindu Mahasabha's, we have
no objection. I'd requested for the use of Dhiren-babu's room near
Amtoli police station, which is a Congress den. I have no problem,
as long as the relief material reaches the people. But Dhiren-babu did
not agree. Kader here offered us space in his shop. It's all very well to
stop us, but it's not as though you're offering an alternative.'

Mukunda Saha crept away, soon after which Boikuntho Giri
arrived, earning Kader's recommendation at once. 'This fellow may
work at Saha's warehouse, Ismail bhai, but he's a good man.' Ismail
Husain not only gave him a cotton shawl and a woollen sweater, but he
also sent another warm sweater for Boikuntho's employer. Boikuntho
accepted the powdered milk but left it behind at Kader's shop.

'Who knows what babu will say when he sees this foreign milk?'
Wrapping the shawl around himself and then putting on the sweater,
Boikuntho strutted about the market.

Tamiz didn't get a sweater, though. 'These people's skins can't
stand sweater.' Kader didn't pass on the tin of powdered milk either.
'This is foreign milk,' he said, 'you can't stomach it. You'd better take
two shawls instead. Give one to your father.' Tamiz gave his father the
green one, and handed his own brown one to Kulsum, who had worn
it just once before putting away inside an aluminium pot.

Wrapped in the same shawl now, Tamiz rounded the Katlahar
Lake to its north and arrived at his own plot of land. It was late at night
in Girirdanga. There were rice fields all around, most of them bare
now that the grain had been harvested, interspersed with pepper fields.
Everywhere there were either dense crops or post-harvest stubbles.
A group of foxes drank some water at the lake before disappearing to
its north. They couldn't drink much at night because of the heat that
Munshi gave out. Tamiz was left alone after the foxes left.

There was the lake and the fields stretching out, above them the
moonlight wrapped in mist going up all the way to the sky. A light

canopy of vapour lay over Tamiz's land like a mosquito net, his sheaves of grain bent with sleep amidst the moonbeams trickling through the covering. The light from the moon did not leave these rice fields once it entered, rubbing its cheeks against the grain and slurping up its colour, while the paddy stalks soaked up the light and slumbered.

Taking in his field as his heart swelled with pride, Tamiz looked away abruptly. He wasn't giving it the evil eye, was he? But his entire being froze when he glanced at the pepper field, though it was difficult to stay stock-still now. Icy air escaped from his lungs, but Tamiz was too frightened to hear its whistle. What was this creature come to haunt Harmatullah's pepper field on this moonlit night?

Had Munshi himself appeared from his station at the northern head of the lake to collect food for his fish? Tamiz had passed that way a short while ago without seeing anything unusual. Perhaps he would have if he had walked beneath the fig tree, but then he hadn't gone as far as the tree, which stood farther to the north. Tamiz could not remember if he had ever actually seen the tree for himself, and because he couldn't remember, he grew even more frightened, for in that case the creature there on Harmatullah's field might not have anything to do with Munshi. Just as Tamiz had closed his eyes in fear of something completely unknown, he was saved by the sound of Harmatullah coughing.

Even on a winter night the old coot was sleepless. Realizing that Harmatullah was here to look over his pepper field, Tamiz remembered that it was at just such an hour of the night that the old man had diverted the water from his rice field. Phuljaan had been with him then. Was she here now? Why not? Standing on the ridge separating his field from Harmatullah's, Tamiz looked around. And Allah's timing ensured that Phuljaan arrived at that precise moment, yelling 'baapjaan,' from the edge of the ox pool. Her cry was a quavering one, perhaps out of fear on seeing Tamiz, who must have looked like a sinister shadow. Her dark-skinned frame looked paler in the mixture of the mist and moonlight, her complexion appearing to border on fair.

When she came closer, Phuljaan was astonished to discover it was Tamiz standing there. But her grouse got the better of her surprise and she said, 'What about my money? You must be earning quite well now considering you're harvesting everyone's field around here. Your arse hurts only when it comes to repaying my loan, doesn't it?'

Leave alone his arse, no part of Tamiz's body hurt on hearing this. On the contrary, he felt a desire to pay her eight annas, no, not eight annas, twelve annas. Hastily he said, 'Tomorrow. I'll pay you back tomorrow. I'll pay interest too.'

'You think these fishermen keep their word?'

Phuljaan walked off towards her father, who said, 'Just a little bit more to clean, it won't take long.' Cutting the weeds with a sickle, he said to himself, 'It's no trouble working when the moon is shining. Allah has given us the sun so that people find it easy to work on their fields. So the nights on which he switches on the moon are meant for working too, work all night when the moon is bright.' His vote of thanks to Allah was cut short by a coughing bout.

Phuljaan grew animated, refusing to listen to him. 'No baapjaan, come home now. You have to leave for Girirdanga early in the morning, Mondol has sent word.'

Harmatullah had decided not to leave till Allah switched the moon off. But Phuljaan squatted next to him and took the sickle from his hand. 'Enough,' she said. 'Didn't you have a fever this morning? No leftover rice for you tomorrow, Nobiton will make you some fresh rice with chillies. Go along home now, I'll bring your things.'

Harmatullah had never received such loving orders from his eldest daughter. He couldn't remember her as the kind who cared when her father caught a cold. It was his second daughter Nobiton who was usually the affectionate one. Harmatullah's cough was a permanent affair, and the occasional fever in winter was nothing new either. But the doting voice emerging from the region of Phuljaan's goitre actually made Harmatullah's health seem important to himself. Getting to his feet, he told his daughter,

'Don't be too long,' and set off for home. It was difficult to tell whether he was tottering because of an imminent fever or because he was unsettled by Phuljaan's concern.

Phuljaan, however, did not leave even after gathering her father's things. When he turned around to look at her she said with the same indulgent authority, 'Go along, I'll be there in a minute.' Either because of his daughter's love or because he really had got a fever now, Harmatullah lurched homewards without protest. Phuljaan began to weed the field.

The clicking of the sickle as it sliced the weeds reminded Tamiz of horses munching on grass, which made the soles of his feet flutter, lending him a stealthy energy that he did not know how to use. The pepper field lay on one side, covered under the canopy of a light mist through which moonbeams had entered only to be trapped in a changed colour. It was vastly different from the rice field. Slipping in through the mist to gobble up the pepper, the moonlight had turned a yellowish green. Crouching awkwardly within the small pepper bushes, it held their growth in check. The crop was growing too slowly now for anyone to make out. Except Harmatullah, perhaps, and, Phuljaan too, thanks to the training she had received from her father. The clicking of the blade clipping the weeds gave the pepper the sense of comfort it needed to grow a little faster. Tamiz wanted to creep in beneath the canopy to share the task of weeding with Phuljaan. The mosquito net was tucked in so tightly that the moonlight would not be able to escape even if he entered. If the light in his own rice field could mingle with the pepper field, the two of them would spend the night in the service of the land. If they could have worked together Phuljaan would have been by his side even after the rice had been harvested. There would never be a shortage of work on Tamiz's fields. When the amon season came he would be taking on more land to sharecrop. Considering the crops he had produced, Mondol would not be able to refuse him. In fact, people would be gratified if he cultivated their fields. With just two or three more harvests he would be able to, if not actually buy back the land adjoining his father's house from Mondol, at least pay back most of the mortgage. The land was part of his home, you set foot on it as soon as you stepped out of the house at the back. Phuljaan could work on it then, she could water the crop, and certainly weed the field. Under the moonlight and the mist, Tamiz's own house and Harmatullah's, Kulsum and Phuljaan, all merged into one. Why shouldn't Tamiz lend a hand on the pepper field in that case?

But before Tamiz could step off the ridge, Phuljaan lifted the mosquito net of mist to emerge into view, allowing the moonbeams to gush out. She was holding her father's hookah and the sickle in one hand, and a basket to collect the weeds in the other. She often carried a much heavier load, so if she was bent over and shivering as she walked home along the ridge, it must have been because of the cold. The pepper field was completely dark now, for Phuljaan had let the entire moonlight out. But the ridge, and the high bank of the ox pool beyond it, were glittering under the moon, as though someone had layered everything in sight with a paste of rice, making the entire land visible without bathing it in a blinding light.

Everything was perfect. Harmatullah's daughter was perfect too, but Tamiz was fidgeting because she was walking along quietly instead of demanding her money back. Had her anxiety vanished now that Tamiz had promised to pay her back the next day? 'Can you take the money a few days later and not tomorrow?' he asked softly.

'How many days later?' asked Phuljaan, throwing Tamiz a look even as a taunting smile appeared on her lips. It was this smile and not her glance that Tamiz kept seeing the rest of the night. He realized that the glow on the land around him actually came from her lips, for the moon up there in the sky did not have enough luminescence. Looking up, Tamiz couldn't even see the moon anywhere, but all this light could not have come without a source. He felt a little frightened of the woman, but he didn't want to leave her either. So he continued softly, 'As soon as the paddy ripens. I'll pay a little extra, all right?'

Still keeping the moon shining on her lips, Phuljaan said, 'These are just promises. I need the money, don't you understand? I have to take my son to the doctor.' She shivered as she spoke, and so did the light around her.

Whether it was the reference to Phuljaan's son's illness or her shivering, Tamiz's heart was thrown into turmoil. 'You're feeling cold, aren't you?' he said, and threw his shawl around her shoulders.

Gazing at him with brimming eyes, Phuljaan drew the shawl closely around herself and said, 'My son won't live.' There were sobs in her voice. 'He didn't eat this evening. He can't eat at all.'

A deep burden of responsibility crowded Tamiz's head, but a breeze blew the weight away the very next moment. Why did he have to keep himself in Abdul Kader's good books? He could take Phuljaan's son himself to Karim the doctor in Chhaihata. Just let the harvesting be completed on his land. How far was it, 4 miles, 5 miles? He'd just go, with five rupees tucked into this clothes. He would lead the way, Phuljaan following with her son in her arms.

For now, though, they were walking side by side. Now that she had wrapped herself in the brown shawl, the yellow cowl she had made for her head with the end of her sari was visible. The light from her lips was falling on his brow. Poor thing. Where had her heartless husband disappeared, leaving her with her sick child? Didn't he ever think of her? She had to slave day in and day out in her father's house. She would feel comforted if her son were treated by a doctor. Teaching that hard-hearted bastard of a husband a lesson would satisfy her too. Tamiz was prepared to accomplish both of these tasks for her. Hardly had he resolved to do these things than a whirling column of wind shot out from the seven currents and forty-nine waves of the Jomuna 12 miles away, weakening as it soared over the Bangali river, shedding some its moisture on the land, and struck the high bank of the ox pool in Nijgirirdanga, its impact making not only Tamiz but also Phuljaan, wrapped in the Red Cross shawl, shiver uncontrollably at the sudden chill. They trembled at the same time with worry for the child with the swollen belly, withered limbs and dying yellow eyes.

Tamiz trembled so much that he could no longer keep himself under control physically. Phuljaan's father's farming tools slipped from his hand, the same hand that fell, still trembling, on Phuljaan's shoulder. He put his arms around Phuljaan to prevent himself from tumbling to the ground. The moonlight was streaming from her lips now, and Tamiz felt the heat from the flames behind those moonbeams. With no white kerosene available, red kerosene fuelled the light from Phuljaan's lips, its pungency making Tamiz's head reel. But the feel of Phuljaan's pert breasts against his chest, along with the agony in her heart, or her nipples, or all of these, together created pandemonium in Tamiz's body. When he tried to press his own lips against her glowing ones, she turned her face away, so that her goitre brushed against the stubble on Tamiz's cheek. The turmoil in his body did not die down at this. He may not have succeeded in sipping the light from Phuljaan's lips, but this probably did not indicate rejection. After all, she hadn't objected to his rubbing his mouth and cheeks with great ardour against her goitre. Tamiz's passion and arousal increased with matching intensity. When he attempted to put his arms around Phuljaan and make her lie down with him on the slope beneath the high bank east of the ox pool, a short distance from the rice fields, she slid out of his arms without applying the slightest force, leaving him bemused about how she had done it. And almost immediately she disappeared somewhere. Had she merged into the moonlight?

'How dare you try to touch the sky?' Tamiz could still hear Phuljaan's voice, but whether she had said this while he was holding her or after she had escaped, he did not remember. There was more. Phuljaan's taunt kept ringing in his ears, its source somewhere on the edge of the ox pool. With Harmatullah's daughter vanishing into thin air, Tamiz staggered back to his own rice field, gasping for breath. Overwhelmed with fatigue, he was feeling numb all over his body now. Even after he slumped to a sitting position, Phuljaan's jibe, now made worse by the fiery flavour of pepper, continued to sting his ears. This did dispel his exhaustion, however, replacing his numbness with burning humiliation. In a fury he uprooted several stalks of rice which, however, refused to be crushed in his fist. Scratching his unshaven cheeks with the pointed ends of the sheaves gave Tamiz a little relief, but when grains of rice fell out of the sheaves, he began to wonder whether he had left it too late to harvest his crop.

Tamiz set off southwards, possibly to avoid going around the northern side of the lake, with the intention of rowing across instead. But Mondol's boat was moored on the other side of the lake, which meant he had to walk along its southern edge. His eyes were fixed on the opposite bank, however, where he could see a shadowy figure walking along. Could his own shadow possibly fall across the width of the lake? No, it was someone else, a dim figure with a fishing net, walking northwards. Looking closely with a combination of hope and fear, Tamiz realized it was not a shadow but his father. Tamiz's father was walking northwards in his sleep. He was muttering some verses that sounded like prayers, and the words swam to the eastern bank, gaining new life in the bubbles made in the water by the exhalation of a variety of fish. Listening carefully, Tamiz could make out his father's voice.

The sun bids goodbye, stricken with cold
The grain in the stalks quivers alone
A red glow appears in the western sky
The water is black, the banks unfamiliar
Fakirs will gather here late in the night
Harvest the crop, farmer; go home, fisherman.

Trying to recall whether he had heard this particular incantation before, Tamiz allowed the sounds to propel him homewards quickly. Opening the door, Kulsum made room for him to enter and asked, 'Where did you go at this hour? Have you got your father's illness too?' Barring the door, she said, 'Your father was saying terrible things about you while you were wandering about in the night.'

'He's at home?' asked Tamiz hoarsely, the air forcing itself out of his lungs.

'Yes.'

About to enter his own room, Tamiz turned back and peeped into his father's room to discover him lying on the maacha beneath a quilt. Then who was it whom he had seen walking along the lake with a fishing net, muttering verses? The sight of Tamiz's father sleeping and Tamiz's inability to recollect a single word of the incantation made the moonlight go out in the tiny yard in front of the house. Entering his own room, he had barely lain down and drawn the quilt over himself when Kulsum shouted, 'My shawl? Where did you leave my new shawl?'

Tamiz responded to Kulsum's plaintive question by dropping his head on his oil-stained pillow, and what Kulsum did as she expressed her anguish and regret over losing her new cotton shawl was to take her nose close to Tamiz's head and sniff loudly. She was going to inhale as deeply as possibly in search of the smells that would tell her the whereabouts of her new shawl. What was this thing touching Tamiz's head lightly? His eyes closed at the sensation. The incantation he had heard a short while ago and forgotten now, his father walking northwards while singing the words, and the same father sleeping deeply in his own maacha—it was probably to avoid acknowledging these confusing things that Tamiz sank deeper into slumber. But before he could travel through one layer of sleep to the next, the moonlight gushed out from the confines of the mosquito net in the pepper field like a paste of white rice, going up in flames on the eastern side of the ox pool, where it was wrapped in a fishing net, and dropped into the depths of Katlahar. Tamiz kept waking up repeatedly as the huge net sucked up the entire water of the lake and began to roll itself up. This was annoying! He turned over on his side, resting his cheek on his palm.

With his hand pressing his three-day stubble back into his cheek, the sheaves of rice began to plant bristly kisses on his face. A mountain of sleep descended on him, leaving him oblivious to whether Kulsum was still sniffing at his head to locate her new shawl. Perhaps she was. Still he slept. Or perhaps sleep overtook him precisely because of what she was doing.

14

Tamiz would have to wait a little longer before harvesting his rice. Meanwhile, the forty-day observance for Humayun was under way. All of Sharafat Mondol's sharecroppers had put in some work for the ritual in exchange for meals. Both Aziz and Kader had been in favour of paying them too, not wanting to skimp on expenses when it came to ensuring forgiveness for the soul of the innocent boy. Spending money now meant investing in the afterlife. But Mondol's longest-serving sharecropper Hamid Sakidar was unhappy. Considering their living came from farming the land owned by Mondol, how could they possibly take money in the family's time of grief? There was Allah to fear, there was their own afterlife to think of. They might be poor, but they would have to answer on the day of judgement. It was on his entreaties that Sharafat decided not to pay the sharecroppers, giving them two meals a day instead. Abdul Aziz was in favour of giving them money because he didn't want to take the trouble of feeding them. Put in work, get paid. It would be more economical to pay them at the rate of daily labourers than to satisfy their bottomless appetites. But it was part of Sharafat's responsibility to take care of his sharecroppers' afterlives along with their earthly existence. So he paved the way for his aadhiars to secure their rewards after death by allowing them to winnow the rice, cut down trees in their own yards, buy seven enormous castrated bulls from the Doshtikar market across the Kortowa and escort them to his house, arrange for several hundred seers of wheat, potatoes and spices, dig huge ovens, fetch colossal pans from Shimultola several miles to the east, and cook and serve the food during the ceremonies.

Considering the scale on which it was all being done, how could Tamiz not join in? Tamiz's father objected. Tamiz was so set against working on anyone's land just for food that he had humiliated his father for working on Shamsher's land in return for meals. But now he had no problems about working for Mondol without payment. Why?

Tamiz's father was a constant thorn in his side. Even at this age he was as obstinate as ever. Abdul Aziz had sent for him so many times before his son died, even Tamiz had pleaded on Abdul Aziz's behalf, because his wife had had a dream that she wanted to talk to Tamiz's father about, but the old man simply refused to go. Even today Tamiz trembled to think of the kind of scene Abdul Aziz might have created had Kulsum not turned up. And Tamiz would have lost face with Kader too.

Tamiz couldn't afford to follow his father's wishes. Abdul Kader depended on him to a great extent. Gofur was capable of looking after Kader's guests from the town, but he couldn't afford to do without Tamiz during the preparations for the fortieth-day ceremony. Gofur manned Kader's oil shop all on his own—it was much easier to sell kerosene in a shop than to extract oil from a press. There was prestige too—you had to see how obsequious people could be just to get their allotted quarter of a litre of oil at controlled rates. The same people used to be disdainful about him earlier because of his line of work. Gofur had other responsibilities too. When the Muslim League people came to the shop for their meetings in Kader's absence, it was Gofur's job not only to make them comfortable but also to keep his ears open for what they said about Kader.

The number of upper-class guests was far lower than estimated. Abdul Aziz's office colleagues lived too far away to attend. Only one of the three friends he had invited at the civil supplies office in town had turned up. Abdul Kader had plenty of guests, but he had invited many more. Sharafat Mondol had no objection to his sons inviting as many people as they liked, for he know only too well how many of them would be ready to make the long bone-shaking journey in a carriage along the unpaved road.

All the Muslim staff at the office in Lathidanga had been invited. Kader claimed with great authority that it was doubtful whether their fear of the manager would allow them to attend the ceremony en masse. He was wrong. Sharafat knew very well that even a few years ago the manager would have made a great fuss about it, but with age he had become religious. He was not a man to come in the way of anyone who wanted to observe a ritual. What he said nowadays was: I have faith in my own religion, but whether your religion is right or wrong, follow it scrupulously. Everything in a man's life is unpredictable, everything in this world is transient, but religion and caste lie at the core of existence. Someone who breaks with these loses all they have.

Not that the manager would have stood for it if they were to invite the Hindus of Kamarpara. Neither god nor the manager could give them permission to stuff themselves with food at the last rites of a Muslim and offend their religion in the process. But then Mondol would have a big feast for his aadhiars from Kamarpara at Kader's wedding. The Muslims of Shimultola followed the practice of setting aside one day during family weddings to invite Hindus for a meal—Sharafat could do it too.

Still, the crowd at Humayun's fortieth-day observance was enormous. From Girirdanga, Nijgirirdanga, Golabari and Chhaihata on one side of the lake to Ranirpara, Paranirpara and Mahishaban on the other, not a single villager was left out. Whether it was farmers or fishermen, oil grinders or weavers, they had all come in droves with their entire families. The entire village rang with their voices, sending all the fish in Katlahar Lake scurrying towards the Girirdanga shore. The prayers were offered in the mosque immediately after the fazr namaz. In fact, it was for this specific occasion that the mosque adjoining the Mondols' house got a fresh set of fences, and began to be called a mosque. Since the mosque nearby belonged to the Jamiat Ahle Hadees, the Milad Sharif couldn't be read there. Although Kader had wanted a moulobi from the town with a formal title to lead the prayers, Mondol hadn't agreed. It had been a tradition from his forefathers' times that the Imam from Motabek village would do the job. The priests from the town could perform the nazaat prayers after the ritual bath and meals, that would be all right.

Sitting on the improvised prayer mat of a sheet laid out in the front room with pillows stacked on either side, Alhaz Maulana Hafez Abu Nasar Barkatullah Pratapuri, Imam of the Jama Masjid in the town, read out the nazaat prayers. Floating on the smoke rising from the incense sticks planted in gunmetal glasses filled with rice grains and balanced on the heads of the pillows, the maulana's melodious voice spread through the huge gathering, mingling with the steam rising from the large pans of beef curry to be transformed into an appetite-inducing fragrance.

Flustered by such a huge crowd, Hamid Sakidar and Gofur began to rush the process of serving the food, ladling out the rice and salt on rows of plantain leaves just as the prayers began. The last part of the prayers was still under way when they began carrying buckets of beef curry to serve the rows of people waiting to eat. Harmatullah, Kolu's father, Hamid Sakidar, Gofur, Tamiz—they were all rushing about with the buckets, paying no attention to the prayers. Suddenly Abdul Aziz issued loud instructions from the veranda adjoining the front room, 'The monazat is under way, raise your hands, everyone.' The maulana's voice rose suddenly.

He was reading the prayers in Urdu, a language of which the collective ignorance of the guests was so high that it instigated their devotion, the sense of mystery helping to close the gap with the Arabic verses of the Quran. Meanwhile, many of the guests who had already sat down to eat got impatient and began to wolf down their rice with salt. Their complaints—'What about the curry?'; 'Are we supposed to eat nothing but rice?'; 'What sort of service is this, where's the meat?'—began to collide with the verses of the prayers.

Irked, Kader came up to stand next to Aziz and bark, 'Khamosh!'
Not knowing that this was merely the Urdu word for 'shut up', even
those in charge of serving the food put their buckets down and raised
their arms, as did many of the diners on observing them. Those who
had already added salt to their rice could get the scent of their food
now, which, instead of satiating half their appetite, as the proverb
promises, only served to induce fresh pangs of hunger. The guests
seated in the front room and the adjoining veranda had joined the
prayers devoutly. Their eyes grew moist at the maulana's ardent plea
to Allah for a place in heaven for the innocent child Mohammad
Humayun, salty echoes of 'amin', 'amin', pouring out of their
throats. Meanwhile, the maulana was using the opportunity offered
by the death of the child to seek forgiveness for the sins of his parents,
grandparents and all his ancestors. The smoke from the incense hung
over the room like a cascade of water, and before they could lose
themselves in the aroma of beef, the people in this smaller gathering
grew united in their remembrance of not just Humayun but also of
his parents, grandparents and even of his unidentified forefathers.
Humayun's elder brother Babur was seated close to his grandfather.
Sharafat Mondol had a weakness for him because of his academic
prowess. He had been weeping ceaselessly from the time the prayers
had begun, and the maulana's plaintive petitions overcame the
unintelligibility of the language to make him sob loudly. Sharafat
Mondol's own eyes misted over, although his tears were confined
to the sockets while his gaze cut through the curtain of briny water
to settle on the dignified Chhotomian from the Mian family. The
fragrance of attar from Chhotomian's off-white kurta and the shawl
of the same colour thrown carelessly over his thighs lent glory to
Sharafat's grief, making him numb with gratitude as he observed the
honoured guest's half-closed eyes.

Sharafat had visited the four aged brothers of Shimultola not once
but twice to invite them, risking the damage that the derisive smiles
on the corners of their paan-and-tobacco-stained lips could cause his
eyes. Kader could have easily secured large pots and pans from the

town. But instead of paying heed to his son, Mondol decided to borrow them from the Mians in Shimultola, who had renewed their traditional affluence with a collection of large and expensive vessels for the kitchen. Sharafat's efforts had paid off, and Chhotomian was here today with the grandson of one of his brothers.

Abdul Kader's guests from the town might be influential people, but could they really give Sharafat Mondol's social standing a boost? They were here in a group and immersed in conversation, making many powerful statements about Pakistan, the Muslim League, the Congress, Gandhi, Jinnah, elections, Jawaharlal, the Krishok Proja party, Fazlul Huq, Suhrawardy, Abul Hashim, Najimuddin, Aligarh, Islamia College and so on. People listened in wonder, overwhelmed even though they understood very little. And after they would say 'slaamaleikum' and leave for the town in their carriage, everyone else would stare at the vehicle till it disappeared from sight, at which point they would promptly forget not only the visitors but also whatever little they had gleaned from their conversation. But what they would not forget was that they had eaten a meal with the Mians of Shimultola, if not sitting in the same row, at least at the same ceremony, in the same building.

The lineage of the Shimultola Mians went back a long way—they were not upstarts. They had been collecting taxes on behalf of the king of Dighapatia for many decades. When it came to bullying the people of Dighapatia, which occupied the entire eastern side of the district, beating them up, or sleeping with beautiful women among them, the Mians had been doing it all. Of late some of the lower-class people had become slightly literate, and didn't want to bow to authority as a result. Still, Sharafat knew the value of tradition. Even if Shimultola had lost its lustre, the names of the Mians continued to have a halo around them. It was only because they had seen better days that Sharafat had mustered the courage to strike up a relationship with them. He had once considered getting Kader married to one of Baromian's granddaughters, and had even sent a signal to that effect through Jagadish Saha, who had returned to say—though he alone knew the truth of what had happened—that Baromian had flared up in a rage on hearing the proposal. How dare this peasant think of having his son marry someone from the Mian family?

Baromian needn't have been so enraged. Sharafat did not plough the land himself any more. Even his father had given up manual labour in his own youth. Admittedly, he couldn't stand up to the Mians when it came to the extent of land he owned or had leased, but if you added up his income from cultivation, the bamboo grove, and kerosene sales in the Golabari market, he wouldn't fall particularly short of the Talukdars. Jagadish Saha visited the Talukdars in Shimultola late at night—did they think Sharafat didn't know the implication of this? Some members of the Mian family were distinctly snub-nosed, but ever since their fortunes went on the decline, they began to keep those noses in the air all the time.

Chhotomian was in fact the decent one in the family. He frequented the town quite often, besides visiting Calcutta every other month, and travelling to Darjeeling once every three years. He had even begun to dress in handloom clothes for some time to signal his political affiliation. Chhotomian was in Darjeeling when Deshbandhu Chittaranjan Das died. He had accompanied the Congress volunteers who took Deshbandhu's body to Calcutta on the train. There couldn't have been too many Muslim volunteers in the group. All this had taken place a long time ago, however. He had given up politics at least ten years ago, but that didn't stop him from mingling affably with everyone. There was another thing about Chhotomian that Mondol liked, which was that he was keen on forging ties with all affluent families, without caring for their lineage. But his problem lay elsewhere—no one was allowed to marry a girl in his family unless they were a graduate. Did he think he was giving out officer's jobs in the government, which no one could apply for without a B.A. degree?

Abdul Kader was not inferior to a college graduate in any respect. Sharafat Mondol was spellbound by Kader's conversation with Chhotomian. His elder son was a government employee, but still he gave important and well-known people a wide berth. All his whispers and gossip were exchanged with the civil service clerks. But look how well Abdul Kader was conducting himself.

'Do tell Ismail Shaheb to lobby for a ticket. His prospects in this area are excellent. And no one can turn down your family's request east of the Bangali and west of the Jomuna.'

Chhotomian was not in the least bit flattered by this, for he was used to hearing such things. But the praise for Ismail pleased him. Ismail Hussain was married to his brother's second daughter, which practically made him Chhotomian's son-in-law. He was doubtful, however, whether Ismail would be chosen to fight the elections. 'How will he get a ticket here?' asked Chhotomian. 'The area is full of old settlers.' Far from being deflated by this,

Kader was enthused even more. 'It is, but they're useless. Ismail bhai is so close to the party leaders in Calcutta. He was a student leader, after all. Those who are spreading the word about Pakistan across Bengal . . .'

Chhotomian was not particularly impressed by the idea of Pakistan. 'Our boy talks of nothing but Pakistan, and I see you're the same. All you young people, it's natural to be worked up at this age.'

Kader felt grateful to Chhotomian for clubbing him with Ismail Husain in terms of age and excitability, using the gratitude for some latitude. 'Muslims cannot survive without Pakistan,' he said heatedly. 'Just think about where we were once and where we are today . . .'

The middle-aged Doctor Amiruddin Akhand, one of the leaders of the League in the town, voluntarily took over the task of explaining the current plight of Muslims. 'Don't you see that everything from education to the courts to business is in the hands of Hindus. And 90 per cent of the jomidars are Hindus too.' He seemed to have rehearsed his speech this morning, or perhaps he had memorized it after making it many times over in his chambers. 'Muslims are the subjects of Hindu jomidars, clients of Hindu lawyers, debtors of Hindu moneylenders, students of Hindu teachers, patients of Hindu doctors.'

Chhotomian staunched his flow of rhetoric with a question. 'Don't you have Muslim patients?'

Amiruddin said, 'Hindu patients never come to me, and all educated Muslims believe Muslims cannot be good doctors.'

'Then why blame the Hindu patients alone? Do you think Hindu patients will shun a Muslim doctor if he is an able one? Both the eye doctors in the town are Muslims, are you telling me Hindus don't go to them to have their eyesight checked? The best-known dentist in Calcutta is a Muslim, have you ever calculated what percentage of his patients are Hindus?'

'These are exceptions. The point is, what is the overall situation?' The doctor also took on the task of answering Chhotomian with a counter-question. 'The businesses are in their hands, they monopolize the senior posts when it comes to jobs. You can give members of your own community a boost when you're in a position of power. Do we have that opportunity?'

'But it's the Muslim League that runs the government. The League has been ruling Bengal for quite some time now. Can you tell me of their accomplishments besides the famine?'

'That's a correct point you've made,' said the doctor, his tone suggesting that he finally had Chhotomian where he wanted him. 'The Bengal government asked the Bihar government for rice during the famine, and the Hindu-dominated Congress government refused. The Hindu leaders of Bengal supported the decision, while the British made off with all the rice on the pretext of war. Who got a bad name? The Muslim League, of course. Once we have Pakistan every Muslim in India will come to our aid. The Muslim business community will have the opportunity to help us.'

'What help are we getting from the Muslim jomidars? Do you think we would have had schools and colleges if the Hindu jomidars hadn't built them? Other than the district school here, every single school has come up thanks to the generosity of Hindu jomidars. The two biggest jomidars in the town are both Muslims—has either of them donated even a single brick for a school or college? This kind of work needs a different mentality, Doctor.'

'The mentality will be created once we have Pakistan. Our own country, power in our own hands. Muslim jomidars will acquire social responsibility.'

But Kader didn't support the doctor's views. 'The system of jomidars will be abolished in Pakistan,' he declared, 'without compensation. In Pakistan the law will decree that the owner must till his own land. There will be no distinction between the rich and the poor in Pakistan.'

Ismail Husain was capable of saying the same things much more eloquently. Sacks of posters and leaflets were arriving from Calcutta with such statements printed on them. There were even books titled *Pakistan*. Kader did read them, but he couldn't articulate all of it clearly. Nobody responded to his incoherent agitation. Amiruddin was in fact annoyed by it. Fearing anarchy over property rights in the absence of the system of jomidars, Sharafat Mondol found himself unable to support his son. It was in fact Chhotomian who said with a tranquil smile, 'So you'll take away the property of jomidars, you'll kill the rich people. What's the difference between you and the communists then? You preach the ways of Islam, but you borrow the language of atheists. Which of these do we consider real?'

'Islam gives every human the same rights. There is no caste system in Islam. Our prophet said this hundreds of years ago. The communists actually took all this from Islam.' Kader's voice was ringing with confidence now. Chhotomian was pleased when he realized that this confidence was borrowed from Ismail, who had obviously built up a following in this area. He would get a lot of votes hereabouts if he could secure the nomination. It would be good to have the eastern side of Kartowa under the control of a relative. An added reason for Chhotomian's satisfaction was that it was he who had made the match between Ismail and Razia. His eldest brother was unwilling, while the middle brother was disinterested. With no land of one's own, it wasn't so easy to marry into the Mian family of Shimultola simply on the strength of a job in the town. Since the difficult task was achieved only on Chhotomian's insistence, he was bound to be pleased at the sign of success of the groom he had chosen for his niece. He responded happily to Kader by echoing Ismail. 'Does Islam allow you to seize someone else's property? Did our prophet Hazrat Hareem Sallallahu Alaihi Wasallam confiscate the property of Hazrat Usman Raziallah Anhu? It isn't important whether you're rich or poor, my son, a philanthrope is a good man no matter whether he is rich or poor.'

Kader did not know these details—how was he to answer these points? If only Ismail bhai had not gone off to Calcutta today! The election for the Mayor of Calcutta Corporation was still a month away, but he had used that as an excuse to run away. He tended to go to Calcutta on the slightest of pretexts. They could have had a marvellous meeting today if Ismail Husain had been here. It wasn't often that so many people were gathered at one place.

'All the big shots of your League are jomidars and wealthy men. How will the party survive if you throw them out?' Assuming that he had established the logic of his long argument with this conclusion, Chhotomian felt vindicated and displayed the victor's generosity by changing the subject to give Kader some respite. Drawing Abdul Aziz's elder son Babur close to himself, he asked his name, which school and class he studied in, and how much he scored in his exams, before setting him an impossible translation from Bengali to English and laughing uproariously at his own wit. A fidgeting Babur withstood Chhotomian's curiosity and affection for some time before escaping from the room. With the boy out of reach, Chhotomian turned to the father. He knew the full story of Abdul Aziz's boss, the sub-registrar, and proceeded to let the cat out of the bag about how the unworthy son of a worthy father from Murshidabad had got his job. But he also informed Abdul Aziz that the sub-registrar's family had been related to his own for three generations. One of Chhotomian's aunts was from that family, while her father was also distantly related to another aunt of Chhotomian's. Aziz was delighted to hear of this connection. He would have to inform his boss about it as soon as he went back to work at Joipur. He went off happily to check on the arrangements to feed the honoured guests. His wife and mother-in-law were cooking for the special invitees. Two goats had been slaughtered for them, since some of them might not be keen on beef. Besides, not everyone could be served just beef curry and rice. Someone had been sent to get curds from Hatibandha, where Gopal Ghosh had promised to deliver it personally, although there was no sign of him yet. It was late, but then the special guests had been served a heavy breakfast immediately on arrival, which meant they had to be given some time to work up an appetite.

Meanwhile, someone could be heard scolding someone else where the ceremonies were being conducted. It wasn't clear who was admonishing whom or why, but it was obvious from the screaming that someone had committed a blunder. The uproar led to an uncomfortable silence among the honoured guests here, while a Muslim League worker took advantage of the lull to start afresh about the indispensability of Pakistan. Just as Abdul Kader was preparing to launch into the subject, he had to leave the room at Sharafat Mondol's signal to find out what was going on.

Running into Tamiz, who was rushing along the wide passage between two of the rooms with a bucket of beef curry, Kader looked at him questioningly. 'Harmat Poramanik is creating trouble.'

Although Harmatullah had started the whole thing, the credit for heightening it went to Gofur. When the yard in front began to overflow with people waiting to eat, Kader himself had instructed that fifty or sixty of them be made to sit in two facing rows here in this passage. Among those who had sat down there were Harmatullah and Tamiz's father. Although he was responsible for serving the guests, Harmatullah hadn't been able to contain his hunger after the first batch of people had eaten, and had forced himself into the group of those who were waiting to eat. But as it turned out, Tamiz's father was sitting right next to him. What are you doing here? All the fishermen are eating behind the cowshed. Do you think you'll get less food if you eat with your kind, or will the bucket of beef curry overlook you? If it wasn't bad enough that Tamiz's father was seated in the same row as Harmat, he was actually touching him. What if the fisherman splashed a drop or two of his curry on Harmat's plate? So Harmatullah began to shout, 'Your caste people are sitting over there, how dare you sit with us?'

Paying no attention to any of this, Tamiz's father wiped his plantain leaf plate with his fingertips, leaving dirty streaks on it, not even heeding the fact that repeated swipes of his fingers were obliterating the green colour, for his eyes were riveted on the cones of steaming rice as he wondered how long it would be before they reached him.

Gofur went up to deal with Harmatullah's complaints. His primary responsibility was to look after the upper-class guests, but since they were still chatting in the room reserved for them, he had taken the opportunity to supervise the meals laid out for other members of his community. The oil grinders were seated beneath the cluster of storks from Shimultola, and he was on his way there to ensure that there was enough meat to go with the curry being served to his clansmen. When he heard Harmat talk about caste, Gofur admonished him at once, 'Muslims have no castes. Don't expect to get a meal here if you're going to talk about caste.'

Chastened, Harmatullah quickly modified his complaint, for he knew how influential Gofur was hereabouts despite belonging to the clan of oil grinders. 'Not caste, it's not just caste. This lunatic here farts all the time during his meal, the smell is making my stomach turn. Tell him to sit somewhere else.'

By rights the fragrance of the meat should have suppressed all other smells. Still, Gofur could not approve of this act on Tamiz's father's part. He spat on the ground and touched his nose, which inspired several others to follow suit out of respect, spitting gobs of sticky saliva rich with beef curry on the ground in front of their plates. By then Harmatullah and Gofur had both been served their rice, along with two ladles each of beef curry. Both of them had dug holes in their respective mounds of rice, putting the pieces of meat in safekeeping and sucking the curry off their fingers. Of course, they had begun eating even earlier, mixing salt into their rice.

Gofur looked directly at Tamiz's father with a frown and exclaimed, 'Didn't you just eat outside the cowshed? I saw your arse stuck to the ground there. Now you're eating again? Get up, get up at once. No one's allowed two meals. Eat as much as you like the first time, eat till your stomach bursts, but you're not allowed to eat a second time, I won't let you put it in a bundle either.' Having conveyed the rules applicable to the forty-day observance, he proceeded to put them into motion. 'You, yes, you crazy old coot. Get out.'

Tamiz's father was deeply involved in extracting the marrow from a thick bone, which made it impossible to comply with Gofur's orders. If anything, the threat multiplied his appetite tenfold, and he postponed the extraction of the marrow to wolf down his rice in gigantic mouthfuls. None of the people next to or in front of him endorsed his second meal, being unanimous that eating more than once at a prayer meeting was a very bad habit. Their condemnation was tame, however. They were keen to please Gofur, but determining that talking too much about it right now was a waste of time, they dedicated themselves to transferring fistfuls of rice and beef curry into their mouths. Some of them may even have been encouraged by Tamiz's father's example to quietly eat a second time themselves.

Despite the two different kinds of objections made by Harmatullah and Gofur, Tamiz's father raised his eyes from his plate and looked around in search of a second helping of rice. Tamiz was walking down the passage to refill the bucket of beef curry from which he was serving the fishermen. Although the beef curry had been cooked outdoors, for the sake of security it had been stored in gigantic pans beneath a canopy erected over a portion of the yard. Tamiz had served his father mountains of meat just a short while ago. The sight of his father sitting down to eat a second time after having stuffed his belly already made him laugh. The old man was a little too greedy when it came to food. But let him eat, Allah alone knew when he'd be invited to a feast like this again. Mondol was a generous host today, and if it took three or four meals, never mind two, to soften his father's heart towards Sharafat, it would be worth it. As he was plotting how to give his father some extra meat, he heard Gofur's harsh order, 'Get out.' At once his indulgence was buried under sharp indignation. The old coot shouted at me because I'm working without pay here. But you, you're as slippery as they come, your tongue is so long that one meal isn't enough for you. Must you be such a glutton? Although Tamiz couldn't say any of this out loud, these were the thoughts that ran though his head. And that Gofur was a bastard; he had begun to think no end of himself just because he had married a whore divorced by a fisherman and stuck like a limpet to Kader's arse. He wouldn't stop till he got the old coot to abandon his meal. Tamiz strode off towards the cowshed, without even bothering to refill his bucket of beef curry, to avoid witnessing his father's humiliation in the presence of so many people. The fishermen's clan would be delighted if he could ensure that they ate to their hearts' content, although the same people would feel a stab of envy when they realized that Tamiz, though one of their own, was considered important by the Mondols. He was being deprived of the glory and pleasure of being able to generate both happiness and jealousy amongst so many people only because of his father's gluttony.

Abdul Aziz's mother-in-law was peeping through a slightly parted door to one of the rooms at the sight of an old man ignoring two different kinds of protests from the two different men and continuing to eat with gusto. She had come here on the day her grandson had died, filled with a fresh grief. This time she had been here for the past three days to join her daughter's mourning and the forty-day observance. At the request of Mondol's second wife, she had supervised the cooking for the special guests. She lived close to the town, which was where her family's income, occasional business deals and daily necessities came from. Once in a while, the women of the family went out together to watch the first show of a talkie before returning home in rickshaws, swaddled in their saris.

Under the influence of urban living, and also because of their strained means, the way they dressed, ate and lived was more or less austere. Even the excitement in their lives was routine. The town was rather small, but because there was no agriculture, the income was predictable, which also meant that daily lives were regular. The sight of the crowds, the uproar, and the unexpected, unimaginable enthusiasm at the forty-day observance of her grandson's death in her son-in-law's house, along with the opportunity to supervise the cooking for the honoured guests, made Aziz's mother-in-law squirm with jealousy as well as happiness while she feasted her eyes on everything around her. She had gone into her daughter's room to pop a paan into her mouth now that the cooking was done, and to provide her daughter with an accurate estimate of the depth of ignorance of the members of this family about fine cuisine. She began to giggle on seeing an old man with a salt-and-pepper beard being harassed outside the window. She watched with great enjoyment, laughing louder the longer it went on.

Meanwhile, Hamida was reminded of her son at regular intervals as she made sure that the women sitting in rows in the inner yard with their skinny or disproportionately fat babies with protruding bellies, festering scalp sores, dirt-rimmed eyes or running noses clinging to them, were being served their meals properly. All these people today were celebrating a grand feast of rice and beef. It was thanks to the apple of her eye, the piece of her heart, that everyone was eating here, but the poor little boy could not be part of it all. Wiping her eyes, Hamida went back to her room and burst into tears. But where was the time to weep? She had to go back into the yard. The more she could personally do to ensure that everyone ate to their hearts' content, the more the soul of her innocent son was likely to find peace and comfort. Hamida was on her feet, about to return to the women outside, when her mother called out to her, 'Look how that man there is eating, Hamida. Seems he ate once already. Do you see how large each mouthful is? These village people can eat so much!'

Hamida was not in the least inclined to watch village people gorge on their rice and beef curry. She was fed up with it, having seen it often since her marriage. It was only because of her mother's interest that Hamida joined her at the window.

That was the moment Tamiz's father looked up from his plate in the expectation of more food, even as Gofur and Harmatullah continued with their respective complaints and condemnation, becoming clearly visible to Hamida and her mother. The sight of his face made Hamida stagger backwards and fall on the bed, from where she could still see Tamiz's father, whose face was tilted upwards because he had not yet got a second helping of rice. Hamida kept staring at him, trembling uncontrollably all the while. Sitting down by her side, Hamida's mother held her tight, asking in anguish, 'What is it, what's happened?'

'It's the same man, Ma,' whispered Hamida, her face ashen. 'This was the man the night before Humayun went, or was it the night before that night, didn't I tell you? This was the man who came.'

Hamida's mother remembered it all. She had heard of Hamida's experience on that apocalyptic night. Everyone in the family had heard. Many of the villagers had heard too, and Hamida had told her mother at least a hundred times.

15

Two days before he died Humayun passed urine three times in all, with blood in it. The fever went on the rampage across his body, much like a drunkard, climbing to 106 degrees, going down only after water was poured over his head for a prolonged period of time. But it was lurking beneath his pillow all the while, burrowing underneath the mattress and leaping back into action as soon as the stream of water thinned. 'Pouring so much water over his head might give him pneumonia,' warned Horen. 'A cold compress might be better.'

Mondol's second wife switched to a cold compress, continuing till late into the night, Aziz and Kader taking turns to sit by her. Hamida refreshed the water in the bowl at regular intervals. Even as he kept reading rakats from the namaz, perched on a stool in his own room, Sharafat Mondol kept tabs on his grandson on a minute-to-minute basis. In the room with the door to the east, Mondol's first wife was matching the rise of the fever with regular invectives directed at her husband, but as the night deepened she fell asleep with exhaustion without eating or even reading the asr namaz. Mondol's second wife could barely move her hands after the namaz, and couldn't keep her eyes open either. Kader had left already. Aziz and Hamida practically forced Mondol's second wife to rest a little, to get a couple of hours' sleep. Abdul Aziz began to doze soon afterwards, and was soon curled up near his son's feet. Hearing his faint snores, Hamida called out to him softly, 'Babur's father, Babur's father.' This made him stop snoring, but didn't wake him up. The room was completely silent now. A dry leaf fell from the guava tree on the tin roof under the weight of three dewdrops, the light, wet sound not breaching the silence in the room.

Hamida alone remained awake. The strip of cloth she dampened in the gunmetal bowl of water before placing on Humayun's brow dried instantly. Could a human body be so hot? Humayun seemed to be giving off fumes that made Hamida's eyes smart. Closing them gave her some comfort. A lot of comfort. 'My darling, my baby, my bird . . .' Hamida touched her son's forehead with her lips, touched her son's cheeks with her lips, planting kisses on him. She would suck up all his fever with her kisses. Allah, make my son well, Allah, give me all his fever, all his illness Allah, make my Humayun well again. Just as she was telling Allah all this, Hamida felt a gust of cool air on her back. Allah had listened to her prayers then, he had sent a cooling breeze to take away the heat from her son's body. Hamida felt a second gust of cool air on her back, her head feeling clear. But almost immediately there was a whiff of incense, which made her heart thump. Raising her head quickly, she saw a man with a salt-and-pepper beard, standing in front of her in spotless white clothes. A long iron chain hung around his neck. Hamida's right hand was resting on her son's chest, clutching the dried strip of cloth she was using for the cold compress. Even if the boy was gasping for breath under the weight of her hand, Hamida could neither move it, nor tear her eyes away from the figure in front of her. The doors and windows of the room were shut; the windows had been kept permanently closed ever since Humayun had fallen ill, and Mondol's first wife shut the doors even before evening fell. How had the man got in, then? But this had not yet occurred to Hamida. Instead, a different question glowed like the first light of dawn all over her: Where had she seen this man before? When? He was looking at Humayun with glazed, reddened eyes. Then he turned those eyes, which had no pupils, towards Hamida. His lips didn't move, but a hoarse voice emerged from his chest. 'It can't go on like this. Let your son rest now, let him rest.' The scent of the incense intensified.

Hamida had heard this hoarse voice before. But where? When? Or perhaps she hadn't really heard it. Giving up her efforts to remember, she said, 'Go away. Go away.' But the words could not escape her lips, as though she had been robbed of speech. The wick of the lantern hanging from a nail in the open door connecting two rooms was burning with a blackish-red light. Hamida was just beginning to think of the man's white clothes as a shroud when the flame flared up suddenly before going out. Before it did, though, Hamida noticed mud stains at several places on the shroud. The man was no longer visible after the light was extinguished, but the low strains of an incantation floated in from the yard. Hamida heard the words clearly, but even before the hoarse voice died down she screamed and collapsed next to her son.

She came to her senses soon afterwards when water was splashed on her face. The room was full of people by then. No one but Humayun slept the rest of the night. In a quavering voice Hamida described the sights, sounds and smell over and over again, her account growing increasingly incoherent.

Sharafat's second wife could tell that all this was Cherag Ali's doing. No one knew where he had disappeared, who could tell where he had died? He often appeared in disguise to lure the young men of the village to where he was now. If there was one person who could extract the meaning of Hamida's dream it was Tamiz's father. He was the only one who used to accompany Cherag Ali everywhere. After he had married the fakir's granddaughter, all of Cherag Ali's learning, wisdom and tricks had passed on to him. Hamida informed everyone repeatedly that it wasn't a dream. How could it have been a dream, considering the lantern had actually gone out? Hadn't Abdul Aziz found the room plunged into darkness when he woke up after she fainted? And then, how could anyone have smelt incense in their sleep? Even Mondol's second wife had got the smell.

Still, everyone was in a pleasant mood the next morning onwards. Humayun's fever was down to 99.5 degrees, and he had actually had half a bowl of barley water with lemon juice. But Hamida refused to budge from her son's bed, still shuddering from time to time.

'Send for Tamiz's father. No one can tell what's going to happen to Humayun till he interprets Babur's mother's dream.' Even Aziz became apprehensive after Mondol's second wife's repeated warnings. How would he survive if his wife was also felled along with his son? Therefore word was sent through Tamiz to his father. Neither Sharafat Mondol nor Aziz liked to involve servants or sharecroppers in their personal affairs, but Hamida had the backing of her stepmother-in-law, which made it difficult for Sharafat to contradict her. And besides, he could hardly allow his wife to die of fear.

Tamiz's father didn't show up, though. He heard the story of what Hamida had dreamt or seen in fragments, conveyed by his son while he was practically asleep, and, having heard it, he continued to sit there drowsily before eating a plateful of rice as soon as darkness fell and then falling asleep on the maacha. Kulsum stayed up late into the night to listen to his mutterings in his sleep. An abundance of sounds emerged from Tamiz's father's lips all the time, but none of them acquired the shape of words as far as Kulsum was concerned, although she could identify traces of her grandfather's incantations. This only gave her a headache.

That night the scent of incense and the humming of a male voice in her ears frightened Hamida all over again. A roomful of people were awake with her all night, their skins prickling with fear when they saw unfamiliar shadows reflected in her large eyes. The next morning Kader pestered Tamiz to get his father to explain Hamida's dream to her, even if it meant concocting an explanation. Tamiz went home to give his father an ultimatum—Sharafat would not allow Tamiz to sharecrop his land any more if his father didn't visit the Mondols at once. Tamiz's father stared at his son uncomprehendingly, and continued the same way without betraying any other reaction.

At this point Kulsum proposed visiting the Mondols herself. That would do too, for she was Cherag Ali's granddaughter, after all. Tamiz knew his stepmother was not to be dismissed, as it was she who had ensured that his father remained under Cherag Ali's spell.

Walking alongside Kulsum, an enthusiastic Tamiz recounted Hamida's frightening experience. When they had gone past Bulu majhi's house, Tamiz looked back to see his father standing nearby, watching them walk and talk together. Tamiz's father stood there while they continued towards the Mondols' house.

Hamida presented a detailed account of the night to Kulsum. She began with descriptions of applying the cold compress on Humayun's forehead in the evening, her exhausted stepmother-in-law going into the next room to rest after the asr namaz, and Aziz going to sleep near their son's feet, taking almost as much time to recount the incidents as they had taken to occur. She interspersed these accounts with information about her son's intelligence, his skills at sports, the influence on him of his uncles from the town, and the similarities and differences in the natures and behaviour of her elder son Babar and younger son Humayun. Although Kulsum didn't understand much of this, none of it appeared annoying or irrelevant to her. She listened to everything that Hamida said with great concentration, her lips clamped together. Sitting ramrod straight, she sniffed deeply without leaning forward, trying to retrieve the forgotten parts of Hamida's dreams by smelling them out. But she trembled when Hamida spoke of kissing her son's fevered brow. When she tried to control this trembling, there was an upheaval in her breast, spreading to her ribcage, where she could hear Cherag Ali clearly.

The mother kisses her son's brow in his sleep
At once the boy jumps into the arms of death
What do I tell you mother about such kisses
The angel of death was lurking in your lips.

Then Kulsum wanted to hear the verses that Hamida had heard in her dream after the man in the shroud had vanished—not that Hamida was willing to acknowledge it was a dream, for how would the lantern have actually gone out in that case? Hamida couldn't remember a word, however, though she tried very hard to recollect them at Kulsum's behest. By then Kulsum could hear the twanging of Cherag Ali's dotara in her head. Softly she said, 'Shall I tell you? Try to remember, isn't this it?' Her voice turned heavy, and possibly it was Cherag Ali himself who sang.

> The bird burns with a fever
> The mother cannot sleep
> Once she closes her eyes
> The bird will fly away
> Listen to me, mother mine
> Cover both your eyes now
> I cannot flutter my wings in the egg
> Only when you close your eyes
> Can I fly away
> Go to sleep now, mother mine
> So that I can say goodbye

Fear and desperation descended on Hamida as she listened. The deep dark night when the lantern had gone out arrived in the middle of the afternoon, enveloping her as she heard Kulsum sing. Gripping Kulsum's hand urgently, she slurred, 'That's the one. Those very words. Sing it again, bubu, sing it again.'

Overwhelmed at being addressed as an elder sister, Kulsum became confused about the words she had just hummed. Stopping, she tried to remember the entire verse correctly, while Hamida pleaded with her, 'You're my own sister, bubu, sing it again.' But Hamida's eyes were closing with sleep. Kulsum continued singing.

The moon rises over the bamboo grove
One by one its lays all the eggs
The yellow yolk is everyone's home
But when I look my fakir is gone.
The mynah bird has flown away
I cannot see it any more.

'Oh yes, it was this one, this was the song he was singing.' The words
rolled off Hamida's thickening tongue, her eyes closed. She would
have fallen off her low stool had Mondol's second wife not grabbed
her, helped her to her feet, and guided her to her bedroom. No
sooner had she lain down by her son than Hamida fell asleep.

After Humayun was buried, Hamida's brother got hold of a
formidable moulobi from the town and had the house cleansed with
prayers. For forty days there was a reading of the Quran Sharif in
Hamida's room. And yet no one was bothered about the man in
the shroud whom Hamida had seen. He hadn't returned since that
night, not even for a stolen glance at Hamida.

16

After signalling her son's death, the same man was here a full month and a half later, having swapped his shroud for a lungi with rust-and-blue checks, to eat at the forty-day observance for the same boy. And eating twice, at that, so shameless. Hamida looked at him, examining him closely. Perhaps it was her eyes that were tricking her, but the man's salt-and-pepper beard swiftly turned white and a chain materialized around his neck. This development made it impossible to keep looking at him, and Hamida's eyes began to close. But her trembling didn't stop, which in turn made her mother tremble twice as violently. But unlike her daughter, she was not robbed of her power of speech. Hamida's mother's laments made many from the inner yard gravitate towards the room. Unable to understand the reason for Hamida's agitation, some of them grew irritated with her, although a few of them were sympathetic too, clucking and producing other moist sounds in their throats. But there was nothing they could do, and their rights to fulfil their responsibilities towards their wives had not yet been established. Their sympathy aggravated the irritation of the rest. Hamida's mother-in-law, Mondol's first wife, was positively enraged. The anger she felt for her daughter-in-law postponed her grief for her grandson, and, released after a long time from anxiety and suffering for Humayun, a pure torrent of rage led her to cancel her regular practice, go back into the room with the door to the east, lie down on her bed, and soon fall asleep.

Abdul Aziz arrived at last after repeated summons. He was both perturbed and anguished by what was going on with Hamida. But since he could not take his wife to task in his mother-in-law's presence, he only scolded her in an affectionately indulgent tone, 'You must be strong, Babur's mother. Allah has taken what he considers his own.'

His mother-in-law had retreated behind the door on his entrance. Being a mother-in-law from the town, she was not shy, and was able to address her son-in-law directly from where she was standing, 'Hamida has had such a big shock, she could fall ill any moment. Let me take her home with me tomorrow.'

Everyone who heard curled their lips—as if Hamida was the only person to lose a son. Why should mourning for a dead son make her fall ill? What kind of talk was this? These old hags from the town really had no sense.

Abdul Aziz couldn't afford to devote all his time to his wife's illness. He left the area, threading his way through the women seated for their meals. Where was the time to pay attention to his wife? There were so many people here, it was the first time that a forty-day observance was conducted on such a scale in their home. It wasn't as though no one else in their family had died. They had invited several fakirs to his grandfather's forty-day observance, but it was still doubtful whether there had been more than twenty-five people. And just look at the size of the gathering for his son's death. Aziz's eyes grew moist when he thought of how Humayun had died to pave the way for such a huge assembly at his house. And yet not a single person from his own office had turned up. He was a mere clerk, who cared for him? But no matter how insignificant his position was, if he could just show the sub-registrar the size of the gathering the man might get over his obsession with pointing out mistakes in Aziz's English. Even if he wasn't ready to attend the ceremony himself, at least one of the office boys could have come and updated everyone on the transformation of the house.

He might be young, but Kader was much sharper in this respect. He had made all the arrangements in advance, so that some fifteen or twenty people arrived together in horse-drawn carriages in a joyful group. As soon as they got off, they rent the air with cries of 'Long live the Muslim League', 'Long live Quaed-e-Azam', and 'We'll fight to get our Pakistan'. Three of them were political leaders in the district. The hospitality they received would greatly improve Kader's status in the town.

But just look at the state Abdul Aziz was in. Alimuddin, the primary school teacher, rescued him from his grief, regret and envy. He didn't arrive till the afternoon, being a man who was late everywhere except to school. He stopped to chat with everyone on the way, getting along particularly well with cultivators. His home was a long way away, somewhere near Shantahar or Adamdighi in the west. Here he lived in the house of a farmer north of Golabari, whom he helped on his fields, or why would the farmer allow him to live in his house? His popularity with peasants had led Kader to talk to him about the League, without much response. Today Abdul Aziz displayed uncharacteristic initiative in striking up a conversation with Alimuddin, whom he escorted to the room for honoured guests. Everyone there had eaten by then, though some of the League workers whom Kader had invited had not. Aziz added Alim to their numbers.

All the illustrious guests got into their carriages hurriedly for their long journey on the unpaved road home. The coachman of Chhotomian's phaeton was waiting for him with the horses already attached. Chhotomian was chatting with Mondol, waving his cane. Abdul Aziz refused to abandon Chhotomian, for people remembered the last thing they were told. He wanted to ensure that Chhotomian brought up Aziz's case when he met the sub-registrar.

Five of Abdul Kader's guests, all of them party workers, stayed back. They would visit people at their homes tonight. Kader had made arrangements for posters and handbills to be fetched from Golabari.

It grew quite cold as the sun set. Standing in the veranda outside the front room where the honoured guests had been sitting, Sharafat

Mondol could see some of his daily labourers warming themselves at a bonfire of dry straw. Hadn't they had their meals yet? Why were they here still? But let them be, the cold is biting, allow them to warm up a little. Sharafat's eyes were misty. Allah would ensure that his little grandson was destined for heaven, and these people's prayers for the innocent child would be the first to reach god. The poor did not have to send their prayers separately, for the satiation of their hunger was enough to please Allah, who couldn't possibly have any greater joy than an impoverished man eating a good meal. It was only because there were so many starving people in this area that Sharafat Mondol had had the opportunity to bring happiness to them in the form of a grand feast today. Yes, let them be. If the warmth of the fire comforted these scantily clothed men, that would bring absolution to his grandson's spirit.

Basking in the heat of the flames, the storks in the silk-cotton tree unfurled their wings slowly, only to fold them again in a hurry. Some of them took lazy, tranquil flight into the thin mist hanging over the lake before breaking into small groups and flying in circles above the water, allowing the chill to seep into their feathers.

Those still walking along the Golabari road were on their way home from the Mondols' house. They were visible from a long distance through the thin curtain of fog. Sharafat Mondol's own land lay across the lake, and the mist was a little thicker over the land he coveted. The bare breasts of the plots from which the crops had been harvested swayed faintly in the fog with the memories of the paddy. The haze hanging over Katlahar Lake was being fattened by the fish-like smell of the water. Looking in that direction made Sharafat's heart, soul and mind overflow.

The winter evening descended abruptly, the darkness deepening in the arms of the mist. A wind from the lake blew all the way to Sharafat's head beneath his traditional cap. Going inside, he put on a woollen cap, wrapped a muffler around his neck and a brown shawl around himself, and went back outside to climb down from the veranda. The lake was no longer visible, although the conversation between the illustrious guests was faintly audible. Chhotomian's cane swayed in front of his eyes. Oh, what prestige his little grandson had ensured for Sharafat by dying—but he was languishing under the earth now, all alone. It was all Allah's will. Tears flowed down Sharafat's cheeks. He wandered off towards the west, past the two ponds at the back of the house, across the eggplant field, to the enormous bamboo grove, next to which lay Humayun's grave.

Grass had grown on it in the forty days since the burial, the blades looking ashen under the intensity of the cold. Over them hung a net of mist, which became thinner as he went forward. Sharafat's father, mother, stepmother, sister-in-law and younger brother were all buried here, their graves scattered haphazardly, but still identifiable. The large expanse of land was filled with nothing but graves, which were hard to tell apart from one another—somehow they had all survived the onslaught of overgrown grass and plants. Kalam majhi sometimes lit a candle at the far end of the field, in the north-eastern corner. Apparently his father was buried there. To light a candle on a grave was an act of profanity, which Sharafat, belonging as he did to the Mohammadi Jamaat, couldn't tolerate. But Kalam majhi was very obstinate, and Mondol's warnings had not worked. He had said, 'We belong to a different Jamaat, this is a Hanafi graveyard, all my ancestors are lying here. I simply have to light a candle.' This plot of land had always been a cemetery, but Sharafat's father had added it to the documents when buying the land hereabouts from the fishermen. Still, dead fishermen continued to be buried here even during Sharafat's father's lifetime. Sharafat extended his landholdings in the west and the north, even purchasing the stagnant pond to the south of the graveyard from a relative of Kalam majhi's. Once he had taken control of the land surrounding the graveyard, he began cultivating it with a ferocity that prevented the people of Majhipara from continuing with their practice of burying their dead here. Sharafat had directed them to a stretch of fallow land on the north-eastern side of Katlahar Lake, which they now used as their graveyard. It was only a pig-headed type like Kalam majhi who protested sometimes, using the pretext of lighting a candle at his father's grave to hatch a conspiracy to reclaim the land for the living among his clan. It was the same Kalam majhi who had proposed that Bulu should be buried here. But he didn't succeed. Sharafat had been generous with money at Bulu's burial, while Kalam majhi had not parted with a single paisa despite running a large shop. Naturally the fishermen had no right after that to choose the burial spot. Kalam had been dying of jealousy ever since Sharafat Mondol had leased the lake. But then what he didn't realize was that the jomidar was the one who picked the lessee. Envy would serve no purpose. Sharafat would allow every one of the fishermen to become a sharecropper on his land so that they could stop seething about the lake. He had made sure not to leave a single one of them out of the guest list at today's ceremonies.

When Kalam majhi hadn't turned up at first, Kader was about to send Tamiz to fetch him. 'He'll be here in good time,' Mondol reassured his son. 'He has a shop to run, he's a busy man, it's not unusual for him to be late.'

He had been proven right. Kalam majhi's son Tahsen, who had got a police job somewhere in Bardhaman, was home on holiday. Sharafat had personally invited him, and he had not only come but also sat among the honoured guests and ate with them. As for Kalam, he had turned up sometime in the late afternoon and sat down with all the other fishermen. Sharafat knew all of this. Kalam's influence was on the wane. His plot to reoccupy the graveyard would be snuffed out today.

With Humayun having been buried there, Sharafat could now seal the plan to turn the place into a family graveyard. Abdul Aziz had been nagging for a gravestone for his son. Sharafat's elder son was far too henpecked—he was desperate to fulfil every one of his wife's demands. Sharafat had declared that adorning the grave was not acceptable in their Ahle Hadis Jamaat.

But as he stood next to Humayun's grave now, his eyes were drawn to the rows of graves of members of the Mian family. Many of them had beautiful headstones. Some had a moon and stars engraved on them, and others had, beneath Allah's sayings, the name of the pure soul who had died, the father's name, and the dates of birth and death. Visiting such a grave filled one with respect not just for the dead but also for their children and grandchildren. It wasn't necessary to meet the living among the Mians to understand how aristocratic their family was, for these eye-catching graves were a silent testimony of their lineage.

What harm would it do to have a gravestone for Humayun? Considering how much honour he had earned them, did he not deserve even this? What objection could the manager have to a gravestone of brick and cement? An effort to clear the land to the north of the lake in order to cultivate it had failed a few years ago, which had made Ramesh Bagchi, the lawyer from the town, consider setting up a brick kiln there. But he abandoned the idea when his nephew Tunu-babu made off with all his money for Bombay or was it Madras. Then Kader demanded that he be allowed to set up the brick kiln. Since it was a forested area, the timber would be available free. They could begin by manufacturing cheap bricks and then build a house of their own. Word of Kader's ambition reached the office at Lathibhanga somehow, whereupon the manager himself sent for Sharafat and said, 'The jomidar is a humble man, Mondol. God makes some people that way. But how will his prestige remain intact if even peasants begin to live in brick houses?'

Getting the message, Sharafat said, 'There's no honour in living in a house of bricks if everyone lives in one. The jomidar is right. Take our case. My father's house was a hut, I replaced it with walls of tin. All I need is your blessing'—Sharafat bent to touch the ground at least 5 feet away from the manager—'so that the house is still standing when I die. I want to die in this house.' At that time he used to take gifts regularly for the manager, who only needed this response to dismiss the rumours.

But why should the manager object if they added a headstone to the grave? A house and a grave were hardly the same thing.

The difficulty lay elsewhere—there were Sharafat's elders to think of. Since his father, his mother and his brother were all buried here, how could he put a headstone on Humayun's grave without doing the same to theirs?

Was there nothing Sharafat could do for Humayun then to ensure safe custody for his corpse? Would that not mean betraying the boy? Worry and anxiety disturbed his prayers, forcing him to concentrate. But he had only uttered a few words when Abdul Aziz appeared next to him. Although he joined his father in his prayers, the fact that he was holding a packet of candles and incense sticks made it difficult for him to raise both hands for the monazat. Abdul Aziz glanced at his father guiltily when the prayers ended. Lighting a candle at a grave was completely forbidden by their Jamaat. 'Babur's mother can't stop crying,' he said faintly as justification. Whether it was to bridge the gap with his father, or simply out of grief, he blurted out, 'She only weeps and says, my son is alone in the darkness. So I.'

Silently taking a candle from his son, Sharafat set it up near Humayun's head, and then planted the rest of the candles and incense sticks in the earth around the grave. Perhaps it was the glow of the candles or the fragrance of the incense sticks that led to his brainwave, but Sharafat realized that neither his parents nor his brother had asked for a headstone on their graves before dying. They were members of the Ahle Hadith. His brother's name was changed from Shetal Mondol to Shamsher Ali Mondol at the behest of Maulana Abdullah. Putting headstones on their graves would actually mean torturing their spirits. But Humayun was a child, an innocent boy. His elders had to decide what his grave would be like. They wouldn't do anything out of the rule book, they would only erect a gravestone so that future generations could identify the child who had brought such honour to their family.

Sharafat did not declare his decision to Aziz immediately. But the knowledge that he could indeed fulfil his responsibility to Humayun cleared the confusion in his head, allowing him to devote his heart and soul to mourning for his grandson. Meanwhile, Abdul Aziz had sprinkled rose water on the grave, and the combined fragrance of roses and incense wafted across the entire graveyard in the tender glow of candlelight. In this way even the graves of all the fishermen buried long ago were added to the jurisdiction of Humayun's grave. This flawless conclusion to the forty-day observance made Sharafat Mondol feel lighter, the briny water pouring from his eyes accepting the pleasant fragrance of the incense and the soft light of the candles to turn sweet and clear.

The darkness deepened. Father and son turned eastwards to return home, but stopped abruptly on hearing a noise in the bamboo grove. Sharafat Mondol frowned: Was the ancient corpse of one of the fishermen about to burst through the earth to patrol the graveyard? Abdul Aziz's thoughts or his capacity for fear had entered the now empty grave of the corpse on the prowl, so that the only thing he could do was to try with all his might to stay on his feet. How were they to negotiate this enormous bamboo grove now? Both of them were rooted to the spot.

But Sharafat breathed in relief just a few moments later. Thanks be to Allah! It wasn't anything like that. Some scum of the earth was shitting in the bamboo grove, releasing the food he had wolfed down at the feast, now subjected to digestion as well as indigestion, to the accompaniment of both shrill and guttural sounds. Relying on his conviction that no matter what ghosts and spirits might be up to, they didn't shit or piss, Sharafat shouted belligerently, 'Who's that? Who's shitting in there? Who are you, you swine?'

Sounds emerging from the defecator's throat could also be heard in the bamboo grove now. His desperate grunts and the liquid expulsion of his turds played a duet as he tried to finish as quickly as possible. But even after a second round of bellowing, Sharafat and his son had to wait some more time before Tamiz's father walked out of the bamboo grove, trembling, while a foul stench emanated from his body. The stink slithered into Aziz's gullet and descended to his belly, so that he looked away and threw up, the liquid drops of his vomit making the flame of the candle placed at the head of Humayun's grave waver and then go out.

Looking at Sharafat Mondol, Tamiz's father said guiltily, 'I was going home but the shit came upon me so suddenly I couldn't control it. So I went into the bamboo grove in our graveyard . . .'

The stench of Tamiz's father's shit had taken over the graveyard. How could an angel possibly visit it now? Sharafat and Aziz themselves found it difficult to enter.

Sharafat's brows furrowed as he walked homewards. Why had Tamiz's father taken this route back home? People from the fishermen's colony had long stopped passing this way. How could the bastard have called this graveyard 'our graveyard'? How dare he? Was Kalam majhi encouraging him?

Meanwhile, Abdul Aziz felt a succession of thorns lodging themselves in his heart, or perhaps it was the same thorn with numerous sub-thorns. Wasn't it the same man who had terrified Hamida this afternoon? Aziz realized that it was Tamiz's father who had appeared wrapped in a shroud that night to take Humayun away. And he wasn't letting go of the child even after death. Could he not have found another spot to shit? Why did he have to squat next to Humayun's grave? Who was he, really? Was Tamiz's father actually nobody but Tamiz's father, or was he someone else entirely? Abdul Aziz shook with fear, which lent him wings, so that he arrived home well before Sharafat did. Tamiz's father's defecation had plunged Sharafat in worry. He trudged back slowly, his body feeling like lead.

17

Well before dawn on the day that the paddy was to be harvested, when it was still dark, Tamiz stood on the ridge bordering his two and a half acres of land, feasting his eyes on it. He wouldn't have another chance this year to see the land with its bosom so full. Most of the stalks were bent over under the weight of the ripened grain, and when they were not, Tamiz had done it himself, so that the ripening was uniform. Each of the plants slept stealthily, cradling the grain in their arms, their slumber deepening with each dewdrop oozing out of the mist to settle moistly on each sheaf. Tamiz sat down on the ridge, reeling under the onslaught of this vision.

Swaying in rhythm with each assault, Tamiz examined the sharpness of his sickle casually, his fingertips tingling at the touch of the fresh teeth of the instrument, the sensation spreading though his blunt fingers to the rest of his body. He had honed his sickle with Dasharath Karmakar the blacksmith's help just the day before yesterday. There was no one hereabouts who could put an edge on a sickle or a spade as well as Dasharath. He was a man of few words, pulling on his bellows all day and honing instruments on the side. His son, however, was always complicating things. The father worked silently with the bellows, but look, Judhisthir the son kept talking continuously. His complaint? That Mondol had driven a hard bargain when the paddy was being stored in the granary. Sharafat kept grumbling, pay for this, pay for that, if you can't pay cash pay from your share of the grains, this is how much you owe me. 'You've got a rich harvest, I saw it for myself, but I doubt how much you'll actually be able to take home,' Judhisthir warned Tamiz.

Was there any need for such ominous talk? Tamiz was rather annoyed with Judhisthir. You think your faith allows you to slander the very person whose land you sharecrop, who is the source of your income?—'Mondol will make trouble when it's time to weigh the grain.'—Look, the glow of the furnace at Judhisthir's house was visible now as the darkness began to be dispelled by dawn, the heat of the flames dispersing the mist gathered over the rice field while the dewdrops dried and were lost in the soil. The sky was turning pale.

Tamiz got to his feet on seeing his father approach with a sickle. The old coot was on time. Father and son could start working on the field at once.

Before they could begin, however, Harmatullah arrived, followed by three daily labourers, all of them from the eastern part of Nijgirirdanga.

'Get going,' Harmatullah instructed them. 'Start work. Every last stalk has to be harvested and stored in my yard before sundown.'

But Tamiz had no plans to hire labourers. That wasn't part of his arrangement with Mondol. What was going on? Apparently he had no choice, for Mondol had given orders. The entire paddy on the field had to be harvested in a single day. If he worked alone, Tamiz wouldn't be able to finish in a week, leave alone a day.

'My father's with me. Do you know he's as good as two hired hands?'

Harmatullah paid no attention. The grains were over-ripe. Half of them would fall on the ground on their own if the harvesting took days, which would rob the crop of its bounty. So Sharafat had summoned Harmat last night and put him in charge of hiring daily labourers.

Once they had all got to work, Harmat's constant stream of instructions—'Tie three stalks at a time', 'Be careful', 'A sickle isn't a fishing net'—echoed Sharafat's commands. But Tamiz regained his predawn spirit at the speed with which his father's sickle was flashing, giving him the chance to fire a few shots of his own about how the rest should learn from the old man's prowess.

Thanks to his father's extraordinary agility and deftness, Tamiz succeeded in stamping his authority over the operations by afternoon, giving him the chance to be overwhelmed by the quantity, form, health and beauty of his crop and to make numerous claims about his own industriousness and technique. His father was silent, making it impossible to tell whether was pleased with his son's prowess at farming. But the pace of his sickle and Tamiz's swagger served to crush Harmatullah's bluster.

Still, Harmatullah's defeat was avenged by his daughter Phuljaan, who made an appearance when the daily labourers began to stack the grain in the yard. She might have gone to the field herself had these labourers not been there.

The labourers left after helping complete the harvest in not one but two days. Tamiz would have to take care of things from this point onwards. His father was at home, having no more interest in the proceedings now that the harvest was done. He might have helped his son had Tamiz requested him to, but Tamiz had not. Phuljaan had no control over her tongue, and there was no telling what she might say in the presence of Tamiz's father. Tamiz gathered courage every morning before entering Harmatullah's house. It wasn't as though he was dependent on Phuljaan or sharecropped her father's field. What did he have to fear? Then again, he felt a burst of compassion for Phuljaan because of her sick child, poor thing, she must suffer so much on account of her son. He would definitely suggest that the boy be examined by a doctor in the town, but first he had to finish stocking the paddy in Mondol's granary. Phuljaan's son sat in Nobiton's lap, watching with glazed eyes as Tamiz threshed the grain. Those eyes, set in his pale face, slowed Tamiz down. Damn it, had he recovered? Now he wouldn't have a chance to escort Phuljaan to the town.

'You have to thresh the rice the right way,' Phuljaan told Tamiz. But instead of demonstrating, she continued talking. 'Brute force isn't everything. You have to use your brains.'

Phuljaan hovered nearby constantly, picking flaws in his work. Sometimes Tamiz lost his temper, making up his mind to throw at the bitch the coins he owed her, saying, 'Count them.' But Phuljaan didn't want the money, and Tamiz told himself it wasn't a good idea to spend so much before he had taken his share of the harvest. But considering how adept Kulsum considered herself at her work, Tamiz wondered what it would be like to bring her here. Phuljaan wasn't the only one who knew about threshing and winnowing. Kulsum had been doing the same work for the Mondols even a few years ago. And she must have boiled countless pots of paddy at Kalam majhi's house before she got married. In any case, this bitch was no match for Kulsum, whose skin was silky smooth at the precise point where Phuljaan's goitre protruded. Kulsum might be dark, but she looked every bit like a woman from a wealthy family. She had never been envious of Tamiz despite being his stepmother. It was true she taunted him sometimes about his ancestry, but that was only when Tamiz himself heaped scorn on her forefathers. If Kulsum were here, Phuljaan would at least stop running Tamiz down. This was the first harvest of his sharecropping efforts. He would have stored the crops at home if Mondol hadn't interfered. Kulsum had even made arrangements for threshing the grain in the yard. Although he hadn't been allowed to do it at home, how could Tamiz accomplish his task without Kulsum by his side?

But Tamiz's father hadn't been particularly enthusiastic about Kulsum's going to Harmatullah's house in Nijgirirdanga on the other side of Katlahar first thing in the morning. 'It's your loose talk that will ruin you,' Kulsum blurted out. But, more than taking part in the threshing, she was keen on hearing scandalous things about Phuljaan, who made her furious. How could a woman be such a bitch? No wonder her husband had deserted her. And now she was chasing Tamiz. Kulsum left before dawn with her stepson without giving her husband a chance to protest.

Tamiz's father was lying on the maacha, looking outside. When they left his wife was following his son, but on the other side of the pond they fell in step side by side. Tamiz's father turned over and went back to sleep.

Still, Kulsum's temper tantrums and snarling were all within the four walls of her own house. She went silent when they entered Harmatullah's yard, throwing covert glances at Phuljaan as though she were setting eyes on her for the first time in her life.

Almost immediately they began to thresh the grain with the help of a pair of oxen. The stalks were being stacked on one side of the yard after being slammed against wooden planks. Phuljaan and Harmatullah had already spread some of the stalks on the ground. Tamiz followed the oxen, who had muzzles and blinders on, with a pan. Meanwhile Phuljaan shouted as she transferred the paddy from the heap to a flat tray, 'Pick up a stick, Nobiton, and help the son of a fisherman.' Nobiton was embroidering a quilt, which she continued to do without bothering about her sister's instructions. Whenever Tamiz saw her she was embroidering quilts—she had no interest in farming. But when Phuljaan screamed at her a second time, she took up a position behind the oxen and Tamiz, holding a stick with a hook at its end, which she used to spread out the broken stalks. They had turned red with all the threshing, which meant that the rice cooked with this paddy would be red too, and not particularly tasty. Tamiz strutted about proudly, he knew that the grain he threshed never had any paddy sticking to it, all of it fell to the ground.

'You have nothing rotting on the stalks,' Nobiton commended Tamiz on his threshing, 'you've got all the grain out.'

But Phuljaan said, 'You must be starving all the time. No wonder you don't leave anything on the stalk.'

Phuljaan refused to acknowledge his threshing skills, describing it as a starving man's greed. Offended at this, Kulsum said, though softly, 'We don't eat rice made from rotting grain.'

'Why not? You beg for food, but you turn down rice made from rotting grain if someone gives it to you?' Phuljaan was addressing Kulsum, but Tamiz was upset that she had got the chance to say this. Stroking the oxen on the back lightly with the pan, he said,

'We don't beg. My father didn't move into the fakir's house after marrying his daughter. We don't eat rotting rice.'

Phuljaan must have been disarmed by what Tamiz said, or else she would have had a rejoinder. There was a lot Kulsum could have said too. She had often had to eat rotting rice in Tamiz's father's household, and she felt more helpless than saddened by what Tamiz had said. Troubled, she stood facing Phuljaan, holding the tray the wrong way. This made Phuljaan break into peals of laughter, the sound changing from a squeal to a croak as it passed through her goitre. The winter wind blew in from the north, making fragments of paddy and straw fly off the tray to the ground, though the plump grain remained on it, which Kulsum had ended up holding the wrong way only because she was facing Phuljaan. Either in protest against Phuljaan's mocking laughter or in annoyance at Kulsum's incompetence—it was difficult to say which—Tamiz struck both the oxen with great force with the pan. This unexpected blow made them break into a run, which in turn almost made Tamiz fall on his face before he recovered. Nobiton giggled at his plight, her laughter retaining its pure notes. Instead of laughing, Phuljaan said, 'Tchah! You're nothing but a fisherman, and still you want to be a farmer.'

Her croaking laughter a few moments earlier had held a hint of indulgence about Kulsum's amateurishness. But Kulsum cared neither for Phuljaan's taunts nor for her sympathy. She had turned the tray around on realizing her mistake, but not even harnessing the northern wind could dispel her uneasiness.

Tamiz observed all of this as he walked behind the oxen. The airy dance of Kulsum's long, dark fingers was flicking the scraps of paddy and straw off the grain to the ground, where they gathered in yellow and yellowish-black mounds, just like her breasts. But the sorting was progressing faster on Phuljan's tray under the light strokes of her fleshy fingers. But why was the bitch with the goitre behaving so aggressively today? Soon afterwards she told Nobiton to take over the tray from her, exchanging it for the stick with the hook, and began to walk behind Tamiz on quick footsteps. Tamiz had to increase his pace as a result, which in turn influenced the speed of the oxen. He managed to control the animals, nevertheless, but his heart began to pound and a shiver ran down his spine. What if Phuljaan poked him in the back with the stick? What if she grabbed his neck with the hook and yanked it backwards? Or, oh, what if Phuljaan stroked him lightly? Would Tamiz's back ever have that pleasure?

But Phuljaan only engaged herself in raking away the hay. She was quick with this task too. Thrusting the hook into the bottom of every bundle, she twisted the stick so dextrously that the sheafs were separated at once to be spread across the ground. The oxen found it comfortable to walk on them, and the hay became softer in the process. Meanwhile Kulsum kept shaking her tray; even after her nails had been at work all this while, the scraps of paddy and straw she had separated were far smaller in amount than Phuljaan had.

Phuljaan was so good with her hands. If only his father's wife had been as good. With someone like her to help him, Tamiz could have cultivated acres of land single-handedly. If he had someone as skilful as Phuljaan when it came to threshing, he could sink his plough deep into the soil and even bring the water up from beneath the surface. He wouldn't need to plead with Mondol for water in that case.

Tamiz cast his eye over the mountain of paddy he had harvested before returning home in the evening. By Allah's grace, it looked abundant. It would be transported to Mondol's house tomorrow, and Tamiz would take his share into his own yard the same day. Would Kulsum be able to boil so much paddy? The last time she had done it was in Kalam majhi's house, when she was young and unmarried. The women at Kalam's house would do all the work, and Kulsum only had to lend a hand. Was she capable of boiling, drying and storing so much grain? What should he do now? Would Phuljaan agree to come home and do it for him?

Why did Tamiz feel so hesitant to harbour such hopes about Phuljaan in Kulsum's presence? Was there any need for him to consider Kulsum's feelings? Was he going to be too frightened of her to ask after Phuljaan's son's health? Defiantly he put the question to

Phuljaan, in a voice louder than necessary, 'How is your son? Let's go to the town after a few days. It's not a good idea to delay things.'

'Why do I need you to go to the town? You think I can't go with my father to have a doctor see my son?' Tamiz tried his best to smile at Phuljaan's response, but without success. It only made his jaws and lips ache.

It was evening, the mist turning a blackish red in the light of the lamp in the veranda. Phuljaan went inside and emerged with her son in her arms, still taking to Tamiz, with a new shawl wrapped around the ailing boy. The lamp lit up the shawl, which Tamiz had no trouble identifying even in the dark glow. He glanced immediately at Kulsum, who was looking at the shawl closely. She turned her eyes away as soon as they locked with Tamiz's.

Kulsum didn't bring up the Red Cross shawl on the way back. She had asked about it at least a hundred times since Tamiz had put it around Phuljaan that moonlit night, getting a different answer each time. Why couldn't Tamiz have told the truth? He bristled—it wasn't as though he was dependent on his father's wife. Why was he frightened of her? He had been right to give Phuljaan the shawl. Was his life going to be dictated by Kulsum? He had to have his own household, he had to double his land from 2 acres to 4, who was there to protect his interests? His father was out of the picture. Day or night, all he did was fish or sleep, besides having strange dreams and sleepwalking. Had Kulsum ever told her husband not to doze or sleep or sleepwalk?

It was because he had fallen into the quagmire of sleep that Tamiz's father had all these dreams and had lost the ability to work. If anything, Kulsum had actually encouraged these habits of her husband's. What kind of woman took her ears close to her husband's mouth to hear what he muttered in his sleep? It was this behaviour of his father's that had destroyed their well-being. Now ask yourself, where had he acquired these habits? Obviously they had come from his practice of attaching himself to Cherag Ali's arse all the time. The fakir had initiated him to the dangerous practice of dreaming, and now he was immersed in them even at this age, home and family forgotten. Imagine a man who had loitered around the Mondols' home till he grew up, who had survived on their leftovers, now being totally unwilling to have anything to do with them. What power had Cherag Ali bestowed on him? Considering how much effort, lobbying and money Sharafat Mondol had put in to persuade the manager to let him lease the lake to him, he couldn't really be blamed for suspecting Tamiz's father of being up to no good when he wandered about there in the darkness of the night. Who knew what magic spells Cherag Ali had wrought when he foisted his granddaughter on Tamiz's father? Or was it Kulsum who used the magic she had learnt from her grandfather to control the old coot? What else could it be? Tamiz couldn't afford to pander to the whims of a woman who was clearly his enemy.

18

A large crowd had gathered at Ismail Husain's house that day. Between two slabs of stone with the words 'Husain Mansion' and 'M.T. Husain', respectively, engraved on them in Gothic letters, a tin gate set in a wooden frame stood wide open. The two orange jasmine trees on either side were hidden behind the open gates.

Inside, close to the boundary wall, stood two moonseed trees along with a medlar and a bayur. Two or three people were clustered beneath each of them. Some of them were familiar faces to Kader, but they continued whispering to one another without paying any attention to him. He walked across the lawn and up the flight of steps between a pair of tamarisks, but there was no room on any of the chairs or benches laid out in the veranda. One of the doors leading into the hall was closed, and the other, ajar. Going up to them, Kader saw Ismail signalling at him. All the seats inside were taken too. Several people, who appeared to be party workers, were milling about. Kader had to stand as well.

Shamsuddin Khondkar, once a doctor by profession, was seated on the sofa, talking incessantly. A veteran Muslim League leader in the district, he had become an MLA on a Proja party ticket in '37 before joining the League three years later. Even if he was not forbiddingly solemn, he was usually a taciturn man, seldom speaking either in the assembly or outside it. Having no desire to get into conflicts with patients, he had given up on a career in medicine two years after getting his MB degree. He was busy running a rice mill, a soap factory and a kerosene dealership, and had no links to speak of with the League office. Whatever political thoughts or responses he had, those he presented at the court of Khan Bahadur Syed Ali Ahmed, the district president of the Muslim League.

Today, the same man had not only appeared at Ismail's house but also become so voluble that everyone was listening to him in silence. The rapt attention of his audience elevated his statements to aphorisms. 'One can walk beneath the noonday sun. Am I right? But walking on hot sand will burn our feet. Yes or no?'

Interpreting the silence of the listeners as acquiescence, the speaker explained his enigmatic utterances. 'Don't you understand?' His eyes sweeping across the listeners to gauge their ability to understand, he said, 'The jomidar's tyranny can be tolerated. Why? Because it has rules, it has a logic. But the low-class people do not follow any systems or laws. Am I right? Impudent rogues, all of them, and their oppression is unbearable. Yes or no? Now if the Muslim League workers side with these people, will you be able to stay with the party? Will you?'

'But doctor shaheb, you're talking of the tebhaga areas,' Ismail tried to placate him. 'Here we don't divide the grain three ways like in those places. Our workers are sharecroppers, all of them. How can they oppose their own kind?'

Sadeq the lawyer took the opportunity to give Ismail some advice. 'Call them here, tell them about Islam. Talk to them about the need for Pakistan without losing your temper. Islam makes sure the poor get what's due to them. We'll introduce the zakat in Pakistan. All those who have been made wealthy by Allah will contribute two and a half per cent of their wealth to the zakat. Islam is a full code of life. Does any other religion give so many rights to the poor? But Islam doesn't approve of anyone's property being ransacked either. The Quaed-e-Azam's motto is live and let live. That is to say . . .'

For Sadeq, to talk was to deliver a speech. Before he could translate his own English sentences into Bengali, Shamsuddin the doctor expressed his agreement with the lawyer and with the Quaed-e-Azam. 'That's exactly what I'm saying. What these louts are doing will make it impossible for decent people to stay in our party.'

Majid Sarkar of Adamdighi was seated next to Shamsuddin, enjoying his protection to some extent. Ismail turned to him with a smile. 'Is your relationship with party workers really so bad? Don't you have any control over them? Surely they will listen to you at least.'

The doctor was delighted at the opportunity to corner Ismail. 'But aren't you the one who recruited all of them?' he said, and repeated his analysis of the situation. Abdul Kader had missed the explanation the first time around, but the other listeners were no less attentive. The aadhiars had been harvesting the crops in the western part of the district and taking the grain home. Let them. They wanted to keep two-thirds for themselves and give one-third to the jotedar. This nuisance had been going on for quite some time. Why should Ismail, who lived in the town, be affected? But what was worrying was that many of these sharecroppers were Muslim League workers—they were known to everyone as members of the League. Why, even the room with the Muslim League signboard 2 miles east of Adamdighi in Shantigarh market was under their control. Not only were they not giving the jotedars their due, but they had also joined hands with the communists to instigate ordinary villagers to hold on to the entire harvest. The campaign for Pakistan was taking a beating as a result. But how was the party to survive without the support of the upper class?

Giving up all hope of completing his speech, Sadeq had angrily begun to read yesterday's *Daily Azad*. He had read every word as soon as the newspaper had arrived on the Darjeeling Mail. His pieces on local problems, the necessity for starting schools, and solutions to various ambiguities within Islam were published in the Letters to the Editor section of this paper at least once every three months. Having reassured himself with a sidelong glance about which page Sadeq was reading, Shamsuddin was in full flow now, but this time the interruption came from elsewhere. Majid Sarkar had been trying to get a word in edgeways for some time. Now he took advantage of the doctor's coughing fit to declare, 'They have bankrupted us. Can you believe it, our sharecroppers took the crop from our land into their own homes, and now they say they belong to our own party. Everyone's laughing at us, what kind of party is this? I held up the train at Akkelpur station to get Tamizzudin Khan to give a speech, I gathered a crowd for him from the village, fed the workers too. And now those same traitors are encouraging the sharecroppers. We've lost everything.'

The listeners appeared deeply worried by the possibility of the owner of 3000 acres of land becoming bankrupt. Their collective sigh was also a form of protest against Ismail, who, they believed, had opened the doors of the party to the lower classes in the area. Ismail Husain was actually from the eastern part of the district, and besides, his family had lived in the town for two or three generations. He himself had been living in Calcutta till recently—what did he know of the situation in the district? He had been warned earlier that allowing all and sundry into the party just to expand its ranks could prove dangerous. That was exactly what had happened.

The realization that Ismail had been cornered added elation to the doctor's excitement, but, restraining himself, he explained to Ismail, as he would to a child, 'Majid Sarkar, Ali Mamud Khan, Altaf Mondol, Abul Hossein, Mohammad Hossein Paikar—these are not the new rich, their influence runs across the entire jurisdiction of police stations. The police don't arrest criminals in their areas without consulting them first. No one here can earn a living without working on their estates. Even the farmers from the east harvest the crops on these people's lands to earn extra money. If you break the backs of all these important people who will be left to keep the Muslim League going? Pakistan will disappear in thin air if the League is pawned off to these arrogant low-class people.'

Ismail had gathered his thoughts by now. 'Don't tell me all this. Joipur, Adamdighi, Panchbibi, Akkelpur—we went to all these

places in '41, didn't we? Abul Hashem shaheb came too, don't you
remember, Doctor shaheb?'

Without waiting to verify the doctor's memory, Ismail continued,
'None of the jotedars cooperated. With Shyamaprasad and Huq
controlling the cabinet the rich are afraid to lean towards anyone
else. It's impossible to even conduct a meeting nowadays, you know.
Over in Panchbibi Nasir Mondol is a powerful man, he's sided with
the communists.' Ismail grew animated as he recounted events from
three years ago. 'Eventually we met Kiran-babu, the lawyer from
Natore, Kiran Maitra, an old Congressman, he said, go plead with
Nasir Mondol, you can have your meeting if you win him over. So
we went to him. But do you suppose the old fool agreed?'

The story was making both Shamsuddin and Sadeq
uncomfortable, since Nasir Mondol had not allowed either of
them to enter his territory. To hide his discomfiture Sadeq the
lawyer said, 'I gave your Nasir Mondol a piece of my mind once
in Santohar. I told him, you people are waging a war against
Allah, while we go to battle to fulfil Allah's commands. Islam is a
complete code of . . .'

This time too, Ismail cut him off. 'Wait, let me finish. I told the
old fool, if you can give shelter to the communists even after reading
the namaz five times a day, why do you ignore us, what harm have we
done? You can preside over our meeting, you can say whatever you
want to against us. But you must let our leaders speak too. The old
fool agreed, and even had his people organize the meeting. Hashem
shaheb spoke for a full hour and a half, and the response was terrific.
We spoke of nobody but peasants. Several young men, all from
farmers' families, joined us. We formed a local committee with them
as members, had a feast at Nasir Mondol's house at night and then
took the Darjeeling Mail to Shantahar.'

'Fine, but did those young men actually understand the ideology
that . . .'

Ismail interrupted Sadeq again, for his story wasn't over. 'Wait,
there's more.

At Shantahar we found Kiran-babu waiting for us. He was delighted to hear of our meeting, and treated us to lunch at the entertainment room in the station. Why was he delighted, you ask? Because this meant the Congress could also have as many meetings as it liked now. Let them. How did it matter to us? Let the Hindus hold as many Congress party meetings as they like. The Muslims are all with us. You think we could have got those young men to leave the Communist Party if we hadn't held that meeting of ours?'

'But what use was it?' Sadeq Ali led the effort to dismiss Ismail Hussein's achievement. 'You couldn't persuade them to change their mind, could you? Has any of them accepted the ideology of Pakistan?'

'All you did was put upper-class Muslims in trouble. Here you are, a member of the Muslim League, intent on creating a division between Muslims.'

But Altaf Mondol from Chandihar prevented the doctor from repeating his allegation. 'What Muslims are you talking about? They practically live with Santhals. The Santhals used to farm our fields so efficiently earlier, their fingers were pure gold, and there were no disputes over sharing the harvest. Now thanks to your boys they take the entire crop home. Santhals, Muslims, aadhiars—they've all joined hands, what Pakistan are you talking about? We had no choice, so we asked doctor shaheb and lawyer shaheb here to get us an audience with Khan Bahadur shaheb. And he said . . .'

Not pleased with this information being divulged, the doctor interrupted Altaf Mondol. 'He's an aristocrat. Do you expect him to talk to these arrogant low-class young men?'

But unless Altaf Mondol could stop these same arrogant low-class young men, he stood to lose his crops, the land he had leased, and even his prestige. He was ready to clutch at straws to survive. 'But Khan Bahadur seemed worried. They're all Ismail's people, he said. Tell Ismail to calm them down.'

A betrayal of Khan Bahadur's ineffectiveness was tantamount to personal humiliation for Shamsuddin Khondkar. Vexed, he responded, 'What are you so afraid of, Altaf Mian? It's not Khan

Bahadur who's worried, it's you people who're dying of anxiety. What are you so afraid of? Wait and see, Nazimuddin shaheb will be coming to Balurghat within a week. Our Khan shaheb will be going too. If Khan Bahadur can get Nazimuddin shaheb to conduct a meeting at Joipur or Shantahar on the way back to Dhaka, that will do the trick. A successful meeting will allow us to drive these louts out of the village.'

'Forget it!' Ismail slapped the table forcefully to dismiss the doctor or Nazimuddin or perhaps both of them. The cup and saucer sitting on the table rattled at the impact, lending a strident note to Ismail's voice. 'You think your Nazimuddin can get off the train at Shantahar if those boys turn hostile? I'd like to see him even pass through Joipur. In fact, they are our best workers in the entire district.'

Altaf Mondol made to get up and leave. 'There's nothing to discuss then. You people can remain surrounded by those louts. The rest of us cannot stay on.'

The doctor forced him to sit down again. 'You can't afford to be in politics and be short-tempered. Don't leave.'

But Altaf refused to calm down. 'Who says we're in politics? We're village people, what do we know of politics? You told us about Pakistan, it will honour Islam, Muslims will hold their heads high, Allah will be happy, our souls will be at peace. So we left the Krishok Proja Party to join the Muslim League. And now what do we see? People who don't even believe in Allah, leave alone read the namaz or observe the roza, are the heroes of this young brigade to whom you've handed over the keys of the League. Very well then, let them run the party.'

Mahmud Khan was pleased to see the audience being stirred by Altaf Mondol's vehemence, although he also felt envious of Mondol's ability to continue with his diatribe for such a long time. 'Those riff-raff with the red flags will be of no use to the League,' he began. 'There's a farmer who's a sharecropper on my uncle's fields in Goneshtala, his son, name's Budha, he and his friends have all been carried away by this tebhaga wave. Son of a ploughman, doesn't even believe in Allah, the lord will judge him, he's ruining his own future, but that's none of my business, that's not the important thing.' Mahmud Khan lowered his voice to get to the point. 'You won't believe this, but my uncle told me himself. My uncle has been on the Haj, he's not one to lie.' His voice went another octave lower as he prepared to disclose the information provided by his truth-loving uncle. 'That Budha even eats turtle meat,' he whispered. 'The bastard eats haraam food.' Lifting his voice to its normal level, he continued, 'These are the people who are considered leaders by your Muslim League boys.'

'All of them will be expelled.' The doctor attempted to re-establish his authority. 'This isn't a joke, after all. The elections are coming, how many votes do these aadhiars have anyway? How many of them pay six annas out of every rupee in taxes?'

'But the farmers' demands have the highest priority in the Muslim League's programmes,' said Ismail. 'Getting rid of jomidars without compensation . . .'

'Take our Majid Sarkar or Altaf Mondol or Ali Mahmud Khan—is any of them a jomidar? Or even a moneylender? They can barely pay their taxes to the jomidar, and the jomidars have to pay an education cess too, where will they get the money?'

They had recently heard Khan Bahadur Syed Ali lamenting helplessly about the jomidars' backs being broken under the burden of the cess imposed on them to widen the reach of primary education. They were saddened by the crisis in Khan Bahadur's life. But an additional reason for their regret was that the jomidar would raise the money for this extra tax from the farmers. However, the peasants were not his only source of income, the jotedars would have to pay, too. Couldn't Ismail explain to those louts that the jotedars were also victims of exploitation?

Majid expelled a long-suffering sigh, bottled up from the time he had met Khan Bahadur. 'We're exploited by both sides. The jomidar makes us pay taxes regularly. The Floud Commission has presented its report, but who's implementing it? And then we're caught in a pincer, the aadhiars are taking away all our crops. What are we supposed to do? And then Kabir Tarofdar shaheb says, the Krishok Proja Party takes care of the farmers as well as the taxpayers. Who are the biggest taxpayers? You know the answer.'

Sadeq was alarmed. What if these people joined the Krishok Proja Party? 'You call that a party? If Huq shaheb goes, that'll be the end of the party. There's just one party for Indian Muslims, and that's the All India Muslim League.'

'Of course.' Ismail jumped into the breach. 'The majority of Muslims are farmers. And the majority of the League's demands are for farmers too. It's their children who will go to school if primary education becomes compulsory and free. Or take the demand for withdrawing the toll on selling agricultural products in markets— that will benefit them too. Naturally their sons will grow up to become party workers.'

'But won't your party have to fight the elections if it wants to implement its programme, Ismail shaheb?' Shamsuddin had regained his confidence. 'You won't earn votes by opposing the influential people in the village. The Hindu candidates will all be put up by the Congress, there's unity among them. The jotedars may not support us in the Muslim constituencies, how do you expect them to be on our side when our workers loot their crops? The Congress and the Krishok Proja Party will both put up Muslim candidates, won't they? If the Muslim vote is divided, can you be sure who will win? Who will direct the voters in the village? Who? The influential people, am I right?'

Ismail looked grim. Sadeq said, 'Does the Muslim League's programme include looting the jotedars' grains? Has robbery been legitimized in Islam?'

Ismail looked at him in silence. The Communist Party was accomplishing its tasks through the best workers in the League— this was not right. And the village elders were an important factor in the elections. When he had worked for the mayoral elections as a student, he had seen that even the educated people of Calcutta

voted as a block. They too had their distinct groups, subgroups
and leaders. All these things had to be taken into account during
elections. The voters here were rural people, with only those who
paid taxes being eligible. From weddings to burials, from animal
sacrifices to mourning, everything was done according to socially
acceptable norms.

He was happy that the young men who had worked with the
communists had joined the League. The tebhaga movement was quite
strong in the western part of the district—if the party couldn't hold
on to these young workers they were bound to join the communists
again. Why couldn't these old idiots understand this? And then, if he
could help impoverished Muslims with the help of the communists
without being a communist himself, it was the Muslim League that
stood to gain. His childhood friend Ajay and Ajay's sister Pratima
had helped him distribute the milk provided by the Red Cross.
Where were all these interfering busybodies when Ismail was burying
all those bodies during the famine? It was Biren and Samir and
Sukumar who had helped him. In Golabari the Red Cross material
was handed out from Kader's shop, which had a signboard of the
Muslim League, and the Congress had even complained about this.
When the British officials of the Red Cross came to investigate, it
was Ajay who had defended Ismail. Which was all very well, but if
these people were going to use the young men in his party to divide
the Muslims, then, leave alone creating Pakistan, even keeping the
League intact would be difficult.

Ismail's silent, troubled reflections were accompanied by the
lawyer's confident conclusion. 'Don't worry, just organize meetings
in your areas. We have to explain Islamic ideology properly. That will
cure this practice of looting jomidars.' Noting that Ismail was looking
worried, he uttered a long monologue in English, dripping with
satisfaction at his own accomplishment. 'Let us earnestly hope and
trust that the most noble teachings and examples of our holy prophet
will be followed by all Muslims, from land-tillers to sharecroppers,
from jotedars to jomidars, by the poor and the rich, by the educated

and the illiterate—not only from the area we are talking about but throughout the length and breadth of India. Brothers, never forget that Islam is a complete code for living. It gives us everything we need. It offers us the option to fight for Pakistan, which remains our goal until we achieve it.'

Having decided that Ismail Husain had been cornered sufficiently, Shamsuddin tried to bring the matter to a close. Ismail was a loose cannon who often sounded impudent in Khan Bahadur's presence. 'The Muslim League has to be brought out of the pockets of the nabobs and knights,' he thundered. The real achievement would have been to put him in his place the same way in front of Khan Bahadur. Ismail had shown a shocking lack of respect for a man with a lineage like Khan Bahadur's. The Muslim League office used to be in Khan Bahadur's house before Ismail had insisted on renting a new office in Jhautala. Khan Bahadur had to gasp for breath trying to climb up the spiral staircase to enter the cubbyhole on the first floor, his face turning red with exertion. Ismail would have to be taught a lesson one day in Khan Bahadur's presence, but for today, this was enough. It was best to call things off while he was still licking his wounds. The rustic jotedars and party workers were reeling under the onslaught of Sadeq's speech in English, but allowing Ismail to retaliate in the same language might neutralize the advantage. Why risk it?

When everyone got to their feet, Shamsuddin drew Ismail aside and whispered for a long time into his ear.

19

About a week later Ismail gave Abdul Kader the secret information that Shamsuddin Khondkar had passed on to him. Kader, who was on his way to the town after seeing a Kuber Bank advertisement for an auction in *People United: The Only Weekly Mouthpiece of the People of North Bengal*, had entered Husain Manzil for a consultation with Ismail. Ismail was about to go out, dressed in khaki trousers and a grey coat with a sola topi in his hand, but on seeing Kader he turned around, ordered two cups of tea, and drew up chairs on the veranda.

'Auction? Auction for what?'

'In order to recover dues owed to The Kuber Bank Ltd, items stored in packing cases (usually oil, soap, tea, ink, powder, vermilion, scent, etc.) in the shop named "The New Swadeshi Bhandar" located on Thana Road in the town, and top-quality English lamps will be sold to the highest bidder in open auction on the date and time indicated below. Prospective buyers are invited to attend the above-mentioned auction.'

Ismail did not care for the *People United*, which a few of the wealthy people connected with the disintegrating Krishok Proja Party had continued to publish with the Muslim League as their target. Huq shaheb still cast a long shadow on them. Kader's father was bound to be a subscriber. Ismail read it regularly himself, but furrows appeared on his brow if he happened to see any of the party workers going through it. Sliding the paper across the table, Ismail said, 'Swadeshi Bhandar meaning Akhil-babu's shop, Akhil Kundu. The sons divided the property after the father's death, I think the youngest son Pratap runs this one. Couldn't keep it going.'

Ismail's familiarity with the matter gave Kader some hope of being able to bid at the auction, but Ismail said, 'What are you going to do with all this? Have you started using scent? How much oil and soap can you use personally?'

'It's not that,' stammered Kader. 'I was thinking of selling these things from my shop at Golabari market.'

'A stationery shop in the village? Who'll buy all this? Is there anyone in your village to buy English lamps? They'll break the chimney and cut themselves too in the bargain.'

The lamps were meant for Abdul Kader's own home. Every room in Ismail's house had these lamps, the bulbs glowing a soft white, transforming the surroundings when switched on. It was thanks to all these lights that the people of the town were not afraid of jinns and spirits. The municipality people came with ladders to turn on the lamps at street corners. Electric lights powered by a dynamo shone in front of the cinema hall, and every shop had gaslights hanging from the ceiling. How were jinns to show themselves in such brightly lit places? If only there had been a gaslight in Humayun's room the other night—the man in a shroud would never have dared to enter.

'What do you need vermilion for? Are you planning to get married or something?' When Abdul Kader smiled shyly, his eyes on the floor, Ismail dismissed the idea. 'It's not like the women in your family use it.'

'How can we? We belong to the Mohammadi Jamaat, we can't possibly break the rules.'

Ismail burst into laughter, the kind that Abdul Kader had never succeeded in mastering despite practising at home. These things were probably hereditary. 'Haven't the Mohammadis and Hanafis stopped feuding yet?' asked Ismail after quietening down. 'Do you people want to a start a caste system among Muslims or something?' He could have continued to taunt Kader about this, but he didn't forget his visitor's desire to buy fancy goods in the auction. 'What's the vermilion for, then? Are you going to use it for some sort of ritual for the jinn or whatever it is that's supposed to live in that lake of yours? Doesn't that mean breaking the rules too?'

It was Kader who had told Ismail stories about Katlahar Lake. His father had leased it, which now made it their family property. Munshi was perched on the fig tree at the northern head of the lake, keeping a watchful eye not only on the water but also on Girirdanga and Nijgirirdanga on either side. They were thriving only because they were in Munshi's good books, they survived dangers and misfortunes only because Munshi looked after them. Even the flock of storks on the silk-cotton tree in their yard were Munshi's pets. They took wing at his command, and returned after investigating the lake at his signal. Kader used to be upset initially when Ismail joked about Munshi, but these days he felt not only a sense of discomfort but also a stab of fear—what if Munshi became angry with Ismail?

It was Ismail's penchant for making fun of things that made the elders reluctant to talk to him. Many of them disliked him, in fact. But when he went to the village to chat with the poor people or with League workers, they didn't mind if he laughed at them. They knew they would get his help and support if only they could bear his caustic comments. Ismail was an expert at putting in a word to people who mattered, whether it worked or not. Despite all his barbs about Munshi, he was now saying as he lit a cigarette, 'Gopen-babu is the manager of Kuber Bank, his father was a friend of my father's. They're from Birbhum, when we lived in Suri my father and Gopen-da's father Nalinaksho-kaka were inseparable. Let's go and talk to him. What's all this nonsense about bids? The manager can sell it to whoever he wants to.'

It was after they went out that Ismail told Abdul Kader the secret that Shamsuddin had whispered in his ear the other day. There was a man about whom Kader would have to dig out some details.

The man had escaped soon after the riots in Joipur a fortnight ago. The jotedars' people had had a skirmish with the aadhiars over the division of the crops grown on Ali Mahmud Khan's fields. Ali Mahmud's sister's son, or was it his brother's, or perhaps his sister's daughter's husband or maybe brother's daughter's husband, or it might even have been his sister's son or brother's son who was also another sister's or brother's son-in-law—someone had had his skull split by the aadhiars and was now fighting for his life. Ismail made long-drawn-out jokes about the relationship between the victim and Ali Mahmud. His theory was that the jomidars were so greedy about their property that they ensured that their children married within the family, which meant that the man who had been beaten up must have married his own cousin. Now if he were to die, Ali Mahmud would lose two relatives instead of one, losses that he would find it difficult to get over. Would either Shamsuddin or Sadeq be able to activate their cliques to extricate him? Or did Khan Bahadur already have his antidote ready? But Ismail also said that as long as their property was intact, the jomidars would remain unmoved by sorrow.

'If the tebhaga system does materialize all these people will die of heart attacks. Already they're beginning to camp at Ali Ahmed shaheb's house whenever they come into the town. How can such cowards be involved in politics?'

It wasn't as though Kader's father would be pleased if the tebhaga system were to be established. Kader couldn't respond to Ismail's jokes about Ali Mahmud's predicament. In any case, it was obvious Ali Mahmud was not a reliable sort. He was lamenting loudly the other day at Ismail's house, but he didn't mention that his people had been beaten black and blue by the aadhiars. He wouldn't rest till he had eliminated the best workers in the area from the Muslim League. Still, it wasn't right for Ismail to talk this way about the trouble the man was in.

Since Kader couldn't afford to antagonize Ismail, he was forced to hear a long story about Ali Mahmud's avarice and apprehensions. Exaggerating his account, Ismail turned him into both the devil incarnate and a complete buffoon. Then, when they neared the market and got into a rickshaw, he brought up the matter of the absconding person.

Not that he was exactly absconding, but he had been spotted with the aadhiars during the rioting. Ali Mahmud Khan had even named him in his police complaint. Shamsuddin knew everything, however. The man lived on the eastern side, east of the Bangali river, either on the bank of the Jomuna or perhaps on an island in the river. He had been to western Khiyar to work on the fields during the famine. An itinerant vagabond, he apparently used to follow the leaders of the tebhaga movement around in Joipur, Panchbibi and Akkelpur, instigating the farmers. The police hereabouts were not putting in much of an effort to capture him, but if anyone could provide genuine information of his whereabouts, they would definitely take him in. According to Shamsuddin, he had been spotted somewhere on the western side of the Bangali river.

Abdul Kader thought deeply but could not identify anyone who fit the description.

Ismail offered some more clues. 'He's a singer, apparently. He sings to the tillers. Ali Mahmud had himself heard him sing.'

'An old man? There used to be a fakir, his name was Cherag Ali. He used to live somewhere on the eastern side too, but moved to our area after the Jomuna flooded and destroyed his house. He had his granddaughter married to one of the fishermen in Girirdanga. You've seen the fisherman's son, Tamiz, his first wife's son. The old fakir has been missing for a long time.'

'No, this man's young. Ali Mahmud told me the other day to keep my eyes open for him.'

'Should I inform the police if I get any information?'

'Inform the police?' Ismail was in a quandary over the best course of action involving the absconding peasant-cum-singer. He had managed to organize the people in the area between Shaorapara and the western bank of the Jomuna, on the other side of the Bangali river. Hashim shaheb and Suhrawardy shaheb were very pleased with the reports from this part of the state. There was no trouble over the tebhaga movement in the east. The jotedars in the area were not particularly powerful, and the Talukdars of Shimultola owned huge tracts of land. That was also where Ismail's in-laws lived. Everyone who had a grievance against the Talukdars was close to Ismail. There were several schools hereabouts, with most of the students working for the Muslim League. Those who were in college in Rajsahi or Calcutta or right here in the town also championed the cause of Pakistan when they came home. But if this absconding criminal was moving about in the villages to foment trouble among peasants, how long would it be before the whole thing erupted? Once farmers had their back up about something it was hard to change their minds. Ismail had told all the workers in Joipur and Panchbibi and Akkelpur to be patient, for the jotedars would be put in their place once Pakistan had been created. Along with the abolition of the system of jomidars, a bill to institute the tebhaga system would also be introduced in the assembly. They had written as much in *Millat* magazine. Once the bill became an Act, the jotedars would have no choice but to let the aadhiars take two-thirds of the harvest. Nor would they be allowed to evict any of the aadhiars. But if only anyone listened! These things couldn't possibly be announced at public meetings, after all. They had to keep the jotedars on their side at least till the elections. Then, once the tebhaga system had been established by the law, who would dare mess with the peasants' rights? But still they wouldn't listen. Ismail had convinced the students, but the peasants continued to create trouble. And Ismail had to face the brunt of it all from the party leaders, who didn't realize that unless these people were mollycoddled they would all defect to the red flag party. But here was something new. Ismail began to think afresh about the absconder. It would be useful to win him over. Having someone like him on his side would mean securing the support of the aadhiars.

Kader asked again what he should do in case he learnt anything about the whereabouts of the man.

'Come and tell me quietly. It's best not to involve the police immediately.'

20

'One for one. Two for two, two for two. Three for three, three for three. Four for four, four for four.'

Hamid Sikdar was sitting in the yard outside the Mondols' house, measuring the harvested grain. Sharafat Mondol was seated nearby in his easy chair. Forcing his sleep-laden eyes to stay open, Abdul Aziz was watching the needle on the scales, often jumping to his feet to stop himself from dropping off. He had to return home frequently during this period, when the harvest was stored in the granaries. But how was he to get so many days of leave? He took the train from Joipur on Saturday evening to the town, and then a carriage, to arrive home at about nine-thirty at night. Having missed the connecting train at Shantahar by a few minutes, he hadn't reached home till the early hours of the morning, and hadn't slept more than an hour. Still, it was a matter of just a few days. The whole thing couldn't possibly be left to the family. His father was ageing, how much pressure could he take?

Sharafat wasn't paying attention to the measuring scales, for he knew he could trust Hamid Sakidar. His eyes were trained on the silk-cotton tree. The storks had flown off towards the lake early in the morning, and most of them had returned in small groups to perch on their favourite branches. They were staring at the grain in the yard.

Aziz's son Babur kept drifting towards the lake absently, nibbling on a home-made sweet. Sharafat had asked the boy several

times to come to him, coaxing him to sit on the handle of his chair.
But the child slid off as quickly as possible. A quiet, studious boy,
he had all but stopped talking after his brother's death. Sharafat
couldn't concentrate on the grains being weighed. His eyes misted
over, while the storks took turns to fly tight circles above the heaps
of paddy. Sharafat was relieved, but a fog of grief for his dead
grandson and sorrow for the unhappiness of the living one gathered
in his eyes.

Harmatullah was seated beneath the silk-cotton tree, along with
the barber and the blacksmith, Shamsher Pramanik and Judhisthir
Karmakar. All of them had clay pots of home-made sweets in front
of them, and puffed rice to munch on. Tamiz was standing close
to Hamid Sikdar. He was not interested in either the sweets or the
puffed rice—he was intently watching the movement of the scale,
every fibre in his body tense. The mound grew higher in front of his
eyes. Not just Shamsher and Judhisthir but also Harmatullah gazed
in wonder at the eighteen mons and 12 seers of paddy produced on
land just over 2 acres in size. Tamiz's eyes were fixed so firmly on the
scales that they would probably bleed if he tried to tear them away. If
only he could show Phuljaan this mountain of grain. You taunt me
constantly for being the son of a fisherman, but show me any bastard
who can grow so much rice on a field this size. Just take a look, you
bitch, let your eyes feast on the sight.

'Have your sweets before you divide the crop. Take your time.'
Sharafat's instruction to Hamid Sikdar robbed Tamiz's gaze of half
its intensity. They would now take an axe to this magnificent stack of
grain and split it. Couldn't it be maintained this way for another day,
just one more day? He could give Phuljaan a glimpse of it. What did
Mondol have to lose? Tamiz would be a little more confident if the
division were made tomorrow, in Abdul Kader's presence. But how
was he to say all this with so many people listening?

Sharafat issued his next instruction when Hamid Sikdar was
done eating his sweets. 'Before the division we have to calculate the
costs of the ploughshare, the oxen, all other equipment, the wages

for the daily labourers who worked on the field, and the work done at Harmatullah's house.'

Sharafat knew the calculations like the back of his hand, but still he began to add up the numbers. After adding, subtracting, multiplying and dividing, he asked for a certain amount of the grain to be set aside in lieu of payment for all of these. When Hamid Sikdar began to weigh the grain again, Tamiz mumbled with a sinking heart and a falling face, 'Can't the cost of the equipment and the oxen be reduced a bit? And . . .'

Sharafat accepted this at once. 'All right. You're a new aadhiar on my fields, you've done very good work. Give him 5 seers more from my share, Hamid. I'm asking you to do it, go ahead.'

Still Tamiz fidgeted. His dark face reddened till it couldn't turn a deeper shade of purple. 'What's the use of scraps? And you're accounting for daily labourers, but it was you who chose to employ them. My father and I would have done the work ourselves if you hadn't.'

Pulling on a length of straw, Tamiz threw a sidelong glance at Judhisthir. It wasn't clear whether the blacksmith's son's eyes held a message for him, but even if they did, Judhisthir was looking the other way. Sharafat's eyes were trained on Tamiz now, all the mist in them gone. Sounding much more gentle than his glare suggested, he said, 'I've given you more than your fair share. You can check for yourself.'

Abdul Aziz was wide awake now. 'You didn't account for the water,' he reminded his father. 'You should.'

The proposal to include the cost of the water turned Tamiz's throat into a wasteland, making him gasp for breath. Abdul Aziz's explanation: a canal had been dug to bring in water from Katlahar Lake to the plot of land—it would never have yielded such a rich crop otherwise. So the cost had to accounted for. If the owner of the lake had to be paid, half had to come from the jotedar and half, from the sharecropper. Sharafat Mondol would get the money as the owner, half of which he would pay himself, being the jotedar, while Tamiz had to pay the other half.

Everyone listed to Aziz's explanation in astonishment. It was up to Aziz to dispel their disbelief. 'The manager would have to be paid if we had got permission to dig a canal out of the ox pool. You can pay the manager happily, but you get heartburn when it comes to paying the Muslim jotedar. Isn't that the truth?'

'If you're going to account for the water, babu,' countered Judhisthir, 'you have to consider my point too.' How was he involved? 'I have personally watered your field with water from the Kamarpara canal. The labour was all mine, and the water was from our area too. Shouldn't you be paying me for it?'

Sharafat could not endorse Abdul Aziz's argument about the water. There really hadn't been any need to bring up the matter of the Katlahar Lake. But there was no going back now, which meant he had to take control. First he had to take care of Judhisthir. 'The Kamarpara canal runs through the middle of the field. It was just a matter of dipping a pan in and watering the fields, wasn't it? What labour are you talking of? And is the canal your personal property? Most of the land on either side of the canal is mine. Don't talk about accounting for the water, it'll only mean more losses for you.'

Aziz, however, was on Judhisthir's side in this dispute. To government servants the law was equally applicable to everyone. Just as the sun never set on the British Empire, it was also the British government's sacred duty to ensure that it shone equally on everyone. Inordinately pleased with himself for having applied such a suitable metaphor, Aziz assured Judhisthir that if the calculations showed that he was owed some money, he would be paid down to the last paisa.

But it was doubtful whether Tamiz had registered any of this. He said, 'I dug the canal all by myself. Bulu's son came to help but I told him, you're too young for this. I dug the whole thing myself. I don't understand how you can make me pay for the water.'

'I hired Bulu for the work, he didn't look after the cattle all those days. What you did with him is your business.' Sharafat wiped his now-dry eyes and continued, 'You talk too much, Tamiz. You begged and pleaded with me, so I gave you the land to farm on. That was how you began sharecropping. You can keep doing it, just get your own plough and oxen. Who's stopping you? Don't come creating trouble here.'

Tamiz was deflated by the reference to the plough and oxen. Sharafat was threatening him. He fell silent, afraid of losing his chance to grow onions and garlic on the same land.

'His lawyer is absent today, so the accused has no choice but to speak up himself.' Tamiz was furious with Abdul Aziz for hinting at Kader's partiality towards him. Kader had left early this morning, and would not be back before evening. Couldn't he have chosen some other day to go into the town?

After Mondol had claimed some more of the grain by way of payment for the water, Tamiz found it hard to collect his own share. Aziz would now concentrate on the grains sent by the other sharecroppers. Azfal the driver was unloading the cart. 'Do you need a cart?' he asked Tamiz. 'I can deliver your grains.'

Tamiz answered, 'There's hardly any, I don't need a cart.' He hefted his sack.

When Afzal sat down beneath the silk-cotton tree after unloading the paddy, Abdul Aziz asked Judhisthir, 'It's not even past Poush, and you're here to borrow rice already. What's going on?'

'What I get from sharecropping on your land barely serves us for two months. My father asked me to borrow a few seers, we'll pay for it with cash after the Nishan fair in Joishtho.'

'I see.' Not just Abdul Aziz but everyone else understood too. Plough blades, spades, axes, sickles, kitchen blades and other metal implements were greatly in demand at the Nishan fair. Peasants travelled long distances to buy them. From the east of the Kortowa to the west of the Jomuna, all the blacksmiths made most of their earnings at the fair. But Sharafat brushed aside Judhisthir's request. You can't have run through your share of the crops already. Come to me later.'

'No babu, I need it now.' Judhisthir struggled not to reveal the reason. 'I have to buy things for my father's workshop.'

'What are you lying for? I know why you need so much money, you want to bid for Ganesh Karmakar's land.' Caught out, Judhisthir remained silent. 'Why don't you go to Jagadish?' advised Abdul Aziz. 'Same caste, try your luck.'

Judhisthir looked stricken. 'How can you say that, babu, they're a much higher caste. How can he and I be the same?'

'Are you saying the Sahas are high-caste people? But your family and ours, we're the same caste, is that what you're saying?'

Judhisthir had an expression of dismay on his face. 'No, how can you say that?' But there was nothing more he could add.

Sparing him further interrogation, Sharafat said, 'Come back in a few days, all right? Let me get all my grains first.' After Judhisthir had left, trailing behind Tamiz, Sharafat admonished Aziz softly. 'Why did you keep telling him to go to Jagadish? Don't you understand Judhisthir will take a lease on Ganesh Karmakar's land as soon as he gets some money? Let him keep looking for cash, Ganesh will come to us on his own meanwhile.'

Back home, Kulsum came running as Tamiz put his load of grains on the ground. Not knowing what she should do now that they had some paddy of their own, she thrust both her arms inside the sack. 'How beautiful this harvest is.' 'This will last us an entire year and more. 'So much, there's so much in there.' Kulsum kept muttering as though in a delirium.

Tamiz was squatting on the ground by now, while Judhisthir stood on the other side of the pond, talking to someone. When Kulsum had babbled on for some time, Tamiz said, 'All right, enough. Empty out the sack, let me get the rest of the grain.'

Having stacked the grain, Kulsum put the sack back in the container in which Tamiz had brought it and went up to him. Even in the winter chill his neck was coated with perspiration, and stiff after having carried the laden sack. Wiping Tamiz's neck with the end of her sari, Kulsum said, 'You're sweating so much! Rest a little.'

Emerging from the room, Tamiz's father picked up the sack and set off towards the Mondols' house. 'Yes, rest a bit, let me bring the next lot.'

The end of Kulsum's sari returned to her hand as Tamiz shot to his feet. His father might lose his temper when he saw the quantity of paddy set aside for Tamiz, there was no knowing what he might say to Mondol. If Sharafat or Aziz took umbrage at this, Tamiz wouldn't get the land this time. No, it was best not to let his father go there. Tamiz lengthened his strides to catch up with his father on the other side of the pond. What was the old coot walking so quickly for? Was it for the joy of bringing the grain home, or out of some kind of obstinacy? Tamiz decided to be more obdurate than his father. 'Can you put the grains out to dry? I'll bring the rest while you do that. Judhisthir will help me.'

After the paddy, they brought some hay too, with Judhisthir and Shamsher lending a hand. The short winter afternoon came to an end meanwhile. The three of them took a dip in the pond, shivering in the cold. There wasn't enough water for a proper bath, and in the bargain the icy water froze their limbs. But then this shivering was enjoyable too, and the sensation persisted even after the other two had left. Equating the bath at this odd hour of the day with a celebration of bringing the paddy home, Tamiz's father drew on his hookah for a while before setting it down for this son. Then he said softly, 'Mondol hasn't parted with much. When we were harvesting it, I thought . . .'

'You sold the oxen, you didn't keep the plough or ploughshare, how much paddy do you expect after that?' Tamiz directed his ire at his father before turning to Kulsum. 'And you, remember that we must buy oxen and a plough first, we mustn't eat up all the rice ourselves.'

Such a sweet scent.' Kulsum breathed in the flavour deeply. 'I can smell it everywhere, inside and outside the house. Even the stench of the pond has disappeared.'

Not in the least overwhelmed by the information that the bad smell from the pond had receded, Tamiz's father snarled, 'Never mind the scent. Who can eat this kind of rice every day? We have to sell this and buy aush.'

Tamiz overruled both of them. 'Not rice, we're not buying rice. I'm going to boil all this and sell it at Gokul's market.' When he saw neither his father nor his stepmother paying attention, he continued, 'All you two can think of is food. Stop salivating. I'm going to sell the rice and then go to the cattle fair 10 miles to the north the same day to buy oxen.'

Still delighted by the grain in her yard, Kulsum giggled, 'Give your tongue a rest now.'

Tamiz obeyed her, and tried to measure out a space in his head for the cowshed. His own room stood now where the cowshed used to be before the draught. If he could just put up a roof over a small space to the north-west of his room, it would do for two oxen. The oxen, the plough, the yoke, the harrow—he would have them all before the next sowing season. His father's appetite was much too large, though, and that Kulsum was too frisky as well. She had already gathered some of the paddy in a five-seer basket with the words, 'Let me take this to Kalam chacha for husking. I'm going to make some sweets today, there'll be no blessings from fresh rice at home till the sweets are made.' Kulsum left for Kalam's house, where husking was in full flow. Fragments of her laugh were strewn all over the house, mingled with the sweet breath of oxen. There was also the sound of a pile of grains raining on the mound of paddy in the yard. Couldn't Tamiz take Abdul Kader's help to wangle a little more grain out of Mondol? Sharafat had not been inclined to deduct the value of the water from the lake, he had merely accepted his elder son's argument. But would he not listen if Kader explained? Surely Tamiz would find Kader at Golabari now.

'It's market day, let me see if I can get some fish.' But there was no one to respond to Tamiz, for Kulsum was at Kalam majhi's house. Tamiz slipped inside the house and emerged with a basket for the fish, only to go back in again for the bottle of mustard oil.

As he approached Golabari it was obvious the market was about to close. Darkness had descended, and people were returning home, most of them carrying a bag or a basket in one hand and a bottle of oil in the other. Some even had two bottles, one for mustard oil and one for kerosene. All of them were discussing the price of fish and rice. Tamiz asked everyone he met what the price of rice was, responding with, 'Looks like the price won't go up. I'll make losses.' He tried to import the despair of jotedars into his voice.

The gaslights were still on in Kader's shop, which meant it must be full of people. There was a new stool next to the cash box, large and high. On it were arranged mirrors, combs, vermilion, powder and many other cosmetics that Tamiz was not familiar with. Gofur was standing behind it. Sales were closed for the day, what was that bastard doing there? Perhaps he was guarding the shop. All right then, you bastard, go on and be a guard. Tamiz had seen similar arrangements in shops in the town, but the shopkeepers didn't dress in lungis like Gofur. They looked completely different in their dhutis. But along with the kerosene there was a faintly pleasant scent too, which he had got earlier when walking past those shops in the town.

None of the people inside was a customer, they were all members of Kader's party. Kader was explaining to some of them, 'The majority of Muslims are farmers. How many of them are well off? If a party of Muslims don't look after the interest of peasants, who will? Do you understand? There's no doubt Huq shaheb is a great politician. Muslims considered him their leader without question all this time, obeying him faithfully. But he has chosen to ally with the Hindu Mahasabha. Considering that Hindus won't drink a glass of water offered by a Muslim, in fact, Hindus hate the very sight of a Muslim, haven't you seen how contemptuously the manager talks even to our elders, how are we to consider Huq shaheb our leader if he's going to join hands with the same Hindus? You have to explain all this properly, all right?'

Someone from the Ranirpara school asked a question which made Kader pause before replying. Then he continued with renewed fervour, 'Don't you understand that it is for the benefit of the poor that we're demanding the creation of Pakistan? In Pakistan the police will arrest any rich man who does not donate to the zakat fund. A law will be passed. The poor won't starve, they will have a right to the money in the fund.'

'Why all this talk about the zakat, about farmers having to beg? All it needs is that peasants be paid their dues. Considering how hard they have to work, tell me, is getting only half the crops a fair deal?'

Kader jumped up from his chair when Alim the schoolteacher spoke from one of the benches at the back. 'Oh it's master shaheb, come up, come up, why are you sitting with the riff-raff at the back?'

Alim went forward to one of the benches in front. 'But answer my question, my boy. Why do we need the zakat just because people are poor?'

'No, all I'm saying is, the few rich men that there are will have to part with their money for the poor. A law will be passed in Pakistan to allow the farmer to demand his due. The jomidar system will be abolished. Who will be the owner of the land then, tell me.'

'The Muslim jotedars will do what the jomidars used to. How will peasants benefit?'

'How can you say that? The peasants' rights will be established as soon as the tebhaga Bill is passed.' Realizing that he hadn't answered the schoolteacher's question, Kader tried a new angle. 'Wait, let me give you a booklet. See what it says here, primary education will become free, there will be compulsory free education. That will help farmers, won't it?'

'Hmm. But whether you make it compulsory or free, no aadhiar peasant will ever be able to send his children to school. Give the farmer his due, he will pay his children's school fees. Why is it that jotedars send for the police whenever this matter of giving the farmer his fair share is raised?'

Kader wondered which side the schoolteacher was on. Grimly he said, 'Don't you think what the aadhiars are doing in Khiyar is destroying Muslim unity?'

'But there's no lack of Muslims among the jotedars. How can they send for the police when the Muslim farmer demands a fair share of the crop?'

Kader repeated his ultimate solution. 'Once we have Pakistan the peasant will get his entire dues. Creating trouble now will hurt everyone.'

Tamiz was fired up by whatever little he had understood of the exchanges. Now if he could only get even a few seers of paddy by asking Kader to intercede on Tamiz's behalf with his father. He was too worked up to wait quietly. But there was no telling when the young men would leave Kader's shop. Going out, he saw the lamp still on in Kalam's shop. Kalam was busy storing the grain in his yard and husking the paddy, so his nephew Lalu was manning the shop. It was too late to buy fish now, but Tamiz could at least get some mustard oil and chickpea daal from Lalu. They hadn't had chickpea daal in a long time. If Kulsum made rice cakes they could have them with the daal. But Boikuntho called out to Tamiz before he could get to Kalam's shop.

A lamp was burning on the paved circular platform going around the base of the banyan tree, with a tray of tiny sweets boiled in sugar syrup next to it. Whoever was selling this nokuldana had probably left the tray in Boikuntho's care, but the way he was wolfing it down meant the vendor would only get an empty tray. 'Don't eat any more of those,' said Tamiz and went closer—and his head began to reel. Was this Cherag Ali himself? The stranger's dark, elongated face had blended into the fog and the darkness, as had his flowing locks. But Tamiz felt the darkness swaying before his eyes. Mukunda Saha's godown was just a few shops away, the scent of spices wafting out of it made the flame of the lamp shoot up, and the space beneath the banyan tree rode the blackened beam into the distant past when a slim young girl's voice harmonized with a man's in the darkness. The dotara in his hand couldn't be seen in the darkness—had he hidden it in the folds of his flowing red-and-black patchwork robe? Where was the iron staff he always carried? The dark-skinned girl kept the song going whenever Cherag Ali paused for breath. 'When your son weeps in your dream he will go missing.' Tamiz was laughing at the sight of Cherag Ali opening his mouth wide to sing, but someone was scolding him. Who was it? He clearly recalled the girl looking at him angrily and tearfully. Had Cherag Ali travelled through time to arrive here with the same girl?

'Where's your father?' The image in the darkness did not dissolve at Boikuntho Giri's question, but its colours began to fade. 'I'll tell you,' Boikuntho answered his own question. 'Tamiz's father doesn't come to the market any more. He's become something of a mystic himself. People say he stays home all day, preparing bait for the fish, and walks out at night to the fig tree. Do you recognize this man, Tamiz?' Boikuntho told Tamiz who Cherag Ali was. 'You don't, do you? He was Cherag Ali's pupil, his companion. He doesn't live hereabouts. He used to know Cherag Ali, but they got close to each other only in Khiyar. Isn't that right, fakir?'

As soon as he realized this wasn't Cherag Ali, the figures of the fakir and the slim young girl vanished from Tamiz's view, taking with them the cloudy afternoon from the past. Boikuntho gave out bits of information about the man—apparently Cherag Ali had instructed him to go to Girirdanga village and meet his granddaughter and her husband. He was going to pass on many secrets to Tamiz's father, wisdom which could not possibly be revealed here and now.

'Where are you from?' asked Tamiz.

'From the east.' But before he could continue, Boikuntho interrupted to explain who the stranger was. During the famine he had deposited his wife and children near here, in Nijgirirdanga, to go off to Khiyar. Music was his passion. He was a very popular singer among the people in Khiyar, and there was great demand for him to sing in the town too. That was all he did for a living now.

Tamiz immediately suspected him of being Phuljaan's long-lost husband. Now Tamiz saw yellow moonbeams beginning to drip from the lamp, and the narrow ridges between the rice fields were immersed in this moonlight. When Tamiz tried to touch the bubble of light balanced on the ridge, it slid away to hover over the ox pool, its dark face reflected in the pinkish glow on the water. Taking on the indistinct shape of a goitre beneath the chin, it curled up into a tiny point before disappearing within the sheath of the mist. And the Red Cross shawl that Tamiz had offered Phuljaan fluttered across the sky. Was it Keramat Ali's shawl then? Tamiz kept staring, which made the man squirm. In an attempt to shed his unease, he asked, 'You're Tamiz? There's so much I have to tell your father. There's so much I have to tell his wife too. I'll go to your house tomorrow or the day after.'

'Of course, you can go with me, I'll show you the way,' proposed Boikuntho. 'Sing that song again, your voice is beautiful.'

Meanwhile, a boy of fifteen or sixteen appeared and picked up his tray of nokuldana. 'You've eaten it all, Boikuntho-da. Aren't you going to pay for it?'

Boikuntho was still holding some of the tiny sweet balls. 'You should count yourself lucky that the fakir ate your sweets,' he scolded the boy. 'Give him four paise, Tamiz.'

When Keramat handed him a two-anna coin, Boikuntho said resentfully, 'Your father steals nuts from people's trees, but you, Jagatbandhu's son, are taking money from a fakir.'

'We aren't fakirs,' protested Keramat Ali. 'It's no easy matter being a fakir. We compose songs, we sing, we sell them. We're no fakirs.' It was difficult to say whether he was being modest or boastful.

'Same thing.' Boikuntho tugged on Keramat Ali's arm. 'Come in here. They have meetings every day. Lots of people. Sing a song.'

Ignoring the discussions in Kader's shop, Boikuntho called out from the door, 'Look dada, see who I've brought.' Annoyed by this unwarranted intrusion into an important conversation, Kader turned towards Boikuntho, who all but shouted, 'It's our son-in-law from Nijgirirdanga.' Looking at Keramat, however, he added a question, almost as loudly, 'Oh, but you've divorced that wife of yours, haven't you? You people can do it by word of mouth, you can get married by word of mouth too.'

The League workers should have been angered at this reference to their religion. But this man could do no wrong where Kader bhai was concerned. Still, everyone was irritated. Even Keramat Ali frowned when Boikuntho mentioned his in-laws, before introducing himself to the people in the shop. 'My name is Keramat Ali, I live in the east, on the western side of the Jomuna, my village is called Atamari.'

'Atamari?' someone asked. 'One of those islands in the river?'

'No, ours was on the bank. Most of the people in our area died during the famine. And after the famine took the people, the river ate up the deserted village. Don't think of us as those who live on one of those islands in the river, this is my respectful request to all of you.'

People smiled at his humility, Boikuntho most of all, for he was immensely proud of every achievement of Keramat Ali's. 'He's not an ordinary man,' he said, 'he's fakir Cherag Ali's pupil. You can tell them by their names, Cherag Ali the teacher, Keramat Ali the student. Now the pupil has become a fakir himself and sings everywhere.'

'Actually, no, we're not fakirs, we don't sing the songs of fakirs. We write our own songs, set our own tunes, we sing at fairs and festivals, we sell our songbooks too.'

'You write songs?' said Kader. 'How nice, do you have a songbook?'

'Yes, I have four books out in the market. But I don't have any with me right now, I never have them in stock, those who sell them take fifty or sixty at a time. By your parents' blessings and his grace, my books never remain unsold.'

'Excellent.' Kader wanted to be a patron to this poet. 'Come tomorrow afternoon, we'll listen to you sing. If we like your performance I'll ask you to write a song about Pakistan. If it's really good I can get Ismail shaheb to print it.'

'Why not sing a song for us right now?' requested Alimuddin the schoolteacher.

Although Kader considered Alim was overstepping his authority, he wasn't in a position to protest. To maintain his authority, he had to issue a firm instruction. 'Go on, let's hear you.'

'That one,' urged Boikuntho, 'the one you sang for me.'

Reaching into a sling bag beneath his shawl, Keramat Ali pulled out a four-page booklet, held it open, shook his flowing locks and pushed them back, and began to hum:

Bismillah says Keramat as he begins
May Allah have mercy on every countryman
Listen everyone, be you Hindu or Muslim
The farmer's sorrow will break your heart
He grows his crop with blood sweat and tears
And still his days pass in starvation.

'A song about farmers?' Kader interrupted him. 'Very good. Come tomorrow, let's see if you can write a suitable song for us.' Yawning, he said, 'Look how late it is, and no work to show for it.' Turning to the party workers, he said, 'Come early tomorrow, in the afternoon. Later in the evening we can hear him sing. What do you say, poet?' What he was saying did not suggest he was either enamoured of or indifferent to Keramat's music. Since his empty stomach wouldn't let him belch in satisfaction at having stopped Keramat Ali from singing as soon as he began, thus neutralizing the schoolmaster's request, Kader resorted to yawning long and noisily.

Although Keramat had been prevented from singing his song in its entirety, Tamiz had been paying close attention to the bounce of his flowing locks of hair. Keramat flicked his head during the first line to sweep his hair from the back to the front, hiding his face behind a curtain of darkness, and then flicked it again during the next line to sweep the locks back so that his eyes lit up like gaslights after the clouds had dispersed. How could those curls flow so smoothly with a simple flick of the head? Keramat had sung only a line or two, and Tamiz's heart longed to hear the rest. He had not understood the lyrics entirely, their meaning having eluded him because he was concentrating on the singer's wavy hair. But the few words that he had heard had penetrated his skull to gnaw at his brain. The uncomfortable sensation might have spared him if only he could have listened to the entire song.

21

Abdul Kader accepted that Tamiz deserved a larger share of the harvest—that he had definitely been overcharged for the water from the lake and for the hired hands' wages. 'What you're saying is right. But bhaijaan made things difficult.'

His bhaijaan wasn't even home six days a week, but still Kader couldn't do anything about it. His brother might be absent, but his sister-in-law was there. Tamiz was aware of Abdul Kader's problems. Abdul Aziz's in-laws lived near the town, Tamiz knew the type. Bhabijaan was tight-fisted. And when his elder son was away, Mondol took his daughter-in-law's advice before offering largesse to a sharecropper or a daily labourer. Even though his first wife moaned about it, it was his daughter-in-law whom Sharafat let himself be guided by. Even when it came to his second wife, no matter how much she softened his toughness by day with her gentle sarcasm, or how much he softened her at night with his sweet words, she played no part when it came to calculating the payments for the crop. Which was why appealing to her would serve no purpose for Tamiz.

With no other option left, he took his courage into his hands, muttered a prayer to Allah, and went to the Mondols to present his case to Sharafat with Kader as witness. Sharafat rejected his appeal bluntly. 'Kader speaks up for you every day. How will an illiterate fisherman like you understand the calculations? If you check the figures you'll find out you've got more than your fair share. And you, Kader, you're an educated man, how can you not understand this simple calculation?'

Kader had interceded only once on Tamiz's behalf with his father. But Sharafat's exaggeration made Tamiz hold him in greater esteem. Preening at this extra honour, he told his father, 'How can you charge for the water, baapjaan? As for the hired hands . . .'

'It's not good to get anything free of cost, my son. You're going to water your field, but you won't consider whose water you're using. Why? Did I not pay to lease the lake?'

When Kader didn't respond to this, Mondol assumed the matter of the water was sorted, and switched to the cost of the hired hands. 'Aren't you the ones who hold meetings to uphold the rights of the daily labourers? The Quran Hadith says we must settle the worker's dues before the sweat on his skin has dried. How can you now tell me not to pay them?'

'That's not what I'm saying.' But it took Kader some time to work out what he was actually saying. Eventually he reasoned, 'Since Tamiz's father was there at the time of harvesting, there was no need to hire anyone else. And then if the grain was taken to Tamiz's house first, his father and his stepmother would . . .'

'The two of them wouldn't have been able to harvest the crop in less than a week. The paddy was so ripe it would have rotted by then. That's why I had to get hired hands.' Since this had been settled too, Sharafat went on to the next point. 'And the entire crop would have gone bad if it had been taken directly to Tamiz's house. His father is a fool, and a devil on top of that, and his stepmother is from a family of fakirs, what do they know of grains? If it's Harmatullah's daughter you were talking of, or his wife, or even Harmat himself, all of them work on the field. You think there would have been so much paddy if I hadn't asked for it to be taken to their house first?' Sharafat paused to let Kader reply, but since his son didn't use the opportunity, he continued with his explanations. 'After all, Tamiz is the son of a fisherman. He will learn the ropes eventually, but only after a few more years of farming. Leave him to learn, why are you jumping in on his behalf?'

Not that Kader himself had time to jump in. Preparations had begun for the festival in Poradaho where holy men came. People from different places were gathering there already. Ismail shaheb was taking a carriage to Shimultola today—he would stop for an hour at Poradaho for a meeting. Kader would come too, from Golabari. Ismail was on his way to his in-laws', but the real objective of his visit was to persuade the supporters of the Proja party in that family to join the League instead. Without the Mians of Shimultola on their side they wouldn't get a single vote from the area, neither from the rich, nor from the poor.

Tamiz lapsed into silence after Abdul Kader left. When Sharafat rose to his feet, Tamiz suddenly feared he would never have the chance to bring up the subject with Mondol. Squatting at Mondol's feet, Tamiz said, 'I want to grow onions on that land.'

'Let Harmatullah do the farming,' Sharafat told him. 'You'd better get your plough and your oxen first.' But he praised Tamiz's work, saying he knew how to work hard, which Allah had rewarded him for. But to sharecrop without his own equipment and oxen would only lead to trouble, with both sides claiming not to have received their fair share. Mondol did not get angry or scold Tamiz or use foul language. On the contrary, he had become gentler after his grandson's death, he spoke deferentially to everyone ever since the forty-day observance of Humayun's death. But his behaviour with Tamiz had changed, and a distance had sprung up between them. Tamiz could not even look directly at Sharafat any more.

Still, Mondol offered him a solution. 'Why don't you work as a daily labourer on my fields? Harmatullah farms a lot of my land on the other side of the lake, you're sure to get some work. You can grow onions and garlic if you like, who's stopping you? Working with Harmatullah will help you learn.'

Tamiz collapsed at this new proposal, he could even be said to have been destroyed by it. Realizing this, Sharafat lowered his voice as though he was saying something confidential. 'If you're there, Harmatullah can't play any tricks. His daughter practically lives in the field, who's going to catch her if she makes off with baskets of onions and garlic?'

Tamiz lurched back home. He had to pour his anger out on his father and Kulsum before he could regain some strength in his legs. But by then Kulsum had put a pot of paddy on the clay oven, the joy of having grains at home was visible on her face through the smoke like eczema on the skin. Taking in the mark with a glance, Tamiz entered his father's room, who also appeared at the same moment with a fishing net. Happiness gleamed in his eyes and his beard. Walking across the yard, he said, 'Kalam gave it to me. It's from his father's time. Has a few holes, patch them and it'll last a lifetime.'

Tamiz's regret and suffering were buried under a mountain of anxiety. 'Are you going to Katlahar again for fish? Isn't Mondol going to break both your legs?'

The possibility of his father's legs being broken made Tamiz shed his fatigue. If Mondol's stick really did strike his father, he could also force himself out of Sharafat's control. Meanwhile, Tamiz's father seemed to have become possessed by the ferocity of the catfish in the lake, a ferocity that lent power to his tongue. 'Is there no water anywhere else in the world besides Katlahar? Has Mondol taken possession of all the lakes in the world? What about the Bangali river? What about the Jomuna? What about the Kartowa in the west?'

This long speech made Tamiz's father drowsy, but his vehemence was not in the least diminished. 'How many months do you think we can live on the money from the paddy you've brought home?' His rumbling began to fade into a muttering now. 'If I can get a catfish at Poradaho . . .' Without completing what he was saying, he asked in a louder voice, 'So Mondol won't let you sharecrop now. Are you going to work as a daily labourer?'

How did Tamiz's father know what Mondol was plotting? Had the old coot been to the fig tree north of the lake last night? Was it there that he had acquired all the belligerence he was displaying now? If he was on such good terms with Munshi, why couldn't he put in a word so that Mondol could become favourably disposed towards Tamiz? What use was all that walking around the lake till the early hours of the morning if Tamiz's father couldn't even inform Munshi that Tamiz had been dispossessed of the land he was sharecropping on? Couldn't Munshi hear the bare plot of land mourning for Tamiz, could he not respond to its sighs? What use were all his powers?

In the afternoon, the plot of land next to the ox pool in Nijgirirdanga was sunbathing happily in the nude, stripped bare of all its crops. Not even the green-and-red glow from Harmatullah's pepper field next door could make it shiver. It was Tamiz instead who was moving about restlessly. Perhaps he could plead with Harmatullah to intercede on his behalf with Mondol and get him sharecropping rights to the plot even though he did not have his own equipment.

But Harmatullah's house was deserted. Tamiz had been standing quietly for a long time outside the makeshift curtain of plantain leaves before he heard a child's moans. He cleared his throat, at which Phuljaan emerged. The little boy's groans had imposed the rhythm of a wide, empty field on the house. Tamiz needed to talk to Harmatullah desperately—but that was forgotten now. His heart began to beat faster, was no one else home?

'My son won't live any more.'

Without responding to her anxiety, or perhaps to prepare a suitable response, Tamiz asked her, 'Where's your father? Nobiton? Your mother?'

'Bajaan's gone to the Mondols. I don't think he had even got as far as the lake before the boy began to vomit. The vomiting has stopped, but he's groaning in pain. I doubt if he's breathing.'

Since it wasn't possible for a child to groan without breathing, Tamiz had no doubt that the boy was alive. After scanning the empty kitchen and yard, Tamiz bent over the child to examine him, touching his forehead and stroking his cheeks. Then he said, as a doctor would, 'No, he'll be fine. It's not rare for children to vomit. Where's your mother? Isn't Nobiton home?'

'My uncle came and took away my mother, Nobiton and Felani went along.' Perhaps Phuljaan was reassured by Tamiz's learned pronouncement. 'They took the boat. The Poradaho fair starts in two days, my uncle told me, your husband isn't coming back, but your father is our son-in-law, I'll take him to the fair.'

Tamiz did not laugh at the thought of a son-in-law of advanced years being ceremoniously invited home by his wife's family. But a faint flush of happiness appeared on Phuljaan's lips, its touch turning the tears for her ailing son into large drops in her eyes, which encouraged Tamiz. 'Why didn't you go too?'

Phuljaan couldn't go with her son being so sick, and her father couldn't leave her alone at home either. Her tears rolled down her cheek as Phuljaan revealed this information to Tamiz, but they didn't dry. Once he had assured himself that there was no one at home besides Phuljaan and her son, Tamiz was overcome by a new anxiety: Did this mean the responsibility for taking advantage of this absence of the others had been imposed on him? But what responsibility could that possibly be? What was Tamiz to do now? Would it help in any way to tell Phuljaan that Harmatullah was about to grab his land? If not, what should he tell her? He had to say something, after all. Phuljaan's son released him from this tense situation by vomiting in his mother's lap. He did it in silence, spewing out liquid from his mouth. Then he lay back in her lap, seemingly shorn of the power to live.

'Has he fainted? Let me see.' Tamiz took the boy into his arms. Phuljaan's son's distended belly had swollen even more, and although his eyes were closed there was a gap beneath his lids—he even appeared to have lost the ability to shut his eyes properly. The dark-yellow hue of his skin had deepened, and his hair was sticking to his skull like strands of jute. Tamiz planted a deep kiss on his cheek, which was still smeared with threads of his vomit. His skin was so hot that Tamiz felt as though his lips had been scalded.

The boy's hot breath cleared his confusion—he responded to Phuljaan's wails with a firm command. 'Your son's got a high fever, we have to pour water over his head, get a bowl and a mug.'

When she brought him a pitcher filled with water, a bowl and a mug, Tamiz sat down on the floor with the boy in his lap. After Phuljaan had poured the cold water on his head for some time, the boy opened his eyes and began to cry. But Tamiz signalled to her to continue, and she obeyed. When the pitcher had run out of water, she stopped at Tamiz's bidding and wiped her son's head with the end of her sari. Tamiz laid him down on the sheets spread on the maacha and said gravely, 'The fever's better now. I'll take him to the doctor tomorrow. We'll have to leave early.'

Phuljaan's son was probably feeling comfortable now, or perhaps it was because he was so weak, but he fell asleep after moaning for a bit. 'He's feeling cold, can't you tell?' Tamiz admonished Phuljaan. 'Where's the shawl I gave you?' Maybe because she had no idea what a shawl was, not even the way Tamiz pronounced the word, or maybe because Nobiton had taken it with her, Phuljaan covered her son with one of her sister's embroidered quilts. As Tamiz gazed at its floral pattern, Phuljaan began weeping. 'No medicine, no charmed water, why do you suppose my son is dying? No one cares.'

'Why are you crying?' Tamiz scolded her. 'What's there to cry for? You're like a maidservant in your father's house, how do you expect to get your son treated?' Tamiz's consolation-cum-rebuke made Phuljaan burst into tears.

Sobbing uncontrollably, she said, 'I have wretched luck. The boy might as well not have a father. Never bothers to find out if he's alive or dead.'

'You're talking of your husband? He's there all right. Travels around singing, haven't you heard? Visits all the fairs, hasn't he been here?'

Phuljaan went back to sobbing and then stopped crying. 'Who told you that? Why are you lying?' Tamiz didn't find it difficult to assume that Phuljaan knew of Keramat's whereabouts. But her attempt at pretence was charming.

Throwing a casual but confident smile at her, Tamiz said, 'Why should I lie? I met him yesterday at the Golabari market, he said he had married you, but that he's divorced you now. I said, you can't divorce your son, can you? He's seriously ill, aren't you going to see him? He didn't answer. Everyone was there.'

Phuljaan looked at Tamiz with wide eyes before lowering them. Tears began to roll down her face. Tamiz roused himself swiftly to wipe them away with his palms. He couldn't stop—how could he take his hands away if she was going to keep weeping? 'Are you going to be your father's maid all your life?' he asked. 'Don't you want to marry?' When Phuljaan began to sob with double the intensity, Tamiz pressed her head to his chest, and then began to kiss her salty cheeks and briny eyes, even raining kisses on her goitre all the way down to her breasts. The fervour of his kisses made Phuljaan slump on the bed next to her son. 'Your son will be mine too, I'll take care of him,' said Tamiz, trembling, and what he had just said made him tremble even more. It was to stop himself from trembling that he had to lie down too, with his arms around Phuljaan.

She tried feebly to stop him, but failed, for she was trembling uncontrollably herself. Her son woke up and began to cry. Tamiz was on the rampage all over her body. It was not just her nostrils but also her eyes, ears, neck, goitre, breasts, belly, thighs, legs, feet and soles, back, buttocks and every other part of her body that was filled with the smell of fish from his.

Even after Tamiz got to his feet, Phuljaan remained on the bed, drawing her son into her arms. 'Where's your father?' asked Tamiz. 'Shall I talk to him at once?' He knew it wouldn't be easy. But Harmatullah didn't realize that if he let Tamiz marry his daughter, his newly acquired son-in-law would grow the kind of crops on his field that the old coot couldn't even have dreamt of.

Harmatullah was heard coughing outside the house. As he hacked away, he demanded to know from his daughter why the oxen hadn't been fed yet. Tamiz rushed out into the yard, walking up to Harmat as though to welcome him.

'So you're here at last. I've been waiting hours for you.' His voice was flat, but its unnecessary loudness evoked a hot gust of wind as on an afternoon during a famine.

'Mondol wouldn't let me go, I got late.'

No sooner had Harmatullah explained than Tamiz asked him, 'You went to get permission to plough my land, didn't you?'

'Why should I have to go? Mondol sent for me. He's insisting that I sharecrop on that plot. I can't turn down the jotedar if he asks, can I?' To change the subject, Harmatullah turned towards the house and shouted, 'Are you dead, Phuljaan? Why haven't you fed the calves?'

Phuljaan emerged with her son in her arms. 'My boy was about to die,' she said, without making the slightest effort to offer an explanation or an excuse for neglecting the oxen.

'We have to go to the doctor tomorrow,' Tamiz reminded Phuljaan with needless severity. 'We won't get to see him unless we leave early.'

Harmatullah was thrown into doubt by Tamiz's sharpness towards his daughter. Squatting in the yard, he told Tamiz, 'Why don't you talk with Mondol about the land next to your house? He might let you have it if you beg for it.'

'I have no wish to beg Mondol. Do I depend on him for my food?'

Softening, Harmatullah said, 'But the fact is that sharecropping is a difficult business without your own tools and animals. Mondol asked me to tell you to work with me as a daily labourer. I don't need helping hands, my daughters . . .'

Tamiz flared up in rage. 'Don't try your tricks with me, old man. You think it's good for a man's wife and daughters to work on his land? You cannot make your daughters work on your land any more, I'm warning you.'

Striding away, Tamiz turned his eyes to the north when he was close to Katlahar Lake. The head of the lake was not far from here, it was in fact quite close by after rounding the ox pool and walking through the bushes. That was where Munshi collected the entire lake into his fishing net from his position on the fig tree. The murrel swam in the water all night after being transformed into sheep, and then guarded the lake deep beneath the surface when they had been returned to their original form before dawn. It was under their watchful eyes that all the other fish thrived in the lake. And what did Munshi do all this time? He would perch on the top branch of the fig tree, turning himself into the narrowed eye of the vulture, and watch the journey of the sun across the sky, or become the sunshine in an instant and spread himself across the water to warm the chilled bodies of the fish in the water. And what else? What else would he do? When he was tired of all this he would turn himself into the fine fur within the fur beneath the wing of a wedge-tailed pigeon hidden in the dense foliage of the fig tree to sleep uninterruptedly till evening in the warmth of the tender flesh of the bird.

Was Munshi sleeping all day and night then? Had he taken a monthly lease on sleep like the annual arrangements that Mondol made with his daily labourers? Tamiz felt a sudden urge to walk up to the fig tree and shake it violently to wake Munshi up from his death-like slumber. He did in fact go round the ox pool and walk through the bushes in search of the fig tree. There were so many trees here, large trees and small trees, across the grassy expanse and in the thicket of kaash on the other side. Even when he had reached the kaash he could not identify the fig tree. Tamiz's skin began to prickle then, and his determination ebbed away. But how could it be that he could not spot the fig tree? He looked around again. Where was the tree?

22

'I couldn't wait any longer for you, Tamiz. Why couldn't you come earlier?'

A fog of masticated puffed rice rose in front of Boikuntho's mouth as he spoke. He scooped up a huge fistful from the heap of puffed rice he was cradling in a fold of his dhuti, but did not stop speaking while transferring it to his mouth, and went on talking as he picked up a piece of jaggery from the plantain leaf on the ground.

Having managed a dip with great difficulty in the knee-high water of the pond, Tamiz was sitting on the veranda next to Keramat. He threw a sidelong glance at Boikuntho. Kulsum had been frying rice flakes till late into the night, and here was this bastard Giri dispatching them to his belly. And then there was Keramat Ali next to him, to whose plate Tamiz's father was transferring pawfuls of rice. At this rate these two were going to finish off everything Tamiz had brought home from his land. Meanwhile, Tamiz's father might have his mouth clamped shut now, but soon he was going to demolish platefuls of rice with a little fish curry. How was Tamiz ever going to get his plough or his oxen if basketfuls of rice were going to disappear in their bellies? He vented his anger on Kulsum, who kept serving him rice. Even as he ate it, Tamiz scolded her, 'Who can eat all this rice you're giving everyone?' Not that that stopped anyone present from gobbling up whatever they had been given.

After they had eaten, the intoxicating fragrance of Boikuntho's tobacco seemed to make the veranda close in on them. Even the small yard seemed to squeeze in with them, bearing the aroma of the paddy husk. When Tamiz's father's room also wanted to join them on the veranda, Tamiz's foot came into contact with Keramat's knee. He felt a tingling of fear in the foot: all it would need was for Keramat to visit Harmat's house tomorrow and talk to his wife for Tamiz's lies to be exposed. How would Tamiz face Phuljaan then?

'Now for a song, why not the fakir's song?' Boikuntho ended his request with a sigh. 'Now that the fakir is gone we will never hear him sing again.' Adding a sprinkling of water and a salty gust of wind to this sigh, he said, 'We followed the fakir everywhere all our lives, but he chose to die in your arms. Strange are the ways of god!'

When suppressed groans from somewhere inside the room made the briny air hanging over the veranda heavier, Tamiz peeped through the door. Kulsum was lying on the maacha, wrapped in a quilt. Her body was convulsed with sobs she was trying to hold back.

'Don't cry, Kulsum, don't cry,' Boikuntho said from the veranda. 'How can anyone's grandfather live for ever?' His voice thickening, he changed his instructions. 'Weep then, weep to your heart's content. You haven't said a word since you heard the news. Cry now, lift the load off your heart. Cry.'

Kulsum did not follow either of Boikuntho's instructions. She neither stopped sobbing, nor showed any signs of crying her heart out. Tamiz's father drew on his hookah in silence. With the sunshine waning in the yard, it became colder in the veranda. There were very few people on the road across the pond. The fields on the other side of the road had halted their journey to the sky to contract and slip into the scabbard of the late afternoon. The sky was looking blurred now.

Keramat Ali was speaking slowly. 'The fakir said, Keramat, 12 miles east of the Kartowa is the Golabari market, a couple of miles south of it is the village of Girirdanga. My granddaughter lives there, she loves me, tell her about me if you ever go there.'

After a pause, he continued, 'About Tamiz's father, he said, my granddaughter married a simple man. The villagers say he is a fool. Let them, there's something special about him, he's like a fire smothered by ashes.' Having passed on Cherag Ali's final comments on the couple, Keramat sat with his head bowed. The wave of his words turned Kulsum's groans into a thin sobbing, and she kept crying. Her grandfather had vanished long ago, so long that she had nothing of him she could feel with her senses besides the smell in that tattered book of nonsense he had left behind. When she heard the news of her grandfather's death, there was not even a twitch on Kulsum's face. It was only after she had fed the bearer of the news, Keramat, and the bearer of Keramat, Boikuntho, that she climbed on the maacha in the room, taking in the smell of her grandfather's book, which made her nose, and then her eyes, moist. Drowning in the flow from her own nose and eyes, she begun to hum, a humming that had been converted by Boikuntho's instructions into an unending stream of tears which had now began to drench the men sitting outside. Clearing his throat in an effort to stop his own tears from welling up in his vocal cords, Boikuntho said, 'Sing a song of the fakir's.'

'There was a song that the fakir sang often before he died. I don't remember it clearly.' When Keramat began to demur, Boikuntho pleaded, 'Try to remember. Once you start I'll remind you of the rest. I know all the songs of the fakir.'

Keramat Ali sat up straight, his eyes closed as though he was meditating, in an effort to recollect Cherag Ali's last song. The other three people on the veranda lapsed into silence on seeing him in this pose, and Kulsum's constant sobbing took advantage of this opportunity to subsume the entire house. The pond in front of the house, the road across the pond, and the late-afternoon fields shorn of crops were all captured by the sobbing to fuse into a single mass. Tamiz's father looked upwards with a little fear and a lot of hope: had Munshi cast his net even before sunset today? Would the murrel in the lake be turned into sheep, float across the water, climb on to the land, and traipse across it to Girirdanga? But suddenly Keramat Ali's voice lent words to Kulsum's sobbing:

Make no noise, the fakir is sleeping
Ohhhhhhh make no noise, the fakir sleeps.

The strumming of a dotara from within the room kept time with the singing. Keramat's strange melody found its rhythm in the strumming, and he sang, flicking his hair, 'The fakir is sleeping, make no noise.'

But who was it who was playing the dotara? The very thought of who it might be made Keramat's voice falter in fear. Boikuntho, who had joined in the singing, also stopped. But the song did not, and Cherag Ali's deep voice could be heard inside the room. Tamiz's father and Boikuntho had their heads bowed, their eyes flowing with tears on hearing Cherag Ali singing after such a long time. But Keramat Ali fidgeted—how could Cherag Ali be here? Did they not believe he was dead? He was thrown into doubt himself—whose corpse had he buried then behind Nazir Manda's house north of Panchbibi? Now that he could hear the same voice, Keramat's eyes were fixed on the sight of Cherag Ali slumping slowly to a sitting position while singing on the platform of Panchbibi railway station, his song slowing down. Cherag Ali died two hours after lying down on the platform, at exactly the time Keramat had gone off to eat. But his claims that Cherag Ali had died with his head on Keramat's arm had brought things to a point where his own right arm sometimes felt heavy in his sleep. What else could it be but the weight of Cherag Ali's head? But there was no weight on his arm now, for Cherag Ali was singing to a slow rhythm inside the room. Was it Cherag Ali, though, or his granddaughter Kulsum? But if it was Kulsum, who was playing the dotara? Between these jabs of doubt, the melody, rhythm and pace of the song grew clearer.

Each of the four men could hear the song, some of them when they looked inside the room, the others not even having to look.

Make no noise, the fakir is sleeping
His throat perforated by a gunshot
Riding his sleep, the fakir rows slowly
His wavy hair a canopy for his head
A lamp sits on top to show the way
No light in the lamp, the boat has sunk
Injured by the Company's cannonball
Make no noise friends, the fakir sleeps
The perforated throat is parched
The water in the river is muddied
It cannot satiate his endless thirst
Riding his sleep, the fakir rows slowly
Make no noise, the fakir is sleeping

As the song ended, the voice drifted away. Traversing the expanse outside the house, raising a handful of bubbles in the knee-high water of the pond and absorbing their burbling in its own form, the sound crossed the road and shed all the words, after which, acknowledging the whispers of the dew, it nestled within the sheath of the evening before turning the darkening pink sky suspended in the mist into a pitch black, concealing both the sky and itself this way. To tell the truth, it was the rolling notes of Cherag Ali's song that made the night descend a little early on Girirdanga that day.

And at once a wave of sleep claimed Tamiz's father. He was lying flat on the ground, his head resting on the doorstep, even before Cherag Ali's song had emerged on the other side of the pond. In his sleep the wound he had acquired on his thigh when Tamiz's mother was alive and the wound on his knee from Kulsum's era began to itch, while his preparations for walking out in his sleep continued amidst the pulsing of the song.

On the way back to Golabari, Boikuntho felt the intoxication of the fakir's song getting more intense with the beat of his footsteps. And Keramat Ali felt Cherag Ali's restless gaze bore into his prickling skin. He could not free himself of the look in those eyes even after sitting in silence for a while with Boikuntho in the Golabari market and then walking up to Alim the teacher's ancestral home. Unable to sleep all night, Keramat took himself off to Mukunda Saha's shop in the Golabari market at the crack of dawn.

He could not rid himself of his fear even during his breakfast of flattened rice and jaggery with Boikuntho beneath the banyan tree. 'I think the fakir took possession of his granddaughter yesterday,' he said tentatively. He was sure Kulsum was not capable of singing with Cherag Ali's voice, which was deep and gruff, even hoarse at times. But listening to it made the entire body respond, so that no one could go away. Try as hard as he might, Keramat was incapable of summoning that quality to his own smooth voice. And Kulsum's voice was positively sweet—how could she possibly overwhelm the listeners the way the song had? She had to have been possessed by her grandfather yesterday.

But Boikuntho dismissed Keramat's theory, sounding, if anything, angry. 'What's all this you're saying? How could she possibly be possessed by him? Didn't we see the fakir ourselves on the maacha? Who was playing the dotara if it wasn't him?' His temper rose when he saw that Keramat still had a doubtful look in his eyes. In a fit of rage he took a huge mouthful of flattened rice, speaking through it despite the risk of choking. 'My eyes aren't ruined yet, all right? Your kind is used to eating any and everything, we're not like you. I saw the fakir with my own eyes, sitting on the maacha wrapped in a quilt, singing and moving his head in time. Did you understand the things he said about dreams in his song? You people are nothing but peasants from islands in a river, what do you know of Munshi?'

'Why shouldn't I understand? The fakir predicted his own death. Riding on sleep . . .'

Boikuntho smiled through a mouthful of flattened rice. 'It's not so easy. The fakir never spoke about himself. It didn't matter to him. Anyone who lives near the Katlahar Lake knows that the fakir's pillar of strength was Munshi on the fig tree. Do you understand now?'

'Are you sure?'

Reading surrender rather than scepticism in this question from Keramat, Boikuntho tucked into the rest of his flattened rice with enthusiasm, washing it down with a long drink of water from a cupped hand at the handpump, and popping a pair of paans into his mouth before saying, 'Who can explain all this to you if not me?' He elaborated on his rights. He was from the Giri line, for heaven's sake, the blood of one of the ten most renowned families was flowing through his veins. All these places nearby, Girirdanga, Nijgirirdanga, the land on which the Golabari market had been established, the grounds of the Poradaho fair—all of these were part of their kingdom. They were Bhabani Pathak's people, they had fought against the British of the East India Company on his orders. When Bhabani Pathak drowned in the water of the Manosh river after being struck by a cannonball, his associates scattered around the country. Keramat was always travelling about, had he not heard of Bulan Giri Goswami, the jomidar of Mahikhali? His grandfather's father, or perhaps his grandfather's grandfather— who could tell for sure—was a member of Bhabani Pathak's squad. Boikuntho's grandfather's grandfather's father, or perhaps *his* father, had accepted this swine as his spiritual guru, but the traitor that he was, the fellow pleaded with an East India Company magistrate to get hold of some land and become a servant of the British. As for Boikuntho's grandfather's grandfather, or was it *his* father, or perhaps even his grandfather, he, who was in fact a hermit, went away south of Sherpur. The area was densely forested at the time, with packs of tigers, lions and wild elephants being the only inhabitants. He cleared the jungles, killed the wild animals, domesticated the elephants, farmed the land— acres of land, in Akhundia and Mirzapur. Boikuntho's father became impoverished when his grandfather's stepbrothers conspired against him, and when he died, Boikuntho left home to eke out a living from a minor job at a shop owned by the Sahas, a family of oil traders. They were hermits by origin, Kshatriyas by caste, and look at the state they were in now. But it was not for nothing that Boikuntho was languishing here. If he were to file a case today, his relatives would have no choice but to hand his land back to him. There was a different reason for his living here, a completely different reason.

Pleased by the wonder and curiosity in Keramat's eyes, Boikuntho felt himself in a quandary about whether or not to reveal the reason for his living here. 'You're not one of us, would it be right to tell you?' But he had no choice now. So he explained. This fair at Poradaho had been established by Bhabani Pathak himself, it had been very close to his heart. He had departed for Kailash after his death, but he made an appearance here on one day every year. But whom did he show himself to? Not to people of every religion or caste, obviously. The area had been overrun by Muslims, and by Sahas and Kumars and blacksmiths and fishermen and oil traders. How could they hope to catch a glimpse of the great man? He wouldn't allow Brahmons and Kayasthos to see him either. They might be godly, but Brahmons and Kayasthos had also sold themselves to the British during the war. Only if a man from a lineage of hermits were to stand beneath a palm tree on the high bank of the ox pool, dressed in clean garments and with a clean heart, Bhabani Pathak might show himself to him. Boikuntho's dead father had repeatedly told him that if only he kept his wits about him, he would never lack for food or clothes. Everyone in this life would honour him, and as for the rewards in his afterlife, well, he wasn't one to say it himself. Only Bhabani Pathak knew.

Boikuntho's explanation did not dispel Keramat's puzzlement. What was the connection between Bhabani Pathak and Cherag Ali's posthumous singing? The person whose influence he had observed west of the Jomuna had in fact been Majnu Shah and not Bhabani Pathak. Each and every inhabitant of Madaripara, which the Jomuna had consumed, used to behave as though they were members of Majnu Shah's army. The beggars that they were, they were starving, with no land of their own and even their buttocks uncovered, but there was never any meekness in their voice. They did their begging with sticks in their hands, cursing and threatening those who did not give them alms. Cherag Ali belonged to this tribe. Keramat had heard him say that all the land to the east and the west of the Kartowa was under Majnu's control till the British occupied it forcibly.

'That is true,' agreed Boikuntho, accepting this partially. 'Munshi was Bhabani Pathak's general. Haven't you heard that song, Bhabani goes to battle, his general by his side. Do you know who this general was?'

Equating Keramat's silence with ignorance, Boikuntho grew more confident. 'Munshi on the fig tree was the general. Even now on the night of Kali Puja Munshi launches a sacrificial stake on the water of the lake on Munshi's orders, if you can sacrifice a black goat at the stake all your sins will be written off. Even children know all this.'

Keramat said, 'The fakir would often say, even in his songs, that Munshi was close to Majnu Shah.'

Boikuntho had no objection to this. 'You're right. Majnu had sent word to Bhabani Pathak. And what was his message? You may have Kali, but I have Ali. Your strength comes from Kali and mine, from Ali. Yes or no? Let us join hands. If Ali and Kali fight together, the Company won't be able to withstand us for even a minute. Then the two armies became one. So naturally Munshi had to obey Bhabani Pathak.' Boikuntho even offered evidence. 'Otherwise why would Munshi still be launching the katra on the water of the lake?'

There could be no more debate after such proof. Meanwhile, Mukunda Saha had arrived at his shop. But Boikuntho wouldn't stop. 'All your doubts would have been cleared if fakir Cherag Ali were here. Didn't you hear him sing yesterday? Didn't you understand the details of the dream in the song?'

What details? Boikuntho sneered at Keramat's inability to grasp the song. 'You're a songwriter yourself, how is it that you don't understand? A mop of flowing hair, on it the lamp. Meaning, a lamp in the boat that doesn't burn. Why not? Nothing to light it with, how will it burn. The boat is sinking, the fisherman is swallowing the filthy water. Before he was shot dead by the Company soldiers, this was the dream that Munshi had. The fakir always said that everyone is informed through a dream when death is imminent.'

Keramat followed him as he set off for the shop, saying, 'Maybe Cherag Ali had that dream himself before dying, so he wrote that song.'

'You're a fool.' Boikuntho stopped, annoyed. 'The fakir never wrote songs, these are all verses that he received. Why should he be speaking about himself? How could he possibly speak about himself and not Munshi? He wasn't as arrogant as you are. How much time did you actually spend with him? We're the ones who walked around with him, who spent hours in his company. People would come and tell him of their dreams, the fakir would tell them the meaning. We heard him.' Boikuntho was outside Mukunda Saha's shop now. 'Tamiz's father knows some of these things now. The fakir even left his book for Tamiz's father. There has to be a reason behind it, don't you see?'

'Whom were you eating with first thing in the morning before coming to the shop, Boikuntho?' Mukunda Saha's voice emerged from within. He didn't approve of anyone eating with people from other castes or religions before entering the shop in the morning.

'Coming, babu,' said Boikuntho.

Looking up at the leaves of the banyan tree, Keramat Ali noticed a multitude of red fruits through the gaps. Each of them was like the look in Cherag Ali's eyes. Apparently this was the spot where Cherag Ali sang for the first time when he arrived here. It was an auspicious location, as the fakir's success had proven. Over on the other side, from Joipur, though Panchbibi, Akkelpur, Adamdighi, and Hili all the way to Paharpur, and even farther, to Shantahar junction, crowds gathered wherever Cherag Ali sang. The fakir was so wise, and though Keramat made fun of him, he had never been able to acquire Cherag Ali's rustic voice. And then Cherag Ali could interpret dreams. No one knew what happened after that, but Boikuntho had told him that he had given up analysing dreams on Munshi's instructions and left the land. In Panchbibi, the fakir had told Keramat several times about this Munshi. Keramat had paid no attention, however, saying, 'Never mind all that. Maybe you have cordial relations with your Munshi or your jinns or your deities, but they won't give you the words of your songs, you'll have to write them yourself. I write my own songs.'

But Cherag Ali had never responded to these jibes. One day, however, he had turned to Keramat after a song that Keramat was overwhelmed on hearing, and said, 'You think you can write a song like this? You think I can? It's one thing to write a song, and another to be given your verses.' He had himself said he had written a book of explanations of dreams, which he had left with his granddaughter. Keramat had met his granddaughter's husband, but was he even a man? He had not seemed affected at all by the news of his grandfather-in-law's death. A dead man could appear in his room in a dark corner, singing and playing the dotara, but the idiot only slept like a dog on the floor. To think that Cherag Ali's book was entrusted to such a man! It was the fakir's granddaughter who was the quick-thinking one. From what little Keramat had seen of her behind the veil of her sari, she was clearly pretty. How beautiful her long, tapering fingers were! Far from reacting when told that her grandfather had died, she had cooked for them and taken care of them, and listened with attention to all that Keramat had said about Cherag Ali. Then, after ensuring everyone had eaten, she had lain down on the maacha in a corner of the darkened room and begun to weep softly. The kind of weeping that seemed not to come from high up in the room, but from the depths of the earth, the last tears of the roots of trees before dying from a lack of water. If only Keramat Ali could write a long poem about her, he wouldn't need to write another word ever again, the book would earn him enough money for a lifetime. It would be worth having a look at the fakir's book. Tamiz's father knew neither to read nor to write. An illiterate fool, who apparently sleepwalked to a distant place, which Boikuntho marvelled at. Come on, if people could do all their work in their sleep what had Allah provided such a large sun for, and why did the sun give out so much light, for that matter?

But Tamiz's father was not to be found at home. It seemed he had gone off to sleep for a bit in the early hours of the morning after having wandered about all night. Kulsum told Keramat from inside the room that he had woken up a short while ago and walked off to the east with a net, along with Kalam majhi's nephew. They would be back after visiting the fair at Poradaho.

Kulsum was speaking from inside the room. Yesterday she had taken care of them personally, even though her head had been covered with the end of her sari. Why was she behind a curtain today? Keramat said, 'Isn't Tamiz home? I have something to talk to him about.' This worked.

Still keeping herself hidden behind the door, Kulsum opened it a crack to put a low stool out for Keramat. 'Please wait outside,' she said, 'he'll be back.'

Sitting on the stool in the yard, close to the door, Keramat said loudly, 'Fakir Cherag Ali talked about your often. I must tell you what he said. It is my duty to pass on the instructions he left before dying.' Kulsum displayed no enthusiasm to listen to her grandfather's last advice or statement. But Keramat felt he had no choice but to fulfil his responsibility. 'The fakir had regrets about you. I have just the one responsibility, he would say. My orphaned granddaughter.' Realizing that Kulsum had come up to the other side of the door, Keramat lowered his voice. 'Tamiz's father is a wonderful person, pure of heart. But your grandfather said, I don't know, it was he who said it, Tamiz's father is a little too old. Allah has not given him much intelligence either. Nor has he learnt to read or write. What do these things mean to fishermen anyway? He can't be blamed for that. But it was to him that Cherag Ali bequeathed his book. Can Tamiz's father even read it?' When Kulsum didn't reply, Keramat continued after a pause, 'I was thinking of taking a look at the book. The fakir told me, you're a writer, Keramat, you'll understand what's in my book. I write books, I read them at fairs and markets, people buy them for the songs in them, wholesalers buy them in large numbers to sell them to others. And the verses in the fakir's book have all been passed on to him, they're from another era, nobody wrote them. If I could just have a look . . .'

'You can't have the book right now,' Kulsum answered from within. 'Let him return.' Still Keramat wouldn't leave. He was fed up of hearing about Cherag Ali from everyone ever since he had arrived here. Boikuntho kept asking Keramat to sing, but his heart

was devoted to Cherag Ali's songs. Even when charmed by one of
Keramat's songs, by the time he began to hum it, it had become a
completely different song—his mind had been taken over by one
of Cherag Ali's verses. Alim the teacher enjoyed Keramat's lyrics.
But he said, 'People hereabouts aren't ready for such songs yet, they
haven't united yet against the jotedars.' It was Keramat's songs that
had galvanized the aadhiars of Panchbibi and Joipur into action
when taking away the crops by force. In Dhalahar, bullets fired
by the jotedar's mercenaries struck Palani Barman's mother in the arm,
the blood was streaming from her elbow—slumping to the ground,
the old woman saw Keramat standing in front of her and said, 'Why
have you stopped singing, don't stop, keep singing.' But Keramat had
run out of an audience for his songs in these parts because they were
frightened of the jotedar's guards. He had run out of money, and had
to stay with Alim, who himself was a tenant in an aadhiar peasant's
house. He had been allowed to stay there because he gave the farmer a
hand on his land. It was thanks to him that Keramat was still getting
two meals a day, but how long could he count on this hospitality? The
farmer was giving Keramat food because of the harvest, but when he
himself would begin starving a few months later, and if the teacher
had to hand over his entire salary to him, Keramat was unlikely to get
his two meals a day any more. If instead he took Boikuntho's advice
and sang Cherag Ali's songs, he might be able to keep body and soul
together. These were local songs, which everyone was allowed to sing,
he wouldn't be breaking any rules. Boikuntho claimed that the fakir's
soul would rest in peace if his songs continued to be sung. Keramat,
however, would prefer the fakir to make his own arrangements for the
peace of his soul. For now, he just wanted to leaf through the book.

'He won't be home for two days. Why don't you come back
after the fair has ended?' Keramat was forced to leave after Kulsum's
instructions from the room. But he made another attempt before
that. 'I'm thirsty, may I get some water?'

Kulsum brought water in an earthen cup and set it outside the
door. The sight of her long, tapered fingers, appearing slightly pale

on her dark hand, made Keramat's thirst spread across his body. As he walked along the road after emptying the cup, his wish to sing began to grow, while the desire in his body crossed all limits. What was Keramat to do now?

It was rather late by the time Tamiz went to meet Phuljaan.

He had not been frightened to hear Cherag Ali's song from a dark corner of his father's room, but then he wasn't the kind of person to be overwhelmed by it either. Cherag Ali was the right-hand man of Munshi from Katlahar—dead or alive, there was a lot he was capable of. Kulsum had gone to bed weeping after the song, wrapping herself in the quilt. There wasn't a single grain of rice in the pot. Tamiz was too hungry to go to sleep quickly, and then Gofur was at the door at dawn. 'Tamiz, come to the market quickly with me. Kader bhai has asked us to go. There's a lot of work.'

At the market Kader set him to work with Gofur. What was this—did Tamiz now have to follow Gofur's orders? It was to avoid Gofur that Tamiz chose instead to follow Kader to the office at Lathidanga. From the office there he carried a load of chairs, red felt, and fabric for a marquee back to Golabari.

The Poradaho fair was starting the day after tomorrow. All the married women nearby had come back to their parents' homes for the occasion, and their husbands were on their way. The villages around Poradaho were full of people, presenting an opportunity that Ismail didn't want to miss. The Muslim League was holding a meeting the day before the fair at the Golabari market. Ismail Husain would obviously give a speech, and Shamsuddin had promised to try his best to bring Khan Bahadur shaheb, though it was Allah who would decide. The stage would be erected close to the banyan tree, with Mukunda Saha contributing a bedstead to act as the dais, while the manager would provide the chairs.

The manager not only provided the chairs, but also paid for the marquee on being told that the Khan Bahadur was coming. He even asked Kader to sit on a chair. 'Go on, take a seat. Khan Bahadur shaheb is a childhood friend of babu's eldest son, they're perpetually to be seen together in Calcutta. If he comes I simply have to be there myself.'

Lowering his voice, the manager continued, 'Here all of you are screaming about Pakistan, no one's stopping you. You're saying there won't be jomidars any more. Very well, take that away too. But will you be able to retain your own holdings? If you don't get the harvest from your own land, there'll be no difference between it and the jingle. You know very well what's happening in Joipur and Panchbibi. If you can't stop such things here you will be wiped out with your families. Today the peasants are looting the jotedars' granaries, tomorrow they will want to marry the jotedars' daughters. Don't forget any of this.'

Propelled by the weight on his shoulders, Tamiz was trotting instead of walking, which enabled him to reach Golabari quite quickly. But then he had picked this pace by choice, though it was difficult to say whether it was because he had to take Phuljaan's son to the doctor in the town or because of the pressure applied by the peasants of Panchbibi and Joipur.

Lowering his load in front of Kader's shop, Tamiz set off without a word to anyone. Looking up at the sky after a few steps, he saw that the day had progressed a good deal already, but there was still time. Phuljaan would be ready, she wasn't one to dally. Why should a woman like her have to suffer so much? Considering the state her son had been in yesterday, Allah alone knew how he was today. Maybe he would take a carriage from Golabari. Tamiz had left home this morning with six and a half rupees, some of which would surely be left over after paying for the journey and the medicine. Perhaps they would take a rickshaw when they reached the town. He would ask Phuljaan to take a sari along to use as a curtain for the rickshaw. He could save two annas if they didn't take a rickshaw, but what if Phuljaan found it difficult to walk with an ailing child in her arms? Proshanto the compounder might agree to waive his fee if Tamiz pleaded with him. But he must make sure not to touch the compounder

when throwing himself at his feet, because Proshanto would
create a scene in case of actual contact. Afterwards, Tamiz could
buy Phuljaan some nokuldana or peanuts outside the cinema hall.
Wouldn't she want to see some of sights in the town? It would
be her first visit, after all. On his way back after harvesting the
crops in Khiyar, Tamiz had stopped in the town in front of a large
garden, the people there called it a park or something, it was filled
with trees and flowers and benches to sit on. He hadn't dared go
inside. It was best not to try, though, he might be humiliated in
front of a woman if refused entry.

No one answered when Tamiz cleared his throat outside
Harmatullah's house. Yet he could hear voices inside. Had Harmat
taken his daughter to weed his pepper field? All this had to be stopped.
Or had Phuljaan's son taken a turn for the worse? Was there still time to
go to the doctor? Was Tamiz going to ruin his life chasing the Mondols?

It was a rather apprehensive Tamiz who parted the curtain of
plantain leaves to enter the inner yard. He could hear the conversation
in the room clearly now. Whom was Phuljaan talking to? Tamiz came
to an abrupt halt outside the room. It was he himself who was sitting
on the maacha inside the room, with Phuljaan's sick son in his lap
and Phuljaan next to him. Tamiz returned from yesterday to today
in a flash to discover Keramat Ali sitting in his place. Everything else
was unchanged from the day before.

Phuljaan covered her face with the end of her sari and looked
away when she saw Tamiz. Keramat Ali looked at him in surprise.
'You here? What news?' Then his tone acquired the authority of being
in his father-in-law's house. 'Come on in. I went to your house, you
weren't there, and your father is off somewhere to the east. He's gone
fishing, hasn't he?'

Phuljaan said softly from behind her sari, 'What else will they
do but fish?' Then, rising to her feet and making to leave, she told
Keramat, 'Tell the son of the fisherman here to step aside.'

When Tamiz obliged, Phuljaan went out and turned towards
the kitchen.

Stroking his son's brow, Keramat said, 'This boy of mine is very ill. There are no doctors to speak of in the village. These people have no idea of how to get him treated, they have been neglecting him. I see no option but to take him to the town. But how?' His forehead creased with worry. 'How do I do it? There's a meeting at the Golabari market, I'm supposed to sing there. I can't turn down so many people.' Neither his statements nor his behaviour suggested he was meeting his wife and son after many years. Tamiz was unable to look at Keramat. Had Phuljaan told him everything? But what he was saying suggested Phuljaan had not passed on Tamiz's lies about Keramat's having divorced her.

'You're the one who sharecropped Mondol's field, aren't you? But he's given you less than your fair share.'

Tamiz spoke finally. 'Who told you that?'

'I know everything. It's my business to know. Phuljaan's father is a simple man, he takes whatever Mondol gives him. This can't go on. Have you heard what's happening in Khiyar?'

Tamiz was both exhilarated and frightened by such news. 'Where's Harmatullah?' he asked.

'My father-in-law has gone to his father-in-law's house.' Keramat followed this disclosure with a rhyme about a father-in-law visiting his father-in-law and laughed uproariously. Then he explained, 'The son-in-law is visiting during the Poradaho fair, right? So my father-in-law has gone to fetch my mother-in-law and sister-in-law. Who visits his father-in-law's house if his sister-in-law isn't there? Don't you get it, every day you have your wife, her sister is the joy of life.' Having demonstrated his wit, he returned to the subject of the harvest. 'I hear you had a very rich crop. Which is all very well, but how much of it did you get for yourself? Less than half, right? But the tillers in Joipur and Panchbibi and Akkelpur are raiding the jotedar's granaries unless they're given two-thirds of the crop. Did you know?'

23

Despite issuing a call in Bangla to plunge into a jihad for establishing Pakistan in order to lead the ideal life prescribed by the Quran and the Sunnah, Sadeq the lawyer's own professional practices and the fact that he had memorized nearly half of Syed Amir Ali's *Spirit of Islam* ensured that most of what he said was in English. His concentration, care and devotion to broadcasting the victory of Islam while at the same time preserving the grammatical purity of the official language of the state were absolute. But in spite of the presence of two gaslights, the unfortunate absence of the primary source of illumination for the night, Khan Bahadar Syed Ahmed Ali, compelled Sadiq Ali to speak in Bangla about the missing luminary's generosity, sacrifices for Islam, and strength of character. When he lapsed into English soon afterwards, Shamsuddin the doctor, aware that the subject of the lawyer's eulogy was shifting, and that the audience, intimidated by his English, were unable to understand a word of what he was saying, gently tugged at the edge of Mir Mohammad Sadeq Ali's long striped sherwani, and when this tugging turned into pulling at his garment, the lawyer was forced to pull out of his encomiums and curtail his speech to the relief of his listeners.

Finally, Khan Bahadur Syed Ahmed Ali appeared before the gathering. Thanks to several generations of feudalism, his grandfather's status as a minister, followed by his own elevation to deputy ministership after the gap of a generation, three generations of

romance and sex with English and Anglo-Indian women, including
wives and not-wives, and assorted other reasons for consorting with
pure-bred Britishers, the Bangla language was distorted considerably
as it flowed from the Khan Bahadur's tongue. Speaking in a mixture
of halting Bangla, broken Urdu, and an English better than that of
Englishmen, his voice grew heavy with grief as he related the tyranny
of Hindu jomidars and moneylenders on Muslim peasants, which
made it impossible for his oration to last beyond eight minutes.
Besides, he had to travel onwards to the town at once on an important
mission for the party. So, brimming with regret, the Khan Bahadur
humbly sought permission to desert the site of the meeting. His milk-
white hands, with the palms joined in supplication, looked reddish
under the gaslights, their complexion and his courtesy combining to
captivate the audience. Overcome by his apology for having to leave,
some of the aged listeners risked exposing their chests to the cold
while using the ends of their shawls to wipe the corners of eyes about
to be attacked by cataract.

The manager was standing behind the stage. The jomidar's
eldest son was at the Lathidanga office today, where he was waiting
to accompany the Khan Bahadur to the town. At the manager's
signal the Khan bahadur gestured to him to join him in his car.

Since the beginning of the war, cars had driven through the
Golabari market at least five times over the past few years. But
because this was the first time that one of them had been parked here
for such a long time, the local people as well as the sons-in-law who
were visiting on the occasion of the fair were all quite excited. No
sooner had the wheels of the Ford started rolling with the manager
and the doctor seated as passengers along with the Khan Bahadur
than the energy of the spectators descended to their respective feet,
so that nearly half of them began to run behind the car. The other
half, or perhaps a little more than half, of the people gazed at the
moving car, and, after it had disappeared from sight in a short
while, engaged themselves in a crucial discussion about its power,
beauty and speed. From the stage Ismail Husain shouted into his

megaphone, 'Brothers at this gathering, sit down, all of your, sit down, the meeting is being resumed, do not run about, brothers, take your seats.'

But the spectators were still too interested in the echoes of the growling automobile engine, now vanished, to pay any attention to Ismail's appeal. Even when Abdul Kader began to shout, at Ismail's orders, the slogans 'Naraye takbir..', 'Ladke lenge . . .', 'Pakistan . . .' and 'Quaed-e-Azim . . .', he was the only one to respond to them with 'Allahu Akbar!', 'Pakistan!', 'zindabad!' and 'zindabad!', respectively, because all the party workers were temporarily lost in the dust, smoke and mist left behind on the road by the Ford.

'What's all this?' Ismail complained to Kader. 'No discipline. Go get your workers. Where's that poet of yours? Get him. The public will come back if there's singing. Go.'

But since Keramat Ali had not yet succeeded in writing a song about Pakistan, Kader, annoyed by his intimacy with Alim the teacher, had just a short while ago withdrawn the invitation to sing at the meeting. Perturbed by Ismail's instruction now, he stammered, 'But Keramat Ali's song says nothing about Pakistan. I told him over and over again, but he hasn't written the song.'

'Just listen to what I'm saying. Any song will do.'

Setting off in search of Keramat at Ismail's urging, Abdul Kader found him in front of Mukunda Saha's shop, where he was engaged in a deep conversation with Alim the teacher and Boikuntho. Kader practically dragged him on to the stage. At once Ismail said, 'Take your seats, brothers. Here to present a song about Pakistan to all of you . . .'

Asked for the poet's name in a low voice, Kader whispered, 'But he hasn't composed a song about Pakistan.'

Ismail barked at him, 'Never mind all that, just tell me his name.' Once informed, he turned to the spectators to complete his announcement,' . . . is the poet Keramat Ali.'

Keramat began to gulp in panic. He had performed his songs in Joipur, Panchbibi, Akkelpur, Adamdighi, Hili, and even as far afield

as the Shantahar railway junction, and sold his songbooks by the
dozen. But the gathering here was ringing with the sound of Sadeq's
perfect English, the Khan Bahadur's halting Bangla, broken Urdu
and an English better than that of Englishmen, and, most of all, the
roar of the Ford. The heat from all of these produced drops of dark
perspiration on Keramat's face, and he could only gaze blankly at the
people, possibly without actually seeing any of them.

But Boikuntho Giri was standing on the ground, right next to
the stage. he told Keramat encouragingly. 'Just start singing. Sing
the one the fakir sang in Tamiz's father's room.' When Keramat still
remained silent, Boikuntho reassured him, 'All you have to do is
start. The fakir will help you sing.'

This flustered Keramat even more. He looked over his shoulder
in fear, where the banyan tree stood. It wasn't out of faith in Cherag
Ali but to prevent him from possessing Keramat, he began:

Bismillah says Keramat as he begins
May Allah have mercy on every countryman
Listen everyone, be you Hindu or Muslim
The farmer's sorrow will break your heart

He repeated the final lines several times, and the crowd began to
reassemble. The Muslim League workers made the spectators sit
down. 'Take your seats, everyone, the song is beginning.'

From the ground Boikuntho continued with his reassurances.
'The fakir is here, Keramat Ali. I can tell he is in you now. Sing his
song. Don't your remember? Make no noise, the fakir sleeps. Just
begin, put your trust in god and start singing. The fakir is always
there, in case you forget.'

Keramat Ali was paying no attention to any of this. He walked
about from one end of the stage to the other, pulling out a slim four-
page book from beneath his shawl and prepared to read it. Usually
he could sing without having to refer to the book—in fact, he didn't
even have to look at the pages. But holding the book increased his

confidence. Besides, the book needed some publicity. Holding it open, he continued in a baritone, shaking his head violently:

> The one with the plough, the man with the plough
> Who makes crops grow, gets no rice on his plate.
> The jotedar lives in comfort with a lease on the land
> The farmer toils to sow the seeds under a noonday sun
> After four months of labour he is all but dead
> When it's harvest time, the jotedar divides the crops.
> Less than half goes to the peasant, his family has to starve

As he listened, Alim the schoolteacher went closer to the stage, standing next to Boikuntho, and began to signal with his eyes to Keramat. But it wasn't clear whether he was encouraging Keramat or warning him. Keramat didn't look at him—his eyes were set on the darkness in the road that lay beyond the spectators.

The audience was taking its seat now. The complete silence that had persisted during Sadiq the lawyer's and the Khan Bahadur's speeches some time ago had been broken. The people were nodding in time to the song, some of them rising to their feet to surge forward, some edging in the same direction without standing up, a few comparing Keramat with Cherag Ali, others humming along with the singer even without knowing the words. Keramat's song swam through their low-voiced conversations, their enthusiasm at this new song, and their tuneful as well as tuneless humming:

> The farmer puts in all the labour, the jotedar gets the honey.
> In two months the peasant visits the man who lends him money.
> The jotedar and the moneylender, how they love each other!
> Both of them rob the farmer of his food and life.
> These two are the greatest enemies of the poor tiller.
> Like the cage is the enemy of the bird, like the moon
> Is the enemy of the thief, like the owl is the enemy
> Of the worm. Like Ravan's enemy is his brother Bibhishan

Ram's follower, who became moral after his own immorality.
Like sickness is the enemy of the body, and weeds of plants.
The jomidar and the jotedar are the enemies of the farmer.
So let us get a law, a law that evicts all the jomidars
One-third for the jotedar and the farmer will get two-thirds
So let us raise a cry for tebhaga, for peasants' rights.
Everyone knows the world cannot survive without tillers.
Look, Burman's mother! The police have shot Burman's mother
But even with bullets in her leg, her heart is still strong.
The peasants will no longer take the tyranny of the jotedar.
The peasants' blood will flow no more for the jotedar's benefit.

The ranks of listeners began to swell swiftly. Some of the people who had been running behind the car had gone home directly without bothering to return, but most of them had come back as soon as the singing began. The audience nodded in time with the jerking of Keramat's head. A group of workers led by Gofur kolu kept swinging their heads, although Gofur himself was throwing glances at Kader from time to time. Kader gazed wanly at Ismail, whose reaction to the song was proving difficult to gauge. He was more intent on watching the audience than the singer. A little later Keramat began to sing the final lines.

What Keramat says, what Keramat says, let it not fade.
If farmers are united the enemy shakes with dread.

When Keramat moved aside, Ismail addressed the crowd. 'Brothers at this gathering, it is to save the Muslims from jomidars, from moneylenders, from jotedars, that the Muslim League, under the guidance of Quaed-e-Azam Mohammad Ali Jinnah, leader of a hundred million Muslims, has thrown itself into the battle to secure Pakistan for us. It was the Muslim League that the poet Keramat Ali just told us about. We have sacrificed our nights' sleep and days' leisure to . . .'

'More songs, more songs!' Ismail paused in response to the demand from the audience.

Sadeq nudged Ismail unobtrusively, whispering, 'Let him sing. If the public turns unruly . . .'

Paying no attention to his suggestion, Ismail all but shouted at the spectators, 'Silence! Mark my words. We can't sit here listening to songs all day. We have to work too. All of you toil day and night to make a living, and when you're exhausted, you listen to songs, you sing yourself, you chat with one another to get some respite. Would you succeed in growing crops on your fields if you frittered away your hours?'

He waited a few moments for an answer to the last question. No one responded, but everyone was silent. Ismail said, 'Of course we'd feel better if we could listen to songs during breaks in our work. Let me tell you some important things, after which we can have some songs again.'

Now there was complete silence among the listeners. Ismail gave an hour-long speech, taking his time, raising and lowering his voice alternately for effect. The interest of the audience deepened when they realized that what he was saying was similar to Keramat's song in some ways. Ismail said that the Muslim League was not an organization of jomidars, how many jomidars were there anyway among the Muslims in Bengal? The few jomidars and jotedars that there were had joined the party after accepting its ideology. The Muslim League wouldn't hesitate to expel anyone who betrayed it like Mir Zafar. Having acquired his listeners' absolute attention, he declared, 'If necessary we can even expel our leader, the president of the Muslim League in the district, Khan Bahadur Syed Ali Ahmed.'

The audience was dumbfounded at first. In a moment their astonishment was converted to excitement and ecstasy, and everyone burst into applause. Even those whose eyes had misted over a short while ago at the Khan Bahadur's humility now took the risk of catching a cold a second time to take their hands out from beneath their shawls in order to clap.

Having brought the meeting under his control, Ismail raised his right hand in a gesture asking for the applause to cease. Once there was complete silence, he told the audience that the rising resentment among peasants in some parts of the state was justified. A solution, however, would be possible only in Pakistan, where no one would have the right to oppose laws in favour of farmers. What had to be examined now was: these people under whose leadership cultivators had begun their conflict—which religion did they belong to? It was Hindu jomidars who had oppressed farmers since the beginning of British rule. From the time that Nawab Siraj ud-Daullah had met his downfall in the mango orchard of Plassey, these people had licked the boots of the British to prevent Muslims from leading honourable, affluent lives. And now they were creating dissent within the community by pushing Muslims towards conflict. Whose purpose was being served here? If Muslim peasants avoided the path of bloodshed and joined the movement for the formation of Pakistan, and if the new country of Pakistan could be established, all their problems were bound to be solved.

When Ismail completed his speech with a number of instances to prove his point, Kader led a wave of slogans, with even Keramat Ali joining in.

As they climbed down from the dais, Sadeq the lawyer said in Ismail's ear, 'The meeting went off well enough. But a song about the tebhaga movement was out of place in a Muslim League meeting.'

Ismail answered him with the loud authority of success. 'It was tebhaga today, but the same man will sing a song for Pakistan tomorrow. You will be able to do neither.'

Keramat was walking with Alim the schoolteacher, with Boikuntho by his side. Judhisthir Karmakar appeared from somewhere and fell in with them. Waiting for an opportunity, he asked softly, 'You mentioned tebhaga in your song, will we get it?'

'Understanding the mystery of a song is no easy matter,' Boikuntho answered on Keramat's behalf. 'When the fakir sang, we used to hear his songs often. People hereabout have known his songs for years. But how many of them understood the meaning? Keramat's song is a new one, you think you can understand it fully the very first time you hear it?'

But Keramat's song had left its mark on Tamiz too. He had himself seen the tebhaga movement in action in Khiyar. 'Never mind the song,' he said. 'Songs say so many things, you can't take all of them seriously.' Tamiz looked at Keramat from the corner of his eye as he spoke, concluding that he had taken him down a peg or two, and felt bolder. 'I saw it for myself in Khiyar. The bastard jotedars were beaten up so badly by the aadhiars that they bared their arses in fear and didn't know where to hide.'

Everyone laughed at this. The wave of laughter could have been on account of the vision of jotedars being stripped naked or because this provided some respite from the pressure of the homilies they had been subjected to at the meeting. Pleased with his success at making so many people laugh, Tamiz shed all his anger with Keramat, and even tried to please him. 'Your singing was marvellous today. I've heard of Burman's mother from Joipur too.' Tamiz was overwhelmed by Keramat's performance.

He kept glancing at one of Kader's party workers, but the student in question did not smile at him. Instead, he spoke in the same vein as Ismail. 'Talking of fighting will do nothing but create schisms. And if Muslims are divided, Hindus will benefit. The tebhaga system will be established in Pakistan in any case.'

Which was all very well, but how would Judhisthir benefit from it? Would he get a fair share of crops if these people established the tebhaga system? A few days ago the manager had asked Judhisthir's father how he could spend so much time with people from the Muslim League. If this area became part of Pakistan, they would have to eat the leftovers from Muslims' plates, eating beef would become compulsory, and the Muslims would treat them badly. Didn't they know any of this? Would any Hindu girl be allowed to remain chaste in Pakistan? If they wanted to maintain their religion, they should stop consorting with Muslims.

Still Judhisthir had come to the meeting, on Tamiz's request. He was feeling a little reassured on seeing the manager getting into the Khan Bahadur's car. And the song about tebhaga had been positively scintillating. But now it appeared that the tebhaga system would be established for Muslims alone. He only stood to lose if Pakistan was formed—he would not only have to break with his religion but also get no benefit from tebhaga. But Jagadish Saha had said the other day that all this talk of Pakistan was a sham, that Muslims would have been blown away by now if only Mahatmaji had been a little firm. Muslims had no leaders—the lower classes couldn't become aristocrats just by making money or becoming ministers.

Judhisthir was confused. He was friends with Tamiz, but he couldn't bring himself to be as enthusiastic about tebhaga as Tamiz. Coming up to him, Alim the schoolteacher said, 'If there's a law it will apply to everyone. Do you know the things that are happening in Joipur? Try to understand Keramat's song properly. All right? Try to understand it.'

But then Judhisthir came from a family of blacksmiths. He was used to being oppressed. Even his attempts to sharecrop on Sharafat Mondol's land had failed. How was he to penetrate the mystery of this song?

24

Tamiz's father couldn't make much headway on the Jomuna with Kalam majhi's boat and brother-in-law. The people around the river were disdainful of fishermen—even those who had left Girirdanga during the famine avoided their former relatives with the hope of forging relationships by marriage with the fishermen who operated on the Jomuna. The locals had used nets 500 or 600 feet long to capture as much of the waters as possible. Since there was nowhere to cast Kalam's discarded net, now stitched to his own tattered one, which did not run beyond 72 yards, what could Tamiz's father do but to reel his net in and row down to the double bend in the Bangali river? Depositing its tears at the spot, which was no more than 15 or 20 yards deep, the dried-up channel of the Manosh had run as far as the District Board road before disappearing altogether. Many years later, the Bangali river had taken a ride from the east on the water overflowing from the Jomuna to flow along the channel for a few miles to the south, and a narrow distributary from it had lost its way to run past the large field at Poradaho and though the kaash grove to join the Katlahar Lake.

Tamiz's father cast his net close to the edge of the double bend in the dead Manosh nestling in the arms of the Bangali river. Bhabani the hermit had died at the hands of the British troops all those years ago at this very spot. Everyone knew that the Manosh had dried up out of grief for Bhabani, only leaving its tears behind to conceal the corpse, which was why the double end brimmed with water round the year. The fish from the Jomuna, the fish from the Bangali, and even the descendants of the fish from the Manosh before it dried up all swam here to fulfil the purpose of their existence by guarding Bhabani or turning into his food. As luck would have it, Tamiz's father moored his boat at this very spot. After casting his net in the evening, he stood in the waist-deep water, muttering unknown verses. Kalam's nephew Budha felt frightened as Tamiz's father's voice became softer—was he going to fall asleep? Then, unbelievably, not even the first three hours of the night had passed, and the evening star was yet to climb to the zenith, when a devil catfish threw itself into Tamiz's father's fishing net like a baby hurling itself into its mother's arms. The two of them nearly died hauling the forty- or fifty-seer fish into the boat. The small craft tilted from side to side as the devil catfish thrashed about. Budha waved his arms and legs, twisted his hips, and banged his head without being able to release even a fraction of his joy at having netted such a gigantic fish. 'Not less than 60 or 70 seers, I tell you, Nana. How old must this fish be, five hundred years? Or even more? How much do you think we can sell it for, Nana? Everyone at the fair will die when they see its size. All of them will come for a look, I'm telling you.' This long monologue, the happiness of catching a mammoth fish and the exhaustion from the effort of hauling it into the boat was making Budha sleepy. He quietened down, as Tamiz's father stroked the fish all over, mumbling an incantation, but the fish kept wiggling its tail the way a rich man wiggles his knee, making the boat rock, which in turn made Budha fall asleep.

The boat travelled all night, but Budha knew nothing of this. In the early hours of the morning, when it was still a little dark, a commotion woke him up, and he discovered that they were moored on the southern side of Katlahar Lake. Tamiz's father was standing in the mud on the bank, facing north. A flock of white storks from the silk-cotton tree in Mondol's yard was circling overhead. Glancing around the boat, Budha found it empty, with the devil catfish gone. Standing close to Tamiz's father on the dry land was Sharafat

Mondol, with a lantern in one hand and patterned wooden clogs in the other. Abdul Aziz was shining an electric torch on Tamiz's father's face, the beam moving over the water in a vast arc from time to time.

Unlike his usual practice, Sharafat Mondol was saying the same thing over and over again. What was he saying? That the arrival of his nieces and their husbands, along with their children on the occasion of the Poradaho fair had forced him to sleep in the front room, this change of bed robbing him of a good night's sleep. When he had gone out into the veranda for his ablutions before the fazr namaz, he had noticed a bloody fish thief netting a huge fish in the lake. As soon as he had shouted, 'Who are you, you bastard?' the thief had thrown the gigantic fish back into the water. Mondol had realized at once that it was none other than Tamiz's father. Going up to the man with the lantern, his suspicions had been confirmed. Sharafat had spent a fortune, besides imploring with the manager, to get this lake on lease—how could he allow thieves in the night to plunder what was rightfully his?

Sharafat Mondol's wrathful screaming served to wake Budha up completely, and the same screaming made it impossible for him to keep his head. All he remembered dimly was that the two of them had hauled the fish up on board, after which he had become so exhausted that he had lain down. He could not recollect whether the devil catfish had been put beside him, or stowed away. 'Where's the fish?' Budha asked in confusion.

'You bastard son of a bitch, you're a thief too, you're the servant of a thief.'

No sooner had Sharafat Mondol lifted his arm with the intention of bringing the clogs down on Budha's head and neck than Kader restrained him. 'Don't. The house is full of people. It's the day of the fair. What do you think you're doing?'

Lowering his arm, Sharafat continued to repeat himself, asserting that he had long been warning everyone that Tamiz's father stole fish from the lake, but unfortunately no one had listened. It wasn't for nothing that the wretched fellow went to the lake every night with a fishing net. He was such a skilful thief that he hadn't been caught yet. But it was the day of the Poradaho fair, which meant Munshi's eagle eye was on the entire lake today, so any bastard who tried to harm the lake was certain to be caught.

Boikuntho rushed up a little later as the sky lightened. He had maintained a vigil over the location of Bhabani Pathak's ancient home since midnight beneath the palm tree on the high bank of the ox pool. Bhabani was scheduled to arrive in the afternoon on Tuesday to possess the idol that had been set up in his memory beneath the banyan tree in the large field at Poradaho. People would gather to worship him at that hour. Bhabani would accept the offerings of the faithful till the hour after midnight, and then, on his way back to Kailash, he would pass the ox pool, glance at the fig tree momentarily and then take his place at the appointed time directly above his ancient home. Now the sun god would start smearing the sky with vermilion, and Bhabani would turn into sunlight himself to disappear in the sunlight. Knowing full well that Bhabani would be unhappy not to catch a glimpse of the descendants of his followers, Boikuntho had stayed on here, allowing his grandfather's stepbrothers' sons to cheat him and take over acres of land that were rightfully his. How could he have slept that night? But then not once during his vigil over all these years had he seen even a shadow of Bhabani Pathak and his blade. What was this a portent of, he wondered. Had he done something wrong? Setting off on a quest for his own possible wrongdoing, Boikuntho had seen a boat entering Katlahar Lake from the north along the narrow distributary of the Bangali river which had lost its way. His heart had begun to quake—was Bhabani Pathak taking a boat back home this time? But the boat was travelling south, how would he reach his own ancient home? Boikuntho was perplexed. But with the blood of the Giris running in his veins, he could not allow himself to be frozen with astonishment. The urge to perform his duty towards Bhabani Pathak had made him run around the fig tree and race southwards along the western bank of the lake, calling out to Harmatullah along the way when passing his house.

But what he was seeing now near Mondol's house was a different story altogether. Could someone like Tamiz's father actually be capable of such a thing? But then, ordinary people could not expect to unravel the mystery of Tamiz's father's actions. Cherag Ali would have known whose bidding Tamiz's father was following. But then the fakir was not here any more, so who was going to explain?

Harmatullah had also turned up at Boikuntho's call, but how could he bring himself to believe Mondol? But then again, was Mondol capable of fabricating his statements? As for Tamiz's father, since he wasn't saying anything, Boikuntho had no way of knowing what he had actually done. Harmatullah began to fidget, for he had to go to the fair at once, where he was planning to sell the water-chestnut and radish seeds he had bought. Nobiton had knitted twenty wall hangings of jute, with beautiful patterns on them. They were bound to fetch a good price—well-off buyers would definitely appreciate them. It was difficult to secure a good spot at the fair unless you went there early.

It was just that it was the day of the fair, and Sharafat Mondol's house was full of relatives. And then the young men from Kader's party would be visiting the fair too, some of the leaders might be there as well, which meant he would have to arrange for food for them. Without these distractions Tamiz's father could have been trussed up and packed off to the Amtoli police station on a bullock cart. The bastard could have spent his time breaking rocks in jail.

Meanwhile, Sharafat's elder son got his father in a spot of bother. Since there was no need for the torch after sunrise, he had made a quick trip home to deposit the expensive three-cell affair, returning with his son instead of the torch. Taking his father aside, Aziz whispered to him, 'It's best not to annoy this fellow, he has many tricks up his sleeve.'

Seeing that Tamiz's father was trembling, either because of the cold or fear, or for some other reason, while Sharafat's wooden clogs were in his hand instead of on his feet, Babar put his arm around his father's waist and burst into tears. The sight of a grown-up boy crying angered Sharafat. Not even his own son and grandson seemed interested in protecting his honour. Aziz was completely under his wife's thumb. He had probably received instructions from her when he had gone home to deposit the torch—for all he knew, Sharafat might now be asked to wash Tamiz's father's sore-ridden feet with milk. Whatever nonsense it was that Aziz's wife had dreamt before Humayun's death had stricken her with fear when it came to Tamiz's father. Sharafat drooped under the combined weight of his resentment, unhappiness and anger with his sons and only grandson, and was no longer able to nurture his rage against Tamiz's father.

Tamiz heard about his father at the Poradaho fair. Carpenters from Kamalpur, Aolakandi and Amtoli had been transporting their beds, bedsteads, clothes racks, benches and stools in bullock carts since midnight. Tamiz had arrived even earlier to work for them as a hired hand. He could earn some money unloading the furniture from their carts and then loading it on customers' own carts or boats. This meant he couldn't afford to waste the day, but now, having heard about his father, he had rushed to the spot. Sharafat was on his way home, muttering, 'Not today, we'll see after the fair.' His sons, grandson, and an assortment of relatives and their relatives, besides servants and daily labourers, trailed behind him.

Tamiz's father was still standing ankle-deep in the mud, facing north. Taking his arm, Tamiz felt the touch of ice on his rough, calloused palm. How could a human being's arm be so cold? Tamiz trembled—was his father still alive? He tugged on the frozen arm to haul his father to dry land, practically prising the old man's feet out of the mud. Up on the bank, Tamiz's father threw a single glance at his son and then at Boikuntho. Fresh blood was sloshing about in his drowsy eyes. When he began walking, Tamiz said, 'Come home, bajaan.'

Tamiz's father didn't look at anyone. He didn't appear to be seeing or hearing anything at all. Taking his lips close to Tamiz's ears, Boikuntho said, 'Don't say anything, Tamiz. Let him go. Let's go back to the fair.' Boikuntho was staggering, his breath reeking of ganja.

Tamiz had to get to the fair as quickly as possible, for the carpenters would engage other people if he was late. Tamiz ushered Boikuntho into Kalam majhi's boat, where the devil catfish had left signs and smells of his enormous body. Budha couldn't utter a word for a long time, finally managing to speak only when the boat had left the Katlahar Lake and began to move up the narrow stream from the Bangali river.

Returning home in the afternoon, Tamiz's father lay down on the floor at once, resting his head on the doorstop.

'What's all this I hear?' said Kulsum. 'Apparently you went to the lake to steal fish, and Mondol beat you up with his clogs? Did he tie you up? Where did he hit you, was it on your head? They're saying he clobbered you with a pan. What is it, why don't you speak? Why aren't you talking to me, Tamiz's father?'

Still Tamiz's father didn't respond, and a whistling sound emerged from his nostrils. Its intensity dropped a little later; he used the faint but deep sound of his snores to gather the entire room inside his sleep as he walked. He always walked in his sleep, but why was he trembling uncontrollably? Tamiz's father walked around the room in his sleep, possibly muttering verses too. He put his arms around Kulsum in his sleep, and then pushed her away, still asleep. But Tamiz's father had never trembled so in his sleep. He simply couldn't stop trembling now, and as he trembled his body alternately curled and stretched. His head rolled off the doorstop on to the floor, and then rolled back up on the doorstop on its own.

25

What was Kulsum to do with this man now? She sat down next to her husband and touched his forehead—her palm was scalded. Tamiz's father was being roasted by the heat of his fever. Could a man's skin possibly be so hot? Kulsum could boil an entire pot of rice on it. But what she placed over Tamiz's father instead was his old overshirt, his lungi, a tattered sari of her own, all the quilts in the room and even a frayed fishing net. Still he wouldn't stop shivering. Kulsum made several trips into the inner yard to bring armfuls of hay to cover her husband with. Finally, when he still wouldn't stop shivering, she lay down on top of him, but when he turned on his side to deposit her on the floor, there was nothing more she could do. Still, he stopped shivering in a while, although the fever remained. After he was beaten up by Sharafat Mondol, had Tamiz's father spent the entire morning and afternoon stealing all the fire in the world and in the skies and gathered them in his body? Kulsum sniffed all over him, but she could smell nothing. Had the permanent stench of raw fish and raw flesh on his body vaporized in the heat of his fever then? Even when she sniffed deeply, with her nose near his slightly parted lips, Kulsum could get no smell of any kind. She felt a dread—was the fire raging inside his body too? Putting a little distance between her nostrils and Tamiz's father's open mouth, Kulsum felt her head reeling. The medium-sized opening between his lips looked like he was asking a question.

He seemed to have parted his lips in an effort to find out something. Kulsum had often seen this kind of question mark in open mouths, but when had she last seen lips parted with such surprise while asking a question, she asked herself. When? And where?

'Oh, the cotton pillow lies at the head . . .' As Cherag Ali stopped singing, Kulsum took up the refrain. 'The cotton pillow lies at the head.' There it was—a dark, round face beneath thinning hair, the beard not particularly thick either, though unkempt, thick lips parted in the centre of his beard. He was kneeling on the floor, listening to the song, his eyes fixed on Cherag Ali, his mouth opened to swallow the fakir's song. That was such a long time ago—it would need great strength to swim against the current so far back in time. Kulsum was not as young as she used to be. But perhaps it was the tremendous heat in Tamiz's father's body that gave her strength, who knew, perhaps her arms sprouted wings on which she flew to those days when the Jomuna was flooding its banks. When it saw the tattered book and Cherag Ali drawing rectangles on the floor to interpret the dreams of the entire clan of fakirs of Madaripara, that fucking Jomuna destroyed Cherag Ali's unshakeable self-confidence and his infallible prophecies to consume the entire village. Taking shelter on the Akandas' land for a month and a half, they moved into the Dargah Sharif in Dargahtala. But the shrine was occupied at the time by caretakers of a different sect. Despite asserting that it was his forefathers who had fought with the British for the right to conduct their ceremonies in the shrine, Cherag Ali and his family could not find a foothold there. Whether it was to maintain the sanctity of his own lineage, or out of fear at the prospect of having to maintain the roza according to the Shariat as demanded by the new caretakers—or simply because of the attraction of a life of getting leftover food for chanting verses, Allah alone could tell—Cherag Ali set off west with his granddaughter. He wouldn't live in the east any more, he would go beyond the Kartowa to where all the fakirs gathered. That was where Majnu Shah had run his jihad from. But travelling this great distance was no easy matter. Once they had gone past several villages

on the other side of the Bangali river, the number of people they
saw began to fall. The humidity and heat of the Bhadro afternoons
robbed Kulsum's legs of whatever strength they had. Unable to find
a suitable spot to sing, Cherag Ali grew restless. The few people they
passed were all busy washing the harvested jute in knee-high water.
Some of them were resting beneath large trees on the wide District
Board road—when they saw Cherag Ali with his dotara, they said,
'Keep walking, fakir, it's market day at Golabari, lots of people there.'
Both of them were encouraged by this reassurance, and when they
saw a crowd of people in the distance after taking a bend in the road,
Cherag Ali all but broke into a run.

There was a handpump outside the primary school in one corner
of the Golabari market. Putting her tin plate down on the ground,
Kulsum cupped one hand under its thick spout while pumping the
handle with the other and had a long drink of water. The damp smell
from the mud was not as strong as usual because of the rain. The
metallic flavour and taste of the water took away Kulsum's appetite.
Meanwhile, Cherag Ali deposited his iron staff, dotara and sling bag
on the large platform of bricks circling the banyan tree to stake his
claim to the spot and returned to the handpump.

There weren't too many people near the tree, for business was
in full swing in the marketplace, and most people were busy buying
or selling. Strumming on his dotara beneath the banyan tree, Cherag
Ali hummed, 'Oh the cotton pillow lies at the head.' As he kept
repeating the same line, Kulsum joined in. She might have been
young, but still she had to draw her homespun towel over her breasts
repeatedly, because the handful of people who had gathered were
paying as much attention to her breasts as they were to Cherag Ali's
songs. Only one man was kneeling on the ground, gaping at the
fakir. Now Cherag Ali began to run through a succession of songs,
strumming in the gaps between them, giving Kulsum time to hold
out her tin plate to the listeners. But whoever she went up to with
the plate either became distracted or slipped away. Only the man
with the thinning hair and beard squatting on the ground didn't

pretend to be busy or walk away furtively, though he didn't put any money on the plate either. All he did was listen open-mouthed to Cherag Ali's songs, taking in the singer's beauty. A boy of about the same age as Kulsum walked up to him, saying, 'Let's go, bajaan. We won't get any fresh chilli seeds if we're late. They're all wilting.' The man didn't seem perturbed at the prospect of the chilli seeds losing their freshness because of the sun. He kept gazing at Cherag Ali. Perhaps to answer his unasked question, or at the sight of a small crowd gathering around him, or to attract a larger audience, Cherag Ali kept singing, alternately opening his mouth wide and pursing his lips, widening his eyes or closing them altogether.

> Your wife sleeps by your side
> The moon is awake in the sky
> Your son weeps in his dream
> The pillow languishes near the head.

He was singing and grimacing at the same time. The dark-skinned young boy standing next to the man gaping at Cherag Ali began to laugh so uncontrollably that everyone turned to look at him.

Cherag Ali continued singing without a change of expression.

> He gave up bodily comforts and sleep was forgotten
> In his blood and his bones the fakir wanted to go
> No one knew his whereabouts once he had left

When he stopped, just strumming his dotara and shaking his head, Kulsum sang the final line by herself, 'Oh the cotton pillow lies at the head.'

Although the singer's fearful grimace did not reflect his tearful voice when parting with the vital information that the fakir's son, the chances of whose being his parents' only child was 100 per cent, was weeping in his dream at the moment the father left the house, everyone except the dark-skinned young boy listened mournfully to the song.

Meanwhile, Obayed Sarkar of Narchitola could be heard speaking on the other side of the banyan tree. For Sarkar, to speak was to make a speech, and he was now announcing that Fazlul Huq had proposed the law, which had been drafted as well and was now only waiting for the governor's signature, that would end the tyranny of jomidars, giving the common people ownership of the land. Fazlul Huq would resign as Prime Minister of Bengal if the governor refused to sign. Obayed's declaration injected belligerence into the people at the market, who used it to listen to the fakir's song. A well-built young man, barefoot and dressed in a clean vest and a dirty dhuti, strolled up a couple of times, listened to the song for a few moments, joined in effortlessly but tunelessly, and then vanished again. Between his visits he scolded the dark-skinned boy, 'What's so funny? Listen to the song.'

The boy explained the reason for his mirth, still laughing, 'Why's the old coot making all those faces?' Cherag Ali continued singing:

The horse came up to the door and bowed
The fakir leapt on its back and disappeared

When it was over, the man in the dirty dhuti and the clean vest said, 'I used to listen to these songs often at the Poradaho fair.'

Still shaking his head though the song had ended, Cherag Ali said, 'So many people from the other side of the Jomuna used to come to the Poradaho fair. Poradaho, Bagbari, Nungola, Jorgachha, and then Chandandaha, Koritala, Royadaha, Kutubpur over on the other side—fakirs used to visit the fairs everywhere. They're the ones who sang these songs. But after the flood the people scattered, who knows where they went. That's why you don't hear these songs any more.'

The young man protested, 'Of course not, fakir. Everyone hereabouts knows these songs. The Poradaho fair is named after Bhabani Pathak, he's the one who started it, didn't you know that?'

When Kulsum walked around with her plate after the singing, the clink of coins being thrown on it was echoed sweetly by the dotara. Kulsum was frightened when she saw the dark-skinned young boy coming towards them again, what if he made a face at his father now? But no, he only leaned towards the man and said, 'Prices seem high at the fair today bajaan. It's market day at Joragachha the day after tomorrow, if we leave right after eating we can come back home before sunset with the chilli seeds.'

But the boy didn't leave his father alone even after securing his approval for this plan. Now he began to hurry him to go home. 'Can't you see it's going to rain, bajaan? Let's go.'

By then another song of Cherag Ali's had rolled on for several lines before returning to the opening one.

My heart was so sick
There was no comfort, nooooo . . .

To keep the final syllable going, Cherag Ali pursed his thin lips and contorted his body so violently that it seemed the last line and his last breath would emerge simultaneously. But soon his unharmed body returned to its original form, and he paused for breath, strumming on his dotara. This time the song was not a success, however. Seeing that the sky was turning cloudy, Cherag Ali gathered his dotara, his iron staff and his sling bag and appealed to the audience, 'My Hindu brothers and my Muslim brothers, nomoshkar to you, salaam alaikum to you. We are wandering fakirs, we make a living from your alms. We eat leftovers, any money you give us won't go waste. Give it to us for the sake of the lord, one paisa for us will bring you seventy paise's worth of good deeds, my brothers.' But the audience didn't seem keen on a seventy-fold increase in its good deeds. While there were clinks of coins being thrown on Kulsum's plate, Cherag kept his ears pricked for a clanging.

When the raindrops grew fatter, Cherag Ali made to set off homewards. But Kulsum began to moan, 'I'm hungry, Dada, I'm hungry.'

Not that Cherag Ali was any less hungry, but, putting the thought away, he urged his granddaughter, 'Keep walking, my love.

We'll have piping hot sweets at the dargah. They said they'd made khichuri today, they've promised us some.'

'No, I want jilapi.' Kulsum kept repeating her demand till the rain came down in torrents. There was commotion everywhere as people ran about, the sold and unsold cattle began to bleat and moo in unison, and the sellers raced for shelter with their goods. But still Kulsum didn't stop, continuing to demand her jilapi. Cherag Ali was furious with her for going on and on about it. The shop where the jilapi was being sold was visible from everywhere in the market. They had been frying the sweets in the open earlier, but now that it was raining they had shifted inside. Still the fragrance and the smoke were in the air. Cherag Ali was enraged with his granddaughter for her clever ways. But he was not one to be angry for long—many of the men mentioned in the verses were heroes who ignored their sleeping wives and their children weeping in their dreams, whose roars on the battlefield made the enemy's knees shake. Yet Cherag Ali's own ability to nurture his rage was quite poor. Never mind anger, his limbs began to quiver if he felt even a strong attack of anger's younger sister irritation, and he often collapsed on the ground. Moreover, his desire for anger was not very deep right now, for he himself wanted some jilapi too. But how could he take the grand decision of having it all by himself? He had just the one granddaughter, an orphaned little girl, she hadn't asked for anything but a little jilapi—with these thoughts he bought six-paises worth of the sweets, disregarding the fact that he was being soaked to the skin. The shopkeeper asked him not to go inside, for the shop was teeming with people. What was Cherag Ali to do now? Kulsum had wrapped her arms around herself, trembling uncontrollably. Suddenly a cry came from a structure with tin walls opposite them. 'Fakir, fakir.' In the torrential rain the call sounded like the clinking of coins to Cherag Ali, while Kulsum's eyes roved in desperation. But the force of the rain made it difficult to identify the person who was hailing them, although it suddenly seemed to Kulsum that it might be the man in the dirty dhuti. She ran off in the direction of the voice, followed by Cherag Ali. Both of them climbed the two steps to the wide veranda, and then walked into the large tin-walled room, with Kulsum sneezing at least a dozen times as she entered. The room was packed with sacks of chilli, stacked next to piles of cumin, ginger and garlic. It was a very familiar smell. Soon after crossing the creek at Madaripara, the roof and yard of every house was to be found covered in red chillies. She could eat a plateful of rice at any of those houses while taking in the scent. But this was such a peculiar place that she couldn't stand the same smell here. She no longer remembered now how she had felt back then, but Kulsum used the chilli godown to transfer her annoyance at having to leave their hut in Kalam majhi's bamboo grove and travel upstream. What had actually happened, though, was that, in order to avoid the sting of the chillies which was invading her brain through her nose, Kulsum was standing on the doorstep, facing outwards, getting soaked in the rain neck downwards, though only a few drops splashed on her face. 'Why are you getting wet in the rain? Come inside.' When the man spoke to her she turned around and identified him—it was indeed the person in the clean vest and dirty dhuti, but the vest was no longer as clean after being exposed to the rain, which was why Kulsum summoned up the courage to go inside and stand shivering in the cold and a little fear.

'Where do you keep disappearing, Boikuntho?' Someone shouted from the corner of the enormous room.

'Nowhere, babu. Where would I go in the rain?'

'It's only been raining a few minutes. But you're never there when there's work to be done. It's so dark in here, why can't you light the lantern?'

'We're out of oil, babu.'

'Take the lantern and get it filled, go.'

'No money, babu,' Boikuntho replied at once.

In the dim light of the single lamp that was lit, a fat man, looking shorter than he was because of his girth, came up to the door before returning to his seat in the corner to open a cash box and count out a few coins. He counted them again before handing them to Boikuntho. Without lowering his voice, he said, 'Pay the five and a half annas we owe the fisherman's shop and then buy some kerosene and a matchbox with the rest.' Then, wrinkling his nose in Cherag Ali's direction, he added, 'We don't give alms at this hour. Leave.' Throwing a sidelong glance at Cherag Ali and Kulsum, who were standing close to the door, he declared regretfully to an unknown person, 'See how it's raining, Gobindo-babu? If they don't have the sense at home to move the chilli I put out to dry on the roof, it'll all go bad.'

As he was leaving with a large lantern, Boikuntho scolded Cherag Ali, 'It's time for evening prayers, you can't stay here now.'

Cherag Ali responded by following him out in the rain towards the grocer's, with Kulsum clutching the tail of his robe, and resuming her whining, 'What about the jilapi, dada, the jilapi?'

It was a mid-sized shop, but with a veranda in front, in one corner of which was placed a sewing machine, with a rush mat next to it. Pointing to the mat with his left hand, Boikuntho told the shopkeeper, 'Will you let the fakir sit here for a bit? He'll sing for you. Babu will throw a fit if a Muslim is in his shop during evening prayers.'

A tall dark man was lighting a lantern in the shop. Instead of agreeing, he said, 'Why should I? We don't let Muslims in here either. You want oil? Wait.'

Paying no attention, Boikuntho asked him, 'How many sacks today?' Without waiting for an answer, he told Cherag Ali, 'You have a wonderful voice. I've heard that song of yours so many times at the Poradaho fair. Sit down there. We'll listen to that song today.'

Boikuntho filled his lantern, while the shopkeeper counted the money Keshto gave him and said, 'There's five and a half annas to be paid from yesterday.'

'Take it tomorrow. Babu said to tell you, I don't have the money to pay you today.'

The shop was brightly lit up now by the lantern. It was stuffed with things. Several sacks of rice sat on a low table, along with two or three sacks of daal, a pitcher of jaggery with bees clustered around it, containers of salt, tins of flattened rice, and large bottles of coconut oil, while tins of kerosene oil lined up on the floor. An intense smell hung in the air like an invisible mosquito net, passing through Kulsum's nose when she inhaled, entering her eyes and mouth and striking her brain like a dull object. In fact, Kulsum didn't even have to breathe it in, for it was so thick that it demolished the sensations of hunger and thirst in her head before entering her belly and bringing them back to life all over again. Cherag Ali could not make up his mind whether to sit on the mat or not—perhaps he was hesitating because he wasn't sure whether Boikuntho's employer's anger had percolated down to this shopkeeper as well. Kulsum held her hand out, saying, 'Where's my jilapi?'

The tall dark shopkeeper stepped into the veranda and said without looking at anyone in particular, 'Give me a hand.' Cherag Ali and he picked up the sewing machine, each holding one end of it, and carried it inside. Two tins of kerosene had already been put behind the wooden bedstead to make room for it. At the shopkeeper's gesture, Cherag sat down in the space vacated on the veranda. The shopkeeper weighed out some flattened rice in a leisurely manner, wrapped it in a banana leaf, held it out to Kulsum and told her to eat. He went back inside and brought some sugar cane jaggery out without weighing it, handing it to Cherag and saying, 'Have it with this.' Then, settling himself comfortably on the bedstead, he said, 'Where do you live?'

Feasting on the flattened rice with jaggery and the jilapi, Cherag Ali took advantage of the shopkeeper's detached curiosity and said, swallowing his food, 'We're victims of the flood, we have no home to live in. I have this granddaughter, her father is dead, her mother has married someone who lives in an island in the Jomuna, this girl travels around with me.'

The man was annoyed. 'So what if there was a flood? If you didn't have a home to begin with what damage could the flood have done? You say you don't have a home, did your mother give birth to you on the riverbank?'

Cherag Ali named his village and had just begun a detailed account of the devastating flood when the shopkeeper spotted someone he knew and said effusively, 'You haven't gone home yet, Tamiz's father? Listen, you have to do something for me.'

It had almost stopped raining. All the people who had been stranded were now leaving, chattering loudly. When the cries of 'is that you, Gedu's father?', 'bajaan, bajaan', 'Raees mamu!', 'Keshto-da, listen' 'Ramesh!', and 'Jetho, it's me,' began to collide with one another in the darkness, Cherag Ali and Kulsum began to wolf down their food as quickly as possible. Tamiz's father climbed up to the veranda, and the shopkeeper seemed rather pleased to see him. 'There you are, I thought you had gone home. I saw Tamiz walking towards the river before it began raining. Why didn't you go as well?' Without waiting to find out the reason, the shopkeeper held out a sack. 'They were slaughtering an ox in front of the school, I took some meat, about 2 seers, take this to my house, tell them to simmer it tonight and cook it tomorrow morning. And tell them I won't be home tonight. Afsar won't be coming, and I can't leave the shop unattended, it might rain again.'

Tamiz's father took the burlap sack and sat down near the mat. The light from the lantern seemed to have coated his dark-skinned face with yellow dust. Kulsum stared at him, yawning. She was feeling sleepy, but still she stared. She didn't know whether she could lie down right here. Her unseeing eyes stared at the man. Tamiz's father's eyes were as drowsy as they had been that afternoon, and his mouth was agape as before. The same question mark was written both in his glance and on his lips. The glow from the lantern seemed to have robbed his eyes and his teeth and tongue of all colour. When he mumbled, 'No more songs?' Kulsum, who was nodding off, was startled. So he knew how to speak?

Before her surprise could turn into fear, the shopkeeper scolded the man, 'Have you gone mad, chacha? The fakir has to go home, doesn't he? Do you know how far he has to travel? Or are you offering him shelter for the night?' The shopkeeper's indulgence of Tamiz's father was evident in his manner of scolding him.

Cherag Ali mellowed his gruff voice as much as possible. 'We don't have a home or anything, baba. You know the Dargah Sharif near the village, our forefathers' forefathers had earned the right to use it, but now people from a different sect have occupied it, they don't let us stay there. They point to my granddaughter and say women are not pure, they cannot be allowed in here. So we have nowhere to stay.' Realizing that the shopkeeper was softening, he continued, 'It's pitch dark and raining, how can I take a boat with a little girl now, baba?'

Suddenly Boikuntho leapt into view from across the road. Standing at the door, he reached out for the pot of jaggery, taking a little on his fingertips and licking them, saying, 'What's a meal without sweets afterwards?' Wiping his fingers clean on his dhuti, he sat down on the mat and began to pluck the strings of the fakir's dotara. Letting go of the instrument in a minute or two, he said, 'You might as well sleep here, fakir. But you must sing for us first.' Then he told the shopkeeper, 'Kalam majhi, majhi kaka, give the fakir some food. Do you expect him to starve with his granddaughter?'

'Why don't you feed him if your heart is bleeding for him, who's stopping you?'

'You belong to the same religion, he will eat with pleasure if you give him some food. Won't be the same thing if I do.'

Without waiting for the shopkeeper's response, he requested Cherag Ali, 'That one, fakir. The pillow lies at the head. How beautiful it is, I've heard it many times.'

But Tamiz's father was silent through these exchanges, gazing at Cherag Ali with the same sleep-laden eyes, eyes that made Kulsum's skin prickle. Did the man sleep with his eyes open? Was he gazing at her grandfather in his sleep? But her own drowsiness prevented Kulsum's fear from escalating. Was the man at the other end of the mat transferring the sleep from his own eyes to hers? When Cherag Ali began to sing, Kalam majhi said, 'What are you waiting for, Tamiz's father, go home now.' But still he wouldn't budge, his eyes fixed on Cherag with such intensity that a sleepy Kulsum felt he was dreaming of her grandfather. What kind of man was this? How could he be dreaming happily in the presence of so many people? Or was

it Kulsum herself who was dreaming? Must be—or how could there
be an iron chain around her grandfather's neck? He had given up
the chain several years ago at the order of the new caretakers at the
Dargah Sharif. And how had he acquired that black turban? But then
if Kulsum was dreaming, how could she clearly hear the shopkeeper
say, 'So you're sitting here listening to songs, Boikuntho? Wait till
Saha catches you.'

Boikuntho couldn't care less. 'No chance, kaka. Babu is going
to lose 20 seers of chilli, he's rushed home, you think he will come
back in this rain?' And the sound of Cherag Ali singing rose above
the conversation, but was that in her dream too?

'Your wife falls asleep soon, in the bamboo grove, a moon.'
Kulsum was bored of listening to Cherag Ali's account of the river
swallowing up hundreds of acres of land, but this did not prevent her
from watching her grandfather shaking his head and Tamiz's father
gazing at him with dreaming eyes.

Suddenly Boikuntho said, 'Weren't you talking of hiring
someone, kaka? I hear Asimuddi majhi is creating trouble over your
bamboo grove. Why don't you let the fakir take care of it? You will
have a guard and you can hear his songs too.' The wind whistling
through the bamboo grove ate up Boikuntho's words, and the same
bamboo grove appeared in front of Kulsum's now-closed eyes, with
a white moon above it. The moon lodged itself on the tallest of the
trees in the grove and shuffled a little. Your wife falls asleep soon, in
the bamboo grove, a moon. Then in the bamboo grove, a moon, it
laid an egg and gave a boon. In her sleep Kulsum began to confuse
the words of a song she had heard and sung many times. She moaned
with the same discomfort that assailed her head when the coins in
her tin plate refused to add up properly no matter how many times
she counted them. But when Cherag Ali, still singing, laid his hand
on her head gently, she sank into the safety of sleep. But still she
saw, perhaps still listening to her grandfather sing, beneath the moon
above the bamboo grove which had laid an egg, a bearded man in a
black turban striding across the yellow-streaked land that looked like

the yolk of the cracked egg, an iron staff in his hand, a chain around his neck. Traversing the bamboo grove, he was now on the edge of a deserted sandbar on which stood a tall, milk-white horse, every part of its body pierced by arrows, with drops of blood like large beads of sweat marking the spots. It began to gallop as soon as the man jumped on its back. Kulsum moaned again. The Jomuna lay ahead, it could be heard flooding its banks, the sound making Cherag Ali's dotara shake uncontrollably. The horse pierced by arrows would fall into the water with its rider any moment now and drown, they would never be found again. When Cherag Ali stroked her head, Kulsum sank deeper into the quicksand of sleep. But who was going to stroke her head right now so that she could fall asleep? Kulsum's dream had now burrowed into the tunnel of Tamiz's father's open mouth. There was no trace of a bamboo grove anywhere, but the sounds of the Jomuna flooding its banks could be heard in his snores. Shivering, Kulsum tore her eyes away from the gap between Tamiz's father's lips, sat up, and put her hand on his brow. The fever was still high. Meanwhile, Kulsum's blood flowed through her veins and arteries, coursing through her palm and tickling Tamiz's father's forehead lightly through her skin. Now she could feel the beat of the verses on his fevered brow. And in his delirium Tamiz's father could hear:

All you Madari fakirs, Majnu roared,
Wrap those turban rounds your heads
Put your chains around your necks
Line your eyes with strips of kohl

26

Tamiz's father opened his eyes at the behest of Cherag Ali's singing of Munshi's verses, brought alive by the pulsing of Kulsum's palm on his brow. But no sooner had his eyes opened than they closed again, and he began to see his boat being rowed along the narrow stream leading out of the Bangali river towards Poradaho. But narrow or not, the stream now had a current that was making the boat laden with a sixty-seer devil catfish and not one but two able-bodied men dance like a whore. As the boat bobbed up and down his slumber deepened, but Tamiz's father was the only one awake, along with the devil catfish caught at the double bend in the river. What a huge fish it was—not less than 70 seers. There were stories that Tamiz's father's grandfather Baghar majhi had once netted a hundred-seer devil catfish. Never mind, let his grandfather's feat be greater than his own. Was this devil catfish the grandson of that one? Or perhaps the grandson's son? In that sense Tamiz's father was certainly related to the fish in some way. He examined its body carefully. Its stripes looked yellowish in the moonlight. Its age was evident in its ashen scales, the fish had one of its eyes fixed on the stars. Whether it was because of its advancing years or kinship, it had accepted the authority of Tamiz's father. Who knew why the fish was so quiet, though? It wasn't as though Tamiz's father was entirely in control of the boat he was rowing—he didn't even realize when they had crossed the banyan tree on the field at Poradaho. The rituals for Bhabani Pathak were in full swing beneath the tree, with pairs of pigeons that had been pledged by boon-seekers piling up at the feet of the idol. Hermits with matted locks who had travelled long distances to gather here were already smoking ganja. Why didn't any of this catch his eye? Why? Budha was sleeping in a corner, wrapped in a sheet, while the devil catfish occupied the rest of the bottom, plotting something which escaped Tamiz's father's attention. The District Board road ran for almost half a mile next to the stream, bullock carts piled with all kinds of fish creaking along it all night, but still Tamiz's father had no idea of any of this. The squeaking and the groaning of the wheels were playing the sounds of one of the fakir's verses, and Tamiz's father, you never knew, may well have joined in tunelessly in his hoarse voice. It was hard to tell whether Budha had heard it, but the devil catfish must have, for there was no other reason for it to have stopped thrashing its tail. Or it could also have been the fish which had transferred the chill of its cold blood to Tamiz's father's body, making him oblivious to the world so that he could keep rowing.

Leaving the field at Poradaho behind on his left and gliding past Shankar's Ghat, Tamiz's father steered his boat into Katlahar Lake. Since the Bangali river joined the lake near its northern head, that was the route Tamiz's father took, and yet the fig tree didn't catch his eye. This was Munshi's doing, of course. All the people of Girirdanga were part of his extended family. Day or night, summer or winter, flood or famine, he had been keeping watch over his family from the fig tree for a very long time. The boat passed through the secret fishing net that Munshi had strung up, and Tamiz's father spotted a flock of grey sheep swimming alongside at the same pace and rhythm. The boat sped across the lake, and only after it had reached Fakir's Ghat did the sheep turn around and swim back on the reverse current. They could no longer be seen, but the waves on the surface of the lake made it clear that they had regained their original form of murrels and would now swim underwater towards the fig tree. By the time the boat reached the southern end the mist hanging over the water had taken on a pinkish hue and the entire lake was shimmering, which meant that Munshi had begun reeling in his invisible fishing net. It was dawn now. Each of the fish in the lake would be frozen in its spot while Munshi drew in his net. Nothing around the lake would move an inch, not the cattle, not the ducks and hens, not the people, not even the blades of grass or leaves. Tamiz's father was thrown into doubt—was he late? How was he to turn the boat back in the direction of Poradaho without showing Munshi the fish he had caught?

The sound of the fazr azaan made him breathe a sigh of relief. It was time for Munshi to fly off from the southern end of the lake to the northern one. Picking up the fish, he laid its enormous head on the bow of the boat for Munshi to see it. As soon as the azaan ended Tamiz's father saw, in the half light and half darkness, Munshi—yes, who else could it be but Munshi—appear beneath the silk-cotton tree in Mondol's yard, close to the lake, asking through its perforated throat, 'Caught a fish?'

Tamiz's father gazed gratefully at Munshi through the pink mist. His beard, turned white by the fire, had blended into the vapours, for what else could the swagger of the pink mist on either side of Munshi's sunken cheeks and beneath his chin be but his beard? The power of his black turban made the mist overhead look a little dark. Rattling the iron chain dangling on his chest, Munshi shouted, 'Who is it that's taking fish from the lake, who?' Tamiz's father's heart quaked at this, but not with fear. Why, then? Was it because he had caught a glimpse of Munshi? Not that either. For Tamiz's father knew that if they were at the right place at the right time with a clear heart and unclouded vision, those who lived in Majhipara in Girirdanga were certain to see Munshi. He was actually trembling because he had been caught in the net that Munshi used to snare all of Katlahar Lake and then release it at his will. Why shouldn't he be furious then? The fish, the water, the residents of Majhipara, were all his family. If one Sharafat Mondol had come from nowhere to lay his claim on the lake now, it was natural for Munshi to be enraged.

It was just yesterday that the fishermen on the Jomuna had paid a rent to Munshi and mopped up all the fish in the lake so that they could sell them at the fair today. The children of the fishermen of Girirdanga had not had a single slice of fish on their plates. Was Munshi supposed to dance with joy at this? All the fish belonged to him—not just the fish in Katlahar Lake, but also the fish in the Jomuna, in the Bangali, in the double bend of the now-dry Manosh, even in the Kartowa, which had dried up in shame and despair when the Company had demanded taxes from Shah Sultan's dargah—all of them were his property, all of them were under his control. Cherag Ali used to say that Munshi's iron pan had fish motifs carved on it. Which meant that this enormous devil catfish was also his by rights. Tamiz's father sighed—what was the use of netting such a huge fish if he couldn't take it to the fair to sell? Munshi had never been kind to him, he was not in Munshi's good books. No, really, say what you like, Munshi was a little too greedy. He had been so benevolent when it came to Cherag Ali, he had been unendingly merciful when it came to the fakir—Tamiz's father knew the reason. Which was?

Just that Cherag Ali had actually flattered Munshi constantly by singing his verses in markets and villages, on the fields and in trains, twanging away on his dotara all the while. Munshi was hungry for praise. Since Tamiz's father could not sing those verses, how was he to shower praises on Munshi? He had wandered around the lake all this time without making an offering to Munshi—no wonder Munshi had not appeared before him. But because Tamiz's father had an enormous fish today, Munshi had appeared of his own accord on the southern side of the lake. Oh well, everyone had to be given their due. Even before he had finished sighing, Tamiz's father returned to Munshi what was his own. He pushed the devil catfish towards the edge of the boat, and then a loud splash was followed by an upheaval in the water, the pink mist taking on a whitish hue, and in an instant the enormous fish dived deep into Katlahar lake with its mossy striped body, beginning to swim towards the north bank. Maybe Munshi would ride the light beams to reach the northern head of the lake before the fish in order to catch him, and then, perching on the fig tree, he would slip into the eye of a vulture and watch the motion of the sun across the sky, or merge into the sunlight to become the sunlight. And when he was tired of this, he would turn into a tiny ball of fur beneath the wing of a pigeon behind the dense foliage of the tree to sleep all day in the warmth of the tender flesh.

But Munshi had not taken wing yet. From the bank of the lake he yelled, 'You, son of a bitch, come here, come ashore at once.'

Munshi's ways were unique, he summoned people to him with invectives. Distraught, Tamiz's father moored his boat and stepped on the mud, and was at once struck by a blow on the head from an iron pan with fish motifs carved on it. Continuing to smash the pan on his head, Munshi said through his perforated throat, 'You bastard, you son of a whore, you swine, you dare steal fish from the lake? You think I don't know that you lurk around here all day? You think I spent all that money and pleaded with the manager to take the lake on lease so that I can feed you all the fish you want, you bastard?'

Tamiz's father's head began to spin from the blows from the iron pan, so that he could not understand most of what Munshi was telling him. But he did notice with his blurring vision that Munshi's turban had slipped off, revealing a cap underneath, and that the chain dangling on his chest was now concealed beneath a warm shawl, while the perforation in his throat was covered by a muffler. Even the iron pan had been transformed into wooden clogs. Munshi had disappeared from view, leaving Sharafat Mondol in his place. Which was why storks from the silk-cotton tree were flying overhead, for Munshi had installed Sharafat Mondol on the bank of the lake and flown off himself towards the fig tree. Sharafat's elder son Abdul Aziz was standing behind him with a torch. Abdul Kader suddenly gripped his father's arm, the one with the wooden clogs. There were probably others there too. Where did Harmatullah spring from? Someone resembling Boikuntho seemed to be standing on the bank. And was that Tamiz next to him?

Tamiz's father could not make sense of any of this. Munshi had appeared here, and Tamiz's father's head was still ringing from the blows he had delivered with the iron pan. Had he gone off to the fig tree afterwards? Tamiz's father could remember nothing. He grew exhausted with this turn of events, his body beginning to shake. He could find no warmth even beneath several layers of quilts. Not just him, everything from the fig tree in the north to the silk-cotton tree in the south covered in white storks shook too. And neither the water nor the land was still.

27

It was very late by the time Tamiz returned from Poradaho. Even at that hour Majhipara was ringing with the conversations of the people going home from the fair. The women, who had fallen asleep, woke up to take the shopping bags from their husbands, while the children went back to sleep and slipped into new dreams amidst the smell of deep-fried jilapi and fritters. Kalam majhi was the only one to enter with Tamiz, peeping into Tamiz's father's room from the door to tell him, 'Come to the mosque tomorrow, chacha. Mondol has beaten you up, we're going to try the case. You've heard, haven't you, that our Tahsen is being promoted to havildar, they'll announce it next month, that's why he couldn't come to the fair. One letter from him and the inspector will personally come from Amtoli to arrest Mondol. Come tomorrow.'

The room plunged into silence when Kalam left. Kulsum didn't even spare a glance for Tamiz. No one but Allah knew how the day had passed with worry over Tamiz's father's fever, and there wasn't any need for anyone to know, either. Tamiz had enjoyed himself at the fair, deigning to return late at night. He had brought packets of food, along with a basket of fish that was rotting already. But Kulsum didn't care for any of this.

But there was no doubt that he was strong. He hoisted his big-boned father single-handedly on the maacha, while Kulsum watched his prowess covertly. And this when he had been away from home

since yesterday, who knew whether he had eaten. He worked like a
dog even without food.

Tamiz filled a pitcher with water from the pond. Putting a bowl
on the floor, he poured water over his father's head, grumbling, 'He's
burning with fever, but has anyone thought to pour even a single
mug of water over him?' Kulsum had no opportunity to fire off an
angry reply, for she had to step up to take the mug from Tamiz when
the water began to soak the bed. This wasn't a man's work. After she
had poured water over Tamiz's father's head for a long time, Kulsum
wiped his head dry and rose to her feet to go towards the inner yard,
when Tamiz handed her a packet of the fritters he had brought. But
Kulsum wasn't going to eat all this at midnight. Throwing them
into a corner of the maacha, she picked up the basket of fish to wash
and slice them in the yard, while Tamiz sat near his father's ribs and
finished the jilapi.

He had a nagging ache in his shoulders, which, far from hurting,
actually gave him a sweet pleasure. He had carried several loads on
these shoulders today. From beds and bedsteads of mango wood and
jackfruit wood to clothes racks, benches, stools and chairs—all of
them heavy. There were many other labourers on hire, but no one
had borne the load that he had, and this had earned him a good
deal of money, which he was going to set aside. Today he had learnt
of other places where he could offer his labour for money. In the
next two months there would be fairs at Bagbari Nishan, at Elangi
over in the south and then of course there was the fair for fakirs at
Royadaga. And west of the Kartowa there would be fairs every week
till the month of Chaitra. If he could get work at some of these,
no bastard could prevent him from making some more money. He
wouldn't contribute a single paisa out of it for the household—
instead, he would buy a pair of cows at the Doshtika market. Each of
the cows would be as good as an ox, and once he got a plough made
at Dasharath's furnace, he would use the oxen to sink the blade 6 feet
deep into the earth. Not just amon, the aush he would grow on an
acre of land would be of the kind that no farmer in this area had even

dreamt of. He would take the land next to their house on a mortgage, the soil was very fertile, as soft as butter, rice would sprout on it like grass after the first two crops. All he needed to get hold of the land was to save some money. And why shouldn't he be able to save enough? He didn't throw his money around like other cultivators, he wasn't going to squander his earnings. Take that bastard Keramat Ali, who used to be a farmer on an island in the river in the east, now he claimed to earn a lot of money from his singing. What earnings? What use was he putting them to? Hadn't he just thrown away a fortune on a prostitute? What use was it to make money if you were going to waste it?

Tamiz was carrying a wooden clothes rack on his shoulders from the Bottola market towards Kathpatti through Maachhati when he ran into Harmatullah. 'Have you seen my son-in-law, Tamiz?'

'Your son-in-law? You mean Keramat? He's at the fair most of the time.'

'Did you see Keramat buying fish?'

'No.' Tamiz had not seen Keramat anywhere near the fish market. But Harmatullah said he had given Keramat four rupees to get a juicy Rui from the Jomuna or some succulent Pabda from Katlahar, so that he didn't have to buy expensive fish himself. But his brilliant son-in-law couldn't care less about any of this. Tamiz had heard from Judhisthir that Keramat had been loitering near the circus, behind the tent on the northern edge of the field where the fair was held. Although it was difficult to stop with the clothes rack on his shoulder, Tamiz deliberately said, 'I heard your son-in-law is over on that side, there, near the fence.' But how was Harmatullah to go there? Pleased by his crestfallen expression, Tamiz continued, 'There, near the tent . . .'

Harmatullah hurried along. He was accompanied by Dasharath Karmakar, who was not particularly happy with his own son-in-law either. He kept no contact with them through the year, and even when Judhisthir's mother, who was dying, had grown desperate to see her daughter the hard-hearted man had not allowed his wife to go home till she had actually died. But now he was here with his entire family three whole days before the fair, even bringing his sister and her husband along. Which meant Judhisthir had to get gifts for all of them, from dhutis to saris, not to mention feeding them fish and fancy sweets two evenings in a row. He had even had to give his son-in-law seven rupees in cash on the day of the fair. Now, Judhisthir had spotted the man in the gambling den. He had not bought any fish or curds, nor was there any likelihood that he would.

Although Dasharath and Harmatullah did not tell each other about their respective sons-in-law's exploits, both of them blamed their own fate. Going into the jilapi shop, they were driven by similar regrets into buying half a seer of jilapi each.

Tamiz's mood worsened when he saw the new bamboo fence beyond the circus tent. Couldn't he visit that part of the fair too? What use was all this hard work if there was no pleasure to be had at the end of it?

Since there wasn't much work to be had after sunset, Tamiz did in fact go over. The door was shut, but it opened as soon as Tamiz pushed at it impatiently. There were about four people inside, and Keramat Ali could be heard singing.

Kusumlata she has three bright spots of red on her pretty nose
A man who hasn't visited her has wasted all his time and life

Tamiz felt a stab of envy when he saw that Keramat was the centre of attraction. No matter where the bastard went, he could make up verses to captivate everyone. But then Tamiz nipped his jealousy in the bud, for it was Keramat Ali after all, whose singing at Abdul Kader's meeting had rejuvenated the audience. When he saw Tamiz, Keramat shouted in welcome, 'Is that you? Come in, come in. Kusum, Kusumrani, we have family visiting us. Give him a seat, give him paan, let him have a smoke.'

Everyone sitting on the sheet spread out on the floor was dressed in a clean dhuti and a shawl. One of them was wearing a black coat, though he had a dhuti on too. Keramat was in a dhuti as well, and looking like a real gentleman. Tamiz was flabbergasted at the sight of a thin young woman with large breasts sitting next to an employee of the jomidar's office in Lathidanga, but no one asked him to sit down. And how could he anyway even if they did? His knees were shaking as he stood there. Keramat Ali was his only hope. The lines in Keramat's songs about the woman's eyes and her lover's passion were like fingertips on his skin, and the aftertaste of betel nut in his head. Tamiz was telling himself that since Keramat Ali was here, since he was the singer, surely Tamiz could sit, if not on the sheet, at least on the floor, when Keramat sang, 'She called me to her, gave me a bitter sweet, a bitter sweet she gave me.'

When the employee of the jomidar's office burst out laughing, so did everyone else, and one of them asked, still laughing, 'How can a sweet be bitter? Really, this poet can sing all kinds of things.' Tamiz tried to laugh too in response to their mirth and one man's appreciation, but he didn't dare. Still, he went forward a few steps. Bowing his head slightly to acknowledge the laughter and praise, Keramat continued singing with twice as much zest.

> Her lover is the son of a fisherman, now who will tell him
> Grasping Kusumrani's twenty-seer breasts is not like going fishing
> Holding her heavy breasts is not like netting a devil catfish

The guffaws of the audience nudged the fingertips of the song off his skin, and it was the song that turned into collective laughter and threw Tamiz out of the room. As he opened the bamboo door to leave, Tamiz could hear the next line of Keramat Ali's song rising above the laughing voices to ask plaintively whether it was fair of the fisherman to have deprived the woman of her payment.

Since then Tamiz's temper was running high while his body was at a low ebb. How dare Keramat Ali humiliate him this way in the presence of a prostitute? He had a strong urge to go directly to

Nijgirirdanga from the fair, drag that bastard Keramat's wife out of her home and lie down with her on the sloping eastern bank of the ox pool. But his body wasn't responding. It was not so much his body as his mind that all but drove Tamiz out of the fair, but it was time to load the furniture again, this time on the boats of the big customers who were done with the pleasures of the fair by now. So Tamiz had to stay on for more work, but it was because he did this that his earnings eventually went up to just three annas short of three rupees.

But not even this windfall could make him happy, for he could not forget how he had been disgraced by Keramat with a whore looking on. Kusum's high breasts added no heat to his desire, the cold made him shiver instead. Why? As he was loading a huge bedstead on a boat, the buyer poured his scorn on Tamiz in a muffled voice. 'Do you know whose room you went into, you son of a bitch? I was there to listen to Keramat sing, that didn't mean you had to go too. Your father should consider himself lucky that you came back alive from Kusum's room.' Tamiz hadn't realized it then, but now he saw that it was Mafiz Sarkar from Jorgachha. The man didn't berate Tamiz any more because he had his son with him, or else he would probably have used his fists to teach Tamiz a lesson.

Tamiz's father suddenly began to feel horribly cold, and his fever came back with a bout of chills that penetrated his sleep, possibly because of which he turned over on his side restlessly and began to moan. Touching his father's brow and his coarse, bearded cheek, Tamiz asked, 'Bajaan, how do you feel, bajaan?'

Speaking for himself, Tamiz had no idea whether he had ever called out to his father with so much concern. It was doubtful whether Tamiz's father could himself recollect another occasion when his son had sounded so anxious. He did not respond to the unfamiliarity in Tamiz's voice. Or maybe he had sunk into a deeper sleep because of his rising fever. Tamiz transferred his palm from his father's face to his body beneath the quilt, soaking up the warmth and allowing it to spread from the fever-ridden frame, through his hands, which were cold with all the water he had dipped them in, all the way to his heart, which had been broken by Mafiz Sarkar's harsh words. Perhaps it was this warmth that obliterated Kulsum and the prostitute's room, along with Keramat's figure. Tamiz lay down next to his father, appropriated most of the quilt, and put his arms around his father to warm himself.

Cocooned in this comfort, he may have actually fallen asleep, when Kulsum called him from the yard to come and eat.

When there was no response even after she had called out several times, Kulsum came into the room, grumbling, and gazed for a long time at the sight of the father and son lying down with their arms around each other. Taking her face close to the quilt, she sniffed deeply. Kulsum alone could tell what she was smelling, and for all anyone knew, her nostrils were singed by the heat from Tamiz's father's body. But her sharp intakes of breath made Tamiz surface from his deep sleep to a lighter one. Dozing, Tamiz heard Kulsum muttering to herself, 'How can they beat him up? Imagine beating up an honest man like him with clogs? Mondol, you old vulture, your arms and legs will fall off, you'll die of leprosy, you vulture, everyone in your village will become a leper.' She made several appeals to unknown and unidentified authorities to ensure that Sharafat Mondol was affected by leprosy. Eventually, deciding that even a permanent disease like leprosy was not sufficient punishment for Mondol, she demanded imminent and unnatural death for him. 'Not even three nights will pass, take my word for it, not even one, the old coot will die tonight. Never mind his lake, never mind his land, his skull will be shattered. Shattered.'

Tamiz began to wake up now, Kulsum's curses ringing in his ears like incantations. Her curses had the power and edge of Keramat's songs. She might be Cherag Ali's granddaughter, but the things she was saying were nothing like Cherag Ali's verses. How could they be, anyway? Fakir Cherag Ali had not written the songs he sang. As for who had written them, whether it was a deity or a devil, a fakir or a hermit, a jinn or an angel, and how they were passed on—these were things that, leave alone other people, Cherag Ali himself did not know. Unlike him, Keramat wrote his own songs. The strength and the mood, the violence and the compassion, the contempt and the respect, the joy and the sadness, in all of those verses were all Keramat's creation. Had he never been told of Mondol's tyranny?

28

'Why don't you speak, Tamiz's father? The gathering is asking, answer them.'

Perturbed at being unable to identify anyone called the gathering, or in search of the question from this unidentified person, or to cast off the shadow of sleep from his eyes, Tamiz's father gazed wide-eyed at the rusted tin roof of the mosque in Majhipara.

Kalam majhi was feeling light-headed after savouring the account of Tamiz's father being beaten up by Sharafat Mondol, which had released him from the rigid devotion with which he had been reading the namaz a few minutes ago. So Tamiz's father's silence did not annoy him. Friday came two days after the Poradaho fair, and it took another week for next Friday. For eight hours each over eight days, Kalam had left Afsar in charge of the shop, abandoning business and visiting all the houses in Majhipara. Moulobi Kuddus had been on the job, and Kalam had had to spend a good deal of money. It wouldn't have been possible to collect such a crowd on Friday otherwise. It wasn't as though fishermen were pious followers of Allah Rasul. But since so many people had been induced to gather here, it wouldn't do for Tamiz's father to be silent for too long. So Kalam had to urge him, 'Come on, speak up. Didn't Sharafat Mondol hit you on the head with wooden clogs? Or did he hit you all over your body, do you remember?'

Tamiz was getting impatient. 'Why don't you say something, bajaan? What are you afraid of? What's the use of being frightened?'

Kuddus echoed Tamiz's belligerence. 'Allah alone can judge you. Why are you afraid when Kalam mian himself is supporting you? Kalam mian is faithful to Allah, he has pledged to put up a permanent mosque. When you have such a pious soul on your side . . .'

Kalam majhi fidgeted. It was true he had mentioned putting up a permanent mosque, but it hadn't exactly been a pledge. 'The tin roof leaks, so I've promised to have it repaired. If Allah gives me strength, I will buy some tin. But why bring all that up now?'

Interpreting Kamal majhi's statement as modesty, Kuddus was even more inspired. 'Now that you have promised to repair a house of Allah, your place in paradise is assured. More and more people will come forward to serve Allah's cause once we broadcast the news of your pledge. Isn't that so?'

Paying no attention to him, Keramat Ali leaned a little closer to Tamiz's father. 'You're an honest and simple man, Chachamian, you don't go in for intrigue, you don't tell lies. Tell us truly what happened.'

Absorbing the current of the Bangali river on the brown roof of tin, or perhaps it was the tears for Bhabani stored in the double bend in the dried-up Manosh, or maybe the image or the sound of slow waves on the surface of Katlahar Lake, Tamiz's father said softly, 'I caught a devil catfish that day. Must have been 50 or 60 seers, maybe more. When I got it into the boat it was so powerful that . . .'

'Get to the point. What did Mondol do to you?' Tamiz's sharp interjection made his father turn towards him, but what he saw on his son's face was not impatience.

At Keramat's gentle prodding he continued, 'My grandfather had caught a devil catfish once. I think it was he who caught this one for me. All the fish belong to Munshi after all, whether it's catfish or carp, large fish or small fry, they're all Munshi's property. I saw the sheep swimming north when it was so dark inside the lake that you couldn't see a thing.'

'We'll hear about the north later.' Kalam majhi prepared to edit the account. 'First tell us the details of what happened in the south.'

Now Tamiz's father sat up straight, looked at the gathered devotees, and said, 'On the southern bank of the lake stands the silk-cotton tree, and he was standing just a few feet away from it on the edge of the water, holding an iron pan with fish motifs carved on it. It may have been in the boat, but the catfish kept thrashing about.' He kept lowering his voice to a point where it became indistinct.

The listeners grew impatient, and one of them shouted, 'Speak up. You speak so softly we can't hear anything.'

But Tamiz's father continued just as softly, mumbling, 'I'd never seen him before, he'd never come down from his fig tree. But now Munshi was standing near the silk-cotton tree. So tall!' He paused for a few moments. 'His beard was absolutely white, it kept flying, it was like he was whipping the sky with his beard. His beard was like a shaft of flame, it set the mist on fire to clear the sky. The silk-cotton tree seemed to be on fire too. He was furious when he saw the devil catfish in my boat. He shouted at me, so you've caught a fish in my lake?'

Only the last eight words were intelligible. Keramat Ali offered his commentary loudly. 'Listen, it was Mondol who was standing by the lake. When he saw Tamiz's father he screamed at him, how dare you take my fish, you bastard, do you think the lake belongs to your father?'

Scanning the attentive faces of the audience, Tamiz's father lowered his eyes. A black mist like burnt earth peeped through the gaps in the rush mat. His throat felt parched in the heat of the flames from Munshi's beard. 'He said, you dare catch my fish?' he rasped. 'Then he hit me on the shoulder with the iron pan, and I threw the devil catfish back into the water. When he hit me with the pan, I could see the motif of the same fish on it. The chain around his neck was rattling.'

Tamiz's father fell silent suddenly, for Cherag Ali's voice was ringing in his ears, 'Iron pan in his hand, a chain around his neck.'

It was doubtful whether anyone else could hear Cherag Ali sing, for Keramat interpreted Tamiz's father's inaudible testimony loudly.

'When Tamiz's father got off his boat, Mondol hit him on the head with his wooden clogs as soon as he set his feet on the mud and said, you bastard, you low-class fisherman swine, you can't live without stealing fish, can you?'

'What, he said that? Mondol said that to you, Tamiz's father?' A middle-aged fisherman jumped to his feet, his agitation dislodging his cap from his head. Several others leapt up as well, shaking with anger, and in the absence of caps, the homespun towels wrapped around their heads flapped furiously, inducing some of them to tie them around their waists instead. For now, they directed the entirety of their rage into constructing sentences like ,'The bastard is nothing but an ordinary farmer, now that he's come into money he thinks he's the king', or 'The swine's father used to walk around naked, couldn't even afford a shirt in winter', or 'The bastards ate nothing but rice all their lives, would they ever have got to taste fish if the fishermen didn't give it to them free?', or, 'The swine didn't even rinse their hands after eating, only wiped them on their loincloths'.

Everyone felt a sense of relief after the poverty, poor manner of living, and disgusting taste of Sharafat Mondol's forefathers had been announced, and many of them returned to their seats. Finally Abiton's father began to speak. 'Shut up, all of you, you were born just the other day, what do you know?' He assured them of their imbecilic ignorance and, doubly sure of his diagnosis, he said that peasants ate rice for their meals during only two months a year, Poush and Maagh, a period when they also ate flattened rice and puffed rice and sweets. And there was something else that they did. 'The farmers invited our forefathers home, fed them sweets, and made them hand over the ownership of their land. If not for this, all the land and trees around Katlahar would still have been ours.'

'And now he's even bribed the manager to take control of the lake,' said Kalam majhi, preparing to take the general anger to its climax. 'It's all very well for the jomidar to lease out the lake if he wants to, but who has the first right to it? One of us fishermen, isn't that so?'

Everyone agreed, but no one was bothered about whom the lease should have gone to. The lake belonged to the fishermen, they were going to fish in it, what was all this about taking a lease?

Everyone spoke at the same time, and though they didn't listen to one another, the decision that emerged from the clamour and commotion was this: Let's go to the bastard Mondol's house, let's get torches and burn the swine's house down today. That bastard Sharafat is planning to add a raised terrace to his house, we saw bullock carts piled high with bricks yesterday, let's go take care of his desire for a terrace once and for all.

Although he was as worked up by the collective anger as everyone else, Kalam majhi also felt frightened of their determination. They were his clan, his race, his blood, Kalam knew them only too well. A volatile set of people, they made a living from killing innocent creatures of the water. There was no telling what they could do. Kalam's first wife's son had got a job with the police, and was posted in Kalna in Bardhaman district. He had been home only once after getting his job, when Kalam had appraised him of the unfair lease on the lake. His son had said that there was no question of bending the government's rules. Under the British, the judge could be swayed but not the law. But then the law had loopholes too, and if you knew them it was very easy to disregard the law. But what did these fishermen know of the law, leave alone understanding the loopholes? If they descended on Mondol's home and set it on fire, who knew what section of the law Kalam's son might invoke against them? Who was going to handle it then? And given Abdul Kader's influence, he could persuade the leaders in the town to do anything at all in retaliation. Softening his strident tone, Kalam majhi pleaded, 'Wait a couple of days. Let me send a telegram to Tahsen, he'll be here within three days of receiving it. He works for the police, taking his advice before doing anything will ensure we don't get into trouble.'

'Bhaijaan will come with the force if necessary.' But Kalam did not support this confident claim of Afsar's. A constable couldn't exactly summon the entire force at will. Kalam was in some distress now, wondering how to stop the crowd from acting out its plans.

Suddenly Keramat Ali jumped to his feet, his lips quivering. He had written a song after hearing Kamal majhi's stories about Mondol's tyranny over the fishermen during the past eight days. The poem was in his pocket, but he would prefer not to have referred to it, even though he couldn't remember a single word right now. So he had to rely on a prosaic version. 'Listen, let me tell you something.' When the listeners quietened down, he said, 'Listen. The aadhiars till the jotedar's land, right? They put their blood and sweat into their work and get half the crop. Now they want two-thirds instead, and they're fighting the jotedar for their rights. The aadhiars are not afraid. In Khiyar over to the west . . .'

'We know all this. Never mind about all these stories of yours.'

When Afsar jumped up to cut him off, Kalam vented his annoyance on his nephew. 'Why can't you listen to what Keramat has to say?' Clapping Keramat on his back, Kalam reassured him and sought a way to dispel his own fear as well. 'Go on, tell them. You have a sensible head on your shoulders. Tell them that burning a man's house down is a sin. Explain properly.'

Kalam majhi's patronage lent Keramat courage, and the poem he had written about the fishermen began to fall into place in his distracted mind. But because he still could not recollect all the words, or perhaps out of modesty or even hesitation, he stuck to plain prose. 'You know everything, but you don't learn anything. What's the use of knowing without learning? What is the value of such knowledge? In Joipur I saw how Burman's mother did not lose heart even after she was shot by the police. The peasants fired arrows from their bows on her order. And here in Girirdanga village I see people from another caste occupying the lake owned by fishermen over many generations, and all the fishermen can do is tear out their own pubic hair.'

Keramat Ali kept speaking, and the fishermen in the mosque all stood upright. Even Tamiz's father rose to his feet and looked out through the open door, his eyes searching for the northern head of

Katlahar Lake. The rusted tin roof of the mosque rose a yard or so in the air, and a bell began to ring loudly. But even the pealing of the bell was drowned by Tamiz's scream. 'Why? Why should we sit here tearing out our pubic hair? Let's go, let's all go. Bring all your fishing nets from home. On to Katlahar!'

29

When the fishermen lined up raggedly on the western side of Katlahar Lake to cast their nets, the upheaval stretched from Fakir's Ghat near Kalam majhi's house all the way to the ghat near Bulu majhi's house in the south. Most of the fishermen had modest-sized nets attached to triangular bamboo frames, which could be used to catch small fry at best, but the flourish with which they were handling them made it appear that they wouldn't settle for anything less than giant fish. As for those who had larger nets, their behaviour suggested that not even crocodiles were safe today. Some had even brought two or three pieces of the nets used for fencing—they couldn't be cast into the water, but the gaps were so fine that they patched them together in the hope that no fish would be able to escape them. Some had brought baskets, while small boys had turned up with fishing hooks, casting them into the water at the end of fishing rods without any bait, and being forced to shift constantly because of the uproar, which killed any possibility of their catching any fish.

The afternoon hours remained suspended between the trees on both banks amidst the tumult. Tamiz's father trudged northwards with the net for catching carp that his son had given him. What use would such a net be in winter? Tamiz really had turned into a peasant, he had even forgotten how to match the net to the season. Who knew who had given him this net that he had dumped on his father!

The water was a little deeper in the southern half of the lake, but in the north it was very shallow, except where the thin stream from the Bangali river flowed in. Fresh land had begun to appear here, some parts of which Mondol's hired hands had already ploughed for the first time and planted kaun paddy on.

But then Tamiz's father was not interested in what lay below his feet. Shading his eyes with his palm, he searched for the topmost branch of the fig tree at the northern head of the lake. Although the tree wasn't visible from here, the tinkling of the chain hanging around the neck of its only inhabitant could be heard, giving audible form to Cherag Ali's voice:

Munshi's voice is like the breath of gunpowder.
Their hearts quake, those who live in this world.

Tamiz's father went forward, ignoring the fire-breather's hot exhalation on his skin. A group of fishermen followed his example and began to walk northwards, if not exactly trailing behind him. There were far fewer people on the northern side of the lake, which should mean greater chances of catching fish there.

But moulobi Kuddus remained on the southern side, near the ghat next to Bulu's house, which delayed the azaan in the mosque in Majhipara. He had been getting late every day of later. Kuddus's beard was beginning to look more pointed in the pink sunshine, but because the hour for the asr namaz was almost past, he lost some of his poise and told Keramat, who was standing nearby, 'The fishermen have risen to your call, now let's hope Mondol doesn't have the whole lot arrested. He belongs to the Rafadani jamaat, this is one chance he has.'

The storks from the silk-cotton tree in Mondol's yard beat their wings slowly over the lake, faint shadows dripping from them, which they used to guide the dusk towards the water of the lake. Taking advantage of Keramat's wide open eyes, the shadow of the winter evening slipped into his head, the beating of the storks' wings raising waves of darkness in his brain and making his shaggy mop of curly hair stand up straight. If he was indeed the one who had instigated the fishermen to plunge into the water of the lake, he wouldn't be spared in case they were arrested. In fact, they would nab him first. His name was already in the police records, and even if the police were not on his tail now because he had moved away from the trouble in Joipur, Panchbibi, and Akkelpur, they could well get after him again, using this uprising as a pretext. What should he do then? Should he steal away around the southern end of the lake to his in-laws' house in Nijgirirdanga? But the commotion of the fishermen in the north forced his feet in that direction. Their frenzy gave him fresh energy—it was his simple speech that had drawn the fishermen to the lake. But then why were they ignoring him now? None of them was nearby, even Kuddus had gone off for the azaan. Was it Tamiz's father who was leading them to the north? Perhaps they considered him their leader. Had he got the position by dint of having spent some years in Cherag Ali's company and marrying his granddaughter? Or perhaps it was the blow from Mondol's wooden clogs that had become the crown on Tamiz's father's head. Had the iron pan with fish motifs that he spoke of landed on his head in the form of the clogs, or was it the clogs that had changed their shape to become the iron pan when it hit his head? Although Keramat had found in the crown a metaphor for the beating that Tamiz's father had taken, he couldn't fit it into his verses. Now that he had been by himself for a while, he could recall every word of the song he had written about the fishermen, but he was finding it impossible to fit in the metaphor about the crown. Meanwhile, the horde of fishermen kept receding in the distance, looking indistinct in the faint darkness and the light mist. Suddenly fearful, Keramat lengthened his strides.

Those of the fishermen who had captured nothing but small fry were being forced to listen to the young boys' jeering rhymes about the lack of nobility in the lineage of their catch. The fishermen from the Jomuna had paid a rent to Mondol on the day before the fair and emptied the lake of big fish. Meanwhile, the water level had

gone down, and even the middle was not very deep any more. Small
fry were in abundance. The stomping of the fishermen wading into
the water turned it into mud, which looked murkier in the shadows
dripping off the wings of the storks. Who knew, maybe it was at a
signal from these shadows that the evening glided in on the mist.
Although the entire lake looked unfamiliar in the ghostly light of the
waning moon, or perhaps it was because it looked unfamiliar, the
fishermen's urgency grew a hundredfold. They swooped with their
baskets on the shadows cast by the storks' wings, confusing them
for schools of fish. The storks felt their wings being tickled by the
pressure against the shadows, and slipped away. 'You sons of bitches,
you fucking bastards, you think you can escape us? You can sit on that
fucking Mondol's lap and lick his arse but you won't allow yourself to
be caught by us?' Such harsh words forced the fish of Katlahar Lake to
renew their familial ties with the fishermen of Girirdanga, and some
of the smaller fish leapt into the fishing nets held out for them.

Moulobi Kuddus was back after giving the call for the maghreb
prayers and leading three or four aged devotees in prayers. Walking
alongside Keramat, he informed the fishermen, 'Apparently Mondol
and his son are on their way here with a group of people. You'd
better leave now. Take whatever fish you've got and go home.'

Far from abandoning the lake, someone shouted back at the
moulobi, 'Give us your blessing, *huzoor*, give us your blessings. Let
Mondol bring his father too. Does he think he owns the lake, or
does he think it belongs to his father?' Encouraged by such bravery,
someone else resolved, 'Let the bastards come. We'll stick these
baskets up their arses.'

Their gradual shift to the north had brought the group quite
close to Tamiz's father by now. It might have been in response to
a signal from the north, no one knew for sure, but Tamiz's father
summoned them hoarsely, 'This way, all of you.'

Not that anyone heard him, but Budha shouted out to him, 'I'm
sure the devil catfish you caught the other day is right here, nana, the
water seems pretty deep.

Although Tamiz's father didn't reply, Tamiz prepared to cast his net, assuring everyone, 'Mondol's holed up in his home, he's not going anywhere tonight.'

None of this commotion was audible to Tamiz's father, who could hear Munshi's own voice emerging through his perforated throat from the fig tree:

Majnu shouts, now listen, my friends.
They've banned the Urs at the Darga Sharif.
The Christian Company is arrogant and sinful.
And the devils even dare to tax the shrine.

Presumably no one else could hear Munshi sing, for Abiton's father told Keramat, 'If you could perform at the Golabari market on Mondol's son Kader's request, why can't you sing a few verses now?'

Keramat was watching the lines on Tamiz's father's face rippling in the faint light from a ghostly moon. Keramat began to belt out the song he had written a couple of days ago just to ensure that the old coot didn't start singing all those secret songs of Munshi's again:

Mondol occupied the fishermen's Katlahar.
The destitute fishermen lamented their loss.

'We've found our poet,' screamed the fishermen in joy. 'Go on, keep singing.' But Tamiz didn't approve of all the words in the song. 'Who are you calling destitute? We'll make Mondol destitute.'

Keramat could now recollect all his verses without having to consult his notebook. The swishing of the fishermen's nets and their cheers and Tamiz's protest added a new vigour to his voice:

Mondol strikes the aged fisherman on his head.
And in the sky the moon sets at once.
But the sun does not rise in Girirdanga.
In the lake the lotus does not bloom.

Tamiz's father was a little surprised at this altered reverberation of Munshi's song. How could a mediocre poet-singer like Keramat be echoing Munshi? No sooner had Keramat ended than the voice from the fig tree informed everyone:

> Sultan Hujoor lies in his glorious grave.
> All the world knows him as Mahisawar.
> The Christian Company disrespects him.
> In shame and rage the Kartowa dries up.

Because Munshi's voice had gone lower by the time it emanated from Keramat's throat, Tamiz's father could not tell whether it was expressing satisfaction or anger. Keramat sang without any instruments:

> A lake without fishermen and water without fish.
> Are a mother without child or tree without flowers.
> If a woman doesn't get a kiss from a man.
> Even the best jewellery will not bring her sleep.

'What wonderful lines!' the fishermen shouted in elation. Some of them sang the last two lines themselves, getting the lyrics wrong. 'Can you come this way, bajaan?' yelled Tamiz. 'Help me cast the net. I'll have your devil catfish back in your arms.' Considering Munshi had taken back the fish himself, Tamiz's father was not pleased by his son's greed. On the contrary, he considered it audacious, and felt apprehensive.

Certainly on account of their long familial relationship with fishermen, not to mention the attractions of Keramat's song, and it could even be because of the warmth of Munshi's verses as heard by Tamiz's father, the medium, small and tiny fish began to leap out of the water, first into the nets and then out again to frolic on land, playing hide and seek and leapfrog at the same time. As soon as the little fish vaulted out to the bank, the little boys began to run after them. Watching the scene, Tamiz's father could hear Munshi sing:

Madaris go to battle with their swords.
The Company's soldiers die in droves.
The British Taylor picks up his own gun.
The sight of the Madaris makes him quake.

Once again Munshi's song found an echo in Keramat's voice. Listening, Tamiz's father reflected, just see how all those songs handed down the generations are being distorted by this useless man:

If the lake doesn't get the fisherman's touch.
Its water dries up, its currents recede.
Keramat says, listen to me closely.
Katlahar weeps, says, come, fishermen.

Suddenly Tamiz's father yelled at the fishermen's children, 'Don't go there, don't go there.' But none of them could hear his low voice. What was the matter, though? An adolescent carp had been flung from someone's net, at least a couple of seers in weight. The naughty fish had buried its nose in the sand on a patch of land newly risen from the lake where it curved.

The children were running towards it, chased by moulobi Kuddus who kept shouting out warnings, 'Don't go there, you'll drown in the quicksand.' But no one was listening. Disobeying Kuddus, Abiton's father's grandson, that is to say, Bulu's son, the stupidest of them all, shoved the others out of the way and leapt to grasp the fish by its tail. But the baby fish sucked not just its own tail but also Bulu's son's arm into the sand. The boy, who was on his knees when he made his final grab, sank up to his waist. Still he refused to let go of the fish. 'The boy's going to die, can't any of you see?' shouted moulobi Kuddus, racing through the mud. Watching, Tamiz's father could hear the verses from the fig tree once again:

Majnu shouts out to Bhabani Thakur.
Catch the British and hang them all.
The clan of Giris pick up their swords.
And dispatch the British to their graves.

About to descend from the high bank to rescue Bulu's son, Tamiz's
father stopped so that he wouldn't lose the strain of Munshi's
song. And then he stopped again on hearing the distorted echo in
Keramat's voice:

Cast your nets, says Keramat to fishermen.
Catch all the fish, let Mondol burn.

No one had any time for Keramat now, for everyone was running
towards the patch of quicksand that had appeared next to the lake.
Someone from the crowd tossed a net towards Bulu's son's head—it
was the same net that Tamiz's father had brought. The boy's head
caught in it. 'Afaz, don't be frightened, my boy,' everyone told him.
'Keep swimming in the sand, keep swimming. Keep your head in the
air.' But when they began to draw the net in, it didn't come back,
tearing under the pressure of the quicksand or perhaps because the
devil catfish lying in ambush in the quicksand was biting the threads
off.

'Stop, don't pull on the net any more,' yelled Tamiz, making a
lasso with the rope at the end of his own net and then flinging the
net towards the boy. Afaz's head was caught in it too. Perhaps Afaz
had died already in the sand, or perhaps it was this noose that killed
him. His body was dragged out of the quicksand somehow on to
solid land.

Abiton's father's wailing made all the other sounds of Katlahar
pause, and the lake clumsily gathered around Afaz's corpse, complete
with both its banks.

Abiton had not been allowed anywhere near her father's
house after marrying Gofur kolu. Even the fishermen maintained

a distance. Abiton had no chance of meeting her son from her first husband. No one in the neighbourhood allowed her, and Gofur kolu couldn't even stand the boy. Afaz had got work with the Mondols, which was why he had to spend all his time there. Whenever she cooked something special, Abiton's mother would call Afaz over to feed it to him, while also looking for an opportunity to engineer a secret meeting with Abiton. But, what else could it be but fate, Afaz had gone on his own today to meet his grandmother, probably for a meal which he hadn't been able to eat because of the commotion all around. So instead of returning to Mondol's house to resume his work, he had followed his grandfather to Katlahar Lake, even carrying Abiton's father's net. Recounting the events in fragments, Abiton lost the thread and began to weep.

Stacking the fish near the prows of their respective boats at the edge of the lake, several yards south of the quicksand, everyone gathered around the corpse. Afaz's death became a palpable reality when moulobi Kuddus sent someone to fetch a cot and began to recite the prayer for the dead. Some of the people present began to sob, and Abiton's father broke down in tears. But the desultory patterns of the ayat from the Quran and the unrestrained weeping broke down when a rumble was heard in a gruff, coarse voice, 'You dare steal my fish? You swine are here to kill my fish?'

Tamiz's father glanced at the northern head of the lake. Wasn't it Munshi himself who had instigated everyone with his verses and with their stuttering echoes to launch an assault on the lake? And now here he was to punish them too. What kind of behaviour was this? At this moment the waning moon scraped the murky glow off its own body to focus a white beam on the fishermen. And riding on that beam came an echo to the question, 'Who's allowed you bastards to fish in the lake?' Tamiz's father looked alternately towards the water and the land. In his head writhed a sexually aroused virgin, while his body trembled with the desire and the fear of being hit with Munshi's iron pan with fish motifs.

The first person whose face was lit up by the three-cell torch was Tamiz. 'Tamiz? Is that you?' exclaimed Abdul Kader with all the astonishment at his disposal.

'Fucking traitor, you fucking bastard traitor, it was his fucking father the other day. Wasn't he supposed to be a fakir? He's no fakir. The bastard has been stealing my fish for a long time now. Seven days from last Wednesday, and then a Thursday and a Friday, it hasn't even been nine days since I caught the swine stealing a devil catfish. And he's here again today with his entire tribe.' Now Sharafat Mondol shifted his attention from the father to the son. 'You son of a bitch, is this what I let you sharecrop on my land for? You weren't satisfied stealing my crop, now you want fish from my lake to eat with the rice made with grain from my land.'

Abdul Aziz arrived, and immediately busied himself with Afaz's death. Those who had been to the mosque to collect the cot had informed Aziz of the incident. Aziz made fresh inquiries and issued a grim announcement. 'It's a case of murder.'

Gofur kolu had never been fond of his wife's son with her first husband, but now his love for the boy welled up at the sight of his father-in-law. 'You made the boy suffer terribly, you didn't even let him meet his mother. And now you've taken your anger out on your daughter by drowning her son in the quicksand. You call yourselves human beings? You'll find out the joy of choking to death on the gallows.'

Sharafat was annoyed that the theft of the fish was losing significance. He ordered his men, 'Harmatullah, Kolu's father, Gofur—tie them all up. They'll be sent to the police station in the morning.'

However, the fishermen weren't frightened by the prospect of the police, for wasn't Kalam majhi's son a policeman himself? Who would dare touch them at the police station? But when they looked around, Kalam majhi was nowhere to be seen. Someone asked Budha, 'Where's your mamu, Budha?'

'Mamu didn't come, he went off somewhere with Afsar.' Some were reassured by Budha's response. Kalam must have gone to send a telegram his son, which meant that Tahsen would arrive with a police force before dawn.

But moulobi Kuddus said, 'Kalam mian has gone to Sabgram. It's market day there.' That was when everyone recalled that neither Kalam nor his nephew had accompanied them when they left the mosque.

A confident Tamiz said, 'What's all the fuss about? Katlahar belongs to the fishermen. Why shouldn't they catch fish here?'

This enraged Mondol so much that his orders emerged as an incoherent mess. 'What did I tell you, Harmatullah? Tie him up, tie up the swine.'

Taking a step forward to comply with Sharafat's orders, Harmatullah began to tremble, so much so that he found it difficult to keep his feet planted on the ground. Seeing the state he was in, Hamid Sakidar tried to pin Tamiz down without a rope. 'Stop,' said Abdul Kader, and then lowered his voice to address Tamiz. 'What have you done? If the fishermen have a problem all you have to do is to take it to the League office in Golabari and have it resolved. But now you're accused of stealing fish, and then there'll be a murder case against you too. What do you think you're doing just before the elections?'

Sharafat ran out of patience again at this theatrical dialogue. 'Don't complicate matters, Kader. The boy died because of his father's fault. He will have to answer for it. Forget all this love talk. They've stolen fish from my lake, it's up to me what to do with them. For now tie them all up, they'll be dispatched to the police station tomorrow.'

Even Aziz was irked because Kader kept up his conversation with Tamiz in a low voice. He had had an inkling yesterday of what the fishermen were up to when he was bringing a load of bricks home in a bullock cart. He had been busy all day today having his son's grave paved by workmen. He had saved on bricks and cement only because he had supervised the work himself. It had taken him some time to put things in order before getting here. Being a government employee, he wasn't one to say anything before understanding the ramifications and ensuring that the law was being followed. Now he had come to a conclusion from his investigation. 'This bastard Tamiz is the root of all trouble. He can be accused of several crimes. The murder alone will ensure he is hanged. Anyway, there's no need to take the law into our own hands. For now the swine must not escape.'

Abdul Kader professed surprise on spotting Keramat Ali. 'What a traitor you are! Didn't I give you a chance to sing the other day in the presence of all those leaders at the meeting? And now you're instigating the fishermen. Are you a professional troublemaker?'

'Take the body away, be quick,' instructed moulobi Kuddus fearfully.

Gofur kolu wanted justice for Afaz's death on his wife's behalf. 'We must file a general diary against Tamiz's father, Tamiz, Budha, Abiton's father, Kalam majhi, all of them, at the police station. Everyone here will be counted among the accused.'

Abdul Kader wanted to postpone the involvement of the police. The fishermen accounted for no small number of votes. 'Take the body home for now, Gofur. Aren't you going to give your wife a chance to see her son?'

But the fishermen might create trouble if the corpse were taken to an oil grinder's home. So Sharafat Mondol ordered, 'No, let Abiton's father take the body.' Finally he expressed his grief for Afaz's death. 'Poor boy, he was always to be seen here. There'll be no more scolding for him tomorrow for not feeding the cattle.' Wiping his eyes on the end of his shawl, Sharafat said ruefully, his voice salty, 'This innocent boy had to pay with his life to Allah for all the endless sins you people have committed. You've seen for yourself how quickly Allah's justice strikes. He has done his job, now the judge will do his.'

Abdul Kader drew Keramat aside. 'Isn't there a police warrant against you? I know everything. I asked for a song about Pakistan, but you didn't write it. You can eat your meals in jail now.'

When Keramat continued to look grim, Kader relented a little. 'Come over tomorrow, let's see what Ismail bhai has to say.'

Once the fishermen set off with the soaked and mud-stained body, moulobi Kuddus's non-stop recital of the kalima shahdat wiped out everything but the unnatural death from the minds of those present.

The water settled down at last, and the mist took the opportunity to lie down on it, holding the lake in an intimate embrace. When Munshi's pet jackals howled their farewells to the fishermen on his behalf, on behalf of the lake, and on their own behalf, the sounds struck the departing fishermen on their buttocks. Finally they began to feel the cold. Their nets were wet, their clothes were wet, and the corpse on the cot was wet too. As the procession with the dead body advanced, the tight grip of the jackals' farewell over them began to be loosened. Soaked by the mist copulating with—or rather, raping—the lake, frozen by the chill, and melting in their tears, the howling of the jackals turned into ceaseless lamentation. This made sleep descend like lowering clouds on Tamiz's father's eyes. The dark-red glow from the lamps in Majhipara faded into the smoke from kitchens or from hay stacked in yards. But the continuous howling of the jackals did not die down, merging instead with the wails emanating from Abiton's mother's house. The unbroken sounds and the spreading half-light made Tamiz's father's sleep even deeper. In his sleep he continued to walk, sometimes in front of the corpse, sometimes behind it. No one paid any attention to his lurching gait. The low farewells from the creatures of Katlahar suddenly exploded into Abiton's mother's shrieks of grief. Not even this could induce a crack in Tamiz's father's sleep. Instead, even without his attempting to capture a fish that had vaulted on to the land, his feet began to sink in the quicksand. But instead of going in deeper, they continued to move forward. There were no questions or complaints in Tamiz's father's footsteps, which only rang in silence with an indistinct resentment: How could Munshi have drawn the fishermen to himself, both inciting and exciting them, only to snatch the little boy away? What kind of sympathy was this? Was Munshi's heart made of stone? Tamiz's father's tears pooled in his eyes with bewilderment and rage, filling them with briny water. But because both his eyes were closed, his tears did not roll down his face. The heat generated beneath the closed eyelids thickened the briny water into a thin gruel of mucus which would emerge as solidified rheum in the morning.

30

'So the red turbans didn't arrest you after all? Seems you read out some verses or incantations or something at the mosque in Majhipara that made all of them run to Katlahar Lake with their nets. Seems you read the namaz too at the mosque there. Shame, shame on you!' In reading the namaz with a gathering of fishermen, Keramat Ali had apparently lowered not just his father-in-law's but also his father-in-law's daughter's prestige. The crime of causing this humiliation, besides the fact that it was at Keramat Ali's instigation that the fishermen had decided to occupy Katlahar Lake, had perturbed Phuljaan deeply. Because Tamiz, provoked by Keramat Ali's stirring verses, was now in jail, she glared at Keramat, even if it was only out of the corner of her eye, a glare that was difficult to distinguish from the look she gave him because he had read the namaz along with a gathering of fishermen.

But Phuljaan's frighteningly stern glances melted when her son suddenly cried out on his bed inside the room, and to dissolve it further she took the child into her lap and slapped him twice. Weakened by his illness, the boy could only gasp for breath instead of crying louder, and he began to hiccup.

'What are you hitting him for? How dare you hit my son, you bitch?' Ending several days of passivity, Keramat Ali tugged hard at his wife's hair and delivered several blows on her back. The resultant rocking gave the child new strength to cry, while Nobiton yelled from the kitchen, 'Ma, he's hitting bubu, he's hitting her.'

No one responded to Nobiton's appeal. Her younger sister was gathering pumpkin leaves from the kitchen garden and her mother was busy instructing her daughter. As for Harmatullah, he had gone to work on his land at the crack of dawn.

Holding her son close to her breast, Phuljaan wept, sneering, 'So now your heart is bleeding for your son. Did you ever think of his illness when travelling the world? Have you ever got him even a grain of medicine? Ever brought him any charmed water? The son of the fisherman wanted to take my son to the doctor, and all you did was to first incite him and then have him arrested. Now he's serving time in jail and you're downing three meals a day. Aren't you ashamed of yourself? To hell with such men.'

Ever since the red turbans had arrested Tamiz, he had become a hero for the people on both sides of the lake, which had become a source of heartburn for Keramat. He was smarting now at Phuljaan's barb. But then he had a chance now to attack her too. 'The son of the fisherman is your lover, isn't he, you whore? Your goitre is itching for the smell of fish on his body. They say I have broken the rules by reading the namaz with fishermen, but there's nothing wrong with going to sleep with the fisherman's tongue buried inside your goitre, is there? You think I don't know anything, you bitch?'

Phuljaan's goitre had been subsiding slowly, but now it began to swell again, to a point where it came into contact with her son's disproportionately large head, and quivered in the heat from his fevered body. There would probably be no opportunity to take the boy to Proshanto the compounder any more. Phuljaan sobbed twice as piteously when Nobiton took her child away forcefully from her. Unknowingly, or perhaps knowingly, she made marvellous use of the chance to express her grief for Tamiz. Keramat squirmed, sensing a conspiracy brewing against him in the silence of Phuljaan's mother and two sisters in the yard and in his son's gasps and tears. He had never suffered from this particular disease before. He had been so full of vitality when singing his verses amongst the peasants of the tebhaga movement—why had he left suddenly? But then things had gone well enough here at first. He hadn't felt lethargic when he had got involved with the fishermen, but the trouble started once he began to visit his in-laws. It would have been better if Sharafat had not saved him from the police because of Harmatullah's request and Kader's kindness. A poem about the bravery of the fishermen had begun to form in his head—in fact, some of the lines had been composed already. But it was nipped in the bud by Phuljaan's account of Tamiz's audacity and arrogance. Why should he stay here any more?

'Fakir, is that you?' Calling out to Keramat from the back, Boikuntho corrected himself at once. 'How silly, I went and called you fakir again. But where have you been? Alim the schoolteacher said the other day you're writing a song about Tamiz. Is it done?'

It was these very people who had ruined his songwriting, they could talk of nothing or nobody else but Tamiz. Judhisthir joined them a little later. This bastard was no better, he had some news to give them too. Which was? That the blacksmiths were also furious with Sharafat Mondol. No one who had made someone like Tamiz go to jail could come to any good. Not only had Tamiz been cheated of his fair share of the harvest on Mondol's land, but Judhisthir also had got far less than he should have. In the west the sharecroppers got two-thirds of the harvest, but Mondol had parted with less than half of his. The old coot had kept most of the grains on the basis of some spurious calculation or the other. Would he dare do this if everyone got together like they had over in Khiyar?

Keramat frowned. 'It's different there. The farmers are united and fight collectively. They're supported by educated people. And here the fishermen steal fish. Do you expect the police to kiss thieves instead of arresting them?'

This should have silenced them. But perhaps because they couldn't accept that Keramat Ali could think this way, or perhaps it was because of the vehemence with which Boikuntho responded, this observation elicited no reaction. Boikuntho said, 'Tamiz's father is a fakir. Mondol hurt him. If Cherag Ali had been alive it would have taken just one verse from him to make Mondol's entire family shit in their clothes. Oh, that fakir could sing. He still can, actually; his songs are still powerful.'

How could a mere song achieve such results? Keramat said, 'You keep talking of Cherag Ali. All right, he was a good man, I'll grant you that. But how can you say his songs were about fishermen? How would Cherag Ali have known about the farmers of Khiyar for that matter? He didn't write the songs himself.'

He stomped off, leaving them behind. He was sick and tired of hearing about Cherag Ali's songs. When the police sided with the jotedars and attacked the farmers, no one paid any attention to those airy verses of Cherag Ali's. Burman's mother had kept fighting even after she was shot by the police, only because of Keramat's song. From tillers to people like Nasir Mondol or Chitto-babu or Purno Bose or Sunil-da, all of them used to listen to Keramat singing. Why, even an eminent personality like Haji Danesh was supposed to have told Chitto-babu, don't let go of that Keramat, we need him. When the police began to arrest people indiscriminately Chitto-babu had sent word that Keramat should go away for some time. Let him go eastwards and sing his verses there, they would prove useful. But then the people here were all crazy about the songs of Majnu or Munshi or some jinn and of Bhabani Thakur or his ghost. Some sort of secret songs had apparently been passed on to Cherag Ali—no one cared for anything else. What songs could Keramat Ali possibly sing for them?

Since it wasn't market day, the earthen mounds with thatched roofs overhead were unoccupied. But Mukunda Saha and Kalam majhi had opened their shops. As for Kader's shop, it was now a full-fledged election office. Posters with Ismail Husain's name written in large letters were stuck diagonally on the tin walls of the shop. Several student workers were gathered near the door, collecting their megaphones, posters and bidis while Kader talked to them. He went up quickly to Keramat when he saw him, drawing him aside to say, 'Didn't I ask you not to leave home for a few days?' It was difficult to tell whether his suppressed excitement concealed anxiety or pleasure. 'The manager has added your name to the people accused of theft at the lake. I can't tell what my father is planning. We're making arrangements to have Ismail bhai ask the police to remove your name. Why don't you stay with your in-laws for some time now?' When Keramat was silent Kader continued, 'You seem eager to go to jail.'

Keramat certainly had no desire to be in jail. He might have been arrested if he hadn't slipped away from Joipur. The police had detained all the leaders, whether they were gentlemen or not, and given them a beating. Not even the women had been spared. It was this news that had broken Keramat's back. He no longer had the courage to go on, which made his head spin, and when that happened he could no longer compose lines. These weren't like Cherag Ali's songs where all you had to do was strum the dotara and sing the lines that came down from the skies on the rhythm of the strings. No, if Keramat went to jail his songwriting would end forever.

'Now that you're here you might as well come in for bit.' Kader ushered him in on second thoughts. 'All these people here are League workers.' Then he asked Keramat softly, 'Have you finished the Pakistan song?'

One of the young men said, 'We're not being allowed into Majhipara. Your people have filed cases against the fishermen for stealing fish . . .'

'That's the problem.' Abdul Kader adjusted his tone in response to the speaker's belligerence. 'We've taken a lease on the lake. Naturally my father will stop anyone who tries to fish there without his permission. But our relationship with the fishermen goes back a long way, many of them are sharecroppers on our land. We wouldn't imagine taking them to court. It's all the manager's doing, he's the one who bullied my father into filing cases. This is an old ploy of theirs, don't you see, make Muslims fight one another so that their power is intact.'

He brought up Keramat's own case. 'Take Keramat here, the poet Keramat Ali, even though he doesn't live in Majhipara they hold him in great respect. When they were stealing fish the other day . . .' Kader paused, gulped, and continued, we're giving him shelter. Talented man, composes songs, a young Muslim, Ismail bhai says he must be saved at any cost.' Then he handed Keramat over to the gathering. 'Why don't all of you take him to Kalam mian? Go on, take him.'

Keramat trailed behind everyone, though. Kalam majhi didn't entertain the contingent from the League. His shop was the election office for the Krishok Proja Party, whose posters were plastered on its tin walls. Although there weren't too many people there, most of those who were present were grey-haired, with grey beards, and caps on their heads. Two or three of the young men had megaphones. The other youngsters were all from Majhipara in Girirdanga.

One of the young League workers who was here from the town said, 'Assalam Aleikum. We have come to you as those in service of the Muslim League. There's only one party of Muslims in India, only one Jamaat, and that's the All India Muslim League. The elections are coming, and for Muslims these elections . . .'

'We're Muslims too,' Kalam majhi interrupted him. 'But then we're fishermen and all of you are gentlemen. Your job is to hand over our sons to the police, to turn us into criminals.'

The young canvasser sidestepped the issue of the court case. 'All the Muslims of India have united today under the leadership of Quaed-e-Azam. Who will benefit if you start creating divisions between fishermen and peasants, between the rich and the poor? Even the farmers agitating for the tebhaga movement have abandoned the path of conflict to unite under the flag of the League, and . . .'

Keramat was thrown into doubt. It had been a long while since he had had any news from the western side. Could the peasants there abandon this battle so easily? The oppression they had been subjected to had left no avenue open for escape. What about that? But this young man was saying with conviction, 'This isn't the Muslim League of the upper class any more. The farmer and the fisherman and the labourer will all get their rights in Pakistan.' Then what's the bloodshed for, Keramat reflected.

The young man went on to talk about jobs. Muslims would have no difficulty securing employment in Pakistan. They would no longer be deprived of government jobs because of the crime of being Muslims. 'All these educated Hindu gentlemen mock the faith of Muslims, they taunt our communities, their books are full of contempt for Islam. We cannot possibly live with them. In Pakistan the laws will follow the Quran and the Sunnah, the administrators will live like the Khalifs of Islam did. They will have to live off whatever they can earn by sewing caps and making copies of the Quran.'

Keramat felt overwhelmed hearing all this, as did the young men from Majhipara. But one of the Talukdars of Shimultola who was present kept frowning, even trying to cut the speaker off. 'These people don't listen to anyone, they just spin their own yarn.'

The dedicated League worker narrowed his eyes and smiled. 'You're one of the elders of the community, you're dressed like a Muslim, but you parrot the Hindu line. What can you have to tell us? After Huq shaheb betrayed Muslims and Islam . . .'

Putting his Rampur cap back on his head, the aged Talukdar said, 'Have you taken a sole agency for Islam? How much of Islam do you understand? Does your Jinnah know the routine of the namaz? Be it Jinnah or Liaquat Ali or Suhrawardy, have any of them ever prostrated themselves to Allah? And these are the people who are supposed to take charge of our religion.'

Talukdar's middle-aged companion agreed with him. 'These people spend all their time with the bottle, chacha, how will they have the time to bow for the namaz?'

The other League workers began to turn red with anger, but the young man continued as before, 'You must understand that the Islam of the mullahs and the Islam of Quaed-e-Azam are not the same. The mullahs want to use religion to keep Muslims backward, it is their fundamentalism that is responsible for the current condition of Muslims . . .'

'Then why blame the Hindus, my boy?'

'Many of the maulanas are also pandering to the Hindus. Maulana Azad is the show boy of the Congress, it is to save Islam, to save Muslims, from such mullahs and maulanas that we need Pakistan.'

Before he had finished, there were slogans of 'Pakistan zindabad', 'Quaed-e-Azam zindabad', and 'Vote for Ismail Husain', mingled with the growl of a motor car. The young men ran in that direction. The canvassing for votes was going on from a vehicle with a canvas roof. Getting out of the jeep, Ismail Husain offered salaams left and right with a smile on his face as he walked towards Kader's shop. 'Come on, Kader, let's go to Majhipara,' he called out.

Abdul Kader was astonished to see him. Ismail was supposed to have spent three more days in the east, along the banks of the Jomuna where fresh land had sprung from the river. He was scheduled to arrive here the day before the election, when Suhrawardy shaheb was also expected at a meeting. Had he completed campaigning along the Jomuna then?

Entering the shop, Ismail said, 'Do you people spend all your time here? Do you know what's going on in your own village of Girirdanga? Tell me what the situation is at Majhipara. Call Kalam majhi, let me hear it from him.'

'As you can see, Malek Talukdar has turned Kalam majhi's shop into his election camp. Why will Kalam come if I call him?'

'Do as I say. He'll come when he's told who's asking for him.'

But Gofur kolu came back with the information that Kalam had left just a minute ago. Kader realized that he had slipped away to avoid Ismail Husain. 'What have you people done, Kader?' whispered Ismail to him. 'Was there no better time to take the fishermen to court?' Kader made to reply, but Ismail Husain cut him off. 'And yes, what's that fellow's name? Tamiz, yes. Tamiz and his father may not have voting rights, but there's no lack of people in Majhipara who pay enough taxes to vote. Their votes are not insignificant. The entire area will be affected if Majhipara's votes go into Malek

shaheb's box. Over by the Jomuna the fishermen are already angry,
apparently we Muslim League people have turned them in to the
police for robbery. There were no Krishok Proja workers in those
areas earlier, but after Tamiz was arrested Malek shaheb's people are
happily doing their propaganda there. Did you have to brand these
harmless people criminals?'

'I wasn't keen on taking them to court. But the manager
convinced baapjaan somehow . . .'

'I've heard all the stories. Come on, let's go to Girirdanga. We
have to discuss things with the fishermen.'

'But Malek shaheb's people are campaigning there now. Is this
a good time to . . .'

Gofur kolu sprang to Kader's defence before he could finish.
'Forget about those fishermen. An obstinate race if there ever was
one. They'll always swim against the tide. A different Jamaat too.'

'What do you mean, different Jamaat?' asked Ismail Husain
gravely.

Kader answered, 'The majority of the people around here are
Mohammadis. But all the fishermen belong to the Hanafi Jamaat.
Majhipara in Girirdanga is the only place in the Union with a
Hanafi mosque.'

Ismail Husain's rage shot up at this explanation. 'This is what
will finish Muslims off. You lot are still playing Hanafi versus
Mohammadi. Forget all this, Kader, just forget it. Don't even
think of bringing it up during elections at least. I'm going to read
the namaz at the Hanafi fishermen's mosque today. There are
no distinctions between Muslims. Quaed-e-Azam is not a Sunni
Muslim, in fact even amongst the Shias he belongs to a specific
Khwaja community. Think of the support we're getting from the
district school headmaster Tarbak Ali shaheb. Are we going to leave
him out because he's an Ahmadi?'

This made Kader even more apprehensive. There would be
trouble if the people in the villages here found out all this about
Quaed-e-Azam. Ismail Husain took leave of his senses sometimes,

there was no knowing what he would blurt out. Not only did he not bother to read the namaz, but he also made jokes at the expense of priests whenever he had the chance. Everyone in his family mixed freely with Hindus. Once Pakistan was formed, perhaps Kader would also have the chance to consort on equal terms with Brahmons and Kayasthos. But then it was one thing to keep the company of Hindus and be on good terms with them, and completely another to read the namaz at the fishermen's Jamaat. In any case, Ismail Husain didn't even pray in the normal course of things, yet today he was determined to read the namaz at the fishermen's mosque.

The car remained at the Golabari market, while Ismail toured all of Girirdanga on foot, his anger with Kader increasing progressively. The fishermen were deeply aggrieved at Tamiz's arrest, which meant their votes were destined for Malek shaheb's box. When he reached Kalam majhi's house, Ismail called out, 'Kalam mian, do you want us to go back without entering your home?'

Kalam majhi had been plotting to slip away, but Ismail's arrival had ruled it out. The only chair in the house with armrests was rather heavy. He lifted it with both his hands and placed it in front of Ismail, while Budha responded to his signal by fanning Ismail furiously. Ismail made a demand. 'We've been invited to eat at Kalam mian's today. Since you didn't invite us, we accepted your invitation on our own.'

This worked. Moulobi Kuddus had to postpone the zohr azaan to slaughter a couple of large roosters. The sounds and aromas of cooking wafted in from somewhere inside the house.

Abdul Kader had accepted the situation by now. All the fishermen seemed frightened when he visited their houses, which made him even angrier with his father. Some, like Abiton's father, actually made snide remarks, in response to which he offered excuses on behalf of his father, blaming the manager. Their prospects for getting votes here were not high. Now that the scum had got the upper hand, he had no choice but to appease them. It was all very well to do what it took to get votes, but how could Ismail be allowed to visit Girirdanga and eat at a fisherman's house instead of Kader's? Kader had sent word home before leaving Golabari, a goat had been slaughtered, and fresh fish had been procured. Now his prestige was in tatters. On top of which, if he had to eat at Kalam's as well, it would be too humiliating to go home afterwards. He glanced helplessly at Ismail Husain. 'But I sent word home, bhai. Lunch is ready.'

'Dinner will be at your house. After lunch I'll tour the village with Kalam mian. Then I will take your father to the other side of the lake and eat at your place at night when I'm back. After that we'll have to finalize the programme for Wednesday with the party workers, we must organize at least three meetings for Suhrawardy shaheb in this area.'

Kader gave up and observed the excitement among the fishermen. None of them was paying much attention to him—they were speaking directly with Ismail Husain. Gofur hadn't even turned up, but then it was not safe for him to be here. Even Keramat Ali had things to say, once directly to Ismail, and at other times while taking up a position next to Tamiz's father. Allah alone knew whom the bastard was passing on his verses to.

Meanwhile a large pot of rice pudding and sweets of different kinds appeared although it was nearing lunchtime. Kader could not help himself, he said, 'I'll just pay a quick visit home. The rest of you can eat these and have lunch later, I'll have lunch at home.'

'Help us with these now,' said Ismail. 'Lunch must be some time away. You can come back and eat with us.'

'No bhaijaan, I'm not eating any of this at this hour, it'll just ruin my appetite. I'd better go home for lunch instead.'

Budha winked at Afsar in response to this demonstration of urban strategies for staying healthy. 'Kader bhai will never eat at our house,' said Afsar.

Kalam majhi got Kader into trouble now. Gratified by the opportunity to play host to Ismail, he gripped Kader's arm. 'Please eat with us. We've eaten at your house so many times, are you going to become an outcaste if you eat at ours?'

'What caste are you talking of?' Abdul Kader sighed. 'Does it even exist any more?' The poor man could neither accept nor refuse the invitation. Many of these fishermen may have grown up eating at the Mondols', but did that mean he would have to eat at their house too? It was one thing to taste the sweets, but an entire meal? But it was looking like he would have to defy both his caste and community thanks to Ismail. He stole a look at Ismail and modified his statement immediately. 'Not that Muslims believe in caste. Islam is a religion of equality.'

It wasn't out of pity but out of some other consideration that Ismail gave him a respite. 'All right, you'd better go home and eat then, give my salaam to your father, you'll have to take the trouble of going with us across the lake in the afternoon, no, in the evening.'

As soon as Abdul Kalam had left, the yard of Kalam majhi's house filled with the people of Majhipara. Ismail Husain was sitting inside the house. The party workers ate their sweets in the veranda outside, while the fishermen stood in the yard, watching. After he had eaten, Ismail Husain occupied the chair with the armrests in the veranda and chatted with the fishermen, inviting them to do away with all distinctions between fellow Muslims. The manager had plotted to have Tamiz arrested. Ismail Husain was convinced that the fishermen had lost control of Katlahar Lake because of the Hindu jomidar's greed and conspiracy. If Ismail won the elections the fishermen would be given the lease for the lake, this would be his first task. These detestable and barbaric systems would not exist in Pakistan, where everyone would get what was due to them.

The fishermen listened to him in rapt wonder. Tamiz's father was among them. Budha pushed him forward so that Ismail could see him. 'This is Tamiz's father,' he said.

Ismail rose from his chair to put his hand on Tamiz's father's shoulder. 'You don't have to introduce him. Tamiz has been framed in this complaint of robbery. It's a tough case. We'll provide a lawyer, our Sadeq shaheb is the best criminal lawyer right now. We will free Tamiz, inshallah.' Then he told the gathering, 'Your lake will be returned to you. There are some legal complications, the jomidar owns it at the moment. But once we abolish the very system of jomidars, the lake can only go to all of you.'

Ismail Husain's promise evoked a response in Majhipara that even buried the joy of the news that Tamiz would be freed. By evening Muslim League posters appeared on all the fences and trees. Several of the younger men rushed off to Golabari straight after lunch to get posters from the office and put them up on the walls of Kalam majhi's shop.

31

Keramat Ali had blundered into a circle of fire that he could not get out of. In the light cast by the flames, one particular face looked familiar—in fact it was because he had turned to look at it that he had found himself trapped, or else he might have had a chance to escape. Who was it? There was a fiery glow on the dark-skinned, oval face, and the eyes were blazing. Was it those eyes where the fire had started? Keramat was woken by Alim the schoolmaster before he could identify who it was. 'Gofur has told you to be there early. There's a meeting in the Paranirpara school field.'

This made Keramat worry. He was supposed to sing a song about Pakistan, but not a single verse had popped into his head. He had spent the entire day with Ismail's campaign team before going to sleep next to Alim. He didn't mind the bustle preceding the election. Golabari market was alive till late into the night—an atmosphere he could immerse himself in. But as soon as he fell asleep these days he had a dream of being trapped in a fire. At first he had thought the blazing eyes were Phuljaan's, for who else but the goitre-ridden bitch would try to singe him? But her face was neither oval, nor one he couldn't tear his eyes away from. Even Alim the schoolmaster had told him before going to bed, 'Keramat, you have no choice now but to write a song about Pakistan. You've been saved from the police only because Ismail shaheb has put in a word for you. Either you must follow his orders and give him the song he wants, or you must get away to Joipur or Panchbibi. You have plenty of songs about the tebhaga movement. Let the League say what it likes, I cannot believe the aadhiars are on the run.'

But every time he tried to compose a verse he was singed by a tongue of fire from an oval face, and perhaps in the hope of seeing it clearly, Keramat felt his eyes grow heavy with sleep, which made him go to bed at once. Waking up at Alim's call, he finally had two lines after a lot of effort:

A Pakistan from India's soil will set us free
All the woes of Muslims will end finally.

But they didn't satisfy him. The lines that followed either had the right words but the wrong rhythm, or followed the correct rhythm without the words being good enough. Was he going to have to depend on songs handed down from other people then, just like Cherag Ali? Not a chance! You couldn't whip a gathering into a frenzy with these fakirs' songs. Still, if Keramat had been his apprentice maybe he would be able to sing spontaneously. But how? Tamiz's father used to follow Cherag Ali about everywhere, but it was impossible to tell what he was actually good at. The imbecile had mumbled a strange tale at the fishermen's mosque the other day, but had anyone actually understood whether Sharafat Mondol had indeed beaten him up and humiliated him, or how he mistook Sharafat's clogs for an iron pan? It was because Keramat had twisted into proper lyrics the babble that Tamiz's father was relaying that the fishermen had been fired up. What other skill had Cherag Ali passed on to Tamiz's father besides the ability to walk in his sleep without stumbling? But that couldn't be the only reason the people of Majhipara held Tamiz's father in such reverence. Cherag Ali had left his tattered book with Tamiz's father, perhaps it was the book that gave him all his strength. Cherag Ali had repeatedly announced in Joipur that he had never had the chance to be educated. Even if the old coot was bent over with humility, when it came to announcing his illiteracy he used to brim with pride. 'All of you are educated people, you write your own songs, you have printed songbooks. Allah didn't give me such powers. All my songs were handed down to me, they live in my heart thanks to the blessings of my ancestors and my teacher, they jump to my lips whenever I touch the dotara. I cannot tell how this happens.' The fakir knew many tricks. When singing for a large audience he used to pause for breath without warning and tell Keramat, 'Go on, make up the rest of the lines.' When a perplexed Keramat simply kept standing there, he would say, 'You can't, I know. I can't either.' Keramat was certain now that all his secrets were concealed in the book. If he was so proud of being illiterate, did he use the book just to wipe his arse?

Going up to Tamiz's house in the middle of the afternoon, Keramat called out softly, 'Are you home, Tamiz's father?'

'He isn't home,' answered Kulsum from within.

'But he asked me here.' Keramat's voice shook, for he had seen Tamiz's father at the Golabari market just a short while ago. With just one day to go, Kalam majhi was campaigning for votes with a group of people from Majhipara, paying for their food and everything else.

Kulsum knew this. 'Kalam majhi is getting food for everyone today. The old coot is so pleased his son's going to be released from jail after the elections that he doesn't come home till night.'

'Yes, I did see him at the market.' Keramat made sure he wouldn't be caught lying. 'But then I thought he'd be home by now.'

'He isn't coming now. There's no one at home.'

'But you're at home.' Frightened at what he had said, Keramat added, 'Tamiz's father said, eat with us this afternoon.'

'You want to eat?' Kulsum opened the door and retreated into the yard, from where she could see Keramat was looking sick with hunger. Covering her head elaborately with the end of her sari, Kulsum piled all the rice he had kept for herself on to a plate and said, 'There's some daal from yesterday, that's all there is.'

Keramat ate, stealing glances at Kulsum. Even from a distance he could tell that her dark face was inflamed by the sun. It would get warmer still and soon there would be flames. He couldn't identify the face he saw in his dreams every night nowadays—was there any resemblance with Kulsum? He ate slowly, his eyes constantly swivelling towards Kulsum's cheek as she sat in the veranda behind the door. A verse seemed to be poking at him in his head. Keramat did not look away, afraid of losing the dark-skinned face. 'In my dream the world and the sky are burning.' There, the lines were coming to him. But no, these were his own thoughts. He would probably never write another song in his life. The rice sated his appetite, but suddenly he felt a shooting pain in his head. Looking out the door, he saw the silk-cotton tree aflame under the noonday sun of summer. The flowers bled in the heat, and then burst to release white cotton.

Another line popped into Keramat's head when he turned his attention back to his food. 'The fire has never looked lovelier anywhere.' No, it wasn't working. Rinsing his hands using the same plate he had eaten off, Keramat said recklessly, 'I wanted to take a look at your grandfather's book.'

'Sit near the door. I'll get it.'

Squatting on the doorstep outside the room, Keramat looked at the summer afternoon again. 'In the dream the world and the sky are burning.' He muttered quietly, trying to work out a suitable second line, but a rustling from the maacha inside made his heart thump. Was the fakir himself here again? He had sung for a long time from the same spot the other day. But Keramat felt hopeful too—if the fakir's shadow fell on him perhaps he would be able to sing again. With a mixture of fear and optimism he reflected, no, how could the fakir arrive so suddenly? Kulsum was on the maacha, sniffing hard at her grandfather's book. Keramat felt a dryness in his throat—was Kulsum sucking out all the words in her book with her nose? Would she inhale everything written in there and hand him an empty shell? Was Kulsum planning to wipe out the words with her sniffing and display a set of blank pages to prove that Cherag Ali was illiterate?

Keramat reached out for the book when Kulsum climbed down from the maacha with it. Handing it to him, she said, 'Take a look and give it back.'

Suddenly mustering courage, Keramat said, 'And if I don't?'

'No, the book stays here. What will you do with it?'

Leafing through the book, Keramat discovered there were no verses on the pages. A cover of khaki-coloured paper had been sewn to the pages, the first of which carried the words *Khwabnama Falnama O Tabeer* written in an inexpert Bengali hand. Such books for explaining dreams were easily available. But this one had nothing printed in it. More than half of the pages were covered in squares and rectangles, further divided into smaller boxes, each occupied by a single Arabic letter. That he had touched the Arabic script with an unclean body frightened Keramat slightly, but performing the ritual cleansing now might mean having to let go of the manuscript. He turned the pages carefully, worn pages that had to be handled with great care, for the paper could tear easily. The squares and rectangles were followed by descriptions of dreams in large-sized Bengali script. What a particular dream might lead to, what the outcome would be, how to interpret it—all of this was explained. Was this how Cherag Ali could tell people what their dreams meant? But there were no verses anywhere. Keramat had seen plenty of books for interpreting dreams, there was a man in Shantahar who sold not only Keramat's poems but also books like these, as well as compendiums of Islamic practices. But then all of those were printed books, published in Calcutta. Was this book so valuable because it was handwritten? Or were the Arabic letters a code for Munshi's verses? Keramat stared at the squares and rectangles, desperately seeking clues to the songs handed down by Munshi. But overshadowing his concentration was Kulsum's face, glowing brightest of all. One look at the book and he had realized that the face in his dreams of fire was clearly Kulsum's, the flames emerging from her eyes to set his house ablaze. As he surveyed the grids drawn in the book, the words slipped out of his mouth, 'In my dream the world and the sky are burning, this is where Allah has sent us beauty.' But the verse was not to his liking.

When a corner of a page tore under Keramat's impatient fingers, Kulsum leaned over his head. 'What are you tearing up the book for? Give it back.' But Keramat's head was throbbing now, he would not survive without composing a verse he could approve of. The fire from his dream had spread to his mop of hair, its heat making him squirm. He kept muttering the two lines although he didn't like them. No, it wasn't working.

His mumbling made Kulsum turn her eyes towards the maacha. 'Give me the book,' she whispered. 'Dada is here, he wants it.' But instead of holding her hand out for it, she gaped at Keramat.

'I've seen that face in the fire somewhere,' muttered Keramat. 'The face in the dream is in front of me.' But still it didn't please him. The lines creaked and groaned in his voice, they didn't roll off like oil.

'Dada never sang these lines,' said Kulsum. 'Where did you get them?'

But all his efforts couldn't get Keramat the lyrics he wanted. Listening to his frustrated recitation, Kulsum trembled and said, still trembling, 'Dada never sang these lines. They must have come to him after his death. Did he hand down the songs he got after dying to you?' Kulsum was thrown into doubt. Had Keramat Ali also become the inheritor of Cherag Ali's songs, just like Tamiz's father? Could he now claim his rights to this book? What was she to do now? Had Cherag Ali sent her a signal to let Keramat Ali have the book? What should she do?

But Keramat rescued Kulsum from her quandary. He was already stricken at the lack of supply of satisfactory verses, and now someone else was being given the credit for his quest for the right lines. He replied with some rancour, 'How would your grandfather get these lines? I composed them. I was happy to see you, so I wrote these lines.'

Oh, so this was not a song handed down to Keramat Ali, not even through Cherag Ali. But what sort of a man was this who confessed to composing his own verses? Her grandfather Cherag Ali was the only one who knew the secret source from where his songs came. And it was in search of that source that Tamiz's father wandered around the fig tree at the northern head of the lake every night. And here was Keramat Ali, sprung from nowhere, who was passing off as his own the verses that had popped up in his head from signals he had got from Kulsum's grandfather's book. Leaning over farther, Kulsum grabbed the book from Keramat's lap.

Keramat felt the fieriness of her rage on his face, its bite in his eyes. His head slumped with pain. Climbing back on to the maacha with the book, Kulsum levelled a look at him that made her eyes blaze. The heat from those flames reached Keramat's body and gathered in his head. When a thin shaft of sunlight entered through a crack in the roof and actually lit up Kulsum's face like a fire would, Keramat realized he was dreaming. His usual dream was being repeated, this time in Tamiz's father's house. But the side effect of today's dream was a splitting headache. His brain was melting in the heat and dripping down his face. His entire head throbbed with fear, pain, suffering, anxiety and worry.

Keramat lowered his maddened head, and as soon as he did two lines emerged, setting off a turmoil in his mind:

If ever I've seen beauty in my life
It's a fiery face I saw in a dream.

32

'Ma Bhabani has made the double bend in the curve of the Bangali river, so the fish there is for the goddess herself, isn't it?' The manager did not bother to wait for a reply. 'And that rascal of a fisherman, that Muslim, how dare he steal it? How can we tolerate this as children of the goddess? And all of you are his friends. Shame!'

The manager spat his rebuke directly at Boikuntho, whose defensive demeanour changed at this claim. 'No babu,' he said, 'This is Bhabani Pathak's double bend, Bhabani Pathak, who fought against the soldiers of the British company. The rituals every year on the day of the Poradaho fair are in his honour.' After a pause, he continued, 'He passed away near that spot.'

'How can a goddess and a man be the same, you fool?' Purnochandra Chakraborty was annoyed, but he didn't raise his voice. In fact, he softened it and said, 'You know of Bhabanipur, don't you? Bhabanipur, near Sherpur . . .'

'I do, babu. Our relations . . .'

'Then you know it well enough to know there's a temple to the goddess there. It's under the jomidar of Natore. But the temple was not named after Queen Bhabani, was it? When Ma Durga died of rage after her father Daksha's refusal to invite her husband Shiva, he became furious and began to whirl her body, holding it over his head. Narayan realized that the air would be poisoned if Durga's body were to decompose. So he used his sudarshan chakra to slice her body into pieces and let them fall on different parts of the earth. Where do you think the goddess's left ear fell? On the bank of the Kartowa, in Bhabanipur.'

As Satish, the attorney from the town, kept nodding with his eyes closed, Purnochandra's enthusiasm increased. 'That was how the place became important and was named Bhabanipur. The goddess's ear is enshrined there, devotees worship every day and get the food offered to her. So the ear remained there, and the fish meant for the goddess was let into the double bend in the Manosh river. The Manosh has dried up, but the double bend is always full, the Bangali river curves around it to protect it. It's sacred, the water at that spot.'

Dasharath, Judhisthir and Keshto Pal from Palpara were speechless at this commentary. Satish the attorney from the town and Anil Sanyal from Serpur nodded silently. But Boikuntho began to fidget. What were these people trying to say? Everyone in the neighbourhood knew, from Brahmons and Kayasthos to the Sahas and the Pals, and even the Namashudras and Muslims, they all knew that Bhabani Pathak was shot dead next to the double bend by the Company's troops. He was accompanied by his general, a Pathan. It hadn't exactly happened the other day. Boikuntho's grandfather's grandfather's father, or perhaps *his* father, was there with Bhabani Pathak. What about that? How could the manager suddenly bring the goddess Bhabani into this? Softly he said, 'No babu, the Poradaho fair is held in Bhabani Pathak's memory. His idol is placed beneath the banyan tree on Tuesday, the day before the fair, and he himself appears early on the morning of the fair.'

'Don't tell me about the fair. It's just a place where everyone goes to have fun, people of all sorts of castes turn up. You don't know yourself what your rituals are for. There's nothing wrong with devotion, but how can anyone tolerate the fact that the goddess herself isn't worshipped so close to the double bend in the Manosh. The goddess is the mother of the world. How can we endure her humiliation?'

Mortified by the injustice of it all, Purnochandra howled, 'Ma, ma, ma!'

Never mind the mother, his ardent cries would make even the mother's father run away. Everyone looked around warily out of fear and hope of the arrival of the mother or the grandfather or both. The manager paused briefly to allow their apprehension and their devoutness to solidify. Then he continued with aplomb, 'If a Muslim fisherman steals what belongs to the mother, the touch of a Muslim means the water isn't sacred any more. My goddess is compassionate, she didn't harm him. But what about us, her worthless children? What did we do? We sat back, while the bloody Muslim was encouraged even more, so that his son decided to steal fish from the lake. The lake belongs to the jomidar, he can lease it out to whoever he pleases, what right does anyone else have to interfere?'

'But the fishermen of Girirdanga have always fished in Katlahar Lake, babu.'

Dasharath's observation displeased the manager, who said, 'Just because things were lawless in the past, it doesn't have to continue the same way. If the jomidar doesn't go by the law, if he does not care for the good of his people, how will they prosper? Are you suggesting that everyone should do as they please while the jomidar watches? Should he just sit and watch?'

None of the listeners was in favour of a jomidar who sat and watched. The blood began to flow faster in their dark-skinned bodies on hearing of the jomidar's powers from his manager. Now Purnochandra Chakraborty unsheathed his actual grievance. 'That Tamiz's father, he dares besmirch the body of the goddess and instigates his son to steal fish from the lake, how can you people even consort with him? But you go to his house, you even drink water there. What is your religion? Does your blood not boil at the humiliation of your mother?'

A rueful smile, like the moon at dawn, appeared on Anil Sanyal's thin lips. His heavy sigh dismissed the moon, keeping only the regret, on the strength of which he said, 'They're partitioning the country, and you're talking of a mere double bend in the river. All this is just . . .'

Satish the attorney burst into a fiery rage. 'You think the humiliation of the goddess Bhabani is nothing? Will you tolerate the desecration of your own mother? And Durga is the mother of the world, the universe should explode in flames if she is insulted. This is how you people have handed the country over to them. Would things have come to such a pass if the Congress had concentrated on protecting our faith from the beginning? Just consider how they've indulged the Muslims over and over again.'

'The country includes everyone, Satish-babu,' Anil Chandra Sanyal, who was the joint assistant secretary of the Congress in Sherpur, offered an explanation. 'Mahatma Gandhi is who he is because he has made room for everybody in his heart, irrespective of caste or creed.'

'And now we're paying the price for it. They're ready with swords to slice up the nation. It is our own religion that is about to be defiled thanks to the Mahatma.'

'No, Satish-babu.' Anil Chandra was inspired by love for his religion. 'Why should the Mahatma consider his own faith unimportant? He cannot possibly do anything that goes against the religion and the interest of Hindus. He has said it himself, I'm a Hindu first and then a patriot. His ideals come from the Bhagavad Gita.'

All these political discussions were preventing the manager from getting to the point. It would be difficult to bring it up openly once Sharafat Mondol arrived. So the manager interrupted the crucial conversation between Satish the attorney and Anil Sanyal to say, 'Let me tell you, that bastard Tamiz's father is the root cause of all trouble. He pretends to be an imbecile, but he's as evil as they come. I'm going to have him arrested. The people of Majhipara might create trouble, and Kader won't dare say anything because of the elections. You people have to take care of them.'

His listeners were quiet—Dasharath, Judhisthir and Keshto Pal out of fear and Boikuntho Giri, out of both fear and unhappiness. Everyone in Girirdanga, Nijgirirdanga, Golabari, Palpara, Ranirpara,

Paranirpara and even in Sabgram and Chhaihata knew of Tamiz's father's direct relationship with the fig tree via Cherag Ali.

'Can I say something?' asked Dasharath hesitantly. 'It would be best not to touch Tamiz's father.'

'Why not?' The manager sounded acerbic. 'Sharafat Mondol beat him up, but I didn't notice his arm falling off.'

'No, babu,' Boikuntho corrected the manager. 'It was Munshi from the fig tree who beat up Tamiz's father. He punished him for taking the fish meant for Bhabani Pathak.'

'Really, if such superstitions are going to persist even in the twentieth century, what will we do with self-rule, and what use is the freedom movement for that matter?' Anil Sanyal was deeply disappointed by the backwardness of the ignorant.

But Dasharath informed everyone, 'Kader mian apologized to Tamiz's father personally after Mondol behaved badly with him.'

'No, you really can't trust these Muslims.' Satish the attorney sat up straight. 'What possessed him to apologize to a fisherman? You can be educated and well off, but you cannot stop behaving like a Muslim.'

But the manager knew the truth. 'Of course not, what do you mean, he apologized? Kader was in Majhipara to canvass for votes. He met Tamiz's father too. Ismail promised to have Tamiz released, but it isn't so simple. He's been charged under section 387, he won't get bail.' The manager wasn't remotely dispirited. It was on Mondol's suggestion that Boikuntho and the blacksmiths had been called here today. But the idea of severing the association between Bhabani Pathak and the double bend in the dry Manosh river was the manager's own, though Mondol had given his approval, for he could not stand the antics of Muslims at the Poradaho fair. The place would be rid of the people of Majhipara if a Hindu goddess could be established there. The manager's dream was that the people of the town would start visiting Poradaho not just for the fair but also to enjoy Durga Puja festivities. If a ritual for the goddess could be instituted to free the people from the superstition of worshipping a ghost, not just the people nearby but also the affluent people from the town would be drawn to the area. The manager didn't have the courage to have the news published prominently in the *Anandabazar Patrika* without the townspeople on his side. But it was obvious now that Boikuntho Giri could be a troublemaker. So the manager vented his anger on him. 'Why do you keep going to Majhipara, Boikuntho? Stop this. I'll see how those bloody Muslim fishermen enter the Poradaho fair once I've put an end to this worship of ghosts.'

Judhisthir walked on leaden feet after leaving the office. Not only the manager but also Mondol would be upset if he consorted with the people of Majhipara. No matter how much Mondol squeezed his share of the crops, what choice did Judhisthir have but to request him to be taken on as a sharecropper? Kader might even come to an understanding with the fishermen thanks to the elections, and once Tamiz got out of jail perhaps he could find him something to do. But where would that leave Judhisthir? If he didn't get sharecropping rights, he would have to sell his own land to Mondol just to pay the interest on the money he had borrowed from Jagadish Saha. And if he insisted on holding on to his land, he would hand over his house, his utensils, his father's furnace and bellows and everything else to Saha. It was either Jagadish Saha or Sharafat Mondol. Judhisthir was helpless, but by god's grace he had a brainwave. He might be able to ingratiate himself with Kader if he followed him about during the canvassing of votes for Ismail shaheb. Now that Mondol had charged the fishermen with stealing from his lake, he was unlikely to allow any of them to sharecrop his land. Neither Judhisthir nor anyone else from Kamarpara had been anywhere near the lake, so he could well use this opportunity to snatch the sharecropping rights away from the fishermen. All he had to do was to follow Kader everywhere.

There was a big crowd of people in front of Kader's shop and at Kalam's and Mukunda Saha's godowns. The tin walls of Mukunda Saha's store were covered by the Congress tricolour. People from the party were here from the town. Even though he had left the jomidar's office in Lathidanga after Judhisthir, Anil-babu had arrived already, having taken a carriage. Judhisthir had no business with any of them. 'What are you doing here?' someone asked when he merged into Kader's team. One of the student workers of the Congress dragged him off to Saha's shop, saying, 'What were you doing with them?'

Another worker said with a smile, 'Ismail shaheb's constituency is Mohammedan. You have to vote for Suren-babu, Suren Sengupta, our Congress candidate.'

Judhisthir was deflated. Being part of Kader's entourage might get him Mondol's land. And then Ismail shaheb was a decent sort, apparently he would pass a law to increase the aadhiars' share of the harvest even more. Suren-babu could well be a good man too, but Judhisthir didn't know him. Anil Sanyal stepped forward to clear his confusion. 'There'll be one MLA for Muslim voters and one for us.' Finally Judhisthir realized that voters from each religion would get their own representative.

In the afternoon Mukunda Saha drew Boikuntho aside to ask, 'What did the manager tell you this morning? Sharafat mian told me yesterday the manager is very upset with you. Why do you have to keep going to Majhipara? Tamiz's father is an old man, what do you have to say to his young wife? Weren't your ancestors supposed to be holy men? What do you have to do with those Muslim fishermen then?'

There was a commotion inside the market. The seeds on the silk-cotton trees standing on the east and the north of the market had burst in the heat of the last of the sunshine, obscuring Boikuntho Giri's vision with tears of cotton. Closing his eyes, he could at once see another pair of eyes, narrowed, and the words uttered through lips curled in contempt rang in his ears to the accompaniment of Cherag Ali's dotara, 'Considering your religion doesn't allow you to drink water in our homes, how can you eat our mangoes? Give my mango back to me, take your religion and go home.' But Mukunda Saha had confused him today. On the day of Kulsum's wedding Boikuntho had eaten his fill of the different sweets and curds served to guests before going to the shrine of Bhabani Pathak in Poradaho.

He had begun to sing in his tuneless voice after several rounds of ganja. Those lyrics came back to him today after all these years. To quench his thirst for the entire song, or perhaps on some other impulse, Boikuntho left the uproar of the market behind to walk towards the Poradaho field. He had barely arrived at the shrine when he heard the same song even without the effect of ganja.

The Manosh is red with the ascetic's blood
She is glittering in full bridal dress
The groom wants no wealth for himself
The only dowry is people's devotion
His only possession, the clay idol

Joining in completely out of tune, Boikuntho felt tears flooding his eyes at Bhabani Pathak's noble death and his detachment from the world. His face and mouth and tongue began to smart at the saltiness of the tears. Bhabani had come to possess his idol, and though it had been immersed in the river after the end of the rituals on the last Wednesday of the month of Maagh, the clay with which the idol had been made flowed along the thin stream of the Bangali river to the double bend in the Manosh. If the manager were to evict Bhabani Pathak out of rage at Muslim fishermen, where was Bhabani to go? The manager wanted to install the goddess Durga instead. Bhabani Pathak couldn't compete with such a powerful goddess. Where are you, Ma Durga? You are the slayer of the demon, the saviour of the world, the earth mother, the giver of sustenance. You are full of strength, you are swathed in the devotion of your followers. You are Ma Tara, you are Ma Kali. Had a goddess like her, mother of the world, decided to use the manager to oust Bhabani Pathak? Would the manager make the Muslims pay for their sins by evicting Bhabani Pathak and installing Durga in his place? That would stop the advent of Muslims to Poradaho, and the high-class people from the town, the Brahmons and the Kayasthos, would come here to worship the goddess. Even the tears of the Manosh nestling in the arms of the Bangali river would not belong to Bhabani Pathak any more, they too would be captured by the goddess with her ten fists. And Boikuntho would have no right to stay here either, for he would have no other identity besides being an employee of Saha's. And the tale of his property in Sherpur having been usurped by his grandfather's stepbrothers would remain just that, a story. An anxious and agitated Boikuntho stirred restlessly in uncertainty. Trying his best to work himself up into a fit of anger against Tamiz's father but failing, he set off once more for the Golabari market, in case he ran into Tamiz's father there.

But Tamiz's father was nowhere to be seen even on voting day. All of Majhipara was present, with Kalam majhi having shepherded his flock. Only Tamiz's father was missing, but then he wasn't eligible to vote anyway. Most of the people who had turned up were not voters, for how many could afford to pay the necessary taxes?

It was another month and a half before Boikuntho finally met Tamiz's father. He was carrying a message from Mukunda Saha to Girirdanga that day. Mondol's elder son Abdul Aziz had built a brick kiln farther north of the northern head of the lake, from where Mukunda Saha meant to buy several thousand bricks. He was supposed to have gone himself with the advance payment, but the poor fellow hadn't been able to make it because his nephew had died. The tears hadn't even dried in his eyes when he said, 'Be quick, Boikuntho, Aziz mian will create trouble if you're late. Tell him I will go myself with the advance payment the day after tomorrow.' But when had Boikuntho ever rushed anywhere? He inevitably took a circuitous route. Sharafat Mondol had leased 2 acres of land this year where the sloping southern bank of the ox pool ended. Harmatullah had been engaged to sow aush. He was running his harrow through the freshly ploughed land, and, with all her modesty forgotten early in the morning, Phuljaan was walking behind her father.

Boikuntho paused. 'Looks like you've ploughed your new land well.' Lowering his voice, he added, 'Isn't your son-in-law here? He's been singing everywhere in the market. Is he at home?'

Harmatullah did not reply. Was it because he had a coughing fit every time he tried to speak, or out of embarrassment because his son-in-law never visited? Boikuntho walked along the edge of the pool, humming Keramat Ali's new song, 'The darkness of the Muslim's night is ending'.

It was on his way back from the Mondols' that he ran into Tamiz's father, who was sitting in the yard outside Kalam majhi's house. Kalam was saying, 'Arrangements will definitely be made for Tamiz's release since Ismail shaheb has given his word. But the lawyer must be paid. I'm spending freely, but have I asked you for a paisa, tell me.'

When Tamiz's father shook his head, no, Kalam majhi continued, 'But if you don't contribute how will I manage alone?'

'What have I got of my own? I even had to sell the land behind the house to Mondol in the year of the famine.'

'Do you consider Mondol your master? Are you going to sell him your house too?'

Tamiz's father had never considered selling his house. Where would he live? 'Your house will remain yours,' explained Kalam majhi. 'If you lose your home I'm the one who will have to make arrangements for you to live somewhere with your wife and son, isn't that so?' When Tamiz's father agreed, he said, 'It's just that I'm the one who's paying, but the son is yours, so surely you have some responsibility too, yes? My son can look after himself, he has a job, and he writes to me, have you single-handedly taken the responsibility for everyone in Majhipara? So think about what I told you.'

After Kalam majhi left Boikuntho fell in with Tamiz's father. Walking a few steps together, he said, 'What you did wasn't right, Tamiz's father.' At this Tamiz's father turned to look at Boikuntho, who lowered his voice to continue, 'All of us are having to pay for your sin of catching a fish in Bhabani's double bend.'

Tamiz's father's dull eyes turned even more turbid at this. 'Sin? What's sinful about catching fish?'

'You took away fish meant for Bhabani Pathak on the day of the ritual, didn't you? That's why he's refusing to stay here any longer. The manager has said he's going to stop all and sundry from going to Poradaho to worship Bhabani Pathak's idol. Why is this happening if not because of your sin?'

'I took the fish from the water and put it back in the water. How is that a sin?'

Now Boikuntho was in a quandary. This was true, Tamiz's father had indeed returned the devil catfish to the waters of Katlahar Lake. And the fish must have swum northwards along the narrow stream of the Bangali river to reach the double bend in the Manosh. How could Tamiz's father be said to have committed a transgression any more?

Gazing at an unidentified object in the north, Tamiz's father said, 'Munshi came down from the fig tree and scolded me, so I returned the fish to the water. What crime did I commit?'

33

Everyone had thrown themselves at a copy of *Anandabazar Patrika* from a few days ago. Muslims were decimating Hindus in Calcutta. Suhrawardy was himself on the streets with a pistol to kill Hindus. Despite the rasp in his voice, Satish the attorney had to take on the responsibility of reading out the newspaper and commenting on it. But his indignation did not inflame Boikuntho, for he knew that these people could not take their anger very far. What people needed now was a spirited fighter like Bhabani Pathak, who would have his Pathan general get rid of a hundred Suhrawardys if necessary. Boikuntho would visit his shrine at Poradaho after sunset today.

After a smart shower had washed away the humidity to make way for a bright evening, Boikuntho popped a paan into his mouth and sauntered off to Kader's shop to listen to Keramat sing.

But there were no melodies in Kader's shop today, where the owner's chair was occupied by Abdul Aziz. His reddened eyes and the quivering stubble on his unshaven cheek made him look like a stranger. Some of the people in the shop glared at Boikuntho and one of them suddenly shouted, 'We'll fight to get our Pakistan.'

'Not now, Boikuntho,' said Abdul Aziz. 'Come later.'

Boikuntho retreated but lurked near the door to hear how Abdul Aziz's brother-in-law Ahsan Ali had been murdered by Hindus in Calcutta. Aziz himself had been there, and had barely managed to escape with his life. There had been a huge meeting of the Muslim

League at the Maidan that evening. Attacked by Hindus on the way back, Aziz had tried to run away, pulling his brother-in-law with him. They had already heard at the meeting that riots had started in many parts of the city. Both of them had left before the meeting had ended. As soon as they had reached Dharmatalla they had seen shops being looted. Aziz had wanted to stop in front of a shop owned by a Hindu, but it was Ahsan who had dragged him along farther. At Taltala, just as they were about to jump into a shop owned by a Muslim, a group of Hindus had stabbed Ahsan in the stomach with a knife. He had collapsed at once. A Hindu shopkeeper had rescued Aziz by pulling him into his shop, from where Aziz had seen the killers knife Ahsan in the chest several times more before turning their attention to a boy of fourteen or fifteen running a paan-shop. What could Aziz possibly have done in this situation? The Hindu shopkeeper had hidden him behind a cupboard, where he had stood for two full days before being released on the street. Aziz was gasping for breath now as he recounted the incident. Who could have known there would be riots in Calcutta? Aziz had gone to the city to buy some goods for Ahsan's shop. All the shops were closed on the 16th, so they could buy nothing. They had planned to get everything they needed the next day and take the Darjeeling Mail at night. Ahsan would get off at Shantahar and take the metre-gauge train, while Aziz would travel all the way to Joipur. But who could have told this was what Allah had in store for Ahsan? Eventually Aziz had spent a few days at a tailor's shop in Koolootola before arriving at the town this afternoon. He had managed to inform his in-laws and was planning to take a carriage home. His wife was there, but Aziz had come to the market because he didn't have the courage to break the news to her. He was not able to speak coherently in any case. But Gofur kolu broadcast a description of Aziz's brother-in-law's murder that suggested he had personally taken part in the events. Listening to his account, Abdul Aziz began to sob suddenly, and although it was difficult to gauge how much of it was out of grief for his brother-in-law and how much out of fear of his brother-in-law's sister, the weeping brought forth a response from Kader's youthful workers. 'Why are you crying?' said one of them. 'We will avenge this.'

Abdul Kader scolded Boikuntho, 'You haven't left yet? Go home at once.'

There was no question of Boikuntho's budging from there, because Bhabani Pathak's blade was dangling in front of his eyes now. He had met Abdul Aziz's brother-in-law three or four times—no one would have said from his fair skin and sharp nose that he was not a Brahmon. And he was so polite too, always addressing Boikuntho courteously instead of dismissing him as one of Saha's employees. He was addicted to paan, and to the same brand of tobacco as Boikuntho. He had even pressed his own tin of tobacco on Boikuntho once, saying, 'Keep it, I get it all the time in the town.' Who could have murdered such a man? If Bhabani Pathak's blade didn't descend on their necks, what was the point of his having it in the first place? Was it just going to hang from his fingers like a whore's ornament? He had been hearing for several days now at Mukunda Saha's shop about violent riots in Calcutta. Muslims were abducting Hindu women and carving Hindu men into pieces. But then these bastard Muslims were very hot-headed, the swine had no rules about their food, they even ate off one another's plates, the men were constantly looking to get married. But Abdul Aziz's brother-in-law, such a good man, why did he have to be killed like this? Boikuntho's thoughts began to ramble. He was rooted to the spot, waiting to see Bhabani Pathak's blade hanging over the murderers' heads. Bhabani would be here any time, and Boikuntho didn't move for fear of missing him.

Abdul Kader practically pushed him outside, shoving him into Mukunda Saha's shop and saying loudly from the veranda, 'All of you had better stay indoors tonight, Mukunda-babu. There's no reason to worry, but it's still safer not to go out. Young people are angry at the news of Muslims being killed in Calcutta. Anyway, our workers will be in the market, there's nothing to be afraid of.'

Mukunda Saha felt his fear rise on learning that the Muslim League workers would be in the market. He was no less informed than anyone else about events in Calcutta. Kader read the *Daily Azad*, which Satish the attorney habitually sneered at. An educated Brahmon, he was right when he said that the bastard Muslims didn't even know how to use the language properly, and here they were, boasting of their own newspaper. Such ignorant people could only tell lies while mangling the tongue. When Abdul Kader had left, Mukunda Saha whispered, 'Lock the door, Boikuntho, bar it, and prop up the bamboo basket against it.' Dragging a couple of sacks of rice to the door, he said, Prop these up against the door too. Let any motherfucker come, don't open it. I have a crowbar, I'm leaving it here, don't be afraid. I have to go home now, the house is empty. If only Haripodo was still here . . .' Reminded of the recent death of his nephew, his voice grew heavy with grief. But he became fleet of foot as soon as he stepped outside, and rushed homewards.

Boikuntho made a bed for himself on the cot in the corner by the light of the lantern. Whether it was out of his desire to dream of Bhabani Pathak swinging his blade or to hear Cherag Ali's song in his head as an accompaniment to the sudden drizzle outside, or perhaps because he was sleepy already, he fell asleep as soon as he lay down. Taking advantage of this, a pair of rats crept into the sacks of rice propped up against the door. The sounds of their scurrying about inside woke Boikuntho, who searched the room thoroughly. No, no rats anywhere. The rain must have stopped, for he couldn't hear water dripping on the tin roof any more. But as soon as he fell asleep again, there they were, the rats. Meanwhile, some people had lit up the room, but still the fucking rats showed no signs of hiding. They had cleared out the sacks of rice. As the lights kept growing brighter, the rats finally disappeared. Why so many lanterns, though? What were all these lights for? Why were all these people here with torches? Even with the dazzling illumination and the people and the groom's headgear on Boikuntho's head, Cherag Ali looked solemn. 'What is it, fakir, why don't you talk?'

Cherag Ali smiled at his anxiety. 'You're getting married, haven't you understood yet?' But why was the fakir so forlorn at Boikuntho

getting married? 'You won't stay with us any more after you're
married, and we won't let you, either.' No sooner had he finished
than he began to strum his dotara:

> Musa smiles on seeing himself as a groom
> On Majnu's face there's nothing but pain
> The wedding is a union the wedding a union
> A union that takes you away from your own

Cherag Ali's sharp observations woke Boikuntho up, his blood
curdling with fear. Dreaming of marriage was ominous, the fakir
had told him as much. But was this the first time, or had he sung
these verses before too? If only he could go to Tamiz's father—if
Boikuntho pleaded with him, either he or Kulsum would explain the
dream to him.

'Is that Boikuntho, come on in.' Hearing him in the yard,
Tamiz's father left his maacha to escort Boikuntho in cordially.

Entering, Boikuntho said, 'The fakir came to me in a dream,
sang a verse. I thought I'd come to you for an explanation.'

Tamiz's father strolled off to the pond, seemingly in no hurry.
It was Kulsum who sounded distraught. 'How could you think
of coming here at this time? Haven't your heard the news from
Kamarpara?'

No, he hadn't. Last night someone had set the houses in
Kamarpara on fire, marching through the neighbourhood shouting
slogans and returning with chants of 'Naraye takbir, Allahu Akbar'
after starting the fires. But the blacksmiths got together and gave
chase, yelling 'Bande Mataram'. Since blacksmiths did not lack for
weapons, the assailants could not remain on the spot very long.
It didn't take Kulsum very long to recount the incidents. All that
Boikuntho asked was, 'What did they light the fires with?'

How would Kulsum know? Lowering her voice to a whisper, all
she said was, 'The attackers were from this area. There was a large
gathering at Kalam majhi's house yesterday. We could hear them

talking late into the night. They didn't ask Tamiz's father to join them, he was asleep. I think Budha called out for him, but then I heard Kalam majhi say, who wants that old fool? There are enough of you.'

Back from the pond, Tamiz's father bent over to wipe his face with the end of his lungi. 'Never mind all that,' he said. 'Tell me about your dream, Boikuntho.'

But Boikuntho was confused now about the dream he had had just a few hours ago. First he said rats dripping from the tin roof got into the sacks of rice and ate up the grains. Then, when he saw the room lit up, he asked Cherag Ali what the lights were for. Cherag Ali said these were fireworks to celebrate Boikuntho's wedding, following up with a verse that Boikuntho couldn't remember any more. He felt hesitant in Kulsum's presence about recounting a dream featuring his own wedding. The bitch still lusted after the details of others people's dreams. She was just the way she had been when her grandfather was alive. And she had inherited his trait too, she needed to be paid to explain other people's dreams. Brazenly she said now, 'Can't do any of this without money. My grandfather wouldn't take less than a paisa to explain anyone's dream.' When Tamiz's father raised his arm to stop her, she grumbled as she went into the inner yard, 'Take him out of the village. Not only will they kill him, they'll set your house on fire too.'

Kulsum's response changed the details of Boikuntho's description of his dream. After a pause he said, 'The rats kept scampering around in the rice sacks. And then . . .'

Suddenly Kulsum's mutterings turned into a verse.

When rats eat grains it's not a good sign
You can be sure a man will lose his life.

This single verse of Kulsum's brought Boikuntho's entire dream back to him. He now recounted it from beginning to end, while Cherag Ali put his book in front of him and drew squares and rectangles on the floor with a twig. Meanwhile, Kalam majhi was heard saying,

'We'll fucking carry weapons tonight. Won't let a single Hindu survive.' Someone else said in a deep voice, 'We'll get that bastard manager too. The swine doesn't consider us human beings.' It was difficult to say whether Tamiz's father had a reaction to any of this— he just kept drawing diagrams on the floor.

'Are you there, Tamiz's father? Chacha? Tamiz's father?' Startled by Shamsher's voice, Tamiz's father invited him in nevertheless.

Standing at the door, Shamsher said, 'Mondol's elder son has sent for you, you have to come at once.'

'Why?' Kulsum practically charged at him. 'Why should he go there? How dare he ask for someone whose son they have sent to jail?'

'Haven't you heard? Mondol's son's brother-in-law or father-in-law or someone has been murdered in Calcutta. But Aziz mian's wife won't believe him. Says you left my brother in Calcutta and ran away. He isn't dead. Only Tamiz's father can say for sure. She's from the town, keeps fainting ever since she heard. Can you come?' He offered a bait to make Tamiz's father agree. 'You'll have a chance to bring up Tamiz's matter too.' Suddenly noticing Boikuntho, Shamsher looked a little abashed. 'Oh, is that you?' he said. 'We hear Hindus are catching hold of Muslims in Calcutta and killing them. You shouldn't be here, either go to the market or stay at Saha's house for a few days.'

But Tamiz's father wouldn't let Boikuntho go. 'Come with me. Difficult dream. Let's go to the Mondols' first.'

However, Hamida's loud wails struck at Tamiz's father's heart even before they could enter Mondol's house. Her son had been taken from her just a few months ago, and now the Hindus had taken her brother too. Couldn't Munshi see what was going on? Calcutta was probably too far away for him to keep an eye on.

Sharafat Mondol's temper rose on seeing Tamiz's father. 'How dare this old fool enter my house? First you stole my fish, now you want to rob my house? You fucking traitor!'

Abdul Aziz felt somewhat perturbed and rather frightened. He feared Tamiz's father's curses much more than he feared his father.

Before he could speak, Abdul Kader told Kalam, 'We sent for Tamiz's father. Bhabi keeps fainting, so bhaijaan sent for him to convince her of Ahsan bhai's fate.'

Sharafat was disgusted by these histrionics of his daughter-in-law. Allah was the lord of life and of death, he had decreed death for the boy. It was a sin to think of the dead as alive or to make an attempt to bring the dead to life. Allah's messenger had never lobbied with Allah about anyone's life or death. And this bastard from nowhere, this Tamiz's father, who had accepted Mondol's hospitality and then tried to steal fish from his lake, this fucking criminal, had dared to investigate a dead man. And these profanities were being committed in his own house. His elder son's wife had ruined the prestige of his jamaat. She was from the town and fair-skinned, the family income had risen since her arrival, and she was bringing up the children well, too. He couldn't scold her, but he couldn't stand her either.

So he had to vent his anger on Tamiz's father. Sharafat Mondol found fault with him again. 'You people from Majhipara set fire to the houses in Kamarpara last night. And the very next morning you're walking around with Boikuntho. What are you up to? Are you planning to kill this boy too?'

Kader was a trifle displeased at this. 'Does anyone know for sure how the houses in Kamarpara caught fire? Their furnaces are burning all the time, one of them could have caught fire and sent Dasharath's house up in flames, couldn't it?'

Instigated by Kader's vehemence, Gofur kolu said, 'Muslims are dying like cats and dogs in Calcutta. And all that Dasharath Karmakar has lost is an ox or two. Don't the Hindus consider the cow their goddess? Were they so afraid for their own lives that they couldn't even go to the cowshed and set their goddess free?'

'Couldn't you have got hold of the oxen? You sell oil, your lives depend on them. Will you be able to tap the trees for oil without cattle? Did you go with the fishermen too? I thought they didn't let you into their neighbourhood.'

'Baapjaan!' Kader found it difficult to control himself now. 'Muslims of all castes are being killed by Hindus these days. Muslims don't have castes anyway. But are the Hindus in Calcutta leaving any Muslim unscathed?' He described Ahsan Ali's murder almost tearfully. When he had asked for a drop of water before dying, the Hindu rogues had urinated on his face. Even the Hindu women were supplying arms from the roofs. His agitation softened Sharafat Mondol. 'But Aziz was saved by a Hindu shopkeeper, you have to keep that in mind too.'

'We do the same thing, don't we? Take Boikuntho Giri here, I've been telling him since last evening to be careful. We know him, we're not going to let him come to harm.'

'What about that Hindu shopkeeper?' Sharafat argued in desperation. 'Did he know Aziz?'

'If you're going to talk about specific people that's another matter. But now it's a matter of religion. Hindus and Muslims are fighting because of their religion.'

It didn't occur to Sharafat to point out that religions consisted of people too. But this was the moment Aziz chose to usher Tamiz's father inside the house, which also irritated him. In fact, he was more annoyed by this than anything else, and told his elder son, 'Keep an eyes on the women's quarters.'

By then Tamiz's father was seated in the inner yard with his wife's grandfather's tattered book and a twig. This was the first time he was entering the house since it had been rebuilt as a permanent structure. Hamida was seated on a low stool in the high veranda, with Sharafat's second wife next to her. Hamida's head was not fully covered. Her stepmother-in-law interpreted her incoherent wails. Like Hamida, she too believed that Ahsan Ali was not dead—maybe the Hindus had locked him away, or perhaps he had been stranded somewhere while trying to escape.

Tamiz's father made marks on the ground, muttered incomprehensibly, consulted his book, and then delivered his verdict. 'I cannot say where he is now. If he had died, then . . .'

'I told you, didn't I tell you?' Hamida screamed as though Tamiz's father had announced that her brother was alive. Sobbing, she declared that a crow had been cawing constantly on the western side of the house for the past few days. She knew some terrible danger was at hand. But it had never occurred to her that her brother might be involved. Still, he was someone who said his prayers five times a day and observed all the rituals, he could not possibly have an unnatural death. He was from the town after all, so he must know his way around Calcutta much better than Abdul Aziz. Tamiz's father knew so much about this life and the next—could he not divine her brother's current location?

'There's nothing more I can say before Purnima,' said Tamiz's father as he left.

On new moon nights there was a greater possibility of getting a glimpse of Munshi beneath the fig tree at the northern head of Katlahar Lake. Everyone knew this. Aziz began to doubt his memory—had he actually seen his brother-in-law die and his body dumped in the drain? All right, they could get hold of Tamiz's father again on the night of the new moon, which was still about twenty days away.

Before evening fell Aziz put his wife in a carriage and took her to the town, where he would deposit her with his in-laws before going to Joipur, where Babar was alone right now. Aziz would return to his in-laws' with his son in a week, and pay a visit home as well. His brick business was suffering because of these interruptions. He was supposed to supply several thousand bricks to Mukunda Saha, but he hadn't even had the time to speak to him.

Sharafat exchanged his clogs for pumps after his son and daughter-in-law had left and set off towards Kamarpara. Judhisthir had sharecropped his land to grow aush—the blacksmith had produced a decent harvest. But both his oxen had died in the fire last night. Mondol was deeply troubled, wondering how he could allow Judhisthir to sharecrop his land again.

34

All the villages nearby threw aside the chill of the winter night to jump out of bed as, starting in Lathidanga, slogans of 'Naraye Takbir' and 'Allahu Akbar' shook Golabari on one side and Girirdanga on the other. Sharafat Mondol practically ran all the way to the Golabari market. He had to commandeer Kader and his forces to stop these people somehow. But Kader was not at his shop. Wrapped from head to toe in a Red Cross blanket, Keramat Ali was fast asleep on the quilt knitted by Nobiton, lying across several chairs and a bench put together. He had to be shaken awake. 'Kader bhai left for the town a long time ago, he'll be back tomorrow afternoon.' Why wasn't the door locked then? Rubbing the sleep out of his eyes, Keramat realized that Gofur was gone. He had unlocked the door and then shut it carefully from the outside without waking Keramat up. Sharafat expressed his dismay loudly. How could Gofur have left the shop unlocked when the man inside was sleeping like the dead? Even if he had to scold Gofur a hundred times over, Mondol wouldn't be able to recover the value of all the goods stolen from his shop. But the second reason for Sharafat's unhappiness was even more important. So Gofur had joined the attack on the jomidar's office, which meant that Kader had given his approval. The manager wouldn't spare a single human in the villages around Lathidanga if even one person from the jomidar's office was harmed. Kader moved around with the political leaders from the town but did not realize that the jomidar's

348

eldest son was Khan Bahadur Ali Ahmed's drinking partner. Khan Bahadur would use all his ministerial powers to please his friend.

'Come with me, Keramat,' said Sharafat, 'we have to stop the fishermen. We'll have to pay a very high price if the office is damaged.' But by then the people from the villages nearby had joined the fishermen. It was obvious even from Kader's shop that everyone was rushing towards the jomidar's office in Lathidanga, shouting at the top of their voice. Sharafat went out, only to run back inside, trembling, at the sound of gunshots from the jomidar's office.

Kalam majhi's nephew Afsar retreated with his people when the gunshots rang out. Still, it was beyond him to stop the crowds following him, and it was doubtful whether he even wanted to stop them. They did start running in the opposite direction, but not before demolishing all the eight shanties in Muchipara, which lay a few yards beyond the road, and killing a dozen pigs with the large harpoons used to kill fish. Some of them came up to the Golabari market, and even from inside Kader's office-cum-shop Sharafat and Keramat could hear shouts of 'burn down that bastard Mukunda Saha's shop', which, however, died down when Kalam majhi barked, 'What's the point? Don't bother. Just wait, let me get a fucking gun tomorrow, I'm not going to sleep till I shoot that bastard manager.'

It was market day at Golabari the next day, but the shops were closed, and the few people who were there exuded suppressed tension. Apparently the manager was supposed to have been at the office last night, but he had probably been tipped off in the afternoon and had slipped away. There were rumours that, briefed by the manager, the jomidar's eldest son had presented a report to Ali Ahmed shaheb. The market was rife with speculation—the police were arriving, what would happen after that, who were the people most likely to be arrested? Abdul Kader, who didn't know about the attack on the jomidar's office, had given Gofur a piece of his mind. But he flew into a rage when he heard that the manager had informed the police. Seated in his office-cum-shop, he began by venting his anger on his absent father. 'Baapjaan goes too far. Why does he have to lose his head if he hears the jomidar's office is being attacked? It's not as though the manager can touch his property. How long will this manager last anyway? The bill for eradicating the system of jomidars is in the assembly already, it won't be long now before the jomidar himself has to run away without even the clothes to cover his arse, where will that leave the manager, he's only his servant anyway.'

Alim the schoolteacher expressed his opposition to the bill. 'But why are arrangements being made to compensate the jomidars? That amounts to buying the property from them. How can this be called eradication of the system?'

The issue had come up at the Muslim League office in the town the other day. On being told that the government had been roundly criticized by *Nation* magazine, Shamsuddin the lawyer had said, 'Surely the government has not been given the right to make anyone insolvent.' Under the influence of Ismail Husain's speeches, Kader too had been opposed to the idea of offering compensation to jomidars.

But because this Alim never acknowledged that the Muslim League did anything good, Kader echoed the lawyer. 'Islam has no law to confiscate anyone's property, did you know that? How is it justice if the government takes away someone's property without paying for it?'

'The jomidars have been exploiting their holdings and the people for a hundred and fifty years now. Are you saying they have still not received a fair price? Some people protested at the jomidar's office, and now we're being told the police is planning to arrest all of them.'

Kader evaded Alim the schoolteacher's first question because it was difficult to answer. Besides, Ismail had said exactly the same thing a few days ago. But he answered the second point emphatically. 'Never mind the police. It's not so easy to get the police to enter Golabari.'

He sought support from Keramat. 'Isn't that right, poet? Didn't the aadhiars teach the police a lesson? The police got a thrashing in Joipur, didn't they?'

Keramat perked up at Kader's question, and had a song ready the very next day. He even got an excellent opportunity to sing it. Sadeq the lawyer and Shamsuddin the doctor were present in Golabari that day—perhaps they had come to conduct an on-the-spot investigation of the attack on the jomidar's office on Ali Ahmed's orders. Keramat began singing after getting Kader's approval.

> Invoking Bismillah I write these verses
> I bring good news, listen everyone
> Dark days are gone for the poor and the helpless,
> Here in India we'll have our free Pakistan.
> All will be equal there, the law will be passed
> For the good of the people jomidars will be removed.
> Noblemen and commoners, middlemen and farmers
> Will all have the same seat, the poor will be saved.

Keramat had many more lines to sing when Sadeq raised his hand to stop him. 'Enough. There's something you people don't understand. Who will gain if we create a division between rich and poor Muslims? The entire Muslim nation will benefit from the existence of affluent Muslims if they are allowed to remain solvent. The government belongs to us now. There should be no agitation against our own government. Nazimuddin shaheb pointed out correctly the other day that our fight now is against the Hindus.'

Even Kader took Sadeq Ali's side. 'You heard? I don't hear anything about Islam in your song. Write about the greatness of Islam, write powerful songs, mian.'

Keramat's enthusiasm had waned with the failure of his song. He could no longer write songs properly. Alim the schoolteacher had been right when he said, 'Your best songs are the ones you wrote about tebhaga.' But then in Joipur and Panchbibi he used to witness these things for himself, he had seen the spirit of the people, and the lines would flood his nib with such force that he didn't even have the time to dip it in ink.

Why was he in such a sorry state today? But Keramat had seen for himself how Cherag Ali would quickly start singing when explaining a dream, verses that fit in perfectly with his analysis. Cherag Ali probably deceived his listeners when he claimed that the songs had been handed down to him. They were not to be found in his famous book. Where were they written then? But maybe there were clues to the verses in the Arabic letters or numbers written inside the squares and rectangles on every page of that book of his. Even Tamiz's father, who was nothing but a mere fisherman, a fool among fools, an imbecile, was revered by everyone because of the book. His habit of sitting in a trance, of wandering around in his sleep near the fig tree or whatever the swine called it at the head or wherever it was of the lake—what great significance could any of this have? The bastard was ill, that was all, what else was it but an illness? But how could anyone earn so much respect because of a disease? His real strength was that book of the fakir's. It was the book that let him sit in a daze all day, that gave him the power to attract people. If only Keramat could get hold of the book, he'd compose a string of verses every day—all of them his own compositions which would easily outshine the songs handed down to Cherag Ali. People would listen with rapt attention, and even Boikuntho would admit, 'Now that's a song. Even our fakir never sang anything like this.' Keramat felt his skin breaking out in goose pimples—was there not a way to get the book? But then the goose pimples could have been because of the chill too, you never knew.

It was extraordinarily cold that night. At Golabari market the people inside the shops had shut each and every door and window tight and gone to sleep. Seated on the paved circular ledge beneath the banyan tree, Keramat Ali couldn't see anything more than 2 feet away. The door frame of Tamiz's father's room materialized in the thick translucent fog, as viscous as mud. Kulsum was kneeling on the floor on the other side, reasting her bottom on her tapering ankles. How tall she looked even in that position! The line of her neck was breathtakingly beautiful. Without the hint of a goitre on her throat, her breasts were blossoming like two enormous flowers. No, not like flowers, they were like twin domes. Keramat's head bowed with the desire to pay homage to the spot between the twin domes and to the tips of the domes. Not just his head but also his entire body began to shake so much with the lust to display his devotion to the pair of domes, no, the twin domes, that he feared he would fling himself at those two domes sculpted out of stone in the turbid fog there beneath the banyan tree and ravage them. He moved a little farther away so that he could control himself. He felt a tingle on his tongue, where verses were bubbling up like tiny pimples. Keramat felt a burst of joy, perhaps he would be able to compose a spirited song about Pakistan this very moment. If it was powerful enough Kader himself would pay to have it printed in the town. If the song became popular so many copies would be sold that they would not be able to provide enough supplies to the vendors. As Keramat muttered and hummed in his head, assuming he was about to come up with potent verses about Pakistan, an entire line of the song presented itself:

Twin domes are carved on my heart.

But this was not followed by a second line. What sort of verse was this? Was it really something he had composed? For that matter, he wasn't even sure whether it was he who had composed the two lines that had forced themselves out through his lips like vomit the other day outside Kulsum's house. This line didn't seem to match anything he had written earlier. Had it come from a clue in the fakir's book then? Would Kulsum never give him the book?

Visiting the Mondols' house sometime later, Keramat suddenly sensed the possibility of seizing the book. Kader was not at home, but he ran into Abdul Aziz, who was fretting morosely. He had brought his wife home as he always did during the harvest, but Hamida had no interest in supervising the weighing of the crops. Her suspicion that her brother Ahsan Ali had not died in a riot in Calcutta had now hardened to certainty. Aziz had taken her to the pir at Khanjan Lake near Joipur, who had informed her that Ahsan Ali was not dead—he was being held prisoner in a house in a narrow lane in a large city to the south. It was obviously Calcutta, but the pir had not provided an address.

Since then Hamida had been having a particular dream twice a week to begin with, then four days a week, and, for the past fortnight, every day: Several plump bare-bodied men in tight dhutis with tufts on their heads were gathered around Ahsan, their leader had a red sandalwood paste streak on his forehead, and the blade in his hand was dusted with vermilion. As the blade descended, Hamida woke up just before it fell on Ahsan's head or neck. She was woken up by her own shriek, after which she would sob quietly for an hour. On the first night after she returned to her husband's house, she had spotted a hint of a tender young face superimposed on Ahsan's, which she had observed closely. Oh, but this was Humayun! True to the proverb that a boy took after his maternal uncle, there had always been similarities between Ahsan and Humayun in appearance and behaviour, long before Hamida's dream series had materialized. Discovering that they were indistinguishable in her dream had frightened Hamida, but also pleased her a little. Maybe the uncle and the nephew, occupying a single body, would be able to stave off the attack from the blade.

All this strengthened her fear and her confidence while she slept. When awake, however, she was confused. Ahsan was alive, after all, so how could he be united with Humayun when he hadn't died? Hamida set off for the graveyard behind the house at every opportunity in the hope of a sign from the dead Humayun. But the people at home kept a strict eye on her, for it was not legitimate for a woman to visit a graveyard. And so Hamida's confusion could not be cleared, which was perhaps why her head throbbed during her waking hours, forcing her to bathe regularly every afternoon and even every evening despite the fact that it was winter. She neither caught a cold, nor developed a fever, however. This displeased her mother-in-law, who felt that a daughter-in-law with a body of stone was not auspicious for the household. Mondol's second wife tried to label Hamida a madwoman, calling her the insane wife. 'All these are signs of madness, madwomen don't feel the cold, their bodies are hotter.'

As with everything else, Mondol's first wife was not in agreement with her. 'Madness nothing, it's all pretence. How can a madwoman sleep so much?' This was true. Barely had the sun set when Hamida's eyes began to droop and she started yawning, often going to bed without eating. She had no other way to find out how her brother and her son were today.

All this had made things extremely inconvenient for Abdul Aziz. Not only was he a government employee, but he had also been transferred to the town with a promotion a month or so ago. How could the head assistant at the sub-registry office in the town tolerate such problems at home? The inquisitiveness, amusement, irritation and despair that his wife's behaviour elicited from everyone turned into barbs directed at him.

Then again, Kader gave him a mouthful if he didn't visit them at home frequently. His transfer and promotion had undoubtedly come about on his brother's recommendation. Kader had taken a smallish house on rent in the town and become a contractor, which meant that Aziz had to manage all the household affairs. He stayed at his in-laws' house in the town, but Kader became upset if he didn't go home every other day. Even the responsibility for the brick kiln was his. The trouble was that it was Aziz himself who had started it. It had begun when he paved the area around the bathroom with the bricks and cement left over from building Humayun's grave. The water from the bathroom began to flow towards the latrine as a result, which also happened to be on the way to the graveyard. So two rows of bricks were laid out from the cemetery all the way to the yard. After this the brothers decided that they would build a house with brick and cement. Sharafat was hesitant, fearing an adverse reaction from the manager, but this only increased Kader's determination tenfold. 'The manager even has a problem with a Muslim family living in a proper house?' Kader had wanted to get the bricks from the town, however, but this was both expensive and troublesome. So Aziz leased some land to the north of the lake and built a brick kiln. The house was built, but the brick kiln didn't close down. This business was a matter of luck—even after untiring effort and tremendous attention, many kilns still yielded third-class bricks which were completely useless. But Aziz had not yet turned out a supply of poor bricks. At first people would say it was not an auspicious spot, that things would go wrong. That insolent thug who worked at Mukunda Saha's shop had told Aziz to his face, 'Munshi won't stand for it. There's no knowing what Bhabani Thakur will do if he gets a signal from Munshi.' And now Mukunda Saha had started his own business of supplying bricks which he bought from Aziz's kiln. All the bricks that Kader needed for his work came from here. Whether it was with his job or with his enterprise, by Allah's grace Aziz was going through a good phase.

But how could he savour his fortune if his wife was going to behave this way? He dismissed Keramat Ali at first, saying, 'Kader isn't home.'

'Isn't he supposed to come today?' Keramat smiled, adding, 'I heard bhabi's ill.' Aziz couldn't take this village-wide curiosity any more. He was about to go back into the house without replying when Keramat said, 'I heard the pir shaheb at Joipur said the same things that Tamiz's father had said after consulting his book.'

Abdul Aziz wheeled around. 'What did Tamiz's father say? He did say something after drawing all those lines in the yard, didn't he?'

Like everyone else in the neighbourhood, Keramat knew the answer to this. 'Tamiz's father checked his book and said it wasn't clear whether bhaishaheb is dead. He had said he would find out on the night of the new moon, but none of you sent for him.'

Now Aziz was worried. Should he send word to Tamiz's father? But Sharafat was unwilling to spread the news of his daughter-in-law's sickness. And Kader was vehemently opposed to the charmed water of pirs. Aziz fell in step with Keramat, saying softly, 'The problem is that baapjaan cannot stand Tamiz's father. Tamiz is rotting in jail for no good reason.' What he couldn't say was that such oppression on Kalam's part ensured that someone or the other at home would always be ill. What he could say, though was, 'Maybe Tamiz's father can tell us the reason for the illness . . .'

Keramat both agreed and disagreed with him at once. 'Yes, your father will be angry if Tamiz's father comes here. All his tricks are thanks to that book. If we could get hold of it . . .'

'That tattered book of his? Tamiz's father is illiterate, he just glances at the book and draws lines on the ground.'

'The book has clues. I'd be able to make them out if only I could get my hands on it. So would you.'

'Then why not ask for the book? But will he part with it?'

'He'll have no choice if you order him to.'

'No, there's no need to force anyone.' Aziz was a little apprehensive of Tamiz's father's powers. 'Only if he hands it over on his own. Why don't you try? Don't take too much time, I doubt if Babur's mother can be kept here much longer.'

'No, it won't take me long, I'll get the book.'

'I heard at the Mondols' that Tamiz will be released. People are trying to get him out.'

'Who told you that?' Tamiz's father's cold response did not reveal either hope or doubt. Kalam majhi was trying his best, going to the town every other day to meet Ismail Husain and reminding of the promise he had made before the elections. He had spent plenty of money on lawyers too. But how was Tamiz's father to repay this debt? Kalam majhi had taken Tamiz's father's thumb impression by way of a signature on a piece of paper to appropriate his house and land. Kulsum had objected mildly, wondering where she would live after the old coot died. Kalam majhi couldn't contain his laughter. 'What will I do with this house anyway? It will remain yours, you can continue to use it. But there must be a document when money is spent. Else that bastard Mondol will say one day, remember you sold me the land behind the house? You sold the house to me too at that time. It won't take him a minute to forge the documents.'

Having signed over his house and land, Tamiz's father was now hopeful that his son would be released. Cherag Ali used to say, when a man makes a loss here it means he's made a gain somewhere else. He would sing:

> When the flood destroys your crops
> Don't let it break your heart
> It means the next crop that you grow
> Will be two times as bountiful

When Tamiz's father and Kulsum didn't respond, Keramat was silent for a while. Then he said, 'Aziz bhai is very upset about Tamiz. His wife is not her usual self, all she tells me is, nobody but Tamiz's father can identify my illness.'

'There's nothing to check, she sees her brother in her dreams every night, but her brother is dead.' Keramat was deflated by Kulsum's cold statement. He wasn't pleased with her certainty. What harm would it do anyone if a mistake in the analysis of Hamida's dream soothed her heart?

'That's just what I told Aziz bhai about, her dream. The fakir's book is not just a book, you people cannot understand the secrets of dreams that are written in it. It would be best if Tamiz's father could go there, but if not, give me the book, I can spend some time with him first to learn how to read the book.' When Kulsum didn't respond to this long speech, Keramat pointed out that Aziz was a government officer, after all, which meant he could also make efforts for Tamiz's release. Such opportunities didn't come easily. How much longer should Tamiz have to spend in jail?

'One month twenty-two days more and it'll be a full year in jail.' Keramat was reassured by Kulsum's brief sigh. In desperation he said that Aziz might succeed in pleading with his father to withdraw the case against Tamiz if Keramat could take the book to the Mondols' house. Kulsum said nothing. Although Tamiz's father fidgeted, she was carved out of stone. Keramat was not perturbed—on the contrary, the weight of the stone with which the domes of her breasts were made urged him even more strongly to get hold of the book.

But neither his vocal nor his silent entreaties worked. Kulsum walked into the yard in silence, looking away, her breasts pointing away.

Tamiz's father was aware that any more pressure would mean Kulsum wouldn't cook and lie down in the yard, which would mean he wouldn't get anything to eat. 'I'll see,' he said softly. 'Not today.'

35

It was the night of the new moon, but even when he walked in his sleep Tamiz's father had no difficulty getting his bearings right. Why couldn't he locate the fig tree tonight then? He couldn't do without it. He had to lock eyes with Munshi beneath the fig tree. Tamiz was imprisoned, it had been almost a year. Why wasn't his son being released? Had he done something to offend Munshi and Bhabani Pathak? There was so much trouble early in the morning of the Poradaho fair last year, or was it even earlier, Tamiz's father hadn't been able to pay even a brief visit. He hadn't even had the chance to check whether Tamiz had managed to make the ritual offering of a pair of pigeons at Bhabani Pathak's shrine. And then he had caught the fish meant for Bhabani, but then he had released it back into the waters of Katlahar Lake. Couldn't Bhabani let Munshi have even a single fish to celebrate the fair? Who knew what sin he had committed, surely Munshi could send him a signal from the fig tree. And then take Dasharath, he went back such a long way, his grandfather's, or perhaps *his* father or grandfather, had arrived here with the Giris, it was at the same time that Tamiz's father's grandfather, or *his* grandfather's grandfather, or was it *his* father or grandfather—Tamiz's father couldn't keep track of all this—the very same Dasharath Karmakar had had his house burnt by the fishermen. Who knew whether Munshi was sulking because of this? As soon as

Tamiz's father reached the fig tree he would look up at the highest branches, surely Munshi would send him a signal about what he had done wrong.

The Mondols' brick kiln had expanded to the north, and was advancing to the south as well, encroaching a little more on the lake every year. But where was the fig tree? Many of the trees had been cut down hereabouts, all the large trees had been gobbled up by the brick kiln. But surely the fig tree couldn't be among them. Any axe would melt before its blade could strike the trunk. Wandering around the lake all night in the cold and the mud, in his sleep and in his dreams, Tamiz's father began to freeze from his toes upwards. When one of Munshi's verses—'Creatures of fire are Munshi's servants, seeing him makes their hearts flutter'—played in his head, he ran even farther northwards in hope. But no, there was no fig tree to be seen.

As Tamiz's father wandered about, the pressure of his feet, or perhaps it was the look in his eyes, brought forth a winter dawn, and when the sun had risen a little higher, the workers at the brick kiln discovered that he had knocked off several rows of unbaked bricks while wandering around in the darkness. One of the men charged at him, shouting, 'And who might you be, you silly old coot, don't you have eyes?'

Arriving a little later, Gofur kolu got a chance to scream at Tamiz's father for ruining the unbaked bricks. 'Do you know how old you are? Will you never behave sensibly? Just wait till our boro shaheb and chhoto shaheb get here, then you'll see.'

These days Aziz was addressed as boro shaheb and Kader, as chhoto shaheb. But Tamiz's father, who did not know this, looked around for these revered figures. Was Gofur talking of Munshi and Bhabani Pathak? Tamiz's father cast his eyes towards the pile of broken unbaked bricks, scouring the debris in the bright morning light for a trace of either of them. But leave alone the fig tree, he couldn't even see a large tree anywhere.

The fakir went out no one knew where
The horse came up to the door and bowed
Then it took wing no one knew where

But what was the source of these lines? 'You've been wandering about all night, you old coot, what if you fall into the quicksand?' Gofur warned him.

Tamiz's father looked in the direction Gofur was pointing, where the quicksand had been walled in by rows of bricks about a foot in height, but it made no impression on him. 'Where's the fig tree gone, Gofur?' he asked.

'Munshi's fig tree? But that's at the northern head of the lake, what are you looking for here?'

'Isn't this the northern head? There's the Bangali entering the lake. This is the northernmost point.'

'That's true, this must be,' answered a troubled Gofur kolu. 'I don't see the fig tree anywhere.'

Meanwhile, Boikuntho Giri arrived, animating the stilled moist air over the lake with the fragrance of the tobacco he was chewing, saying, 'Babu said he needs some bricks the day after tomorrow.' Spotting Tamiz's father, he smiled widely through the paan in his mouth. 'Have you been walking around here all night?' Lowering his voice, he asked, 'Did you talk it over?'

Tamiz's father asked, 'You're here often on work, Boikuntho. Where's the fig tree gone? I've been looking for it all night, I can't find it.'

'But the fig tree is at the northern head of the lake, how will you find it here?'

Whereupon Gofur kolu and even some of the workers at the kiln said, 'But this *is* the northern head.'

Learning that Munshi's fig tree was missing, the paan in Boikuntho's mouth turned to ashes. His words came out like chewed cud. 'That's true. Gofur, all those trees you people cut down for the kiln, the fig tree wasn't one of them, was it? Not that Munshi's seat will fall to anyone's axe. Wasn't Munshi our Bhabani Pathak's general? Bhabani will not stand for any harm being done to him.'

'You'll never change your habits, Boikuntho. Munshi never worked for Bhabani Thakur, it was Majnu Shah who . . .' About to protest against Boikuntho's attempt to prove that Munshi was subservient to Bhabani Pathak, Tamiz's father stopped himself. No, it wouldn't be right to be arrogant; where Bhabani was concerned, both of them were important people.

Boikuntho looked everywhere for the fig tree, without paying any attention to Tamiz's father. He had forgotten all about reminding the people at the kiln about Mukunda Saha's requirements. Boikuntho looked high and low, but where had the fig tree gone?

But then what was there to look for anyway? The entire expanse had been cleared out, and any tree that had existed a few months ago had been gobbled up by the brick kiln. But Gofur kolu and the other workers at the kiln claimed that one black siris and about four white siris trees, several pithraj trees, and half a dozen arjuns, besides a number of jackfruit trees and about three mango trees on the high ground on the north-western bank of the lake were all that were chopped down. Not a single tree was to be seen nearby from the northernmost tip of the lake, the only treelike thing visible being the shaggy foliage of the banyan tree in the field at Poradaho. Where was the fig tree, then?

Abdul Aziz looked worried too when he arrived. It had been wrong to have cut down Munshi's seat, if that was indeed what they had done. His son had died last year, and this year his brother-in-law had been murdered. If, as the pir at Khonjondighi had suggested, Ahsan was indeed imprisoned in someone's house in Calcutta, Munshi's curses would now ensure that he was killed with a slash of the vermilion-streaked blade that Hamida saw in her dreams. Considering her behaviour these days, she could well go mad at the news of the disappearance of the fig tree. Abdul Aziz returned home deeply disturbed, and had barely said, 'Baapjaan! The fig tree at the northern head of Katlahar Lake . . .' when Sharafat, who was reading the zohr namaz, stared at him coldly, at which he hastily took his position next to his father for the prayers.

Sharafat said, 'Clean up, lay out a prayer mat, and read the namaz.'

But even before they had finished, word went around the Mondol household that the fig tree at the northern head of the lake was missing. Abdul Aziz said, as though providing justification, 'But not a single fig tree was cut. I was there when the trees were chopped down for the kiln.'

Abdul Kader had arrived from the town, had a bath, and asked for a meal several times. He skipped the namaz frequently these days. But Sharafat was finding it increasingly difficult to upbraid his younger son for this as easily as he could his elder son, the government employee. 'Where's my food?' Kader shouted suddenly. Frowning, he continued, 'What does it matter whether the fig tree is there or not? It's not as though Munshi lacks for a place to live in. The brick kiln is big enough for him to sit wherever he likes, sleep as he pleases.'

Abdul Aziz was startled to hear his brother joke about Munshi. But because his fear was greater than his rage, and because Kader's social and familial influence were growing by the day, he exercised his lips in a furious effort to produce a smile which would signal that what his brother had just said was a joke.

But his smiling exercises were brought to a halt when Sharafat Mondol said, 'Has anyone ever seen a fig tree on the northern side of the lake? When was it ever there?'

Even Abdul Kader was stunned at this. How could the old coot make such a claim? Seated in the tin-walled room with the door facing east, Sharafat Mondol's first wife was busy expressing her regret at her tired sons still remaining unfed. Mondol's second wife, who was serving the food on a mat in the kitchen, honed her tongue to contradict her husband harshly. Hamida was sitting next to her quietly. Although she didn't understand everything that passed between her husband, brother-in-law and father-in-law, she had an inkling of something ominous about to take place, and asked that she be given her food quickly, so that she could take a nap. She had no means of knowing what had happened to Humayun and Ahsan except by burrowing into the warmth of sleep.

Sharafat Mondol smiled woodenly at this beleaguered anxiety on everyone's part, and said with a rough edge in his voice, 'There's not an inch of land on the west and north and south of the lake that I haven't seen for myself. I've been around the entire area with the manager, and by myself as well. Was there ever a fig tree there? I never saw one. People who lived before us may have seen it, but I never set my eyes on one.'

36

'Kader, you do realize this place is mine, don't you? I've been elected from here, right?' When Kader nodded, Ismail asked, 'I'll have to answer in the assembly if there are riots in my constituency, won't I? What possessed you to set Kamarpara on fire? Why don't you stop people from attacking the jomidar's office at night?'

'But they haven't left a single Muslim alive in Calcutta. If Muslims are going to die this way under a Muslim League government . . . If our families are going be killed by Hindus . . .'

Ismail wasn't accustomed to this sort of response from Kader. Despite his surprise, however, he responded at once, 'Did the people of Kamarpara kill your brother-in-law? Are you going to get your relative back by ensuring that an old man like Dasharath is burnt in his legs while you kill his cattle?'

He introduced his companions to the gathering in Kader's shop. 'This is my friend Ajay Dutta, he's like my younger brother. Dedicated to the Communist Party. We're from the same neighbourhood, we grew up together. This is Ajay's sister Minu, Minoti Dutta, both of them work for the Communist Party. They're going with me to Kamarpara today.' Turning to Kalam majhi, Ismail said, 'Obviously you're coming too, Kalam mian, and so will your people from Majhipara. Arrange for lanterns, Kader, it'll be late by the time we return, we'll eat at your house on the way back.'

Kader felt a sharp pang. In his own neighbourhood in the town Ismail was closest to the Hindus, they seemed to be part of his family. But before the elections he wouldn't utter a word about anything but the glory of Islam and the plight of Muslims. As for Kalam majhi, he didn't support the idea of visiting Kamarpara at all. 'Things are heated up there today. Might lead to trouble.'

'That's exactly why we must go,' said Ajay Dutta.

Despite a niggle of worry caused by Minoti's presence, Ismail Husain insisted, 'Why don't we go and see what happens?'

It would be difficult for Kader to object now. He proposed an addition to the programme. 'All right. But since you're here, people have gathered, you must give a speech.'

The conversation was going on behind closed doors which, when opened partially, revealed a large crowd outside the shop. The sight of a well-dressed young woman from the town arriving in a carriage on market day had made buyers and sellers abandon their business to gape at her.

There was no time. Ismail Husain began without a preamble, 'Brothers, the jomidar and the moneylender will not be able to oppress anyone if we succeed in creating Pakistan. All distinctions between Hindus and Muslims will vanish. We Hindus of Bengal, Muslims of Bengal, are independent-minded. The kings and rulers of Bengal never accepted the dominion of Delhi. Today there is a conspiracy to carve up Bengal. The backbone of Bengalis, be they Hindu or Muslim, will be broken if Bengal is broken up. Traders from the west will plunder our land. You must not allow brothers to fight their brothers, to riot against them, and thus break Bengal into pieces.'

The people here had never heard anyone speak like this, not even Ismail Husain himself. They wanted to hear more. But Ismail ended his speech quickly. 'My friend, my brother, Ajay Dutta will address you now. Ajay had helped me a lot when distributing relief material from the Red Cross a few years ago. I'm sure you remember him.'

As soon as he was pushed forward Ajay Dutta began, 'Hindu farmers and Muslim farmers have fought shoulder to shoulder against the tyranny of the jomidar and the jotedar. We in the Communist Party are still fighting alongside Hindu and Muslim peasants against the jotedars to secure two-thirds of the harvest in the tebhaga movement. But now, instead of battling British imperialism and its agents, the jomidars and the jotedars, we're involved in rioting against our own brothers. We have to desist from this lunacy of hastening our own demise. We are ready to work with any party to stop this fraternal war. That is why, despite our political differences, we are here today with Ismail Husain. He is our brother, we want to join hands with our brother to stop the conflict between brothers.'

Ajay continued his solemn speech, while Kader whispered in Ismail's ear. Kamarpara was in turmoil, for Dasharath Karmakar had died this afternoon. He had burnt his legs while trying to rescue his cattle from the fire. This was nothing serious, causing only a few large blisters. But a burning piece of the roof of the cowshed had fallen on his chest. Horen the doctor had treated his legs but not taken the burn on the chest seriously. Since yesterday Dasharath had been having trouble breathing—apparently a portion of his lungs had been burnt too. The people of Kamarpara were seething after his death today, even some of the blacksmiths who had sold their land and left for the east during the famine three years ago were back with cleavers and spears. A frightened Kader was hoping that Ajay Dutta would keep talking long enough to ensure that it would be too late to visit Kamarpara today. But Ismail whispered in Ajay's ear, 'Hurry it up. We need to get there quickly. The situation is very bad.'

Ajay Dutta was winding up by then. 'We're making a heartfelt appeal to India's two main leaders, Mahatma Gandhi and Quaed-e-Azam Jinnah, to unite in an effort to stop this communal violence. Let the rioting between Hindus and Muslims stop.' He led the audience into a slogan, 'Gandhi Jinnah come together, stop this Hindu-Muslim slaughter.'

It had been a very hot day. The long summer afternoon began to turn pink on the way to Kamarpara. Ismail, Ajay and Minoti were sweating profusely. Drenched in perspiration, Ajay shouted the first line of the slogan, 'Gandhi Jinnah come together,' but only Keramat and Boikuntho responded loudly with the second, 'Stop this Hindu-Muslim slaughter.' The rest couldn't pick up the refrain.

Kader had more or less forced Mukunda Saha and Keshto Pal to accompany them. Keshto Pal was quite enthusiastic, but Mukunda did not want to let Boikuntho get too far away, pausing when he lagged behind, speeding up when he strode ahead. Kalam majhi had been trailing the group before slipping away, telling Budha that he had had an attack of dysentery.

The people of Kamarpara had just returned after cremating Dasharath Karmakar, settling down beneath the arjun tree outside the dead man's incinerated cowshed following their ritual baths. Some of them were still perspiring. They had been informed of the party on its way, but in spite of their restlessness at the sight of all these upper-class people, none of them went up to greet the group. A little later one of the older blacksmiths shouted, 'Get a stool from the house.'

Minoti went inside directly. Judhisthir burst into tears when he saw Kader, and broke into loud sobs with his arms around Boikuntho. A loud echo emerged from within the house. The wailing of the women, especially Judhisthir's sister's shrieks, made evening descend on Kamarpara a little earlier than usual. With no moon in the sky, the sound of the women crying gathered in the sky like a loud covering of clouds, preventing the laments from rising upwards and forcing them to whirl around the arjun tree. The humidity intensified.

Many of the men were wiping their eyes, but Dasharath's son-in-law was not one of them. The flames from his father-in-law's now-cold furnace glowed on his face, lending a charred flavour to his voice. 'So you're here now to spread your love and affection. Mondol has already made half of us homeless by buying our land dirt cheap, and now the Muslims of Majhipara are plotting to burn down the rest. What are you people here for?'

Despite the situation Gofur kolu flared up in rage. 'If Mondol hadn't bought your land Jagadish Saha would have confiscated all of it.'

'What's the difference?' said Dasharath's son-in-law. 'Our land isn't ours any more. At least if Jagadish Saha had taken it the land would have remained with someone of our own religion.'

'Let's not go into all that today,' said Ajay Dutta. 'You may bring up religion, but is the moneylender really one of your kind?'

'Is Sharafat one of us if the moneylender isn't?'

'No, the jotedar isn't one of you either.' Ajay Dutta spoke slowly to explain things simply. 'Neither the moneylender nor the jotedar can be your people. We're fighting against them. Our battle hasn't ended.'

Keramat had been loitering near Ajay Dutta. Seizing the opportunity, he stepped up. 'I was in Joipur and Panchbibi during the tebhaga movement. My songs about tebhaga were very popular in those parts. You must have heard some of them.'

'Don't you sing here?'

'No.' Keramat's response could be interpreted as either a complaint or an excuse. 'The people hereabouts don't have the fire of the tebhaga movement. How can I write songs without this fire?'

'Aren't the people in this area concerned about tebhaga?' Ajay Dutta asked Ismail. 'Have you implemented it already, Ismail-da?'

'None of the jotedars in these parts has a large holding,' answered Ismail, 'so there aren't too many aadhiars. The Tenancy Bill has been moved in the assembly already. The tebhaga system and the abolition of jomidars will be introduced together.'

Budha, Shamsher Poramanik, and even Judhisthir himself sidled up closer to Ismail and Ajay to listen to their conversation. Ismail was part of the government, he would definitely be able to confirm whether the tebhaga movement was going to be implemented or not. But he changed the subject. If the blacksmiths now decided to kill some of the fishermen to avenge Dasharath's death, then the fishermen would also strike back one day. They also had to think of the people of Palpara. No one would be left with a livelihood if the killings continued, and if everyone nurtured violence in their hearts no one would be able to live in peace either.

'Who's benefiting from the riots?' said Ajay Dutta. 'The poor are killing one another, the rich are savouring the whole thing.'

Everyone listened quietly, without adding their own views. The fire in Judhisthir's brother-in-law's eyes didn't die, he remained sitting at a little distance from the rest.

At night everyone gathered at Kader's house, which was lit up with lanterns. Ismail, Ajay Dutta and Minoti rebuked Kader lovingly for making such elaborate arrangements in the height of summer, but they did not desist from stuffing themselves with rice pulao and meat korma. Sharafat was thrilled at the opportunity to host educated upper-caste Hindus in his home. He was genuinely unhappy with what had happened in Kamarpara, saying, 'These fishermen will never change their ways. They can make all the money in the world, but a fucking lower-class person will always stay that way, he will never become a real human being. Look at what they did in Kamarpara.'

There was still a crowd in the yard outside the Mondols' house, with the carriage waiting there. As Ismail was about to follow Ajay and Minoti into it, Tamiz's father came up to him. 'My son is still in jail. I pawned my house and land for the money to get him out, but he hasn't been released yet.'

Before Ismail could respond, Kader jumped in to scold Tamiz's father. 'Do you know how late it is? Is this the time for such talk?' As Kader made to join Ismail and the others in the carriage, Boikuntho appeared in front of them, reminding Tamiz's father of the fig tree. 'You didn't ask about the fig tree? No one can find it . . .'

'Have you gone mad, Boikuntho? These people are busy trying to prevent brothers from killing one another, and you want to bring up such irrelevant things?'

37

The jomidar's manager Purnochandra Chakraborty was deeply mortified by the Kamarpara massacre. Two days after Dasharath's death, he had summoned the inhabitants of Kamarpara through Mukunda Saha to the office. Keshto Pal, who had also been informed, had brought a few people along as well. Besides Satish the attorney from the town and Anil Sanyal from Sherpur, two other gentlemen were sitting in the office smoking. One of them was wearing a pair of sleek glasses, while the other had an English newspaper.

'We could have had him treated properly if you'd informed us in time. Your father's life might have been saved too. But then all of you are friendly with people from the other religion, you'll even die at their hands but you won't take help from your own.' The manager sighed and held up two crisp ten-rupee notes. His exhalation sent them flying to the floor. As he stooped to pick them up, Judhisthir heard the manager say, 'He was such a good man, your father. But they didn't spare even someone like him.'

'But now the bastards are chanting unity.' Satish the attorney spoke slowly and deliberately in a bid to conceal his irritation and rage. 'Suhrawardy kills Hindus with his own pistol, he gets Meena Peshawari to kill so many Hindus, he even gets policemen from Punjab to come to Bengal and kill Hindus. And now he's putting up a smokescreen with all this talk of a sovereign united Bengal. These slitcocks are up to all kinds of tricks.'

'But Subhash Chandra Bose's brother is also in favour of a united Bengal,' said Anil Sanyal, not without trepidation. 'Sarat Bose, Kiranshankar Roy, Satya Bakshi, and then take our Surendranath . . .'

'Never mind those people. Subhash Bose's brother is not Subhash Bose.' Satish could no longer contain his anger. 'First you kill people, then you claim to be a saint. Are you telling me Suhrawardy didn't murder Hindus? How can these people join hands with them? Our Shyamaprasad is right, we demand a divided Bengal even in an undivided India. We must not live with these barbarian Mohammedans any more.'

Taking a fresh cigarette from his tin and lighting it, the gentleman with rolled gold spectacle frame said, 'It's not as though religion is a major factor. But they belong to a different cultural level. We cannot live together, it's impossible.'

'Ajay Dutta had brought his sister to Golabari with Ismail the other day. He put on a big show of sympathy in Kamarpara and then ate dinner at the Mondols. Look how a Dutta is degrading himself.' Satish's temper rose as he spoke. 'You actually ate at the house of the people who set fire to Kamarpara?' Now he vented his ire on Anil Sanyal. 'I heard the Congress held a public meeting with Ismail in Sherpur. Hats off to your taste in people.'

How could Anil Sanyal blame Ismail, considering he had himself delivered a passionate speech in favour of an undivided Bengal at the Sherpur meeting? But he was crushed by a letter he received soon afterwards from a cousin, who had written, 'Do you Hindu Bengalis wish to immolate yourselves? Forsake your perverted inclination for cohabiting with converted lower-caste uncultured barbarians within the same nation. Should you not cure yourself of this insanity, the injustice you will inflict on your progeny will be unpardonable.' This cousin was a learned man whose English composition had astounded even the Englishmen in Britain. He was currently engaged in writing English scripts for the radio in Delhi. He seldom wrote in Bangla, and even when he did, he never strayed from a high diction. But even such an erudite man had allowed his unmitigated rage to coarsen his tone. 'Do you wish to abandon the education and culture you have acquired thanks to the grace of the British government in order to share your bed with these filthy peasants?'

The letter had left Anil deeply dejected. Even if he had a few Muslims in his team, not all of them were poor farmers. But then who in this area would read his brother's letter in English in any case? Ismail's father was the only admirer of his cousin's English skills among the people Anil Sanyal knew. Still, this man was the pride of the family, which meant Anil did not dare ignore his diktat. He listened to Satish in silence.

'A united sovereign Bengal means accepting the permanent majority of Muslims. Their numbers grow much faster than ours, each of them marries three or four women and produces children by the dozen. Can we reduce ourselves to their level? Should we? Does Sarat Bose understand any of this? Does he have the far-sightedness of a Patel or a Nehru?'

Satish kept talking and the manager offered advice to the blacksmiths in a low voice. 'We must be united now. The jomidar will organize a Durga Puja where the shrine of Bhabani Pathak stands. All Hindus will gather there irrespective of caste, devotion will bring them together. Haven't you seen the Muslims, how the hordes collect at the same spot for Eid or whatever they call it. Do they let you in there?'

'But all the Muslims hereabouts come to the Poradaho fair,' protested Keshto Pal. 'There's a horse race from Golabari to Bhabani Thakur's shrine in Poradaho, most of the riders are Muslims.'

'But did you know that Bhabani Pathak's clan was an enemy of the Muslims?'

'No, they weren't, babu.'

'You think you know everything?' Satish the attorney shouted at Keshto Pal. 'Do you know they burnt down the Muslims' houses? Have you read *Anandamath*?'

'No, babu,' said Keshto Pal, and proceeded to convey the information that he had not read *Anandamath*, as well as his rejection of Satish's claim. 'Our Bhabani Pathak had a Pathan as his general.' His confidence grew so much that he added history to his narration. 'Fakir Majnu Shah was the king of his clan and Bhabani Pathak was the king of his.'

'The king of which kingdom? You may not have read novels but you seem to have read a lot of history.'

Not understanding, or perhaps ignoring, the jibe from the gentleman with the English newspaper, Keshto Pal continued, 'They fought together against the British soldiers of the Company. And I've heard that Munshi from the fig tree was with Majnu. But Boikuntho says no, Munshi was Bhabani Pathak's general, who made the fig tree his home after his death. You know the katra that floats up on the surface of the lake on the Purnima night in Asharh every few years or so? Munshi also sends the goat to be slaughtered at the stake. The murrels in the lake turn into goats.'

'That Munshi of yours must be a magician.' Despite his barb, the gentleman was in fact deeply worried for his backward countrymen. 'Independence will be meaningless if people are so superstitious. Listen, those people you're talking about were neither kings nor freedom fighters. They were just criminals. You see, Purno-babu,' he turned to the manager, 'when the East India Company tried to restore law and order in the country, there were clashes with these people.'

'They weren't criminals, babu.' Even Judhisthir felt it necessary to speak up now. 'They weren't criminals, they had renounced earthly life. Munshi flew away with his fig tree when Mondol's son built a brick kiln. All the bad things that are happening are because of his curses. It's been two years since Bhabani Pathak came to the Poradaho fair as he used to.'

Keshto Pal picked up the strain. 'Boikuntho used to see Bhabani Pathak every year, his ancestors came to this area with him. But now he has not seen him in two years. Our lives will be destroyed if some other ritual is started at the spot that belongs to him.'

The manager couldn't remain silent after this, he had a responsibility to fulfil. He said, 'And what if the system of jomidars is abolished? This land belongs to the jomidar, you think you can continue with your rituals if he is removed?'

'Why not, babu?' said Keshto Pal with confidence. 'Check the documents. It says there that this part of the land is earmarked for the use of the people.'

Purnochandra Chakraborty knew this only too well. 'Is your Bhabani Pathak so powerful that he has turned your blood cold?'

'No, babu.' Judhisthir's taciturn brother-in-law was moved to respond. 'Our blood is as hot as ever. Your protection will give us strength.'

The manager glanced at the young blacksmith through narrowed eyes. 'You mustn't be hot-headed, you understand?' he said. 'Meet me before you go. We have to kill two birds with one stone.'

38

Afsar majhi began to face a series of troubles after being involved in setting the Kamarpara houses on fire. A thief had broken into his home a few days ago, but didn't seem to have taken anything, leaving behind nothing but the signs of his intrusion. However, Afsar's wife realized the day after Dasharath died that the thief had found the tin in which she had hidden more than forty rupees. She was in an advanced stage of pregnancy at the time, but three days later, either out of grief for the stolen money or because of Kamarpara's curses, she gave birth to a stillborn son. A boy after two girls, but he didn't survive. Suffering as she did from post-partum complications, Afsar's wife was in a terrible way now. She had to keep going to the bamboo grove to defecate, and one day she had fainted with her sari still hitched up above her hips, a condition in which one of Afsar's young nephews had seen her. She lay on the maacha all day, groaning and scolding Afsar for attacking Kamarpara and causing this crisis.

Unable to confide in anyone, Afsar avoided his wife as much as he could. He had suddenly become very conscientious about reading the namaz. When he was home he made it a point to visit the mosque, and even at Kalam majhi's shop he used it as an excuse to close the shop and say his prayers. Meanwhile, moulobi Kuddus broke down in Allah's court during the Friday namaz over the plight of Muslims in Calcutta and Bihar, complaining vehemently against the fact that Muslims were being butchered today in a land which had once been under their rule. This made Afsar feel lighter, for killing a Hindu was not an unforgivable sin when Muslims were being killed everywhere. But the very next day the same Kuddus told Afsar when they met at Fakir's Ghat, 'What is all this you people are doing, Afsar? What harm did the old man of Kamarpara do for you to burn him to death? He may not have been of the true faith, but that is for Allahtaala to judge. He never betrayed or oppressed you, what made you set fire to his house? You think you won't have to answer for this on the day of judgement?'

The day of judgement was a long way away, his life was being torn apart at this every moment. What was Afsar to do now? One afternoon Boikuntho went to Kalam majhi's shop. Since it wasn't market day, there weren't many people around, and Kalam majhi himself had gone home. Making sure they were alone, Boikuntho said, 'Afsar, be careful, all of you from Majhipara. I've seen Narod from Kamarpara and Judhisthir's brother-in-law from the other side both visiting the jomidar's office every day. The manager has won those two over, they're determined to organize a Durga Puja at Bhabani Pathak's shrine.' Boikuntho had never seen Afsar so forlorn.

The manager had told Mukunda Saha, 'Let the fair go on as usual. If they want their rituals during the fair let them have it. But the area around the shrine will be paved and goddess Durga will be brought there once a month.' The manager was an educated Brahmon, why was he fishing in troubled waters? The same man was also going to ensure that the people of Kamarpara would have the chance to attack Majhipara one of these days and avenge the killing of Dasharath Karmakar.

Afsar's mind drifted as he listened. The time for his asr namaz went by, but he paid no attention. Suddenly gripping Boikuntho's arm, he said hoarsely, 'I'm ruined, Boikuntho-da. My afterlife is doomed, my life is falling apart too. It was I who set fire to Dasharath's cowshed.' An incoherent Afsar described the crisis in his household—he believed that he was personally responsible for the murders of both Dasharath and his own stillborn child. What should he do now? He read the namaz as often as he could, but even so he wasn't hopeful of being pardoned by Allah. Even moulobi Kuddus had informed Afsar of his own displeasure as well as Allah's.

Boikuntho was assailed by a fresh bout of worry. If Cherag Ali had been here he would surely have shown a way out. Bhabani Pathak hadn't set foot in the area in the past two years—it was in fact his dissatisfaction that was behind all the trouble. Even the fig tree had disappeared, making it impossible to take Tamiz's father there to seek Munshi's advice. But perhaps he should consult Tamiz's father anyway. 'No, don't do that,' said Afsar apprehensively. 'Chacha is bound to hear if you talk about all this in Majhipara.'

Boikuntho suggested an alternative. 'Why don't you come with me to Kamarpara?' When Afsar jumped in alarm at this, Boikuntho said, 'Judhisthir's mother is a good person, Judhisthir himself is a straightforward man. If you touch her feet and beg pardon she will forgive you. And Kamarpara will no longer be angry with Majhipara. Let's go.'

After a silence Afsar said, 'If you take me along they'll get after not just me but you too.'

'Me? Which fucking blacksmith dares touch me?' Boikuntho was defiant. 'I'm a descendant of the Giris. Girirdanga, Nijgirirdanga, Golabari—do you know whom these places belonged to? Have you any idea?' After a brief description of the indomitable might of his forefathers, he modified his decision slightly. 'All right, I'll go by myself one of these days. Let me talk to Judishthir's mother and Judhisthir, with Narod and Gourango and that bloody brother-in-law, then I'll take you to meet them.'

But there wasn't a peep out of Boikuntho for the next three days. Meanwhile Afsar's wife had taken to her bed, and both daughters had developed jaundice, their skins turning yellow, with frequent bouts of fever and vomiting. With everyone ill at home, Afsar had asked to be let off early from the shop and was walking home when he spotted Boikuntho, who stopped on seeing him. 'Go along home. I'm going to Kamarpara now. Meet me in the market tomorrow afternoon, beneath the banyan tree.'

Afsar felt his skin prickle. 'What if they do something to you?'
At once Boikuntho seized the opportunity to boast of his ancestral
courage and his own bravery, which reassured Afsar. With no boats
available, Boikuntho walked along the western rim of the lake.

'Go home, isn't your family ill?' he said to Afsar, who insisted on
walking along with him instead.

A slim moon had risen and had set soon afterwards. Since the sky
was cloudless, the lake resembled a giant expanse of sand in starlight.
Several storks flapped their wings at intervals to fan themselves as
they flew around the silk-cotton tree near Mondol's house. Maybe
this brought some comfort to them, but the heat their bodies gave
off in the process made it warmer on the ground below them. Afsar
panted, overcome with fear, tempted to tell Boikuntho not to go to
Kamarpara. But this fear did not grow because Boikuntho talked
constantly, even though Afsar was not enjoying the monologue. He
felt mildly angry with Boikuntho, and was occasionally pricked by
suspicion: What if this man dressed in a dirty dhuti was leading him
into a trap? A few acres beyond the Mondols' house lay Kolupara,
after which they had to walk miles along the southern bank of the
lake, across Mondol's land, to reach the creek. Its narrow channel
was completely dry. Across the creek, to the east of the lake, lay
Kamarpara. When they reached the edge of the creek Boikuntho
suddenly fell silent, and the fear that Afsar had been experiencing
grew a hundredfold to smother him. 'Let's not go today,' he said
tentatively. 'Another day, perhaps.'

Boikuntho did not reply. From this side of the creek both of
them could see shadows approaching from the southern end of
Kamarpara. Someone was heard shouting, 'The bastards are coming,
they're here to set fire to our houses again.'

Identifying the voice as Dasharath's son-in-law's, Boikuntho
said, 'You're right, Afsar, let's go. I think they have weapons.'

The beam of a torch lit up Boikuntho's and Afsar's faces from
across the creek. Dasharath's son-in-law screamed, 'Those Majhipara
bastards are here. Judhisthir, Narod-kaka, Gourango-khuro, come

quickly. The swine have come to burn our houses down again. You fucking fishermen, we won't let a single one of you escape with your life today.' In no time a crowd of blacksmiths had gathered with choppers and spears. Boikuntho began by protesting against his inclusion among fishermen.

'What fishermen? I'm Boikuntho, Boikuntho Giri, don't you know me?' But he couldn't say it loudly enough. Instead he urged Afsar, 'Run, Afsar, get out of here.'

Afsar's feet were rooted in the dry earth on this side of the lake. He was standing behind Boikuntho, resting his hand on his companion's shoulder. At least nine or ten blacksmiths ran up to them in a flash. 'Bande Mataram,' screamed Dasharath's son-in-law at the top of his voice. Not everyone responded, but three or four of them shouted 'Bande Mataram' loudly enough for their cries to resound on both sides of the lake. Some of the blacksmiths said, 'Didn't I say the bastards would attack us again? You see now?' An iron spear raced faster than them through the air, but because Boikuntho and Afsar began to run at that precise moment, it overtook them and went farther. By the time they were close to Kolupara, one of the blacksmiths had caught up with them, and a blade landed on Afsar's neck.

Boikuntho had run even farther by then, but he stopped short on hearing Afsar scream, and, returning, put his arms around Afsar, who was still running, before roaring, 'Watch out! I'm one of the Giris. I am cursing all of you blacksmiths, your clan will die out.' But instead of being afraid of this outcome, or perhaps being indifferent to the need for keeping the bloodline going, either Dasharath's son-in-law or Narod Karmakar—Boikuntho wasn't sure which of them it was—thrust a large dagger into Afsar's stomach, twisting it with so much expertise that Afsar's innards fell out at once. As Afsar slumped to the ground, Boikuntho fell as well, and another blacksmith slashed at Afsar's chest with his blade to ensure his death. Boikuntho raised his left arm to ward off the blow, as a result of which the blade sliced his thumb off neatly, but lost some of its force in the process and could only effect a glancing blow on Afsar's chest. By then the cries of 'Bande Mataram' could be heard much more loudly, in response to which gunshots were heard from Mondol's house. There weren't too many people in Kolupara, but a handful of young men, possibly Gofur's brothers and nephews, leapt out of their homes with shouts of 'Naraye Takbir' and 'Allahu Akbar', forcing the blacksmiths to retreat.

The inhabitants of Kolupara and the Mondols' hired hands picked Afsar up bodily. 'Who is it from Majhipara?' asked Sharafat loudly from the veranda outside the front room. On being told, he came up to them and ordered his hired hands, 'Bring him into the house, though I doubt he'll live.'

It took a long time for Karim the doctor to arrive from Chhaihata. Horen lived close by, but no one could bring themselves to suggest that he be called. Kalam majhi glared as Boikuntho kept up his ceaseless commentary, saying, 'You tricked my nephew into going there, you bastard, we should get you.'

But Afsar mumbled, 'I took Boikuntho-da there, dada . . .' When the people of Kolupara and Mondol's hired hands repeatedly explained how Boikuntho had tried to save Afsar, Kalam finally piped down and, gripping the doctor's arm, burst into tears. My nephew, he means more to me than my son. I'll pay you whatever you want. I can get a doctor from the town if you want me to.'

Tamiz's father came up to Boikuntho and took his hand. 'Come to my house.'

Afsar died about an hour after the doctor arrived. Kader advised burying the body before the police was informed, because if the corpse were taken to the police station, it would have to be sent to the town for a postmortem and not be returned before a week. By that time the body would have rotted with its entrails torn out. Afsar was buried immediately after the fazr namaz in the old graveyard of the fishermen. Sharafat Mondol was strongly opposed to this, but given the situation, and taking into account Kader's capitulation before Kalam majhi's insistence, he had no other choice.

Kulsum made a paste of some tender grass which Tamiz's father applied to the stump of Boikuntho's severed thumb. She tore off strips of cloth from an old sari of hers, but since Tamiz's father couldn't wrap it properly around the wound, she said, 'Enough, give it to me.' The wound didn't stop bleeding even after she had wrapped several layers of the makeshift bandage around it. Handing Boikuntho one of Tamiz's lungis, Tamiz's father said, 'Let me put this on you. You've got blood all over yourself.'

Kulsum intervened suddenly, 'This won't mean breaking with your religion, I hope?' She continued a pause, 'Are you mad? What made you take Afsar to Kamarpara? He was the first one to set fire to their houses the other night.'

Instead of responding to this, Boikuntho declared that now that the blacksmiths had dared touch him, the bastards would find out for themselves whose descendant they had attacked. The swine would be wiped out. Then he explained that he had told Afsar not to go, but Afsar had wanted to seek forgiveness from Judhisthir's mother. The poor fellow was dejected after a string of troubles at home. Dasharath couldn't possibly have remained angry with him from heaven if the family forgave him.

'Be quiet, Boikuntho,' said Tamiz's father. He was worried. Boikuntho had to be taken away from Majhipara as soon as possible.

Budha had already announced at the top of his voice, 'We won't spare a single one of those fucking Hindus.'

Either out of fear of becoming an outcaste or because of the pain in his hand, Boikuntho refused any food. Lying on Tamiz's father's maacha, he groaned and talked at the same time. On the floor Tamiz's father was looking up something in Cherag Ali's book by lamplight. 'Is that the fakir's book?' asked Boikuntho.

Kulsum stayed in Tamiz's room, but peeped in frequently. When Tamiz's father went out at the first cry of the birds in the morning, Kulsum said, 'Take Dada's book with you.'

Tamiz's father returned after a long time, his face looking like thunder. 'Let me take you across the lake, Boikuntho,' he said.

Kulsum held out the book again when Boikuntho rose to his feet. 'Take this.'

Tamiz's father didn't say anything at first. Then he mumbled, 'There's nothing more to find in the book. Even the fig tree is gone. Take it, Boikuntho, I can't keep it any more.'

Putting his arm around Boikuntho's shoulder, Tamiz's father led him out through the back door. Kulsum held out *Khwabnama* to him. 'Aren't you taking the book? Here it is.'

'No, I can't take it.'

Kulsum lost her temper suddenly. Her grandfather had used the book to explain many of Boikuntho's dreams, which he had had both when asleep and when awake. Why, Boikuntho had even tried to find out Bhabani Pathak's intentions and whereabouts from this book. How could he refuse to take the book now? Kulsum understood clearly—despite all his troubles, he would never be rid of his obsession with religion. 'You dare insult my grandfather?' she said, her voice thick with anger.

Boikuntho paused for a moment to cast a loaded glance at Kulsum, but did not reply.

Kalam majhi slaughtered an ox a day later and invited everyone to a feast. Moulobi Kuddus came to read the entire Quran. Allah's words rang out across Majhipara from the school set up adjacent to the prayer house under Kalam's patronage, recited plaintively by young students in their reedy voices. After eating his fill of beef curry with rice at Kalam majhi's feast, Keramat Ali was walking past Tamiz's father's house, immersed in the rhythms of the Quran. Looking around for a glimpse of Kulsum, he suddenly heard someone call him, 'Listen.'

To his surprise, Kulsum herself opened the door and appeared in front of him. She held out Cherag Ali's book to him. 'Weren't you asking for Dada's book? Here you are.'

Keramat was overwhelmed. Holding Cherag Ali's tattered book in his own hands was so overwhelming that he even lost his ability to be overwhelmed. Wondering what to say and how to say it, he looked up to see the door closed and Kulsum gone.

Going to Alim the schoolteacher's house, Keramat smiled widely. His head was crammed with verses. Now that he had Cherag Ali's book, he had nothing to worry about. Thinking up lines about Gandhi and Jinnah coming together, he said, 'Masterbabu, Ismail shaheb brought over a tebhaga leader the other day, Ajay-babu, he spoke so beautifully, did you hear his speech? Gandhi Jinnah come together, stop this Hindu-Muslim slaughter. We need slogans like these.'

'Forget it, mian!' Alim was not remotely interested in Ajay Dutta's speeches. 'After all these years they've woken up to the need for Gandhi and Jinnah to unite. Considering the trouble they're causing from opposite sides, if they come together they won't let a single person in the country survive. Ajay Dutta is a tebhaga leader, can't he find someone else to unite Hindus and Muslims? Do we now have to bow and scrape to Gandhi and Jinnah?'

Keramat barely heard any of this. Picking up a sheet of paper and a pencil, he opened Cherag Ali's book. Ismail Husain visited again the next day on hearing of the turmoil in Majhipara. This time Ajay Dutta and his sister were not with him—he was accompanied by Suren Sengupta of the Congress. The sudden arrival of two MLAs had brought the inspector of Amtoli police station too, besides a circle officer from the town. But none of them had to go to either Majhipara or Kamarpara. Ismail led Suren-babu straight to Kalam majhi's shop. Kalam broke down in tears when Suren-babu embraced him. 'Afsar was not my nephew, babu, he was my son, you could call him my son.' Boikuntho was sent for as well, but he had no opportunity to declaim the history of his ancestors. Suren-babu listened to him closely and then embraced him too. Boikuntho's eyes misted over. Bringing his grief under control, Kalam majhi brought up the business of the lease on the lake. Suren Sengupta said that it hadn't been right to deprive the fishermen of their right and lease the lake to someone else. But he would have to hear the jomidar's side of the story too. However, Ismail promised that they would request the jomidar, even put government pressure on him if necessary, to have the lake returned to the fishermen this year.

Kalam majhi had already made arrangements for a huge gathering of fishermen at the Golabari market. Since the veranda in front of Mukunda Saha's shop was higher than all the others, Suren Sengupta and Ismail Husain used it as a dais to deliver their speeches from. The diminutive Suren-babu, dressed in just a dhuti and a shawl, spoke about Hindu-Muslim unity so sweetly and simply that everyone was entranced. When both of them had left for the town after Ismail's speech, Keramat Ali began singing. He had been flooded by verses after getting Cherag Ali's book. Bowing to the audience, he began:

> Bismillah says Keramat as he begins
> The country will now get a just government.
> First, the supreme being rules the world.
> Next, the god of death will take over
> When Israfil blows into his trumpet
> Neither houses nor the land will survive
> Don't anyone forget what you have been taught
> League-Congress violence hasn't ended. Why?

The audience cheered with joy, their applause drowning Keramat's voice. Alim jumped up, shouting at them to be quiet. Keramat continued singing:

> Namrud was jealous of the prophet Ibrahim
> The barbarian Namrud made his own heaven
> Where is Namrud now, where his opulence?
> League-Congress violence hasn't ended. Why?
> What the Muslim League demands from India
> Is the right to create their own Pakistan
> The Congress says we won't let you have it
> And so the two parties battle it out
> This is how they destroy the tender fruit

League-Congress violence hasn't ended. Why?
Four League and Congress leaders are invited
With joy and pleasure they depart for London
The honourable League leader Quaed-E-Azam
Sets London on fire with his fiery speech
Liaqat Ali Khan goes along with him
Lord Wavell represents the Indian government

Baldev Singh is one of the Congressmen
Jawaharlal Pandit makes up the team.
The visit to London yields no benefits.
League-Congress violence hasn't ended. Why?
We've suffered always, we Hindus and Muslims.
Waiting for independence we're laid to waste.
This land is ours, make no more trouble here.
League-Congress violence hasn't ended. Why?
This is what Keramat tells his own people.
Try to understand what fate has in store.
Selling milk for tobacco will cause you harm.
Try to understand what Keramat tells you.
Hopes of freedom are driving us mad.
League-Congress violence hasn't ended. Why?

The cheers of the audience overflowed their throats. Many of the listeners began to sing the refrain. A moved Keramat took Cherag Ali's book out of his sling bag and touched his forehead reverently with it. Abdul Kader called him into his shop. 'Come with me to the town tomorrow. Ismail-bhai will be delighted with the song since it mentions Pakistan. And so will Ajay-babu and his comrades, because you've talked about the League and the Congress coming together. Let's go tomorrow, let's not delay.'

Aziz called Keramat outside now. 'Excellent song. Come to my house in the town with Tamiz's father. Babar's mother just won't get better. Not even all the money I've spent has had any result.'

Lowering his voice, he added, 'Kader hates all this talk about fakirs and songs. My wife's maternal uncle is a theologian, if he can have a chat with Tamiz's father and consult the book to . . .'

'What do we need Tamiz's father for?' Keramat rejected the idea with conviction. 'I know all his tricks.'

'What do you mean?'

'His wife's grandfather Cherag Ali's book is with me now. His wife told me, my husband is illiterate, poet, what can he make of this book? Why don't you take it and use it for the good of the people?'

'The book's with you?' asked Aziz in excitement. 'You've got hold of Cherag Ali's book? Really?' Keramat offered it to him, and continued boasting, while Aziz leafed through the frayed pages. When Keramat finally paused, he said, 'Let the book be with me for now. I'll give it to my wife's uncle to read tomorrow morning. He's a theologian, a famous priest, spends all his time with fat books.'

'I need the book badly, bhaijaan,' implored Keramat. 'Tamiz's father's wife wasn't willing to give it to me, I had to go to great trouble to get it. I have to return it to her too.'

'It's the same thing, whether I keep it or you do,' said Aziz, tucking Cherag Ali's book into his bag. 'I'll show it to my wife's uncle. A theologian. He makes more than a hundred rupees a month just supplying charmed water and amulets. He can appreciate a book like this.' Handing Keramat a ten-rupee note, Aziz said, 'Get that songbook of yours printed. Won't this pay for it?' As Keramat took the currency note and stared at it, Abdul Aziz said, retreating into his shop, 'Give me a couple of copies when it's printed. Don't forget.'

39

Triangular banners in red, blue, green, purple and yellow were strung across the roads in the town; flags fluttered on rooftops, a white moon smiling against a green background. People were brimming with joy. So was Tamiz, with two rupees and twelve annas in his pocket. The deputy head clerk had taken his thumb impression on a piece of paper when he was released from jail, saying, 'The government is giving you this money for your travel back home.' The clerk was happy too. 'Independence will be announced tomorrow. We have been ordered to mark the occasion by releasing some convicts before their sentence is completed. Ismail Husain shaheb recommended you to the DM. Meet him before you leave.'

But there was a huge crowd at Ismail Husain's house. Of course, there were a few village elders amongst the well-dressed people, but no one whom Tamiz knew. He didn't dare enter.

After paying a full three annas for a meal of rice and beef curry near the railway station, Tamiz felt sleep descending on him as soon as he lay down on the platform. But he woke up well before dawn at the medley of whistling trains. Everyone was running towards the main road. Tamiz had meant to buy a lungi for his father and a rolling pin for Kulsum when the shops opened in the morning. Kulsum loved ruti, and had even learnt to make them at the Mondols, but she needed a rolling pin. There was no sign of the shops opening, however. The streets were choked with people.

He paced around near Akbaria restaurant next to the police station, savouring the aroma of pulao, meat curry and parathas, but didn't have the courage to go in. The crowd of people in panjabis and pyjamas, dhutis and shirts, and dhutis and panjabis at the Oriya restaurant tucked inside a lane meant he couldn't eat there either. Buying peanuts for two paise outside the cinema hall, he found out that all the shops would be closed today, and there would be a procession soon.

And what a procession it was! Overflowing with people. There were even two motor cars with their hoods down. In one of them a group of young men were dressed like the British, saying goodbye to Indians, pretending to speak Bangla in an English accent as they announced their return after two hundred years of ruling the country. People couldn't stop laughing at their antics. In a clearing in the centre of the parade, a few strapping young men in shirts whose pockets had flaps, just like police uniforms, were marching to a beat. 'The Pakistan National Guard,' said a man next to Tamiz. Oh, wasn't that Abdul Kader with them? Had Kader bhai joined the police? If only he had joined a year earlier—Tamiz wouldn't have had such a hard time. Some people went by in carriages with flags of Pakistan, shouting slogans, 'Long live Pakistan.' A group of boys were swaying and dancing on a bullock cart, saluting passers-by. The procession kept moving. Now a tall elephant appeared, with an upside-down bedstead on its back. A flag of Pakistan was flying from each of its four legs, while some people sat on a mattress in the middle. Wasn't that Ismail Husain? But how was Tamiz to push through this crowd and approach the elephant? He was still willing to try, but there was a sudden commotion near the police station. What was it? A young man of eighteen or nineteen, clad in a lungi and vest, was trapped on a tall lamp post which he had scaled to hang the flag of Pakistan from the tallest point. He was screaming now, while people shouted advice from the road. 'Jump into the first-floor balcony behind you.' 'Jump, we'll catch you.' Ignoring all the suggestions and requests, he plunged to the street.

The people had moved back despite the crush to make room for him. The young man's skull broke on impact with the surface of the road. He hadn't let go of the flag, and his blood reddened much of the green and white on the fabric.

The procession continued on its way after a few people took the corpse into the police station. It crossed the railway lines to proceed towards Jhautola or Badurtola or whatever the area was called—Tamiz found it hard to remember the neighbourhoods in the town. He couldn't go any farther. The young man had died trying to take the flag higher, and the colour red had triumphed over the flag. How could something like this have happened? In jail Tamiz had become friendly with some people who swore by the red flag. They had said that if the jotedars and jomidars and moneylenders remained, then neither Pakistan nor independence would make any sense. Tamiz could tell from the numbers in the procession that Pakistan was bound to get the tebhaga system. Were all these people fools? The young man who had died of electrocution trying to make the flag of Pakistan fly high was just as poor as Tamiz. He hadn't climbed up there without a good reason. Tamiz responded lustily to the slogans with 'Long live Pakistan!' and 'Long live Quaed-e-Azam!'

Seeing the sky clouding over, Kulsum was gathering all the branches and leaves from the yard and putting them in Tamiz's room. She gaped on seeing Tamiz, who went up to her and said, 'All well?' When Kulsum didn't reply, he continued, 'I was released yesterday.'

Kulsum hid half her face behind the end of her sari. Tamiz stared at her in surprise. He had never seen her weep like this. His own eyes grew heavy with tears at the sight. Possibly to control himself, Tamiz asked, 'Where's baapjaan?'

His voice sounded deep, and he spoke evenly. Wiping her eyes, Kulsum gazed at him, breathing rapidly. Tamiz smelt different now. She spoke after a long time. 'You've grown so thin, you're all skin and bones.'

On the contrary, Tamiz had in fact put on a little weight thanks to regular meals in jail. Accepting Kulsum's observation, he smiled. 'I'm hungry. Make some rice.'

Kulsum talked ceaselessly once Tamiz sat down to eat. Tamiz's father was seldom home these days, spending most of his time wandering around the northern head of the lake. He brought home some money from Kalam majhi at regular intervals, maybe he had sold the house to Kalam, who could tell? Kalam was an important man these days, he had declared he wouldn't rest till he had wrested the right to the lake for the fishermen. This sounded reasonable, since Tamiz also knew that no one would be denied their rights in Pakistan. Kulsum talked late into the night, recounting everything that had happened in the past year.

When he went into his own room to sleep, Tamiz found the thatched roof worn out, and the floor littered with leaves and branches. It had rained a little while earlier, leaving the floor slushy. Living in a properly constructed building during the year he had spent in jail had changed his habits. Still he fell asleep the moment he lay down on his maacha.

Tamiz's father returned in the morning, his feet caked in mud. A little later Tamiz came in and handed him two rupees. 'They gave me this when I got out of jail.'

Sleep was dripping from Tamiz's father's eyes. 'Have you heard?'

'You've taken money from Kalam bhai and sold him the house.'

'Why should I sell it? I've pawned it. What could I do, fighting your case needed money. But that's not what I was taking about.'

'You're talking of Afsar chacha? I heard. About Judhisthir's father too.'

'No, not that. There's been a disaster.'

'Boikuntho-da's thumb . . .'

'No, not that either. A disaster. The fig tree at the northern head of the lake can't be found. The fig tree is gone.'

'Gone? They must have chopped it down.' It seemed simple enough to Tamiz. 'Didn't the Mondols make a brick kiln?'

'You think it's so easy to chop down Munshi's tree? Who can be so bold?'

'Munshi has flown off with the tree.' Despite his reckless answer, Tamiz seemed a little worried. 'I think they've cut the tree down without realizing it.' But he didn't have the time to discuss all this. 'Let me go look for some work.'

Phuljaan wept like a brief shower when she saw Tamiz. 'So you've come at last? You didn't take my son to the doctor, I don't have a son any more, why have you come now?'

Tamiz had heard of Phuljaan's son's death from Kulsum, who was not particularly concerned by Phuljaan's grief. 'The bitch killed her son,' she had said. 'Her lover doesn't show up either. Who's the whore with the goitre going to marry now?' Ever since he had heard Kulsum worrying about this, Tamiz had been very keen to pay Phuljaan a visit.

'Enough!' Phuljaan's mother scolded her daughter. 'Must you start crying the moment anyone visits?' Then she began complaining about her husband Harmatullah. The old coot thought of nothing but land, although he had spent his entire life sharecropping for someone else. This time he had got more of Mondol's land for sharecropping, for it was difficult to find anyone to grow aush these days. Wages had risen, and most of the people in the village had left in search of higher earnings in Khiyar. The aush had been harvested on some of the plots, but the old coot was now preparing to sow amon there. But he still hadn't made up his mind about what to grow on his own land. He spent all his time working on Mondol's land, and paid no attention to his own.

No matter whose land it was, the rhythm of Harmatullah's sowing and harvesting reverberated through Tamiz's body—he remembered the time with Phuljaan by the ripening paddy field in the mist. His fingers curled in anticipation, though it was difficult to say whether it was because he wanted to hold Phuljaan or a plough.

Mondol had leased more land, nearly 4 acres that lay between the sloping bank of the ox pool on the east and the spot where the shrine to Bhabani Pathak used to be. 'Recognize me, old man?'

Without looking at Tamiz as he harrowed the land on the sloping bank, Harmatullah answered, 'Why shouldn't I? It's important to recognize people who've been to jail.'

Despite the heat rising in his face, Tamiz restrained himself and said, 'It was you people who sent me to jail. Mondol's slaves. He gave the order, and all of you came at me with sticks. Those days are over. You won't have Katlahar to yourself any more, it belongs to the fishermen, it will come back to the fishermen.'

Harmatullah felt intimidated, the rascal seemed to have become even more aggressive. Since he had been in jail once, there was no trusting him any more. Realizing that Harmatullah was frightened, Tamiz said, 'I heard you're sharecropping a lot of land. Let me know if you need a hired hand.'

Helping Shamsher Poramanik's nephew up on the hoe, Harmatullah said, 'Mondol won't let you sharecrop any of his land. He might get upset if I let you work as a hired hand on his land.'

'Pack your fears away in your trunk. Let me tell you something, Mondol's son sticks to Ismail's arse all the time. Have you heard of Ismail Husain?'

'I voted for him.'

'Yes, all of you voted him into the council. He drove in his own motor car to the jail and had me released. Now it's up to you. You're sharecropping the land, I'll work on it, you'll pay me. What's Mondol got to do with it?'

Tamiz harvested Harmatullah's aush and took standard wages. But he wanted to set a different condition for harvesting the amon on the adjoining field. If Harmatullah wanted to pay wages, he could pay the prevailing rate, but he could compensate Tamiz another way too, by giving Tamiz a portion of his own share of the crop that he would get after Mondol had taken his own due. What was he getting at? Tamiz said with conviction, 'The tebhaga system will be in place by then. The jotedar gets one-third, you get two-thirds. If you give me even an eighth of your share, you'll still have plenty for yourself.'

Harmatullah didn't understand. But then he didn't mind accepting Tamiz's condition on the assumption that he would get two-thirds of the crop. Instead of confirming, however, he said, 'We'll see. Do the work first.'

He liked the way this young man worked. Not only was he from a family of fishermen, he had also been in jail for a year, when he hadn't even set his eyes on a rice field. But just look at the way he sowed the amon. He planted the seeds in such perfectly straight rows that Harmatullah's own lines of seeds looked ragged. And now even Phuljaan had started coming to the fields to work, which she had stopped doing when Keramat had scolded her. What a bastard this son-in-law of Harmatullah's was. He'd disappear for months at a time to wander around from one market and fair to another, staying in the houses of all sorts of people, and he issued threats from time to time asking why a woman should work on the fields. There was no need to bother with someone like him.

Now that the amon stalks were turning plump with sap, Tamiz even checked on them at night. Phuljaan threw her weight around unnecessarily, annoying Harmatullah. There was no need to supervise Tamiz's work, there was nothing he couldn't do on his own. But despite her sarcasm, Phuljaan seemed to be in good humour when Tamiz worked on the fields.

Keramat spent a lot of time chatting with Tamiz when he ran into him at the market. All the tebhaga leaders whom Tamiz had met in jail were Keramat's friends, after all. It was Keramat's songs that had inspired the peasants to rise in protest. With the tebhaga system about to be introduced, Keramat's stock would rise even higher. It wasn't as though Tamiz believed everything that Keramat said, but then he didn't seem to be lying either. And he composed excellent songs. Still, sales of Keramat's book *League-Congress violence hasn't ended* had fallen after the formation of Pakistan. On Ismail's advice he was now thinking of writing a song titled 'Our New Land Pakistan'. But it wasn't coming to life.

Keramat wasn't a bad sort, but why did he behave badly with Phuljaan? Tamiz had wanted to ask her about Keramat, but he kept postponing it. By now the paddy stalks had become quite fleshy. Winter had come early this year. Wondering if this would affect the crop, Tamiz was weeding the land on the east of the ox pool when he heard the sound of a chorus of female voices sobbing in Harmatullah's house. He raced off in that direction.

Gofur kolu had come with his wife. The women were weeping because of the piece of paper Abiton had brought. Although he couldn't read, Harmatullah turned it over in his hands grimly. Tamiz practically snatched it from him for a look. But Abiton was herself relating its contents. 'It's better for the son of a bitch not to be here,' Harmatullah shouted at his daughter. 'If he's divorced her the curse on us is lifted. Good riddance.'

Tamiz was upset to see Phuljaan writhing in tears on the maacha. Why did she have to break down at being divorced by Keramat Ali? Maybe Phuljaan's unhappiness had made him unhappy too, he didn't know, but Tamiz did a poor job of the weeding when he went back to the fields. Phuljaan herself had told Tamiz many times that even if Keramat pretended to be a good man, he wasn't human, the bastard was the spawn of the devil. The swine wasn't divorcing her deliberately, she had said. Harmatullah had nobody but his three daughters, who would inherit all his land. It was because of his greed for this land that the devil wasn't divorcing Phuljaan. She would have sent him the talakhnaama herself if Islamic law had allowed it. But in that case why was she weeping inconsolably now that he had divorced her? Did Keramat really have his eyes on the land all this time? But whoever married Phuljaan now would get the land, and surely she wouldn't have any objection to marrying Tamiz. In fact, Tamiz could expand her property. If he married Phuljaan, and if Harmatullah gave him his own land to sharecrop, Tamiz could make enough money from his share of the harvest in three years to buy back the land behind his own house from Sharafat. Of course, he would have to pay back Kalam majhi before that to reclaim the house and the land it stood on. Harmatullah had taken a lease on the land to the east of the ox pool, Tamiz would take the land on the west. Since the system of jomidars was being abolished, the people would get all these prime plots of land. All they would have to do was to plough the soil, sow their seeds and reap the harvest. Phuljaan wouldn't have to work so very hard. One snarl from her was all it would take for Tamiz to produce a harvest so bountiful that there wouldn't be enough people to eat all the grain. It would take him less than three years to be the owner of 6 acres of contiguous land.

40

Boikuntho came late one night, leading Tamiz's father by the hand. Tamiz had only just returned home. 'Your father was wandering about in search of the fig tree in his sleep,' said Boikuntho. 'He didn't recognize me. I've brought him back.' Up on the maacha Tamiz's father continued sleeping without interruption. 'Keep an eye on your father, Tamiz,' said Boikuntho. 'I thought I heard Munshi today. The fig tree is gone, I couldn't make out where he was calling from.'

'There's just one Munshi who might get bajaan,' said Tamiz, 'but there's no lack of people who want to get you, Boikuntho-da. Best to be careful.'

Mukunda Saha had said the same thing. 'It's not a good time for you to be moving about at night, Boikuntho. Two things you cannot trust are the sky and Muslims—clear now, clouded over the next moment. Sunshine here, darkness there. Kader mian said the town is overflowing with refugees from India. Why does he have to tell me all this?'

Judhisthir had burst into tears one day in Mukunda Saha's shop. 'What kind of tyranny are we living under, babu? Three rascals from Majhipara took two spades and an axe from me the other day. When I asked them to pay they shouted at me, we'll use this axe to avenge Afsar's murder. What do I do now, babu?' One of Judhisthir's two companions was not as much of a coward, he wanted to go to the manager for justice. It was on the manager's assurance that they had been preparing to avenge Dasharath's killing. So Mukunda Saha had no choice but to accompany the three of them to the manager, who, it turned out, was not at the office and had not been there for a few days. On the blacksmiths' demand, Mukunda had to take them all to the town, but the manager was not there either. He had gone to Jalpaiguri with his family. According to his servant, he was arranging to exchange houses with a Muslim there. The manager would return from time to time, however—he had no choice. Who else was going to look after the jomidar's affairs? But neither Mukunda Saha nor the blacksmiths felt they could depend on him any more.

'Don't forget our Bhabani Pathak,' Boikuntho reassured them. 'Even the Muslims are devoted to him.'

Kalam majhi provided some comfort too. 'There's nothing to worry about, none of these bastards can do anything to you.' But then he himself was worried. 'Trouble is that they're slaughtering Muslims in Hindustan, the people in the town are ready to explode.'

Trains were leaving Pakistan for Sealdah Station in Calcutta every day with their bogies stuffed with Hindus' corpses. Mukunda Saha was hesitant to tell the others what he had read in a three-day-old copy of *Anandabazar* that had just arrived from the town. It was difficult to predict Kalam majhi's mood. A week later Kalam returned from the town and asked the owners of all the permanent shops in the market to meet him at his shop. Handing Boikuntho a ten-rupee note, he said, 'Get some sweets from Gopal's shop. Use the entire money.'

What was he celebrating? Kalam majhi had struck a deal with the manager today in Ismail Husain's presence to have the lease for Katlahar Lake to be transferred to him. The documents had been signed. Mondol's lease would end in the month of Choitro. The manager hadn't been very keen—after all, he had pocketed plenty of bribes from Mondol. But Ismail Husain had got a letter from the jomidar in Calcutta. The manager had no choice but to sign the lease over to Kalam.

The news spread to Majhipara. The fishermen gathered at
Golabari to hear it from him first-hand, even though they knew
he wouldn't be back till late that night. On being told that the
fishermen's lake had been returned to them, some of them wanted to
cast their nets in the water at once. 'Don't do any such thing,' Kalam
majhi stopped them. 'The paperwork is final. All that's left is for
Mondol to hand over the lease.'

Tamiz had also rushed from Harmatullah's fields on hearing the
news. His father had come too. Helping Tamiz's father up into his
shop, Kalam majhi said, 'They humiliated this old man, now justice
will be served. I want Tamiz's father to be the first to cast a net in our
Katlahar Lake. Mark my words. He's not a nobody, he's Baaghaar
majhi's grandson.'

41

But Tamiz's father never did get the chance to cast his net in Katlahar Lake. He was late getting back home that night after having sweets at Kalam majhi's shop in Golabari. He was hungry by then. All he ate was rice with salt and chillies, but Kulsum couldn't even provide this meal more than once a day. Still, Tamiz's share of the paddy would be here soon, which meant they wouldn't have to survive much longer on one meal a day. For at least the next two months there would be platefuls of rice. And once the lake was under their control in a few months, there would be large slices of fish to go with the rice. A fresh breeze played in Tamiz's father's belly at the possibility of eating rice and fish every day, and with the breeze sleep descended on his eyes. When the deep sleep turned into a light slumber sometime later, he climbed down from the maacha and started walking towards Katlahar Lake. With each step his sleep intensified further, which was why he didn't stray at all when making his way along the familiar path to the northern head of the lake.

Many of the inhabitants of Majhipara had been up and down the banks of the lake that evening, but none of them was there when Tamiz's father arrived. The workers at the brick kiln were asleep beneath a thatched roof of straw. Stopping at the edge of the lake, Tamiz's father raised himself on tiptoe and craned his neck to gaze as high up as possible. Behind him the smoke rising slowly from the kiln had mingled with the mist to obscure most of the sky. How was he to see the fig tree, then? Taking advantage of the invisibility, someone cleared their perforated throat, sounding like a child playing hide and seek. Tamiz's father felt a thrill run down his body. There was a piercing pain in his arms, his legs, his chest. His half-filled belly twisted with the same pain, and his thighs and the wound below his knee began to throb, while his eyes, mouth and cheeks tingled at Munshi's voice.

But the verses were indecipherable. It couldn't have been anyone but Munshi, for Cherag Ali had never sang verses without words, and it wasn't his voice either. The sound was coming from the north, so Tamiz's father had to retreat a few steps to locate its source. Multicoloured lights appeared, piercing the curtain of the sky. Munshi's face was indistinct, or perhaps it couldn't be seen clearly because of the glare of the illumination. His black turban was caught in black flames, and his throat, perforated by a bullet, was glowing red from the flames. The mist was burning in his white flowing beard. The iron pan with the fish motifs was ablaze, and so was his fig tree. Was his own fire burning his throne in the heavens? Tamiz's father retreated farther when he felt the heat of the fire on his skin. Farther south to his left, there was a large expanse of sand next to the lake. When he saw the ash from Munshi's burning tree fall on it, he gathered his courage and looked up. The sight of the storks on Mondol's silk-cotton tree increased his fear—was it the shadows of their wings that he could see on the sand? Or was it the ash of the burning fig tree that was dripping from their wings? To save himself from the ash, or perhaps to smear the ash on his body, Tamiz's father turned his left foot eastward. It struck the bamboo pole planted by the brick kiln workers to demarcate the edge of the quicksand, and his frightened momentum uprooted the bamboo pole. Tamiz's father plunged headlong into the quicksand.

The workmen at the brick kiln were the first to spot Tamiz's father's left foot in the morning. His folded knee was trapped beneath the uprooted bamboo pole, a layer of sand covering the wound beneath it like ointment. One of the workmen who had come from the west said that when he had woken up late at night to check on the fire in the kiln, he had noticed the half-mad fisherman staring at the sky and talking to spirits. But then the man came every day. Since the furnace was working, the man had gone back into his shanty to sleep. Then, when he heard the sounds of a struggle in the early hours of the morning, he had assumed it was two people having a fight.

The news spread as the day advanced. People thronged to the spot—from Girirdanga, Nijgirirdanga, Golabari, Palpara and even the jomidar's office at Lathidanga.

Harmatullah was standing very close to Tamiz, he seemed terrified, and did not want to let Tamiz go. Tamiz was silent, only staring at his father's knee. Boikuntho alternately wept with his arms around Tamiz and ran towards the quicksand. Keshto Pal prevented him from going farther, with Keramat Ali also lending a hand. But Keramat kept thinking it was more important to convey his sympathies to Kulsum. He was longing to do anything he could to dispel the grief a shocked wife must feel on this unnatural death of her husband's.

The primary reason for Kalam majhi's lament was, 'I had wanted Baghar majhi's grandson to be the first to cast the net in my lake. Allah did not let me fulfil my wish. Fate!'

Abdul Aziz and Kader were both in the town. But Sharafat Mondol was here with all his hired hands. It was he who made arrangements for them to haul Tamiz's father's corpse out of the quicksand, but every time they tried, the body sank farther. The ripples on the surface made it seem that the corpse was going in deeper with every tug.

Boikuntho kept putting his palms together, one of them with the thumb severed, in a gesture of supplication to request everyone, 'Let Tamiz's father remain there. He chose his own resting spot, who are we to change it?' His voice choking with tears, he continued, 'How do we know where Tamiz's father has gone? Can anyone tell us where Munshi went with his fig tree? Tamiz's father has joined him. Let his body be where it is.'

'What are you talking so much for?' said Sharafat Mondol angrily. 'The dead body of a Muslim must be bathed according to the Shariat. He needs a shroud, prayers have to be said.'

Kalam majhi agreed with Mondol. He also proposed that Tamiz's father should be buried in the fishermen's old graveyard, where his ancestors had been buried too. A graveyard couldn't just become the sole property of someone who had taken possession of it. Pakistan was not an anarchic state. And a shrine to Tamiz's father would be erected in the centre of the graveyard. He wasn't a nobody, everyone held him in high respect hereabouts.

But Tamiz's father's corpse could not be recovered. So Kalam majhi proposed that he would pave the area bordering the quicksand with bricks.

That would mean a large chunk of the brick kiln going into the possession of the dead fisherman. Still, this meant a smaller loss compared to the plan to bury Tamiz's father in the old graveyard. So Sharafat announced that he would supply the bricks.

Within three days that quicksand was walled off with the best bricks from the kiln. The edge near the water remained unprotected, of course. Moulobi Kuddus brough his students to read the entire Quran near the wall. Kalam sent stocks of incense sticks every day from his shop.

42

What was taking Tamiz so long tonight, why wasn't he home yet? Kulsum opened the door and sat down on the floor, her vision blocked by a thick mist. If she gazed at it long enough, it seemed to lift a little under the murky moonlight, even swaying in the gentle breeze. If the accursed moon had to rise after all, why couldn't it have risen a few days earlier? It was the shape of a woman seven months pregnant now, but if the moon had been this way ten days ago, her husband would never have fallen into the quicksand. But then what difference did light or darkness make to a man who walked in his sleep? Maybe he had confused the quicksand for water and jumped in with the hope of riding Munshi's sheep. There was no other way he had of tracking Munshi down, since there wasn't even a trace of the fig tree any more. From which part of hell did Munshi rule over the lake now? Deep within the quicksand, was Tamiz's father still in desperate search of Munshi in his black turban and flowing beard? Surely he could lurch back home sometimes.

Eight days from one Sunday to the next, and then a Monday and Tuesday had passed, how many days was that? Couldn't Tamiz's father at least pay Kulsum a visit in her dreams? If Munshi could cut all his ties with Katlahar with Girirdanga and Nijgirirdanga, with all of them, and even uproot his fig tree and disappear into thin air, why did Tamiz's father still have to be so attached to him?

For several days now they had only been eating rice left to soak in water overnight. The fermented rice slowly turned sour, its aroma suspended over the house. When Kulsum served herself the rice and bit into a slice of onion, her teeth remained stuck in it, for she didn't have the strength to chew. Tamiz's father was used to finishing off five onions with two plates of rice—what was he eating now? Kulsum's dry eyes felt itchy. The moonlight sucked up all her tears, turning them into dewdrops that fell on the yard, on the roof, on the pile of fresh hay. The tears could not gather in her eyes, although one reason for this could be the long breaths she kept drawing. Kulsum went mad sniffing everything, but no, she couldn't smell Tamiz's father anywhere at all. Had he left with the fishlike smell on his body, the smell of rotting fish in his mouth, the smell of pus on the fresh wound above his knee, even the stale smell of the old wound below his knee, with all of these, to give them as gifts to Munshi? Not once had he appeared in Kulsum's dreams during these past ten days.

And what sort of behaviour was this from Munshi? Did he love Tamiz's father so much that he couldn't spare a thought for the granddaughter of his devotee Cherag Ali, who had spent his entire life singing Munshi's verses? And then again, what kind of man was Tamiz's father himself if he couldn't ask Munshi, your own throne in the fig tree has disappeared, maybe it's been swallowed by the brick kiln or has just flown away, where will you make room for me? Couldn't he ask Munshi, how will you feed me? After spending so many of his days in a state of starvation, he could have eaten fresh rice now from his son's harvest on Harmatullah's land. Could he not say, my wife is going to make sweets with amon and jaggery, I'll go home now?

Perhaps it was because of his craving for the sweets made with the newly harvested grain that Tamiz's father approached suddenly through the mist, his head wet with dew, his shadow cleaving to the vapour lit up by moonbeams. Kulsum closed her eyes, lest the fluttering of her eyelids made him disappear.

'Why are you sitting on the doorstep? Have you eaten?' Even when she realized it was Tamiz, Kulsum trembled, with fear, with happiness. After his death Tamiz's father's spirit had entered his son's body to return home.

Tamiz didn't get a great deal of paddy this time, however. It would have been better to have worked for a wage. Harmatullah was unhappy, for his share of the crop had not changed. 'People talk nonsense, and you think it's all true,' he complained to Tamiz.

Harmatullah Poramanik was no more than a peasant, the Golabari market was as far as he could go.

Abdul Kader had said so. Keramat had sung about it. An important man like Ismail Husain had said repeatedly that there would be no jomidars or moneylenders in Pakistan. About the tebhaga system he had claimed that it would come into effect automatically with the birth of Pakistan. It wasn't for nothing that the Muslim cultivators had stopped their movement. The tebhaga leaders had expressed their regret in jail, so many young Muslims had joined the Muslim League because of the promise of Pakistan, there was a reason all this had happened.

When Tamiz asked Kader about it in Golabari, he said grimly, 'Never mind all that now, ours is a new nation, India's pimps want our people to protest, so that they can take advantage of the turmoil and swallow our country.' He explained India's problem too. 'Those who led the agitation over farmers' rights were sent to jail. Jawaharlal spent so much time in jail, now as prime minister he's sending communists to prison.'

Tamiz was confused. It was the same party, but in Pakistan they were accepting payment from Hindustan to create trouble here, while in Hindustan they were going to jail. What did this mean? And why should people have to create trouble here? Didn't Ismail shaheb say just the other day that as soon as the new law was passed sharecroppers would get their just share of the harvest?

'Ah, I see.' Now Kader understood what Tamiz was talking about. 'The government has just brought in a bill to abolish the system of jomidars. One of the clauses says that the jotedar cannot evict sharecroppers arbitrarily. Yes, there's a bill in Parliament.'

Tamiz was happy now. 'Whether it's from the lake or the land, whether it's the fisherman or the farmer, all we want is our due share.'

Kader did not have patience to correct Tamiz's mistaken assumptions about the bill. 'Why are you asking so many questions?' he laughed. 'You're not sharecropping now.'

Even if not this season, Tamiz intended to go back to it in the next. Jagadish Saha had sold two and a half acres of land to Hamid Sakidar. Apparently he was planning to sell nearly 12 acres of contiguous land, all of which Kalam majhi was going to buy. If he went to one of them, surely Tamiz would not have to come back empty-handed. And once he got lifelong rights to sharecrop on a particular piece of land, how long would it be before he also got the benefits of the tebhaga system?

Reassured, Tamiz remembered his father. It had been three or four days since he had been to see him.

Standing on the edge of the quicksand, Tamiz felt a chill. His father was somewhere in there, and his own body longed for the warmth of his father's. He might have spent all his life wandering around the lake, but Tamiz's father was a storehouse of heat. In some senses it was not a bad thing for him to be resting here, for he belonged to this lake, after all. He had wanted Tamiz to live on the water too, he had never wanted a descendant of Baghar majhi's to wield a plough. But he wasn't one to insist on it either. If there was one person in the world whom Tamiz's father feared, it was Tamiz himself. When he returned home after working in the fields in Khiyar, Tamiz would speak to him sharply if he found his father asleep or wandering around the lake all night. He had said mean things about his father's appetite too. Tamiz's father loved to eat, he was always in search of feasts he could be invited to. The knot in his lungi would open up as he ate, he had even vomited and earned the wrath of those eating next to him with his farts. Now during this winter there was no more eating or shitting or vomiting. Before his death he was often half-starved. He used to come here every night, wandering about in search of the fig tree. What was he doing now inside the quicksand? Neither his fig tree nor his Munshi were in there. Was he in search of a feast? Who knew where he had dug through the sand to follow the scent of food?

Tamiz was both startled and frightened to see his father sitting at the doorstep to his house across the pond. His father was gazing at him. The newly harvested grains were being cooked at home these days—overnight rice in the morning, and freshly made rice in the afternoon and at night. They would have rice three times a day during these two months. But Bajaan wouldn't be able to eat any of it even if he spent all his time here.

As he entered, however, Tamiz realized it was Kulsum. But when he saw her eyes, they looked like his father's, and he lay down at once on his father's maacha. 'What will you eat, bajaan?' he said, and began to sob, shedding the tears that had been gathering in his eyes when he was standing at the edge of the quicksand. Through his tears he continued asking his father about his preferred food. Sitting next to him, Kulsum put her hand on his shaggy mop, and then buried her nose in it to sniff loudly, taking in the scent of Tamiz's father's hair, which used to smell like strands of jute. After all these years she finally succeeded in identifying it as the smell of a bird fluttering its wings. Sniffing Tamiz all over his body, Kulsum began to sob as well, and soon she began to cry loudly. In a bid to absorb the warmth from his father's body, Tamiz buried his face in Kulsum's high breasts. Weeping, Kulsum said, 'He never got a full meal, where has he gone now to answer Munshi's call, he didn't even tell me before leaving.'

'Bajaan is wandering around in the quicksand in search of a feast.'

'He didn't have the chance to eat a single sweet this season. He went to listen to Munshi's verses, and he never came back. He used to finish an entire basket of sweets on his own.' Tamiz burst into tears.

'What a scene he had created at the Mondols' feast.' Kulsum told him, 'He had wanted some koi from Katlahar with his rice the other day, he didn't get the chance to have it.'

Trying to take in the heat from his gluttonous father's half-filled belly, Tamiz touched Kulsum's back, drawing her close to bask in the warmth of his father's body. Kulsum ran her hand over Tamiz's knees and thighs to smell his father's half-starved body through the two wounds on his legs. And far away, Tamiz's father stretched out his long arm from the quicksand next to Katlahar Lake, or perhaps he extended his arm to make it longer, to lightly remove Tamiz's lungi and Kulsum's sari. Trying to take in the warmth and the smell of the one who was missing, the two of them entered each other.

43

Was it midnight? Or dawn? Was it afternoon or evening? Who knew, it could be a cloudy day. What was it that was rolling along in the dim darkness? Kulsum had not realized all this while. Wasn't it Tamiz's father? He looked thinner than before. Poor man! Went on a half-empty stomach to the northern head of the lake, never came back. His hair was like strands of jute before he left, but it had grown into a shaggy mop in just a few days. Something glittered in his hair and beard, were those shards of his smile? She had never seen such drops of joy on Tamiz's father's face before. Not even a feast of mounds of rice with beef curry had made him so happy in the past. What was he so happy about? Was it because he was savouring the pleasures of the flesh by entering his son's body after dying? Was that why Tamiz was moving about with laughter glinting in the jungle of dark hair and dazzling sand of his beard? If Cherag Ali had been here Kulsum would certainly have asked, 'Can people dream after dying, Dada? What dreams does Tamiz's father have now?'

Kulsum heard Cherag Ali's dotara being strummed. She joined in as he began singing:

Death is strange, we don't understand it.
Sleep is strange too, the brother of death.
The brothers love each other, they're never apart.
Entwined together like body and heart.

'Don't speak in riddles, Dada. Does Tamiz's father have dreams now?'

Without interrupting the twanging of his instrument, Cherag Ali said, 'When did Tamiz's father ever have dreams? He lived inside a dream.' When Kulsum looked at her grandfather in astonishment, he said, 'How will he have dreams? He's appeared in your dreams after his death.'

Cherag Ali sang, without caring whether Kulsum understood or not:

Sleeping creatures wander into other people's dreams
The dead bring dreams to those whom they loved

Cherag Ali strummed his dotara furiously as he sang, making the world ring. Swaying in time to the verses, Tamiz's father set off for the bamboo grove, fragments of laughter glittering in his beard and hair.

Tamiz woke up even though he didn't hear the song. Arranging his lungi beneath the quilt, he threw a sidelong glance at Kulsum. Even in the darkness he could see the sliver of a smile sticking to her lips like a thread of saliva. One of her arms was draped around Tamiz. When he sat up it fell back on the quilt, which was warm from Tamiz's body. But Tamiz felt restless about what had happened before they had fallen asleep. He hung his head, unable to look at Kulsum even in the darkness. He stood up, his eyes still on the floor, and went out of the room, shutting the door gently behind him. He lay down in his own room, but couldn't sleep. He left the house before the sun rose.

Tamiz's scythe fell with such force on the rice field on the east of the ox pool that soon there was a mountain of stalks. Harmatullah said, 'Who would say you're not a farmer by birth?'

Happy with this praise, Tamiz felt an urge to tell Phuljaan he wanted to marry her. She was looking at the crop from a distance. Her goitre was disproportionately large today. This part of Kulsum's throat was so silken that resting his cheek against it gave Tamiz great pleasure. But as evening approached, his feet refused to take him home. Despite her smooth skin, he felt frightened to look at Kulsum. He took on more tasks in the yard of Harmatullah's house, and when he finally began to count the bundles of grain that he had already counted earlier, Phuljaan came up to him. 'Aren't you going home? Your mother's alone, don't forget.' Tamiz felt a chill run down his spine at Phuljaan's referring to Kulsum as his mother. His face paled, his throat went dry. 'It's not yet been forty days since your father died, isn't your mother going to be afraid all alone? Go home.'

There were always people now in the area where the fig tree used to be, since the brick kiln was perpetually active. But Tamiz skirted the area to avoid the quicksand. What if the same arm that had untied his lungi grabbed him by the throat now? As Tamiz stood in silence on the other side of the brick kiln, two of the workmen from the west expressed their sympathy: the poor boy came here every day out of love for his father. One of them told Tamiz that his father turned rather noisy every night—he had not yet severed his bonds with the world.

Tamiz rushed back home on being told of his father's continued fondness for the world of the living. He was still too frightened to look at Kulsum. 'The rice is ready. Eat.'

Rejecting Kulsum's invitation, Tamiz said, 'I've eaten already,' and went into his room. When Kulsum began to follow him, he shut the door in her face.

Tamiz's father visited home every day from the quicksand now, even holding desultory conversations with Kulsum. He was the same as he had always been, a taciturn man. But he was becoming thinner, although he looked happy. Tamiz didn't return till late in the evening, but he had no choice but to listen to Kulsum's account of her day when he sat down to eat. He was not in the least pleased on being told that his father seemed happy. Why should a dead man be visiting the living in their dreams every day? It was ominous. Was Tamiz's father planning to draw Kulsum into the quicksand too? If it was punishment he was intent on, Tamiz wouldn't be spared either.

Tamiz ate with his eyes fixed on the floor, and, pretending to yawn as soon as he had finished his meal, went to his room and shut the door, resolutely resisting his strong desire to stare at Kulsum's smooth throat.

A few days later, Harmatullah looked very pleased after he came back from Sharafat Mondol's house. Mondol had brought 12 acres of contiguous land from Jagadish Saha, dirt cheap. The sale had been registered. Mondol had taken Aziz to the sub-registry office and finalized everything before Kalam majhi could find out. His success had brought a smile to Harmatullah's face after a long time, which persisted through his coughing fit.

But Tamiz looked grim. When the coughing had died down he said, 'If it was so cheap, couldn't you have bought some of it yourself?'

After a pause Harmatullah said, 'I can't fight against the person I depend on for a livelihood. Didn't you see what happened to Majhipara after they tried to take away Mondol's lake?'

Not that Tamiz was trying to see. Instead, he explained his plan to Harmatullah. Harmat would now be busy with Mondol's newly bought land, which was to the east of the creek. So he could let Tamiz sharecrop the land behind his house, the entire land. It was more than 4 acres, Tamiz would get gold out of it. Harmat would be able to sell the crop to buy even more land. In fact, what Tamiz would get as his share would let him retrieve his house from Kalam majhi, even if he couldn't buy back the land behind his own house from Sharafat Mondol. Harmatullah would see for himself just how big a harvest Tamiz could produce.

Harmat's eyes shone as he listened. Sighing, he said, 'I could do it too once upon a time, now my body has given in.'

'Why should you have to do it? You take care of Mondol's land,' Tamiz assured him. 'If your daughter helps me, you'll see what I can do.' Saying this gave him courage. 'You can't let your daughter live like a widow, you'll have to get her married soon. Why not to me then . . .'

'What will people say if she marries a fisherman . . .' But Harmatullah no longer sounded determined. He needed Tamiz on his side to ensure a good harvest on his land. His daughter had had wretched luck, his heart broke to look at her. Her spirits would be lifted if she were to marry Tamiz. 'You must understand,' he said softly, 'our society has its own rules. Let me talk to everyone . . .'

But when he went to Sharafat Mondol for permission Mondol said grimly, 'She's your daughter, Harmatullah, you can beat her or carve her up or give her to whoever you want, it's got nothing to do with me.' Then he began to shout, 'But will anyone respect me if he becomes your son-in-law?' Pausing, he continued calmly, 'Allah has given me prosperity now, but I cannot cut off my blood relationship with you. Who will respect me if you let Tamiz marry your daughter? You look after my land. Why do I give it to you? Because you're my relative. But how will I maintain my relationship with you if he becomes part of your family?'

Harmatullah didn't relay this conversation to Tamiz, for he couldn't bring himself to turn Tamiz down outright. The fellow was improving the yield on his land, why not let him continue? How long could he pursue Phuljaan, after all, he would give up on his own eventually. It would have helped to have had him as his son-in-law, but Mondol wouldn't stand for it. Harmatullah couldn't be evicted from his house, but he would no longer be allowed to sharecrop Mondol's land or supervise the other sharecroppers. And besides, Harmat's heart was overflowing with the warmth with which Sharafat had spoken about their blood relationship. This meant Abdul Aziz, Abdul Kader and he belonged to the same family. Kader's sons would become officers in the government, and they would be Harmat's relatives too. How could he sacrifice the honour of his family by allowing Tamiz to marry his daughter?

Not that Harmatullah was particularly perturbed by any of this. The responsibility that Mondol had thrust upon him meant he had to spend most of his time outdoors, even at this age. After buying some of Jagadish's land, Hamid Sakidar had become a jotedar himself—several cultivators sharecropped his land now. Harmatullah had a lot on his plate.

So he had no choice but to depend on Tamiz, who not only sharecropped Harmat's own land, but also put in most of the physical labour needed on Mondol's land on the eastern side of the ox pool. Shamsher was Harmatullah's main hired hand, but he had to return home before sunset, for he got a fever every day when darkness fell, and found it very difficult to walk. They had grown onions and chillies on the land, and were busy now preparing it for the sowing of aush. Because it was so hot during the day, Tamiz quite enjoyed working on the land in the evening. No one else would be there at the time, so Phuljaan lent him a hand sometimes, though her primary task was to point out his mistakes. One evening, standing on the sloping bank of the ox pool, Tamiz said, 'Is that all you're going to do—just humiliate me? I do so much work on the land, but will I always be a fisherman to you?' Phuljaan was sitting on the slope. Since she didn't snap back instantly, Tamiz was both disappointed and encouraged. He brought up the subject of her dead son. 'You think he would have died if I'd been looking after him? You've been married to a man from a family of farmers, that too someone who's educated, who composes songs, who sells his books. What did he ever do for you?'

For the first time, Phuljaan was shaken. She felt the ground beneath her feet quake. 'It's my fate, why did you have to be the son of a fisherman?' she said, weeping. When Tamiz sat down by her side, their bodies touching, she suddenly hammered her fists on his chest, complaining, 'Why did you have to be born in a family of fishermen? Why? Why? Why?'

Tamiz didn't bother answering this difficult question, wrapping her in his arms even as she continued to rain blows on him. Lapping up Phuljaan's salty tears with his thick lips, he felt his entire body smarting at the brine. Rubbing his face continuously across Phuljaan's cheeks, lips and goitre, he lay down with her on the sloping bank of the ox pool. The bristly ploughed land of summer was just a few yards away. Harmatullah's pair of bullocks grazed near their heads. Stars came out in the sky. Arranging her sari, Phuljaan said, 'You tore my sari.'

After many days Tamiz had a long chat with Kulsum without avoiding her eyes when he returned home. Apparently, his father visited Kulsum late in the night, every night. But Tamiz was no longer afraid to hear this—on the contrary, he asked her for details about his father.

44

After moulobi Kuddus had completed the Milad prayers in the mosque, all the fishermen got sugar crystals, besides the jilipi fried in butter that Tahsen the police inspector had brought from the town. Munching on their bounteous blessings, the fishermen lined up at the edge of the lake. Everyone cheered as Budha began to sing Keramat Ali's song from three years ago, and some of them joined in tunelessly with Budha's incorrect lyrics. Abiton's father was the only one who looked glum. 'My grandson died here. Pray for him, Munshi.' Kuddus had prayed for Tamiz's father after the Milad, but no one had reminded him of Abiton's son. Now he raised his hands to pray for the innocent child, but the fishermen were not interested in raking up that particular memory. In fact, Kalam majhi's proposal that the first net be cast near the spot where Tamiz's father had died was also rejected by his own son Tahsen. 'Absolutely not. No need to go there today. There's no point creating trouble at the brick kiln.'

But Kalam majhi did make Tamiz cast the first net. 'After all, we have to see whose son he is. And then he's Baghar majhi's grandson's son too, our work will go well if we begin with the blessings of his great-grandfather.'

Many of the fishermen had laughed at Tamiz when he cast a net to catch koi in summer. What was he going to do with such a net, considering how shallow the water in the lake was now. But Baghar majhi's descendant did catch as many as a dozen fish, nine of them in the prime of their life. They cast a reddish glow on Tamiz's dark skin.

However, by the time he had finally trapped a koi in his net, Abiton's father had already netted some mid-sized carp. Most of the fishermen caught some fish or the other. Those who didn't get much of a catch in their nets used baskets and hooks to snare small fry. The fishermen were about to spread out all the way to the missing fig tree, but Tahsen stopped them. 'Not today.'

Even before the afternoon had passed Kalam majhi's nephew Budha told everyone, 'Stop now, all of you. No more fishing.' Spreading out plantain leaves on the ground beneath the young mango trees at the ghat next to Kalam majhi's house, he shouted, 'Deposit your fish here, all of you. Half of whatever you've caught.'

Busy catching fish, the fishermen paid no attention to this invitation at first, but because Budha kept repeating it, with the hint of a command in his voice, they were eventually forced to take note of it. Now what? Did they have to part with the fish they'd caught?

Kalam majhi, who had been with them all this time, had gone into his house. Returning, he said, 'It's the first day that the fishermen have got the lake back. There's no need for rent. Just give me half, or a quarter, or at least an eighth, of whatever you've caught.'

Abiton's father remembered casting his net in this lake three years ago in defiance of Mondol's ownership. Since his attempt to rekindle grief for his grandson's death had failed, he sought revenge now. 'What do fishermen have to pay a rent for? Who's going to take a rent from fishermen?'

What would Nula Bhiku be left with if he had to part with three of the six small fish he'd caught? He provided lukewarm support to Abiton's father. 'Rent for what? Didn't Kalam mian say the fishermen were going to fish in their own lake? Are we still supposed to pay Mondol?'

As everyone gathered beneath the sandpaper tree at Fakir's Ghat, their shouts made it difficult to decipher individual opinions.

'Mondol had bribed the manager to lease the lake. The bastard manager has run away. There's no manager now, no lease either.'

'Manager? Don't forget there will be no jomidars in Pakistan. Who has the right to grant leases any more?'

'Who's going to take permission from the jomidar and his manager in Pakistan?'

Police inspector Tahsen arrived amidst the commotion. Although barefoot and dressed in a lungi, he had a watch and a packet of cigarettes in the pocket of his white shirt. Without raising his voice in the slightest, he told everyone, 'My father has leased the lake. Its ownership . . .'

'Let me explain,' Kalam majhi cut in. 'I've leased the lake, I've paid money for it. The lease starts in Boishakh. It's not been cheap, getting the lake out of Mondol's grasp. How will I manage if you don't pay rent?'

'We'll pool our money to pay you back,' said Abiton's father. 'What do you want a rent for? That will mean paying you whenever we fish here.'

Irked by their ignorance, Tahsen said, 'What's the dispute about? My father has leased the lake. He's paid for a two-year lease. Why should he let anyone fish here without paying rent?'

Despite his discomfort at his son's bluntness, Kalam majhi endorsed his statement. But it wasn't right for Tahsen to play police inspector here. Fishermen were of troublesome stock, you never knew how they'd react. It would be better to win Tamiz over to their side and ask him to explain. Drawing him aside, Kalam whispered, 'Tamiz, see what's going on. Can't you explain to them?'

But what was Tamiz to explain? He was confused himself. With Mondol's lease ending, the lake was supposed to have been returned to the fishermen in the month of Boishakh. What was all this business of rent? 'Is the lake being returned to the fishermen or not?'

'Of course it is, of course it is,' shouted Kalam majhi. 'I'm a fisherman, my ancestors were fishermen. All of you are fishermen, all of you are my blood. If I've leased the lake, doesn't that mean it's been returned to the fishermen?'

Interrupting his father, Tahsen said, 'All property has to have an owner. My father has bought the lake for two years. One of you can buy it after that. For now, just leave a small portion of the fish you've caught. In future you can pay rent if you want to fish. Be quick, no one wants unnecessary trouble.'

The fishermen were taken aback by his crisp words and manner of speaking. No one spoke for a few minutes. Tahsen opened his umbrella. Suddenly Abiton's father stepped up and emptied his basket on the plantain leaf. 'Why are you giving me your entire catch?' said Kalam majhi. 'Take your share.' Paying no attention, Abiton's father strode off homewards. 'Abiton's father,' called out Kalam majhi, but he didn't turn back. Although two or three more fishermen deposited a portion of their catch, the rest, sensing an impending storm or taking advantage of it, set off for their respective homes with their nets and baskets. The small boys suddenly began to run, and at least two of them tripped and fell over, spilling the contents of their baskets on the ground. The storm broke as Tamiz vacillated, wondering whether to part with his fish or not, and then he ran homewards too.

The storm was raging now. Tahsen could be heard shouting from the veranda of Kalam majhi's house, 'Why didn't you note down which of them didn't leave any fish, Budha? You'll have to collect what they owe us the next time any of them go fishing here . . .'

Releasing the koi into a pot filled with water in Kulsum's room so that they would stay alive, Tamiz gave her instructions on how to cook the fish the next day. Meanwhile, the storm was followed by a shower. The aroma of moist earth made Tamiz's head reel, but also whetted his appetite. However, he had to go to Harmatullah's land now. He could plough the stretch on the sloped bank of the ox pool before sunset after such a fine spell of rain.

'You're going to work now?' said Kulsum. 'Eat before you go.'

He had had a meal of dry leftover rice before going to the lake. The prospect of a plate of hot rice held Tamiz back.

After his meal Tamiz transferred five of the fish from the pot to a basket. As he was leaving, Kulsum said, 'Where are you taking the fish?'

'Have to pay rent to Kalam majhi,' said Tamiz, amending his lie the very next moment. 'But why should I? Is it his family property? What rent is he talking about?' With this emphatic declaration Tamiz sealed his decision not to pay a rent. Then he said, 'That old Poramanik had wanted to eat some koi.' Tamiz left, his face radiating a faint black glow of happiness.

45

Keramat Ali had no trouble identifying Abdul Aziz's new home in Kalitala. He only had to mention Kartik Bhaduri's house to be taken there directly by the rickshaw driver. But he felt hesitant getting off the rickshaw outside the wooden gate smothered in Rangoon creepers—perhaps it was too audacious to take a rickshaw to this place. Beyond the gate lay a small field of grass and then a veranda where about twenty people were sitting on a sheet. Abdul Kader smiled at Keramat, who tried to compose himself as he looked up at the roof. The railing was high in the middle, with the Om symbol carved into the cement. Below it were the words 'Srishankaralaya' and '1307'. None of this had been obliterated by recent efforts to whitewash the walls. The only way to remove them was by demolishing the railing.

'Come in, come in, sit down. Babur has come first in his tests. There are sweets for all his teachers.' Abdul Kader shifted to make room for Keramat.

After the sweets there was tea. After delivering brief eulogies to Babur's merit and application, along with advice, the teachers proceeded to express, both individually and collectively, their anxiety and despair over the rapidly deteriorating education system in the country. With the best teachers all leaving for India, would schools and colleges have to shut down? Abdul Aziz was particularly worried: Babur used to take mathematics lessons from Akhil Basu, whose front door had been sporting a lock for the past fortnight. People were saying he had left for Balurghat after exchanging houses with a Muslim, a retired sub-deputy judge.

The tall and thin headmaster, ceremonially dressed, complete with a Jinnah cap, was particularly affected. None of his personal friends were here, and he was struggling to maintain standards in his school.

Niren Lahiri, a young man of twenty-five or twenty-six who taught geography in the higher classes, was seated at a slight distance from the headmaster. He was Babur's favourite teacher. Niren kept glancing at the beams on the ceiling, the wall, and the different varieties of hibiscus and jasmine near the veranda. Soon he was strolling about in the garden, in the area where several flowering plants had been crushed by the bamboo scaffolding used to repair the building. 'Come inside, sir,' Babur kept telling him, 'come and see where I study.'

Abdul Kader said from the veranda, 'Why don't you go in, Niren-babu?'

When Niren returned to the veranda Abdul Aziz said, 'Babur talks about you all the time. Please go and see his study.' He continued after a pause, 'You haven't been to this part of the town before, have you? You live in Malotinagar, don't you? You people don't like crossing the railway lines.'

Niren looked at him for some time, his eyes bereft of expression. Then he said, 'This is my aunt's house.'

'Really? Then Kartik-babu . . .'

'He married my father's eldest sister.'

'Indeed?'

'My aunt died in '41, he married again. We used to visit even after that. When my aunt was alive we used to come here almost every day. She had personally planted these hibiscuses and jasmines. She had a green thumb, anything she planted thrived.' Niren Lahiri seemed to have been afflicted by verbal diarrhoea. He seemed desperate to compensate for all the hours he had spent in silence, his head bowed, in the presence of his favourite teacher and current boss, the headmaster. 'My uncle planted the bayur over there. He transplanted two of them from Calcutta, one died, the other survived. The flowers used to be beautiful. Over on that side, but it's gone now.'

As he looked around for it, Abdul Aziz explained, 'It used to be there, a tall tree. We couldn't keep it when building the wall.'

'How could you kill such a beautiful flowering tree? Such a lovely fragrance. Ismail bhai has a couple of them in his house.'

Although upset at his brother's anguish, Abdul Aziz justified his decision. 'The house had not been whitewashed in years, all the walls were rotting away. There was a boundary dispute with the house next door, which is why there was no wall in between. When the wall was built . . .'

Niren had no interest in repairs and house improvement. He remained where he was, not moving despite Babur's urging.

Meanwhile cries of 'Naraye Takbir' and 'Allahu Akbar' were heard from the main road. The people in the veranda grew restless. Many of them had been aroused, even inspired, by these slogans a year or two ago. Abdul Kader rose to his feet. 'That bastard Shukkur Sheikh must be here, the swine is trying to create trouble over refugees.'

'Refugees have been thronging to the town these past few days,' said one of the teachers. 'Jotin Roy's house is filled with them.'

'Jotin Roy? Our Jotin-babu? Has his house been requisitioned?'

Kader responded to the headmaster's worried question. 'There's no choice. So many refugees, they have to be given shelter somewhere.'

Dissatisfied, the headmaster murmured, 'He's a great leader. Taking his house away is . . .'

Ignoring his misgivings, Kader instructed the gathering. 'Some of you must come with me. This is a Hindu neighbourhood, Shukkur Ali is capable of doing something terrible.' Then he reassured the Hindus among the teachers, 'You'd better go inside the house, you'll be safe there.'

He left with a small group, which the headmaster joined.

In response to the loud cries of 'Naraye Takbir' and 'Allahu Akbar' from the street, a female voice screamed sharply, sending an ominous shriek through the pleats and folds in people's clothes, through the reddish glow from the marigolds bending over in the veranda, and even through the missing shadows of the chopped down bayur, 'Listen, Babur's father, listen, Babur. They're coming, they're coming. They're slashing bhaijaan's throat. Save Humayun, Babur's father.'

Niren was the only one among the outsiders who knew of Abdul Aziz's wife's illness. He had commiserated with Babur on hearing of his mother's suffering. But actually hearing her screams shook him now, disorienting him completely. The thought of sympathizing with his student didn't occur to him as Hamida's screams rose in competition with the cries of 'Naraye Takbir'. Abdul Aziz said, 'The problem is that Babur's mother becomes unstable with the slightest uproar in the streets. The Hindus killed her brother in Calcutta . . .' He stopped on seeing the fear on Babur's teachers' faces.

'Did you get her an amulet, bhaijaan?' Keramat Ali whispered in Aziz's ear. He was here to take Cherag Ali's book back. Keramat hadn't been able to meet Kulsum ever since Abdul Aziz had taken the book away from him. Her husband had died, and Tamiz spent most of his time outside the house. There were plenty of opportunities to meet Kulsum and talk to her.

But there was just the one thing she would say, 'You sold my grandfather's book. You'll pay for it.' Keramat could no longer compose verses. There was something in *Khwabnama* that could change his fortune. He had been looking for an opportunity here to get the book back. When Kader asked people to accompany him, Keramat hid behind a pillar because it wasn't safe to go out.

He asked Aziz about Babur's mother, and Aziz replied with ill-concealed irritation, 'From medicines to amulets from her uncle, I've tried everything. She's just getting worse.'

Although Aziz's knitted brow didn't give him confidence, Keramat Ali gathered all his courage and said, 'I could try if I got the fakir's book back. Will you give it to me?'

'Book? What book?' Abdul Aziz paused for thought. 'You mean that tattered book of yours, the one that belonged to Tamiz's father? It's the nonsense in that book that has got her in this state. Her uncle said . . .'

Without disclosing his wife's uncle's opinion, Aziz said that the book had disappeared when they were moving to the new house. 'We lost many valuable things, who cares for your book?'

When Abdul Aziz went into his house to check if his wife was better, Keramat took another chance. Drawing Babur to himself, he said, 'Do you know where you father has put the book, my boy?'

Babur had to ask him a few questions before identifying the book. 'Oh yes, it's called *Khwabnama* or something like that, isn't it? Abba doesn't let anyone even see it. Apparently he got this house so cheaply only after the book came to him. And then . . .'

'You don't know where it is?'

'No. What will you do with it? It's a peculiar book. All sorts of absurd things about dreams. Full of squares and triangles—can't make any sense of it.' Babur's smile held the contempt of a scientifically minded teenager. Besides, the conversation was proving difficult to continue. Cries of 'Help! Help!' from the north of the house and Hamida's screams of 'They're killing my brother, Babur's father' in response had forced everyone else into silence. Someone ran along the road, shouting, 'They're ransacking the Bose house.' One of Abdul Kader's employees arrived and told them, 'Don't go out, any of you. You're safe here. The police have been informed.' Before returning he said that Phonindra Bose was lying on the steps, stabbed in the chest by Shukkur's people while trying to prevent the family house from being robbed. His elder brother Monindra Bose had run away earlier, he was probably still in hiding.

News of this sort kept floating in. Sometime later Kader returned with a throng of children, elderly people and women in tow. Aziz had no idea what to do. His brother appeared to hate his new house, and seemed intent on doing all kinds of annoying things here. And soon after Monindra Bose, his sons and his cousin arrived, led by the headmaster, carrying an old woman. She was Monindra Bose's widowed aunt, who had cracked her skull when trying to jump down the stairs. She was paying for the piety of keeping the parting in her hair bare for some thirty or thirty-five years—her hair was flowing with liquid vermilion today. As soon as she was laid out on a bedstead inside one of the rooms, Hamida abandoned her common sense about the difference in age, gender, and, most important, religion, to throw herself at the old woman, screaming, 'Bhaijaan, bhaijaan!' But she fell on the floor instead, losing her senses as well as her common sense. Because the two unconscious women had not come into physical contact with each other, Monindranath Basu was relieved that his devoted and staunchly religious aunt had remained free of the touch of a Muslim even at the moment of her death, and used the opportunity to express his anxiety about the valuable asset that his stately mansion, handed down over three generations, represented. The target of his anxiety remained unchanged for twenty-five minutes, until he got the news of the death of his younger brother Phonindra.

Babur had already taken Niren into his study. Niren was hesitating at the doorstep, for he had not been allowed to enter this room during his aunt's time. It was her prayer room. As a young child he had once crept into the room in silence and leapt on his aunt's back. Abandoning her prayers, she had taken him in her arms and returned him to his mother, saying, 'You naughty boy, I'll have to cook for the gods all over again because of you.' Ever since then Niren had been a little jealous of the gods, but the envy and anger had drained away as he grew older. You had to believe in the gods to be jealous of them. Niren was always mocking the gods in the presence of his students at school. He had told Babur and his fellow students that anyone who did not respect the sacred thread of the Brahmon would invite a thunderbolt on his head. But then as soon as he had started college, he had used his own sacred thread to stitch the pages of a notebook together. No one had tried to even hold a matchstick to his hair. And now his favourite student's wall had a map of the world on it, there was a globe on the cupboard, and a geometry box on the desk, along with colour pencils, books and exercise books. Despite the abundance of all the things he loved, Niren's heart wept for his aunt.

After the police had taken away the living, the injured, the all-but-dead, and the dead, Hamida's screams became even more conspicuous. Regaining her consciousness had not helped, for she kept lamenting at the top of her voice the fact that Humayun or perhaps Ahsan had been taken away from her.

Sick of his wife's illness, Aziz went up to the gate of his house, where Abdul Kader followed him. 'Have you heard the news from home?' he whispered in his elder brother's ear.

The question was a barb at Aziz's indifference to family matters. Although a little perturbed, he hinted at his suspicion that Kader might be trying to grab the newly gained family property by asking, 'Is the key to Mukunda Saha's house with you? Are the documents safely with you?'

'The keys are with Bajaan. The documents are in his safe. I've set guards outside the house.'

Out on the road, Kader discovered Keramat walking alongside him.

46

Having heard the rumours, Keshto Pal went to the Golabari market to find out the truth. 'Well, Boikuntho, where's your babu? What's all this we're hearing?'

Keshto Pal was accompanied by several others from Palpara. Flustered by their interrogation, Boikuntho began to stammer. 'Babu is in Ranaghat. His father-in-law was attacked by Muslims on the way from Shirazganj to Ranaghat, his back is badly injured, it's doubtful whether he'll survive. Babu has gone to see him.'

'What about his family?'

'He's taken everyone. Who knows if his father-in-law will live.' When the Pals looked astonished he assured them, 'They'll be in Ranaghat for a few days before going to Calcutta. They'll be back in about twenty days.'

'Never mind all the details,' Keshto Pal said sharply. 'We hear he's sold his house.'

Boikuntho had heard the same rumour yesterday afternoon. Alim the schoolteacher had said that Mukunda Saha had apparently sold his house, which included two separate structures on 2 acres of land, along with two jackfruit trees, about twenty high-quality mango trees, four litchi trees, and one each of hog plum, java apple, and star fruit, besides an orchard of jujubes and a pond, to Sharafat Mondol for a thousand rupees. Mondol was not only a Muslim but also a formidable figure, which meant no one would dare loot the property.

'But they took the keys by force,' began Arjun Pal, only to be stopped by Keshto Pal.

'What arrangements has he made for the shop?' he asked Boikuntho.

'Look after the shop properly,' he told me. 'Sell as much as you can if you get a good price. I'll place new orders in Calcutta before I return.' Boikuntho's faith in Mukunda Saha was still intact. 'He's not one to give up on his shop. It's his life. Give him a few days, see what happens, let all the trouble die down. I don't even know what's happened to his father-in-law. Let me wait a few days. He might send a telegram if he's delayed.'

Moving on to Kader's shop and discovering Gofur was alone over there, the Palpara contingent asked him for the facts. Initially unwilling to divulge any information, he finally told them the truth. 'Chhoto shaheb assigned two members of the National Guard to escort them to the border.'

'So the thief has become the protector?' Despite inverting the popular saying to convey his dissatisfaction with the initiative taken by the National Guard, Keshto Pal remained as anxious as before. 'Did he manage to take away everything he had here?'

'Every last thing. Babu had plenty of gold. And then the gunmetal utensils, the copper utensils, the idols—there's nothing left behind. He may have sold the house cheap, but all told he's made a profit.'

Keshto Pal's anxiety, disappointment and resentment increased manifold. His plump legs began to shake so much that Gofur had to pat him on the back and console him. Boikuntho, however, kept saying, 'Let a couple of days go by, Babu has a full-fledged business here, after all.'

It was doubtful whether Keshto was even listening to Boikuntho. Gofur said that Saha had had to sell his house in secret, or else Kalam majhi would have grabbed his property without payment.

What was Keshto Pal to do now? When he suggested going to the office in Lathibhanga, Gofur said, 'The manager doesn't go there any more.'

'Let's go to the town,' urged one of Keshto Pal's younger companions. 'Satish the attorney will be there even if the manager isn't.'

'The town is on a short fuse,' Gofur warned them. 'Refugees are coming in droves from India. There's no knowing what they'll do.'

'What can they do?' But Arjun Pal's bravado was halved by his next statement. 'Three days to go to the Poradaho fair. The jomidar's office hasn't given any money, Saha-moshai isn't here either.'

Kalam majhi went up the steps to Mukunda Saha's veranda that same afternoon. He told Boikuntho, 'Your employer is a traitor. He was supposed to have sold his house to me. We had agreed that my son would have the police escort him and his family to the border. Now Keshto Pal has told me a different story altogether. I paid five hundred as advance for the shop, the house, everything. He wanted five thousand, I was ready to pay three. How much did Mondol pay?'

Boikuntho had just woken up from a luxurious nap after smoking some ganja when the Pals had left. He had given up these addictions a long time ago, except during the fair. But something had got hold of him today, and his employer wasn't there either, so he had taken a few drags with great relish and was still feeling happy. He spoke through a mouthful of paan, pursing his lips to prevent the juice from escaping, 'That's impossible, majhi-kaka. Babu's grandfather started the shop, how can he give it up? We're in business as usual. Tell me if you need something, I'll give it to you cheap.'

Kalam majhi wasn't going to succumb to the lure of cheap groceries. 'Don't talk rubbish.' He began to mock Saha and Boikuntho's patriotism. 'You people eat your meals here and rinse your mouths across the border. Is this right? You think you can run your business in Pakistan while your children live in India.'

The shop was bound to come under his control, declared Kalam majhi, but he would wait a little longer. If it took too long, he would send Boikuntho to fetch Mukunda Saha, he would pay for the trip himself.

Boikuntho did not agree. 'How will that be possible? Who knows where babu is? I've never been to Calcutta in my life, I have no idea where babu's in-laws live.' Spitting out some paan juice, he said, 'Wait a little longer. Hindustan or Pakistan—let's see where we end up eventually.'

Kalam majhi's love for his nation was dented by Boikuntho's doubts about the permanence of Pakistan. 'Mind your tongue, Boikuntho. Don't bite the hand that feeds you. You'll pay for it.'

Boikuntho remained in his ganja-induced haze, or perhaps it was the paan and tobacco. When Tamiz told him the next day, 'People are going mad, Boikuntho-da, they're behaving like dogs in mating season, you must be careful,' his ancestral blood began to rage.

Swallowing his paan juice, he thrust his chest out and said, 'What do I have to be careful for in these parts? Have you any idea who founded this market?' Tamiz couldn't care less. Instead of naming the founder of the Golabari market, Boikuntho brought up his usual tale. 'My grandfather's grandfather, or perhaps his father or his grandfather . . .' Boikuntho wasn't bothered about identifying the correct generation, but he didn't stop till he had boasted of his forefather's bravery against the British troops under Bhabani Pathak's leadership. Bhabani's general, or perhaps Majnu the fakir's general, was Munshi from the fig tree. 'There was so much news your father would get from Munshi up in the fig tree . . .'

'The fig tree is gone.' Tamiz sounded dismissive. 'There's no fig tree there any more, we didn't even realize when it had been chopped down.'

'It's not so easy to chop down this fig tree, you mad boy.'

But the road from Golabari to Girirdanga ran past the northern head of the lake, running straight and true, with the undergrowth having been cleared after the brick kiln came up. Tamiz had scoured the area without finding a single leaf from the fig tree.

But how did Kulsum get all her news then? Tamiz had gone home a little early the other day when it got extremely cold in the middle of the evening. Whom was Kulsum talking to in the pitch dark behind closed doors? It wasn't Keramat Ali, was it? Kulsum couldn't stand him, but still he turned up whenever he could and talked utter rubbish. Had Kulsum decided to indulge him today? What was she talking about with him inside the dark room? Eavesdropping, Tamiz heard Kulsum say, 'Can't you say it yourself? You took over his body the other day, even if you can't do that again, you can at least explain it to him.' A short silence. When Kulsum resumed speaking, it was obvious she was replying to someone. But Tamiz's heart trembled although he couldn't hear the other person's questions or complaints or protests, for Kulsum was clearly talking to his father. He was too frightened now to pay attention to the conversation, although he could hear Kulsum's voice. Much later, he didn't know how long it was, Kulsum said goodbye, 'Come again tomorrow. Don't you get hungry over there?' When she opened the door and saw Tamiz, she warbled in joy, 'Now the father and the son can sort things out between themselves.' Tamiz felt a gust of wind brush across his body. Who was it? He couldn't see anyone.

Whatever little light had filtered through the mist, took advantage of the open door to slip in. So did the mist, taking on a new shape to suspend itself in the small void inside the room, stretching all the way to the maacha. To overcome his fear, Tamiz snarled, 'Why haven't you lit the lamp?'

'Your father won't come in if there's a light in the room. He left a moment ago, didn't you notice?'

'What's all this you're saying? You've gone mad.'

Tamiz was frightened to look at Kulsum after she lit a lamp. He squatted on the floor of his own room to eat, while Kulsum sat opposite him, telling him about his father without a pause. 'Your father's been saying the same thing these past few days. Tell the boy to be careful. Katlahar Lake will go up in flames, the fire will spread to the houses.'

'You've gone completely mad. What is this rubbish you're saying?' Tamiz's effort to cut her short was buried beneath his own fear. 'Stop this nonsense. Bring me some more rice.'

Refusing to be intimidated, Kulsum brought him some rice from the pot. Then she conveyed his father's latest complaint-cum-warning to him. 'Have you married that goitre-ridden daughter of Harmatullah's? Your father says, let the boy marry whom he likes, but he mustn't live with his wife.'

Tamiz was startled, almost choking on this rice. After a drink of water, he mixed the daal into his rice again and told himself, that bastard Sharafat Mondol had terrorized Harmatullah with his threats. Mondol wouldn't let the old coot sharecrop his land if he let Tamiz marry his daughter. But why should Tamiz bother about Mondol's land? He would get an acre and a half from Harmatullah as Phuljaan's share of the family land, and he would farm the land belonging to the other two daughters too. Harmatullah would be there to do what he did well, which was to supervise everything. The crops that Tamiz would grow on these four and a half acres, along with his portion of the crops he would get from sharecropping on someone else's land, would be more than enough for himself and his father-in-law and Kulsum. In fact, there would be more grains than they could consume, and Tamiz would use the surplus to retrieve his father's house and land.

But how was he to convey all this to his father? Tamiz tried to go to sleep quickly, so that his father would visit him in his dream. But no sooner had he fallen asleep than he began to dream he was swimming across Katlahar Lake, diving into the water at Fakir's Ghat and moving in a north-easterly direction. At the other end was the ghat which would lead him to the ox pool. Phuljaan was standing beside a mound of termites beneath the palm tree on the edge of the ox pool. The child in her arms seemed to have been cured, and was taking in the surroundings attentively. But Tamiz was only halfway across the lake when he woke up. Kulsum was still talking to herself in the next room. Tamiz tossed and turned for a long time before he fell asleep again.

47

Never since opting for a posting in Pakistan, being promoted to assistant sub-inspector, and getting his father to lobby with Ismail Husain for a transfer to the district headquarters, nor earlier in his career, and not even at the hands of his Hindu bosses, had Tahsenuddin faced the kind of trouble he was in now. His mood was soured by the uprising of the fishermen that began in early Boishakh, and his temper spiralled by the day, by the month, by the season. What kind of unreasonable behaviour was this? My family has leased the lake with its own money, with a proper receipt for payments made—who will fish there or row their boats or draw water is entirely my business. No one else can interfere. Tahsen had told his father many times to get the fishermen from the Jomuna to come and fish at Shimultola, followed by Fakir's Ghat, the area where the fig tree used to stand, and at the ghat next to Kalam majhi's house. However, Kalam kept saying the same thing—be patient, be patient. But even patience had its limits. Ever since Mondol's lease had run out, someone or the other kept fishing in the lake at least three times a week, either in the morning or the evening, or in the afternoon during the rains. His father would say, 'They're our own people, we can't live in the village if they get angry. We'll never be able to teach Mondol a lesson unless we have our people with us.' At other times, he assured his son, 'Give it time. Fishermen are like that, they will fight with you one moment and be on your side the next. Now fire, now water. I'm one of them, I know our clan.'

Tahsen did not like his father's frequent declarations of belonging to the line of fishermen. But he couldn't bring himself to hurt his father either. His stepmother had treated him so badly that Kalam majhi had taken him away from home and deposited him with a distant cousin of his first wife's. The cousin's husband used to be a constable in Khetlal, and was later transferred to a distant location—the Englishbazar police station in Malda district. Tahsen had managed to continue with his education in the face of many adversities—having to draw water from the well, do the shopping every day, be bullied by his cousins. He used to fail in his class every other year, but his father never failed to send him money. When Tahsen failed in class nine, his uncle persuaded a senior police officer to let him join the force, and also had his own daughter marry him. Although Tahsen's wife was from the clan of fishermen too, she had grown up far away from them. Her diction was almost upper class, she could speak broken Urdu, and she wrinkled her nose at the goings-on in her in-laws' house. The children had taken after their mother. Would they not be unhappy to hear their father and grandfather identify themselves as fishermen?

Besides, this bunch had got Kalam into trouble many times. He knew them only too well. If you got into a conflict with farmers, they would support you all the way, denting the skulls of a dozen peasants at the smallest of signs. If you wanted to set fire to a colony of oil grinders, the slightest hint was all they needed. Then again, they were a soft-hearted lot, their knees shaking at the prospect of hurting any creatures other than fish. But once they were provoked, they could use their harpoons to kill a dozen in an instant. Kalam didn't expect Tahsen to understand any of these things.

Moreover, it was getting harder by the day to understand what Tamiz was up to. Kalam had depended on him. Tamiz's father had made a big contribution too—it was the humiliation he had faced at Mondol's hands during the Poradaho fair last year that had led to Katlahar being returned to the fishermen. Tamiz had proved to be his father's son every inch of the way, even going to jail after his conflict with Mondol. It was essential for Kalam majhi to have Tamiz on his side.

Tamiz finally appeared after Kalam had peeped in several times. He was standing at the doorstep, rinsing his mouth out noisily after his meal, while Kulsum stood behind him with a lamp, its flame flickering in the breeze coming in through the open door. The woman was in the prime of her life, and she was living alone, with her stepson for company. But before he could pursue this line of thought, Kalam got a whiff of catfish. Stung, he said, 'So you're stealing fish, Tamiz? You could have just told me you wanted to eat some fish, I don't like it when people call you a thief.'

'How is it stealing if I get my fish from Katlahar Lake? Doesn't it belong to all the fishermen?'

'You know how it is.' Kalam majhi had come here to make him understand, but the aroma of catfish from the lake and the sight of Kulsum's face lit up by the trembling flame lent an aggressive edge to his voice. 'Are you asking me to send for the police? I've managed to keep Tahsen in check, but are you now suggesting I ask for my own relatives to be arrested?'

Tamiz went back inside the house without answering. Kalam majhi said, 'Look, you're living alone with your dead father's young wife, but I haven't objected. Now you're stealing fish from the lake too. How much do you expect me to tolerate?' As he went back home, Kalam majhi kept muttering about Kulsum and Tamiz living in the same house, but Tamiz paid no attention.

Tamiz's mind was occupied with thoughts of Phuljaan. He had been standing on the sloping bank of the ox pool the other evening after harvesting a huge pile of grains. Like every day, Phuljaan was there too. But instead of pointing out mistakes in his work, she suddenly threw herself on his chest. Fortunately the scythe slipped out of Tamiz's hand, or else Phuljaan might have injured some part of her body. Lifting her head from his chest, she began to weep, weep ceaselessly. 'What are you crying for?' Tamiz asked in astonishment.

After he had asked several times, she said, 'Ma beat me up with a stick today.' Why? Why did her mother do that? Phuljaan went back to sobbing, and stated that she had lost her appetite these past few days. She couldn't even eat fresh rice with mustard oil, onions and chillies, it nauseated her. All she wanted was the tart taste of tamarind.

Was that all? It wouldn't be difficult for Tamiz to get hold of tamarind. There was a pair of tamarind trees on the southern bank of the ox pool. Normally no one plucked their fruit, for ghouls and banshees lived in those trees, but then Tamiz was even willing to battle with ghosts for Phuljaan's sake. It was a frightening thought, though. Why not just quietly buy some in the market? Phuljaan wasn't going to ask where he'd got them. But here she was, shouting at him, 'You foolish son of a foolish fisherman, don't you understand anything? I have no option now but to hang myself. You'd best buy me a rope.'

Finally guessing the truth, Tamiz began to tremble. Was it his father who had come into Phuljaan's womb soon after dying? There was no cause for concern then if the fig tree was gone forever, for his father had clearly found a space for himself. Euphoric at the possibility, Tamiz pressed Phuljaan to himself with all his force. Rubbing his mouth across her face, eyes, forehead, goitre and breasts, he reflected that Harmatullah had no choice now but to let Tamiz marry her. But he would sort out the matter of the land before the wedding.

But this evening, when Tamiz lay down after Kalam majhi's diatribe, his left eyelid began to flutter uncontrollably. This was ominous. The fair was just two days away. Everyone in Majhipara would line up to cast their nets at Katlahar the day after tomorrow. Tamiz's problems would end if he took Kalam's side—Kalam majhi would protect him and Phuljaan if he brought her home.

But early the next morning he returned from Kalam majhi's house without meeting him. Perhaps it would be best not to tell him directly. He could send word through Keramat, but would it be wise to tell Keramat about his marrying Phuljaan? What about Budha? His thoughts were interrupted by moulobi Kuddus, who expressed his regret on seeing Tamiz. 'Kalam mian has built a new fence around the mosque, but still none of you ever show up. You can work as hard as you like, but eventually you will have to go there one day. What do you plan to take with you then?'

Tamiz promised at once to read the fazr namaz at the mosque every day before going to till his land. But for now, nobody but Allah could rescue him from the danger he was facing. Moulobi Kuddus felt shaky at the thought of danger, but his desire to be another human's saviour was not insubstantial either. He did offer charmed water when people fell ill in Majhipara, but when it came to pledging money, nothing but the Poradaho field would do for the traitors. Looking at Tamiz, he sighed heavily. 'It's no use helping anyone. Everyone is ungrateful, they won't even look at you once they've got what they wanted.'

Tamiz informed him that he would pay in advance. What would Kuddus have to do? Tamiz would be deeply obliged if he were to be allowed to marry Harmatullah's daughter. Poramanik didn't have the courage to annoy Mondol, but if Kalam majhi supported Tamiz, it could be done. Moulobi Kuddus looked grim. Combing his beard with his fingers, he said, 'All right. Kalam mian can never say no to me. Come to the mosque after the maghrib namaz.'

In the afternoon Harmatullah's wife glared furiously at Tamiz when she saw him. But her angry eyes turned tearful in an instant, and, looking around to make sure her husband wasn't there, she began to weep. 'You have destroyed us,' she said. 'This is what comes of Phuljaan's father allowing a lower-caste man in. It doesn't matter to you, but we're ruined.'

'Why do you say that?' replied Tamiz, staring at the floor. 'I'll marry your daughter. Today, if you like. Tell Phuljaan's father.' But since Phuljaan continued weeping silently, Tamiz had to reassure her, 'I'd always said I would marry her.'

'How will we live here if she marries a fisherman?'

'Fine, let her not marry me. What do you suppose will happen if I tell everyone at the fair?'

Tamiz rushed out when he saw Harmatullah entering, but Nobiton ran behind him to stop him. Softly she said, 'I don't know what bubu sees in a stupid fool like you.' Gripping his arm, she added, 'You have to marry her. She'll kill herself if you don't. I'll explain to baapjaan, he'll listen to me.' Phuljaan had complained of her father's partiality towards Nobiton. Tamiz approved of it, now that it was working in Phuljaan's favour. 'Go home now,' said Nobiton. 'Dress well tonight. The wedding must take place today.'

Tamiz carried sheafs of grain all day to Harmatullah's house, depositing them in the yard. The counting went on in Nobiton's presence today. Phuljaan was nowhere to be seen. Nobiton had protruding teeth, but her nose was sharp and her throat held no hint of goitre. But because he didn't see Phuljaan anywhere, Tamiz made mistakes, and his stacking went awry. How could he go on without her?

It was late by the time Tamiz got to the mosque. The devotees were on their way back after the asr namaz. Kalam majhi only grinned soundlessly when he saw him, or was it actually a kind smile? Or perhaps he was reassuring Tamiz, it wasn't clear. Moulobi Kuddus said, 'You were supposed to have been here after maghrib, look at the time now. Why are you so hesitant about reading the namaz? What will you have to show on the day of judgement?'

Tamiz looked intimidated, so moulobi Kuddus got to the point. 'Consider it done. How can Kalam mian turn me down? He said you can get married and take your wife home, you don't have to be afraid of Mondol. He even wept a bit when he mentioned your father. His son, he said, I have a responsibility too. He even wants to pay part of the expenses. Don't worry, you have Allah above you and Kalam mian by your side.'

'Come with me, then.' Tamiz had more or less been expecting just this from Kalam majhi, and displayed no particular elation.

He needed the priest now. 'Come with me to Nijgirirdanga. The wedding has to be held today. Nobody from Mondol's jamaat will agree to preside. You'll have to come with me.'

'Now? How can I?' Kuddus had been invited to dinner at Abiton's father's house tonight.

'Not possible today. Kalam mian said, let's get the fair over with. You'll have to be with him on the day of the fair, you'll have to take care of the fishermen if they create trouble. After the fair.'

Tamiz was committed to supporting Kalam majhi. But he said, 'I've given my word to old Harmatullah. The wedding must take place tonight.'

'He's going to be your father-in-law, how can you address him by his name, and then call him an old man on top of that? Your name may be Tamiz, but your behaviour doesn't suit your name.'

Either to fall in line with courtesy and protocol, or simply out of irritation, Tamiz was silent for a few moments. 'There's nothing to say you have to keep your word,' said moulobi Kuddus. 'Allah understands everything, he knows the difficulties his servants face.'

'No, huzoor, it's different for you. You read the namaz every day, Allah is aware of your difficulties. I don't read the namaz, I don't pray, why should he consider my problems? I've given my word, I have to marry her today.'

Kuddus was sympathetic about Tamiz's situation. 'But we have to talk to Kalam mian,' he said.

'There's nothing to talk about, huzoor. All you have to do is get the wedding done today. I'm not taking my wife home tonight.'

'You know the expenses, don't you?'

A rush mat was spread out on the floor, and on it lay one of the quilts Nobiton had knitted, with patterns of flowers and fish. Another, smaller quilt was laid on top of it for Tamiz and the priest. The youngest of Harmatullah's brothers-in-law was visiting, he wanted to take his nieces to the fair. He was reserved at first, but was soon caught up in the festivities thanks to Nobiton and Fellani.

Although it was late, Harmatullah sent him to the Golabari market for some sweets.

Sitting on the smaller quilt with motifs of a minaret, the moon, and stars, Tamiz made an odd demand. He would not go through with the wedding unless Harmatullah transferred his elder daughter's share of his land to her at once.

Harmatullah felt somewhat hurt at his would-be son-in-law's demand, even more anxious, and, most of all, angry. Sharafat would take away his sharecropping rights for letting a fisherman marry his daughter. Now if he got to know that he was also transferring part of his land to his son-in-law, Mondol would get the farmers of Nijgirirdanga to evict Harmatullah and his family from their own house.

Kuddus was annoyed too. 'You'll go away to your own home in Majhipara with your wife. How will you ensure the land is safe here?'

'It's not so easy to take away my land, huzoor,' Tamiz insisted. 'I've been to jail, not even Mondol's father will dare to make an enemy of me.'

Kuddus was running late. There were no other houses nearby. The farmers lived on the other side of Bhabani's field. If Mondol found out, it would need only a sign from him to make sure that, leave alone Tamiz, even the priest would probably not make it back home alive. He attempted a compromise. 'Harmatullah Poramanik has no sons. Who will get his land and property if not his three daughters? We're here, Kalam majhi is no less powerful than Mondol, inspector Tahsen is his son. Mondol just hands out empty threats. You don't have to worry.'

Even if he wasn't completely reassured, Tamiz accepted this argument. Referring to his daughter's well-being and Mondol's concerns about the marriage, Harmatullah said, 'Mondol and we are the same clan, but letting your daughter marry someone from a lower caste means spoiling the bloodline. That's why Mondol objects. Don't forget, Sharafat Mondol's grandfather's uncle and my aunt's mother-in-law's sister were cousins, or was it my uncle's . . .'

He gave up trying to identify the precise relationship, after which
Kuddus began to hurry everyone, 'Enough, let's get it done now.'

After the sweets, everyone had a meal of specially cooked fish
curry and rice. Tamiz had been planning to go back home with the
priest, but Nobiton had decorated the room she shared with Phuljaan
beautifully. Phalani more or less shoved him in there late at night.
Tamiz found Nobiton putting a thick layer of kohl under Phuljaan's
eyes, while Phuljaan ran her fingers over her goitre absent-mindedly.
It was difficult to say whether she was trying to flatten it with her
fingertips. Nobiton giggled and left the room when Tamiz entered.
Before locking the door, she said, 'Don't go mistaking my sister for a
fish and putting a hook in her mouth, dulabhai.'

48

Abiton's father went to Fakir's Ghat with his fishing net after the zohr namaz on the day before the Poradaho fair. Bhiku, who was Abiton's cousin as well as brother-in-law, joined him. Because of his habit of disappearing from home without warning for three or four months at a stretch, because he was always dressed in a dhuti and a dirty and oily cap, and because he frequently attempted to speak in Urdu, he was considered mad hereabouts.

It was the last Wednesday in the month of Maagh, but still very cold, which was inevitable at the time of the Poradaho fair. Abiton got his cousin-cum-brother-in-law to stuff his hookah for him, took a few long drags on it, murmured Allah's name in his head, bowed his head in deference to Munshi at the now-vanished fig tree at the northern head of the lake, and flung his net out in a diagonal arc. There was a cavity in the lake here, which meant a perpetual supply of fish. His ancestors had said that a long time ago, an earthquake had made the waters of the Jomuna swell so much that they had spilled into the Bangali river. The water then overflowed the banks of the Bangali to flood the villages of Girirdanga and Nijgirirdanga. That was when Munshi had stretched his foot out from the fig tree to deliver a mighty kick to a small pond that used to exist here, transforming it into the huge Katlahar Lake. Since this had created a receptacle for the water from the flooded river, the people of the two submerged villages got much of their land back. Ever since then, there had been a bounty of fish at this spot. Catfish caught at Fakir's Ghat fetched high prices at the Poradaho fair.

Today, too, Abiton's net filled with fish quickly. When the large basket he had brought was full, he handed it to Bhiku. Bhiku was hauling back the fishing net with Abiton when someone gripped his right wrist. 'Assalamu alaikum,' said Bhiku, without checking who it was. 'What's all this, let go of my hand,' he said in his makeshift Urdu.

It was Ali Mamud, a leader of sorts of the Jomuna fishermen. Without bothering to respond to Bhiku's greeting or his instructions delivered in Urdu, he said quietly, 'Take your net and go back home.'

By then the Jomuna fishermen had begun to gather at Fakir's Ghat and across the lake. Ali Mamud was not someone who liked trouble. Despite his large, fearsome appearance, he spoke politely to Abiton's father. 'You people are fishermen and so are we. I doubt whether there are any other Muslim fishermen in this land. Why do we have to fight with one another?' Letting go of Bhiku's wrist, he said, 'Kalam mian has officially leased the lake from the government. After he showed us the papers we paid him a rent and are here to catch fish. We're going to fish in this lake today, it's reserved for the Jomuna fishermen. You've got a basketful already—you'd better hand it over, take your net, and go home.' Seeing the disappointed expression on Abiton's father's face, he added, 'When we're done I'll give you some of our fish.'

Whether it was out of rage and sorrow, or on the assurance of getting a share of the fish, Abiton's father set down the basket and left for home with his net. But Bhiku picked the basket up and told Ali Mamud in his trademark Urdu, 'What is all this drivel? You may be fishermen from the Jomuna or the Ganga or who knows where, you think you can come here and fuck with us? Are you saying the Girirdanga fishermen are not going to sell fish at the Poradaho fair?'

It was neither possible nor acceptable for the leader of a group of Jomuna fishermen who had paid the rent to fish for a day at the lake to stomach this. Ali Mamud was not one to strike at anyone.

He threw a glance over his shoulder, and at once a short and stubby companion of his shoved Bhiku violently into the lake. He was submerged in the water from his head to his belly, although his body from the waist downwards remained on dry land. Shamsuddin, the cripple from Uttarpara, jumped into the water to help Bhiku, but because his left arm was useless, he could do nothing with his right arm alone. But by then Bhiku had crawled entirely into the water, swum a few strokes, and dragged himself back on land. His cap had flowed away, however, and his dhuti was in a state that rendered its basic purpose ineffective. Wrapping it tighter around himself, Bhiku kept touching his head, though it wasn't clear whether this was out of grief for his cap or to shake the water out of his hair.

Abiton's father strode off towards Kalam majhi's house, grumbling to himself, what's going on, how can outsiders invade our village, how can they fish at the lake where our forefathers have always fished, and beat us up as well? Isn't Kalam majhi going to do something about this?

But Budha, who was standing outside Kalam majhi's house, said, 'Mamu has gone to visit Tamiz's father's grave.'

Bhiku had followed Abiton's father to Kalam majhi's house. He was surprised. 'Tamiz's father's grave? But he's in the quicksand . . .' Informing them that that was indeed where his uncle had gone, Budha joined them.

As Abiton's father ran towards the quicksand, Bhiku called out for Tamiz when they were passing his house. Kulsum came out to tell them that Tamiz had left with his fishing net a little earlier for the northern head of the lake.

Standing at one corner of the three low walls fencing in the quicksand, moulobi Kuddus was reading the prayers that accompanied visits to the grave, his hands raised in the air, while Kalam majhi stood next to him, tears dripping from his eyes into his beard, which had not grown very long yet, but was already proving to be luxuriant. The cap on his head was conspicuously placed. A few yards away, another of the leaders of the Jomuna fishermen,

Ali Mamud's brother Shaker Mamud, was pacing next to the row of bricks in the brick kiln, looking for a suitable spot to cast his net. He was surrounded by several other fishermen. The largest of the nets was held by at least three men.

Budha walked past them, walking farther to the north, where Tamiz had just launched an enormous fishing net. As soon as it splashed on the cold, wrinkled water of the lake, Kalam majhi looked in Tamiz's direction, his hands still raised in prayer. Budha ran up to grab Tamiz's arm. 'Chacha, Tamiz chacha, not today. Mamu has taken a lot of money from the Jomuna fishermen to let them fish today. Not today, chacha, don't go casting your net today.'

'Pull in your net, pull in your net.' Tamiz didn't even acknowledge Shaker Mamud's stern order. But Kalam majhi came running, his visit to the grave incomplete, or perhaps he had completed it already.

'Have you gone mad?' he asked Tamiz. 'I prayed at the spot of your father's death to start my lease of the lake. It's thanks to him that we fishermen have got our lake back. The Jomuna fishermen will fish here today, they've paid me the rent. Pull in your net.'

'These Jomuna fishermen are always ready for a fight,' Budha warned Tamiz in his ear. 'And Tahsen bhai has informed the inspector at Amtoli. The police will come in their vehicles if they find out there's trouble. You'd best go home.'

But by then Tamiz's arm muscles were straining. He must have netted a big fish. A huge one, in fact. 'Budha, didn't baapjaan catch a devil fish?' Tamiz whispered. 'You were with him, weren't you? I think it's the same one.'

Budha lapsed into silence, his spine tingling. Realizing he wouldn't be able to haul the fish in from the bank, Tamiz waded into the cold water, which didn't feel as chilly as the air did while he was on land, and besides, his thighs could still feel the warmth from Phuljaan's. But right now he concentrated on pulling his net in. Mad Bhiku, the crippled Shamsuddin, and Shamsuddin's nephew Monglu had also waded in with Tamiz at the possibility of a large catch. All of them were gasping for breath as they tried to pull the net in. No one knew how big the fish might be.

Shaker Mamud decided to confront Kalam majhi directly. 'Kalam mian, your people from Majhipara are casting their nets everywhere in the lake. What's going on? Return our money, we're not going to start a fight just to be able to fish. Give our money back, we're going.' But they were showing no signs of going back. On the contrary, the Jomuna fishermen were now brandishing weapons that could be used to kill not just fish but other creatures too.

Kalam majhi noted everything and shouted, 'What are you Majhipara bastards doing? All of you will die.'

Shakur Mamud insisted, 'Never mind, just give our money back. We paid a rent to Sharafat mian earlier and fished here, no one came in our way. You're only making things difficult for us.'

'Come up here, Tamiz,' Kalam majhi bellowed again. 'You bastards don't behave unless Mondol beats you up.'

The fish was now gasping under the combined strength of mad Bhiku's and Monglu's two plus two four arms, crippled Shamsuddin's single arm, and Tamiz's two arms—seven in all— and the entire strength in Tamiz's body. It couldn't be allowed to escape. 'Must be a very big rohu,' said Bhiku in Urdu.

'No, a devil fish,' said Tamiz softly. 'Don't talk.' His voice quavered. Had his father slipped into the water from the quicksand and caught the fish for him?'

Kalam majhi couldn't take it any more. 'You son of a bitch, your father fell in line after Mondol beat him up, looks like you need the same treatment.' It seemed that Kalam majhi no longer felt the need to revere Tamiz's father. When Tamiz still didn't let go of his net, Kalam majhi fired his most deadly arrow. 'Didn't you give your word to moulobi Kuddus yesterday? If I tell Mondol you married that bitch with the goitre last night he will throw Harmatullah out of his house at once. Where will you go with the whore then? Your house is pawned to me, I'll evict you right now.'

For support Kalam turned to Kuddus, who mumbled, 'Take a fish and go home, Tamiz.'

'Shut up, moulobi,' Kalam majhi shouted at Kuddus. 'How dare you take my money and speak against me? Go to your mosque, don't you have to read the namaz?'

Anxious that he might be demoted from the mosque, moulobi Kuddus screamed at the top of his voice, 'Didn't you promise to do as Kalam mian says, Tamiz? And now . . .'

Before he could finish, a spear struck Monglu on his back. Because it had slowed down on impact, it glanced off his shoulder and fell into the water. But when Tamiz and mad Bhiku still didn't let go of the net, another spear embedded itself in Tamiz's elbow. Now the ropes of the net slipped through his slack fingers. Had Munshi's pan turned into a spear to hit his elbow? Whether it was Munshi or not, Tamiz wasn't going to spare the attacker. Looking over his shoulder, he found the assailant standing a few yards away in the water, quaking with fear. A frail-looking man, at least fifty years old. It was obvious the bastard had no net or boat of his own, the swine worked for other people. He hadn't even learnt to throw a spear properly—there was no difference between a spear and a pan for him. Plucking the spear out of his left elbow, Tamiz took a deep breath and hurled it at his attacker in a head-high arc. The man jumped in the air, because of which the spear struck him below his throat. He fell into the lake at once, and a large pool of red appeared in no time. As the enormous fish trapped in Tamiz's net shook its ancient tail, stomach, back and head, waves rose in the water, and the currents in the bloodied water made the lake look as though it was on fire.

The Jomuna fishermen hauled the man with the spear in his throat out of the water. Shaker Mamud dispersed the crowd gathered around him, shouting, 'Are you here to see the fun? Go cast your nets. There's no one there beneath the silk-cotton tree, all of you can catch fish there.'

The man struck by Tamiz's spear was unconscious. He had been lain down close to the low wall around the quicksand. Kalam majhi had sent someone to fetch Doctor Karim. But Ali Mamud said, 'What do we need the doctor for? Let the police see the wound first. How will there be a strong case unless they inspect the wound?'

'Don't worry, the Amtoli inspector will do whatever my son tells him.' Neither Ali Mamud nor Shaker Mamud was convinced by Kalam majhi's confidence.

'You don't know these inspectors, they don't spare their own fathers.'

Meanwhile, several of the Jomuna fishermen had charged at Tamiz. Led by Abiton's father, Monglu and mad Bhiku staved them off, but Tamiz had to weather a powerful blow from a bamboo pole on his back. However, the leaders of the Jomuna fishermen weren't willing to get into a fracas now. 'Catch your fish. It's getting late, light the lamps, catch your fish.'

'Tahsen can't be present, but he has ordered the Amtoli inspector to gather with his force at the Golabari market,' Kalam majhi assured them. 'The police will be here soon.'

'No, not now,' Ali Mamud interrupted him. 'Let us get our fish first and dispatch it all to Poradaho. Or the fucking police will take half of it.'

Kalam majhi was so angry with Tamiz that he felt capable of stamping on his neck till he died. But then this rage was also mixed with anxiety for Tamiz. While he wished he could truss Tamiz up and throw him into the quicksand like a fishing net so that the son of a bitch could choke to death, he was also worried that if the police arrested Tamiz he would spend the rest of his life in jail. Meanwhile, the people of Majhipara had begun gathering in Uttarpara. If all of them rushed here now, these bastard fishermen, there was no trusting them, they were fully capable of setting Kalam majhi's grand new house with the tin roof on fire. What should Kalam do now?

Tamiz was on his way from the northern head of the lake to Uttarpara, supporting himself with his arms around mad Bhiku and Monglu's shoulders. Kalam drew him aside, along with mad Bhiku.

Lowering his voice, he said, 'You've betrayed me so badly that I won't be able to stop them even if they want to hang you, Tamiz.'

'We can deal with all this later,' said Monglu. 'Let's go to Abiton's father's house first.'

Once Tamiz reached Abiton's father's house the bastards would form a group and return. 'You'd better get away from here, Tamiz,' said Kalam. 'The police won't listen to anyone when they arrive.'

Mad Bhiku was flustered at the prospect of the police. 'We'll tell the police the truth,' he said in Urdu.

It was late at night now. With Budha's help Kalam majhi more or less forced Tamiz into his own house. 'The rest of you go to Uttarpara,' he told the others.

A little later Budha set off for Golabari with his hand on Tamiz's back to guide him. Tamiz's head and body were wrapped in a grey shawl. Mad Bhiku was still standing in Kalam majhi's yard. Budha winked at him.

The Amtoli inspector arrived before dawn with two constables. The Jomuna fishermen left for Poradaho at almost the same time, their boats loaded with fish. The injured fisherman remained at Kalam majhi's house, and Ali Mamud stayed back to handle the police.

It was the day of the Poradaho fair. Every house in the village was hosting their married daughters and sons-in-law. All of them had risen well before dawn to get ready for the journey to the fair, which meant that the police did not have to trouble themselves to wake anyone up. Since they were in full uniform, the chilly wind sneaked in beneath their shorts to make their lower halves freeze, to compensate for which they used the mouths in the upper halves of their bodies to deliver a fusillade of swear words. The three pairs of feet belonging to the three policemen, including the inspector, stampeded all over the village, arresting two persons per foot, or twelve in all. They were all trussed up and made to sit in front of Kalam majhi's house. Tahsen arrived in plain clothes, his plan being to deposit his wife and children here and leave before 10.30 a.m. He kept expressing his regret to his father, 'The main culprit has not been caught, what's the use?' The police left no house unsearched in their hunt for Tamiz, even checking his own house thoroughly at Tahsen's behest.

With his son continuing to throw sidelong glances at him, Kalam majhi looked crestfallen, saying, 'This is that bastard Mondol's doing. He must have given Tamiz shelter because of his enmity with me. How about searching his house?'

'Have you gone mad?' answered Tahsen. He had never been in favour of his father's entering into a conflict with Sharafat Mondol. Kader was a very powerful man now. His elder brother's son was going to take his matriculation examination this year, apparently he was a very good student. The boy's younger sister went to V. M. Girls' School with Tahsen's daughter, where she did very well in class too. Aziz had bought a house in the town in Hindupara, a beautiful house at that. And these were the people his father had made enemies out of, while rubbing shoulders with lower-class people. 'I'd better go,' said Tahsen glumly. 'I have to go to Kahalu at 2 p.m. with the force, those tebhaga devils might attack Moyez Sarkar's granary today.' Bidding goodbye to the Amtoli inspector, he said, 'You could search Golabari too. But then the bastard had a full night to get away, I doubt if he's going to be there.'

49

Keshto Pal was observing the goings-on at the Poradaho fair with a thunderous face and reddened eyes that had a dark, murky look in them. After the ritual of bringing Bhabani Pathak's idol to life on the Tuesday before the fair, he had gone home with a dismal expression and blazing eyes, and spent the next day at the shrine beneath the banyan tree instead of visiting the fair. His heart pounded in anxiety: If Bhabani Pathak was going to be worshipped so disdainfully, how long would it take for his benign glance to turn malevolent? How long, for that matter, would people's devotion to him last?

Mukunda Saha had run away before the Durga Puja, and even if they had somehow managed to get an audience with the manager, the things he had said about Bhabani Pathak would have immediately invited divine wrath on him had it not been for the fact that he had been born in a Brahmon family. Being lower-caste people, they had committed a sin so heinous by being within earshot that it was doubtful whether the scriptures could offer them any form of atonement.

But then what did the manager care? He had already taken his family across to India, where he would himself go in a year or two. Once in India they could worship all the important gods and goddesses to their hearts' content. They had Kashi, Vrindavan and Mathura in India, they had Kalighat and Nadia too. There was no counting the number of active deities. But if Bhabani Pathak were to be displeased, what would that mean for the people in the village here?

The Muslims could not be trusted. Those who had come into even a little money or barely read two pages of a book would immediately object to Bhabani Thakur's being worshipped. Sharafat Mondol had said he did not mind the fair being held, but Muslims must not frequent the spots where religious rituals were held. Muslims must follow the Sharia scrupulously, he had warned. He did not approve of the long-established practice of holding a horse race from Golabari to Bhabani Pathak's shrine on the day of the fair. Kalam majhi had, however, wanted to go one better by getting hold of big horses from Khondkartola, to the west of Sherpur. Apparently five or six horses had even arrived, but the riders at the race were all from Majhipara, and half of Majhipara had been arrested by the police early in the morning of the fair. So the horse race was eventually called off. Would Munshi tolerate this? It was his general, Majnu Shah, who had come riding up on his horse, and Munshi had been on the side of the fakirs. He was definitely going to heap curses on them if people forgot all of this.

This time there were far fewer people from the west at the fair. The ganja offered to the idol was going to waste. Keshto Pal was an old-timer, who tried to maintain his composure, but he was deeply dismayed. It would be hard to keep Bhabani Pathak happy if everyone ignored him.

After the fair had ended Boikuntho Giri appeared late at night and sat down beneath the banyan tree. This year too he had been deprived of a glimpse of Bhabani Pathak early at dawn. Boikuntho was on his way back to the shop last night, on the eve of the fair, when the shrine was buzzing with visitors and rituals, ganja and bells, blacksmiths and potters, oil grinders and weavers. With the fair starting the next morning, most of the Golabari shopkeepers would spend the night at Poradaho. 'Why don't you go to Golabari?' Keshto Pal's younger brother Bishtu told Boikuntho.

'It's best not to leave Mukunda Saha's shop unattended, people have their eyes on it.' Before sleeping, Boikuntho had eaten some of the eatables offered to Bhabani Pathak and then distributed amongst the devotees. Suddenly hearing someone whisper, 'Boikuntho-da', he opened the door to discover Tamiz standing outside. He had been hiding in a bush near Muchipara all evening. On arriving at the Golabari market later at night, he had found it deserted.

'I heard,' said Boikuntho, without allowing Tamiz to finish. 'I heard everything at Poradaho. Come inside.'

Tamiz's left elbow was impossibly swollen, though the gash on his back was not serious. Wilting without food, he gulped down the leftovers from the offerings to Bhabani Pathak that Boikuntho gave him before collapsing on Mukunda Saha's mattress with groans. Boikuntho discovered that Tamiz was burning with a high fever. All he could do was fetch water from the handpump outside and put a cold compress on Tamiz's forehead through the night. There was a soft sound at the door of Mukunda Saha's shop before dawn. 'It's the police,' whispered Boikuntho. Tamiz gripped his arm. Boikuntho was planning to go out soon in the hope of catching a glimpse of Bhabani Pathak. This was no time for physical contact with a Muslim, but what choice did Boikuntho have? The police would torture Tamiz mercilessly if they got hold of him.

Meanwhile there were muffled knocks on the door. 'Boikuntho, are you there?'

Guiding Tamiz to a spot behind the sacks of chilli at the farthest end of the shop, Boikuntho laid him down on the floor. As soon as he opened the door, Gofur kolu rushed in and bolted it behind him. 'Get rid of Tamiz,' he whispered. 'The police are marching towards Majhipara. Tamiz is the main culprit.'

'Tamiz isn't here.'

Gofur flew into a temper at Boikuntho's statement. 'The police will kill you if Tamiz is found here. Kalam's son has informed the Amtoli police station. You're the last man standing between Kalam and this shop, he's desperate to get you out of the way.' He strode to the back and pulled Tamiz to his feet behind the sacks of chilli. 'You're in luck.' Elaborating, he said that Kader had informed Gofur a short while ago that Tamiz should not try to escape on his own, that if Gofur located him, he should take him to Kader's house in the town. Since Gofur was supposed to go to the town anyway to escort Kader's friends to the fair, he could just take Tamiz along at the same time. 'Come with me, I'm taking my cycle, just wrap yourself in the shawl. Don't be afraid. The police are approaching from the east, but we're going the other way. Let's go.'

Boikuntho regretted not having fled for the town earlier with Tamiz, who was standing close to him now. Was he afraid of Gofur kolu? Perhaps he was wondering whether Gofur would actually take Tamiz to Kader's house, or just hand him over to the police. What was Kader's intention, for that matter? Could he be plotting to use Tamiz to instigate the people of Majhipara against Kalam majhi? He couldn't stand Kalam, after all. Boikuntho wondered what he should do.

'The fucking fishermen,' said Gofur in annoyance. 'You can't even try to help them. Stay here then, you bastard, if you think you'd rather trust a Hindu. I'm going to kill the fucking Hindu too.'

Tamiz put his arms around Boikuntho, who told him gently, 'Go with Gofur, Tamiz, Kader has a lot of influence.'

Tamiz staggered along with Gofur, throwing a single glance back at Boikuntho with his hot and reddened eyes. Something exploded in Boikuntho's head: it was like Tamiz's father gazing at Cherag Ali while the fakir explained someone's nightmare.

Gofur indicated that Boikuntho should lock the door carefully. But Tamiz didn't give him another glance.

Soon the sun came up. Boikuntho had missed his chance with Bhabani Pathak again, although his need had been particularly great this time. If only he had taken Tamiz to the ox pool before sunrise! He had more or less thrown Tamiz out eventually—Tamiz had the expression of someone going from the frying pan into the fire. If Boikuntho could have had a glimpse of Bhabani Pathak from the bank of the ox pool, the ascetic would personally have protected Tamiz. Had Tamiz's father's son been angry with Boikuntho when he left? Why hadn't he looked back even once?

The visitors to the fair had left, and some of the shopkeepers were asleep inside their shops. The lights in the brothel were on. About half a dozen of the people from the west were sleeping beneath the banyan tree, sharing four blankets, while the rest had left. All six of them were wrenching their souls out of their navels and ejecting them rhythmically through their noses. The variations in their snores sounded like a cacophony to Boikuntho at first, but after some time the divergent sounds made way for a certain harmony, which, by Bhabani Pathak's grace, banished the noise of the snores. The new and unfamiliar tune and beat told Boikuntho that Cherag Ali's song was about to begin. Touching the edge of the shrine reverently with his forehead, he murmured, 'Have you composed a new song, fakir?'

'Do you consider humans capable of composing such verses?' How could Cherag Ali suddenly speak in such a high language? Startled and a little frightened, too, Boikuntho lifted his head, heavy with uncertainty and anxiety, inebriation and disquiet, excitement and dread, to discover an enormous idol of Bhabani Pathak in front of him, its locks matted, its arms raised, its body smeared with ash. The three prongs of his trident had pierced the mist to enter the sky, while all three hooks in his hand glowed at their tips, the fish motifs glittering on them. Was he intent on spearing the lightning with his trident? Had he borrowed the fish motifs from Munshi's pan? Or had Munshi borrowed them from him? Why the fish? Was the lightning partial to them, so that Bhabani Pathak was using them as bait? With Bhabani Pathak's enormous head fixed to its own, the ancient banyan tree had spread out across the Poradaho field. Boikunthonath closed his eyes and heard the words:

Forsake ye thy sleep
Awake like the lion
The fish awaketh
The trees awaketh
Awake, ye Giris.
Ye sleepeth supine

> The foe doth enter
> Binding sleep in chains
> Bhabani awaketh, thunder roars
> Awake, ye Giris.

Boikuntho's entire body trembled, for this was not Cherag Ali's scripture. Even if he had stored such magniloquent expressions in his stomach, they must have melted away before they could have risen to his throat, so that they could not mount his tongue. Cherag Ali's voice was heavy, but the signs of its being broken were evident in the currents in the river, in the air and the water and the heat and the cold. It did not hold the angry crack of thunder. This voice was coming from somewhere far above the banyan tree. Standing beneath it, Boikuntho realized that it was travelling to the north-west. He started walking beneath it.

He had barely taken a couple of steps when his feet encountered the fruits from the tree, and tender banyan saplings touched his knees and hips. One, two, three saplings, whose touch made a chill run down his spine. To avoid contact with them, but also to draw strength from them, Boikuntho uprooted one of them with great force. How could he travel unarmed on this dark and misty night?

The song had traversed the Poradaho field on its way to the north-west. It wafted over the thin stream of the Bangali river, casting a shadow on it, taking in exchange the burbling of the water. The song was echoed back from the northern head of the Katlahar Lake, where the fig tree used to stand, its words acquiring the finely rustling speech of the leaves and the air moistened by the waves on the lake and the water in the Bangali river.

> Arise now in droves everywhere
> In Girirdanga and Katlahar
> Join forces, your enemies won't survive.
> Join forces, break those chains on your hands
> Let them vanish in the sunlight like dewdrops.

Here at last was Munshi's song, fired by the blazing sun, soaked in the rain, made lighter by the wind, dripping from the sky in Cherag Ali's ragged, heavy voice. Reeking of the fish, large and small, in Katlahar Lake, and of the fur on the murrel transformed into sheep, Munshi's song, in Cherag Ali's voice, collided repeatedly with Bhabani Pathak's shrine beneath the banyan tree. Boikuntho could delay no longer. Tamiz hadn't looked back at him even once when setting off to surrender to Kader. He must have been upset at not getting the shelter he had sought from Boikuntho. Tamiz's father must be fidgeting restlessly beneath the quicksand at his son's suffering. Boikuntho had no choice now but to go and sit down next to him. He set off towards the quicksand with long strides, the banyan sapling in his hand.

50

A scarf was draped over her kamiz, and though it was dirty, a closer look revealed that the woman had a breast missing. Having sucked and licked both her breasts to their hearts' content, a group of Hindus in Bihar had cut off one of them. Everyone in the refugee camp was aware of this, because of which her relatives' share of the relief material was disproportionately high. When, following Kader's orders, Keramat Ali held a sari out to her, it was instantly grabbed by someone else. The woman looked up from behind her scarf, her veil shifting slightly. Keramat's ears rang with the sound of her breathing, and this sound, or perhaps the ringing in his ear, disturbed the flowing locks on his head. Was she also going to sniff people's secrets out of them? But this woman was fair-skinned, her nose was sharp. Her eyes were not as wide as Kulsum's, they were more like almonds. Where was the similarity, then?

The woman's severed breast and the vehemence of the refugees' indignation, rage, laments and accusations, expressed on the ground and first floor and the roof of the Kundu residence, wiped out the incomprehensibility of the Urdu and rustic Hindi in which they were articulated, piercing the sheen of Keramat's coiffure to poke at his head. They turned into the seed of a poem that lodged itself in his skull—a seed that refused to sprout, however. As he distributed relief material across the house with Kader's guidance, what blossomed in Keramat's head instead of a poem was Kulsum's face, planted on the body of the woman from Bihar. One of Kulsum's breasts had been sliced off by a blade.

Collecting two large tins of milk powder for the refugee camp for which Jotin Roy's house had been requisitioned, one of which he deposited at Kader's house and loaded the other on a rickshaw, Keramat Ali set off for Badurtala, Kulsum's severed breast turning into a blur in his mind's eye. Which was why it took him a long time to realize that someone was calling his name at the railway gate. Startled, he looked to his right to see Kalam majhi using a small mirror to choose a pair of glasses from a box. He too had a packet meant for refugees. When Kalam joined him on the rickshaw, Keramat said 'Slamaleikum' to him twice, for he was seeing Kalam bespectacled for the first time in his life. 'All well?' he asked with as much deference as possible.

'All well, you ask?' One by one, Kalam listed the evidence of things not being well. Ismail was furious with him for no good reason, only because the police had arrested some ruffians from Majhipara. Had he leased the lake with the money he had earned with his own blood and sweat simply to make it easy for thieves to catch fish? Ismail was so angry that he had not even given Kalam any of the relief supplies. But he didn't care! If anything, it had made him more valuable to formidable leaders like Doctor Shamsuddin Khondkar and Sadeq the lawyer. Even though the doctor hadn't been able to help with the milk powder, he had made sure that Kalam had got a number of saris and lungis. Trouble was that Ismail was an MLA and had consolidated his position in Girirdanga, Nijgirirdanga and Golabari. But Sharafat Mondol's son Kader had poisoned his mind about Kalam. Kader wanted to bring Majhipara under his own control. Kalam thought it was the bastard Kader who was shielding Tamiz, and entreated Keramat to put in a good word on his behalf with Ismail.

But Keramat was deeply troubled by his vision of Kulsum's severed breast and her fair skin, which prevented the verses in his head from flowering. Absently he asked, 'There aren't any refugees in Golabari, are there?' and 'Hasn't Tamiz been arrested yet?'

Although the questions were unconnected, Kalam majhi answered them both. 'Not yet, but how long can it be?' and 'The bastard is accused of murder, but he's gone into hiding.'

How would Kulsum be safe on her own now? What if Kalam majhi's son the inspector swooped on her with his force? Had the police stabbed her in the breast? Was it the milk and blood from her severed breast that had splashed on Kulsum's dark-skinned face to give it a pink glow? Since it wasn't possible to ask Kalam majhi any of these questions, they remained strewn across his heart, which was not protected by breasts. Kalam majhi said without prompting, 'His son might be a convicted criminal, but Tamiz's father was sent to us by the angels. We belong to the same clan. I'll have to take care of his wife. It's my job to look after her, considering she lives in a house that belongs to me.'

A man who had promised to take care of Kulsum during her crisis was definitely going to improve his chances of securing Allah's mercy. Keramat gazed gratefully at the newly bespectacled Kalam, although he also felt a stab of jealousy that the opportunity of looking after Kulsum had fallen on Kalam majhi. When Keramat had filtered out the envy, Kalam majhi recompensed him for his devoted gaze by displaying an interest in his poetry. 'We hardly see you these days, Keramat Ali. Don't you compose songs any more?'

'There's no time, Kalam bhai.' The glory of his busy life dispelled Keramat's melancholy, anxiety and jealousy, or perhaps he looked for ways to be busy in order to dispel them. 'Where's the time? Ismail shaheb says Keramat must handle the relief material so that nothing goes wrong. And then Sadeq the lawyer said the other day, this is the time for you to write songs, poet. If we continue to read Hindu poetry even after we have our Pakistan, what was the point of building an Islamic state? Go to Dhaka, compose songs about the Islamic spirit to cleanse people's minds. But do I have the time to go to Dhaka?' Still, Keramat had to make the time to ensure that the seed of his new verses sprouted. He continued, 'But I've finally written a song after a long time. It's about refugees.'

'Come over one of these days, we'll have you sing for everyone.'

Although he was pleased with Kalam majhi's proposal, Keramat played hard to get. 'Is there anyone in Majhipara who wants to listen to songs?'

'Why should you sing in Majhipara, there's no one there.' Kalam majhi had no faith in the poetic sensibilities of fishermen. 'You'll sing at the Golabari market. I'm taking Mukunda Saha's shop, I've paid him an advance. Plenty of room in front of the shop.'

Keramat felt a deep desire to sing his verses to a large audience. Abandoning his attempt to not give in easily, he said, 'Why not today? I can be there as soon as I've delivered this tin of relief material to Jotin-babu's house. Won't take any time at all.'

'They need milk at Golabari too. How about taking it there?'

Kalam majhi's wish to present both Keramat Ali and a large tin of milk powder intensified. He had become isolated in Majhipara. His own wife put on a long face whenever she saw him. The brother-in-law of one of her cousins and the son of another cousin were in custody now because of the incident at the lake. The only place in Majhipara that gave him some relief was Kulsum's house. She never brought up the subject of the lake. Kulsum was not from the clan of fishermen, after all, she was Cherag Ali's granddaughter. Apparently Tamiz's father visited her quite frequently. Normally Kalam didn't pay much attention to such talk, but for the past few days he had been listening to Kulsum closely. Kulsum's oval face glowed when she talked of Tamiz's father. Kalam had known this distantly related aunt of his for a long time—she had practically grown up along with her brother in his own bamboo grove, and then even got married to the man he considered an uncle. But he had never noticed this glow on her face.

And yet the glow frightened him too, for he wasn't sure of himself when he visited her alone in her house. Kalam majhi was losing his stature in front of the people of Majhipara by the day, and he felt he was losing his self-control too. He sought Keramat Ali's company constantly these days, and had even made arrangements for him to live in a new front room he had added. The makeshift shack that had been erected for Cherag Ali behind the bamboo grove was still empty. Kalam could easily have built a small house there for Keramat, but this fucking poet never settled down anywhere, and there was no knowing when he might disappear—for all you know he might run away like a dog the first time Kader called out to him. Let him live in Kalam's own house, in the new front room. The longer he stayed here, the better it would be. Kalam majhi could chat with Keramat whenever he wanted, and take him along to the market or to fairs. He could even throw his weight around in the presence of other people.

Kalam wasn't unhappy about Keramat's attraction for Kulsum. No matter how much he enjoyed his private conversations with her, they frightened him too. He would be safe if Keramat was around.

Keramat's days passed eating leftover or dry rice in the morning at Kalam majhi's house, hot rice with fish curry in the evening, and wandering around with him at all hours of the day. But still no poetry bloomed in his head. He would have had a song ready by now if only he had met Kulsum. As they walked side by side, Kalam majhi suddenly said, 'Carry on, I'll join you,' and entered Kulsum's house, while Keramat strolled towards the front room of Kalam's house. But then Kalam also talked to Keramat about Kulsum, asking whether he was going to remain a vagabond all his life and never get married. How long should Kulsum remain unmarried at this age, for that matter? Kalam didn't say it in as many words, but the hint was obvious. Then why didn't he allow Keramat into her house?

One cloudy morning Keramat began to feel wistful as he was shitting in the bamboo orchard, facing Cherag Ali's empty house. Kalam majhi was still at home—it would be some time before he went out. Rinsing his hand carefully in the pond, Keramat set off for Tamiz's father's house.

Sitting at the doorstep of Kulsum's room, he appealed to her, 'You know all of your grandfather's verses. I can write them down if you tell me.'

'I already gave you the book, and I heard you've sold it to someone? Dada looks for it every time he comes, but he never finds it.' Keramat had no hope of retrieving the book. Why couldn't Kulsum understand that he was perfectly capable of composing songs of his own, which would be no less than the ones in *Khwabnama*? His books were actually printed, which people paid to buy, and hawkers lined up to collect.

But poetry was eluding him now. That tattered book was at the bottom of it all. Who knew what gift it had bestowed on him, or what spell the book had put him under—but now that it was no longer with him, his pen had dried up completely. If only Kulsum were to help him out by singing Cherag Ali's songs, he would be able to write his verses as before. In desperation he said, 'I can compose my verses if you're there. You're the fakir's granddaughter, after all. I'm writing a song, it isn't finished though. Want to hear it?'

Although he had no pen or paper, the seed of the verse burst in his head anyway:

Refugees thrown out of family homes
Have gathered together in Pakistan.

As he recited he looked directly at Kulsum, but her eyes were trained outside the door. Instead of defiance, they held a hint of a smile. She didn't seem to be listening to Keramat's lines. Whom was she gazing at outside the door? Keramat couldn't see anyone out there. Turning to him, Kulsum suddenly said, 'Don't block the door, let him come in.'

But there was no one there. Whom was Kulsum telling, 'Your son's wife is pregnant, did you know? I was there the other day.'

Someone did seem to enter through the door, his movement working up a breeze that brushed past Keramat, who shifted a little. But why couldn't he see who it was? Kulsum kept talking to him. 'She might have a goitre, but she's a good woman. She gave me fish curry and rice.' Taking a light quilt out of an aluminium pan on the maacha, Kulsum held it out. 'She gave me this. It's slightly torn in the corner, but it'll easily last two winters.' A corner of the quilt rose in the air and then fell, as though someone had lifted it and let go. 'Her sister stitched it,' said Kulsum. 'It's beautiful, have you seen the pattern?' The invisible man saw, as did Keramat, a design in red, blue and yellow, interspersed with moons and stars. Three stars per moon.

Guessing, or to be more accurate, realizing the presence of Tamiz's father, Keramat gulped, his throat dry. There was a smell of the water and the mud from the lake everywhere in the room, along with the stench of fish.

Keramat practically racing out of the house without another word, running straight into Kalam majhi, who suddenly turned grim. When Keramat said he had been to Tamiz's father's house, Kalam looked at him coldly.

That same evening Kalam told him, 'It's Wednesday tomorrow, isn't it? Market day. You can sing tomorrow.'

'Tomorrow? But I haven't written the entire song yet. Isn't it market day on Friday too?'

'Fuck your song. Make sure you write the whole thing tonight.'

A bed frame without a headboard was laid out on the veranda of Mukunda Saha's shop. Boikuntho put it out himself. Going into the shop, Kalam gauged the stock with his eyes. 'Didn't I see eight sacks of chillies the other day? Why is it down to six? And just the one sack of cumin? Have you sold the rest?'

It wasn't so much what Kalam said as the fact that he would have to provide the accounts to Mukunda Saha that made Boikuntho look defensive. Because of his employer's delay in returning, he had been selling the goods at whatever price people were willing pay. He was living extravagantly too, having flattened rice with sweets for breakfast, and rice with large fish for lunch and dinner, not to mention snacks all day. There was no lack of food at the market. The other day he had been to the Gosaibari fair, where he had lavished his money on the women at the brothel.

But Kalam was threatening him for a different reason. 'Saha has taken an advance, he's giving me the shop with all the stocks. I'm going to lose money if you sell everything recklessly.'

But Boikuntho didn't pay too much attention to Kalam. He was busy doing up the stage for Keramat. Lighting two lanterns, he hung them from the tin roof of the veranda. Kalam got Budha to fetch him a chair with armrests from his own shop. When Boikuntho brought another, Kalam said, 'One will do. It's not like the poet will sit and sing.' Gesturing with his head, he added, 'Clean those up.' Boikuntho didn't understand, so Kalam pointed to the sponge-wood plates and mango leaves tied with strings, both used to worship Lakshmi.

'But those are for Lakshmi puja . . .' began Boikuntho.

'Do as I say. Get rid of those, Budha.' As Budha was about to comply with his uncle's orders, Boikuntho jumped up in protest. 'What are you doing, what do you think you're doing? Not everyone is allowed to touch those.'

'Are you suggesting we can't touch your door? It's the door to my fucking building, are you saying my nephew can't touch it?'

'That's not what I'm saying. But these are used for the puja. If someone from a different religion . . .' Boikuntho removed them himself.

Kalam majhi bellowed again, 'Where are the incense sticks, Budha?'

Wedging the joss sticks into pots filled with rice, Budha placed them in the front half of the stage. 'Naraye takbir,' yelled Kalam majhi. Getting only a lukewarm response, he shouted at the audience, 'Why do you hesitate to call out Allah's name? Say it out loud.' When he followed this up with cries of 'Naraye takbir' and 'Pakistan', he received a satisfactory response. 'My Islamic brothers,' he began, and launched into his speech. Holding a month-old copy of the *Daily Azad* in front of his bespectacled eyes, he began describing the atrocities on and the arbitrary killings of Muslims by Hindus in India. But finding it difficult to spell each word in his head before reading it out loud, he put the newspaper aside and presented his own version of the merciless murders of Muslims. Not being used to giving speeches, he conveyed what he had heard from people and at the refugee camp in the town in a haphazard manner. But although his language wasn't fiery, his accounts of Muslim women's breasts being cut off, their being raped on a wholesale basis, rampant massacres, and eviction from homes not only excited but also provoked the audience. They kept turning to glare at the listeners from Palpara, who hung their heads so low that they all but scraped the ground. Finally Kalam majhi gestured to Keramat, 'Begin your song.'

Keramat had been fidgeting at Kalam majhi's unrestrained descriptions. Would his song make any impact after this? So he started singing from memory, 'He who wields the plough has no food on his plate.'

'Drop that nonsense. Sing about the refugees.'

Boikuntho seemed to have woken up. 'Have you written a new song?' he asked from where he was standing in front of the stage.'

Although Keramat had indeed written a new song overnight on Kalam majhi's orders, he was unhappy about it. But what could he do now? Fishing out a sheet of paper torn out of a ruled notebook, he began to read:

Listen to me now, Hindu and Muslim brothers.
I will tell you something about refugees.
Refugees evicted from their family homes
They had houses, fields and little ponds too
By Allah's grace they owed no one money
They kept their faith in god and his prophet
For which thousands sacrificed their lives

Making a 'tchah' sound with his tongue, either to stop Keramat or because he was inspired by his song, Kalam said, 'Muslims lay down their lives for the sake of their faith. So many people are dying.' In the absence of music, Boikuntho swayed his head to the monotonous rhythm of the lines. Even if the metre broke at times, interrupting the movement of his head, his concentration did not flag. Keramat continued with his verses.

Mothers and sisters lost their honour to infidels
Everything gone, they came to this country
Our Hindu brothers have left their homes
Everyone suffers to leave their motherland
The place we're born in is heaven on earth
We kiss the soil our ancestors lived on
Their suffering makes Allah unhappy . . .

Even without knowing whether Keramat had got any of the facts
wrong, Kalam majhi interrupted him because his own desire to
speak surged. 'Enough!' Then he concluded his speech, saying, my
brothers, Pakistan is not just a country for Muslims but for Hindus
too. If our Hindu brothers do not consider this country their own, if
they dispatch their assets here across the border, it is like plunging a
knife into Pakistan's heart. Don't you agree? Whether it is a Hindu
or a Muslim, there is no room on Pakistan's soil for anyone who
damages the wealth of the country.

But because the listeners began to leave without paying attention
to any of this, with the people of Majhipara in particular telling one
another, 'There's rain on the way, let's go,' Kalam was forced to stop.
Boikuntho alone sidled up to Keramat to ask, 'Aren't you going to
finish your song?'

'If the touch of a Muslim defiles your shop, isn't listening to a
Muslim's verses going to make your ears rot?' Kalam majhi snapped
at him.

'Of course not, nothing like that,' Boikuntho justified himself
quickly. 'But those things are used for Lakshmi puja, if someone
without faith touches them . . .'

'So Muslims have no faith? What are you saying, you son of an
infidel?' Kalam majhi shook with anger. 'How dare you eat off the
soil of Pakistan and yet abuse Muslims?'

Bishtu Pal hurried up and screamed at Boikuntho, 'Be careful
what you're saying, or I'll knock out all your teeth.' Then he

apologized to Kalam majhi on Boikuntho's behalf, 'We don't take this fucking madman seriously.'

'Why should *you* have to take him seriously? He doesn't say anything about your faith.' Rejecting Bishtu Pal's apology, Kalam glared at Boikuntho again. 'Son of a Hindu bitch, you think you can live on my property and abuse my religion? Out, you bastard, I'm throwing you out right now. I'm going to put the Kalma up on that fucking door of yours, let me see what your Lakshmi can do to me.'

Keshto Pal's brother Bishtu retreated. With no one else either opposing or supporting him, Kalam majhi turned to his nephew. 'What is it, Budha, don't you have blood in your veins? How can you stand there watching the fun while the swine of an infidel abuses our religion? Throw the bastard out right now.'

Boikuntho was frightened now. 'Babu's sent word, he'll be back in a few days.'

'Fuck your babu in the arse. Fuck your entire tribe in the arse.' Kalam had been declaring his intention of establishing a homosexual relationship with Saha ever since he had heard of his return. He was furious because none of the Muslims present was speaking up for him. Gofur kolu went up to Kalam majhi.

'What's all this temper for, majhi? Kader bhai has warned us of trouble if any harm comes to Mukunda Saha's shop or to his people. Be careful what you say, all right?'

As he came closer, Kalam majhi stepped away. 'Don't come near me, you bloody oil grinder, don't you dare.' Retreating to prevent Gofur from touching him, he said, 'You think you're a bigwig now just because you married the daughter of a fisherman? Not so easy. The moment I saw your fucking face I knew something would go wrong.'

Unhappy with this bad omen, Kalam majhi strode off homewards. Leave alone keeping pace with him, Budha had to run all the way just to trail behind him. But he could hear everything his uncle was saying. 'Mondol has grabbed Saha's home, now he wants his shop too. We'll see.'

Kalam majhi poured out his woes to Keramat the next morning. How were fishermen going to get a better life for themselves? Take that bastard Gofur kolu, even the other day the people of Majhipara wouldn't go anywhere near him out of contempt. And now the same fucking oil grinder had insulted him yesterday, which the fishermen of Uttarpara were sniggering about. How were they to improve their condition if they fought amongst themselves? Tamiz's father used to be a genuine leader among them, actually allowing himself to be beaten up by Mondol for the sake of his brothers. And now even his son had betrayed him, betrayed his clan. Tamiz's father's spirit visited Kulsum at home at least once a day, talking to her, listening to what she had to say. Kalam majhi yearned in his heart to go to Kulsum and tell her how he was suffering.

51

Tamiz was now treated most cordially in Ismail Husain's home for his success at inducing the ochnas and moonseed in front of the house, the orange jasmine on either side of the gate, and the pair of medlars by the pond to bloom colourfully on twenty-five-year-old trees by hoeing the soil, mixing in manure, and watering the roots twice a day. A pair of bayur grafts had been brought from Calcutta, whose growth Yakub used to measure with a scale every day for four years. With Tamiz's help Yakub had now got after the bayurs with such dedication that they had no choice but to bloom at the beginning of monsoon. Even before the trees had shed the seasonal flowers in winter, Yakub labelled them wild growth and had them cleared. Circular, square and triangular flower beds had been made there now. Yakub brought so many different kinds of fertilizers to be added along with cow dung to the soil that Tamiz could not remember their names despite being told hundreds of times.

It was doubtful whether he even tried. If he could have put this labour into rice fields, the cultivators of Girirdanga and Nijgirirdanga would have gazed in wonder at his harvest. Tamiz could not understand the eccentric townspeople. Not paddy or jute or onions or garlic or potatoes or vegetables—they wasted their money on flowers. Why? Tamiz's hands slowed down as he mixed the manure into the soil. After harvesting the onions and garlic he had grown on the land behind Harmatullah's house earlier this year, he had planned to sow aush. But the time for preparing the soil was slipping by. Harmatullah had never grown anything but onions and garlic on that patch of land. They might boast of being farmers for many generations, but Tamiz was the first one to have identified from the colour of the soil that it would yield a good crop of aush. He had told Phuljaan on the wedding night about ploughing the land. It would help if she remembered.

'Use those farmers' hands of yours gently,' Yakub Husain explained to Tamiz. 'This manure must be used as a fine mixture.' Tamiz looked at Yakub with grateful eyes for identifying his farmers' hands; but was he doomed to expend all his abilities on keeping these flowering trees happy?

Yakub used the fair, tapering fingers radiating from his palm, which was attached to a wrist with a watch on it, to demonstrate the art of making a fine mixture of the manure. 'Ask Nibaron to come and show you one of these days,' he said.

'Why are you soiling your fingers, bhaijaan? What's Tamiz here for?' Turning around to identify the source of the allegation, Yakub found Abdul Kader standing behind him. But his concentration remained focused on Tamiz. Pointing to the uneven lines of the fresh flower beds, he said,

'Didn't I ask you to draw a line in the soil with a trowel before using your spade?'

'Yakub bhai was in the military, Tamiz,' said Abdul Kader, 'you can't fool him. You'll learn many things if you stay here for some time, you won't have to go back to the village and take up the plough any more.'

Yakub offered a quick smile to Abdul Kader before pursing his lips. He didn't give these people the time of day. It was because his elder brother had such guests through the day that the garden was in such bad shape. But Yakub's cold message, delivered with a smile, 'Borda is in Dhaka,' made no difference to Kader.

He was here for an audience with their father. 'Actually, it's your father I wanted to meet. That is to say . . .'

'I see.' Kader was relieved when Yakub strolled towards the veranda and disappeared inside the house. This brother of Ismail bhai's was a decent sort, polite too, but he couldn't have a conversation with people from the villages. If it were Hrishikesh Maitra's son Anil now, or Doctor Aziz, Yakub's laughter would be audible from the centre of the town. Still, Kader wasn't budging today until he had had a chat with M.T. Husain.

'Did you talk to Phuljaan's father, bhaijaan? He had promised the land to me . . .'

Kader responded to Tamiz's entreaty with a second rebuke in the space of a few minutes. 'Forget it. Just stay here as long as you can. It took a lot of pleading with the SP shaheb to keep the police away. They'll arrest you the moment you step out. Meanwhile Kalam majhi has dropped out of sight, the people of Majhipara hardly see him. He's eyeing Mukunda Saha's shop, but none of his own people are with him.'

It wasn't clear whether Tamiz was listening to any of this. 'Won't it be too late to sow aush if we wait?' Kader was irritated by this, but he also felt a twinge of compassion for him. Ismail Husain had a soft spot for this young man. How could he have promised to secure Tamiz's release from jail before the elections if Tamiz hadn't been arrested in the first place? It was thanks to Tamiz that everyone in Majhipara had voted for Ismail Husain. And now Kalam majhi had made him a target. The way Kalam was spreading his wings might not make any difference to Ismail Husain, but Kader certainly had to be careful. The district board elections were coming up—Kalam majhi was the only one who might stand as a candidate against Kader. If Kader could keep Tamiz on his side, Kalam wouldn't even get his family's votes, never mind the villagers'. Which was why Kader had brought him here, even though it had meant begging and pleading with Ismail bhai and giving him many explanations. Now it was clear that Tamiz was in everyone's good books here. Not only did he tend the garden with Yakub, but he had also been given charge of the two Multan oxen that Ismail Husain's mother was extremely fond of. If Tamiz could secure even a fraction of her affection, there was no one who could displace him from this house. And yet Tamiz's father's foolish son was impatient to go home. If anything, it made Kader angry.

'Who's going to give you land to plough as soon as you go home? You may have married Harmatullah's daughter, but no one knows if baapjaan will allow Harmatullah to sharecrop his land? Harmat will have to grow crops on his own field in that case.'

But Tamiz wasn't giving in easily. 'Didn't all of you say there would be a law to give sharecroppers the right to the land they work on? How will your father evict Phuljaan's father from his land in that case?'

Despite his rage, Kader couldn't help laughing. 'Honestly, the things you remember! You should become an MLA.' He burst into laughter. Even though he was yet to achieve the volume of Ismail's or Yakub's or their father's guffaws, his laughter was growing stronger these days. Practising the announcement of such aristocratic mirth, he said, 'It's true, something about sharecroppers' rights was included in the bill to eradicate the jomidar system two years ago. The bill's back again, it came up just a few days ago, but they've left out sharecroppers' rights this time.'

'Left them out?' The fine mixture of fertilizer and earth slipped through Tamiz's fingers to fall on the grass. How could the same law be presented in different form the second time? The lawmaker may change but not the law—were the elite going to prove their own saying wrong?

'Go tell the old man I'm here,' Kader hurried Tamiz, who paid no attention.

'Even the tebhaga system will do. Tebhaga at least is coming, isn't it?' Tamiz asked.

'Is there nothing else you can talk about?' Kader scoffed at Tamiz's single-mindedness. 'All that is over and done with, all right? Although some hot-headed youngsters over in Natore . . .'

'Natore?' Even though he had heard of the place, Tamiz didn't know exactly where it was. But he wasn't going to admit that.

'Nawabganj, right? Of course I know it. When I was harvesting in Joipur all the jotedars were running away there with bare arses.'

'All those days are over. Now go tell the old man. I'm waiting in the veranda.'

Tamiz went around the building to enter the house through the back door, while Kader took a chair in the veranda and admired the lawn. It was beautiful. A wide unpaved road ran past the open gate. A ten-minute walk led to the river, which could be crossed on a ferry to reach the bustling town on the other side. It would have been nice to have bought some land here and built a house. Abdul Aziz had bought a house, but it was in a congested part of the town, on the other side, and surrounded by Hindu homes. Before the Partition Muslims couldn't even rent a house there, but now one or two Muslims had made inroads, buying or at least occupying houses. But Sharafat Mondol was right, it was good to have Hindu neighbours. The presence of high-caste educated Hindus in the area ensured that the children didn't become wayward. In any case, Hindus were bound to have an inferior position in Pakistan, and no one would have to tolerate them throwing about their weight. Most newcomers would be loot-and-grab hooligans who were certain to vitiate the atmosphere.

M.T. Husain lived with his head held high in this suburb. Here too the residents were dominated by Brahmons, Kayasthos and Boidyos, but the neighbourhood club was run from his house, and it was high-caste Hindus who frequented it for the most part. Yakub Husain's relations with young Hindu women were so elegant!

'He's asked you to sit inside.' Abdul Kader entered the large hall in response to Tamiz's message. With Ismail Husain being in Dhaka, the room was empty. Kader had never seen it quite so unoccupied. The shelves were packed with Bengali and English books. Discovering one of the doors open, Kader went up to it, picked out a volume and leafed through it. Several issues of an English magazine had been bound in leather, with M.T. Husain's name embossed in gold letters. If Kader built a house in the town he would have such bookshelves too.

'Oh Kader, you're here? Sit down, sit down.' The first thing M.T. Husain did on entering was to shut the open door of the bookshelf and lock it. Although he was taken aback by this, Kader had managed to get a good look at the display.

M.T. Husain asked Kader how things were back in his village, although he already knew all the news from Girirdanga, Nijgirirdanga, Golabari and nearby areas. Abdul Kader's father had bought Mukunda Saha's house dirt cheap, while Kalam majhi was eyeing Saha's shop—there was nothing the old man didn't know. His regret was that Ismail Husain had not bothered to get a house in the town or in Dhaka. Hindus were deserting their large residences, this was the time to buy, by all means pay a fair price, but don't neglect the opportunity, for it wouldn't come again. If you didn't have enough money he, M.T. Husain, would provide the rest. But no, Ismail Husain wasn't interested. If you're so upright, why can't you stop your followers from stealing people's homes? What's the use of such righteousness?

Kader was among the five or six closest followers of Ismail Husain's. To ensure the old man didn't bring up Kader's father's exploits as an example of such theft, he quickly echoed M.T. Husain's regret. 'Bhaijaan has no time for himself. People like Doctor Shamsuddin or Sadeq the lawyer or Samad Khan or Mofizul Huq are all amassing property freely. Take the case of . . .'

Interrupted by the arrival of parathas and a meat curry, Kader devoured the entire thing practically by himself, belching twice with the satisfaction of his meal and in preparation for his petition. Which was . . .? Kader said that a match had been proposed for him from the Talukdars of Shimultola. His father Sharafat Mondol would visit the bride's family today to meet the girl, make a formal offer, and finalize things. It wasn't going to be a large group. Sharafat himself, of course, and then, since Kader had two mothers—here he lowered his eyes and smiled sheepishly before overcoming his embarrassment and continuing—both of them would go, besides Abdul Aziz, some four people from Aziz's in-laws' family, including

Aziz's mother-in-law and, possibly, his eldest brother-in-law's wife. Interrupting this recital of the abbreviated list of members of the party bound for the bride's home, Ismail's father said, 'Which of the Talukdars of Shimultola is her father?'

'She's part of Ismail bhai's father-in-law's clan. You know her father. Azhar Talukdar. Old family.'

'Old family indeed! If you have money you can become an old family overnight these days.'

Despite his disappointment at this, Kader pleaded humbly with his palms joined together—if only M.T. Husain would take the trouble of joining his relatives on their visit to the bride's house, he, Kader would have a blue-blooded, wise and judicious elder on his side. His father Sharafat Mondol would escort M.T. Husain personally. It would take about an hour in all.

When M.T. Husain agreed at once, Abdul Kader broke the tradition of his family's mazhab and bent to touch M.T. Husain's feet. Kader's eyes misted over, which didn't happen very often. Tears may have gathered not just in his eyes but also in his ears, for he did not hear anything else that the dignified old man said after this.

Kader's emotions swelled again when he saw Tamiz sitting beneath the orange jasmine tree. 'Now that you're here, Tamiz, consider yourself lucky,' he said. 'Ismail's brother's father is like an angel. You won't get such people in your life easily. But be on your guard, let me see what I can do for you. I'm trying my best to have the case against you withdrawn. Let Ismail bhai come back from Dhaka. And listen, keep this.' About to hand over an entire eight-anna coin he had taken from his pocket, he changed his mind and put it back. 'No, let me keep this, it's a new eight-anna coin of Pakistan's. The government has released new currency, the old one will be withdrawn gradually.'

Gazing at the gleaming disc with fascinated eyes, Kader handed Tamiz two four-anna coins instead, adding two annas as an afterthought.

Tamiz pulled out an entire five-rupee note from a knot in his lungi. Counting out some coins along with the note, he gave it all to

Kader, saying, 'I had returned seven rupees less three annas earlier, now you've given me ten annas, and I'm giving you eight rupees and six annas, so what does it all add up to? Seven plus eight fifteen, and then . . .'

'Fifteen rupees and eleven annas,' Kader got the calculation over and done with quickly.

'How?' Tamiz began calculating all over again, feeling reassured only when his figure tallied with Kader's. 'Yes, fifteen rupees and eleven annas. If you gave me five annas more that would be exactly sixteen rupees.'

Kader did so at once, which Tamiz returned to him immediately. 'I don't need very much more to take back the house from Kalam majhi. Since Phuljaan's father has given his word, he has to give her the land. If I can produce two crops on it, can't I buy back the land behind my house? You just have to say the word, bhaijaan. The land will produce a very good crop of amon, it's perfect for it. Just needs to be ploughed several times . . .'

'I'm going now. You'd better stay here.'

As Kader made to leave, Tamiz continued, 'Will you give Phuljaan two rupees out of the money I gave you? And buy a dress for my daughter for ten annas or less from the market in town. How much does that leave?'

'You've had a daughter?' Tamiz was so surprised that Kader did not know this important piece of news that the words bubbling up in his throat—I haven't even got to see her, I have no idea what she eats, what clothes she has—sank into his stomach instead of emerging through his lips. What came out instead was, 'Ten annas for the dress and two rupees for Phuljaan, no, it's best you give her eight annas more. What does that work out to?'

But Kader was in a great hurry. His father was probably at Aziz's house by now. Kader would have to bring him back here by the afternoon, after which they would go to Namazgarh to the bride's house. Sharafat had bought a ring from Rupmohol. They would have to take some sweets along, plenty of it in fact—they were going to visit one of the Shimultola Talukdars, after all. Kader had been lukewarm at first on hearing that the prospective bride wasn't fair-skinned, which more or less meant she was dark. But Sharafat Mondol was adamant: leave alone dark-skinned, even a lame one-eyed bride from the Talukdar family for his son would enhance his prestige in the eastern part of the district. Maybe Azhar mian was from a distant branch, but he was a Talukdar nevertheless. All of them got together for weddings, birthdays, Eid, burials and funerals. The bride's family even had an equal share of the immaculate graveyard of the clan. There was no point antagonizing his father any more, Kader told himself. No further grounds for objection remained once he was told that Azhar mian's daughter would inherit his earthen two-storey house in Namazgarh. Moreover, the marriage would also make him related to Ismail Husain in a roundabout way.

His father had probably arrived at the town by now. Kader couldn't pay attention to Tamiz's calculations any more. But he channelled some of his brimming devotion for M.T. Husain into anxiety for Tamiz. 'I have to tell you something, Tamiz. Baapjaan will come to this house today, after the asr namaz. Ismail bhai's father has invited him, he will be upset if baapjaan doesn't come. You must stay out of sight when he's here. If he sees you he'll fly into a rage, you know what he's like.'

But Tamiz continued with his calculations. 'Let's say you spend twelve annas on the dress for my daughter. How much will that leave after you've given Phuljaan the money? I need some more to have my land released. And if you can explain to your father . . .' Kader set off for Aziz's house without finalizing the accounts.

52

It was impossible to stand at Bhabani Pathak's shrine beneath the banyan tree; the Poradaho field had collapsed under the raging current of the Bangali river. Who had lent such force to the frail stream? How had the dead Manosh come to life and overflowed into the Bangali? Boikuntho's grandfather's grandfather, or perhaps it was *his* father, or even *his* father, had arrived here with Bhabani Pathak—was the Manosh looking to regain the muscle and power it used to have back then? Or was it the Jomuna's pride at being a creek transformed into a wide river by the earthquake that had propelled it all the way to Poradaho to gobble up the Bangali? And now you're flicking your tongue, you bitch, at the shrine of your father, not even your father, you slut, your father's father Bhabani Pathak. Just look at the audacity of the whore. But Boikuntho did not have the power to stop it in its tracks. Now that he was standing erect, his head was touching the mosquito net, which had draped itself around his body and limbs all the way down to his knees. He couldn't see anything because his eyes were covered; no matter how sharply he scrutinized his surroundings, not a living creature was to be seen anywhere. Bhabani Pathak's ancient shaggy banyan tree loomed over his head, the fig tree entwined with it. So the fig tree had taken wing from the northern head of Katlahar Lake to insert its roots into the banyan tree and wrap itself around it. Bhabani Pathak's incantations were resounding from every leaf of the fig and the banyan, but not even a fragment could break through the mosquito net to touch Boikuntho. Not a soul was around. Had the fair ended much earlier, then? Or had the manager ordered its closure so that he could establish an idol of Durga? Or perhaps Sharafat Mondol's family was too frightened of him to visit the fair any more.

There wasn't a human being to be seen. It wouldn't have taken long to split open the mosquito net with the help of others. It wouldn't have taken long to pin down the coils of the Jomuna had there been some people to help him. The 3000 square feet of land 'set aside for the use of the common people under the ownership of Bhabani Pathak' beneath Boikuntho's feet was shrinking visibly as the waves lapped at it. The water reached Boikuntho's soles, rising beyond his ankles to his knees in a matter of moments. Boikuntho Giri woke up at its whistling sound.

The room was pitch dark, and his knees were wet from the water dripping through the holes in the tin roof. It took him a long time to make out whether the sound outside was coming from the currents of the Jomuna or the torrential rain. The dream he had just had reverberated chillingly from the drumming of raindrops on the tin roof, and his fear from having had that particular dream swelled so much that it began to swallow up the dream itself. He felt apprehensive: What if the dream frightened him to the point where he forgot the very dream that was causing this fright? How then would he be able to seek the meaning of the dream at Cherag Ali's house? Boikuntho's throat was parched out of fear—either of the dream or of the possibility of forgetting the dream. Groping for the earthen pitcher of water, he filled a brass tumbler, drank it down, and sat down on his bed, his heart thumping. How could a man have such a dream? Could a man who had such a dream survive? What did a dream like this mean? That was when he heard Cherag Ali singing from the other side of eternity:

The fakir keeps dreaming in his eternal sleep
Fire rages, ashes drop, and the water churns.

Those who are born and die on this earth
Without courage have dreams such as these

Perhaps it was the glass of water that stopped Boikuntho's trembling.
But the pride of having had a dream that no living being on earth
could dare to have did not blunt his fear—on the contrary, it pressed
down on him even more emphatically. For a few moments Boikuntho
thought he was having a hangover from his dream, and he shifted his
bedstead and lay down again in the hope that another dream would
dispel this hangover.

But sleep eluded him. Every time he looked at the door he could
tell even in the darkness that the rain was splashing through the cracks
in the windswept door, soaking the sacks of cumin. Boikuntho had
already sold several sacks of chilli and cumin and pocketed the cash,
but his employer wouldn't spare him if whatever was left was spoilt
by the rain. Mukunda Saha had put him in a tight spot by delaying
his return. Kalam majhi had come to the shop this afternoon despite
the drizzle, accompanied by a group of louts from Majhipara, and
threatened him. 'Vacate the shop, you fucking Hindu. I'm going to
take possession before your babu returns.' He left when Gofur kolu
turned up because of all this screaming, but not before telling Gofur,
'How much more is that bloody Mondol going to gobble up? His
belly will burst one of these days.' He had issued a stern order to
Boikuntho, 'The number of sacks here had better not change, I'm
warning you.'

As he was pushing the sacks out of the way of the rain, Boikuntho
heard someone scraping at the door. With the torrential downpour
muffling the sound, Boikuntho realized that the stray dog which
roamed around the market was probably getting drenched in the
rain—what harm would it do if he were to give the dog shelter
behind the cumin sacks? It wasn't as though his employer would
be checking. Moreover, Boikuntho needed to urinate. He hadn't
realized it because of the dream and the associated fear, but as he was
shifting the sacks one of them bumped against his lower abdomen,

which felt painful. As soon as he unbolted and unlocked the door
and lowered the crossbar with the intention of pissing from the
doorstep and bringing the dog inside, he was assailed by gusts of
wind and rain. And before Boikuntho could unknot his dhuti, two
pairs of arms slick with rainwater wrapped themselves around him
and knocked him to the floor.

Boikuntho Giri's head, laden with the dream and his fear of the
dream, fell on a plump rat, which emitted a faint cry of death as it
was flung to one side.

'Urghhh!' Boikuntho's scream was lost in the violent storm. A
bolt of lightning struck the double body of the fig and the banyan,
bypassing the trident in the idol's hand, and the earth shook at the
sound. But couldn't Cherag Ali turn Munshi's pan into a rod and
make himself be heard over the deluge? With no help forthcoming,
Boikuntho gathered all his strength and jerked his body violently,
which loosened the hold of one of the two pairs of arms. But when
he tried to free himself, they returned at once, one hand clamping
itself on his throat and the other on his mouth. One of the assailants
sat down on his chest. Boikuntho gasped in agony, but even gasping
proved difficult and soon became impossible. His suffering finally
ended when the entire length of a heavy dagger was plunged into
his neck. The hand covering his mouth moved away. Boikuntho
tried his utmost to keep his eyes open, but once the blade had found
its way in, he could not see anything although his eyes were wide
open. With the weight off his chest, he felt light in his body as well.
Since his eyes were no longer functional, his glance turned inwards,
capturing a young woman in a soiled, red-bordered sari, her head
of black hair lit up by a line of vermilion. She scolded him, 'Where
do you roam around all day, baba? Where do you go, what do you
eat? Must you go to the gods as soon as you enter home?' Drawing
Boikuntho to herself, she wiped his face with the end of her dirty
sari, muttering constantly, 'This boy, always in the sun, always in the
sun.' She wiped his face with the end of her dirty sari, kept wiping
it, continued to wipe his face, sticky with sweat, and with every time

she wiped his face it shrank. Perhaps to keep pace with his face, his chest, stomach, arms, legs, fingers, everything began to shrink too. Lying back in the young woman's lap, Boikuntho gazed at the round moon on her brow. The end of the dirty sari cast a shadow on the moonlight, but made it tender too. Sleep descended on Boikuntho's eyes, riding those moonbeams. He could hear the sound of music from the west, and the young woman matched her voice with it, singing of the death of Bhabani Pathak and exhorting the Giri clan to weep.

> The Giri clan is in the water
> To pick him up with love and care
> Like Radha holds Krishna in her arms.
> Let your hearts turn to stone today
> Weep, you Giris, weep all you can
> Bhabani Pathak is in this world no more.

The music and the singing both faded, while his sleep-laden eyes saw her face clouding over, becoming darker and more elongated, the round red moon on her forehead disappearing behind an immense tree. Still she continued humming.

> The moon rises behind the grove
> The wife and son are fast asleep.
> Who knows where the fakir has flown
> Bhabani Pathak is in this world no more.

Suddenly the young woman whose face was clouded with shadows stopped humming to glare at him. 'So you can have our mango, but drinking water here means breaking with your religion?' Who was she now? The face was familiar? Who was this who was scolding him? When Boikuntho's tears mingled with his blood, he extended his arms towards her slowly from his side of the red curtain drawn over his eyes, but they did not rise at all. He had left it too late to find out who she was. As more blood gathered in his wide-open eyes and congealed there to turn black, everything finally disappeared from view

In the morning the rain stopped, but the clouds refused to leave. Wading through the ankle-deep water towards the handpump, Gofur kolu called out on seeing the door to Mukunda Saha's shop open, 'What a storm, Boikuntho!' Rinsing his mouth out and filling his pot with water to drink, he called out again on his way back, 'Where are you, Boikuntho?' Getting no response, he was about to leave, but spotting the sacks of cumin and chilli lying scattered beyond the open door, he climbed into the veranda and entered the room. There were large clots of blood on Boikuntho's chest and face—he was lying on one side of the sacks, with the pulverized body of a plump rat on the floor near his head.

53

'Boikuntho, can you hear me, Boikuntho?'

As the storm wreaked havoc through the night, Tamiz's father entered his own room to call out, 'Why can't you hear me, Boikuntho?' While he continued to shout, the top of the jackfruit tree broke off and crashed on the roof of Tamiz's unoccupied room. It was obvious now that Tamiz's father had informed everyone of Boikuntho's death by snapping the head of his favourite jackfruit tree. But why did the old coot also have to visit Kulsum to recount the tale? Even death had not managed to make a sensible man out of him. Was it a very long way from the quicksand near the fig tree to Mukunda Saha's shop?

The clouds had deserted the Srabon sky, leaving it crackling in the sunlight. The heat crept into the room though the wilting straw roof so relentlessly that keeping the door shut couldn't keep the room cool. Kulsum could neither sit nor lie down in the sweltering heat. She wandered around, sniffing at everything, the room bereft of one particular smell—Cherag Ali's *Khwabnama* was missing. It was this book that had brought Boikuntho in here ever so often. 'Look up your book, fakir.' 'What's the matter?' 'Late last night, around ten, no, more like eleven, actually, not before twelve, that was when I fell asleep. I had just about lain down when I saw . . .'

As Boikuntho began recounting his dream even before he had entered, Cherag Ali raised the twig with which he was drawing lines on the ground. 'Wait, wait, give me a moment.'

Cherag Ali was busy listening to the story of a helpless man from the town whose wife had been possessed by a jinn. 'He's been to every doctor possible, but nothing's worked. So he's come to me. Let's see what Munshi can do.'

The pride of having a client from the town, the pleasure at the failure of the doctors, and the joy of seeing Boikuntho all at once made Kulsum's grandfather emit a sound like rice boiling over. Boikuntho had completed half his story even before the patient, or was it the patient's husband, had left. Cherag Ali asked a series of questions, and with each answer Boikuntho took more than the opportunity he was given to expand on his dream. He went into a trance as he recounted it, as though he was having the dream at that very moment. As the fakir added lines on the floor, Boikuntho's dream grew proportionately longer. He was in fact addicted to Cherag Ali's verses—hearing them made him change the story of his dream. Whether it was thanks to those verses or not, he had even accommodated Cherag Ali in his dream. Apparently Cherag Ali was perched on the topmost branch of the fig tree, demanding the pan from Munshi, who, far from being angry, was twinkling with laughter. Why would Munshi stand for anyone taking the pan with which he ruled all of Katlahar Lake, the instrument at whose signal the murrel in the lake turned into sheep? Surely the fakir knew this, but he was happy making his demand. For in Boikuntho's dream Munshi's smile was cutting through the white beard on his face. He was delirious with joy. But what to say about this descendant of Bhabani Pathak's? He could have dreams of the white-bearded man with missing teeth, but why did he never see Kulsum in his dreams? Kulsum knew the extent of Boikuntho's ability to have dreams. He was afflicted with the virus of religion. He would visit their house, eat his fill of mango or jaggery, sucking his fingers for every last trace, but he had never taken even a sip of water here. How far could anyone's dreams stretch with this virus? Kulsum had personally pleaded with him to take Cherag Ali's *Khwabnama*. It was this book that used to draw him to Cherag Ali, but still he turned it down. What was his problem? Would keeping *Khwabnama* in that miserly bastard Mukunda Saha's shop defile the premises? She had made a mistake—she should have forced him to take it. Had Cherag Ali's book lain at the head of Boikuntho's bed, the dacoits would never have succeeded in hacking him to death. They had forced themselves in on the stormy night and slaughtered him. Slaughtered him. Kulsum's eyes filled with tears.

Whenever Tamiz's father came he left behind a trail of sand, which was why sand dripped from Kulsum's eyes in this room. But now all the sand melted under sprays of Boikuntho's blood. The room filled with the vapour of blood, obliterating everything from view. Kulsum groped her way to the door to open it.

When the sunlight had dried the red waves in her eyes, Kulsum heard someone say, 'I got some fish for you, here it is.' Slipping back into the room, she took the basket made of bark from Keramat Ali from behind the door and set it on the floor. 'You live alone here,' Keramat Ali continued, 'it's not safe for a widowed woman.'

But since yesterday Kulsum had no longer been staying here at night. Kalam majhi had been telling her the same thing for several days, 'You're a young widow, it doesn't look right for you to be living alone, people say things.' Yesterday afternoon Kalam had spoken to her for a while, after which his wife and Budha's daughter had more or less forced her to accompany them. Their reasoning was that it wasn't as though she was giving up her home, she could still pass the entire day here. But they couldn't allow a nubile woman to spend the night alone.

Kalam majhi had spoken to her quite gently in the afternoon, though. 'I have no quarrel with you. You're Tamiz's father's widow, I make the moulobi say prayers at his shrine every Friday. It was Tamiz who became my enemy, which he still is. But then Tamiz is not even your son. Why should I blame you? There's something I have to talk to you about, though.' What? 'People say Tamiz visits you every day. How can you be so bold as to let someone on the run come in here? How will I manage things if the police come here?'

'Tamiz?' said Kulsum in astonishment. 'Tamiz never visits me.'

It was difficult to disbelieve her. But Kalam majhi was fed up with the behaviour of the people of Majhipara. He had gone to so much trouble to bring them the relief supplies meant for the refugees. Nobody objected to accepting the clothes, but the tins of milk powder remained untouched. Budha had personally heard Abiton's father, the bastard—the old coot had happily taken the saris and lungis—telling everyone that drinking the milk Kalam majhi had brought would mean certain death. Considering he had handed over his own kin to the police, he was eminently capable of feeding poisoned milk to those who had slipped through the police's hands. Consider too the fact that the fishermen's children cast their nets in the lake all the time. They drew back their nets and ran away when the saw Kalam majhi, but some of them pretended not to have seen him at all and went on with their leisurely fishing. How many guards could Kalam deploy? As for the very small children, the moment they saw him they retreated a few steps and chanted, 'In the lake the big fish, small fry on your dish.' Kalam majhi had been hearing something like this since childhood, they were among the verses women sang while husking the rice. But the lines had been altered for him in particular—why? Had the devil fish Tamiz's father caught now taken control of the children's tongues?

Kalam couldn't tolerate their fathers' misbehaviour any more. Not only did the people of Majhipara never buy anything at his shop in the market, but they also announced while walking past, 'Everything in this shop is adulterated.' His own son, who was a police inspector in the town, paid no attention when he complained about these things. He claimed he could not afford to antagonize Kader mian. He was close to MLAs and ministers, he even had the power to shelter people accused of murder. But Tahsen hadn't helped Kalam majhi with his efforts to grab Mukunda Saha's shop. He did say, though, that since it was Hindu property, if Kalam could find a way to get rid of the current occupant, Tahsen would ensure that his father could keep the shop—which he had done. The very next afternoon after Boikuntho was murdered, the Amtoli police sealed the door of the shop, unsealing it only the next day on Tahsen's instructions. Kalam had the idols of Ganesh removed and celebrated Milad. Tahsen was present, but afterwards he went to Kader's shop and chatted with him too. Very few of the people from Majhipara attended the Milad, but a huge crowd of the bastards turned up when the jilapi was being distributed. Budha, who had overheard their conversations while they were eating their jilapi, told Kalam, 'No one but Tamiz could have taught the fuckers all these tricks, mamu.' One day Keramat Ali let slip, perhaps accidentally, that he had heard the hum of conversations in Kulsum's house late at night.

Kalam frowned at once. 'Do you visit her at night?'

'Oh no. I was passing that way when I heard people talking in Tamiz's father's house.'

'Who was it? What were they saying?'

Keramat was prepared to make up a story about Tamiz in straightforward terms, but he decided not to because he wasn't sure what trouble he might get into. 'No,' he said, 'I didn't stop to hear.'

Kalam majhi hadn't disbelieved Kulsum that afternoon, but he had continued, 'You say Tamiz doesn't visit you, but then whom do you talk to late at night? Lots of people have heard conversations in your house.'

'Tamiz's father visits me,' Kulsum answered at once.

Startled at Kulsum's casual response, Kalam majhi looked around in alarm. Gulping, he said, 'How can a dead man visit you? What are you saying?'

'He does. Late at night.'

That very day Kalam decided that Kulsum could not be allowed to spend the nights alone at home. He told his wife, 'Dead or alive, it isn't right for a man to visit a woman at night. Make arrangements for her to stay here. She can't be allowed to live in a haunted house.'

Kalam majhi's wife agreed to bring Kulsum over—in fact, she proved quite enthusiastic about it. But she was unwilling to take possession of Tamiz's father's house. They had already been ostracized by their family, and grabbing the house would incense the people of Majhipara. Tamiz's father could create trouble too from beneath the quicksand. Although Kalam majhi said, 'We'll see, that's my business,' Tahsen's stepmother realized that her husband had accepted her warning for now.

But no matter what anyone said, Keramat was convinced that it was Tamiz who visited Kulsum late at night. On the morning after he had heard voices in Kulsum's house, there was a glow of happiness on her face. He was a poet—if he couldn't tell a woman's needs and pleasures from her expression, who could? He hadn't been writing verses all these years just to pass the time. What had Kulsum ever got from Tamiz's father anyway? She was making up for it now with the old coot's young son, with interest added. Moreover, those young louts of Majhipara mocked him with his own verse now, 'A lake without fishermen, water without fish in it, a woman without a man is a tree without fruit on it.' Hearing the lines he had written frightened him, for who but that bastard Tamiz could incite the fishermen so effectively?

One day even someone like moulobi Kuddus had said in Kalam majhi's presence, 'I saw a group of thugs gathered together today at the Shimultola ghat. They had nets with them, and all of them were chanting Keramat's verses.' Keramat's throat was dry with fear. He couldn't stay here if he incurred Kalam majhi's wrath, and if he was forced to move from Majhipara Kulsum would never be his.

Instead of responding to Kuddus, he offered an excuse to Kalam, 'I stopped singing those long ago.'

But Keramat's problem was with Kalam majhi. Not only did he not bring up the subject of his marrying Kulsum any more, he had also lapsed into a sullen silence whenever Keramat broached the subject. Keramat could neither compose new verses nor sing his old ones until he called Kulsum his own. So he had decided that he might as well offer her the fish and make the proposal himself. Sitting on her doorstep, Keramat presented his case, telling her that people would say all kinds of things if she went on living alone here, and he couldn't stand anyone criticizing her. But all of them could be made to shut up if Kulsum agreed to marry him. Kalam majhi was in favour of the wedding, he had even been to the quicksand to seek Tamiz's father's blessings. He would let both of them live here—he would never evict Keramat if he stayed here with his family.

'Does Kalam majhi think this house belongs to his father?' Although startled by Kulsum's first statement after a long silence, Keramat marvelled at her spirited response. 'Tamiz's father had pawned the house for money to Kalam majhi. It will all be settled as soon as Tamiz pays him back.' The tip of Kulsum's tongue, the rise and fall of her lips, and the knotting and unknotting of her brows all transported Keramat into a state of wonder; even if only for a moment, he wondered whether he was awake or whether he was asleep and dreaming.

'I've never worried about where to live. I won't starve so long as I have an income. Kalam majhi has already given me the job of keeping the books at his shop, and now that he's got Mukunda Saha's shop, I'll have to take care of that too. I'll be earning well enough.' He also reminded Kulsum of the popularity of his songs amongst the people in the town. Marrying her would bring his vagabond-like existence to an end. 'I'll be able to compose songs again.'

'You can write your songs in the books you'll be keeping at the shop, isn't that so?' Keramat was a trifle hurt to imagine that Kulsum didn't distinguish between bookkeeping and songwriting.

Containing the pique of the poet, he said, 'If Kalam majhi doesn't want you here I'll get a house in the town for us. I can earn enough from my songs to get a house there.'

Kulsum had no objection to moving to the town. But she had heard they had lights there at night too, and there were crowds everywhere, and shameless hussies roamed around the streets in rickshaws.

'Will you come live in the town?'

After some thought Kulsum said, 'Tamiz's father won't go to the town. He doesn't even know the way.'

Keramat Ali was deeply disappointed. What if this illness of Kulsum's that made her see dead men wasn't cured even after their marriage?

He might have brought this up with her, but Budha's daughter appeared meanwhile. 'Chachi you've come away from the husking, how am I supposed to manage it all alone?'

'Let's go.' Putting the catfish Keramat had brought into a large pot of water to keep them alive, and covering the mouth with an earthen dish, Kulsum shut the door and went off to Kalam majhi's house. Harvesting was in full swing since this morning. Not only did they need rice for the family, but they also had to send 40 seers of it to Tahsen's house in the town.

Kalam majhi's wife was a kind woman who did not make Kulsum work very hard. Kulsum did a good job of the husking, and it did not tire her out even if she laboured all day. On this pretext she could get lunch at Kalam majhi's house, where fish was included. Tahsen's stepmother had a soft corner for her, in fact. There might be something else to it too. That evening, finding herself alone with Kulsum, she had said, 'Why don't you marry Keramat, Kulsum? He's a good man, but you never know with men, it doesn't take them long to change their minds.' But it appeared that the real cause of her anxiety was a different man. This morning she had said, 'Don't sleep in the veranda, Kulsum, sleep in Budha's room instead, make your bed there.' Kulsum didn't quite understand. She had in fact been quite pleased to see a tall shadow next to her bed on waking up in the middle of the night—so Tamiz's father was visiting her here too. Tahsen's stepmother had asked her to sleep in Budha's room within hours of being told of this incident.

Would Tamiz's father be able to find his way to Budha's room? Kulsum felt worried. But her mind was cleared of all doubts when a cool breeze wafted across her body in the evening while husking the grains. There had been a shower soon after she had arrived here with Budha's daughter in the afternoon. This was followed by humidity, a sultriness that refused to be dispelled. Everyone was perspiring profusely—everyone except Kulsum, who felt a pleasant breeze blowing around her body. What could this mean? Was it the fakir's doing? No, Munshi was the only one who could conjure up a breath of fresh air amidst such heat. But then his supply of breeze came from the vicinity of the fig tree, acquiring a light, sweet, fishlike smell from the carp and catfish swimming in the lake. Today the fragrance of tobacco had been added to it. With the two scents mingling, Kulsum could no longer tell them apart. Her feet slowed on the husking pedal, and Budha's daughter said, 'What's wrong with you, Chachi? The hammer was about to fall on my arm.' Her bones would have been shattered if it had.

'In the lake the big fish, small fry on your dish,' chanted Budha's younger daughter. Kulsum's head reeled as she listened—but was it at the aroma of the tobacco, or the fishlike smell of the devil fish, or the words of the childish rhyme?

Not sure of the answer, Kulsum said, 'Let's stop for a while, let me catch my breath.'

54

Everyone was drenched to some extent in the early-morning rain. Considering the fury of the night-long storm, it was doubtful whether they would be able to leave at dawn. The three suitcases—eldest, middle, youngest—the trunk, the holdall and the basket of food did get a little wet while being unloaded from the district magistrate's jeep at the station. The water jug overflowed despite the caution and care with which Kader was handling it. The train was nearly half an hour late. The rain had stopped meanwhile, but the sky remained overcast.

Kader had been entrusted with the responsibility of escorting Ismail Husain's wife, one son, two daughters and maid to Dhaka, a responsibility he had willingly accepted. He would use the trip to shop for his own wedding. The sari, jewellery, other clothes, cosmetics and suitcase would be purchased under Ismail's supervision. Sharafat Mondol had personally requested Rizia Begum the other day at Husain Manzil, 'We're bringing the girl to your house, ma, please buy everything as you see fit.'

Abdul Kader had taken the opportunity to smuggle Tamiz away to Dhaka. The police would not dare touch him once he was ensconced in Ismail Husain's house there. Tamiz could be brought back to Girirdanga after they lobbied successfully to have the case against him withdrawn. Then they would see how Kalam could be elected to the district board.

At Ismail Husain's house in Dhaka they needed a servant they could trust. Rizia Begum had generously given Tamiz an old twill shirt of her husband's, an almost new lungi, and even a formal grey coat with only a small tear in it. She had also bought a sari and a blouse, and a frock for his wife and daughter, respectively. Rizia Begum was so pleased with Tamiz that she was more or less plucking him out of the arms of her mother-in-law and brother-in-law, ignoring their glum expressions.

But then Tamiz attended to her needs as much as his intelligence allowed him to. He grabbed the smallest suitcase from the porter in a bid to save it from the rain, and, because he was clutching it to his chest and stomach all the way to the waiting room, he tripped on the weighing scales and then on a pile of rice sacks on the platform. It was in fact to please Rizia Begum that he had made an attempt to put on the grey coat before leaving Husain Manzil, but thanks to observations and advice like 'what's this, why are the sleeves hanging loose?', 'why are you wearing this in summer', 'people at the station will mistake you for Ismail bhai in that coat and salute you', 'take it off and put it in your luggage', he had packed it away in his sack, which he was refusing to let go of.

Arranging the luggage in the first-class compartment and making sure Rizia Begum, her children, and the maid were properly seated, Kader pushed Tamiz into the third-class compartment a few carriages away. Before returning to the first-class compartment, Kader told him repeatedly, 'Come to the other carriage when the train stops at Bonarpara, bhabi may need something. But don't get off the train before that. You won't be able to get back on at those small stations.'

Tamiz had travelled often enough by train not to need all these warnings. But gentlemen were amused by the way peasants and fishermen floundered during rail journeys. So Tamiz didn't say anything about being a seasoned traveller, and that he knew very well what he was supposed to do at Bonarpara, where he would have a chance to put himself to some use for bhabishaheba. She might need tea, or she may have run out of water. She had her own supply of paan, but still he could get her some from a shop. One smile from her was worth a week of happiness for him. And if she happened to say, 'Tamiz doesn't need instructions, a signal is enough,' his happiness lasted a month.

His carriage was extremely crowded, but he managed to find a place to sit on the floor near the door. Just as he was reassuring himself for the third or fourth time that the contents of his sack were intact, a local train stopped on the line next to theirs. A group of policemen got into it with trunks and beddings—not a group, a carriageful of policemen, in fact. Tamiz quickly turned his face away—what if the police identified him as a criminal on the run? In this compartment there was no Kader or Ismail shaheb or Yakub shaheb, not even his father. Being captured now would mean twelve years in jail, maybe more. He might even be hanged. Tamiz was suddenly reminded of Phuljaan. How much had his daughter grown? Was she walking now, or still crawling? Would he be lucky enough to see her? Kulsum probably did not visit Phuljaan and her daughter, or perhaps she had been there once and been at the receiving end of Harmatullah's barbs. Who knew whether Harmat treated his granddaughter with contempt for being the child of a fisherman? Tamiz felt so distraught for his wife and daughter that he forgot his fear of the police. A little later the policemen were no longer visible, having wedged themselves into their carriage. Someone nearby said, 'There's big trouble somewhere, an entire carriage full of police left yesterday, and now here's another one today.'

'What trouble?' asked someone, and the answer came from the crowd. 'The aadhiar peasants are agitating, the police are beating them up and arresting them without even bothering whether it's a man or a woman.'

'Where's that train going?' Tamiz asked.

'Shantahar.'

Shantahar! The train was bound for Shantahar! Its engine seemed to whistle the word, 'Shantahar!' Although he didn't know the alphabet, the first thing in his life Tamiz had learnt to read was the name of this place. From Shantahar you could go to Joipur or Akkelpur or Hili. Or to Dinajpur and Thakurgaon. Or you could take the other line for Natore or Nobabganj. With so many policemen going there, it could only mean the cultivators were claiming two-thirds of the harvest, while the jotedars were on the run with their arses bared to the world, they were trying to hide inside the policemen's arses. Meanwhile the land was being prepared for the sowing of amon, it was being ploughed in strips once, twice, thrice, and now the light-green paddy seeds were laid out in the sun. Once the land was ready there would be a frenzy of sowing. It had rained all last night, the soil must be like butter now, the blade of the plough sinking deep into the earth on mere contact, so deep that Tamiz could draw water from it. Images of the rice fields appeared in the smoke from the engine of the train going to Shantahar. Oh, the land, the land! The stalks began to ripen as soon as the seeds were sown, drooping under the weight of the sap. There was no counting the number of people busy harvesting the fattened grain. The jotedars had arrived with the policemen, who were getting off their trains at every station and fanning out across the fields. They were spreading like cholera, like smallpox. The peasants were giving chase with sickles, the bastards had nowhere to hide however fast they ran.

'Is this train ever going to leave? How late does it plan to be?' Tamiz jumped to his feet suddenly, pushed through the crowd and jumped off, setting off at a run in search of a third-class compartment in the train bound for Shantahar. The wheels of the engine had begun to turn in response to the guard's long whistle. Tamiz jumped into a carriage.

It was not as crowded here. Although there was room on the benches, many bare-bodied men with homespun towels wrapped around their shoulders were squatting on the floor after pushing their balancing rods, baskets and spades under the seats. Some of them moved away at the sight of Tamiz's neat shirt, clean lungi and rubber sandals. About to take a seat, Tamiz suddenly recollected with a shock that he had left his sack behind. But the train had gathered speed by then. So many clothes lost! With as much as five whole rupees in their creases!

There was no going back now. No need to go back, either.

55

The moment Sharafat Mondol entered Kader's shop, closing his umbrella as he crossed the threshold, a fully liveried Tahsenuddin stood up from his chair and bent over to touch Mondol's feet. 'May Allah bless you,' said Mondol with a smile. Although he didn't go so far as to touch anyone's feet, the inspector of Amtoli police station said slaamaleikum and lifted his bottom a couple of inches from his chair before returning to his comfortable position. Mondol had guessed something was in the air when he saw the police jeep in the market early in the morning. But who had authorized the town police to come here in search of Tamiz?

Gofur had already arranged for sweets. As they ate, after the mandatory discussion on adulteration and the quality of the sweets Sharafat said bluntly, 'So you haven't been able to track Tamiz down.'

The inspector from Amtoli looked disgruntled. 'We can certainly catch him, but if bigwigs are going to shelter criminals . . .'

'What are you saying? You must do your work, who's going to stop you?' Kader protested and reassured the police officers too. 'I said as much to your SP shaheb's face the other day. How will innocent people live in peace while criminals are on the lose?'

The police had received a green signal about three weeks ago. Tahsen had been to Tamiz's house and examined it carefully, although in plain dress. He had told the inspector from Amtoli frankly that the criminal belonged to his own clan, and then Mondol was persecuting them; so it wasn't safe for him to raid Tamiz's house officially. The inspector from Amtoli was on his way to Nijgirirdanga now to search Tamiz's father-in-law's house. He wanted to consult the most important person in the area, which was why Tahsen had accompanied him to perform the introductions. Tahsen would have to return soon.

'Harmatullah is a long-standing sharecropper of yours,' said Tahsen. 'If you want they will arrest him, and if you don't, they can just go and conduct their search.'

'Harmatullah is a good man. A simple man, that is. He's in trouble for allowing his daughter to marry Tamiz. I had asked him not to, having a relationship with a fisherman inevitably . . .' Because he wanted to skirt this particular issue with Tahsen present, Mondol said cautiously, 'He's paying the price of having a convict as his son-in-law. I gave him a lot of land to sharecrop, but after he agreed to the wedding I've taken all of it back except a stretch around the ox pool. I'd considered taking it all away, but then I thought, he's an old man. Harmatullah will have his daughter get married to someone else if you arrest Tamiz.'

Tahsen, whose thoughts often included English words, felt encouraged. His determination to capture Tamiz had been increasing by the day. He was certain that Tamiz was the rogue who was instigating the people of Majhipara. And he was definitely in touch with Kulsum. She had a perfect figure, with a soft glow on her dark-skinned face, but she had spent her entire life with an imbecile crippled old man. Now she was sleeping with her dead husband's first wife's ugly hot-headed son. Tahsen had seen enough criminals and more, he had been thrashing thieves and robbers across several districts for over eight years now, having started in undivided Bengal in the British era. One look at Kulsum was all it took to know that there was nothing the bitch was not capable of with that tight body of hers. And even more dangerous than her body was her sniffing. Tahsen had been near her on two occasions, and he had felt himself trembling when she began to sniff—the whore had probably correctly identified Tahsen's brain, heart, and even intestines by now.

The problem was with his father. Kalam majhi did not lack common sense, but why was a man like him drawn to Kulsum? Tahsen simply couldn't convince him that Tamiz was using Kulsum to incite Majhipara. But why did his father refuse to acknowledge any flaw where Kulsum was concerned? Was it out of fear of a connection between Tamiz's father and the jinn or spirit of whatever it was of Katlahar Lake? Was it because Kulsum's grandfather Cherag Ali was the right-hand man of the jinn that Tahsen's father was afraid of annoying Kulsum?

Sharafat Mondol might be able to provide sane counsel. After all, land was his business, and he was as immovable as land. Such people did not have the restlessness of fish that fishermen did. A committed householder if there ever was one, with mature thinking.

'I don't know about Harmatullah's daughter,' said Sharafat, 'but I find it hard to believe that Harmatullah will allow Tamiz to stay in his house. Still, it's your job to check, so you should check carefully.'

'No, it's he who will check,' said Tahsen, pointing at the inspector from Amtoli. 'The area is not under my jurisdiction. I'm going back to the town now. Some of the tebhaga leaders have been captured, they're going to be produced in court today. Now this officer is new in this area, he doesn't even live hereabouts, he's from Pabna. Which means someone well known locally should be present during the search.'

When Sharafat Mondol looked stricken at the thought of being singled out as this well-known person, Tahsen rescued him. 'I've asked my father. He'll probably go to Harmatullah's house directly.'

Soon after Tahsen had left for the town in the jeep, the inspector from Amtoli left for Nijgirirdanga with two constables.

On the road to Nijgirirdanga, the fields of ripened aush and harvested jute, and even the trees were giving off moist waves of fire in the sultry heat of Bhadro. People were harvesting the paddy on some stretches, the harvested jute was being carried to the creek, and some were resting beneath mango trees. At the sight of the police all of them began to run with their sickles and trowels, some of them coming directly in the path of the policemen in their hurry to escape.

Harmatullah was seated beneath the jujube tree on the land he used to sharecrop. The harvest of jute had not been a good one because of the low rainfall. It could never have happened without Allah's intervention. And the storms—every shower of rain had been accompanied by storms during the three months of Joishtho, Asharh and Srabon. It was nearly the end of Bhadro now, but the rain had disappeared. It was so hot that the sorry sight of the field made Harmatullah's head reel. He couldn't harvest the jute for long without wanting to vomit. Karim the doctor from Chhaihata had paused for a minute while cycling past the other day to tell him to drink a mixture of lemon and sugar with water at least two times a day. Harmatullah was usually famished by lunchtime, but the leftover rice he ate was more water than rice, whose grains could practically be counted. He longed for a couple of platefuls of rice with spicy dried fish. But since neither the healthy mixture of lemon and sugar with water nor the unhealthy meal of rice with spicy dried fish was available, and, moreover, the harvest was poor, he was feeling quite miserable. Suddenly Nobiton came running up, trying to catch her breath as she spoke, 'Police, baapjaan. The police are raiding us.' He had been feeling miserable all this while, but now Harmatullah sprang up like a calf and looked southwards, towards the Mondols' house. Judging it the safest place, he began walking in that direction. 'Come home, baapjaan,' said Nobiton, 'the police are here.'

The inspector from Amtoli was seated on a bench outside the house. About to fan him with his sweat-soaked homespun towel, Harmatullah got a mouthful from the inspector instead. 'Never mind all that, bring your son-in-law out of the house.'

Harmatullah frowned on spotting Kalam majhi standing at a distance. But his fear of the policemen was reduced. Hoping to cash in on their relationship by marriage, he tried to cosy up to Kalam majhi, saying, 'Your daughter-in-law is well.' Paying no heed to the kinship acquired through Phuljaan's marriage, he said, 'Why shouldn't she be? Your son-in-law brings your daughter money, clothes and everything else, doesn't he? How does he do it?'

At a signal from the inspector, one of the constables went to the back of the house, accompanied by a union board guard. It was at Phuljaan's insistence that aush was being cultivated on the land here for the first time. The stalks were sweating in the heat, and the constable crunched through them in his boots even as blisters began to appear on his skin from the heat given out by the rice field.

Nobiton appeared unbidden and touched Kalam majhi's feet, saying, 'Please come inside.' Acceding to her request, Kalam glanced at the inspector, who also gestured to him to enter. A constable followed Kalam into the house.

There was nothing they could offer the policemen to eat. The constable searched for the criminal all over the house, while Nobiton and Phuljaan looked around for what they could welcome the policemen with. Crawling beneath the maacha in her father's room in the hope of finding some flattened or puffed rice in the utensils stored there, Phuljaan pulled out an earthen pot and screamed. A silky black snake had lifted its hood in her direction. Disturbed by the entry of strangers, the snake slithered away into the yard even without getting anything to eat. In the yard, Kalam majhi leapt in the air, and the constable said, 'That's a cobra.' The inspector stepped into the yard to find the snake gliding past the kitchen towards the land at the back of the house. Although he hadn't actually seen anything but its tail, he delivered his verdict on the strength of his position in the force, 'This snake has a mate. Do you have pet snakes?' He compensated for his fear of snakes by venting his rage on Harmatullah.

After this, leave alone search the house, no one ventured anywhere near the yard. The inspector sat outside on a bench beneath an ebony tree to complete his interrogation of the members of the family. Phuljaan's mother was unable to answer any of his questions. Instead, in trying to cover as much of her face as she could with her sari, she ended up with a large tear in it near her buttocks.

Kalam majhi joined the interrogation unbidden when it was
Phuljaan's turn. 'When does Tamiz come here to give you money?'
he asked. 'Which of the Majhipara people are present at the time?'

'Who's going to allow anyone from Majhipara into this house?'

Although he was burning with anger at this, Kalam majhi only
asked caustically, 'Who gets you your money and clothes, then?'

Phuljaan was about to snap back again, but Harmatullah
stopped her. 'Kader mian brought money twice, and an old shirt.
Sharafat Mondol is from our family too, when he saw my daughter
in trouble . . .'

'How long will it be before you die, you old bastard?' Kalam
majhi reminded Harmatullah of his advancing years. 'How can you
lie so brazenly? Aren't you afraid of the afterlife? How could Kader
mian have brought you money?'

Kalam majhi tried to establish a connection between the
Mondols and the absconding Tamiz for the inspector's benefit. This
fucking Mondol clan was trying to use Tamiz to foment trouble
in Majhipara. But the inspector showed no interest in the matter
of Kader's involvement. There would have been no question of his
being here without Kader's approval. He threatened Phuljaan with a
different strategy. 'Your house will be auctioned if Tamiz isn't found.
Do you know that?'

The cobra that had slithered away showed its fangs within
Phuljaan's goitre. 'You think this house belongs to him or his father?'

'You're right.' The inspector agreed but didn't change tack. 'It's
your father's house. But you and your sisters will inherit it, which
means you have a share, which means your husband has a share too.'

Harmatullah grew desperate to prevent his property from passing
into other hands. 'I'll be ruined for making the son of a fisherman my
son-in-law, inspector.'

Kalam majhi chafed in the presence of his son's junior colleague.
Phuljaan rescued him. 'What do you mean he has a share of the house?
I don't live on his money. Has he even checked on his daughter?
What sort of husband is he? I won't take anything from him.'

'Are you going to divorce him?'

Harmatullah answered the question. 'Mm-hmm. Whether you catch Tamiz or not, whether he rots in jail or lives on the streets, I'm determined to get my daughter divorced from him. I've spoken to Sharafat mian, he said the same thing.'

Such faith in Sharafat Mondol was not good news for Kalam. He looked away in annoyance. 'We won't find him here,' the inspector said, getting to his feet. 'Come, let's go to Tamiz's house. This is why Tahsen shaheb had asked me to go there first.'

Kalam majhi refused. 'It's no use going there. I should know, it's close to my house.' When the inspector still seemed inclined to pay a visit, Kalam said, 'Even if Tamiz were to come there it wouldn't be till late at night. If you do want to go there we must do it without warning late one night.'

Kalam's proposal was acceptable to the inspector in this tremendous heat. But he couldn't commit a date yet.

Phuljaan felt at times she never wanted to live on Tamiz's money. What use was it to care for a husband who was on the run month after month? She didn't need his support—if she could get a divorce today her father could arrange another marriage for her tomorrow. Harmatullah had said he would insist on a peasant's son this time.

It grew even more humid after the police left, the heat becoming unbearable. And then suddenly it clouded over and there was torrential rain. Not for very long though—it stopped as soon as evening fell. Scattered clouds remained in the sky. Picking her daughter up in her arms, Phuljaan walked through the mud to take a look at the land behind the house where the aush was being grown. The rain seemed to have enabled the grains to have recovered from a long illness. But could the devastation be reversed? Every stalk appeared exhausted and ailing, though there were signs of rejuvenation after the rain. Who knew, a bountiful harvest might still be possible. Harmatullah cursed Tamiz and his parents for the probable failure of the first aush crop on the land. It was Phuljaan who had insisted on aush, it was she who had first told Tamiz that the land was perfect for it.

Maybe the crop would have flourished had Tamiz been there. He might have been born to a family of fishermen, but his plough could tame the land. A long time ago, Tamiz himself didn't know how many years ago, it was apparently Tamiz's great-grandfather's great-grandfather, or perhaps *his* grandfather, who had cleared the jungles in Girirdanga to create farmland. Tamiz must be connected to Munshi in some way.

If you stood on tiptoes on the narrow ridge between plots behind the house, behind the land where the aush was being grown, you could see lights across the narrow stream of the Bangali river where the fig tree was supposed to have stood. There were no large trees, just rows of lights blinking on top of small bushes. People feared them—they were the lights Munshi had left behind—but they liked them too. Phuljaan never thought about them. Where was the time for idle pleasures? But standing here felt pleasant even in this heat. Was it because of a breeze from where the fig tree used to stand? But then the fig tree was gone. Like Phuljaan, her daughter also gazed in that direction. With clouds gathering in the sky again, the view soon disappeared in darkness. Phuljaan hurried home when the first drops began to fall, clasping her daughter close to her breast.

56

With no cloud cover, the Bhadro afternoon sun was sizzling, making the head reel. But that didn't matter, for a light breeze enveloped Kulsum wherever she went. Cool currents of air raised gentle waves around the pores on her skin. There was a familiar scent, but because she couldn't identify its source, she had to draw deep breaths all the time. A light aroma of tobacco mingled with the smoke from a stronger one, but all of these rode in on a breeze from the lake bearing the smell of fish.

Kulsum was startled on hearing footsteps behind her as she put the utensils in her hand down on the floor and went to open the door. Her surprise held the hope of discovering the source of the scents spiralling around her body. But there was nobody outside when she peeped out. So she went back in and locked the door.

Kalam majhi was also startled to see a man standing outside Kulsum's door. His surprise held a different kind of hope, an astonishment rather than hope, and, most of all, pleasure. So Tahsen and the inspector from Amtoli had been right—that bastard Tamiz did visit Kulsum regularly. Since Kalam majhi had arranged for her to stay at his home at night, Tamiz had obviously decided to visit her in the afternoon instead. This meant a man accused of murder, a criminal on the run, could slip in easily past Kalam majhi's house in broad daylight. What an audacious swine. Kalam majhi would regain his pre eminent position in the village if he could only catch Tamiz red-handed. It would also mean winning Tahsen's heart back. His son hardly came home these days—even today he had driven up to Golabari in his jeep before going back to the town. The people hereabouts would have been quiet for a few days at least if he had visited Girirdanga in the jeep. But Kalam majhi found it difficult to even talk to Tahsen, who had suddenly become the dutiful son of his stepmother. And to think it was to save him from the same stepmother that he had been forced to leave the boy at a distant relative's house! Would Tahsen have been a police officer today had Kalam majhi not taken this step? But considering the insinuations he had made at his stepmother's behest about his father's recent habit of dyeing his hair and beard black prompted Kalam at times to bequeath his entire property to his daughter from his second marriage. The girls were devoted to their mother too. And that bastard nephew's wife acted as his wife's spy. Every time he went to the veranda outside Budha's room at night he found her standing close to Kulsum's bed. Kalam majhi had spent an entire rupee on a bottle of tonic in town to revive his libido. It had gone missing the night before. All this was his wife and Budha's wife's doing. But if he had his son on his side, fixing them would be child's play. Now Allah had given him the opportunity. If only he could capture Tamiz, everyone from the inspector from Amtoli to his boss Tahsen from the town would be beholden to Kalam majhi.

This seasoned fucking criminal, this swine of a convict, was here now with a false head of wavy hair and dressed in a dirty green lungi and vest. Because Keramat was standing on the steps, he looked taller than he was, and even someone as canny as Kalam majhi couldn't be blamed for confusing him for a disguised Tamiz in the blinding sunlight. But Kalam majhi's new pumps did not care for his need not to be observed. The man ran off in a flash. Kalam majhi realized he must have entered Kulsum's room from the back. Or had he escaped past the broken-down jackfruit tree towards the northern head of the lake where the fig tree used to stand?

Kulsum's voice filtered out through the door, 'How long have you been here? There's so much work in the other house, you know, I hardly get the time to come.' She couldn't be talking this way with anyone else but Tamiz. Kalam majhi trembled so much as he eavesdropped that he himself couldn't tell whether it was out of joy or anger or excitement.

Kulsum had increased the ferocity of her sniffing on entering the room, intent on locating the source of the smell. She located Tamiz's father with just a few sniffs. He was standing close to his maacha, his hair clotted with sand. Leaving him there, she fetched some ashes from the oven in the kitchen and the kitchen blade and the earthen pot from Tamiz's room whose roof had caved in before returning to her room. She sat down with the blade with her back to the door, hoping that Tamiz's father would sit down on his maacha, and also worried that he might slip out. As soon as she lifted the lid on the pot the catfish inside began to play in the water, either out of fear or out of happiness. Their frolic sent up a fish-flavoured aroma from the pot, while drops of water splashed on Kulsum's face. Pleasure was written all over her face.

Kalam majhi could neither see her slicing the fish nor observe the fish-flavoured water splashing on her oval face, but he could hear every word she was saying. Kulsum was responding to someone, 'It shouldn't be time for husking yet, but they have to send rice to their son who lives in the town. And Tahsen's mother tells me, don't sleep here. Why shouldn't I sleep there, tell me? Is the old coot going to bite my head off?'

Kulsum could be heard clearly, but why couldn't Kalam majhi hear what Tamiz was saying?

But what Kulsum said next confused Kalam majhi completely. 'Where are you saying Tamiz has gone? Tell me clearly. You, still speak like a fool, even after dying. What's he gone to Khiyar for? You son is mad, I tell you. Don't you remember how he kept running off to Khiyar when he was much younger? How can you not remember?'

Kalam majhi's heart began to thump. Was it not Tamiz in there with Kulsum? Who was it then—it wasn't Keramat, was it? That bastard used to compose songs for the peasants over in Khiyar, was he now bringing news of Tamiz to Kulsum? But considering Keramat sang at the top of his voice in public, why wasn't he audible now?

Kulsum changed the subject. 'Even Budha was saying the other day Tamiz has gone off somewhere to join forces with cultivators. All he wants is trouble, your son cannot sleep at night without getting into trouble during the day. He has a wife, he has a daughter, doesn't he have to give them food and a home? I might be a fakir's daughter, no one cares for me, but what about his wife? That bitch with the goitre will definitely marry someone else if he doesn't look after her.'

Now Kalam majhi's ears began to tingle. Who was the man inside the room? He considered going back, but he gathered his courage instantly. He simply had to enter the room if he wanted to find out more about Tamiz. Whoever it was, the man knew what Tamiz was up to. But Kulsum's soft voice was proving to be a deterrent. Her lilting tones were creeping in through his ears and gently massaging his entire body, making it difficult to peel his ear away from the door.

But it was his duty to locate the criminal—he couldn't allow himself to stick to Kulsum's words like an ant caught in a bowl of sugar.

Taking off his new pumps carefully, Kalam tiptoed around Tamiz's dilapidated room to stand in the sun-bathed yard. There he began to plot how to steal into the room, wrestle the trespasser to the ground and grab him. He had no weapons, and his shoes were in a corner of the yard. All he had was his arms.

It was dim and dark inside the room, with sunbeams from the yard lighting up Kulsum's face. She was slicing the fish as she spoke, pausing occasionally to raise her face to listen to the response of the other person in the room before continuing to speak. The other person said something, at which Kulsum concentrated again on slicing the fish. 'Stay for a while,' she said, 'have some fish and rice. Keramat mian gave me some fish.' Her companion in the room said something, and she said regretfully, 'Oh, can't you eat fish any more? It's so sad to live at the head of Katlahar Lake and not be able to eat fish. Don't worry, just have some. The fig tree has been cut down, how will Munshi know what you're eating? No one will see you.'

Kalam majhi trembled again. Who was it? To shed his fear he thought of the inspector from Amtoli and of Tehsan, and that in Nobabganj or Nachol or Thakurgaon or some such place the tebhaga protesters had scattered everywhere when beaten up by the police. Some of them may well have been hiding in the forest near the northern head of the lake. But that was where Mondol's brick kiln was, and there were hardly any trees to offer shelter. Were they pretending to be workers at the brick kiln then? Kalam majhi would capture the criminal and frogmarch him at once to Sharafat Mondol's house. Tahsen was right, to be considered important in the village it was necessary to be on good terms with Mondol instead of feuding with him. Kalam became impatient to identify the criminal clearly. But when he heard Kulsum say, 'So you can't eat rice or fish or meat or anything now that you're dead because that will mean not being released from your grave. But why is it wrong for a dead man to eat fish?' Now Kalam majhi was so frightened that to prevent himself from collapsing on the ground with fear he had no choice but to borrow his son's work language and shout, 'Hands up!' Befuddled by this sudden scream, Kulsum looked up to discover Kalam majhi standing there. She fell silent, her ash-smeared hands rising from the blade. She didn't even remember to cover her head respectfully in the presence of a man so much older than she was. And because she did not know the meaning of the English words uttered by Kalam majhi, she could not comply with the instruction either.

After the last thing that Kulsum had said, Kalam majhi was anxious to meet a living person now, which was probably why he bellowed again, 'Where is he? Whom were you talking to? Where is he?'

He glanced around the room. The way things were arranged in the maacha made it impossible for someone to be hiding there. Enriched by this realization, Kalam ran his hands nervously across the platform before sitting down on the floor suddenly on the fear that

someone might actually be up there, and, maintaining a safe distance
from Kulsum's sniffing, began rummaging beneath the maacha. The
place was stacked with things. From sacks of cotton wool and a plate
stolen from Kalam majhi's house to a stool and lots more. Even when
he crawled in, Kalam couldn't see anyone there. Retreating, he edged
closer to Kulsum, dragging his buttocks across the floor, and asked
gently, 'Where did he go? Whom were you talking to?'

Kalam majhi's swiftness and his conversation dispelled Kulsum's
surprise—she could see him clearly now. The pale-red colour in her
large eyes made Kalam majhi's voice turn even softer. 'Why are you
worried? You aren't a criminal. Just tell me whom you were talking
to. Which way did he escape?'

The blood from the catfish she had been slicing had dried into
a sticky stain on Kulsum's hands. In response to Kalam majhi's
repeated question, 'who was in here with you?' she indicated with her
eyes at the space next to the maacha and mumbled, 'Tamiz's father.'

Kalam majhi trembled again, either at the signal in Kulsum's eyes
or at the dry rustle in her voice or at both. There was no resemblance
with the gentle touch of Kulsum's soft voice that he had felt earlier.
Was Tamiz's father actually here? What a traitor he was. Here was
Kalam majhi visiting his resting place in the quicksand every Friday
and getting moulobi Kuddus to read the entire Quran, but still he
couldn't be at peace, still he couldn't give up his attraction for the
world. When Kalam majhi's attempts to feast his eyes on Kulsum's
jutting breasts and oval face failed, he said, 'Not so easy. Munshi
himself has run away with his fig tree, how will Tamiz's father travel
all this way?' But, feeling a stab of fear because of his own reckless
display of humour, he tried to dispel it by continuing, 'And what about
that infidel Boikuntho, has that bastard been clinging to Tamiz's
father's arse too?' After this Kalam majhi made the atmosphere in
the room heavier by talking of the restless spirit of a Muslim not
buried according to the rites of Islam, and of the unsatisfied soul of
a murdered Hindu. Now he was trapped in his own intrigue—did
this mean he was wedged between a spirit and a soul? Were the scum

sticking together even after death? And as for Kulsum, was she their slave or their queen—or had they appointed her their successor in this world? Still, slave, queen or successor, Kulsum was clearly the only human here among ghosts. No one else could protect him now. Kalam didn't realize when he had dragged his buttocks farther across the floor to sidle up to Kulsum and her kitchen blade.

Suddenly Kulsum said, 'Whom are you looking for here? Tamiz left the village last year, do you suppose he's still in this area?'

A goat bleated outside suddenly, while two people could be heard talking as they passed on the other side of the pond. Kalam gained strength from the sounds made by living creatures, and he longed to escape on the raft provided by their voices. Kulsum was probably afraid of him now, for she was repeatedly casting distraught glances at the maacha. Once the sounds of the goat and the humans had faded in the distance, the silence in the room deepened a hundred times, much like the darkness after a flash of lightning, while Kalam's fear deepened even more, perhaps a hundred thousand times. With invocations to Allah and to his mother, he tried to embrace Kulsum.

Kulsum fell on the floor at the impact, or, more accurately, under his weight, her hand striking the kitchen blade and pushing it away. Smeared with the blood and guts of the catfish, the blade slid all the way to the second of the two poles holding up the maacha. As she fell on her back, Kulsum's head collided with the closed door. Looking at the maacha, she complained, 'Can't you see what this man is doing with me? What are you staring at?' Now Kalam had no choice but to try to wrap his arms around her. He was feeling a little less frightened now, though only a little. Now if only he could get Kulsum in his arms properly, he would be released from the threat from people both living and dead. Kulsum began to hammer blows on his chest and stomach and even his chin. But how much strength could she summon to those blows anyway? In desperation Kalam pinned her arms down and then knelt on the floor with his legs on either side of her body. Once again Kulsum complained, her eyes fixed on a spot in front of her, 'Are you just going to stand and stare? Don't you see what he's doing to me? Can't you stop him?'

Without looking behind him, Kalam majhi said dispassionately, 'I'll organize prayers for you, Tamiz's father, I'll have a feast for a thousand villagers. Don't visit living people again. Everyone in the village will beg Allah for absolution for your spirit . . .' The plea did not appear to work on Tamiz's father. On the contrary, kicks began to rain on Kalam majhi's back—who but a dead man could kick this way without conviction?

As for Keramat Ali with his wavy hair, dirty vest, and green lungi, he had recognized Kalam majhi at once and bolted to a spot south of the broken-down jackfruit tree behind Tamiz's father's room, where Sharafat Mondol's sharecropper Shamsher had planted chillies. Shamsher wasn't there, and Keramat Ali stopped to catch his breath. Then, going closer to the tree, he tried to eavesdrop on the conversation between Kalam majhi and Kulsum, who seemed to be having a scuffle. What should Keramat do now? Kalam majhi was his benefactor, who had given him a place to live in. It was Kalam who had hinted that Keramat should marry Kulsum, although he didn't bring the idea up any more—on the contrary, he frowned when he found them talking to each other. Still, he had no choice but to defer to Kalam Majhi, for Keramat's livelihood depended on him. Without these assured earnings he would never be able to compose a song. Would Keramat have ever sung for a huge crowd from the veranda of Mukunda Saha's shop in the Golabari market had it not been for Kalam majhi's urging? Trying to save Kulsum from his grasp now meant betraying him. What should Keramat do? He squatted beneath the jackfruit tree to piss. But with no pressure on his bladder, he didn't produce much urine. Now he had nothing more to do. The foam and bubbles in his urine were soaked up by the earth, while he felt hot gusts of Kulsum's deep breaths on his neck, making his wavy hair fly. Kulsum might not be able to see Keramat, but she could definitely sniff out his presence beneath the jackfruit tree. It was essential that he enter the room right now. Kulsum would never be able to turn him down if he could come to her aid when she was in trouble.

Keramat took the identical route into Kulsum's room as Kalam majhi from behind the dilapidated house. As soon as he entered, his eyes settled on a perspiration-soaked white kurta on a man's back. Kalam majhi was hunched over Kulsum's breast. Was he trying to kiss her? Kulsum kept kicking him continuously, but that couldn't possibly stop the bastard. In fact, he was probably enjoying it.

'Why are you just standing there?' said Kulsum with all the strength in her voice. But her mouth was covered by Kalam majhi's heavy hand. Keramat realized that it was his help she was seeking to free herself from Kalam majhi, who was saying,

'Forgive me, Kulsum. You're my aunt, I'll give you this house, I'll give you more property if you want, just tell Tamiz's father to go away, I'll have prayers said for him, tell him to go.'

Because his fear of the goings-on around the fig tree had drained him of much of his strength, or maybe to give Kulsum the chance to tell Tamiz's father to leave at once, the hand he had clamped on Kulsum's mouth became a little slack. This gave the opportunity for Kulsum to speak, accompanied by a deep sigh, 'He's going to kill me. Why are you standing there like a fool? You, you . . .'

It was true Kulsum couldn't see him, but she was certainly relying on him. Her 'you, you' armed Keramat with so much joy, suffering, remorse, glory, excitement, incitement, and, you never knew, even inspiration that Keramat shoved Kalam majhi from the back with all his strength before trying to grab Kalam's neck with his hands. Realizing that Tamiz's father had finally responded to Kulsum's appeal, Kalam pressed down on her face with the upper half of his body, suffocating her in a way that, leave alone asking anyone for help, she couldn't even breathe. Keramat wanted to hear Kulsum call out to him again, at least one more time. So he crouched over Kalam majhi's body, reached out over his shoulder and drew the blood-smeared kitchen blade from where it was lying on the floor near the second post supporting the maacha. The pot filled with water, in which live catfish were cavorting, was knocked to the floor on impact with the blade, the water spilling and soaking Kulsum's hair. Three catfish wriggled on the floor, and then, mistaking the water flowing over Kulsum's hair for Katlahar Lake because of the smell of fish, they foolishly crept into those strands of hair. When Kalam majhi noticed this he had another round of palpitations: were these catfish, or was it the cobra he had seen in Harmatullah's house, or perhaps its mate? Like all creatures on both sides of Katlahar Lake, this one too was under Munshi's control. Had he dispatched it here to help Tamiz's father? The fucking snake must have swum the length of Katlahar Lake underwater and arrived here to bite Kalam majhi. Along with Tamiz's father, Boikuntho, Munshi from the past, and Cherag Ali, now there was the cobra from Harmatullah's house to torment him too. Out of fear of all the dead creatures of Katlahar and their colleague, this snake, Kalam majhi pressed down harder on Kulsum's face. There was no pulse of life there. Had the woman died? If that were so, how would he keep this roomful of the dead at bay? And who had picked up the kitchen blade? Tamiz's father was armed now, which meant it was all over for Kalam majhi.

But it took him only a moment to regain his intelligence and remember that anything made of iron was out of reach of the dead of Katlahar. Then it must be Tamiz who was wielding the blade now, and if not Tamiz, one of the united peasants. An alert Kalam swung his head sharply, and the blade missed it and slashed his right elbow. Before the next swipe of the blade Kalam majhi jerked away to the left, and the blade landed in the centre of Kulsum's left breast. Both the breast and Kalam majhi's elbow began to bleed profusely. Their blood flowed along the floor, and the dried catfish bloodstains on the floor came to life in a bright shade of red with the addition of fresh blood from the two humans.

There had been a rattle in Kulsum's throat from the time Kalam majhi had pressed down on her face. Now she groaned loudly after the blow from the kitchen blade on her left breast.

Kalam majhi had jumped to his feet by now. The wound on his elbow was a severe one. Clutching it with his other hand, he glanced at Keramat but could not recognize him at first. Keramat was staring at Kulsum, the kitchen blade still dangling from his hand. For a few moments he detected a pinkish glow on Kulsum's face—he tried to recollect which of the breasts of the woman he had seen at the refugee camp had been severed. Had Keramat now severed the other breast?

Even as he was shocked to identify Keramat, Kalam majhi could not say a thing because of the combined impact of pain, sorrow and fear. Then he got hold of himself and, leaping over Kulsum's body, unlocked the door and ran out, shouting, 'Murder, murder!' But his voice was faint.

Soon the sky turned grey and it began to rain torrentially. Tahsen brought a carriage from the town when he heard, and whisked his father away for treatment—he had no faith in either Horen or Karim as doctors. He instructed Budha sternly that the corpse should remain untouched on the spot till the police came from Amtoli. Keramat was trussed up and deposited in Kalam majhi's front room.

After a long time, all the people of Majhipara swarmed to Kalam majhi's house. Just imagine, a man like Tamiz's father, who had disdained home and family to accompany Cherag Ali everywhere all his life, who had thrust himself into the quicksand because of his agony at not being able to spot the throne of Munshi, the lord of the entire area—Kalam Majhi had been injured while trying to save the life of this very man's wife, the actual granddaughter of Cherag Ali, Munshi's main representative, who had sung Munshi's scripture though his verses all his life. People broke down in sorrow at Kalam majhi's suffering. Even the relatives of those who were still in jail for stealing fish from the lake wept at Allah's court under moulobi Kuddus's leadership to plead for Kalam majhi's injured right elbow to heal properly. People from Chashapara had arrived, as had Keshto Pal, along with his brother and nephew, from Palpara. Sharafat Mondol and Kader paid a visit too before returning home and sending lanterns.

It was eleven the next morning by the time the police from Amtoli
turned up. Tamiz's father's room and its occupant were drenched in
the rain. A dry quilt was discovered beneath an aluminium pan on
the maacha. Several moons, with three stars per moon, occupied the
middle of the quilt, whose borders were stitched with red, blue, green
and yellow thread. Kulsum's corpse was shrouded in it and hoisted
on a bamboo frame, which two strong young men from Majhipara
lifted on their shoulders. Policemen walked ahead of and behind the
corpse, with the last one holding a rope tied around Keramat's waist.
He had handcuffs on, too.

Keramat was tottering after being slapped and kicked by the
young and old of Majhipara alike all night. Beneath his puffed eyelids
he occasionally caught sight of Kulsum's feet, which had slipped out
from beneath the quilt. The soles of her feet were pale and a little
swollen after being drenched all night in the rain. Despite their best
efforts the moon and stars on the quilt could not light them up.
Keramat's head was jammed, with not a verse anywhere near it. But
who could tell for sure that he wouldn't add some lines to that last
verse of his while serving time in jail—or waiting to be hanged—
along with many others thieves and robbers and peasants from the
north who had been imprisoned for being united? Perhaps the verses
would go this way when recited from the beginning:

> If ever I've seen beauty in my life
> It's a fiery face I saw in a dream.
> Munshi's throne is not beneath the tree
> The fisherman weeps, beauty flows away.

Maybe one of the thieves or robbers or united peasants in jail would
ask, 'Where did you hear these verses?'

'They're my own composition. I write my own verses.' Would
Keramat Ali be able to give this answer? Would the area where the
fig tree had once stood, from where the tree was gone now, not strike
fear in his breast?

But as she went home past the northern head of Katlahar Lake, now bereft of the fig tree, Phuljaan felt no fear in her breast, for her daughter's face was buried in it.

Harmatullah had refused vehemently when Phuljaan had wanted to go to Majhipara in the morning to view her stepmother-in-law's body: getting involved in murder cases would lead to nothing but trouble. He grew bolder later on hearing that Sharafat Mondol and Kader were in charge of the police, and, although it was with trepidation, he did take his daughter to Kalam majhi's house where people were thronging everywhere. The corpse had been shrouded in the quilt and placed on the bamboo frame by then. Harmatullah lent a hand with carrying rice and chicken curry for everyone from Sharafat's house and with other tasks. Once the corpse had left he even went to the Mondols' house and had a meal.

Phuljaan followed the body and Keramat from a distance. Then she veered off towards the brick kiln on her left and turned homewards. The bamboo bridge over the narrow stream of the Bangali river had been destroyed in the storm last night. There was much more water in the river now. Phuljaan had to lift her sari almost to her thighs to cross it. The narrow stream of the Bangali river reflected distorted images of Keramat's battered face. But to stop her daughter from crying because she couldn't get her milk, and out of eagerness to inspect the stalks of aush behind the house after last night's rain, Phuljaan had no choice but to lengthen her strides.

57

The train to Shantahar was speeding along. Everyone in Khiyar was in the fields, if for nothing else but the heightened pleasure of ploughing the rain-soaked land beneath an overcast sky. Being a local train, it stopped at every station, sometimes pausing for a rest even when no station was to be found. People got on and got off. Tamiz stared at the new passengers' hands, feeling jealous whenever he saw mud stains.

Shantahar was brimming with people. Four of the five people he asked said 'don't know', running all the while, when he asked which train would go to Hili and which to Joipur. The fifth one proceeded on his way without answering. When he saw that the train on Platform No. 2, on the other side of the overbridge, was the most crowded, Tamiz climbed into one of its carriages, feeling pleased to have found himself a place to sit on the floor. But the train just wouldn't leave. What was wrong? Peasants had fought with the police a few stations down the line and piled trees on the tracks. More police had been dispatched: the signal would turn green after they had cleared the people and the trees and sent word. Only then would the train leave. Still, Tamiz didn't feel impatient, though his hunger did remind him of the sack he had left behind in Dhaka, with five rupees in it. But he did have nine four-anna coins to see him through till he found a job—he would just have to eat sparingly. There were plenty of other people with spades, sickles and baskets in the train, so he could just get off the train with one such group.

Once the train started moving, well into the evening, it gathered speed quickly. The wide carriages on the broad gauge line swayed in time. The passengers in the bunks were fast asleep, others were sleeping in their seats. Several people were sleeping peacefully, curled up on the floor. Some dozed. Others yawned. Their observations on last night's storm, the prices of everyday things, the sharecroppers' excesses, the trigger-happy behaviour of the police, the corruption of the ministers, India's nefarious behaviour, and so on emerged as distorted sounds through frequent yawns. The train galloped, the train galloped on.

Tamiz woke up from his shallow dreams whenever the train stopped for a minute or less at a station. From the conversations between people with spades and sickles he learnt that wages were higher at Hili, rising as high as twelve or even fourteen annas without food. This was because the risks were higher. Some believed it was better to work as daily labourers for jotedars, while others preferred to join the sharecroppers, so that they could stick rods up the jotedars' arses. Why fear the police so much? The cowards ran away with their guns whenever they saw large crowds. These people couldn't speak softly despite their yawns, they grew louder at the slightest of provocations. But some of them began to doze, and a few even fell asleep. Tamiz felt hungry and, awakened from his dreams, listened to everyone intently. Why would the jotedars allow the tebhaga system to be established unless they had rods shoved up their arses? If he couldn't survive the onslaught of the police he would just move on somewhere else. Tillers were needed everywhere.

It wouldn't need much effort to get land to sharecrop on hereabouts. The jotedars didn't trust people from their own villages. Instead, they turned the land over to peasants who had come here from the east and the south, confident they would face no trouble from the immigrants. As a sharecropper it wouldn't take Tamiz long to turn his fortunes around. Once the tebhaga system was instituted, the money he would get from selling his share of the crops, added to what he had already deposited with Kader, would be enough for him to release his house and land. And then many of the blacksmiths of Kamarpara were on the verge of leaving, which meant he could get some land cheaply there. And after that . . . his calculations began to go awry under the advent of sleep and the swaying of the train. Despite the beating they had been getting from the police, the cultivators over at Thakurgaon or Natore or Nachol or was it Hili had not yet broken ranks. Whether the tebhaga system materialized anywhere else or not, it was bound to be established in this area. If he could get some land to sharecrop on here, how long would it take him to buy some cattle? Now Tamiz shifted to the land behind his own house instead of the one behind Harmatullah's. He could grow vegetables on it, potatoes, eggplant. He could build a bamboo platform above the eggplants and grow gourd, snow peas, cucumbers. Phuljaan could be put to work there. And since his daughter grew older with the swaying of the train, she would be there too, playing and then sitting down on the ground beside her mother. Tamiz would not be angry with her even if she uprooted a few eggplants with her little hands while trying to pull out weeds. She was Phuljaan's daughter after all, look, look all of you, how my daughter weeds the field already, though her head doesn't even reach up to my knees yet. Kulsum might be upset, though. As her grandmother she was entitled to speak her mind. How can the daughter of a fisherman grow up without learning about fishing? She spends all her time in the fields. But then Tamiz could speak his mind too. His lips parted a little under the swaying of the train as it sliced through the darkness. It could be passed off as a smile. Maintaining the smile, he said, 'But then you're a fisherman's wife too. Baghar majhi was your husband's grandfather. What do you know of fishing?' The smile disappeared as he slept, or perhaps snoozed. Without moving his lips Tamiz complained, 'All you've ever cared about is your own grandfather.' And at once a new sound emerged through the chugging of the train. Its source? Kulsum, of course. She was chanting verses with Tamiz's daughter in her lap, words that were difficult to understand.

The rhythms of the verses drew Tamiz's father into the train. But no, it wasn't him, it was Kulsum's oval face that the sand was dripping from. Was she going to grow a beard too? Why was Kulsum nodding off this way? Had Tamiz's father wedged all his sleep and scattered dreams into his long-haired second wife's head? And was Kulsum now passing them on through her verses to Tamiz's little baby? No, this wasn't right. But she was going full-steam, look, Boikuntho was here as well, nodding in time to Tamiz's father's sleepy drawl and Cherag Ali's verses emerging through Kulsum's voice. But Kulsum's chanting was incomprehensible. 'What is this rubbish you're listening to, Boikuntho-da?'

Still nodding off, Boikuntho answered, 'Ask your father.' But where was he? When Tamiz looked around in search of his father, Boikuntho pointed at Kulsum with his eyes. Had his father entered Kulsum's body then? There was no option to searching Kulsum's body if he wanted to find his father, no other way, no other means. Which was why one night . . . when was it? The day his father had died, or perhaps later, Tamiz was lying down in his father's maacha like a grief-stricken bundle of salt. Then, just that one time, his father had come to him. Through Kulsum's arms, using her high breasts, leaning on her thighs, supporting himself on her hips, Tamiz's father had drawn his son to his dark-skinned body. When had it happened? How about telling Boikuntho about this trick his father had played? Why did his father never come to him? How fair was it to have to go through Kulsum to reach his father? He could complain to Boikuntho that his father visited Kulsum regularly after his death and whispered with her, but he never bothered to look in on his son.

'Is there no other way to reach bajaan except through the fakir's daughter, Boikuntho-da?' But before he could get an answer, the chugging of the train coalesced in his head and exploded like a thunderclap. Was the shaggy head of the banyan tree in Poradaho on fire? There were nothing but ashes at Bhabani Pathak's shrine. Had Boikuntho been sitting there? Such a bull-headed man, never bothered to be careful.

No sooner did this thought come to Tamiz than Boikuntho said, 'What do I have to be careful for? Who was it who shoved a rod up the Company's arse here in Girirdanga and Nijgirirdanga and Golabari? Do you know who it was? My grandfather's grandfather's father, or perhaps *his* father came here with Bhabani Pathak . . .' Boikuntho slumped against Tamiz's chest before he could finish. His body was burnt to a crisp, but still he had managed to emerge from the pile of ash. Tamiz's chest ached from the weight of Boikuntho's verse-stuffed head. When he awoke, Tamiz removed his neighbour's heavy, sore-ridden foot from his chest. It was almost dawn. The train stopped at Hili station.

Most of the passengers got off. Seeing the man with the sores on his feet collecting his sickle, spade and basket from beneath the bench, Tamiz said, 'Going for work? Is there work to be had here?'

The man hesitated at the sight of Tamiz's spick-and-span long shirt and lungi. 'Let's see.'

But his companion felt bold enough to ask, 'Are you looking for work?'

'Hmm,' said Tamiz, but their doubts weren't dispelled because of the way he looked. They got off the train without another word, but Tamiz followed them out.

The station was crowded, with another train having entered. There were many men in dhutis and women with vermilion in their hair, all of them walking along the railway lines towards the station building, crossing over the tin roof to the other side where rickshaws, horse-drawn carriages and bullock carts were passing. Joining them, Tamiz jumped in surprise—the manager! The manager was here too. If he saw Tamiz he was certain to hand him over to the police. Stopping to let the manager walk on, Tamiz heard the little boy holding his hand ask, 'Where is it, baba, where's India?'

'There, on the other side of the station, where those rickshaws and carriages are standing.' Tamiz realized his mistake when the man spoke, no, it wasn't the manager, it was just that he looked like the manager from the back. Once he was sure, Tamiz had the wind in his sails once again.

The boy holding the man's hand kept whining, 'Where's India, baba, where is it?'

The man's wife, walking on his left, 'There it is, see?' The boy did not believe her tearful statement.

'Where? It looks the same.' Reposing more faith in his father than in his mother, he asked again, 'Where's India, baba?'

Paying no attention, the man asked his wife, 'You've divided those things between the different bags, right? We have to pass through villages where farmers are creating trouble.' So the manager could not be too happy in India. Suddenly feeling an urge to examine the face of the worried man who looked like the manager, Tamiz lengthened his stride for a closer look.

'Here the police have more or less settled them,' a man told his companion. 'Panchbibi and Joipur are clean. Verbal warnings don't work, it needs police batons.' The companion seemed better informed on India.

He said, 'The police are taking action over on our side too. But the leaders have all crossed over, so it's taking a bit of time.'

While the conversation about the enterprise of the police continued, a group of policemen swaggered towards a train with some fifteen or twenty people in tow, all of them trussed up with ropes. In an instant the platform and the railway lines were overrun by policemen. People with sickles, spades and baskets began to run in every direction, dashing against upper-class men and even the women with them.

Tamiz had no idea which way the man with the sores on his feet and his companions had escaped. With the police having arrested so many already, it wasn't safe to go looking for them. But although the policemen went past him, they did not give him a second glance. It was possible that even though his clothes had become creased during the night, Ismail Husain's old shirt still carried the mark of a gentleman. This conclusion about his shirt kept Tamiz from running away, for that would have meant earning the suspicion of the police.

Tamiz found the crowd thinner behind a goods train beyond the platform. Several spades, sickles and baskets lay beneath one of the wagons, and some weeders as well. Selecting a sharp sickle and a strong spade with his eyes, Tamiz stood quietly. 'Those fucking policemen are beating people up here as revenge for what they cannot do over in Thakurgaon,' someone said.

Tamiz asked a blue-uniformed railway porter, 'When will the train for Thakurgaon arrive?'

'Seven Up will be here at a quarter past four,' the porter answered in Hindi. 'It will go up to Dinajpur. You might get a train for Thakurgaon there.'

About three hours later a passenger train arrived, and Tamiz boarded it after asking someone on the platform. He had to be careful now that he had a sickle and a spade. He should have taken a weeder too.

The train was moving. The porter had mentioned the name of the train to Thakurgaon, but Tamiz could not remember it. He had to go, no matter where the train was bound for. With the police having arrived in every village in Hili, he couldn't stay here. Perhaps this train would take him to Natore if not to Thakurgaon. If he couldn't get work in Natore he would take the train to Nobabganj, or he would go to Nachol. If the tebhaga system was established there he would surely find some land to sharecrop on. With his share of the harvest he would release his own house and land. Vegetables could be grown on the plot behind the house. Phuljaan would work on it, Kulsum wouldn't be able to do it. She would sing verses to Tamiz's daughter, who would eat eggplants and play at weeding as she listened. He would take the land from Harmatullah and grow aush on it. His harvest of aush on this two-crop plot would be far richer than the amon. The train was moving.

58

He might be a fisherman, but Tamiz had grasped the nature of the land behind Harmatullah's house correctly. The first aush crop may have failed, but on Phuljaan's insistence they sowed aush again next year. And what a harvest, oh Allah, amon could never be so lush. But Harmatullah was forced to sell half of this land to get his favourite daughter Nobiton married. The old coot blamed it all on Phuljaan. Since she had married a son of a fisherman, no one from a decent family would agree to marry her sister. Still, because it was Harmatullah's brother-in-law, he allowed his son to marry his niece. He had set just the one condition: Harmatullah should do up the groom's stationery store at the Sonamukhi market. Being a good man, he had allowed the wedding to take place without taking anything more than the money that had come from selling the land, but now he was putting pressure on Harmatullah for the rest of the cash.

Maybe Harmatullah would be able to pay some of the money from the amon he was sharecropping. These days he wilted even under the autumn sun. He felt thirsty all the time, but drinking pots of water only made him piss over and over again. So he stayed on the field after sunset as long as his strength permitted. Phuljaan hovered nearby, putting Harmatullah on the defensive every time he paused for breath while weeding. He might be her father, but she unleashed her sharp tongue whenever she saw him rest. 'You run him down for being a fisherman, but he didn't stop work for a moment. His hands flew faster than the wind.'

'You married outside the clan, and what has your man given you all these years? Not a word from him, not an anna either.' Harmatullah's remorse at his wrong decision made the paddy stalks nearby flutter, which restored his energy, so that he could start weeding another 3 yards of the field.

It wasn't exactly the other day that Tamiz had disappeared. Phuljaan had heard a rumour from Keshto Pal, and had been haranguing her father to find out about Tamiz from the Mondols. Harmatullah may have grown old, but he wasn't mad—he wasn't going to risk annoying Sharafat Mondol by asking about Tamiz. He was certainly not willing to lose the little land that Mondol had allowed him to sharecrop on—he had a family to feed, after all, and a second daughter to take care of. Phuljaan didn't care for her aged father's health, or for his food and rest. If anyone in this family thought about him, it was Nobiton. She'd got married in Joishtho, six months had passed, he hadn't been able to bring her home even once. Harmatullah had sold 2 acres of his own land so that his daughter could marry his brother-in-law's son and live happily. His brother-in-law was always anxious about his own sister and her husband and their children. He even used to send his bullock cart to fetch Harmatullah's wife and children for the Poradaho fair. But now that he had become Nobiton's father-in-law, he had changed colour completely. He took all the money from the sale of the land, but said it wasn't enough to give his son's shop at Sonamukhi market a proper facelift. If Harmatullah was short of cash, why didn't he just sell his land? The land would only go to the fisherman anyway, since he had no son of his own. Nobiton's husband would neither visit his in-laws, nor allow his wife to go home, until his shop had been done up the way he wanted it.

Harmatullah was quite pleased to have a shopkeeper as his son-in-law. Nobiton did not care for peasants or daily labourers. She was devoted to needlework—no one would imagine a cultivator's daughter could be so silken with her hands. But who knew if she got a chance to take up needle and thread in her in-laws' house? Such a tender-hearted girl, she hadn't turned into a man like Phuljaan from wandering around the fields. It was best for a woman to remain a woman, her heart turned to stone if she laboured in the fields.

As for Nobiton, she had not wanted her father to go back to the fields when he went home in the afternoon. 'No bajaan, you can't go back under that scorching sun when you're not feeling well.' And this was the daughter Harmatullah could no longer meet. Sometimes he felt, what's the point, might as well sell the rest of the land. But he had another daughter at home, a manly tyrant, the black sheep of the family, the bitch with a goitre who had brought shame upon them. That goitre of hers was brimming with jealousy.

Harmatullah threw a sidelong glance at the eastern side of the lake. Phuljaan was weeding away intently on the sloping bank of the lake. Her daughter had climbed to the top of the slope, where she was standing in the shade of a jackfruit tree. This daughter of Phuljaan's was black as the night, the same complexion as her father and *his* father. She was overgrown too, no one could tell she wasn't even three yet. And why not, for Phuljaan stuffed her with food whenever she could, whether anyone else at home had eaten or not. No wonder the girl was shooting up. At this rate Harmatullah would soon have to worry about her wedding too. But who was going to marry the daughter of a fisherman? On top of which she got out of bed and tried to open the door and go out of the house without even waking up. In her sleep she poked about beneath the maacha, trotting around the room. She had obviously inherited her grandfather's affliction, and it would only get worse as she grew older. Harmatullah lowered his head under the burden of the responsibility of getting his granddaughter married, or of his worry about how to pay Nobiton's father-in-law, or perhaps it was the illness of continuous thirst.

Spotting her father bent over as though he were paying obeisance to Allah while weeding the field to the east of the lake, Phuljaan reckoned that her father's vision was blurred in this fading light. The old coot had better not start uprooting the rice plants. But she didn't feel like talking to him. His overflowing love for Nobiton occasionally gave Phuljaan the urge to set the house on fire, uproot the entire crop from the earth, and go away with her daughter wherever the road took them. His arse seemed to be itching all the time with the desire to give money to his shopkeeper son-in-law. But the old coot never went looking for his other son-in-law, who had been missing for such a long time now. Keshto Pal from Palpara, who was passing this way the other day, had stopped at their door to announce that cultivators in Thakurgaon or Nachol or some such place had been agitating against the jotedars, because of which the police had got rid of some of them with bullets, and put some others in jail. And that there was a tiller from this area among the cultivators. Keshto Pal didn't know any more, which was why Phuljaan had asked her father to pay a visit to the Mondols' house. 'You'll find out everything if you go there, baapjaan,' she had said. She had even given her father a meal of flattened rice that she had put aside for her daughter. But the old coot had refused to go. But then how would it have helped anyway? He was a slave of the Mondols', he would only have licked Sharafat's arse clean of shit, he would never have had the guts to ask about Tamiz.

In the fading light and imminent darkness, Harmatullah looked from this distance like a sick and aged vulture that had plunged to the ground from the silk-cotton tree on the southern bank of the ox pool. The sight slowed down Phuljaan as well, the weeder in her hand striking repeatedly at the same root without real force. In the scraping of the weeder against the weed and the earth, she heard Kader say, 'You don't suppose the police reveal all the information, do you? So many are killed, so many are jailed, who can keep track?'

Since Harmatullah had refused to visit Sharafat's house for information about Tamiz, Phuljaan had had no choice but to go herself, with her daughter in her arms and one of Nobiton's quilts bundled up in her sari. A woman from Palpara had left an old sari to be converted into a quilt but had never collected it. She had probably left for India. Even if she came to claim it, Phuljaan would redirect her to Nobiton's in-laws' house. Her shopkeeper husband could buy her another sari to turn into a quilt.

Kader's wife was delighted to get the quilt. Shimultola was famous for needlework—her grandmother's prayer mats with a mosque and the moon and stars woven with wool on jute were so beautiful that you wanted to say your prayers as soon as you saw one of them. But this peasant's daughter had embroidered birds, fish, handheld fans and flowers in different colours so intricately that you couldn't tear your eyes away from them.

Abdul Kader was not quite so pleased, however. When told of what Keshto Pal had said, his response was that the police had to take action to stop these troublemaking cultivators. Yes, they had had to kill some people in the north and the west, but it was not possible to compile a list of the names and addresses of the victims. There was no need to make a fuss about it. Even a fart from a policeman here led to an outcry in India, which was trying everything possible to strangle our infant nation. And then they got only Indian newspapers in Palpara. Was Keshto Pal broadcasting all this to everyone?

'No, bhaijaan.' Phuljaan was frightened at the possibility of Keshto Pal's being associated with strangling a baby. Desperate to save him from accusations of murder, she said, 'No, bhaijaan, all he said was that one of the people killed in the police firing was from these parts . . .'

'It's possible.' Abdul Kader sounded even grimmer. 'He never shirked work, I gave him a lot of opportunities. Allah alone knows why he went off there.' Looking for a courteous way to make Phuljaan leave, he turned to his wife and asked, 'Do you like the quilt?'

Kader's wife wedged a one-rupee coin into Phuljaan's daughter's hand. Holding out a ten-rupee note at Phuljaan, Kader said, 'I gave you some earlier, didn't I? This is money from Tamiz.' He gave her five rupees more. 'Keep this.'

Phuljaan felt a flutter in her heart at all this money. If he couldn't provide any news about Tamiz, why was Kader being so kind?

She was about to return when Mondol's second wife signalled to her to come into the yard. Given a small banana to eat, Phuljaan's daughter dropped the coin, which her mother picked up immediately and knotted into the end of her sari. Sitting on a murrah close to the veranda, Mondol's second wife gestured to Phuljaan to sit on a stool. 'What's happening to your mother-in-law's murder case, Phuljaan? Apparently that bastard first husband of yours had something going on

with her. Shame. They say your father-in-law stomps about in the mud.
We couldn't keep the brick kiln, it seems there's a fire raging there all
the time. Must be Tamiz's father's doing. You know anything about it?'

Phuljaan didn't have to answer any of these questions. 'What
rubbish is all this,' interrupted Sharafat, walking in with a pot of
water for pre-prayer ablutions. 'A man condemned to stay in his
grave is bound to be restless. What has that got to do with a fire?
Who told you I closed down the brick kiln because of ghosts? Do you
think your prayers will be accepted if you say such things?'

'Why do you have to interfere in a conversation between women?'
One bark from his second wife and Sharafat turned his attention to
his ablutions before the asr namaz. She had become less volatile after
Sharafat's first wife's death a few months ago—she was much more
restrained now. Relieved of the pressure created by the hot and the
cold wars between his two wives, Sharafat swallowed all the rebukes
his second wife threw at him, savouring the pleasures of living with
just one wife after a long time.

Once Sharafat had begun his prayers inside the room with loud
cries of 'Allahu Akbar', his second wife asked questions to her heart's
content about Kulsum's murder, her relationship with Keramat, the
disappearance of the fig tree, Tamiz's father's anger and agitation
under the quicksand because of Kulsum's scandalous behaviour,
the fact that a fire sprang up at the spot after sunset every day, the
resultant closing down of their brick kiln, and many such subjects,
going on to answer each of them herself. When Phuljaan finally
rose to her feet, Mondol's second wife handed her a large packet
of flattened rice. 'You made this for me, it's delicious. Give this to
your daughter.' Her affection brimmed over. 'Have prayers said for
Tamiz, all right? I hear the news isn't good.'

After the harvest last Poush, she had sent Phuljaan several seers
of paddy to be husked and made into flattened rice. She had made an
advance payment too. Mondol's husking machines were busy with
the rice, and they were operated by the women of Majhipara, who had
no idea how to make flattened rice. The club fell unevenly under the
inexpert pressure of their feet, making it impossible to get high-quality

flattened rice. It either burst or turned sticky. So the Mondols had their flattened rice made at Harmatullah's house. Phuljaan of course had put aside some of it already before delivering it to the Mondols' house—his second wife wasn't keeping track of the quantity, after all. She had given the flattened rice she had set aside for her daughter to her father instead, putting the rest in a pot beneath the maacha. Since her father no longer slept there after the cobra had been discovered, Phuljaan used it herself. It was just as well about the snake, for no one dared touch the pot now. But she didn't know how long she would have to keep the new bundle hidden in the same spot. This flattened rice would have lasted exactly four meals of Tamiz's, three if there was some jaggery to go with it. How the man could eat! Why were they telling her to have prayers read for him? A man like him couldn't be killed so easily in police firing. Tamiz wasn't going to die just because everyone at the Mondols' house wanted him to, because Kalam majhi wanted him to, because the inspector from Amtoli wanted him to. Phuljaan felt his warm breath from a long way away on her cheeks, her neck, her goitre, her breasts. Sometimes she felt it had been a long time ago, but at other times her body seemed to burn at the heat from Tamiz's exhalation. It was this heat that made Phuljaan look away, towards Harmatullah, who was dozing.

'It's past the hour for the maghreb namaz. Are you laying eggs there?'

Looking up at the sky at Phuljaan's dry reminder, Harmatullah became active once again. It was a full moon night. All the rice fields seemed to have been covered in a thin paste of rice. And milk was dripping from the moon, filling the entire place with its fragrance. Phuljaan's daughter hadn't eaten in a long time. She must be hungry at the aroma of milk. Harmatullah might not be able to get her any milk, but she could at least have some rice. Still weeding, he said, 'Go home, isn't your daughter hungry?'

The old coot was only concerned about her daughter's appetite, even the coarse rice the girl ate was a source of annoyance for him. Phuljaan didn't have to wait too long to launch a barb at her father. 'How can I go without finishing my work?' she said. 'There's no dearth of people who have passed this way since morning, but it's still me who has to do all the work.'

Harmatullah had actually managed to poke at Phuljaan's belly with his comment about her daughter being hungry. Phuljaan had been famished since lunch. The coarse rice had tucked itself in near her back after she had digested it. When she went home she would have to eat the same coarse rice—no more than half a plateful at night. A little daal would have helped soften the rice, but there wasn't any at home. But not even the anxiety of having to consume the coarse rice without any daal could dampen her hunger. So she had to focus all her attention on the weeding. But her daughter's demands would not allow this. The child spoke very little, far less than others of her age, but she was fidgeting about all the time, never willing to settle down somewhere. She had been playing beside her mother just a short while ago, but now here she was, leaning on Phuljaan's shoulder and saying, 'I'm hungry, ma, I want to eat.' After this she proceeded to pester her mother by pressing her hands down on Phuljaan's head. But she couldn't let the girl eat now, for then she would start demanding food again before the night was out. Usually, when she kept pushing at her mother's body but was unable to get a response or perhaps to wake her mother up, the girl would jump out of the maacha and creep beneath it. A cobra had appeared there when the police had come looking for Tamiz. There might be more snakes in there. Phuljaan was frightened. Still, she couldn't feed her child now.

So Phuljaan brushed her daughter's tiny hands away from her head. But this led to more trouble, for her daughter walked off towards the slope leading down to the lake. She was inclined to climb the ancient termite heap beneath the tall palm tree standing on the high bank of the ox pool. There was a clearing about 3 yards wide in front of it, where Harmatullah sometimes read the maghreb namaz. The slope was a steep one, if the girl slipped she would roll all the way down to the water. What would Phuljaan do then? She stopped her weeding and ran after her daughter.

59

Harmatullah was showing signs that Phuljaan didn't care for. He seemed to have decided to sell most of his share of the crop. Phuljaan suspected he would deposit the entire harvest in Mondol's granary, take money in exchange, and set off directly for Sonamukhi to pay what he owed his daughter's father-in-law, so that his son-in-law could do up his shop and Harmatullah could get permission to bring Nobiton home. Their youngest sister Felani had gone to Nobiton's in-laws' house long ago, but the old coot made no noises about getting her back. Apparently she was very happy there. If they were rich enough to let their daughter-in-law's sister stay with them, why were they insisting that Harmatullah pay the rest of the money he had promised. As for Harmatullah, was he aware that financing his son-in-law's dreams of doing up his shop would mean the entire family's having to survive on cheap, coarse rice for several months, and probably half-starve for a month?

But then it wasn't as though Phuljaan would allow her father to give in to his whims. She wasn't supposed to have been on the field today. But Phuljaan couldn't take it any more when he decided to spend the entire day in bed, wrapped in a quilt and moaning, 'It's the time of the fair but she won't be home.' So she was on the field to gauge the harvest—she'd see how the old coot could sell off the grains on the sly.

Arriving just before the evening, Phuljaan found Harmatullah reading the namaz on the high bank of the ox pool with his back to the termite heap. But her heart began to thump when he didn't raise his head for a long time after kneeling to touch the ground with his forehead: He hadn't fainted, had he? He'd been in bed since the afternoon, not getting out of it till it was time for the asr namaz, except to urinate every now and then in between his laments for his absent daughter. She was reassured about her father's health, however, when he did finally raise his head only to bend over again, and then her irritation began to grow. What was all this deference for? Was he praying devoutly or plotting how to gather money to pay Nobiton's father-in-law?

Harmatullah read the namaz beneath the palm tree on the high bank of the ox pool while Phuljaan prowled around the field, followed by her daughter. Rice was growing everywhere, the amon was ripening, the stalks were plump on all the plots. A reassuring sight. But she would have to gauge the quantity of the harvest on the field in the presence of Harmatullah, who would have to state clearly how much rice he was expecting. Only then would the old coot not dare to sell some of it on the sly.

Walking along the narrow ridge between the fields with her daughter in her arms to the bank of the ox pool, Phuljaan saw that Harmatullah was missing. Where had he disappeared so soon after his namaz? His weeder was lying on the ground on the eastern side of the slope leading into the lake. Where was he, then? Maybe he had gone for a rest and would be back shortly.

Phuljaan wanted to sit down too for some rest. With the chill beginning to set in, she was feeling uncomfortable. Wrapping the silk shawl around herself made her warm, but removing it made her cold.

And then there was her daughter's nagging. Immediately after sunset she had started conveying her desire to eat, pressing down on her mother's head with her small hands. 'Want my rice,' she said when Phuljaan glared at her.

Phuljaan had gathered a plentiful supply of taro stems, mixing a mound of coarse rice with it. They had eaten this in the afternoon, and there was some left over for the night too. With the rice being softened by taro stems, everyone had eaten their fill for lunch, which meant it was too soon to be hungry again. Phuljaan was angry with her daughter. When the girl said 'want my rice' again, Phuljaan slapped her twice on her bottom and three times on her cheeks. She raised her hand to continue, but her daughter ran off crying towards the high bank of the ox pool. Was she going towards the termite heap? She might slip and roll into the water. Phuljaan ran after her up the slope. For the past few days her daughter had been intent on climbing the termite heap. It wasn't possible—she was sure to miss her step and fall to the clearing in front of it, and roll down from there into the water. Phuljaan grabbed her at the base of the termite heap, her rage flaring because of the anxiety she had been subjected to for a few minutes, which she expressed by raining blows on her daughter's back. She wasn't about to stop, but her arm stopped in mid-air on hearing her daughter's complaint, 'She's hitting me.' Whom was Phuljaan's weeping daughter complaining to in her briny voice as she gazed to the north-west?

Her laconic daughter was not in the habit of complaining. What was going on?

'Look, ma's hitting me.' Phuljaan followed her daughter's gaze with her own eyes. The rice field that Harmatullah sharecropped on lay directly across the lake. Beyond it were a few acres of untouched land, and then the narrow stream of the Bangali river, which had all but dried up over the past two years. No, there was no one there. A little farther to the west was the northern head of Katlahar Lake, where a round moon was dangling from the sky. Unrestricted by the presence of large trees, it had come down a little lower tonight.

But what had happened to the moon? Wasn't it a full moon just the other night? Yes, the day before yesterday, or was it the day before? The moon had grown a little thinner now, but then even

two nights ago all the fields of amon on earth had been flooded by
the condensed milk flowing from it, which the stalks of rice had
been sipping to gather more sap. But what was this illness the moon
was suffering from so soon afterwards? Its silvery complexion had
turned a blackish red, its yellow glow was all but gone. There were
blood clots all over the moon. Oh Allah, what had brought the moon
to such a state? Horen the doctor, no, not him, maybe Proshanto
the compounder would have been able to diagnose it. Or was it the
compounder who had cunningly avoided contact with Phuljaan's son
by tossing his diseased face towards the moon when it was waning?
But really, how could that be possible? Her son had never had blood
clots on his face.

Was Mondol's second wife's apprehensions correct, then? The
same fear took hold of Phuljaan, making her skin prickle. If Tamiz
had indeed been shot dead by the police, what could have made
him abandon his wife and climb into the sky? But then the son
of a fisherman had always been a proud man—he was willing to
work on his father-in-law's land, which he coveted with all his
heart, but his arse would bite him at the thought of living in his
father-in-law's house. Where else could he live, though? No one in
Majhipara would let him in. Kalam majhi had demolished the ill-
fated house and laid the foundations for a permanent mosque in its
place. There had already been talk about building another mosque
in Majhipara. The wound Kalam majhi had sustained in trying to
save Kulsum had all but crippled him. He found it very hard to
walk to the mosque with the constant pain in his arm. The people
of Majhipara suffered at his agony, and besides, it would be best
for the fishermen if that ungodly house were replaced by a mosque.
Kalam majhi was preparing to make his own house a permanent
structure too. But he couldn't bring bricks into his residence before
building one for Allah.

So Tamiz couldn't possibly go and live there. Was that why he
had entered the round body of the moon with his face full of bullet
wounds? Was that why the moon was looking so ghostly?

Phuljaan's nervousness was dispelled slightly by thoughts of Tamiz. Having her fearless husband nearby, living or dead, gave her strength.

There wasn't a single large tree beneath the moon. The fig tree had vanished long ago, and the rest had fallen the night Boikuntho had died, the night of the storm. All that remained were bushes and shrubs. The other thing visible across the northern head of the lake was light. People said fires raged every night where the fig tree used to stand. But now that Phuljaan was not as frightened as before, she knew from gazing at the lights for some time that it was clusters of fireflies in those bushes and shrubs. The fireflies winked on the vegetation and on the discarded bricks from the kiln—when one set went out, another set, a little lower, came alive, after which the upper row flew farther up and glowed with renewed strength. It seemed as though they would fly off with the bushes from the entire expanse on their blazing wings.

Phuljaan felt it would be best not to stay here now. She was standing on the high bank of the ox pool with her daughter on this night of a waning moon, in front of the termite heap beneath the palm tree that stretched even higher into the sky. But what was this sight she could see north of here, a little to the north-east? Sometimes it seemed familiar, and at other times she felt nervous: she had an inkling of what it was. She tried to shriek, 'O baapjaan!' but she realized her voice was stuck in her goitre and would not make it to her throat. Her daughter had stopped weeping too, but her silent sobs wouldn't let up. It was her sobs, emitted at regular intervals, that gave Phuljaan the strength to remain here. The final phase of every sob reminded Phuljaan that it was her father who had told her that in the absence of large trees, all the fireflies who had lost the branches and leaves and dark corners they used to occupy had spread out across the grass, bushes and shrubs.

When Phuljaan's daughter had emitted her final sob, silence descended everywhere. Phuljaan felt that now that her daughter was quiet, the glow of the fireflies had, even from a distance, checked her pulse to identify her fears and doubts. She felt a tickle on her right wrist.

Suddenly Phuljaan's daughter said, 'The fire's been lit in the kitchen.' Her voice sounded rough from the alkalines in the dried salt of her tears. 'The fire's been lit in the kitchen, ma.'

Now Phuljaan could see swarms of fireflies hoisting, on their flaming wings, the entire area where the fig tree used to stand, and lifting it towards the ghostly moon. Or was it the moon that had descended closer to the fireflies because of their magnetic attraction? In the heat, the warmth, and even the vapours from the fireflies, the blackish-red stains on the moon were being eroded, with only the blood clots remaining. The heat from the kitchen of the fireflies wouldn't burn the moon to ashes, would it?

'The rice is on the stove,' said Phuljaan's daughter, replacing her lisping talk with clear diction. 'They're making rice.'

This was true, she wasn't lying, the rosy aush was being boiled in the heat from the fireflies beneath the moon. And before the watery red starch could overflow, it turned into beams of fire and slid down on the northern head of the lake. Phuljaan's daughter gazed at it and sniffed loudly. Was her daughter getting the aroma of rice? Let it be so, Allah. Let her fill her belly with the fragrance of aush boiled beneath the moon on firefly flames. If her hunger was satiated she wouldn't need to eat again when they went back home, and she would neither wake up before the night was out nor sleepwalk to rummage for food beneath the maacha. And the rice mixed with taro roots would remain to be eaten the next day.

How strange! Soon Phuljaan's nosemouthheadthroatgoitre filled with the aroma of rice. Who said it wasn't real? The fragrance of aush being boiled filled with air. But Phuljaan's brain demurred, just the aroma of this rice couldn't possibly fill anyone's belly. Would her appetite be satiated? And would she ever be able to eat coarse rice with taro roots after such fragrance? Still Phuljaan couldn't stop herself from savouring the scent.

'Want rice, they're making rice, want rice, ma.' So her daughter's stomach was still empty. Shorn of whining, the request, made in a rasping voice, sounded like a demand. How could this tiny girl speak so forcefully when she was starving? Phuljaan's heart trembled. People said Tamiz's father stretched himself sometimes beneath the quicksand near the spot where the fig tree used to stand. What if he was the one playing all these tricks? Whether he approved of his goitre-ridden daughter-in-law or not, maybe it was his wish to set eyes on the only granddaughter in his family, to placate her with the aroma of rice, that had made Tamiz's father whisper into the ears of the fireflies to get the fire going in their kitchen. He must be able to see his daughter-in-law too, along with his granddaughter, from his place beneath the quicksand. Overcome by modesty, Phuljaan quickly drew the end of her sari over her head, perhaps a little more tightly than necessary. Who knew, her father-in-law might decide to admonish her with a verse or two in his sleepy voice if he saw her without a veil. Phuljaan had heard Munshi's verses many times, she had often heard verses about Majnu and Bhabani Pathak at the Poradaho fair. But then she didn't remember any of them, she had never recited them herself. Tamiz used to tell her many things, but he had never mentioned the verses. If she had known a few, Phuljaan would have muttered them under her breath, maybe that would have calmed down Tamiz's father.

But why was her daughter standing there so stiffly? How could this little girl, usually so fidgety, stare at something so fixedly for such a long time? Was her own daughter becoming more intelligent in front of her very eyes? Was she really Phuljaan's daughter? Out of fear of her daughter, to prevent her from becoming a stranger, and partly to re-establish her own control over her, Phuljaan knelt on the ground and put her arms around the little girl, touching her tiny shoulder with her goitre and resting her chin on her little head. At once her chin vibrated with a buzzing sound. Tamiz's father must have possessed Phuljaan's daughter to insert into her head all the verses he had inherited from Munshi.

'Come home, ma,' Phuljaan said softly. 'Don't you want to eat?'
Not even this could arouse her daughter. She kept her small
black feet planted firmly on the ground. Such an obstinate girl!
What Harmatullah said was true, this clan of fishermen were very
stubborn people. Fishing was their traditional profession, and they
moved like fish too, all together. They were on good terms with the
water in the river, swimming in the same direction as the current
in a group. But then the bastards didn't hesitate to fight with it
too—flowing against the stream with the same madness when they
wanted to. So they travelled, downstream when they liked, upstream
when they wanted. The fishermen at Girirdanga across the lake had
come together in solidarity a long time ago. All of them used to
be Munshi's followers, they were his favourites. A long, long time
ago, when, never mind Tamiz, never mind Tamiz's father, when
Bhaghar Majhi's grandfather's father—or was it *his* grandfather—
had barely been born, or not, and even if he had, was only crawling
about on the newly laid earth in the home built by clearing a part
of the forest, Munshi had turned into a ghost after being killed by
a soldier's bullet. After his death, with a chain around his neck and
his body smeared with ash, and holding an iron pan with fish motifs
carved on it, he had perched on the fig tree on the northern side
of the Katlahar Lake. All this had happened a very long time ago.
But Phuljaan wasn't remotely interested in the family history of the
fishermen. Still, people said that Munshi had ruled over the lake
from the fig tree since then. Every night his flock of pet murrels
were transformed into sheep on his orders and swam all around
the lake, gasping for breath when they inhaled water. But with the
fig tree gone, no one knew where Munshi's throne had vanished.
Munshi's position had now been usurped by Tamiz's father. But
then he was a bit of a glutton. Considering his appetite, he may well
have sliced up the murrels and set them on the fire to be cooked in
the kitchen of the fireflies. Maybe the round moon had helped the
fish to be cooked by stretching out its bullet-ridden body. Phuljaan
was reassured—her daughter must be breathing in the sharp tang of

murrel curry. She wasn't one to be sniffing continuously if rice was all she could smell.

Now that might explain the matter of the fragrance of the rice and the tang of the fish, but what was buzzing inside Phuljaan's daughter's head? Was it Sakina then who would weave the sounds that emerged from the buzzing into a new set of verses? But what did the girl know besides food? Was she really capable of weaving poetry? No one knew. What verses could anyone expect of her?

With Munshi gone, it was doubtful that even a fragment of the verses he had left behind could hum in Sakina's head. Tamiz's father himself hadn't known how to write them.

Across the ox pool, across the depths, Harmatullah could be heard calling out in his rheum-filled voice, 'Phooooljaaaaan, Phooooljaaaan.' Phuljaan was startled, her glance wavering. She could see the flock of storks from the silk-cotton tree in the Mondols' yard rising slowly into the air. They didn't venture towards the northern head of the lake out of fear of the fire in the kitchen, but they winged slowly across the lake towards her. After a slight detour they would arrive at the ox pool any moment now.

Frightened, Phuljaan rose to her feet, shaking her daughter by the shoulders. 'Sakina, let's go home, ma.'

The flock of storks might have cast an indistinct reflection in Harmatullah's dull eyes. His plaintive cry oozed through the reddish-black mist, 'Phooooljaaaaan, Phooooljaaaaan.'

How could Phuljaan possibly answer him? She couldn't persuade her daughter to budge. Planting her feet firmly on the parched, hard ground in front of the ancient termite heap under the tall palm tree on the high bank of the ox pool and craning her neck as high as possible, stretching her nerves taut, Sakina gazed with eyes that turned sharper by the moment at the kitchen of the fireflies glowing beneath the wounded moon that had risen above the northern head of Katlahar Lake.